ACCLAIMED ACROSS THE NATION!

The Blue Messiah

James D. Horan

AVON
PUBLISHERS OF BARD, CAMELOT, DISCUS, EQUINOX AND FLARE BOOKS

AVON BOOKS
A division of
The Hearst Corporation
959 Eighth Avenue
New York, New York 10019

First Avon Printing, August, 1972

AVON TRADEMARK REG. U.S. PAT. OFF. AND
FOREIGN COUNTRIES, REGISTERED TRADEMARK—
MARCA REGISTRADA, HECHO EN CHICAGO, U.S.A.

Printed in the U.S.A.

For Gertrude, who Chena insists
is too much competition

author's note

I began this novel long before there was any public discussion of a national police union; obviously my National Brotherhood of Police Communications Workers, Foot Patrolmen and Superior Officers, its officers, and the events in which they take part are all fictitious and have no connection with any living person or organization.

For the record I was not born nor was I raised in the Neighborhood (like my protagonist I insist that the term "Hell's Kitchen" is used more by Sunday Supplement writers than its residents), and its people and the events that take place there, along with the waterfront unions, their leaders, and their activities in this novel are products of my imagination.

For their cooperation I would like to thank Joseph Mordino, the celebrated operatic and concert stage star, who with great patience and good humor recalled for me his early years in the Neighborhood before he became Toscanini's protégé. Mr. Mordino's colorful life rates a book all of its own.

Also Drs. John and Gerta Schwarz, who reviewed my fictitious psychiatric case history of Joe Gunnar and advised me how to treat his savage rages; Harold and Pauline Peters who were never too busy to correct my Sicilian dialect, and Frank X. Smith, former Assistant District Attorney, Queens County, and former New York City Council President, who never fails to impress me with his political expertise and insider's knowledge of what's going on in America's Fun City.

Ancient wisdom claims that the last shall always be the first; this distinction belongs to Gertrude, our typist in residence, who fortunately also possesses a sharp editorial eye. She had the dubious honor of typing this 450,000-word manuscript—not counting the numerous inserts and edited pages—which she did with much patience and tolerance. All authors should be thus blessed.

JAMES D. HORAN

CONTENTS

BOOK 1

the neighborhood—1935

1 THE PEOPLE OF THE NEIGHBORHOOD

Even then the old banana pier was falling apart. A thousand suns had sucked the juice from its planks until splinters stood upright like nails. Rain and the salt air had rubbed away the paint of the corrugated tin roof leaving ugly patches of red lead or jagged holes, while the river had gradually gnawed at the timbers until at low tide some stood out like rotted uppers in a dark green mouth.

The pier used by the banana and coffee companies was sandwiched between two of the luxury sheds that housed the first-class liners. To the dock workers the big piers meant not only eighty cents an hour but tips you could make taking down the passengers' luggage on a four-wheeler. It was understood, of course, that a piece of what you made went to Johnny the Gimp's Pistoleers as they called the gunmen who ran the locals and the waterfront. The big sheds were also excellent for stealing. The fence on Eighth Avenue paid fifty cents a bottle for Canadian rye and a dollar for scotch. Two bottles from every case went to the hiring boss. That was the law. Break it once by keeping any part of the loot you stole and you would probably be worked over; break it twice and you could end up under a fishline hoisting several tons of machinery. The last you would hear would be a shout and the whir of the hoist as the hawser slipped to let the load come crushing down on you.

It wasn't very often anyone bucked the Gimp's Pistoleers. That eighty cents an hour, the tips, and all you could steal depended on making the shape. And they controlled the shape. The old pier didn't rate too much attention from the Gimp's mob. Once a year they put the bite on the companies who paid them for the privilege of docking and unloading on the city-owned stringpiece.

Even though times were desperate, bananas and coffee were not popular cargoes on the waterfront. There were too many bugs in the fruit, and unloading coffee was backbreaking work. You had to be careful not to tear the bags with your hook, and each one had to be carried to the pallet for the cargo net. Coffee dust got into your eyes, ears, nose, and hair and turned the hankderchief you wore to a dirty dark brown color. After a few days in a coffee cargo you came out looking like a Sioux.

It was brute labor. Mostly old men and shenangoes— the drifters of the waterfront—took out those cargoes. After a shenango was taken to Polyclinic with a tarantula bite, even the Gimp's Pistoleers had a difficult time forcing the men to work the banana holds.

I can still see the Pistoleers—young, tough, ruthless— swaggering about the piers, following the Gimp as he headed for his car, nervous minnows in the wake of a cold-eyed shark. Looking back, they weren't far removed from the hoods you see in the old Cagney movies on the late show. I guess in their own way they were playing a role. And we were certainly an appreciative audience.

In the Neighborhood you took your choice of legends, and it was the measure of us all that there were damn few saints we cared about, but sinners we idolized. Father Duffy belonged to our fathers' generation, of muddy trenches, machine-gun nests, rats eating the dead, and Huns. We couldn't have cared less; Owney Madden was real. If you were lucky you caught a glimpse of him through the car windows: tight, thin face, white as flour, Chesterfield coat and pearl gray hat. But it was the Gimp, meaner, tougher, and more ingenious in his fashion of murder who really caught our imagination.

From the first day I toddled out into the street I heard

12

of Johnny Wilson, the Gimp, who had lived all his life in a flat on Fifty-third Street off Ninth. Infantile paralysis, as we called polio in those days, had left him with a slight limp; the gangland wars of Prohibition and the early thirties had fashioned him into an ingenious killer and a racketeer with an instinct for profit. After Repeal he had been the first mobster to view the waterfront with its haphazard unions as his own. There was no question of opposition; those who survived became his stooges, those who made trouble were either disposed of or just vanished.

There was an individuality in his style of murder that appealed to the savagery of the Neighborhood: His killings were never stereotyped. I can still recall as a child studying the newspaper picture of a rival gangster, his throat cut and his body hung from a roof to dangle outside a West Side synagogue. The gangster was Jewish.

I was in grammar school returning from an errand when I saw the Gimp for the first time on Fifty-third Street. Later I learned he occasionally visited his father, a morose little Irishman who spent his days traveling about in a cab visiting the Neighborhood's bars and periodically drying out in Bellevue's psycho ward. As I approached the tenement I saw a group of excited kids standing at the bottom of the stoop staring up at the windows of the second floor. One kid was in my class and I asked him what was going on.

"The Gimp's visitin' his old man!" he said excitedly.

"So what?" I replied, but he gave me an unbelieving look and shouted, "Here he comes!"

Two hard-faced men hurried down the steps. Between them was a younger man who limped slightly. I could see that one of his highly polished shoes was built higher than the other. As he stepped into his car, the hoods tossed handfuls of change into the air. I fought with the kids on the sidewalk and came up with a dime as the car pulled away.

"Does he always do that?" I asked.

"Every time his old man gets boozed up and is taken to Bellevue he comes over to see him," the kid explained. "When he leaves, those guys always throw money in the air. Once he tossed five bucks from the old man's window and he had the whole goddam street fightin' over it . . ."

Even after his father's death, the Gimp continued to

return to the Neighborhood. Tom Gunnar tried to explain why to me:

"In the Neighborhood he not only feels comfortable but safe. He knows every face and if they're reliable or if they're not. He was born here and he lived here all his life. He knows everyone on the street and the avenue, what they do, if they're boozers, if they work on the docks, if they owe money to the shylocks, even if they're good to their families. In the Neighborhood the guy who works on the piers or drives a truck grew up with the Gimp. They went their way, he went his, but that doesn't mean they would talk to the cops about him.

"At the same time, the Gimp protects the Neighborhood. Remember when they caught that guy molesting the little kids? They took him up to the roof and threw him off. It's instinct, Frank, the Neighborhood and the Gimp protect each other . . ."

Wilson was an admired part of the Neighborhood when I was growing up. It was overlooked, of course, that he was mean, deadly, a murderer; to the tenements he was a winner. He had survived the gang war, Repeal, La Guardia's cops, and even Dewey. He still had his Cadillac, his hoods, and his power.

Johnny the Gimp ruled the waterfront, they said and you had better not forget it . . .

A few blocks east of the river the Neighborhood's tenements lined the street like ancient red brick battlements shouldering out the hostile world.

The Howells and Gunnars had lived in its railroad flats since Joe and I were infants. Our families were close as blood relations, sharing everything from tears to the hall toilet. In the winter I guess you could say we kept the seat warm for one another.

We had gone through grade school together, joining Nick Valentino in kindergarten. Two days after I started school, I had my first fistfight with Joe in the schoolyard. We battled every day for a week until the afternoon we joined Nick in beating off some kids from Chelsea who tried to steal his lunch box. From then on we fought back to back. We soon discovered you can't survive alone in the Neighborhood.

Like the Gunnars and the Howells, the Valentinos had lived in the same tenement for generations. Only their section of Ninth Avenue had always been casually called "Guinea Alley." In the Neighborhood the caste system was strictly observed; Irish on Forty-Sixth Street, Italians on Ninth Avenue, Polacks, Hungarians, and Gypsies on Tenth and Eleventh avenues.

Nick's grandfather had jumped ship and later worked in a factory in Queens. Growing tomatoes appeared to be his only passion, and even now I have but to close my eyes to see him, slender, morose, wearing a battered black fedora, staggering under the weight of grape boxes filled with dirt that he had carried across town.

During Prohibition, Gus Valentino, Nick's father, operated the Neighborhood's first speakeasy in a cellar that at first sold only wine to the residents of Guinea Alley. He had a bocce court in the backyard where bets were made on Sunday while his neighbors went crazy with the drunken players shouting, cursing, singing, and wagering.

Later he took over the largest speakeasy in the area on Forty-fourth Street just off Eighth, after its original owner, a German bartender, had been found trussed up like a chicken and burned to death in a Canarsie swamp. Gus, along with several others, had been taken to West Forty-seventh Street for questioning but was quickly released. Even then he seemed to know his way around police precincts.

Gus Valentino had always reminded me of a conceited pirate. He had a swarthy handsomeness and was the only man who ever appeared in the Neighborhood wearing spats and white piping on his vest. He sported a Chesterfield coat with a velvet collar and a fawn-colored fedora slanted to one side in the style favored by Al Capone.

All this, of course, was after the big speak was a success. Before that he was never out of his shiny blue suit and water-stained hat. Then he smoked Italian ropes like his father. One day we saw him take a cigarette out of a silver case and have a flunky give him a light. You could almost hear the Neighborhood sniff: Let a wop get a few bucks and see how it goes to his head . . .

As we grew older Nick was always complaining to us about how his father was demanding he get good marks. Once in sophomore year when he was in danger of not passing, Gus put on a Sunday night show of cheap Broadway talent to help the nuns raise funds to pay for a new church roof. Nick passed that year.

But there was never any question who was the leader of our trio—on the streets, in the river, or in school. It was Joe Gunnar. I was closest to him, in fact with the exception of coloring we were almost mirror twins. A faded snapshot in front of me shows Joe, thick, yellow wavy hair and blue eyes that could become cold as ice, and me with curly brown hair, hazel eyes, and a big grin. We were even dressed alike in the picture my aunt took of us sitting on our stoop, varsity neck, sleeveless sweaters, brown and white shoes, and carefully pressed flannels that were our pride and joy that summer.

We all followed Joe. Looking back I can see he had that magic combination of animal vitality, luck, raw courage, and brilliance that make certain men seem destined for achievement and recognition, good or evil, even in their juvenile years. Women would always be drawn to him, sometimes involuntarily, usually disastrously. Even in those teen-age days when he was after a girl he would turn on the charm like a water tap, and you could almost feel his sensuous magnetism.

I now believe he had inherited these qualities, good and bad, from his father who had been hiring boss of one of the big piers in the 1920s, a legendary union organizer and absolute leader of the waterfront—until the Gimp appeared.

Andy Gunnar, a powerfully built man, was a terror to any Eighth or Ninth Avenue saloon when he was drunk. The legend was old hat before I was born of how it had taken ten cops from the Forty-seventh Street precinct to cuff him and throw him into the paddy wagon, only to find it empty, the door off its hinges, when it arrived at the station house. They found him in the bar he had just wrecked captivating a crowd with his wild songs of the Liverpool waterfront.

No matter how grave were the charges, he always emerged, not as a belligerent, violent drunk but as a helpless victim of the police who had tried to stand up for his God-given rights. The Neighborhood loved him, and, as my aunt never grew tired of repeating, when the docks were booming and the money was floating, Andy Gunnar bought enough drinks to float the *Leviathan*.

In the post-World War I years Gunnar was the waterfront's labor leader, organizing one or more unions that always seemed to meet in the rear of Regan's saloon on Ninth Avenue. He led more than one strike and, if you believed the stories told by the old-timers, Andy Gunnar found as much pleasure in battling the cops when they tried to escort scabs through his picket lines as he did in sitting around a conference table with the shippers.

His background was vague. My aunt Clara once told me he had come from Liverpool, where he had killed a man with his fists, signed on as a seaman, and jumped ship in New York. He worked in steel when Macy's was going up, then moved to the waterfront and married Mary Glynn, a pretty blonde cashier in a department store. She was Joe's mother but I think she was as much mine.

Andy Gunnar was a picturesque figure on the waterfront; physically powerful, handsome, jovial, and without a bit of sense in his head when it came to whiskey and women.

Tammany found him valuable. During the campaigns he would lead parades of his dockwallopers through the Neighborhood, some so drunk they could barely hold the banners upright, while Joe's father, along with the district leader and his latest candidate, sat in an open car waving to the shrilling women who leaned on their pillowed windowsills.

Within the walls of their railroad flat, only Joe and his mother and brother knew the other side of the man the Neighborhood loved and admired; the dark strain of violence that ran deep inside Andy Gunnar, a legacy of evil for his son.

Since I was a toddler I had heard the muffled screams and cries from the Gunnar flat. Whenever they started, my aunt would dress me hurriedly and take me out, even in the rain or snow, to the movies, the Automat for a cup of hot cocoa and one of their delicious glaze cakes, or simply a walk up to Central Park. I can still remember her tight, angry face and the bitter looks she gave Gunnar during the weeks that followed.

As I grew older I came to associate his stumbling, muttering approach up the stairs with the pleading cries that followed. Street kids in the slums become highly sophisticated very young; before long I knew that Joe's father beat his mother when he was drunk.

One Saturday afternoon when my aunt was unexpectedly delayed beyond her usual noon quitting time, Gunnar, who had not come home the night before, made his way up the stairs. I held my breath and pressed my ear against the door.

Before long it started. Dishes shattered, something

17

slammed against the wall. Then I heard Joe's pleading cries followed by painful whimpers.

"Joe," I shouted at the keyhole, "hey, Joe c'mon over . . ."

When there was no answer I crossed the hall and inched open the kitchen door to see the powerful Gunnar smash his fist into his wife's face, driving her across the room. She staggered against the wall, then slumped to her knees without a sound, looking up with pleading eyes at her husband. Mumbling curses, he entwined one hand in his wife's hair then, almost methodically, with the other he began to slap her face, one side then the other. In the small kitchen the blows sounded like pistol shots.

Mrs. Gunnar had always been a pretty woman who never failed to catch the eyes of the men on the stoops as she passed; Aunt Clara's favorite description of her was "neat as a pin." Now the long blonde hair hung about her agonized, bruised face. Blood trickled from her nostrils and her lips were split and swollen. As she knelt almost in supplication, Gunnar grabbed at her dress to pull her to her feet. The dress ripped and Gunnar tore it from her body and stripped away some of her undergarments, leaving her almost nude. The sight of his wife's body seemed to drive him into a frenzy and he beat and kicked her as she cringed in the corner, feebly trying to cover her breasts with her hands.

Then, for the first time, I saw Joe crouched near the stove, his face red and puffed. I waved frantically to get his attention but I couldn't; his eyes were fastened, almost in fascination, on his mother's body.

The furious blows and the whimpering cries made me physically sick. I carefully closed the kitchen door and ran for the hallway toilet. After I had vomited, I sat on the stoop until I saw my aunt turn the corner. I ran to meet her and begged that we have dinner in the Automat. There were few things I asked that she didn't grant, so we ate in the Broadway Automat. To keep her away from our tenement, I even allowed her to drag me to confession at St. Barnabas on the way home.

Over the weekend there wasn't a sound from Joe's flat. Monday morning I entered the kitchen to find Andy Gunnar sitting at the kitchen table. He looked like a ghost with a three-day beard, clutching a bottle with both hands, long dirty fingers wrapped about its neck. Even above the smell of fresh-brewed coffee was the odor of raw whiskey.

"Hello Mr. Gunnar," I said but he only blinked as if he was trying to get me into focus.

"Oh, there you are Frank," Mrs. Gunnar said, "just in time to join Joe." She placed a bowl of steaming oatmeal before me. "Eat it up, you two. Get off to school and let the nuns have you for a few hours."

Her voice was unnaturally loud and her face was swollen and bruised. I mumbled a greeting to Joe and slid in the chair beside him. He just stared down at the table, his oatmeal-filled spoon going up and down from bowl to lips with mechanical regularity. There was a bruise under one eye.

While we ate, his father began to nod, jerking awake and using the back of his hand to wipe away spittle that seeped from a corner of his mouth. All of a sudden his face went slack, his head tilted back to rest on the door of the dish closet and he began to snore, long, rasping, gurgling snores. I started to giggle, but Joe turned and gave me a look and I went back to my oatmeal.

"Now, now, Andy boy, I got to get you to bed," Mrs. Gunnar said as she took the bottle away from the big hand like a mother removing a bottle from a sleepy child. She murmured to no one in particular, "Poor man's been workin' his fool head off for the union." Then she knelt down and took off her husband's heavy work shoes.

"I'll let the poor boy rest a bit," she said as she rose.

On the way to school Joe never said anything to me about his father nor did I mention what I had seen. He only spoke savagely of what he intended to do to some kid who had stolen his pencil. I said I would help him, and we waylaid the kid as he came around the corner of Ninth Avenue and gave him a merciless pounding. It wasn't important to me that the kid had or had not taken Joe's pencil; somehow I felt I owed my allegiance to Joe after witnessing that scene in his kitchen.

Early one Sunday morning Andy Gunnar was found in the gutter on Ninth Avenue outside the old carbarns on West Fifty-fourth Street, mangled and almost unrecognizable. The police said he was a hit-and-run victim but no one bought that. The Neighborhood knew that when Johnny the Gimp and his Pistoleers moved in on the waterfront, Gunnar appealed to the shippers for help, but the shippers were only interested in talking to those with the most power. When he tried to rally his friends on the docks, he found that pistols were more influential than friendship and loyalty.

That morning, full of song and booze, he came out of a gin mill on Ninth Avenue. Someone saw a truck chase him down the street to the block-long stretch outside the carbarns where there was no curb. There they smashed him against the wall again and again. Of course there were no witnesses.

The waterfront closed down for the funeral. The cortege moved slowly up Eighth Avenue to Columbus Circle, then down Ninth to St. Barnabas, three shining Mickey Mouses leading the way to the High Mass. Some crumbling old clippings my aunt once showed me claimed the funeral was the biggest on the West Side, more impressive even than that of Ding Dong Bell, Owney Madden's favorite lieutenant who was caught in the kip by Vincent Coll's gunmen. Incredible as it may seem, I once heard old men in a gloomy Tenth Avenue bar argue about the number of limousines in the two funerals. To the Neighborhood that kind of trivia was important.

Joe and I were eight when his father was killed. I was the only one he would talk to; even his older brother Tom couldn't find him. It was late in October and the air was chilled when I found Joe sitting in the shadow of the pigeon coop we both owned. He looked cold and miserable and his cheeks were wet. I had a sweater which I gave him and we sat there, neither of us saying a word, just staring off in the blue haze that was Jersey. When the darkness closed in, he got up and went downstairs to the crowded flat where we could hear his mother weeping. I followed him. It would be that way all our lives.

As for myself, Frank Howell, there's not much to tell. All my life had been spent in the same tenement and on the same floor as the Gunnars. My mother died during the 1918 influenza epidemic and I never saw much of my father, who was at sea most of his life. As chief steward for one of the Grace liners he made a fairly good living in the Depression. I remember him as a slight man of rather quick movement who constantly smoked cigarettes he selected from a wafer-thin case. Each one was carefully tapped on the case before it went to his lips. He was a fastidious dresser and even before he went out to pick up the morning tabloid at Times Square he carefully surveyed himself in the large mirror that hung in the hall.

It was Aunt Clara who raised me. I still cherish the memory of that gentle, sentimental, Victorian woman who I am sure had never been touched by a man. She was a perfect example of the provincialism of the Neighborhood.

For almost a half century she lived in the same tenement, a truck's length from the Ninth Avenue el, yet the only time she left her beloved New York Public Library, where she had worked since she was sixteen, was to attend wakes and weddings. Her preparations to spend a weekend in Philadelphia were enough for an extended voyage abroad. She didn't sleep for a week before she went and never stopped talking about the wonders of Philadelphia after she had returned.

Yet she was different. I believe she was the only one in the Neighborhood who ever attended the theatre. To my everlasting gratitude, she virtually dragged me to see O'Casey's *Juno and the Paycock* and *Within the Gates* one Saturday afternoon. We sat in seventy-five-cent balcony seats, and I had vowed to leave during the intermission. But within minutes after the curtain was raised I was enthralled.

She was a dumpling of a woman with a bun of graying reddish hair and a conviction that all men were beasts and were not to be trusted where women were concerned, as she put it. I relish the romantic illusion that there was a deep dark secret connected with her hatred of all males, but my father once told me bluntly that his sister was born despising all men including the doctor who delivered her. My father and I, of course, were excluded; he was a giant in the earth and I was her North Star.

She never missed a day of work and I still have the small silver watch the staff of the library on Fifth Avenue had given her for her twenty-five years of service. Every Sunday morning after coming home from Mass she carefully wound the watch. Not one day before, not one day after.

She really was a lost soul in the Neighborhood. The screams, the shouts, and the curses of our neighbors engaged in their routine Saturday night warfare frightened her. Most of the harridans who hung out the windows on their pillows were friendly only because of her seniority on the street. Secretly they regarded the neat little woman who carried a book under her arm as an affront to their toughness and their contemptuous disregard of all things civilized.

My visits with my father between his trips were brief. Although he usually had about a week's shore leave, he would get restless after the third or fourth day and start to prowl the flat. When I was small he would take me down to the pier on the pretext of touring his ship. But once we were there, he would spend the afternoon going over his dining room inventory with his chef assistant, who, he told me privately, was out to get his job.

He had assistants, but each one, my father insisted, knew no more about organizing a ship's dining room than an Eighth Avenue pawnbroker; in addition, they were stealing his tips and lying about him to the purser. Yet he had lived long enough in the Neighborhood to have his own double standard of honesty. Each time we left the ship I practically waddled off with the bottles of cognac he had tied around my waist. They were for a few favored friends, mostly female.

Like most veteran seamen, he was an omnivorous reader and down through the years I devoured everything he brought back with him, including a medical book called *God's Treasure Chest*, which he had thought was an adventure tale.

In 1933 my father died of a burst appendix and was buried at sea. My aunt was hysterical after the telegram came, and for a few days neighbors tiptoed in with plates of food and a great deal of maudlin sympathy. But when his possessions arrived, accompanied by a letter from the line informing us that a small pension would be sent to me as a juvenile until I was twenty-one, she managed to dry her tears. That night she took me to dinner at Gilhooley's on Eighth Avenue and had the first cocktail I ever saw her drink. I never knew if it was a celebration of the money or in memory of her brother's death. I believe it was a combination of both.

I did cry a bit when the news came but secretly I felt guilty because I could not experience a deep sorrow. He had supported me, but for all the times I had seen him he was almost a stranger. I believed that after my mother died he had lost interest in me and buried himself in the sea that he really loved.

While Aunt Clara was my formal guardian, I was almost as much a member of the Gunnar family as Joe and Tom. From the time my father died, Mrs. Gunnar watched

22

over me as she did her own. In fact, she always laugh-ingly referred to me as her third son.

Mrs. Gunnar and my aunt Clara were alike in many ways. Both were devout churchgoers; they had attended every mission at St. Barnabas since I was in the first grade. Their big event was on a Friday night when they traveled to Loew's Twenty-third Street for "dish night." Joe and I were their only crosses. If it hadn't been for Tom, we would have been in more mischief than we actually were.

Tom, pride of the Neighborhood, had reached the unat-tainable; he was what some of the local secular priests contemptuously called "a Fordham man." Early in gram-mar school it was clear Tom was destined for big things. He was captain and star forward of St. Barnabas's wonder team of the early thirties, yet he had refused a basketball scholarship and instead won the Bishop Larkin Four Year Scholarship to Fordham. He had enormous self-confidence, and at twenty was the likely choice for the Judge Graybar Scholarship to Fordham's law school for highest excellence during four years. His picture had been on the *Tribune*'s sports page as leading city scorer; his mother faithfully dusted the big trophy every day and recited his scores to any visitor, even the man who read the gas meter.

I was particularly close to Tom that summer because of the time he devoted to tutoring me for the same Larkin Scholarship he had won. Outwardly, I was casual about college, and I guess Tom was the only one who really knew how desperately I wanted to go.

Aunt Clara and Mrs. Gunnar had already visited our district leader at the clubhouse and had his promise that if I won and went to Fordham he would get me a gofer's job for the summer. A gofer was usually an old drunk or a young kid on the docks who did nothing but go for coffee in the morning, sandwiches at noon, and containers of beer in the afternoon. The leader had done the same for Tom who told me that, between gofering, the coffee bags in the back of the pier were great for catching up on required reading.

Like our families, our gang was a microcosm of the Neighborhood. It reflected its politics, prejudices, igno-rance, and values. We were all the same age and street wise. Our ranks were impregnable—you had to be born to it to be a member. There was as much snobbery on our street and splintery pier as there was in any Englishmen's club. That summer of 1935 we were all seventeen, with the exception of Train who never knew his parents, the day or the year of his birth, and couldn't have cared less. When he entered kindergarten at St. Barnabas, the nuns demanded the day of his birth so his grandmother picked Christmas because, as she explained, she could give her grandson both his Christmas and birthday gifts at the same time. There were never any presents.

Ironically, Train had the gentle name of Latham Dooley. He was huge even then and dull witted as a mule. He followed Joe like a shadow and would do anything he asked. Once when we were stealing the New York Central's coal from a coal car on a siding, a railroad bull surprised us. In the chase he whacked Joe across his rear with a billy club. The next day when we were crossing the tracks, Joe casually ordered Train to push over a caboose. He had it swaying, ready to tip over, when the bulls came. From that day on he was Train.

Danny Williams was nicknamed Spider because of his long, pipestem arms and legs which gave him the speed and agility of a spider as he clambered over the freight cars and piers or fled from an angry store owner whose shop he was looting. He had a cap of curly black hair and a cherubic face that made him beloved of all the nuns in grammar school who were sure he would enter the priesthood. He was a superb dancer, a delight to the girls at our Saturday night dances, and an extraordinary shoplifter.

Spider was not only a skillful thief but possessed a ruthlessness that startled us even in those early days. The brown eyes could be as gentle as a doe's and the smile as wholesome as a choirboy's as he pushed a chimney off a roof, narrowly missing the landlord's rent collector who had harassed his mother.

Spider and Train had left school in their freshman year to work on odd jobs on the piers, in Paddy's pushcart market on Eighth Avenue, or in the Chelsea potato warehouse, where, for generations, kids from the Neighborhood had packed potatoes for fifty cents a day. When the WPA began, the district leader got them on cleaning up lots. Later, Train journeyed to Westchester to work on the highways while Spider became a painter in the Queens courthouse.

We were all an integral part of the Neighborhood where our parents, like our flats, were indistinguishable. From birth the Neighborhood had taught our grandparents, our parents, and then ourselves to regard life as a constant enemy. If you wanted to survive, you had to pin Society to the mat by using the Neighborhood's proven weapons —courage, shrewdness, cunning, and double-dealing. The world beyond Eighth Avenue was hostile and didn't give a damn.

From its very air the Neighborhood gave us a deep and unshakable belief that we best get what we could by any means fair or foul; it never offered us anything else except poverty and despair. Yet there was a wonderful sense of validity about the place; its residents stoically and heroically accepted the worst that life could hand them because they knew that nothing would ever change. It was a place where human relationships were cherished simply because there was nothing else to cherish. Each friend had a value to another: it was a certainty that helped us all to survive those bitter days.

The legend makers would have us believe there was a great love of song and music in the Neighborhood. Nonsense! Unless they were pornographic, books were alien to this world, and music was the three-man combo in Regan's gin mill on Ninth Avenue, where on Saturday night you received a piece of tough roast beef on a bun after buying several beers. Poetry was found on the walls of an IRT toilet. Literature was the comic page—the crude, moronic happenings of "Orphan Annie" and "Bringing Up Father" were a part of the Sunday morning ritual.

When we raided the chicken market on Forty-first Street and came running up the street, a protesting hen under each arm, the women leaning on pillows in the open windows greeted us with cheers. We had struck a blow at "them," those people who in a vague way represented bosses, landlords, banks, railroads, and the police. The market and the Central's yards were hit big around Christmas. We would stalk the provision cars for hours, waiting until they were pulled up to be unloaded for the slaughterhouses on Eleventh Avenue. Steers were too big, but more than once we loaded Train down with a sow while we scooped up the piglets. Then you should have heard the whoops and cries from the windows as we staggered up the block.

Someone would hurry over to Eighth Avenue and find Marny Smith, who had been a butcher in Dublin and who now worked as a porter in the gin mills. He was a little man gnarled as an old oak and possessed of the thickest brogue I had ever heard. He still had his set of butchering knives, each one carefully polished, set in a beautiful handmade wooden chest lined with faded velvet. In a few hours he would have the sow cleaned and quartered. He would take his chunk, the favored neighbors would get theirs, and we would feast on roast pork, fried pork, stuffed pork, and pickled pork from Christmas to New Year's Day.

This then was the Neighborhood and its people. Across the thousand years that separate me from those days, I can see how the monotonous existence of the dreary tenement flats, the backbreaking toil on the waterfront, the daily struggle for survival was marked by a numbing sameness that was in itself a way of hell. Joe and I recognized this and swore that someday we would leave it.

We never did.

2 THE PIER

I have always remembered the remarks Joe Gunnar made about the Neighborhood. Like the time he described us as white niggers born on the bottom rung of the ladder, in the worst of times, in the worst of places, where survival not triumph was important, where the cop was the accepted natural enemy and the Golden Rule was "Do unto others before they do it to you."

I was born there, Forty-sixth Street between Eighth and Ninth avenues. We called it the Neighborhood from the moment we could talk. Not Hell's Kitchen, that belongs to the Sunday Supplement writers. I spent all of my formative years in its dirty, drab streets and tenement flats where rats were so familiar we treated them as members of the family. In the summer the walls oozed sweat like a sick man's skin and became slabs of ice in the winter. By osmosis I absorbed its gypsy-camp mentality, fierce loyalties, bigotry, lawlessness, social indifference, and primitive philosophy.

Joe claimed the only way to beat the Neighborhood was by not letting it get in your way, by sighting on your goal, focusing sharply, and using every means to beat it. As you will see that's exactly what we did.

When I decided to tell this story of my life I vowed to myself it would be truth—all or nothing. I would not lie. I would not evade any questions. I would not expect mercy for myself or others, even those I loved very dearly. Delicacy and diplomacy would be cast aside. In brief, I would stand before a mirror and say, "I don't care a curse for you or your opinions, this is an honest man."

We must begin with that particular Saturday which I have always considered the most unforgettable day of my life. Why? Consider this: I met and fell in love with the most beautiful girl in the world, became the Devil's disciple, had my brains kicked out by a monstrous toad of a cop who was shacking up with the most luscious blond piece on the entire West Side, witnessed a beautiful young life snuffed out brutally and senselessly, then watched the walls of my own world cave in about me. It was like slow motion in one of those early de Mille biblical extravaganzas, when the temple collapses.

And before that day ended, I had left my capacity for hope on the chipped steps of a police station. For the rest of my years, at least in my mind, I would spit at the word *cop*.

It was that blazing summer of 1935; the temperatures are still in the record books. The heat wave began in June as though to guarantee our misery. By the time we had returned to school it had not rained for over two months. I can still recall how the heat rose from the streets, making things wavy, out of focus. It penetrated every foot of the Neighborhood; even the damp moldy cellars were hot, and the roof where Joe and I once flew our homers were acres of melting tar that clung to sneakers and clothes like obscene black mud.

It had been a memorable summer. One July morning a very formal letter from the Chancery Office was hand delivered to our flat. Joe and I had been at the pier all day and when we came home Aunt Clara, Mrs. Gunnar, and Tom were waiting on the stoop. Aunt Clara silently, proudly handed me the letter.

I can still feel the crisp, expensive paper, see the name

of the Chancery Office and its address in flowing copper-plate type, and my name:

Frank Howell, Senior Class,
St. Barnabas High School

I was so nervous I could barely open the stiff envelope. I had been selected as the representative of St. Barnabas High School senior class to take the Bishop Larkin Four Year Scholarship Examination for Fordham University.

I read it twice, then handed the letter to my aunt. I was so numb I couldn't speak. Since my first years as a freshman, when the notice had been tacked up on the bulletin board, I had struggled for this letter. Now at last it had arrived. No trumpets. No bands. Just a soggy towel under one arm, my aunt hugging me, Mrs. Gunnar kissing me, Tom pounding me on the back, and Joe pumping my hand.

"Okay. We start tonight," Tom said. "We're going to hit every goddam book I have upstairs. Thank God I saved all of them—"

"Tom! Watch your tongue," his mother said with a frown.

"Okay, Mom. Do we start tonight, Frank?"

"It's okay with me if it's okay with you, Tom."

"I promised you all four years ago that Frank would take it if I had to saw off the top of his head and pour the stuff in," Tom said. "Tonight we start sawing!"

Three nights a week and every Saturday morning, either in our flat or the Gunnar flat across the hall, Tom and I reviewed the subjects for the examination which he had won four years before.

That summer Tom not only tutored me for the exam but lectured me on labor. Since the previous fall he had been attending an intensive course in labor held at Xavier Labor School and when the nights became so hot we were glued to the kitchen chairs, he transferred our classroom to the roof. Stripped to shorts we stretched out on layers of newspapers spread on the still-warm tar, and I listened to his enthusiastic plans of how he intended to invade and organize the world of municipal labor and its allied unions.

"There's a great old Jebbie down at Xavier," he said. "If only a few of these jerks around here listened to him they could take over any union . . ."

"How can you do that, Tom?"

28

"It's not hard. First of all you have to know the people you're organizing; if you don't know them firsthand it's a waste of time. Then you have to lay out plans, just as if you were planning for war . . ."

"For war? Organizing a union?"

"Advance formulation of contingency plans for invasions," he intoned in a deep voice. "You should hear this old guy, Frank. He sounds like Bismarck."

"What exactly do you do to organize a big group?"

"You detail potential deployment of forces and supply," he said with a grin.

"What the hell is that?"

He laughed but then he became serious, and detailed for me how to organize a union, first to know the people and set the goal, disseminate the propaganda—"the courtship of labor," as he put it—then the big push.

I knew labor was Tom's big interest and I listened politely but at the time I was more interested in radical fractions.

One night I sensed a change: he was thoughtful and grave, completely different from the usual effervescent, humorous, and entertaining personality I knew. I had been looking for him all that afternoon and I kidded him about a mysterious Bronx girl we knew he had been taking to the Fordham dances.

"You see how it goes, Tom? Take them out a few times and they start leading you around by the nose. What did she do—keep you in after school?"

I immediately sensed my try at humor had fallen flat.

"I cut my late classes today," he said shortly.

"What's up, Tom?"

"I took my mother out to the cemetery today . . . it's the tenth anniversary . . ."

I should have known; that morning my aunt's note on the kitchen table said simply she had gone to early Mass with Mrs. Gunnar before she went to the library.

"For the first time in years my mother talked a lot about my father. Oh, we talked about him when I was in high school, but never like today. I know what you're thinking: he was just a drunken bum. He was that twice over. But he was still one hell of a union leader, Frank. Did you ever see him in action?"

The scene came back to me. Joe and I must have been in the first or second grade when someone in the schoolyard said there was a big fight on the piers. To the

Neighborhood the word "fight" was as electrifying as free turkeys on Thanksgiving; we all ran like a flock of frightened does across Tenth and Eleventh avenues, dodging trucks and screeching cars until, breathless and full of anticipation, we reached the waterfront.

A huge crowd of dockwallopers was gathered about the entrance to one pier. Standing on a baggage four-wheeler was Joe's father. I didn't know what he was talking about; words weren't important, only the absolute fire in his voice. There were great bells, the clash of iron on iron and the vicious snap of a bullwhip over our heads in that voice. When he finished a roar went up and Andy Gunnar jumped down and, holding high an American flag, led his cheering mob down the wide, cobbled waterfront street, gathering men like a snowball pummeling down a slope until they overflowed onto the sidewalks. As we followed I could see them cursing, jeering, brandishing their ugly cargo hooks or waving their fists to people looking out the windows of the shipping offices.

We followed the mob to Twenty-eighth Street, where Gunnar vanished inside one of the larger buildings while his shouting followers circled the block.

When I recalled this scene to Tom he nodded. "That was probably about contract time. He would wait until the shippers held a meeting in Chelsea, then stage a walkout at one of the big piers and bring the mob to their front door. On the way down he had his shop stewards scoop up anybody; bums, shenangoes, peddlers, even hot dog men. Once he jammed the elevators and made the shippers walk down. He and his officers were waiting on the third floor. They virtually kidnapped the shippers and pushed them into an empty office where they argued and cursed each other for hours. But they ironed out a contract and got drunk together after signing it . . ."

Talking about his father led Tom to the subject of labor. We lay back on the layers of newspapers, hands clasped behind our heads, the familiar noises of the Neighborhood drifting up to us: the deaf old Swede who always raised the volume on his aged Atwater Kent so high that the Wednesday night Sousa Marine Corps Band Concert from Washington could be heard in Hoboken; shrilling kids in soggy underwear darting in and out of the erratic spray made by slapping a crate against the open hydrant; the battling O'Malleys—my aunt scornfully called them "the drinking people"—hurling plates at each other while

30

their kids huddled under the beds; the old German woman who wore a tiny gold watch on her bosom and who played "The Firefly" over and over until the super banged on the pipes with a hammer.

"The way I see it, Frank," he said softly, "labor can get us out of this."

"How do you mean?"

"I talked to that old Jesuit. He thought it was a great idea to specialize in labor after I get my law degree."

"You mean on the waterfront?"

He gave me a grunt of disgust. "Hell no! I'm not interested in those old racket unions run by hoods and gunmen! I want to get into something new, something fresh . . ."

"Like what, for example?"

He hesitated. "If you laugh I'll kick your teeth in—"

"I promise not to."

"I want to get into the municipal setup, municipal employees who supply the city's services—sanitation, firemen—and cops."

Despite my promise, I couldn't keep from laughing.

"Cops! You want to unionize cops, Tom? A bunch of bastards like those up in the Sixteenth on Forty-seventh Street? You're kidding?"

"No, I'm not," he said calmly. "I hit the old Jebbie with the idea and we discussed it at length. He thinks it has excellent possibilities. After I finish my midterm finals, I'm going to start looking into it." He turned to me. "Let me try to explain the way I see it, Frank, and if you laugh—"

"I'll bite my tongue. Okay?"

"See that you do. First of all let's examine the physical structure of the police department. It now has eighteen thousand cops in the five boroughs. An ordinary patrolman gets three grand a year, a sergeant, thirty-five hundred, a lieutenant four, and a captain five. That's not a bad paycheck to be bringing home these days. However, the wait for appointment to the force is long; the average is about seven years before they select anyone from the civil service list. But it won't be always like that. The city is growing, Frank! And the bigger it gets, the more cops will be needed and the more services the city will have to provide. Now is the time to get a union—not a coffee and cake fraternal organization but a real honest-to-God union—started among these people. Cops. Sanitation, municipal workers. But mostly cops. Maybe I'll have some other ideas when I get my degree, but right now I think that's what I want to do."

"Tom Gunnar, King of the Cops."

"No, I'm serious, Frank. In ten, fifteen years or more this department could be a major political weapon. You must consider the politicians who run this city. They're mostly blockhead Irish hacks who don't judge their actions by ethical standards—only by the test of practicability. To these bastards politics is a fistful of power that belongs to the strongest guy in the clubhouse. Whoever controls the police controls a lot of politics."

He paused. "My idea is not to use this power for any personal reason but to use it for the good of the public."

He rolled over on his side, his face a white, intense blur in the faint starlight.

"Do you know what that could mean, Frank? To control eighteen thousand cops in the largest city in the world? The chowderhead politicians would genuflect every time they heard your name."

He threw back his head and laughed loudly.

"And can you imagine their faces when they find it can't be bought. That I would spit in their stupid faces if they tried anything!"

"Okay, Tom, garbage men I can see, but cops? They're bastards! You know that. Christ, they fanned your ass enough times in the Central's yards!"

"More times than I care to remember," he said fervently. "But what the hell, Frank, that's their job. We were stealing and we knew that if we were caught we got a red ass. That's the way the game has always been played in the Neighborhood."

"No matter how you cut it, Tom, cops stink. They steal shoes from a blind man."

"Maybe I have better reason than most people to believe there are some cops that would," he said bitterly. "But I would be a fool to indict all eighteen thousand cops. You just can't do that, Frank. It doesn't make sense."

"Name an honest cop," I said jokingly.

"Do you remember Supercop?"

"The guy who was always chasing us?"

"His name is Elliot. He's tough but straight as an arrow. That's why the Neighborhood hated him; they couldn't buy him. When that old Dutchman who owned the rendering plant on Tenth Avenue offered him a bribe

32

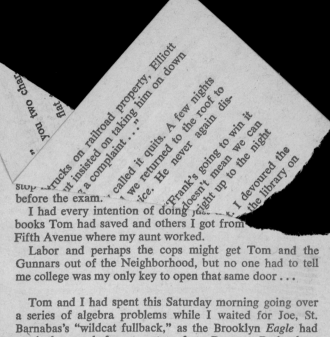

you two char...

...stop trucks on railroad property, Elliott
...ut insisted on taking him on down
...a complaint..." ...called it quits. A few nights
...ice. we returned to the roof to
...ice. He never again dis-
...Frank's going to win it
...doesn't mean we can
...night up to the night
...I devoured the
...the library on

before the exam.

I had every intention of doing ju... ...t. ...
books Tom had saved and others I got from
Fifth Avenue where my aunt worked.

Labor and perhaps the cops might get Tom and the
Gunnars out of the Neighborhood, but no one had to tell
me college was my only key to open that same door . . .

Tom and I had spent this Saturday morning going over
a series of algebra problems while I waited for Joe, St.
Barnabas's "wildcat fullback," as the Brooklyn *Eagle* had
put it the year before, to return from Prospect Park where
the team was practicing.

When he whistled I looked out the front-room window
of the Gunnar flat. There he was in the street, bag in
one hand and cleats hung over his shoulder.

"How do we look?" I shouted.

"We'll take the county this year," he shouted back. "I'm
beat. Tell my mother I'm goin' over to the pier. Everybody's there. You comin', Frank?"

"I'll be over in a little while," I told him. He waved,
threw his gear into the vestibule and ran toward the river.

"You want to knock off now, Frank?" Tom asked.

"Let's finish these problems," I said, "then we can call it
a day. How about coming over to the pier and cooling off,
Tom?"

"I have something more important uptown," he said
and winked. "She's a hell of a lot prettier than a bunch of
bare-assed kids jumping off a dock."

We finished the last of the problems which Tom said he
had found hardest in the test, and I packed up my books.

"Anything you want me to tell Joe?"

"Yeah. Tell him I want to eat early. I have a date.
What are you kids going to do tonight?"

33

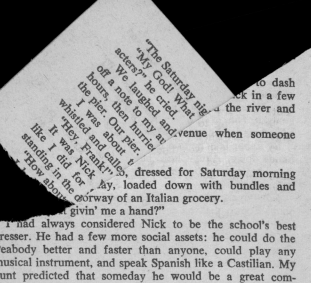

to dash

...ck in a few

the river and

venue when someone

, dressed for Saturday morning

ay, loaded down with bundles and

oorway of an Italian grocery.

givin' me a hand?"

I had always considered Nick to be the school's best dresser. He had a few more social assets: he could do the Peabody better and faster than anyone, could play any musical instrument, and speak Spanish like a Castilian. My aunt predicted that someday he would be a great composer but Joe always told him he would become a one-man band playing spick and wop tunes in backyards for nickels.

When I grabbed some of his bags I realized I hadn't seen him on the pier for most of the summer. Since school opened our only meetings had been brief encounters in the halls between classes.

"Where have you been, Nick?"

"I formed a combo and we've been doin' Irish weddin's on Amsterdam Avenue. Tell me, why the hell do micks drink so much?"

"To pay the rent for the wop speaks—like your old man's . . ."

"No more. Not since he opened the Shadow Box on Forty-fourth Street. Have you seen it?"

"Yeah. Joe and I passed it during the summer. Does your old man own it by himself?"

"He's got some other guy in with him. Do you know who was there the other night—Jean Harlow!"

"Stop bullshitting me, Nick."

"I swear it, Frank, I even got her autograph on her picture. What a piece! . . . When are you gonna take the exam for the scholarship, Frank?"

"In October."

"You got it made. It's a cinch!"

"Don't kid yourself, Nick. There are a lot of kids and only one scholarship. Tom's helping me . . ."

"There's a brain for you!"

"Do you know what he's been doing since last fall?"

"The last time I saw Tom he said he was gonna try for Fordham Law . . ."

"He's going to do that but he's been going down to Xavier one night a week—"

"Why the hell would he want to go down there?"

"He attended a labor school some Jebbie started. He says he likes labor and wants to become a labor attorney."

"Tell Tom to stop playin' with himself, Frank. When he hangs out his shingle I'll bring him to my old man and make him give Tom all his business. Hey, maybe you can go into law with him and you guys can open an office right here in the Neighborhood! How about that? Can you imagine all the creeps runnin' to you guys when they get in trouble?"

"You're smoking hop, Nick. How about coming over to the pier?"

"I'd like to Frank, but I can't."

"We haven't seen you all summer! What's so important?"

"We gotta practice. I've been workin' like hell all summer to buy a fiddle that's out of pawn on Eighth Avenue. It's a beauty! It was pawned by some guy who played in a symphony orchestra."

"How much to you need?"

"Another twenty-five."

"Wow! That's a lot of coin! How many in the combo?"

"Two besides me. Tenor sax and drums. I play the fiddle and the piano. We're not good but we're loud. That's all those Irish bastards want. Play the Peabody and "Tiger Rag" all night."

At the beginning of the summer Nick's family had moved from Ninth Avenue to a luxury apartment on West Fifty-seventh Street between Eighth and Ninth. Their move from poverty to affluence appeared to be linked in some mysterious way to the Shadow Box.

I can still recall how impressed I was by the canopy, the elevator man, a ferret of a man dressed like a guardsman of the King's Own, the lavish mirrored lobby, and the elevator that opened into the apartment. I had been born and raised in a railroad flat and the Valentino apartment seemed as huge as Grand Central's waiting room. Yet despite my awe I thought the furnishings, while obviously expensive, were gaudy. There was a large, bland landscape with misty mountains in an elaborate gold frame, tall silk lampshades, portieres of floor-length beads, simpering marble angels, and heavy, cumbersome furniture. There was also an aroma of Italian cooking, as pungent as in any Guinea Alley flat.

Nick's mother, a slender, attractive woman, whom I had seen many times as a kid in grammar school when I had served the six o'clock daily Mass, pressed on me a small glass of wine and a plate of Italian pastries. I was nibbling at a cake when I sensed someone studying me. I turned to look into the face of a pretty girl slightly younger than myself. She had glossy shoulder-length black hair and warm dark eyes. Even the ugly blue skirt and blouse with the yellow school insignia couldn't hide the perfect legs and superb breasts. There was no question that this was the most exciting girl I had ever seen.

"Remember my sister, Lucina, Frank?" Nick asked. "We still call her Chena. She's been goin' to St. Aedan's up in New Rochelle since the sixth grade. You remember Frank Howell don't you, Chena? I told you he's going to take the Bishop Larkin Scholarship exam . . ."

"Of course I know Frank," Chena said warmly. "Wasn't I his princess?"

Suddenly I remembered. The kid in pigtails Nick always had to mind when we were in grammar school and wanted to play basketball. To keep her quiet I would elaborately fold my jacket, whisper that she was my princess and the jacket was actually a throne and no one else was allowed to sit on it. She never left the corner of the schoolyard until the streetlights came on and we ended our eternal game of twenty-one.

"So that's why you never ran home and told Mama I left you in the street while I played basketball," Nick said with a grin.

"I remember once Frank even came over and gave me some of his soda. The only thing you ever gave me was a belt to keep quiet." She said with mock gravity, "Nicky was a wicked brother, Frank."

"I should have given you more belts," Nick told her. His smiling mother eagerly offered me more cookies.

"You had better eat 'em, Frank, or my mother will

worry all night she did somethin' you didn't like," Nick warned me.

I made a great show of selecting two more, but firmly refused another glass of the sweet but powerful wine.

"Nicky was telling my father the other night that you're the smartest boy in St. Barnabas, Frank," Chena said.

I felt my face grow red. The crumbs of the fragile cake were suddenly cement fragments and hard to swallow.

"I know one thing, Frank, if they give out a scholarship for Spanish, Nicky will get it. . . . It drives my father crazy. He speaks it better than Italian."

"He's been president of the Spanish Club for so long they didn't even have elections," I told her. "I have always wondered why?"

"What did you expect, Frank? There were always good-looking heads in that club," Nicky said with a grin.

We laughed at this, and his puzzled mother asked a question in Italian. Nick answered and they spoke rapidly for a moment.

"My mother said instead of trying to be a *Spagnuolo* I should hang around with you and get some real brains," he explained.

"Maybe you should," an angry voice said behind me.

I turned to face Nick's father, Gus, who had stepped off the elevator. Behind him was a short barrel of a man with a dark oval face and a broad smile for Nick. Cold black eyes flickered over me for only an instant but I felt my measure had been taken.

With his anarchist's smile he looked like an Italian fruit store owner who sold bombs instead of cabbages.

"Is this the kid you told us about?" Gus Valentino asked his son. He smelled of scotch, cigarettes, and expensive shaving lotion.

"This is Frank Howell, Pop," Nick said. "Frank this is my father and Pepe."

"Uncle Pepe," the little man said, nodding at me.

"Uncle Pepe who's not our uncle," Chena said.

"Who took you to the museums and the parks when you were a little girl, eh, Chena?" Pepe asked with a show of mock indignation.

"Uncle Pepe," she said with a smile.

"Nobody else wanted to go, Pepe," Nicky said laughing.

"*Fesso!* You wanted to see Tom Mix." He turned to me and put out his hand. His grip was unusually strong for a

37

small man and, despite his smile, I had the curious feeling he was extraordinarily dangerous.

"You are the smart one, no?"

"The smartest in the school, Pepe," Nick said. "He's gonna win a scholarship to college."

"Bravo!" Pepe said. "And you, Chena?"

"I'm going to New Jersey to college. It's a woman's college."

"How do you like these crazy kids of mine?" Gus asked. "My son only wants to speak like a spick and play the fiddle. The girl wants to go to college. *Ecco!* I tell her, get married—*fare tanto bambini*—have lots of kids like your mother and grandmother. Right, Pepe?"

The little man shrugged. "Not all women, Duchino. Some are smarter than men." He linked his arm with Chena's. She was smiling, but I sensed that almost involuntarily she had stiffened slightly at his touch.

"None of 'em have to be very smart to be smarter than my son," Gus growled. He said to me, "Hey, kid, why don't you take him in hand? Teach him somethin'."

"What's the matter with Nicky, Duchino?" Pepe asked mildly. "He's a smart boy!" He turned to me. "What do you say, *giovinotto*?"

"Nick is as smart as anyone in the school," I said loyally.

"Yeah," his father said dryly. "He hasn't opened a book since school started." He asked his son, "Where are you goin' now?"

"Uptown," Nicky said tersely.

"Uptown! Swimmin' in the river! What the hell's goin' on?" his father exploded. "School's just started, where's the books? What about the algebra? The nuns say you can't add two and two. I want you to go to college to be a lawyer, to be a doctor, not some dumb guinea who has to break his back with a pick and shovel. You be a lawyer, you can be a judge! All you need in this town is connections." He jabbed his finger at his chest. "And I got 'em!" He gave me a look of disgust. "He wants to be a goddam fiddler. What do you think of that, kid?"

"I want to play the violin, Pop," Nick said quietly. "Is there any crime in that?"

"Before I see you playin' a fiddle for a livin' I'll break both your arms," his father shouted. "Do I want a *zìngara* for a son! A *saltabanco*?"

He brushed past his wife, through the bead portieres,

38

and vanished into another room. Pepe looked at Nick, shrugged, and followed Valentino. For a few seconds the click of the beads was the only sound in the room.

"He's got his heart on you going to college, Nicky," his sister said. "Why do you have to get him so mad?"

"I don't want him to get mad," Nick protested. "All I said was I wanted to play the violin."

"You know how that sets him off. Do you want help with algebra tonight?"

"Damn algebra," Nick shouted. He savagely jabbed the elevator button. "Who needs it?"

His mother said something in rapid-fire Italian and Chena nodded and said, "Okay, Mom, okay.... My mother said she's having a big dinner tonight and why don't you stay?" she explained to me.

"I can't tonight," I said, wondering why I was lying.

"Another time?" she asked smiling.

"I'd love to."

"My mother thinks food can cure anything," Nick explained as the elevator slid open.

We stepped inside and I waved to Chena and her mother as the door closed.

As we descended Nick said bitterly, "He keeps telling me I have to go to college. I don't want to go to college. I don't like books and books don't like me. I love music. Do you know old man Lineburger, the choirmaster? He told me he was sure he could get me into Juilliard. One day he went over to the club to talk to my father. Pop almost threw the old man out on his ass. I begged him to buy me that fiddle in the hockshop. I told him I'd do anything, even wash the goddam dishes in the club. But no, all he did was rant like a madman that he'd rather buy me a tin cup and a monkey. But I'm gonna buy that fiddle in Simpson's if it's the last thing I do! I swear it, Frank."

"Aw, he'll come around one of these days, Nick ..."

"You don't know Sicilians. When the old man tells you to do somethin' you do it. Or else."

"How about your mother?"

"She did her best. She wants me to go to Juilliard. She saw Lineburger. He gave her a lot of crap how I had talent and stuff like that. But she can't get anywhere with my old man. You have to be Italian to understand, Frank. What the father says goes. He's the law." He added bitterly, "*Zingara*—a gypsy—*saltabanco*—a bum that's all he calls me!"

To change the subject, I asked him about the short man he had called Uncle Pepe.

"He's not really our uncle," he explained. "We've been callin' him that since we were little kids. His people and my grandparents came from the same village in Sicily. After his mother died and his father was killed by a train on Eleventh Avenue my grandmother took him in. He and my father were raised together. He doesn't look like a tough guy, does he?"

"No, he doesn't."

"Well he is," Nick hesitated. "For crissakes don't ever repeat this but Pepe did time in Sing Sing many years ago."

"For what?"

"Do you remember when my old man ran the speak on Forty-fourth Street?"

I nodded. Who didn't remember that in the Neighborhood?

"Well one night two guys stuck up the joint. Pepe came in and found them workin' my father over with a little baseball bat he used to break ice. He's supposed to have strangled them both." He held up his hands. "One hand on each throat. How do you like that? Then he and my father dumped the guys out on Tenth Avenue."

"Did they get caught?"

"A couple of Micks that had speaks hated my father's guts because he was gettin' all the business. So they turned him in. The cops couldn't get Pepe for the killin' of the stickup men but they found the booze and a gun in the place. Pepe took the rap and went up the river. My old man kept the speak runnin'. When he got enough dough he paid to get Pepe out on parole. He also had to cough up a lot for the cops. He hates their guts. I heard him tell my mother they're always over at the club with their hands out."

"That little guy killed two stickup men with his hands!"

"You better believe it. He's as strong as a bull."

"What does he do now?"

"He's part owner of the club with my old man. He also owns an art gallery on Madison Avenue."

"An art gallery!"

Nick laughed. "It does sound funny but Chena says he knows a hell of a lot about art. She says he learned all about it when he was in the can."

40

"Did he attend some mail order art course or something like that?"

"No. His cellmate was a forger and a painter. He was an old guy and sick; Pepe used to take care of him. Chena says that every night he would give Pepe a lecture on art and teach him how to draw."

"Is Chena his favorite?"

"He can't do enough for her. When we were kids he was always takin' us to museums and art galleries on Sunday afternoons. I used to squawk like hell. I wanted to see Tom Mix."

I don't know why but it blurted out. "I think Chena's afraid of Pepe, Nick."

He turned to me, a startled look on his face. "For crissakes, how did you know that?"

"I don't know—I just guessed. Why, is she?"

"Well, not exactly. When we were little kids, Chena really liked him a lot. But after she got into high school she started to make excuses not to go out with us. Pepe didn't want to be bothered with me. I just kept askin' him to buy me ice cream or take me to the movies but Chena was interested and would listen to him. After a while we stopped goin'. One day Chena told me she was afraid of him . . ."

"Why, did she say?"

"Pepe drags us all over the city for years, then suddenly she's afraid of him." He shrugged. "Who knows dames, Frank?"

"How about you?"

"He treats me fine but he's always sayin' I need more muscle." He held up his fist. "You know—hard-guy stuff."

We stood on the sidewalk for a few moments in an awkward silence. I wondered if Nick regretted revealing so many of his family confidences to me. In all the years I had known him he had never spoken of this little man Pepe.

"Do you want to walk over to the pier, Nick? All the guys are there."

"I have to see my combo up on Columbus Avenue. Maybe I'll see you later."

"Want me to walk you up there?"

"No. No, thanks, Frank," he said hurriedly. "It's sorta personal. Okay?"

"Sure. I'll see you later."

As we started across the street, there was a screech of

brakes. We turned. A cab had narrowly missed a buxom peroxide blonde who apparently had been crossing the street with a small black poodle. As she bent down to pick up the dog the cabbie leaned out his window and made a loud sucking sound. The blonde cursed him with the fluency and originality of a dockwalloper. She would be gone in fat within a few years but in the tight pink sweater and skirt she had a startling figure.

She passed us in a swirl of silk, indignation, heady perfume, and bouncing breasts.

"Wow!" I said. "How would you like a piece of that?"

"That's that jerky Suzy Miller in Five B," Nick said. "Hey do you remember Kidneyfeet?"

"The big dick from West Forty-seventh Street? The guy with the feet like catchers' gloves?"

"That's the one. Believe it or not he's bangin' that dame. He comes here twice a week, Tuesday and Thursday when he's workin' the late tour. I rode up with him once in the elevator. He looks like a mean bastard."

I suddenly remembered the huge detective who had eyes the color of limes moving in and out of the dappled shadows of the Ninth Avenue el as he walked through the Neighborhood.

"Hennessy hates the Neighborhood," Nick said suddenly.

"What do you mean?"

"My old man says he hates it like poison. Did you ever hear the story about Hennessy and Joe's father?"

"Something about Hennessy's brother? All I know is what my aunt told me. She said there was some kind of trouble—"

"Trouble! Christ, and how! I was a little kid when I heard my old man tellin' my mother the story. Hennessy's younger brother was a cop in Forty-seventh Street. One Sunday mornin' a bunch of longshoremen were raisin' hell outside a gin mill on Ninth Avenue. Hennessy's brother came along and told them to break it up. One guy slugged him, then the others piled on. After they beat the hell out of him with his club they threw him through a plate glass window. They all scrammed before the cops came. He was in the hospital for a long time, but the beatin' turned him into an idiot. He died a few years later in a nut house. Everyone in the Neighborhood knew Joe's father was one of the guys, but nobody squealed. They yanked him in but he had an alibi. Hennessy swore he'd get who did it but he never did. But after that anybody from the Neighborhood who got yanked into Forty-seventh Street—look out!

"If Hennessy was around he would make sure to walk all over the guy they pinched. Did Joe ever say anythin', Frank?"

"Only once."

"When was that?"

"A long time ago, when we were kids . . ."

"What did he say?"

"He said he hated Hennessy like poison, but at the time I didn't ask him why—we were running up Ninth Avenue . . ."

For some reason the incident had always remained with me. We were in grammar school and on the way home when we stood on a corner to watch two radio car cops battle a belligerent drunk. It was a commonplace sight in the Neighborhood, and of course we were cheering the drunk when I became aware of the shadow next to me. When I looked up Hennessy towered over us. I was tongue tied. This was the closest I had ever been to the cop whose look was as menacing as the clubs of the other beat policemen.

"You Gunnar's kid?" he asked Joe in a surprisingly soft voice.

I was scared but Joe was defiant.

"Yeah. Why?"

Hennessy studied him for a moment, then, without answering, walked to the radio car whose back seat now held the bloody, subdued drunk.

To my horror Joe began chanting, "Kidneyfeet . . . Kidneyfeet . . ." Then we both ran up Ninth Avenue.

"He doesn't scare me," Joe panted.

"How did he know you, Joe?"

"He knows me," he said fiercely, "and he knows Tom. I hate that son of a bitch like poison!"

"A couple of years ago I met Tom on Broadway when he was comin' home from a basketball game," Nick went on. "We saw Hennessy standin' outside a restaurant. Rather than pass him Tom walked across the street. When I asked him why he just shrugged."

I suddenly remembered what Tom had said about having more reasons than most for hating cops . . .

"Tom and I were talking only the other day about that other cop who worked the Neighborhood . . ."

"Supercop? Who was always tryin' to beat our ass when we were playin' stickball?"

"That's the guy. Elliot. Wasn't he up at the Sixteenth with Hennessy?"

"Yeah. But they weren't buddies. All the cops hated Elliot. My old man said he was so honest they called him St. Peter."

"Tom said he pulled in a guy who offered him a bribe."

"That guy would pull in his old lady! Remember when he had the beat on Ninth Avenue and gave all the cart-men in Paddy's Market tickets for blockin' the sidewalk and they all went up to Forty-seventh Street?"

"Joe and I were coming out of school when we saw them marching up the avenue . . ."

"Supercop didn't back down. He just told the sergeant they were blockin' the sidewalk so he gave them tickets. He made everyone go to court."

"I remember his picture on page one of the News when he killed those two guys on Fifth Avenue after they knocked off that airlines office. Remember that, Nick?"

"Do I? What a picture! Supercop, bloody as a stuck pig, over that guy on the sidewalk, puttin' handcuffs on him. He always was a gutsy guy."

"I haven't seen him around, have you?"

"Last summer the woman in the olive oil store told my mother Supercop's a detective and he's goin' to college at night. How do you like that? A cop goin' to college!"

He nudged me. I turned to see that marvelous Suzy come bouncing out. She gave us a smile and waved delicately at a cab. It slammed to a stop and the driver quickly swung open the rear door. Suzy, breasts and all, hopped in. The cabdriver saw us watching and whistled softly to himself.

Nicky grunted. "What a piece!"

"I can't believe that big fat slob Hennessy is banging her."

"Sully the elevator operator told me. He'll screw any-thin'. One night she was drunk and he went out and got her a pint after hours. When he brought it back she climbed all over him. He told me he left her apartment just before the super came on duty in the mornin'."

"Is Hennessy married?"

"Suzy told Sully he is. She said she's scared to hell of Hennessy's wife who is a nut. When Kidneyfeet was work-in' at headquarters his wife went down there with one of

44

his service revolvers and had a fight with a policewoman she said was goin' out with her husband. Hennessy got in a lot of trouble over that. Sully said that's why he was sent back to Forty-seventh Street."

Nick pointed across the street to a restaurant with a phony brick front and a sign that boasted of its French cuisine.

"Sully says the guy who owns that place also gets a piece of Suzy on the weekends, and"—he pointed to an Italian restaurant down the street—"the wop in there goes up to see her on Monday. Sully says he's just waitin' for the time when they all get their days mixed up."

The elevator door opened and the operator sauntered out into the lobby. When Nick waved to him he joined us on the sidewalk.

"How did you kids like that?" he asked.

"Sully, this is my friend Frank," Nick said. "I was just tellin' him about Suzy."

Sully looked up and down the street. "Hey, don't you kids repeat any of that!"

"Don't worry," Nick said. "You gonna get your end wet tonight, Sully?"

Sully took off his braided hat and carefully ran a hand along the sleek side of his head.

"She just told me she wants a pint tonight," he said with a leer. "I bring up the pint, then when she has a bun on she rings the bell." He made a quick, stabbing motion with his finger. "Three sharp rings. Then I know she's ready for a party."

"Who runs the elevator?" I asked.

"Johnny the night man lives in a fleabag on Eighth Avenue. I call him up and he comes over early. Suzy gives me a buck and I give it to the old guy." He winked again. "An' everybody's happy."

The buzzer rang. "Let 'em wait," he mumbled. "I got only one trouble with that broad. You can't satisfy her."

The buzzer sounded impatient. Sully cursed, then turned away. "I gotta go. I'll see ya."

As he turned away Nick said, "Hey, Sully, tell Frank what will happen if that crazy cop's wife ever catches him in the saddle."

Sully shaped his thumb and forefinger into a pistol and pointed it at his head.

"Suzy says she's a nut—a real nut," he whispered. "If she ever catches that big fat ass . . ." He made clicking

45

noises and cocked his thumb. "She'll kill him! Suzy says she wants to dump him but she's afraid. I gotta go. . . . I'll see ya."

As we waited for the traffic light to change I couldn't get out of my head the picture of Hennessy's screaming harridan wife armed with one of his service revolvers, joined by the explosive Italian restaurant owner and the excitable Frenchman, all rushing together into Suzy's apartment as the huge Hennessy sprawled on the bed with his peroxide love.

When I described the scene to Nick, we doubled up with laughter. We crossed the avenue, slapping each other on the back as we garnished the imaginary scene in Suzy's bedroom.

"Well, I'll see you later, Frank," Nick said with a grin. "Maybe in Suzy's boudoir."

"Tell Sully to fix us up." As he turned away I raised my voice. "Going to the dance tonight?"

He hesitated and the smile on his face faded. "Maybe I'll see you there. Okay?" He waved and hurried up the street.

For a moment I thought it was strange; Nick had always been the spark plug of the dance committee, arranging the music and helping decorate the gym. An excellent dancer, he was a constant favorite with the girls. I suddenly recalled that this was the first year he hadn't tried to con us into helping us with the decorations or hadn't even mentioned the first big dance.

But neither the delicious scenes of Kidneyfeet's complicated love life nor Nicky's unusual reluctance to attend the Saturday night dance occupied my thoughts as I turned to the river.

Only Chena. My princess.

On that Saturday we had opened the pier to our ancient enemies, the Shags from Chelsea. The Shags were invited only on special occasions: to provide a place for a gang-bang when one of their members could persuade a girl to share her favors wholesale, or, more importantly, for a crap game when we heard rumors the Shags had money from stealing lead or fencing a box of hams or a case of whiskey they had stolen from a pier. Stealing from the Gimp's territory could not only be dangerous but fatal. The Shags couldn't invade the Central's yards; that was our undisputed territory, won after a bloody war that reached back to my days in the fifth grade, so they raided the waterfront. Loot from the piers was lucrative, and this Saturday they had arrived, whooping, yelling, and waving money as they raced up the pier.

When I arrived Spider was finishing a detailed account of how he had met and conquered the new girl who had moved into the Neighborhood—two layers of newspapers on top of the coal in his cellar had been sufficient, he explained—and the important business of the morning, the crap game, was started.

For as long as I could remember there had always been crap games, Put 'n' Take, poker, Twenty-One, Banker 'n' Broker—even just tossing pennies in the Neighborhood. We played in doorways, cellars, on roofs, but mostly on the pier.

Joe and I, Spider, and Train had a long-established partnership; win or lose, we always kept ten dollars for a stake stashed away in a hole behind the boiler in our cellar. The grimy bills were at Joe's side when I arrived. After a fast dip I joined him under the stolen strip of canvas we used as a canopy; he handled the dice, I took care of the field, Spider was the money changer, Train was the bouncer. Off to one side of the pot was a pile of Wings—six for a nickel, with four wooden matches. The accepted ritual was for someone to start a smoke and pass it around. After numerous puffs it became soggy, unmanageable, and very unsanitary. But this was 1935, and germs weren't considered important in the Neighborhood, especially on the pier.

For all of us, gambling was a serious, monosyllabic business, marked only by usual street-kid obscenity, bawdy comments on Train's awesome member, the bright red pubic hair of one of the Shags, gleeful howls if a pot was raked in, or anguished moans if a player crapped out.

The game went on until the sun slid down behind the Palisades, its copper light dripping from the roofs along the cliffs. Somewhere in Jersey a bell tolled, its measured solemnity coming to us faint and distant across the water. It reminded me of Tom's warning, and I told Joe. We all agreed on a few final rolls.

The Shags left behind a good part of the bills they had waved so defiantly as they ran up the pier; a revenge session was set for the following Saturday if the weather held. If not the game would take place in the rear of a Chelsea poolroom.

The four of us took a last dip, diving from the string-piece. After vainly trying to duck Train, we started out for the middle of the river. The tide was turning and the undertow was swift and dangerous, but we were all water rats who could swim to the Jersey side with ease. We reached the middle, then turned back. Once out of the swift current, we lay on our backs, faces up to the vivid, dying sky now stained by the rim of the copper-penny sun. We let ourselves drift back to the pier to cling to the mossy hawser, reluctant to leave the cool water, letting our bodies rise and fall with the movement of the tide. The heat was going, and now there was a whisper of a breeze coming across the water. Joe and I agreed: thus far it had been a perfect Saturday; the dance would make it complete.

We clambered up the hawser with Train and Spider behind us. While Joe and Spider divided the profits of the game, Train and I hid the canvas in the shed. We came out to see Joe and Spider facing each other over the neat piles of money. I froze to the planks when I realized Spider was holding a blunt-nosed revolver that appeared new.

"Look what this crazy guy has!" Joe said.

"Jeez, a rod!" Train said.

"Where the hell did you get it, Spider?" I asked.

"Over in the courthouse," Spider explained. "This one cop is a boozer, and every afternoon he comes down to the basement where we're painting the old record room and sleeps for a few hours. Half the time he don't know what he's doin'. Today, when I'm washin' up, I find his holster and gun on the floor and the cop snorin' away, so I put the rod in my overalls and walk out." He held out a handful of bullets. "I took some of these too. It's loaded."

"Let me see it," Joe said. When Spider handed him the gun he weighed it in his hand. It looked evil, dangerous.

"Keep it off the pier, Spider," I warned. "If a Mickey Mouse stops off here and gives us a frisk and finds that, we'll spend the winter indoors."

"Where will you keep it, Spider?" Joe asked.

"For now I'll keep it with our dough in your cellar. I even got some oiled rags so it won't get rusty."

"What are you going to do with it?"

I will never forget the way Spider cocked his head to one side and gave me that choirboy smile.

48

"Who knows, Frank?" he said. "Maybe some day one of us will need it."

We were somewhat subdued as we crossed Twelfth Avenue. There was none of the horseplay and exuberance that usually marked the end of an afternoon on the pier. Although the slight breeze now dulled the edge of the heat, the freshness seemed to have gone from the day.

A strange, hesitating sense of fear crawled over me. I could not understand it, but I instinctively knew it was connected with Spider's gun.

 ## SATURDAY NIGHT

The Saturday Night Dance at St. Barnabas was the big thing, the social apex for the teen-agers of the Neighborhood. The entrance fee which allowed you to stay until midnight when the end of the evening was signaled by the usual "Goodnight Ladies," was twenty-five cents.

The dances were held in St. Barnabas's shabby old gym with the collapsible chairs used for assembly piled up along the walls. The basketball backboards were tied to the ceiling and the art club's posters, usually heralding the current season—Halloween—Thanksgiving—Christmas—were pasted on the windows. The bands were nondescript but loud, and there was the globe in the ceiling that flashed off tiny colored lights and shadows as it slowly revolved. With a girl in your arms, the band playing "Stardust," the gentle shadows and lights caressing soft lips, cheeks, and perfumed hair—it was painfully romantic.

Joe and I had been going to the dances since freshman year and we looked forward to them; they were the peak of our week. There had always been the usual teen-age cliques, but this was senior year and we were kings of the floor; we could sweep any girl we wanted into a fast Lindy or furious, dipping Peabody.

One or two nuns usually fluttered about surrounded by

49

self-conscious freshmen or the girls who knew they would never be asked to dance, while our pastor, Whiskey John— Father John Feeny—hovered about the edges of the floor, sniffing for the whiskey or beer he had heard was being consumed by some of his students.

Whiskey and beer had always been at the dances; I had heard stories from my grammar school days. In freshman and sophomore years we first saw the pints in dark bottles or the cardboard containers of beer emptied by seniors behind the boiler room in the cellar. In junior year we bought our first bottle from a runty super on Ninth Avenue for a dollar. It was horrible stuff that took the enamel off your teeth. But there was a great ritual that accompanied the bottle. After you took the initial slug you usually held your tongue over the bottle's opening and put on a great show of staggering slightly for the shocked, but secretly delighted, girls who shared our evil as we whirled them about the floor.

Across the hall in the Gunnars' apartment, Joe was slicking back his hair when my aunt and I came into the kitchen.

"Ah, the two Romeos," Tom said. He was sitting at the table, the sports page spread out before him, a gaping hole in the page. Mrs. Gunnar came out of the bedroom holding up a clipping showing Tom in a basketball uniform, one arm stretching upward as he leaped for a basket.

"Tom's been elected captain of the team, Frank," she said proudly holding up the clipping. "He never even told us."

"Don't you know your son is a modest hero, Mom?" Joe said.

"Do you have any money, son?"

"Tom's gonna lend me a half," Joe said. "Right, Tom?"

Tom flipped him a half dollar. "When do I get paid?"

"Next week," Joe said. "Frank and I are gonna stack potatoes in Paddy's Market every Saturday after his exam."

"Where? At Fat Freddy's warehouse?" Tom asked.

"Yeah. How did you know?"

"Every kid in the Neighborhood has worked for Freddy Kenton stacking potatoes," Tom said. "What is he paying you?"

"Fifty cents a day."

Tom just shook his head. "I did it for half a buck ten years ago. That old thief must make a mint in the market.

Hey, Mom, doesn't Fat Freddy also work on the piers with the coopers?"

His mother sniffed. "He was always hanging around the piers, but your father never trusted him." She gave Joe an anxious look. "I don't like you working over in that warehouse, Joe—all those heavy bags. You and Frank might strain yourselves—"

Tom gave a loud hoot. "C'mon, Mom! These two kids are strong as bulls. Don't you know they're not little boys anymore?"

She looked affectionately at Tom. "You're all growing up. One of these days you'll be coming to tell me you're getting married."

"When this one gets to college I'll never see him," my aunt said sadly.

"Only a couple of weeks more before the exam," Tom warned me.

"I can't sleep nights thinking about it," my aunt said.

"Don't worry about a thing, Aunt Clara, Frank has it in the bag," Tom said. He gave me a wink. "Unless, of course, he suddenly gets a vocation and goes up to St. Andrew's . . ."

Joe slapped me on the back. "Father Frank! Maybe you can team up with Whiskey John!"

"Joe!" his mother said sharply. "Don't talk about a priest like that! He can't help the size of his nose." She said to my aunt, "Isn't it terrible, Clara, the way they talk about that poor man?"

"With a horn that size and color," Joe said solemnly, "I figger he puts away a quart a day."

"He doesn't drink," Tom said seriously. "He's a great guy—he really is. Maybe you don't know it but it wasn't basketball that got me into Fordham," Tom said grimly. "It was Father John who coached me for that exam. Just like I'm doing with you, Frank, bread cast on the waters . . ."

"He's a saint, that man," his mother said.

"He's not a saint, Mom," Tom explained patiently, "he's just a hardworking priest, with a run-down, bankrupt parish. One night he showed me the bills. I don't know how he does it. He must work miracles every month to keep the doors open."

"They're puttin' in a new boiler and paintin' the trim of the school," Joe pointed out. "We'll be hearin' about that for the next five years—"

"You won't hear about it," Tom said shortly.

"Why not, son?" his mother asked. "The poor man's beggin' every Sunday."

"Because all summer he's been going around with his hat in his hand to every businessman and store owner from Fifty-ninth Street to Times Square, that's why!"

"And he finally got up the dough?" Joe asked.

"He told me every dime."

"I can tell you how he can make a few bucks," Joe told his brother with a choirboy's innocence.

"You give me any crap, pal—"

"You just tell him to come over to the pier next Saturday with tomorrow's collection money and we'll let him in the game . . ."

"Seriously," Tom told us, after his mother and my aunt went across the hall, "don't give Father John any trouble. He's a great guy."

"How are we going to give him any trouble, Tom?" I asked.

"Don't hand me that sweet look, Frank. . . . I know there's boozing going on at the dances."

"Look who's talkin'!" Joe said indignantly. "Are you tryin' to tell us you never went down to the boiler room and took a swig?"

"I was stupid—just like you are," Tom said. "I'm warning both of you—don't get caught. Father John had had a lot of pressure from those cops up at Forty-seventh Street . . ."

"What about the cops?"

"He told me they wanted him to press charges against the kids who messed up the classrooms last spring and they got sore as hell when he refused. If a cop comes in and catches any of the kids drinking . . ."

"Don't worry, nobody will get caught," Joe said.

As we walked to Forty-fourth Street, I told Joe I had seen Nick that morning. "In Guinea Alley."

"Where the hell has he been all summer?"

"He has an orchestra. Two other guys and himself. They've been playing for Polack weddings and the Irish joints on Amsterdam Avenue."

"What's he knockin' his brains out for? His old man made a lot of money in that speak."

"He's tryin' to buy a violin . . ."

Joe looked at me. "A violin? What the hell does he want a violin for?"

"To play, I guess. He wants to become a violinist but his old man wants him to study law."

Joe grunted in disbelief. "A lawyer? I always thought his old man would take him in the place they have on Forty-fourth Street."

"The Shadow Box?"

"Yeah. They must be coinin' dough over there. I saw a picture in the *News* last week. There was a couple of Hollywood stars goin' in there."

"He took me up to his house on Fifty-seventh."

"Fancy?"

"The elevator opens into the apartment. I met his old man."

"Yeah, Tom said he heard Nick's old man is in with some mob. He's a tough dago."

"I also met his sister Chena. Remember her?"

"The kid with the pigtails?"

"She doesn't have any pigtails now. She's real pretty. Long black hair and big dark eyes—"

"Built?"

"Christ, I didn't undress her!"

"Wop dames get fat and old lookin' early," Joe said with an irritating air of authority on Italian women. "You can see 'em sittin' on the stoops in Guinea Alley. Spaghetti eaters."

Chena's no spaghetti eater, I told myself. In fact I had come to the conclusion she was the most attractive girl I had ever met ...

On the corner of Ninth and Forty-fifth we met Train and Spider.

"Do you know that jerky super makes the stuff while you wait?" Spider said. "Look at this!" He held the dark Golden Wedding bottle up against the streetlight and unscrewed the cap. A wisp of smoke slowly curled upward. "I asked the son of a bitch what he put into it and he said only the best ingredients. I bet he meant rubbin' alcohol!"

We passed the bottle around. The raw whiskey exploded in the pit of my stomach and sent tentacles of heat through my body.

"Whiskey John won't be around until late tonight. He's at a county meeting with the coach," Joe warned, "so the nuns will be all over the place. Watch it, Train! No fights and don't get too near the nuns so they can smell you. Understand?"

Train nodded.

When we arrived at the gym, Larry Krug and His Five Merrymakers had swung into a loud and uneven rendition of "The Music Goes Round and Round." The hall was dim—the slowly revolving ceiling globe splashing the walls and floor with dabs of red, yellow, green, and blue like a drunken painter waving a brush dipped into many cans.

"Let's grab one," Joe said. He selected a slender young girl in a cheerleader's sweater. The girl gave him a startled look, then let herself be swept out on the floor. I was searching for a familiar face when someone behind me said, "Is this the smartest boy in the school?"

I turned and looked into Chena's laughing face. A dark skirt, sweater, and a string of pearls had replaced the ugly school uniform. Flickers of colored light slowly moved across her face and were reflected in her dark eyes.

"Is this the prettiest girl at the dance?"

Even though the light was dim I knew she blushed.

"I didn't know you came to the dances," I said.

"This is my first time," she said. "I was supposed to meet Nicky here. Have you seen him?"

"No," I said. "He told me this morning he might come. Care to Peabody, Chena?"

She nodded and we went out on the floor to join the circle of dipping, fast-moving dancers. I was suddenly conscious of her perfume and the smooth, warm skin of her arms. When I whirled her about, the edge of my hand brushed her firm full breast and I could feel the sweat trickling down from under my arm. She was a skillful, graceful dancer and we finished the set with an elaborate flourish that left us both laughing. I got Chena a Coke and we joined Joe and the others on one of the benches.

As the evening passed, Chena and I talked about a thousand inane things, from the eccentricities of ancient nuns to the best place to hold a senior prom. I vowed to myself that before the evening was over Chena would be my prom date. Between dance sets we mixed with the groups of chattering girls and their self-conscious escorts, most of whom I had known all my life, who milled about the floor.

I had completely forgotten Joe. As far as I was concerned, Chena and I were the only kids on that dance floor. Suddenly, Joe was tugging at my elbow and Spider was eyeing Chena with a professional interest.

"Chena," I said, "do you remember Danny Williams?"

"Better known as Spider," Joe said with a smile. "Frank, can we see you for a minute? It will only be a minute, Chena, I promise—"

"If it's only for a minute," she said with a laugh, and my heart jumped.

"What's up?" I asked as we pushed our way past the couples on the floor waiting for the next set.

"Nick's in some kind of trouble," Joe said.

"Nick! What trouble?"

"I don't know. A kid from outside found Spider and told him Nick wanted to see us in a hurry. Spider found me and I went lookin' for you . . ."

The kid was obviously very jittery. He kept shifting from one foot to the other as he anxiously peered over the heads of the dancers. The first thing I noticed were the rust marks on his pants.

Joe said, "I'm Joe Gunnar." He gestured to me. "This is Frank Howell. The other two guys are Spider and Train. We're all friends of Nick. What's up?"

"We gotta move fast," the kid said. "Nick's hurt."

"Hurt?" I said. "Where is he?"

Without answering, the kid hurried to the stairway on the far side of the lobby, beckoned to us, then took the steps two at a time.

"Where the hell are you goin'?" Joe whispered.

The kid leaned over the banister. "He's up on the third floor. C'mon . . ."

When we reached the third floor, the strange kid, his lungs working like bellows, was waiting for us on the landing.

"He's at the other end of the hall," he said hoarsely as he swung open the door.

"Spider, you go down to the second floor landin' and keep your eyes peeled," Joe said.

We followed the kid into the hallway. The only light came from a small red bulb glowing over the heavy fire door that led to the roof. As my eyes became accustomed to the gloom I could see paint cans, splattered tarpaulins, and ladders stacked along the walls and recalled what Tom had told us earlier about Father John making the rounds of the Neighborhood's businessmen. At the head of the stairway was a room with a black and white metal sign: Bookroom.

For years thousands of students at St. Barnabas had run up three flights of stairs to buy pencils, erasers, notebooks, glue, and other miscellaneous school supplies from a tiny, birdlike nun who apparently had come with the school. When she finally died at ninety the supply room was transferred to the first floor. Now the room was used as a catchall storehouse for old hymnbooks, battered Latin, physics, and algebra texts which the nuns repaired during the summer months, and metal file cases of school records that went back half a century. The old storeroom had proven an excellent hideout for skipping classes, luring voluptuous seniors up for some squeals and feels, and sneaking cigarettes.

As we hurried down the hall, I made out two figures in the dim light, one was sitting on the floor, his back to the wall, moaning and holding his leg. It was Nick.

"Nick! What's wrong?" I asked as Joe and I knelt down beside him.

"I think his ankle's broken," the other kid said. "It blew up like a balloon."

"Hiya," Nick whispered. "I told these guys you would come . . ."

"Who are these guys?" Joe asked, "and what the hell are you doin' up here?"

"We don't have too much time, Joe," Nick said. He moaned with pain and punched his knee with his fist. "It was stupid! Stupid!"

"What was stupid, Nick?" I pressed him.

"Do you remember me tellin' you about that fiddle?"

"The one out of pawn? You only needed twenty-five bucks more."

"Well, after I talked to you I went back there. The guy wanted to give me my deposit back. He said if I didn't get up the rest of the dough by Monday he was gonna sell it to some other guy who had the cash. I was desperate. Then I remembered seein' the plumbers bringin' in the lead pipes yesterday to fix the boiler." He jerked his thumb at the two young white-faced strangers. "I talked 'em into comin' along . . ."

"Who are they?"

"Meet my combo," Nick said.

"Hey, is this lead?" Spider said, bending over some burlap bags.

56

"You were stealin' lead, Nick?" Joe said. "What are you—nuts?"

"After tonight? Definitely."

"What happened to your ankle?" I asked him.

"I guess the plumbers put in a temporary hookup or somethin'," Nick said. "We didn't think this one pipe was connected. After we got the lead that was piled on the floor we pulled this pipe—"

"Holy Christ! It was like an explosion!" one kid said. "There was water and steam and everythin' . . ."

"We ran like hell," the other said, "and Nick got hurt."

"One of the bags fell on my foot." Nick said. "I think my—"

The door at the far end of the corridor swung open and Spider ran down the hall.

"There's somethin' goin' on downstairs," he whispered. "There's a Micky Mouse outside and cops. Some of 'em are startin' to come upstairs . . ."

Below us in the street a crowd surrounded a police car. Down the stairwell we could see kids and cops milling about in the lobby. The wail of a siren came closer, then a fire engine roared around Ninth Avenue and stopped in front of the school. Firemen struggling into their coats began unrolling hoses. We ran back into the hallway.

"You guys must have done a job on that boiler," Joe said. "The cops and the firemen are both here."

"How the hell are we gonna get out of this place?" one kid asked nervously.

"There's only one way," Joe said, "over the roofs to Pastore's Truck Terminal on Tenth Avenue. After the school roof there's a drop of about eight feet to the convent roof. Then it's a breeze to the shed where they load the trucks . . ."

"How do you know?" the kid asked.

"It's a short cut to the Paramount for the first show," Joe said dryly. "What the hell do you want—a map?"

"Don't forget the fence around the terminal, Joe," Spider warned.

I added, "And they have a night watchman."

"Nothin' to it," Joe said with his usual air of unshakable confidence.

He pointed to the kid who had found us in the gym. "You go down to the second floor landin' and see what's goin' on." Then to the other one, "You guys go first."

"Over the roofs?" he said nervously.

Joe shrugged. "Then go downstairs and walk out the lobby. Be sure you tip your hat to the cops."

"We'll go by the roofs," Nick said savagely. "What the hell are you arguin' about? These guys are doin' you a favor!"

"We never been over these roofs before," the kid protested. "We could get killed."

"Okay," Joe ruled. "Spider, you go with him. Frank and I and Train and the other kid will help get Nick to the depot . . ."

"Let's go, musician," Spider said. He slid back the bolt of the heavy door and tried the knob. It was locked. He turned and gave Joe a helpless look.

"Bust it, Train," Joe said quietly.

Train stepped back several paces, lowered his shoulders, and charged. He hit the door like a battering ram. I was sure the noise could have been heard across the river. The door shook but remained closed. Three times Train slammed against the door. The last time it started to give. Then at the far end of the hall there was a rush of footsteps and the kid Joe had sent to the second floor landing came out of the gloom to tell us a group of priests and cops were starting up the stairs.

"Hit it, Train!" Joe said fiercely.

Train slammed against the door. This time it flew open sending him sprawling out on the tar roof.

"Okay, you guys. Let's go," Spider said.

Nicky's combo led by Spider hurried off in the darkness across the roofs. For the first time I noticed the orchestra had stopped playing and the building was quiet.

"We'll give 'em a few minutes," Joe said. "We don't want a crowd scene if the watchman's there."

"Christ, I don't know what I would have done without you guys," Nicky said. "I was really up a creek with these other jerks."

"What the hell ever made you think of stealin' lead, Nick?" I asked.

"It was crazy stupid," he said fervently. "I did it on the spur of the moment."

"Why didn't you ask your old man for the dough?" Joe asked.

"I did and we had a big fight," Nick said. "After I left you I went uptown like I said, then I saw the guy in the pawnshop. When I asked my old man for the money,

58

you'd thought I had asked him for the loan of a million bucks. The whole house was in an uproar. My mother was cryin', my old man was shoutin', Chena was cryin' ... Christ, what a mess!"

"Chena's here at the dance," I told him.

"Chena's here? Oh, God!"

"Okay, let's go," Joe said. "Train, you carry him."

Train lifted Nicky as if he were a baby and carried him out on the roof. Under our feet the sun-dried tar crackled like cardboard. We moved cautiously to the edge where the school building joined the convent. It was a drop of about eight feet. I went over first. Joe lowered me to the other roof, he followed, then Train handed down Nicky. It was clear he was in severe pain; he kept clenching his teeth until we put him against the side of the wall. When Train came down like a lumbering buffalo, using our shoulders as a ladder, I felt I was supporting a cement mixer.

There were two more roofs, all on a gradual incline, then the last warehouse adjacent to the truck terminal. Someone whistled in the darkness and Spider came from behind a chimney.

"There's a watchman in the yards. We waited until he went over to the Tenth Avenue side, then I helped those guys get over the fence," Spider said. "I came back to give you a hand."

"How did you get down to the yard?" Joe asked.

"There's a truck under the loading shed. All you have to do is get on the cab ... then ..."

"Oh, Christ! Wait a minute," Nick whispered.

We stood there in the darkness looking down at the white blur of his face.

"I left my jacket back there with the lead ..."

"The hell with the jacket," Spider said. "Who cares—"

"It's got my wallet with my name and everythin'. If they ever call up my old man ..."

"I'll go with you," Joe put in.

"I'll go back and get it," I said.

"Why the two of you, Joe?" Spider said. "Let Frank—"

"How the hell will he get up on the roof again?" Joe snapped. "*You* guys go down now. Spider you go first, then Train will hand you Nick."

"What about you and Frank, Joe?" Nick asked.

"Don't worry about us. We'll see you tomorrow. C'mon, Frank ..."

We ran back through the darkness to the school roof. Joe climbed to my shoulders, hoisted himself over the edge, then reached down and pulled me up.

We lay there for a moment to catch our breath, then returned to the bookroom corridor, frantically searching the floor in the darkness for Nick's jacket. We finally found it after we had lifted the wet, lead-filled burlap bags. We never heard the footsteps on the stairs until flashlights speared the blackness of the stairway and Father John was loudly telling someone this was the third floor and the old bookroom. We were at the far end of the corridor; the doorway leading to the stairs was between us and the open fire door which led to the roof. There was only the bookroom. I reached for the knob, praying it wasn't locked. It was open. We slipped inside. Joe silently pointed to the scaffold outside the window. We carefully raised the creaking, protesting widow. Joe stepped out, tested the scaffold, and waved for me to join him. My stomach turned as the platform slowly swayed. Joe closed the window and unrolled the canvas which had been tied up along the sides of the scaffold. I quickly joined him under the canvas as the beams of a flashlight came through the glass door.

"What's this place, Father?" a man called out.

"The old bookroom," the priest replied. "It's a storage room for our used books. The sisters repair them during the summer. . . . Officer, I don't think they came up here."

"We have to search the whole building, Father."

"A terrible, terrible thing! All that water! I don't know what we're going to do . . . and winter's coming!"

"Don't worry, Father, we'll find them. . . . What's out here?"

"The painters' scaffolds . . . we're having the trim done this year."

The flashlight was pressed against the window, its beam carefully exploring the top of the scaffold. We lay flat on the wooden slats as the light moved across our heads.

Suddenly, on the roof just around the corner of the building, someone shouted:

"They got out by the roof . . . here's the lead, Father."

We heard Father John and the others leave the bookroom. Lights trailed across the roofs. Then the firedoor was slammed shut. There was a rumble of voices in the hall, then silence.

"That was close," I whispered as we climbed back into the bookroom.

"We can't make it across the roofs," Joe said. "There'll be a million cops around the terminal . . ."

"Nick must have made it by now."

"That crazy bastard! Look at the spot he got us in."

"He'd do the same for us, Joe."

"Yeah, but that still won't do us any good now. If we don't get out they'll lock the building! We can't stay here for the weekend—your aunt and my mother will have an alarm out for us."

He cautiously opened the door and we walked out into the dark hallway.

"We'll have to take a chance gettin' to the first floor. Once we reach the lobby we can get to the hall and the door at the far end, you know the one, Frank, the one that pushes out and locks automatically?"

Outside a loud grunting rhythmic sound had begun.

"They're pumpin' water out of the boiler room," Joe said as he looked out the corridor window. "That stupid Nicky bastard!"

I held up Nick's jacket. "What are we going to do with this, Joe?"

He thought for a moment then walked back into the bookroom and pulled open the bottom drawer of a file.

"Nobody uses this place anymore. We'll get it some day durin' the week . . ."

I accepted this. I did not have the slightest doubt we would be back in class the following Monday. Joe was our leader, he had never failed to get us out of a tight spot, and I was confident he'd do it again.

We tiptoed down the stairs. At the first landing Joe held up his hand and we stood still as statues. Below us hoses snaked across the lobby floor. A fireman in a glistening wet coat, helmet, and boots bent over to study a tiny rivulet flowing from a brass coupling, then clomped down into the boiler room.

From the stairway to the first floor hallway entrance was only a few feet, but to get to it you had to cross the lobby.

"Let's go," Joe whispered.

We ran across the deserted, wet lobby, down the dim hallway to the large grilled door. Joe pressed on the bar, we both shoved, and it slowly opened. We slipped outside to crouch behind a wall of garbage cans. Ahead of us was the mouth of the alley and the street.

We were halfway up the alley when suddenly the light over the rear entrance of the convent went on. The hard white light from the single bulb pinned us against the wall.

"Start walkin'," Joe whispered. We had taken only a few steps when the convent door swung open.

"What are you kids doing here?"

It was Francis, the watchman, porter, janitor, and general maintenance man for St. Barnabas. For years I had seen him around the school, a wisp of an old man in sagging overalls. But now, as he stepped into the alley, he was anything but friendly. He was carrying a heavy wrench and his pants were dripping.

"What are you kids doing here?" he demanded again.

Easily and confidentially Joe said, "Oh, hello Mr. Francis, we just came in—well—we had to sort of answer a call of nature . . ."

"Why the hell don't you go home?" he said, coming toward us. "What's the matter with you kids these days?"

"We're sorry, Mr. Francis," I said, pouring it on. "It won't happen again."

We started up the alley but the old man wasn't to be put off.

"Wait a minute," he shouted. "The cops want to talk to anybody that's on school property . . ."

"Look, Mr. Francis, you know me—Joe Gunnar," Joe said quickly. "We only came in here because I had—"

"I wouldn't care if you were Paddy Hayes' nephew," the old watchman said as he brushed past us. "Tell it to the cops!"

At the mouth of the alley Francis frantically waved and yelled to someone. In a moment a cop appeared, listened, and walked down the alley.

"What were you kids doing in the alley?" he asked.

"We told Mr. Francis we only came in to take a leak," Joe said. "We're sorry, it won't happen again."

I can still remember the cold eyes studying us under the leather visor.

"Show me."

Joe's surprise was unfeigned. "Show you, officer?"

"Yeah. Where you took a leak."

Joe walked slowly down the alley and I followed. He waved in a vague way.

"I don't know exactly . . . it was dark and we . . ."

His voice died off. The cop was studying our sweaters and pants. I glanced at Joe. In our excitement we hadn't noticed that our pants and sweaters were smeared with rust and dirt from lifting the lead-filled burlap bags.

"I'm gonna take 'em both in to talk to the detectives," the cop said.

4 HENNESSY

As we passed through the lobby of the school to the gym, a fireman, black hose coiled around one shoulder like a friendly snake, came up out of the boiler room.

He motioned to us. "Are these the kids?"

"It looks like it," the cop said.

"You ought to get your ass broke," the fireman told us.

I think this was the first time Joe and I realized we were the suspects who had caused the flood.

"Look, Officer," I started to explain, "we had nothin' to—"

He used his club like a lance. It drove deep into my back and slammed me up against the wall.

"Give me any of your lip and I'll break your goddam jaw," he warned me. I'll never forget the tone of voice, it wasn't vicious or even cruel, it was casual—like a formality that went with the uniform.

We entered the fully lighted gym, deserted except for a small group of men gathered about Father John. One in a raincoat and boots had a white fireman's helmet with a chief's shield. Towering above them all was Hennessy. Kidneyfeet. They turned as we approached.

"I grabbed these two kids in the alley by the convent," the cop said proudly. "They claimed they went in for a leak but they're lying." He yanked Joe around and pointed to his sweater with his club. "Look at the rust on his sweater." He motioned to me. "This kid's got it too . . ."

Francis pushed past us waving his wrench. "I found 'em, Father. They were—"

Hennessy held up his hand. "Okay, Mr. Francis, you found 'em." The lime-colored eyes fastened on me.

"What were you doing in there, kid?"

Joe said, "We only went in—"

Hennessy turned to him. "Shut up. When I want you to talk I'll ask you a question."

His voice was calm but edged with ice. I stiffened involuntarily against the violence in his hard set face. I knew it was going to be a long night.

"We only went in there because we couldn't get in the school to use the bathroom," I said as humbly as possible. "We—"

The calm even voice told me, "You're a goddam liar." He turned to Father John. "I'm sorry, Father."

The priest nodded in understanding. "Were you in the boiler room, Frank?"

"I swear, Father, we weren't down there," I said fervently.

"Who is he, Father?" Hennessy asked.

"Frank Howell. He lives on Forty-sixth Street. He's one of our finest pupils, Officer," Father John said.

"Isn't the other one Gunnar?"

"Joseph Gunnar. He's another fine boy. I just can't believe they would have anything to do with this dreadful thing . . ."

I saw a flicker in Hennessy's eyes. He turned and studied Joe for a long moment in silence.

"I think they're in it, Father," he said at last. "I'm going to take 'em in and talk to 'em."

"We didn't have anything to do with the boiler, Father," I said. "We haven't been down there—"

"How do you know it was the boiler, kid?" the fire chief angrily demanded. He turned to Father John. "If they're the kids who did this you ought to . . ."

He just glared at us and walked out.

"I'll talk to 'em at the precinct," Hennessy said calmly. "I'm sure they will tell us all we want to know."

"I bet there was somebody with 'em, Officer," Francis said. "It would have taken three or four of 'em to move all that lead . . ."

The cop looked irritated. "Well, these were the only two kids in the alley."

Francis said defensively, "I bet the others got away over the roof." He said to Hennessy, "You'll have to get it out of these two."

Hennessy's lips barely twisted into a smile. "Don't worry, Mr. Francis—don't worry."

Father John glared at us. "The boiler is ruined. It will cost more than two thousand dollars to get a new one. The gym will have to be closed for months. Maybe even the convent."

"But, Father, we didn't have anythin' to do with that!" Joe said.

Hennessy's finger, thick as a sausage, was an inch from his eyes.

"What did I tell you, Gunnar? Shut up unless I ask you a question."

Joe looked up at Hennessy and they locked eyes.

"Just remember that, kid," Hennessy said softly. He turned to the cop. "Get a wagon. . . ."

When Hennessy pushed up out on the sidewalk, two firemen watching the donkey engine spew out its rhythmic mouthful of dirty water turned to watch us. A cop leaning on the open window of his Mickey Mouse called out, "They the kids, Hennessy?"

Hennessy nodded and watched impassively as the patrol wagon backed up to the curb. The driver jumped down, went around to the rear, and swung open the door.

"Get in," Hennessy ordered.

"Wait a minute," Joe said, backing away. "I'm not gettin' in that thing . . ."

Hennessy's hand swooped down, grabbed Joe by the back of the neck, yanked him up one step, and flung him into the wagon. Joe tried to maintain his balance but stumbled and fell on the floor. The driver was not as rough. He jerked his thumb and said to me, "Get inside, kid, or you'll get hurt."

I stepped inside the wagon and the door slammed, shutting out the staring faces of the crowd behind the barricades.

"These crazy cops think we broke the boiler!" Joe said. "Christ, I hope they let us go before someone tells my mother . . ."

"Maybe they won't let us go," I ventured.

"Why? We weren't even in the damn cellar."

"Yeah, but who will believe us, Joe?"

He struck his knee with a fist. "That goddam Nick! He steals lead to buy a fiddle and we're grabbed!"

"We can't tell 'em we saw Nick and those other two guys . . ."

"There's only one thing to tell these stupid cops. We were never in the boiler room."

The wagon jerked to a stop and the door opened. The driver silently motioned us out. As we stepped down, Hennessy came from one side of the steps.

"Okay, Johnny, I'll take 'em," he said. He grabbed us both by the backs of our collars, twisting them until we were gasping for breath, then marched us up the steps. When Joe tried to protest, Hennessy jerked him so hard his eyes bulged.

As we approached a stairway, the fat desk sergeant looked up.

"Who you got there, Hennessy—Dillinger and Van Meter?"

"The kids who broke the boiler at St. Barnabas," Hennessy replied. "I'll come down later and make out an aided card."

"Juvenile?"

"Yeah. Malicious mischief. I'll also have an eight-seventy petty larceny for both of 'em. The captain back?"

"Not yet. He's still on that DOA on Forty-third Street."

"White?"

"Yeah. Female. The guy she was livin' with went nuts and used her for a pincushion."

While he was talking, Hennessy relaxed his grip slightly and Joe suddenly twisted free and ran to the desk.

"We didn't do anythin' to the boiler, Sergeant," he shouted. "We didn't steal any lead. I swear it! We were never even down in the cellar . . ."

Hennessy dragged me across the room, slammed Joe across the back of the neck with a blow that bent him double over the brass rail in front of the desk, then seized him by the back of his sweater and dragged us both up the stairs. He pushed us through a small wooden gate and into a room off to one side. I landed in a large old-fashioned captain's chair and Joe up against the radiator.

A detective who was putting on his jacket looked into the room.

"I'm going to join the captain on that homicide, Hennessy. They found another DOA. That makes three he knocked off. Watch the phones, will ya? If my wife calls tell her I'll call her back. Okay?"

"Okay," Hennessy grunted.

The detective eyed us briefly. "What's this?"

"The kids who stole the lead over at St. Barnabas and busted the boiler."

"We didn't steal any lead," Joe said. "We weren't even down in the basement!"

"All I want from you, Gunnar, are the names of the others—"

"What others?"

"Don't be a wise guy, kid," Hennessy said as he flipped some pages of a notebook. He took out a small silver pencil, turned up the lead, and looked at us.

"Okay. Start talkin'."

We eyed him in slience.

"Now!"

"Up your ass, Kidneyfeet," Joe told him softly, "we're not stool pigeons."

Hennessy was quick on his feet. He swung around on the balls of his feet and the back of his hand caught Joe across the face. It sent him reeling. A clothes tree overturned and a battered old fedora rolled across the floor.

"Pick it up," Hennessy said. His voice was still soft, calm, and deadly.

Joe stared up at him. One cheek was turning a deep angry red and there was a lump over one eye.

"Looks like you have a couple of tough guys in custody, Officer," the detective said with a grin. "Take care of 'em. I'll see you . . ." He waved and left.

Hennessy barely nodded. He continued to stare at Joe.

"I said pick it up."

"Up your fat ass, Kidneyfeet," Joe whispered. As Hennessy lunged for him, Joe scrambled to his feet and the detective caught him in a corner. He threw Joe against the wall, grabbed his shirt and sweater with one hand, and with the other began hitting him on one side of the face, then the other. He was a powerful man, and Joe's head rocked under the studied blows. The punishment seemed to continue a long time. When he stepped away he was breathing hard. My stomach turned when I saw Joe's face. It looked like a red balloon ready to burst. Both eyes were swollen, and a trickle of blood ran from one corner of his mouth. As Hennessy released his grip, Joe slowly sagged to the floor.

"Start talkin'," Hennessy growled.

The battered lips barely moved but I heard it: "Up your fat ass, Kidneyfeet . . ."

Joe apparently saw the big foot arch back. He raised his hand as Hennessy's shoe crashed into his face. When I heard a thick, choked, animal's groan, I jumped up and cried, "Let him go, he's only a kid!"

Hennessy turned with surprise in his eyes, but was quick enough to duck as I swung the heavy captain's chair. It crashed against the wall and a leg snapped off.

Then it was my turn.

I ran for the door but he caught me in the next room and dragged me back inside. He kicked the door closed and gave me the same treatment as he had given Joe. My head was filled with a loud buzzing noise, as though an alarm clock had suddenly gone off inside.

Twice I broke loose, and twice he came after me, lunging and clutching like an angry bear as I dodged and twisted around the desks and chairs. Finally, when I tried to knee him, he gave a grunt of satisfaction, as if my action was the signal to begin. I saw the huge fist, big as a battering ram, coming at me. I tried to roll with the punch but it caught me on the jaw. I could feel my consciousness draining out; the walls began spinning faster and faster.

Then the light in the ceiling winked out.

I awoke to find myself handcuffed to the captain's chair. A telephone book had taken the place of the missing leg. Joe was sprawled on the floor, cuffed to the radiator. He looked worse than I felt. Both his eyes were slits, and a bruise on his forehead was the size of a doorknob. Dried blood caked the front of his sweater.

"Frank," he whispered, "you okay?"

"I guess so." I became conscious of the dull throbbing in my jaw and touched my face. It was stiff and swollen as though I had an abscessed tooth.

"I hope the bastard didn't break my jaw."

Joe held up his hand. The knuckles were puffed and bruised.

"I think he broke my finger, the ring is bent and it hurts like hell."

I could see the bent school ring, the large stone barely visible in the swollen flesh. He gestured to the shattered clothes tree on the floor.

"I threw it at him when he knocked you out. Then he broke it over my back."

He groaned as he cautiously twisted to a sitting position and leaned against the wall.

The pain in my jaw was now like the thuds of a sledge on an anvil. I felt sick to my stomach and swallowed the rising bile in my throat.

"Where is he now?"

"Downstairs booking us."

"For what?"

Joe's swollen lips grimaced. "Beatin' him up, I guess."

I tried to laugh but the pain was too intense.

"He said he would make sure we would go away for a long time."

"It crazy, Joe ... nothing's making sense ... Kidneyfeet's acting like we're gangsters."

"He keeps callin' us a couple of wise guys. Maybe it's somethin' to do with my old man."

"That was almost before you were born, Joe!"

"Maybe he's like an elephant. I don't know. All I know is he worked us over for nothin'."

He raised his hand and groaned. "Christ, this hand is killin' me."

There was the sound of the wooden gate clicking shut, and Joe leaned over to look out through the half-open door.

"Here he comes."

I found myself trembling, waiting for the door to swing open. When Hennessy came in he gave us a swift look and read almost formally from two white cards.

"You're both booked on two charges of violating eight-seventy of the penal code, petty larceny, and of four-forty, striking an officer during the performance of—"

Joe said softly, "You're a goddam liar."

Hennessy refused to be ruffled. "Look, kid, one more crack out of either you or your friend and I'll ram your teeth down your throat." He walked over to me and unlocked the handcuffs. "You're a pretty snorky kid."

"I think you broke my jaw," I said.

He said with mock seriousness, "Believe me, kid, if I didn't I'm sorry because I sure as hell tried to do just that. Next time don't try to kick a cop in the balls."

He unlocked Joe's cuffs. "Get up, Gunnar."

"Still after my old man, Kidneyfeet?" Joe mumbled.

The lime-colored eyes never blinked. "Your old man was scum. Drunken scum. A big bag of shit with a big mouth."

He paused as if waiting for Joe to make a move, but

69

Joe only stared at him, his eyes glittering like water in the deep slits.

"You broke his hand," I said quickly.

"That's what happens to wise guys."

I gently touched my face. "My jaw hurts—"

"Tell 'em at the Shelter," Hennessy said as he sat down in the chair at the desk.

"You fat son of a bitch!" Joe cried. "Maybe his jaw is broken."

Almost casually Hennessy swung around in the swivel chair and knocked Joe against the wall. Joe's hand was caught between his chest and the wall. He pressed his face against the wall and moaned with pain. When he turned, tears were running down his cheeks. It was the first time I had ever seen Joe Gunnar cry. I felt a forlorn sense of anger, it was useless to fight.

"So you're still a wise guy, Gunnar," Hennessy said as he started to fill out a card.

"What's going on?" a voice said.

None of us had heard him push open the door. He had a chiseled face and dark wavy hair. He was a slender man, the type that looks deceptively frail but is hard, wiry, and graceful.

Although he was in plainclothes and carried a folder, he smelled of the law. His face looked familiar, but I couldn't recall it.

"What are the kids in for Hennessy?" he asked.

"Petty larceny," Hennessy grunted. "They ripped out the pipes in St. Barnabas and flooded the whole school. The damage—"

"We were never in the cellar," I protested.

"For God's sake what happened to these kids?" he said, coming into the room.

"He beat us up," Joe said.

"His hand is broken," I put in hastily. "Show him, Joe." Joe raised his swollen hand.

"I had a hell of a time with both of 'em," Hennessy growled. "They jumped me. This one"—he gestured to me—"tried to kick me in the groin. And this one"—he motioned to Joe and the shattered clothes tree on the floor—"attacked me with that. They're two—"

"For Christ's sake, Hennessy," the man exploded. "Can't you take care of two kids without beating their brains out?"

"Wait a minute, Lieutenant," Hennessy said indignantly,

"like the captain told you last week—you walk on your side of the street and we'll walk on ours!"

"You damn fool!" the lieutenant snapped, "Do you want the Workers Alliance or one of those Commie outfits picketing outside like they did last month? You want it again in *The New York Times*? Do you want the shooflies from the commissioner's office up here?"

"Let's wait until the captain comes, Elliot," Hennessy said. "I don't have to take any crap from you while I'm booking a prisoner!"

Then I remembered: it was Supercop, the cop who had broken up our stickball games many years ago. Supercop, the only cop who had refused to come to terms with the Neighborhood. Supercop who went by the book. It was obvious he was no friend of Hennessy.

Through clenched teeth I said, "His hand is broken, Officer."

Elliot turned to Joe. "Let me see your hand, kid."

When Joe held up his swollen hand Elliot gently tested each finger. When he touched the ring finger Joe closed his eyes and moaned.

"Can you open your mouth?" he asked me.

I cautiously tried, but the pain was too severe.

"You either put in a call for Polyclinic or I'll call downtown," he told Hennessy.

"Keep out of my business, Elliot," Hennessy said in a soft, dangerous voice.

"This business is my business," Elliot said shortly. "Are you going to call the hospital?"

"No," Hennessy said, then broke off at the sound of voices and footsteps. "Here's the captain now—I'm goin' to put it up to him."

They both went out and the door slammed shut. Several voices were raised in anger, one was Elliott's. Then the door swung open and a harassed looking white-haired man stared in at us.

"I'm not going to have it on the record that I called any goddam hospital and had an ambulance sent over here to treat a prisoner," the white-haired man said.

"One kid's got a busted jaw, Captain," Elliot protested. "The other one—"

"Hennessy said they went for him," the captain replied in a cold voice. "What do you expect him to do, kiss 'em?"

"Captain, either these prisoners get medical attention or

I'm calling the commissioner's office," Elliot said quietly, almost formally.

In addition to Hennessy, Elliot was surrounded by four other men, all plainly detectives. There was hate and distrust in their faces. The captain was obviously fighting to control himself.

"I have three DOAs, one a woman, and you're bellowing over a couple of kid thieves! What the hell's the matter with you, Elliott?"

"He's been nothin' but trouble, Capt'n," one of the men muttered.

"Do they get a doctor, Captain?" Elliot asked evenly.

The captain stared at him for a long moment, then nodded.

"Okay, Elliott, here's what we'll do. You take these two kids over to the Polyclinic, then drive 'em to the Shelter." He took a sheet from his desk and glanced at it. "Beginning tomorrow night you're four to midnight. From tomorrow night on you're permanently assigned to the morgue." He gave Elliott a tight smile. "Every stiff we send to Bellevue has to be fingerprinted; you know that, don't you?"

Elliott stared back at him. "I'm aware of the department's rules, Captain."

"I'm glad you are. Those floaters smell real ripe. Now take your children over to Polyclinic." He looked at Hennessy. "I want you on this homicide."

Hennessy gave Elliott a look of triumph. "Okay, Capt'n."

"You book these kids?"

"Yes, sir. Petty larceny and assault on an arresting officer. Two of each."

The captain turned to us. "I'm going to talk to Judge Farrell on this one . . ."

Elliott ignored him and waved to us to follow him. I felt shaky when I walked and Joe held on to my shoulder. His face was pale and beaded with sweat.

"You okay?" I whispered; he nodded.

When we came out of the room, two of the detectives didn't move and we were forced to walk around them. Outside the detective bureau the stairway looked steep and forbidding. We both clung to the railing and went down carefully, step by step. Elliott was waiting, and we followed him to the sergeant's desk.

"There's a few questions you have to answer," he said.

The sergeant glanced at us indifferently.

"Where do you live?"

We gave him our addresses.

"Mother's name? Father's name? School? Date of birth? Nationality? Do you drink? Take drugs?" The ritual went on endlessly.

"Get Lotsman out here to drive these kids over to the Shelter."

"I'm taking them over to Polyclinic first, Sergeant," Elliot said. "I want that on the record."

The sergeant slowly looked up and peered at Elliott over the rim of his desk.

"The captain tell you to do this?"

"The captain knows what I'm doing. Put it down please."

In the tense silence, the only sound was the ticking of the big clock on the wall. The switchboard man lowered his magazine and looked over at us.

"Okay, Lieutenant," the sergeant said at last. "You know what you're doin'."

Elliott remained silent as the sergeant carefully scrawled something on the bottom of both our cards. He handed them to Elliott who read them carefully, then signed them. With a good-night nod he turned around, gestured to us to follow him, and walked out the precinct door.

"Over here," Elliott said. We followed him to an old black car.

We drove in silence up to Eighth Avenue, then headed north to Fiftieth Street and Polyclinic Hospital.

"You were over in the Neighborhood, weren't you?" I asked.

"Forty-sixth Street? Some time ago, when I was in uniform," he said.

"We didn't have anything to do—" I began but he cut me off.

"Don't try to con me, kid," he said tersely. "Save it for the judge."

We rode in silence until we reached the hospital. As we got out Joe said, "My mother and his aunt will be worried that we didn't come home. Can we let them know?"

"After I drop you off at the Shelter, I'll notify them," Elliott said.

A cheerful intern examined my jaw and declared that while it wasn't broken it would be swollen and painful for a few days. But Joe had not only one finger but also a knuckle broken. The intern clipped off the bent ring and handed it to Joe, then put his hand in a cast. Both of us would have black eyes by morning he said with a chuckle but there wasn't anything we could do but wait until the swelling went down.

"What did the other guy use—a two-by-four?" he asked jovially.

 ## 5 THE SHELTER

I had lost all sense of time but Elliot told us it was after two when we finally arrived at the boxlike brick building on Fifth Avenue and 110th Street. In the street light I could see the faded gold letters on the front door.

SHELTER OF THE SOCIETY FOR PREVENTION OF CRUELTY TO CHILDREN. Visiting Hours: 1-2 P.M., 7-8 P.M.

A receptionist in a glass-enclosed cubicle touched a buzzer and we passed through a gate.

"Sixteenth Precinct, Lieutenant Elliott," Elliott said, showing his badge. "I have two JD's." He gave the receptionist the aided cards.

The receptionist looked them over. "Okay, Lieutenant, we'll take care of 'em."

"Thanks, Lieutenant," I said.

He nodded. "I'll notify your people," he said and walked out.

The dormitory we entered was dark except for a small light on a desk and a sleeping man sprawled out in a chair. Beyond the rim of light, cots stretched across the room. There was an occasional moan and the sound of heavy breathing. The air was close and the smell of urine so strong I almost gagged.

The receptionist slapped the cards down on the desk. "Got a couple of late ones, Emil."

"Let 'em take the two at the end of the dorm," Emil said sleepily.

"Want 'em to take a shower first?"

"Naw. Wait until they come back from court in the morning."

The receptionist clicked on a pencil flashlight, and we followed him to the far end of the dormitory. The stick of light stopped at the very end and examined two vacant cots.

"There they are, kids; get undressed and hit the hay."

When he walked back up the aisle we stretched out on the hard narrow cots. My head throbbed and my mouth tasted of dried blood.

I heard Joe turn and groan softly.

"I can hardly move. How do you feel, Frank?"

"I can't lay on one side of my face. How long was I out?"

"Only a few minutes. That's when I threw the clothes tree at him."

"It's a good thing Elliott came in. Do you remember him?"

"I don't want to remember any of them! I hate every cop in the United States! They're all no good sons of bitches!"

"Hey, pipe down, willya?" a voice whispered out of the darkness. "You'll bring King Kong down here with his belt."

"Who's King Kong?"

"Emil. That big guy up at the desk. He's the keeper. Waddaya in for?"

"We beat up a cop in the police station," I said. "Then he beat us up."

"No kiddin'? Where ya from?"

"Forty-sixth Street."

"West or East?"

"Between Eighth and Ninth. Who are you?"

"Muzzy Bolinski, they call me Muzzy Blaze. The cops nabbed me and my buddy gettin' into a store on Fifth Street."

"What do they do to you in this place?" Joe asked.

"Hold ya for Juvenile Court on Twenty-eighth Street," the voice told us. "This month we got an old fart from the Bronx named Farrell. Do a little cryin' and tell him you're gonna become a priest when you get out. We better knock it off," he said suddenly, "King Kong's stirrin' . . ."

We could see the figure of the guard as he stood up and stretched. He glanced about the darkened room, then went out.

"He's gonna take a leak," Muzzy whispered. "Ya better get undressed and under the sheet. He's ready to make his inspection."

It was agony to take off my clothes but I finally stripped to my shorts. Joe groaned with pain as I helped him off with his shirt. We were both under the damp sheets when the guard came down the aisle moving his flashlight from side to side. When the shaft of light passed over us he returned to his desk.

As I stared up at the darkness, the events of the day and night seemed far off, unreal. I just couldn't admit to myself that it was my body that ached and that it was really me who lay on this cot in the prison ward of the Children's Shelter.

It seemed incredible that a series of events over which we had no control could have snared us as neatly and effortlessly as a pair of rabbits. And all because of cops! At that moment I hated them so passionately and violently I could taste my rage—mixed with the dried blood in my mouth. I buried my face in the stinking pillow and, mainly to ease the throbbing pain in my jaw, began to dream of ways in which I could avenge the beatings, the humiliation, the injustice. Visions of Hennessy slumping to the pavement under a shower of chimney bricks, the cold, detached desk sergeant falling under a subway train, a bag of fiery, gasoline-soaked rags flung into the patrol wagon— most of the plans belonged in a comic book, and even with the pain I had to smile . . .

Gradually I dozed. It was then, in a half dream, that I heard Tom's voice: unionize the cops—eighteen thousand cops, from Coney Island to the Bronx. I saw long lines of cops, every man perfectly uniformed, every shoe polished until it gleamed like a chunk of black glass; every eye riveted straight ahead—to a platform where Joe and I shouted down our orders; when we told them to left face, right face, present arms they obeyed us.

Stretching from the platform as far as I could see, was a solid blue sea of cops . . .

How did you ever do this? someone asked.

We unionized the bastards, I cried.

Roll over, Joe roared, and thousands and thousands of cops lay down and rolled over.

I woke up laughing so hard the throbbing in my jaw increased.

"Joe," I whispered ...

Only his heavy even breathing answered me. I was surrounded by kids who mumbled in their sleep, turning and twisting, so the old cots creaked and groaned.

I lay back still smiling to myself. A cops' union ... someday we would own all the cops in the country ... roll over, cops ... sit up and beg, cops.... And they would all roll over and sit up and beg, thousands and thousands and thousands, from Coney Island to the Bronx.

Toward morning I must have slept, because it was gray outside when a clanging alarm jerked me awake. I was bewildered for a moment, then I remembered.

"Jesus! They really worked you guys over!"

The voice belonged to a kid about my age. He was thin with a sharp ferretlike face and nervous brown eyes. His thick black hair badly needed to be cut. A lock hung over one eye and he kept brushing it aside. He wore a ragged shirt, ridiculous bell-bottom sailor pants with a wide, rivet-studded belt. There was a hole in one knee and most of the buttons about his fly were missing.

"You the kid we were talkin' to last night?" I asked.

"Yeah. Muzzy Blaze, like I told ya. Did you guys really work over a cop?" He glanced over my shoulder. "Jeez! Your friend looks worse 'n you."

One of Joe's eyes was completely shut, the other was swollen; the skin around both was turning dark. There was dried blood in one corner of his mouth. He had put on his pants, shoes, and socks but was struggling with his shirt. Across the aisle two Negro kids sat on the end of their made-up cots and stared at us impassively.

"Give yer buddy a hand, I'll make the bed," Muzzy said.

He threw the sheet across the bed, smoothed it out, punched the dirty-looking pillow and put it at the head of the cot.

"How do you feel, Joe?" I asked.

"Terrible where he broke that clothes tree over my back, and my head hurts like hell. I hope that guy Elliott told Tom or my mother and your aunt."

"I think he did."

Joe said fiercely, "I would never trust another one of those—"

"Who? Cops?" Muzzy said brightly. "Who trusts cops? They steal your gold teeth. My old man runs numbers on the piers. Every afternoon the Mickey Mouse comes around and the cop puts out his hand. You pay or the bastards lock you up." He touched Joe's cast and whistled. "They busted it?"

Joe nodded. "What do we do now?"

"Wait for King Kong," Muzzy said. "He's takin' his mornin' crap. After he wipes himself he'll shave and then take us down to breakfast." A pack of greasy cards appeared in his hand. "Want a little twenty-one?"

When we both shook our heads he called over to the black kids.

"Hey, Sambo—how about some cards?"

The two boys stared at him dully and didn't answer.

"Goddam shines, they never have any money," he grumbled. "You guys got any dough?"

"Why?"

"Thought you might want a little action while we're waitin' for King Kong . . ."

"Keep your cards," I told him. "Who wants to play with a busted jaw?"

He looked aggrieved. "With this game you don't have to do a thing! You don't have to use yer jaw, just yer head."

"What game is that?" Joe asked suspiciously.

"Just figgerin', you know addin' up numbers." He put a dime on the cot and produced a stub of a pencil and a scrap of paper, then beckoned to one of the other kids. "Hey stupid, come over here and write down these numbers."

The grinning boy who apparently had done this before sat cross-legged on the cot with the pencil and paper. Out of curiosity I put a dime on the cot. Joe eyed Muzzy, then threw one down.

"Okay, wise guy, what's the game?"

"Just add up the figures. You give 'em to jerko here. Whoever gets the total first wins the pot. Okay?"

"In our head?" I asked.

"Of course," he said, surprised. "Anybody can add 'em up on paper. Even King Kong and he's stupid as . . ."

He groped for the proper parallel. The boy with the pencil volunteered, "Stupid as shit," and rocked with laughter.

"Yeah," Muzzy said. He said to Joe, "You give 'em the numbers."

"Any combination?" Joe asked.

"Be my guest," Muzzy said nonchalantly. While I

78

watched the kid record the numbers, Joe rattled off about ten five-digit figures. With a half smile, Muzzy listened attentively, then, when Joe finished, calmly gave him the total. I quickly checked the paper. His addition was correct. After we had lost fifty cents and had used numerous combinations of figures I was sure Muzzy was a mathematical genius.

"The Duchess told my old man I'm better'n an addin' machine," he said proudly.

"Who's the Duchess?" Joe asked.

"A dame on the East Side that runs numbers."

"I never heard of a dame in numbers." Joe said.

"She's like my old man," Muzzy explained. "Numbers is all he knows. How the hell do you think we eat?" The mention of food made him snap his fingers. "I'll tell you what—I'll buy breakfast. Milk 'n' buns. You can't eat that crap they give you downstairs."

He winked and hurried up the aisle, the ragged bell-bottom sailor pants flapping about his thin legs. I had helped Joe put on his shirt and we had both washed in a rusty sink in the corner of the dorm when Muzzy returned. He had a tiny tray with three glasses of milk, a battered tin pitcher, and a greasy bag.

"King Kong's shavin' in the crapper," he explained. "He told me to look after things while he was gone."

"You know him?" I said.

He gave me a look of disbelief. "Know King Kong? I've been here ten times! I bring that slob butts whenever I can ..." He put the tray on the cot and tore open the bag. There were several sugar and crumb buns. I cautiously opened and closed my jaw. One side was very tender and stiff but I could chew on the other. Suddenly I realized that a circle of kids, some younger than we were, others our age, was forming about our cots. Muzzy tossed a bun to the boy who had written down the figures and offered him his glass of milk, silently pointing with his thumb to the amount he could drink.

The boy eagerly downed the milk and the bun. One kid in a torn polo shirt called out, "Hey, Muzzy, how about a piece?"

Muzzy took a swallow of milk and loudly smacked his lips.

"Go shit in your hat and punch it, Chippy," he said cheerfully. " 'Member the last time we were up at the

Proc? You turned me in for snitching that ride to town. Right?"

"You belted me in the hall!" the boy indignantly replied.

"Yeah, maybe I did," Muzzy conceded, "but it wasn't hard enough." He beckoned to one of the blacks. "Hey, Smitty, have a bun—give one to yer buddy." He tossed over two buns, and the blacks jumped to catch them. He looked around at the circle of faces. "Hey, you from Queens, want a bun?"

A smaller boy in torn sagging knickers came to the cot and held out his hand for the bun.

"Have a slug," Muzzy said and offered him his glass and his measuring thumb.

"Thanks, Muzzy," the kid said, wiping his mouth with his sleeve.

"Don't mention it," Muzzy said loftily. He eyed the boy he had called Chippy.

"Hey, jerk—want a bun?"

When the boy held out his hand, Muzzy studied what was left in the glass and gave it to him.

"When we get up to the Proc, you gonna tell me everythin' that goes on?"

The boy nodded. "Sure, Muzzy, I swear."

He motioned in our direction. "These guys are my friends. If they get sent up there you take care of 'em, understand?"

"Sure, Muzzy. Anythin' I hear I'll tell 'em."

"Okay, you guys, just remember who runs this joint." He turned and winked. "Hey, I don't even know yer names."

"I'm Frank Howell," I said, "this is Joe Gunnar."

When the milk and buns had disappeared Muzzy entertained us with card tricks and mathematical feats. From his machine-gun conversation we gathered that he lived on Hester Street with his father who hustled numbers on the East Side piers.

"The Duchess and East Harlem says my old man's the best numbers man on the docks," he boasted.

"Who's East Harlem?" I asked.

"You guys are certainly ignorant," Muzzy said. "East Harlem's the wops. They run the numbers for the coons."

"How about the Duchess?" Joe asked.

"She's like my old man—she's independent. The wops can't touch her."

80

"What is she—young—old?"

"She's an old dame, about thirty," Muzzy said. He rolled his eyes. "Man, is she stacked!"

"How'd she ever get into numbers?" I asked.

"Through her husband, Louie. He was in numbers for years. So after he got killed my old man and some of the runners told her she should take over her husband's business. So she did. The wops like her because she has a good contact—"

"What do you mean, contact?"

"Cops," he said mysteriously.

"Is there dough in numbers?" I asked.

"Plenty."

"How many times have you been up here, Muzzy?" Joe asked him.

He looked thoughtful. "Ten—maybe more. Besides breakin' and enterin', they got me for bustin' out of the Proc." He added hastily, "That's what we call the Catholic Protectory up in Westchester."

"How is it up there?"

He shrugged. "It's a breeze. You gotta have some pull to get in." He said proudly. "My old man had the leader call up someone. I'm goin' back there ... I owe 'em maybe a year. I'll be out in eight months. I'll do it with one hand."

"Why did you run away?"

"My old man was sick. He had pneumonia and they took him to Bellevue." He said proudly, "I helped the Duchess in the drop until my old man came back. Like I said—she didn't need any addin' machine with me around."

"You were in the numbers racket!" Joe said. "You're only a kid!"

"So what?" Muzzy said. "I know numbers backwards and forwards. Where I live that's all you know—numbers and home relief."

"Wouldn't they let you go home to see your father?" I asked.

"Sure. The Brothers up there are okay. I just didn't want to wait for the wagon to come up and take me downtown."

"How did you break out?"

"I found a piece of fence on the far end of the potato field that was busted. So I just walked out."

"Did you have money? How did you get home?"

Muzzy made an upward sweep with his thumb. "Hitch-hike. It's easy. Any trucker'll pick yer up. Lots of kids on the road these days." He looked around the room. "See that kid Chippy?"

"What about him?"

"He's a pratboy for one of the teachers. He hears what's goin' on and tips me off to everythin'. That way I know what the score is up there." He called out, "Hey, Dago, who's yer friend?"

The boy grinned. "You, Muzzy."

"Don't forget it, pal."

"How the hell old are you, Muzzy?" Joe asked.

"Eighteen."

"And you've been up here ten times!"

"They first grabbed me when I was ten," Muzzy said. "That's nothin'. Sammy, one of those coons over there, has been in . . ." He called out, "Hey Sammy, how many times yer been in?"

Sammy showed a mouthful of white teeth as he held up both hands, fingers outstretched, then added two more.

"Yeah, that's right twelve times," Muzzy said. "His old lady hustles her ass on Allen Street. He's always robbin'—"

"When you break out don't the cops pick you up right away?" I asked.

"Naw. The Brothers sometimes don't call the bulls for a coupla days. They think maybe the kid'll come back. A lot of kids do that. They go home, the old man clobbers 'em so they come back. At least you eat up in Westchester. Then some of the kids don't like the highways . . ."

"What's wrong with the highways?"

"Sometimes a queer picks yer up. Like me one time. I get tired of pickin' potatoes so I busted out through my hole in the fence. I get this ride. The guy is drivin' a big car and he keeps grabbin' for my joint all the time. So I finally let him and he gave me five bucks."

Suddenly, the conversation ended.

A man as huge as Hennessy but without his sagging belly walked down the room. He wore gray pants and had a silver shield pinned over the pocket of his gray shirt.

"Okay, you kids," he shouted. "Line up."

After a ragged line was formed he blew a whistle and waved his hand. The line moved past his desk and out of the dormitory. As Joe and I approached he motioned for us to fall out.

"You Howell? You Gunnar?"

82

When we nodded he made notations on two cards.

"Okay. Go downstairs and get your breakfast." He leveled a finger at us. "The captain over at the precinct called me this morning. He tells me you're a couple of wise guys. I'm just warnin' you kids—act up with me and I'll take you down to the shower room and beat your ass blue. I had a lotta wise guys come in here but when they left they wasn't so wise. Understand?"

I held my breath. For a moment I thought Joe would spit in his face, but instead he said very softly, almost humbly, "Yes sir."

"Okay. Get goin'."

"That goddam goon," Joe whispered as we went down the stairs.

"For God's sakes, don't antagonize him, Joe!"

"Don't worry. All I want to do is get out of here."

We joined the others in a large room filled with long wooden tables and benches. On the tables were rows of white bowls containing a gray congealed mess and a glass of thin-looking milk. There were flies everywhere.

"The cooks sell the milk," Muzzy said out of the corner of his mouth. "They mix this crap with water. What did King Kong say?"

"He told us if we're wise guys," Joe whispered, "he'd take us down to the showers."

"That's where he makes ya get undressed, then he belts the crap out of ya," Muzzy said. "Next time ya come in bring him some cigarettes . . ."

"There won't be any next time," Joe said fiercely.

Muzzy gave him a look. "Wanna bet?"

A whistle blew and we took our seats at the table. I tasted the mess in the bowl. Although it was cold and thick as wallpaper paste, I was surprised to see kids on all sides gobbling it down.

After eating as much as we could of the breakfast, Joe and I followed Muzzy's example by folding our arms. When a whistle blew we marched down another flight of stairs, then waited.

"They're pullin' up the vans," Muzzy informed us.

"Where do they go?" I asked.

"Juvenile Court," Muzzy said. "We're gonna be arraigned."

Ten boys, black and white, climbed in each van and sat on iron benches facing each other. When the door slammed shut, Muzzy lit a cigarette and passed it around. We waved aside our turn.

"You guys don't smoke?" Muzzy asked incredulously.

"I play football," Joe explained.

"No kiddin'?" Muzzy said.

The redheaded kid snickered.

"They're nervous."

"Hey, buddy, you want yer mama?" another asked.

"Maybe he's gonna wet his pants," the redhead called out. "Maybe—"

Joe reached over, grabbed the redhead by his shirt, and yanked him forward on his knees.

"Any more shit from you or anybody else and we'll clean up this van. Understand?"

"He was only kiddin' around, Joe," Muzzy said hastily.

"Tell him to keep his goddam mouth shut," Joe said.

The redhead got back on the bench.

"These two guys beat up a cop," Muzzy told the others.

"I'd like to believe it," the redhead muttered.

"They caught the copper under the el on Ninth Avenue and worked him over," Muzzy said. "Then they stole a car. The cops chased 'em down Forty-second Street and shot out the gas tank. Then they kicked 'em around in the precinct. Why do you think they're all banged up? It's true. I heard it on the radio."

For the rest of the trip the redhead and the others eyed us with silent admiration as the soggy butt passed from lip to lip.

When the van stopped we marched out.

"I figgered you guys needed a little buildup," Muzzy whispered.

King Kong marched us into what Muzzy called the identification room where our names and addresses were taken down by several women at typewriters. Then we were ordered to sit on a wooden bench in the hall.

"The judge is upstairs," Muzzy said. "Now don't forget—do a little cryin'. Tell him you're gonna be a priest."

A nearby door opened and a man with several folders under his arm approached the bench and began reading off names. When Muzzy nudged me I realized the man was staring at me.

"Howell?"

"Yes."

"Stand over there."

"Gunnar?"

84

Joe joined me, then several other kids.

"This way," the man said.

There was more marching. We followed him down the hall and up a wide curved marble stairway. He stopped at a large heavy door and gestured to Joe and the others to enter. As I was about to go in he pulled me aside and closed the door.

"You the Howell kid?"

"That's right."

"I have a message for you. Gus says thanks for not fingerin' his kid. He says to sit tight. He's workin' on getting you out."

For a moment I was bewildered. "Gus?"

"Gus Valentino," he said impatiently. "He wants you to know he'll take care of you and that other kid . . ."

The room was large with several somber oil portraits, heavy drapes, and crystal chandeliers. Grouped about a marble table were several men and women who seemed knit together by their own anger, frustration, or sadness. The women were red eyed and apprehensive; the men angry and impatient. When I entered, Joe was in his mother's arms and his brother Tom was standing next to him. Then in a moment Aunt Clara was hurrying toward me, her arms outstretched. Normally I would have been embarrassed, but not now. After the nightmarish night she felt warm, comfortable, familiar. It was only by a great effort that I didn't burst into tears.

"My God, what happened to you, son?" she said in a shocked voice as she held me at arm's length. She gently touched my swollen jaw. "Your face! Were you in a fight?"

Tom echoed her and his mother stepped back, wiping her eyes. "Who worked you over, Joe? What happened?"

"The cops beat us up," Joe said flatly. He held up his hand in the cast. "One of them kicked me and broke my finger."

"Did a cop stop by the house, Aunt Clara?" I asked.

"Elliott—Supercop did," Tom said. "We were all waiting up—we didn't know what happened to you."

"The officer said you and Frank stole some pipes in St. Barnabas's cellar and it caused the boiler to explode," Mrs. Gunnar said.

"Frank or Joe wouldn't touch anything that didn't belong to them," Aunt Clara said stoutly. "I told the officer

85

to his face that they were all liars. And I intend to tell Father John the same thing."

"Father John told me the cops claim they have you both dead to rights," Tom said. His eyes dropped to the rust smears on our sweaters; the question was in his face but he remained silent, waiting.

"We were never in the boiler room. We never touched the damn boiler. We didn't touch any pipe," Joe said, almost pleadingly. "They're lyin' in their teeth, Tom."

"But why did they arrest you boys?" Mrs. Gunnar asked bewilderedly.

"It was Hennessy, Mom," Joe said quietly.

"Hennessy?" Recognition slowly dawned in her face. "Teddy Hennessy?"

"The same one, Mom," Tom said shortly. "Remember when Pop used to say he hated our guts? The big fat bastard!"

"Tom," his mother warned quietly.

"What can we do, Tom?" Aunt Clara said as she clung to my arm.

"We'll see the judge," Tom said. "He can't—"

He broke off, stared over my shoulder, then pushed past me. When I turned, he was facing Hennessy who had come from the judge's chambers, a sheaf of papers in his hand. The others in the room watched him with curiosity.

"You know damn well, Hennessy, neither my brother nor Frank Howell stole that pipe," Tom said loudly.

Hennessy eyed him impassively and walked to where a woman was typing.

"Detective Hennessy, Sixteenth Precinct," he said. "Here's the papers on those two kids."

Tom followed him. "I just wanted to let you know, Hennessy, we're going down to headquarters this afternoon and file a complaint against you . . ."

"File five, kid, for all I care," Hennessy said and pushed past him.

Tom caught up with him at the door and grabbed his arm.

"You're just a goddam bully—"

Hennessy stared at him. "Get your hand off my arm, kid."

Mrs. Gunnar ran over and pulled him away. "Don't make trouble, Tom—please!"

"I'm going to make all the trouble in the world for this guy, Mom."

Hennessy gave him an indifferent look and walked out.

Since I was a baby I had known Tom Gunnar as mild mannered, good humored, and seemingly always happy. This was one of the rare occasions when I had ever seen him mad. He was more than mad, he was seething. His face was flushed a dark red and his eyes were hard and glittering.

"I want to see the judge," he told the woman behind the railing.

"He'll see you all in a minute, sir," she said.

He leaned over the desk. "Ma'am, I want to see him now—alone."

She gave him a severe look. "I told you, sir . . ."

Without a word Tom turned, walked across the room, and yanked open the door of the judge's chambers. A hum of voices broke off as he closed the door behind him. The woman who seemed stunned by his action jumped up and rushed into the room. In a few minutes she came out, glared at us, and sat down.

Mrs. Gunnar said, "I'm sorry my son—"

"He's not going to help any of you acting this way," she snapped and went back to her typewriter. She was so angry the carriage jumped under her touch.

In a few minutes Tom came out. He was pale and there were tight lines around his mouth.

"Just go in there and tell the truth," he told us. Then to his mother he added:

"I'm going up to school and see Dean Franklin."

"Is anything wrong, Tom?" his mother asked anxiously. "What did the judge say?"

"He loves cops and he's an old Tammany hack," Tom said bitterly. "He says he intends to make an example of Joe and Frank."

"Oh my God," Aunt Clara said and held me tightly.

The door swung open. "Gunnar? Howell?" an attendant called out. "Will you ladies please come in and bring the boys?"

6 *HALL OF JUSTICE*

The brief few minutes that we were heard, judged, and sentenced by Juvenile Judge Aloysius Xavier Farrell—a political hack and clubhouse appointee whose claim to fame was a close relationship with some powerful figures in both the Church (Knights of Malta) and Tammany Hall (senior partner in the law firm of the Hall's former leader)—confirmed my growing suspicion, born the night before, that there were two types of law and justice in our country: one for the poor, the other for the rich and politically influential. Farrell, whose pedestrian career included numerous churchly honors and political friendships, was a shocking example, even to me at seventeen, of New York's judiciary at its worst.

To compound his other flaws, Farrell openly avowed his admiration and support of the police in all matters, especially those concerning juveniles in the City of New York.

"I can see, madams," he said sharply after recounting for Mrs. Gunnar and Aunt Clara the shocking, lying testimony of Hennessy, "that had the police broken their night sticks over their rear ends as they did in my day, these boys would not be standing before me now." He ordered the clerk, "Swear 'em in."

After we told our version of what happened, he pointed out the rust and paint stains on our sweaters and pants. When we stumbled over an explanation, he smiled triumphantly at Mrs. Gunnar and Aunt Clara.

In the end, he sentenced Joe and me to a years' confinement in the Catholic House of Refuge in Queens. If we "behaved" ourselves, as he put it, we would be released after six months and placed on probation.

I could only stare incredulously at this fretful little man in the flowing black robe who so casually sentenced me to a year's term in a reformatory for a crime I had not committed. When he asked me if I had anything to say I could only shake my head. I wondered about my classes and the examination for the Bishop Larkin Scholarship. When I looked at Joe, his face was stone and his fists were clenched at his side.

"Your honor," Mrs. Gunnar said hurriedly, "these boys are good boys—"

"I hear it all all day, ma'am," Farrel said wearily. "Every boy who appears before me is, according to his mother, a fine, upright young American who loves his schoolwork."

"It just happens, your honor," Aunt Clara said in a surprisingly loud voice, "that my nephew was chosen by St. Barnabas to take the Bishop Larkin Scholarship test—"

"I knew Bishop Larkin intimately in my younger days, ma'am," Farrell intoned like an archdeacon, "and I am sure that fine man of God would be spinning in his grave if he knew that a boy who assaulted a police officer only doing his duty was taking the test for a scholarship named in his honor."

"Let's not waste time with this slob, Mom," Joe told his mother.

"You see, ma'am," Farrell said, "you see? That's how your son treats a representative of the judiciary—"

"I always thought I might go into law," I blurted out, "but after listening to you, I would rather sell potatoes in Paddy's Market."

"Mr. Hanley! Mr. Hanley!" Farrell shouted.

The court attendant rushed forward. "Yes, your honor."

"Get these people out of my courtroom and turn the defendants over to the correction people!"

He pawed through some papers, found his gavel, and slammed his desk. "I refuse to be insulted by a pair of ruffians who don't know the meaning of respect for the law."

"Bullshit!" Joe said.

"Joe!" his mother cried, "please, Joe!"

As the attendant started to push us out of the room, I called over my shoulder, "You're just what he said you were—a slob."

Aunt Clara gave me a stricken look and tried to reach out for me but the attendant waved her away.

"Get 'em out of my courtroom, Mr. Hanley," Farrell shouted. "Get 'em out!"

The attendant grabbed our arms and pulled us down the hall to an elevator with both Mrs. Gunnar and my aunt frantically hurrying along after us.

"Please—let us talk to the boys for a moment," Mrs. Gunnar pleaded.

"Talk to 'em up at the Refuge," the attendant snapped. When the elevator operator pulled back the door, we were pushed inside. The door closed on the frightened faces of Aunt Clara and Mrs. Gunnar.

"That son of a bitch!" Joe said.

The attendant shook us both. "Watch your language."

Joe gave him a defiant look. "Bullshit, mister!"

"Goddammit! Shut your mouth," the attendant shouted.

"Bullshit," I said, "and in spades."

"Tell 'em up at Refuge to kick their ass," the elevator operator said as he slid open the door.

The angry attendant marched us down the hall and pushed us toward the bench.

"Sit down and shut up."

The man who had spoken to me before I entered the judge's chambers walked across the hall.

"What's the matter?"

The attendant motioned to us. "Here's a couple of wise young bastards. The judge tried to be nice to 'em and they used foul language."

Joe gave him an impassive look.

"I only said bullshit."

"They know how to take care of your kind at the Refuge," the attendant said and walked back down the hall.

Muzzy asked in a whisper, "Waddaya get?"

"A year at the Refuge," I said. "Where the hell is that?"

Muzzy gave us a worried look. "House of Refuge. That's not so good."

"Where is it?" Joe asked.

"In Queens. The food's lousy and the guards are queers and head busters. Do you have any political pull?"

"Why?"

"Maybe ya can get a transfer to the Proc."

The man with the folders was again calling out names and Muzzy and several other boys formed a line, then marched down the hall.

"Nobody's goin' to put me in any goddam House of Refuge," Joe said fiercely.

"See the guy with the folders?" I said softly.

"What about him?"

"Just before we went into the judge's chambers he pulled me aside."

"I noticed that. What did he want?"

"He told me Gus Valentino was working on our case . . ."

Joe looked puzzled. "Nick's father? What can he do?"

"He said Nick's old man was grateful we didn't squeal on Nick. Maybe he can do something."

"Maybe. But I'm not waitin'. As soon as we get out there we're bustin' out." He added intensely. "We're bein' railroaded, Frank, for somethin' we didn't do."

"That crazy judge believed Hennessy . . ."

"Cops!" Joe spat out the word. "I hate every goddam one of 'em."

"Just before I went to sleep last night I was thinking about cops—"

"I hope you threw up."

"How would you like to own them?"

He looked at me. "Own 'em? How?"

"Put all the cops in New York in a union . . . all the dock workers are in a union, why not cops?"

"And who's gonna run it?"

"You and me. When we tell the cops to roll over, they'll roll over. When we say sit up and beg they'll sit up and beg . . . how would you like that?"

He smiled faintly. "Brother, would I like that. To own the bastards. Hey, what an idea!"

"It wasn't all mine," I said. "It's Tom's. We talked about it one night on the roof."

"A union," Joe said softly, almost to himself. "A union of cops. Roll over. Sit up and beg. Wag your tails, you stupid cops . . ."

"Hey you kids," King Kong called out as he walked over to us, "didn't I warn you about talkin'!" He explained in a lower and softer voice. "That son of a bitch Farrell's a bug on kids talkin' in the halls . . ."

It seemed to me that King Kong wasn't as belligerent toward us as he had been earlier in the morning. I wondered if it could have any connection with the man with the folders. For the first time I was beginning to believe that perhaps Nick's father did have some influence.

In a few minutes Muzzy and the others returned. Muzzy looked triumphant.

"I go back to the Proc for a year—" He turned to the redhead. "Watcha get, Red?"

Red licked his lips. "Sixteen months."

"Where?"

"On the Island."

Muzzy whistled softly. "Man, that's tough."

"What's tough about it?" I asked.

"Rikers? The racket guys are the bosses over there and they give the kids to the old cons."

Red looked worried. "I'll break out."

"What—and swim Hellgate? Don't be a jerk."

"Did you tell the judge you were going to be a priest, Muzzy?" I asked him.

"He wouldn't care if I was gonna be the goddam pope," he said. "Today he was handin' out sentences like they was chocolate bars."

At a signal from King Kong we lined up and marched back down to the courtyard and into the van. There was little said during the trip back to the Shelter. Everyone seemed occupied with his own thoughts.

In the morning Red, now a frightened kid on the verge of tears, and the others departed for Rikers Island. Later Muzzy left us for the Catholic Protectory in Westchester.

To our surprise we stayed behind. King Kong became solicitous and let us choose our own cots after the others had left.

In three days we were out. One morning King Kong turned us over to another attendant who drove us downtown to what he called "Probation." There we met Tom, Aunt Clara, and Mrs. Gunnar. After we were smothered with kisses we gave our pedigrees to a bored probation officer who filled out many forms, stamped them many times, put them in folders, and handed Mrs. Gunnar and Aunt Clara two cards.

"Both"—he glanced at the forms—"Frank and Joseph are to report once a month to this office." As if repeating by rote, he added, "If they violate any of the terms of their probation—you can read the rules on the back of the cards—they will be charged with violation of Section 119, Penal Code of the State of New York, Juvenile Chapters five and nine, and returned to the institution to which they had been sentenced by the court . . ."

Tom, who was studying the back of the cards, said, "They can't drink, smoke, or assemble for the purpose of disorderly conduct or criminal activity." He looked down at the clerk. "Are they allowed to walk on the street, sir?"

The clerk gave him a hard look. "They can walk on the street, young man. I'm sure you're intelligent enough to know what this language means."

"I know what the language means," Tom said, "but it's so ambiguous they could be picked up for standing on the corner or talking to their friends!"

"If it's at two in the morning I would say they should be picked up," the clerk said.

"Neither of these boys is ever out late," Aunt Clara broke in. "I can swear to that."

"And they don't hang around with criminals," Mrs. Gunnar added. She put her arm around Joe. "They're good boys, sir."

"Well then, ma'am, all I can say is you don't have anything to worry about," the clerk said with finality in his voice.

"Thank you," Tom said. "Let's get out of here."

Outside it was a crisp, beautiful day filled with a promise of the approaching fall. I almost trembled with the realization I would not have to return to the Shelter and its handful of apathetic, cynical young inmates. For the first time in my young life I really knew the meaning of the word freedom.

I also knew the meaning of two other words that seemed linked with freedom—power and influence. No one had told us why we had not been sent to the House of Refuge but I knew the reason; it wasn't because we were innocent of the charges placed against us by a cold, merciless, blind law or because of the wisdom and compassion of a judge but only because Gus Valentino, a former bootlegger and now a nightclub owner, had issued an order. All the way home in the cab I looked out the window and pondered this. I can still recall the empty feeling I had, as though I had been betrayed by someone.

"What's the matter, Frank?" Aunt Clara whispered. "Don't you feel well?"

I squeezed her hand. "I'm okay."

Mrs. Gunnar shuddered. "All I can say is thank God. I hear that House of Refuge is a terrible place."

Joe asked his brother. "Who got us out?"

Tom shrugged. "All we know is that a man dropped by the house last night and told us to be down here. When we arrived the clerk said the judge had put you and Frank on probation."

"I guess the police finally realized you boys were innocent," Mrs. Gunnar said.

"All they wanted to do was railroad us, Mom," Joe said bitterly. "Gus Valentino got us out. Right, Frank?"

"When we were brought down to the court," I explained, "one of the attendants took me aside and told me Mr. Valentino would help us."

Tom frowned. "Why would Gus Valentino help us?"

"We were always good neighbors," Aunt Clara said.

"That doesn't mean anything," Tom said. "He's a gangster and gangsters don't do anything for nothing."

"Mr. Valentino's a gangster?"

"He's been in the papers," Tom said. "He owns that nightclub on Forty-fourth Street." He turned to us. "Isn't Nick in your class?"

Joe nodded and gave Tom a glance that told him to change the subject.

"Did you see Father John?" I asked quickly. "What about our classes?"

Tom looked uncomfortable. "We'll have to go over to the rectory tonight. He wants to talk to both of you."

The way he said it I knew something was wrong.

"Well, how do you feel about your cops now, Tom?" I asked him when we were alone for a few minutes. "Still want to organize eighteen thousand sons of bitches like Hennessy?"

"I still say they're not all like Hennessy, Frank," he said quietly. "Don't forget a cop named Elliott stopped Hennessy from beating your brains out—even if he had to buck his own captain. And didn't one of you tell me he was put on morgue duty because he stepped in?"

The Neighborhood treated us like conquering heroes. It seemed every resident on our street crowded into the Gunnar kitchen to watch Mrs. Gunnar and Aunt Clara stuff us with stew, large chunks of oven-warm Italian bread, cups of cocoa, and coffee cake.

Friends of Tom who had been "in trouble," the Neighborhood's euphemism for jail, traded reminiscences with us about the Shelter, the Sixteenth Precinct and Juvenile Court. After a time I began to feel like a veteran criminal.

Stuffed with food I took a long leisurely hot bath in our kitchen tub. As I had grown older it always annoyed me that I was forced to take a bath in this narrow iron washtub. But this time it was absolutely luxurious. I filled the tub to the brim and just sat there, knees to my chin,

94

letting the sudsy water seep into my body and drain away the tension, apprehension, fatigue, and bitterness. It was hard to believe I was home. For the first time since Saturday, I thought of Chena. I wondered what stories she had heard and if she would ever talk to me again.

The bath made me drowsy and I threw myself on my bed and dozed off. It seemed only a few minutes, but it was about seven o'clock when I awoke to Aunt Clara's gentle prodding. I felt fresh and vibrant and ravenously hungry. We returned to the Gunnars' where Joe and I finished the rest of the stew and the Italian bread. Aunt Clara had made us a cake which we almost finished by ourselves.

Joe looked much better. The bruises under his eyes were ugly looking but no worse, he assured his mother, than a rough day on a football field. Tom seemed impatient, as though he wanted to talk to us alone.

"Let's go," he said abruptly.

Joe looked surprised. "Where?"

"To see Father John at the rectory. I told him I'd bring you both over there."

"I don't think I want to talk to him," Joe said flatly. "How about you, Frank?"

"Is it something about the scholarships?" I asked.

He nodded silently.

"My football scholarship?" Joe said.

"Let's go," Tom said. "We'll be home in a little while, Mom."

On the stoop Joe reached out for his brother's arm. "What the hell's all this about, Tom?"

"After Mass Sunday Father John stopped me. He said he wanted to see you and Frank."

"Did you ask him what about?"

"Of course. He said it was about the scholarships."

"What about them?"

Tom hesitated. "Apparently someone talked to him."

"Who?" I pressed.

"I'm not sure, but I think some of the dicks over at Forty-seventh Street."

Joe exploded. "Those goddam cops!"

Tom held up his hand. "Easy, Joe, I'm not sure. I'm just telling you what I think happened. We made a lot of trouble down at headquarters. My dean called the commissioner whom he knows and they brought Hennessy downtown. Elliott—"

"Supercop?" Joe said. "He saved us from getting our brains kicked out . . ."

"Elliott's in the soup. He was one of the cops brought downtown and questioned. He refused to lie. He said Hennessy beat you kids around. But two other dicks swore they had seen you attack Hennessy with a chair. What about it?"

"That's true," I said. "You would have tried to kill him if you had seen what he did to Joe."

"No doubt about it. But they didn't tell that part of the story. To get off the hook they transferred Hennessy to Safe and Loft. Father John needed the cops to help him with the insurance claim, and when he went over to Forty-seventh Street the captain really laid it on. As I get it, he pictured both you kids as real troublemakers who should be sent away for a long time."

"Those sons of bitches!" Joe said slowly. "They'd frame their own mothers."

"What about Father John?" I asked. "Did he swallow everything they told him?"

"I don't know. I haven't seen him since the cops paid him a visit. But I think he'll do the best he can."

"I don't know why the hell you're always stickin' up for that guy," Joe said.

"Why not? As far as I'm concerned he handed me the key to get out of this goddam Neighborhood. Nobody else. Not my drunken old man. Not those tinhorn sons of bitches of politicians. Or the guys who spent all my old man's money on booze and broads. Only this priest. He didn't have to do a damn thing for me, Joe."

"He's a priest. That's his job."

"It's not his job to wet-nurse every kid in the Neighborhood! But that's what he's been trying to do for years. Help the kids around here. But most of them don't want any help. They're going to live and die here. Like their old man and old lady. In the same goddam flat. The same rooms. The same stinking job on the pier. Every time a kid goes over to the rectory to get working papers Father John hits the ceiling. He takes time out to talk to their parents but do they listen? Hell no! They want those few bucks the kid can make—"

"What the hell do you expect, Tom?" I put in. "Somebody has to help pay the rent."

"Let the old man knock off the gin mills for a while. There's some families doing it in the Neighborhood.

There's a German kid and a Polack kid over on Tenth Avenue going to college. The Dutchman's father got a second job in the slaughterhouse. He wants his kid to be a doctor." He added bitterly, "He's not like my old man who pissed away his life and money."

"You may think he's king shit, Tom," Joe said, "but I don't think Whiskey John will give us a break."

"He's a good guy with a lot of troubles," Tom replied. "Let's wait and see."

 7 *FATHER JOHN*

St. Barnabas mirrored the Neighborhood, past and present. Even when it was built a few years before the Civil War, the area was poverty stricken, its parishioners the families of river and dock workers. In St. Anthony's Chapel, where the floors are worn and warped, there's a plaque commemorating the bravery of a police captain who held off some of the Draft Rioters in 1863 to rescue two orphans from the Colored Orphanage the mob had burned.

There is no plaque on the sidewalk nearby but many of the older parishioners will proudly point out the spot where Davey Pluckett, alias Little Davey, was gunned down by Owney Madden's mob as he tried to reach a sanctuary—not the church, but a nearby speak where he had stashed his guns.

St. Barnabas always had a core of Irish- and Italian-American families. The old church had an atmosphere of its own; there was always the ancient scent of dust, incense, and the burning wax from the votive candles. Yet as I can remember, in the dim light that came through the high stained-glass windows, the rows of pews never failed to appear as if they had been newly varnished. Perhaps it's because they were seldom used except on Sundays and Holy days.

The rectory we were ushered into by the old Irish

housekeeper had been built in the days when fine wood was cheap; the carpet was threadbare but the halls were paneled from floor to ceiling with heavy, carved oak. It was like walking into a dim wooden tunnel.

We followed the old woman who waved us into a small office. We waited in a tense silence, studying the large figure of the crucified Christ or the bland cheap painting of Gethsemane. Then Father John was in the room, wiping his lips and apologizing for the delay.

In the harsh light, that poor man's nose was more bulbous than ever. It was dark red and full of veins.

He had an extraordinary voice that soared over the congregation and should have been used in great cathedrals instead of poor St. Barnabas.

As Tom had pointed out he was not a cruel man, only a hardworking priest saddled with the enormous debts of a dying parish. I can see now, if I didn't then, that the two thousand dollars' damage to the school's boiler and cellar had been a staggering blow.

There was no sign of anger in his face as he studied Joe and me, only resignation.

"I'm sorry you boys have to be here," he said. "This is a distasteful business . . ."

"We're just as sorry, Father," Tom said.

Joe broke in, "I'd like to say somethin', Father—"

"Yes. What is that, Joseph?"

"Frank and I didn't have anythin' to do with the pipes or the boiler. We were never down in the boiler room the night of the dance."

"If you weren't in the boiler room, what were you doing on the third floor?" He turned to Tom. "You know they were up there, Tom?"

"No I didn't, Father," Tom said, "I haven't had much chance to talk to them." He turned to Joe. "Were you up there?"

"Yes we were," Joe replied.

"Well, at least you didn't lie about it," Father John said.

"How did you know they were there, Father?" Tom asked.

"You didn't have to be a Sherlock Holmes to know that, Tom," the priest said grimly. "They had rust marks on their sweaters and pants. The burlap bags that had the lead were coated with rust. And the bags were on the third floor." He turned to us. "Is that right?"

"We weren't in the boiler room and we had nothin' to do with stealin' any lead," Joe said doggedly.

"That's right, Father," I put in. "We had nothing to do with it."

"Then if you had nothing to do with the business in the boiler room," the priest said, "you must have seen who came up to the third floor with the lead."

"Did you and Frank have anything to do with stealing that lead, Joe?" Tom demanded.

"No, Tom, I swear it," Joe said.

"Did you have anyone else do the stealing while you and Frank waited on the third floor?"

"No," Joe almost shouted, "No, I tell you."

"Then dammit, who did?" Father John thundered. His large bony hand crashed down on the desk. His face now matched his nose in color. "Who is guilty?" he repeated, his pent-up frustration obviously visible.

"They're not, Father," Tom said lamely.

"But they know who is," he said grimly. "And until they tell me the names of the guilty party or parties"—he took a deep breath—"Frank, you will not be permitted to take the Bishop Larkin Scholarship examination and Joseph will no longer play football for St. Barnabas . . ."

"That stinks, Father," Tom said, his voice rising. "You're making them pay for something they didn't do!"

Father John, his face set, yanked open the drawer of the desk and took out a folder.

"The sure sign for any parishioner to start woolgathering at Sunday Mass," he said, "is for the pastor to start talking about money. Most laymen believe that God automatically takes care of rent, water, electricity, plumbing, painting and new roofs." He opened the folder and held up a sheaf of papers. "These are bills. Lord knows how I will ever pay them. Over fifty percent of the men in this parish are unemployed or working on the WPA. There is no money. The total of last Sunday's collection—for seven masses—was one hundred and thirteen dollars and a Philadelphia bus token." He leaned across the desk.

"Do you have any idea of the amount of damage that was done to the boiler and the cellar?" He didn't wait for an answer. "Two thousand, seven hundred dollars and forty-nine cents. I went on my knees to pay for that plumbing job! I may be able to pay the forty-nine cents but now the big sum is impossible."

"You're looking for victims, Father," Tom said. "That won't pay the bills."

"I don't want any victims, Tom," the priest said angrily, "but the police and the insurance company do! Three years ago some seventh graders went on a rampage and wrecked five classrooms. The bills came to three hundred dollars. The kids got their rear ends warmed but I had to pay the bills. The parents sat right there where you're sitting and begged me not to prosecute. What could I do—not show charity? The next week the adjuster for the insurance company was sitting here. He warned me that his company demands its clients prosecute as an example. I talked him out of it. The cops came over and warned me.

"Then that Halloween they broke every window on the west side of the high school. The cops caught the kids and brought them in. It was the same thing. Tears and promises, and I let them go. The adjuster came in this time with fire in his eyes. It would be the last time, he warned me. And it was."

He leaned back and shook his head. "The insurance on St. Barnabas will be canceled if I interfere with the police and if I do not take action myself . . ."

"Take action, Father," Tom said, "but not against the innocent!"

"I'm not a cop, Tom. It's their duty to find the culprits."

"They found the wrong ones, Father," I broke in. "We had nothing to do with it."

He swung to me. "Perhaps you and Joe didn't, Frank, but by God you know who did. Am I right or am I wrong?"

Silence.

"That's what I mean, Tom."

"You're asking them to be informers, Father."

"No Irishman likes that word, young man, but this is no time for semantics. Let's forget our street honor. The adjuster will be here tomorrow morning, and I have to give him a written report on what actions I have taken." He gave us a hard look. "You boys might be interested to know that they demanded you both be expelled. This I refused to do because I feel there may be some doubt as to how much part you both had in this affair—"

"You mean to say, Father, that you know we are innocent and yet you're punishing us this way?" Joe asked.

"Whatever action I'm taking is only because both of
100

you have refused to help me or the police. Now I'm asking you both for the last time, Joseph and Frank, who was in the boiler room and who ripped out the pipes?"

Silence.

He closed the folder, threw it back into the drawer, and slammed it shut.

"There's nothing more to be said. Good evening."

He gave us a brief nod and stalked out of the room. Tom, his face troubled, rose and went out. We followed him. It seemed as though I had been standing in the basement of an empty house and the walls had suddenly collapsed and fallen in on me.

We crossed Ninth Avenue in silence. When we were halfway up the block, Tom whirled around and faced us as though he had suddenly made up his mind. In the glare of the streetlight his face was hard and set.

"Let's cut the bullshit. Who did it?"

"It's none of your business," Joe snapped.

"It's mine now," his brother said, his voice rising. "Don't you realize what you're losing? This is your only chance for college. What do you want to do—be like our old man and die on the docks?"

Joe said evenly, "I said it's none of your business."

Tom swung at me. "For Christ's sake, Frank, use your head! You have more to lose than Joe!"

"We won't play informer, Tom, and neither would you if you were in the same spot," I said.

"But what the hell were you both doin' up there?"

Joe gave me a look and I nodded.

"This much we'll tell you. Someone was hurt and asked us to give him a hand," Joe told his brother. "We did and the cops caught us. That's all there is to it, Tom. I swear it!"

"Then whoever stole the lead got up to the third floor and went out over the roof. But you kids weren't caught up there—"

"We were in the alley by the convent's rear door," I said.

"Why the hell didn't you tell him that?"

"What's the use?" Joe said harshly. "He wants a name and that we'll never give him or the cops. It's the cops again. Those goddam cops!"

Tom slowly turned and started up the block. We followed.

"Hennessy has always hated us," Tom said bitterly. "I remember once when I was on the freshman team and got home late. This big slob pulls up alongside of me in an unmarked car on Fifty-first Street and backs me up to a wall for a frisk. Then he made me open my bag and take out everything, right on the street. He didn't say a word all the time, he just kept staring at me. Then when I was finished he just said, 'You're Gunnar's kid, aren't you?' When I said I was, he got back into the car and drove away."

"I'd like to hit the fat bastard in the head with a brick," Joe said savagely.

"Every night when we're alone Mom talks about how we're going to get out of the Neighborhood once you're in college," Tom went on. "I had it all figured out; by the time you were a sophomore I would be clerking in a law office. My dean says it's all arranged. You aunt will be brokenhearted, Frank . . ."

I knew it and I dreaded the moment I would have to tell her.

"It looks like we'll never get out of this stinkhole," Tom said savagely. "You crawl up the side just so far and then something kicks you back down again. After a while you don't try anymore. You become like my old man, a drunk and a loudmouth until the day you die."

"Christ, I'm sorry, Tom," Joe whispered.

Tom put his arms around our shoulders. "Maybe something will turn up."

"You wouldn't want us to blow the whistle on anyone, would you, Tom?" I asked.

He thought for a moment, then slowly shook his head.

"No, I guess not, Frank. I'm as much of a victim of this goddam Neighborhood as you are."

Like condemned men we walked up the stairs that always seemed to smell of CN and cat dirt from the first floor flat of the old eccentric who fed every stray she could find. We were halfway up when a door opened and Mrs. Gunnar and Aunt Clara came out in the hall, silently watching us. When we reached the landing they hugged us and followed us inside the Gunnar flat. On the table were three steaming cups of hot chocolate and a plate of buns.

"We thought you boys might be hungry," Aunt Clara said with a hesitant, worried smile.

"We might as well give it to you straight, Mom and Aunt Clara," Tom said slowly. "Father John didn't expel them, but there will be no scholarship test for Frank and Joe's off the team."

They stared at us in disbelief. I almost groaned out loud when I saw the deep hurt in my aunt's eyes.

"Does Father John really believe that Frank and Joe did those terrible things to the school, Tom?" my aunt asked.

"No."

"Then why are they being punished?"

"Because he wants us to be informers for the cops, Mom," Joe said harshly, "and before I would do that I would let them twist my arm off and beat me over the head with it."

"Frank—after all the studying and work you've done with Tom," My aunt whispered.

"It stinks," Tom said. "I told that to Father John."

"It's unfair," Aunt Clara said, her voice breaking. "This is the only chance for Frank to go to college. I've been saving every penny, every nickel for years, but without a scholarship I would need fifty times more than I have . . ."

Her voice broke and tears ran down her cheeks.

"Those cops," Joe whispered. "Those goddam thievin'—"

"Joe! Watch your language," his mother said firmly.

"Mary, we'll go and see Father John in the morning," my aunt said.

"It won't do any good," I said.

"I couldn't rest till I did."

"We must see him, Clara," Mrs. Gunnar said. "We were all so sure—"

She looked at us with stricken eyes. "Only the other night Tom and I—"

"We'll work something out for them, Mom," Tom said trying to show confidence that just wasn't there. "They'll be okay. How about some hot cocoa, you guys?"

"I don't want any," Joe said. He hung his jacket on the back of the door. "I'm goin' to bed. Good night, Mom . . ."

He walked inside and we could hear the protesting springs of his old bed. I followed him. He lay sprawled out on the bed, his face a pale blur in the dim light.

"If it wasn't the last year I'd say the hell with it and get workin' papers," he said in a low voice.

"Do you want to work with Spider painting courthouse basements in Queens or breaking rocks with Train?"

"No," he said fiercely, "now more than ever."

"What will you do?"

"I don't know but it won't be sloppin' paint or breakin' rocks." He paused. "I've been thinkin' it over, Frank. Tomorrow mornin' I'm goin' in to see Whiskey John and tell him I was up there with a dame and you had nothin' to do with it—"

"Like hell you will."

He raised himself on one elbow. "Look, don't be a jerk. I couldn't care less if I didn't go. What the hell, all I would be doin' would be playin' football anyway. College is not that important to me. It's different with you, Frank. You don't mind knockin' your brains out over books. With me—"

I hooked my foot around the rung of a chair, pulled it over to the bed and sat down.

"Do you remember when we were in the first grade and tangled in the schoolyard?"

"How could I forget it?" he said. "You knocked out my front tooth and Sister Maria whaled the hell out of both of us . . ."

"But before she came we had beaten each other around the schoolyard."

"I remember," he said with a grin, "you were the only one I couldn't get down."

"Well, I'm warning you, Joe, that before you get into Whiskey John's office you'll have to get me down. You're not going into his office any more than I am. Maybe something will turn up; if it doesn't . . ."

"Okay," he said after a long pause. "Let's forget it."

I got up. "Same time tomorrow?"

"Maybe a little earlier. I still have to copy your Latin quiz."

I was almost out of the room when he said, "Frank . . ."

I turned to him.

"You know that cops' idea you told me about—"

I said half jokingly, "You mean the union where we got them to sit up and beg?"

"I've been thinkin'—we're goin' to steal Tom's idea . . ."

"Sure, Joe," I said. "Someday."

It was hell to finish out the week at St. Barnabas. We were a one-day sensation and most of the kids had heard incredibly exaggerated stories from Train and Spider of what had taken place. I also discovered I had friends. My homeroom Sister, a tough, bossy nun I despised, risked the wrath of Father John to plead for me in a private inter-

104

view which I never knew about until much later. But the combined pressure of the insurance company and the cops was too much for Father John. The precinct commander of detectives had visited the rectory for a personal visit; Tom's dean, it appeared, had really swung his weight through his connections at police headquarters. The commander, Hennessy, and some of the other detectives had been brought down to the chief inspector's office for a tongue lashing. Two had been transferred; Hennessy was taken out of the Sixteenth Precinct and transferred to Safe and Loft, West Side division.

Anyone born in the Neighborhood knew of police payoffs. But I never realized how organized it was and how important to the structure of the ordinary precinct in the city until Tom told us why the precinct commander had been so vindictive: one of the men transferred had been the Inspector's "bagman," the collector for the police hierarchy. While we sat about the table one night he sketched the structure of corruption in the police department as it had been confidentially outlined for him by his dean.

"When a crooked political machine has ruled a city for too long, its corruption remains in its police department for years," Tom patiently explained. "Now there's a reform movement, but even Dewey won't be able to eliminate what's bad in the department. It's too deeply rooted; for many cops, taking money is an accepted way of life." He grinned. "Like stealing in the Neighborhood."

"Taking a few chickens from the market isn't all that bad," his mother sniffed.

"It's fortunate they don't put coins on a dead man's eyes any longer," Tom said drvly, "or O'Halloran's Funeral Home on Ninth Avenue would be broke."

"I would never touch a poor dead soul in his coffin," Aunt Clara said with a shudder.

"No, not you, Aunt Clara," Tom said, "but let's face it there are those in the Neighborhood who wouldn't think twice about lifting them. It's just like the cops, there are some thieves and there are some honest men." He turned to Joe. "Take Elliott, Joe. Didn't you tell us he saved you and Frank from another beating by Hennessy?"

"But what about the other cops who were there?" I put in. "They thought it was a joke. One detective just laughed and told Hennessy to take care of us."

Joe shook his head and said fiercely, "Don't give me

105

any crap about good cops, Tom. None of 'em are any good. They're thieves! They're bums! They only wear that damn uniform because it's a license to steal . . ."

Tom gripped his brother's arm affectionately. "Take it easy, champ! Don't get excited. Maybe when you get older you and your pal here will discover that in this life there will always be two kinds—the good guys and the bad guys. It's never all of one of all of the other. There are just as many saints as there are sinners—even in police departments."

"All this talk about police makes me nervous," Mrs. Gunnar said. "I think I'll make us something—"

"I'll help you, Mary," my aunt said and they went out into the kitchen.

"I'll get even with those sons of bitches," Joe said savagely. "One way or another. Maybe that union . . ."

Tom looked from his brother to me.

"What do you mean a union, Joe?"

"I told Joe about your idea to unionize the cops," I said.

Joe said, "I think it's a great idea! You can tell 'em to roll over and sit up. That's what you need to deal with 'em. Get 'em by the short hairs and squeeze."

"You're on the wrong track, kid," Tom said shortly. "That's not what I have in mind."

"Maybe Frank and I can help you."

"Forget it, Joe, it's not for you."

"The hell it isn't. Someday . . ."

"Okay. We'll talk about it," Tom said quickly. "Someday." Then he raised his voice. "Hey, Mom. We have two big important labor leaders out here. How about paying them off with some hot cocoa?"

When we returned to school one of the mysteries we could not solve was what happened to Nick Valentino. According to the kids in our class Nick had just dropped out of sight; one said he had heard Nick had broken his ankle playing touch football in the street uptown and had been given permission to stay out of school until after the midterms.

I longed for a chance to talk to Chena, to explain what had happened, and after school I would walk up Eighth Avenue and down Fifty-seventh Street hoping to catch a glimpse of her. Saturday mornings I made it a ritual to walk up and down on the side of the street across from their apartment house. Once when I saw Sully the elevator operator come out to empty an ashtray at the curb, I hurried over. He looked vague for a moment when I said hello.

"I was here one day with Nick," I explained. "Remember, you were telling us about Suzy, that piece of tail upstairs in Five B?"

"Oh yeah. I remember now," he said. "How are you, kid?"

"Okay. Have you seen Nick around?"

"No. Come to think of it I haven't," he said cautiously. I knew he was lying.

"I heard he broke his ankle playing football so I thought while I was passing I would drop in and say hello . . ."

"No. It's no use. The kid's not up there. They had to take him to some foot doctor. Or somethin' like that."

When he started to turn away I said desperately, "What about his sister Chena?"

He eyed me with a leer. "You like that kind, kid? Big knockers and soft as silk?"

"She's just a kid," I said awkwardly, cursing myself for even talking to this moron. I knew my face and neck were turning red.

"She's built," he said admiringly, "a real zoftig broad."

"Is she still going to school up in New Rochelle?" I said hurriedly.

He looked bored. "Yeah. She's still up there." He slapped me on the shoulder. "I'll be seein' ya, kid. Don't do anything I wouldn't do." He winked. "With or without Trojans." He laughed uproariously and walked back into the lobby.

 ## THE SHADOW BOX

The first Saturday Joe and I had to go downtown and report to the probation department finally arrived. Tom went down with us. It was a grim, silent journey on the local to Worth Street.

We found our probation officer to be an impatient, hatchet-faced woman who cross-examined us as to how we had spent every hour of the past week. When our answers weren't satisfactory or quick enough she glared at us, tapping the eraser end of her needle-pointed pencil on her desk. She made me feel like a hardened criminal. Joe was in for a long time. When he came out I knew he was raging inside. The woman beckoned to Tom.

"Is this boy hard to handle at home?"

Tom shook his head. "We never had any trouble with my brother at any time."

"Well, tell your mother for me," she snapped, "that she should whack his behind more often." She turned to enter her office but stopped. "You both be down here next month. And I want a better account of your activities. If not, you can always be sent back to the House of Refuge. Do you understand?"

Without waiting for an answer she went inside and slammed the door.

When we got out in the hallway, Joe was trembling with rage.

"That bitch! Who the hell does she think she is, asking me if I go to the burlesque shows and play with myself."

He stood there in the hallway, fists clenched at his sides, his face flushed with shame and hate.

"Come on, Joe," Tom said, "Don't let it get you down."

"Don't let it get me down!" Joe cried, his eyes brimming with tears. "That son of a . . . !"

But Tom put his arm around both our shoulders and walked us outside. The rage slowly drained out of Joe as Tom talked about playing in the Garden for the first time, but all the way home he stared out the subway window at the passing pillars and dirty walls.

"That dried-up old bag!" was all he said as we walked down Forty-sixth Street. "Asking me those goddam questions. And all because of those cops."

In the weeks that passed Joe and I turned more and more to Tom for comfort and advice. When I look back I realize that Tom at twenty was an extraordinary young man. He was intensely devoted to Joe and me, his mother, my aunt, and even the Neighborhood that was secretly proud of him. In its eyes he had beaten "them." The

Neighborhood accepted Tom's determination never to swing a hook on the piers. As the old-timers would say knowingly, he was up at Fordham "with the Jebbies," as though that took care of everything. In their deepest memories he was the only kid who had gone, not only to college, but to law school on his own.

It was expected that someday Tom would move his mother and Joe out of their five-room cold-water flat to a home in Jersey. In those days Jersey had an almost spiritual aura for the Neighborhood. Perhaps it was because of the few families who had left years before to return on Christmas and Easter in an old sedan loaded down with kids and dogs. They looked healthier than the kids on the block, and their dogs wore collars. I can still remember listening with awe as they spoke of large backyards and open fields; the only land we knew in the Neighborhood was in our window boxes.

When we were small Tom helped us fly our pigeons. After the birds were aloft we would sit on the coop and he would tell us about the times he had spent in the country as the guest of some fund that gave slum kids two-week vacations. In fact it was at that camp he learned to play basketball, the game that made his future seem so bright.

It was Tom who talked me out of my deep depression when another senior was selected by Father John to take the Bishop Larkin Scholarship exam; it was he who insisted I write a note to Father John congratulating him on his choice. I had gall in my throat when I wrote the words, but I was proud. I went out of my way to congratulate the kid—a mousy little jerk who I recall always had a cold—then I walked the whole length of Central Park West until the rage left me.

But there was still one glimmer of hope for me. Aunt Clara had told the whole story to Mr. Adams, the curator of the manuscript room in the library, a gentle old man who had bent my ears more than once on his pet subject, the logistics of Washington's army. He was the author of two scholarly if obscure books on the subject, but to his small New England college he was a distinguished alumnus, a published historian. He had written to friends at the college and had received an assurance that I could apply for one of their scholarships which not only paid most of the tuition but assured me of a waiter's job in their cafeteria. Tom was exuberant and we returned to our

109

Saturday mornings of study. But while I was pleased, there still remained deep inside a hard, cold core of bitterness and resentment. The little college in the bleak woods near the Canadian border was fine, and I appreciated all that Mr. Adams had done, but the Lowell Scholarship and Fordham University had been my dream from the first morning that notice had been posted on the bulletin board in my freshman year at St. Barnabas. I could not help but feel I had been cheated by some vicious cops and a spineless priest.

As the fall days grew shorter, Joe and I took to wandering about the waterfront and through the city. I never realized how deep Joe's feelings were about football until one Saturday morning we joined a pickup team in Central Park. Swimming had always been my sport, but I could hold my own in the backfield. That morning Joe was brilliant. The other team was older and heavier, but he tore through their line with such savagery that they protested.

"Hey, Mac, we're not playin' for blood," one called out after one of their linemen, still groggy from Joe's flying block, was helped to his feet.

"You're not but I am," was Joe's answer.

Before the incident at the dance we had been promised a part-time job stacking potatoes in the Thirty-eighth Street warehouse owned by Freddy Kenton, who supplied hotel chains and the carts in Paddy's Market. Fat Freddy was only too happy to let us work, not only on Saturdays but also after school. He was well aware he was paying us coolie wages for brute labor.

If you believed the Neighborhood gossip, Fat Freddy had more irons in the fire than a blacksmith. He not only operated his potato warehouse but also owned several carts in the market, a butcher store on Ninth Avenue, and held a no-show job on the docks.

Kenton had one weakness—booze. He was constantly hurrying out of the warehouse for visits to the nearest barroom. As the afternoon passed, his face grew a deep red, his voice became loud and thick, and his treatment of his help became increasingly worse. His regular employees had to take it but he let us alone. We were bargain labor.

As the potatoes started to come in from the Long Island farms, we worked every day after school and all day Saturday, sometimes until late at night. We soon learned how to fill out the five and ten pound bags with
110

potatoes of marble size and one or two large, clean-looking spuds on top. Each bag also had to contain a few specimens from a pile of rotting, smelly potatoes.

It was dirty work. The packing gangs were mostly from Chelsea, tough and ready to fight anyone who moved in on their warehouse jobs. But after Joe floored one bully boy and I swung a ten-pound bag which caught him in his stomach when he started to get up, we were grudgingly accepted. We realized that we were strangers, and if we wanted to stay we had to fight. The Neighborhood had taught us to survive; it was either stand up or run away.

On weekdays I usually left the warehouse at six. I arrived home shortly after my aunt, washed, had supper, and then tackled the books. Although my heart wasn't in it, I felt an obligation to my aunt, and the old curator in the library who had done so much, and Tom who was constantly urging me on. Joe stayed behind until eight and sometimes later. He was coasting along in school, and routinely copied my homework; I briefed him before every quiz.

We were both waiting anxiously to graduate in June; whatever feeling we had about St. Barnabas had died that night in Father John's parlor.

One brisk fall evening I walked up Ninth Avenue through Paddy's Market, past a hundred stores and push-carts that sold thick, white serviceable plates and cups, shoes, clothes, cutlery, bolts of fabric, tools, sponges, spurious jewelry, and cosmetics. Some carts had strings of tiny pear-shaped Christmas lights strung across their tops while others had colored streamers that stood stiff in the wind like thin flags. What could be burned was burning in the oil-drum furnaces, the flames consuming the trash with the snapping sound of greedy women shelling peanuts; what could be sold passed from hand to hand accompanied by shouts, whispers, curses, and laughter in several languages, including Neighborhood English.

As I turned into my block and neared our tenement, I caught a glimpse of a shiny black car. It was a Cord sedan with radiator edging of gleaming brass and wire wheels—a dream car. I started up our stoop, heard a soft whistle and turned. Framed in an open window of the car was the dark, smiling face of Chena's Uncle Pepe, whom I had met the day Nick took me to his apartment.

"Good evening, my young friend," he said. "Remember me?"

"Chena's Uncle Pepe," I said. "How are you, sir?"

"Fine. Fine," he said. As he leaned out the window I could see the driver, a stocky man in a tilted gray fedora. "I have come to take you to see someone."

"Oh? Who is that?"

"Chena."

"Chena? How is she?" I blurted out almost involuntarily.

"She is fine," Pepe said. "She would like to see you. Also her father. And Nicky."

"Nick? We've been wondering what happened to him."

"There is much to tell. I would also like to bring your friend Joe—"

"Joe Gunnar? He's still working in the Market."

"Good. Then we will pick him up."

He opened the door. "You will sit in the back with me."

"Perhaps I had better tell my aunt. She has supper waiting."

He held up his hands, palms out. "It will be only a few minutes. You will say hello, then good-bye."

"Good-bye?" My heart sank. "Chena's going away?"

"Nicky," Pepe said. "He'll tell you ... and so now we will pick up your friend Joe."

As I got into the car he said something to the driver, then turned to me with a smile. "You are still in school, *giovinotto?*"

"Joe and I graduate in June. Nick was in our class."

"Ah."

More to make conversation, I added, "I hope to go to college."

"Ah, that is good." He said sternly, "You must keep going to school. Do they teach you art?"

"They have an art class but it's not very good."

"Do you like art?"

"Well ..."

"You have been to the Metropolitan?"

"Once when I was in sixth grade the nun took the whole class over there."

"But you never go by yourself?"

When I shook my head, Pepe looked shocked.

"*Marrone!* It is but a subway ride."

"I guess I never got around to it."

He leaned over and patted my hand. "Someday we will go; I will show you what you have missed." He looked out at the passing street. "This warehouse where your friend works?"

"Thirty-eighth just off Ninth."

"Good. You will go in and call him out."

We stopped at the warehouse and Joe, his face covered with brown dust, listened, incredulously, as I told him what had happened.

"He's outside now?"

"In a Cord sedan. Wait until you see this baby."

Joe checked out and we both washed our faces with cold water in the stinking toilet. Then we went out. Pepe greeted him gravely.

"This is Joe?"

"Joe Gunnar," I said. "This is Chena's uncle."

"Uncle Pepe," he said with a smile. "Now we go to see Nicky and Chena."

We went up Eighth Avenue and swung into West Forty-fourth. When we stopped at the Shadow Box, a doorman hurried to open the door.

"This way, my young friends," Pepe said.

The smoky dark Ninth and Tenth Avenue saloons, reminiscent of Dublin pubs, were more familiar to the residents of the Neighborhood than the flashy theatrical clubs on the fringes of Times Square, so we stood in the carpeted lobby gawking like tourists as we waited for Pepe to return. Off to one side was a mahogany bar backed by mirrors and row upon row of glistening glasses and bottles. Beyond the bar was the main dining room and a small dance floor. Every table was set with a crisp tablecloth and shining cutlery. To the left was a smaller room, which we later learned was the famous "Reflection Room," a beautiful, intimate room where celebrities dined around a sparkling fountain and a pool that reflected the soft candlelight. A thick, dark red carpet covered the lobby; numerous framed photographs lined the walls. Joe, who was studying them, waved me over.

"Look, Jean Harlow!" he said. He slowly read the inscription. "To Gus with many happy memories of the Shadow Box." He whistled softly. "Jean Harlow!"

He passed to another. "Here's John Barrymore! Look what he wrote, 'For Gus, who maintains the best watering hole in this lousy town.' Hey, here's Clark Gable. . . ."

"Maybe Gus wrote all of that stuff himself," I suggested.

The voice behind us was amused. "Why would I do

113

that? These people are only too happy to have their pictures hanging in the Shadow Box."

It was Gus Valentino. Standing next to him was smiling Pepe.

"Are all these real, Mr. Valentino?" Joe asked.

"Yeah. Sure. You're the Gunnar kid, right?"

"That's right," Joe said slowly, eyeing him up and down. "I'm Joe Gunnar."

"And this is my young friend Frank Howell." Pepe said with an elaborate gesture. "They're both Nicky's friends."

"I remember you, kid," Gus said to me. "Chena said you were the smartest kid in the school. But maybe she was wrong. Why the hell did you ever do that?"

"Do what, sir?" I asked innocently.

"Go up to the top floor to help my stupid kid! What the hell, maybe it was for the best. You certainly saved me a lot of trouble."

Pepe shook an approving finger. "They're very good boys, Duchino! Very good! The cops beat 'em. But they didn't talk. *Ecco!* They saved Nicky."

"Figlio di butana!" Valentino said savagely. "Those cops."

"They're bastards," Joe said.

"You don't like 'em, kid?"

"I hate every one."

"You wanted to see us, Mr. Valentino?" I asked.

"You kids call me Gus," he said. "Nicky and Chena asked me to bring you over. And besides, I want to talk to you."

We followed him across the lobby and down the few steps into the starched dining room. In the rear was a door that led to a carpeted corridor and a flight of stairs. The top of the landing was guarded by an impassive-looking young man dressed in a skintight dark suit, white shirt, and dark tie. He was reading a scratch sheet but jumped up when we climbed the stairs.

"Stùpido!" Pepe said jovially. All your money goes for horses."

The young man smiled and stood aside as Pepe opened the door. We followed him into a large office. Off to one side was a gray-haired woman at a glass-enclosed switchboard. We crossed this room and entered another one, larger than the first but less businesslike. The thick carpet was a gaudy red. There were paintings on the wall, silk-shaded lamps, deep purple drapes, ivory white lounges, a

114

large oak desk, leather lounge chairs, and a beautiful mahogany and chrome bar.

Seated on the lounge were Nick and Chena. She was dressed in her school blouse and jumper but she was lovely.

Nick looked thinner, more subdued. Instead of his usual sweater, slacks, and sneakers he was dressed also formally in a suit, shirt, and tie. One foot was in a cast. With a smile he jumped up and hobbled toward us, his hand outstretched.

"Hey, Joe! Frank! How are you?"

We shook hands. "Fine, Nick," I said. "What happened to you? We've been trying to find out where you were . . ."

Nick pointed to his foot. "I had a bad break in the arch. I had to go to the hospital to have it set. They're going to take the cast off tomorrow."

But I wasn't interested in Nicky's cast, only Chena. She smiled as I took her hand.

"Hello, Frank."

"You remember Joe, Chena?" Nick asked.

"Well, I only saw him for a minute at the dance . . ."

When Joe gave her an approving look I felt a twinge of jealousy.

"I'm sorry I never had a chance to ask for a dance, Chena," he said. "Maybe next time."

My heart sang when she reached out for my hand. "I cried when I heard about the scholarship exam, Frank. That's terrible!"

"What's terrible?" her father said brusquely as he sat in one of the lounge chairs.

"I told you, Papa," she said. "The priest refused to allow Frank to take the examination for the scholarship to Fordham."

"Oh yeah. I remember. Maybe I'll talk to the priest."

"It won't do any good," Nick said. "Father John has a head like a Sicilian donkey."

"What do you know about donkeys, Nicky?" Pepe jovially asked. "Did you ever ride a Sicilian donkey like your *nònno* had to do to get to school? Duchino—you tell them!"

"Pepe, forget the old days," Valentino said. "Now the donkeys over here are Irish cops. With their hands out."

He turned to me. "Nicky asked me to bring you kids over to say goodbye."

"Good-bye?"

"I'm going to Bologna and enter medical school," Nick said. Bitterness edged his voice. "Me a doctor. How do you like that?"

"It's all arranged," his father said sternly. "There's no problems. You go in, you study, you cut up some stiffs, and they give you a diploma four years from now. You come back and study some more over here and you'll be a big doctor. You'll have respect."

"Are you going, Chena?" I asked, fearing her answer.

She looked surprised. "No. I'll be graduating in June."

"Are you going to college?"

"Why send a girl to college?" her father broke in. "She'll get married, she'll have kids, and live happy ever after." He grinned at his daughter. "With me paying the bills, eh, Chena?"

"When I'm married my husband will pay the bills," she said firmly.

"Where will you go, my young friend?" Pepe asked me.

"I'm taking an examination for a scholarship to a small college in Vermont—"

"That far away, Frank?" Chena said. I thrilled to catch the disappointed note in her voice.

"Why not around the city?" her father said.

"It costs money."

"I never had a chance to say thanks to you guys," Nick put in.

"I heard the cops worked you kids over in the precinct," his father said abruptly.

"They used us for punchin' bags," Joe said. "Do you know Hennessy, the detective?"

"*Pòrco maiale?* The fat pig?" Pepe said.

"I know him. He's a big customer around Christmas. They all are. Did he slug you?"

"Yes, but Joe's brother Tom went down to headquarters and made a complaint. Hennessy's out of the precinct now."

Pepe grimaced. "No, no, no. Never make trouble for cops." He held up his hand and cupped his fingers. "They're like bees. They stick together and suck the honey. You hurt one and the queen bee gives the order. Buzz. Buzz. Buzz. They keep at you until they kill you." He leaned back. "Pay the bums. Keep 'em on your payroll, no, Duchino?"

"As Pepe says, it's easier to have 'em in your pocket. They beat you up and you didn't talk?" Valentino added

116

admiringly. "You didn't tell 'em it was my *fesso*—my stupid son, who went down to the boiler room with two jerks who play the saxophone to steal lead?" He eyed Nick and held out his cupped hand pleadingly, *"Perchè, figlio mio? perchè?"* He said to us, "Ask him why?"

Nicky sighed as though his explanation had been given again and again.

"I told you a million times. Pop, I wanted money to buy a violin. I know it was stupid. I know I was wrong. What do you want from me? I told you I'll go to medical school in Italy. I told you I'll study hard."

His voice rose. "I can't do anymore, goddammit!"

Chena patted her brother's hand. "Okay, Nicky, Papa doesn't mean anything . . ."

"But why is he at me all the time?" Nick said, "every day, every hour—"

"All right, all right, let's forget it," his father said. "Just come home with the *làurea!* The paper that makes me call you Doc. Okay?"

"You said you were going to do something for Frank and Joe," Nick said stubbornly. "What about it?"

"Anything, kids," his father said expansively. "You tell me what you want."

"I don't want anything, Mr. Valentino," Joe said firmly.

"Neither do I," I said.

"You kids took a beatin' for Nicky. You didn't tell the cops."

"They remained silent," Pepe said proudly, leaning over to pat me on the shoulder, "even when the cops put their boots to their heads. They are men!"

Joe said evenly, "We wouldn't have squealed if they had twisted our arms off."

"Bravo!" Pepe said.

"You know the Neighborhood, Mr. Valentino," I said. "It's tough enough living there without informing on each other."

Valentino gave me an unbelieving look. "Do I know the Neighborhood? Are you kidding me? You know Ninth Avenue and Thirty-ninth—the corner where the Esposito Fish Market is? Upstairs, second floor, is where we lived when I was a kid. There were five of us, me, my mother, two sisters and Pepe, who came over to our house after his old man was run over by New York Central on Eleventh Avenue." He got up from behind the desk and came around to stand before us. "Twelve dollars a month

117

my mother paid for that dump. There were so many rats they were part of the family. You want to go to the bathroom, you go out in the shed in the yard. Everybody was makin' a million dollars in Wall Street but my mother and my sisters sewed buttons on cards." He leaned forward slightly, the fingers of one hand bunched together, moving like a piston to underscore his words. "Seven cents a gross! One hundred and forty-four buttons for seven cents! Every day Pepe and I would steal from the yards. You kids steal?"

"Well," I said. Nicky grinned, and his father gave him a hard look.

"Not steal for a fiddle, *figlio mio*—steal to live!" The bunched fingers touched his lips. "Eat. We didn't even have *pasta* or *fogolio*! If we had *scarola* it was a feast! No, Pepe?" Pepe nodded silently. "There was a bootlegger upstairs over our kitchen. So we could deliver the tins of booze and get the tips, we pasted labels on his bottles." He laughed, "Always Golden Wedding. In the front room was the grain and the coloring, in the back the still. The whole goddam house stunk like a brewery. One day my friend here," he jerked his head toward Pepe, "said, 'Let us take this bum's whiskey and sell it.' So we sneak upstairs like two foxes robbin' a henhouse and Pepe takes a little piece of tin and works the lock. Suddenly it opens. Then we go inside, make a hole in the floor, and put a hose down into our kitchen. *Madonna mai!* Was my mother mad? Bang—bang—she gives it to us in the head but we have enough for three tins of booze. What did we get, Pepe? Ten bucks?"

"Fifteen from the butcher and a slice of baloney," Pepe said gravely.

"Yeah. Yeah," Valentino said with a laugh. "The baloney. It was the first time I ever tasted it. Always we had beans and old bread from the bakery on Forty-eighth Street. We sucked out the guy's booze until one day he found the hole in the floor. *Marrone! Pira panel cula!* He lifted me this high off the floor with his shoe." Valentino bent over and held his hand about a foot from the floor. "But Pepe has this stickball bat in his hand and gives the guy a hit on the head. Bang! He falls down and is knocked out. Jesus, the blood! What do we do, run? No, we go upstairs and empty the still and fill all the cans and sell 'em to the speaks on Eighth and Ninth Avenue. A hundred bucks we made that day." He raised his finger and

118

pointed it to Pepe. "But this wise one—this *sbirro*—he calls the cops and tells 'em in his broken English, 'Hey, watsa matter you guys? You no know there is a big still on Ninth Avenue?' " Now the cops love this because this guy ain't payin' off, so we go down and watch outside our house. Pretty soon they come, bang up the guy some more, rip out his still and take him away. We felt pretty good. I showed the money to my mother, but the old lady gives me a shot in the head, takes the money, and puts it in her postal savings."

He faced us, his cheeks glowing with the telling of the story.

"You remember, eh, Pepe? Remember?"

Pepe, a slight smile on his face, shrugged. "It is ancient history, Duchino."

"So it is old but I tell it to this *stùpido* that he should know." He went behind the desk, selected a cigar, cut its end with a small silver cutter, lighted it, and continued.

"This whole place," he said, a wave of his cigar taking in the room, "comes from a few dollars my mother"—his tone became almost reverent—"God rest her soul, gave me. She saved every penny. No banks. Only in the postal savings. 'Governmenti is good,' she always said, 'no government we all die.' My father, like his grandson, was another *zìngara!* A gypsy! Sing, sing, all day. He worked in an olive oil factory but thought he was Caruso. His voice was very powerful. The neighbors banged on the floors with their brooms so he only sang when the el passed. How do you like that?"

"You never told us much about Grandpop, Papa," Chena said.

Her father shrugged with disdain. "What is there to tell? Sing, sing. Nothin' happened. Who wants to hear a guinea with a loud voice? At weddings they threw pennies and nickels like he was a *zìngara*—a gypsy. I had to pick 'em up and put 'em in a hat. Then he began to drink. I spent more time with him on my back with Pepe fightin' off the bums who tried to steal his shoes. He lost his job, then one day he went . . ." On one side of his head he made a series of circles with his finger. "He goes to the cuckoo house and we starve. Then he dies and we get two hundred bucks insurance. That's when my mother takes the money from the postal savings and tells me, 'Your father had a big voice but the brain of a flaxseed. He did not know how to make money. The Americans want to drink so you

119

give 'em good wine and they will pay you.' So I opened the speak. You kids are too young, maybe you heard about it—on Forty-fourth Street?"

He waited hopefully, looking from my face to Joe's.

Joe said evenly, "I think my father used to go there . . ."

"Yeah. Yeah," Valentino said. "I remember your old man. He was a big guy on the docks. He used to come in with the politicians." He said something in Italian to Pepe who nodded and glanced over at Joe.

"I made a little wine and I sold it," Valentino continued. "Nothing big. Just for the Neighborhood." His voice hardened. "Then I got the bigger speak and met my friends, the cops. Soon they were almost partners."

"Horatio Alger," Nicky said.

"Nick," his sister warned softly.

"You laugh but you'll spend my money, *mio figlio,*" his father said gruffly.

"It is over and done with, Duchino," Pepe said softly. "Did we bring their young friends to tell old tales? This is a celebration, no? Nicky is going to the old country to study so we have a glass of wine and a few cakes—"

The telephone rang and Valentino jumped to grab it.

Pepe broke off to study Valentino's face as he listened. Then he said something impatiently, slammed down the phone, and shook his head at Pepe who turned to us, the smile back on his face.

"You like *cannoli? Sfogliatelli?*"

"They're little cakes filled with cream," Chena explained.

"I'm sure we'll like them," I said.

"We will have all kinds, with cream, without cream— everybody will have what they like," Pepe said. He jumped to his feet, opened the door, and said something to the woman switchboard operator, then came back.

"Are you sure I can't do anything for you kids?" Valentino pressed.

"Thanks, but there's nothin' you can do," Joe said and looked at me.

"Nothing," I put in.

"There's one thing I did without asking," Valentino said. "I got you both off the hook downtown. You don't have to go down there anymore."

Joe looked startled. "You mean we don't have to report to probation any more?"

"That's right," Valentino said proudly. "One call I make downtown. Right, Pepe?"

Pepe nodded. "There is no more going down on the subway to see those people."

"They'll send you a letter," Valentino said, "tellin' you to be good boys and that's it. I even had them tear up your file. What the hell is this? I told 'em—treatin' these kids like criminals!"

"How did you do it, Mr. Valentino?" Joe asked.

Valentino picked up the phone and held it to his ear. "I make a call and somebody jumps." He slammed down the phone and leaned across the desk. "That's what I keep tellin' Nicky. That's what counts today in this town, kid—muscle. You don't have it, you're nothin'. They walk all over you. The cops. The politicians. If you let 'em they'll suck your blood until you're dead."

"Maybe you're right, Mr. Valentino," Joe said slowly.

Gus pointed a finger at him. "You remember it."

"Maybe some day you want a little loan," Pepe said, "you come to us."

"Sure. Anythin'," Valentino said. "You're good kids. If the cops had grabbed Nicky, it would have been a pension for the whole Sixteenth. Then if I didn't feed 'em enough they would go up to those goddam reporters at West Side Court and whisper in their ears. It would have been a disgrace to my family."

"It is over," Pepe said getting up, "I will tell them to bring in the cakes."

"Sure. Sure. You tell 'em, Pepe."

Pepe hurried out and Valentino leaned back and lit a cigar. He seemed tense and lost in thought. When Nick began to talk to Joe about the team's chances to take the city crown, Chena whispered to me, "I thought you were mad at me . . ."

"I've walked up and down Fifty-seventh Street until I know every store by heart," I said.

"My father made me stay up at school. He was afraid something would come out about Nicky." She shook her head. "There was so much trouble in our house . . ."

"We would never have told on Nick."

She gently touched my face. "Nicky said the police beat you."

"Well they weren't very gentle."

"I cried when I heard about the exam." She squeezed my hand. "I always told Nick you would win that scholarship. When will you take the exam for that other college, Frank?"

"Right after the first of the year. It's near the Canadian border."

"It's so far away." She shivered slightly. "And so cold."

"Mr. Adams, who works at the library with my aunt, says it goes down to ten below."

"I wish you could go to college around here. I'm going to a girl's college in Jersey." She added hastily, "But it's less than an hour over the George Washington Bridge." She said proudly, "My father's sending me to driving school. I think I can get him to buy me a car so I can drive to school."

"But I thought your father didn't want you to go to college, Chena?"

She glanced at her father who now was speaking softly into the telephone.

"He shouts a lot at my mother but he does anything Pepe wants . . ."

"And does Pepe want you to go to college?"

"He's very proud of me. In junior year, when I was at the top of the class, he took me to the best restaurant in the city and insisted I have champagne."

"Nicky told me he owns an art gallery."

"A very good one. He sells paintings to museums and wealthy collectors."

"He doesn't look like a . . ." I groped for the proper word and Chena giggled.

"My mother says he should be Patsy the vegetable store man and not an art dealer. But he does know a great deal about art."

"How did he become an expert?"

She hesitated for a moment. "He studied a great deal." Then she asked quickly—quickly enough to change the subject I thought—"How do you like the club?"

"It's out of this world. We saw pictures of Jean Harlow and Clark Gable in the lobby. Did they really sign their names?"

"Of course. All the movie stars come in here. It was Pepe's idea to hire a photographer to take their pictures and send them to the newspapers by messenger. The movie stars like the publicity and the club gets mentioned." She made a grimace. "All they do is look at each other. They wear diamonds and furs but I think they're rather stupid."

122

"Pepe seems a nice guy, Chena. Nick said he's part owner of the club."

She nodded. "You heard my father. They've been together since they were kids."

"He seemed shocked that I didn't go to the Metropolitan every weekend."

"Have you been there?"

"Only once."

"Someday we'll go with Pepe. Would you like that?"

"I'd love it."

"This weekend I have to write a paper for extra points in history. I hate that course. The nun makes it seem so dry."

"What is it on?"

"The cotton and slave period before the Civil War. Ugh. There's almost nothing on it in our school library."

"Have you tried Fifth Avenue?"

"The main library? No, I never use it. I've always used the one at school. Do you think I can find what I need there, Frank?"

"Guaranteed. They have the largest catalog in the world."

"Have you used it?"

"It's my second home. You know my aunt works over there—"

The door swung open and Pepe bounced in. Behind him two waiters rolled in a cart with tall glasses of Coke and mounds of pastry and cookies. There were also six tiny crystal glasses filled with wine.

"Now, my young friends, we will have a little feast," Pepe said. "First, Duchino, you will give a toast . . ."

He handed Valentino a glass of wine. Valentino took it and smiled at his son.

"Nick," he said, "come home with the piece of paper."

He raised his glass and we followed. Then Chena slowly clinked hers with mine.

The wine Chena's mother had served me had been sweet, this was smooth and strong. One of the waiters collected the glasses and left, the other spread large napkins across our laps, handed us glasses of Coke, and passed the tray of cookies and pastries.

"These are the best," Valentino boasted. "I got this chef right after he jumped ship in Brooklyn." He chuckled. "In the old country the landlord took his cow for rent, so he shot him. But he's a hell of a cook. Right, Pepe?"

"The best," Pepe said smilingly. "Some night we must have our young friends to dinner . . ."

Valentino said, "Any time you kids want to come over with your girls and have dinner and see the show give me a call. I'll introduce you to some of the big shots from Hollywood that come in here and have your picture taken with them."

"Will you be coming back in the summer, Nick?" I asked.

"No. We'll be going over there," Valentino said flatly. "When Nick comes back he'll be a doctor. Right, Nicky?"

Chena leaned over and hugged her brother. "I'll miss you, Nicky."

"I'll miss you, Chena," he said, resigned. He told us, "You know something? I'll miss that stinking pier."

"It's the Riviera of the Neighborhood," I reminded him.

Chena wrinkled her nose. "That dirty river."

Her father made an explosive noise with his lips. "How many times I went down there to get you?" He asked his son. "Always the river. Always the fiddle. Never the books."

Nick sighed, looked at me, and shook his head.

Valentino's outburst cast a shadow over the room; we ate the pastries in silence and quickly emptied our glasses.

"I don't know about you, Joe," I said, "but I have to get home."

"Me too," he said. We meticulously, self-consciously folded the napkins, placed them on the tray, and stood up.

Valentino came from around the desk and put his arm around his son's shoulder.

"I want to thank you kids again. Don't forget. Anythin' I can do—you call me. If I'm not here ask for Pepe."

Pepe took out a small expensive-looking leather card case and handed me an engraved card. It read, "World's Fine Arts, Sortino Francisco Armondo, Prop." There was a Madison Avenue address.

"Pepe's gallery," Nick explained.

"Some Saturday you will come over with me to the Met," Pepe said, "and I will show you—"

He broke off as the telephone rang and Valentino hurried around the desk to take it. He listened a moment, then whispered urgently in Italian. I caught one word, Dutchman. Then he hung up and gave Pepe a look of triumph. Pepe put his arm around our shoulders and led us from the room. In the hallway the guard glanced at us, then returned to his scratch sheet. In the main dining room waiters were polishing glasses and arranging chairs and tables. A bartender in a red and black vest was serving drinks to several couples.

"We can walk, Pepe," I said, aware of how foolish we would appear stepping out of the gleaming black and brass Cord sedan in the front of our tenement.

"Are you sure, *giovinotto?*" Pepe said. I had a feeling the phone call Valentino had just received was important to both of them and he was anxious to get back upstairs.

"Of course. It's only a few blocks."

He patted me on the back. "Addío—go with God!" He nodded at Joe and hurried across the dining room and up the stairway leading to the offices. I told myself that for a short, heavy man he certainly moved fast. I was happy to see him leave. Now I could be alone with Chena for a few minutes before we left. I was wondering how I could get her away from Nick and Joe when suddenly she nudged me and pointed to one of the framed photographs.

"I'm in that photograph with Eddie Cantor," she said. "Would you like to see it?"

We left Joe and Nick and walked across the lobby to study the photograph that showed her, much younger, standing next to a bug-eyed Cantor. At that moment I couldn't have cared less about Cantor, Clark Gable, or Jean Harlow. There were many things I wanted to say to Chena but I found myself tongue tied. Happily she wasn't.

"I guess I'll go over to your library Saturday morning. Do you know where I should start?"

"Room three hundred, American History," I said. Finally I managed to blurt out. "Look, I know the place by heart. Would you like me to show you around, Chena?"

She turned to me, her large dark eyes glowing. "Would you, Frank?"

My mouth was so dry I could only nod.

"Is ten o'clock too early?"

"That's fine. I'll meet you by the lions on Fifth Avenue."

She smiled, and my head became a pinwheel.

"Hey, Frank, it's gettin' late," Joe called from the doorway.

"Until Saturday," I whispered and she nodded.

At the door I shook hands with Nick, wished him well, and joined Joe on the sidewalk where he was admiring the Cord and its impassive chauffeur.

"Maybe we should have told Pepe to have this guy drive us home."

"I'd feel like a jerk. Every biddy in the Neighborhood would have her head out the window."

"How do you like that guy?"

"Valentino? He's okay."

"I see you got your eye on Chena . . ."

"She's a nice girl," I said defiantly.

We crossed Eighth Avenue in silence, then headed for home.

"How do you like that?" Joe suddenly blurted out. The intense way he said it made me look at him.

"How do I like what?"

"That guy Valentino. A few years ago he was runnin' a two-bit wop speak. Then he moves a couple of blocks out of the Neighborhood, and now he's a big man. Jean Harlow and Clark Gable give him their pictures and people jump when he whistles. How do you like that?"

"So what? He owns a high-class gin mill on Forty-fourth Street," I said. "What the hell's so great about that?"

"I don't mean his nightclub, I mean what the guy can do. Every month we had to go downtown and report to that hatchet-faced dame and listen to the crap she handed out to us. For something we never did, for crissakes! This guy picks up a phone in his fancy office and makes one call"—he held up one finger—"one call to someone downtown. 'I don't want these kids to have to go downtown anymore,' he says. 'Yes sir, Mr. Valentino,' some joker says and that's that. He says we're gonna get a letter tellin' us to be good boys. No more goin' downtown to the old dame. No more record. He said he even had them tear up the goddam file!" He stopped and said fiercely, "You know why he can do that, Frank?" Without waiting for my answer he said, "Because he has it right here"—he held up his fist in front of my face. "Right here. That's why!"

I never forgot his face in the garish light from the nearby stores. His eyes were glowing, narrow slits and revealed an intensity I had never seen before.

"You know what our trouble is?" he asked.

"No. What?"

"Not demandin'. It's the surest way of not gettin'. It's always been that way in the Neighborhood. From now on I'm demandin'—or else!"

126

"Or else what?"

He brooded about this for a moment as the crowds of homebound workers swirled about us. The fierceness slowly faded from his face and a grin twisted his lips.

"You know somethin', Frank? I haven't figgered that out yet."

Two days later Joe whistled in the hall and I opened the door. He was standing in the doorway of his flat, holding a large, official-looking envelope. He had just come from the potato warehouse and his face, hair, and the neck of his undershirt were covered with a light tan dust. A few hours before when I had arrived home my aunt had given me a similar envelope.

"Did you get yours?"

"Aunt Clara gave it to me when I got home."

"How did you like that? No more probation—courtesy of Gus Valentino."

"I think that's wonderful of Mr. Valentino," his mother said as she came out on the landing.

"It certainly is, Mary," my aunt put in from inside our kitchen. "Some official must have realized they made a dreadful mistake."

Joe's mother turned to him. "I guess they finally remembered you were the son of Andy Gunnar . . ."

"That doesn't mean a damn thing, Mom," Tom said as he came out of their kitchen to stand beside his mother.

"Please don't be profane about your father's name, Tom," she protested. "There's no need for it. Mr. Valentino knew your father very well."

"Gus Valentino ran a wop speak on Forty-fourth Street," Tom said exasperated. "The only reason why he knew Pop was because he spent all his money there!"

"Your father was a union leader on the waterfront, Tom," she said, her voice trembling.

"Of course he was," Aunt Clara said moving toward her friend.

Tom gave us a look of resignation. "Okay, Mom. What's important to know is what Gus Valentino wants in return for helping these two kids . . ."

"They're friends of Nicky's," Aunt Clara said. "He and Frank used to serve the six o'clock Mass together."

"Aunt Clara," Tom said weakly, "he didn't get them off simply because Frank served Mass with his kid five years ago!"

"The guy only did us a favor, Tom," Joe said, exasperated.

"Fine. Let it end there," Tom said. "If he wants to see you again tell him you're busy."

"The hell I will," Joe snorted. "Are you nuts?"

"I smell trouble with that guy, Joe," Tom warned.

"I'll take any trouble he will give me," Joe said fervently. "He's got something that I want."

"What's that?"

Joe silently held up his fist.

 PEPE

I couldn't sleep that Friday night; Saturday morning just never seemed to arrive. I tossed and turned until my aunt called in to ask if I was having a nightmare. I put on a sleepy voice and assured her I must have been dreaming. For the rest of the long dreary hours I alternately dozed and watched the window frame of darkness in the front room slowly turn from black to gray. I was up when the first streamers of lemonish light entered that chilly room. I had the universal breakfast for both adults and children of the slums; cornflakes and coffee. Since the NRA had introduced the forty-hour week, Aunt Clara now worked—with a five dollar raise—from Monday to Friday with Saturday and Sunday off. Even the docks were quiet on Saturday; the only gangs working were on time and a half. For the Neighborhood, Saturday morning had become a day for sleeping late. Outside of workdays, getting up early was set aside for Sunday to catch the seven or eight o'clock Mass, push your way into the crowded German bakery on Ninth Avenue to buy the rolls and crumb buns, and then get the *Daily News* Sunday comics at the candy store.

I tiptoed around the kitchen to Aunt Clara's steady snores. It was only a few minutes after seven when I had finished carefully stoking the coal stove and cleaning up my few dishes. Ten o'clock seemed a century off. On an impulse I went up to the roof, taking the steps two at a time.

It was the first cold day of the fall but a beautiful fresh and sparkling morning. Acres of flat tar roofs, chimneys, and clotheslines stretched northward to Columbus Circle and to the south beyond McGraw-Hill, down to the tip of Chelsea. The morning was quiet, windless. Beyond the docks the steely blue Hudson glinted in the strong sunlight beneath the glowering stone cliffs of Jersey. Downriver, a freighter gave two indignant blasts at a fast-moving tug that thumbed its nose with two sharp toots.

When I looked north across the flat, empty spaces I remembered how one day, after a heavy snowstorm, Joe and I had accepted a dare to walk to the next block across the roofs. I closed my eyes and saw again our footsteps, the only marks in the clean deep snow, and recalled the pounding of my heart after we had made the wild leap across the tenement alley before we reached Forty-seventh Street to clamber down a fire escape. Joe and I were still the only ones on the block who had made that leap. Tom had paled when he heard about it, and we had to promise on a Bible never to do it again. But that had been long ago.

Frozen work pants, shirts, housedresses, and underwear hung like crucified figures on the lines. I took down the wash Aunt Clara had done the day before and bent and cracked my pants and shirts so they wouldn't melt on what she called "my clean kitchen floor."

Before I closed the roof door I took one last look. In the short time I had been up there the sun had risen higher and the center of the Hudson glowed like an inner stream of molten gems. I could hear cars on the avenue, and in the harbor at the tip of Manhattan the Statue of Liberty scorched the hard blue sky with her torch. It was a splendid morning, made for living. For the first time in days I no longer felt bitter and depressed.

I left Aunt Clara still snoring and tiptoed down the stairs. Even the Neighborhood looked clean, but it wouldn't last long. Although the garbage had been collected the night before, the sidewalks and street would be littered with fruit rinds, paper, greasy bags, and remnants of pizza crusts which many residents of the Neighborhood made their Friday night meatless meal. The only one on the street was a young kid methodically playing points on

129

his stoop. When he missed a high fly I easily caught it and tossed it back, squeezing the ball to make it spin with English. The kid gave a whoop and threw it back to me, begging me for one more. This time I really gave it English and the ball bounced crazily down the street with the kid in pursuit. The big clock on the wall in Schultz's butcher store on Ninth Avenue told me it was only a few minutes after nine, so I started down the avenue, the collar of my old mackinaw up around my ears. The incident at the school, the beating at the precinct, and the humiliation and disillusionment of our arraignment and sentencing by that miserable clubhouse judge had begun slowly to fade. Only the memory of losing the chance to take the scholarship exam still remained, glowing like a small cinder. I don't know why, but I had nourished the hope that Father John at the very last moment, would summon me to his office and gruffly inform me that I had been punished enough for my foolishness and I could represent the school.

But none of the old resentment was in my mind that Saturday morning. I was going to meet Chena.

At Forty-second Street I smiled to myself as a crosstown trolley passed. A few years before I would have automatically hitched a ride to Fifth Avenue, now I wouldn't think of it. Who was it said the first sign of aging was the discarding of frivolities? I walked briskly across town rather pleased with my philosophising.

I was early, so I went to American History and with the help of my old friend Mr. Adams piled a number of source books on the table. Then I took up a station in the lobby and anxiously peered out the glass doors.

The old Negro guard stationed at the door loaned me his copy of the *Daily Mirror*. The enormous headlines told me Dutch Schultz, the famous gangster, had died in a New Jersey hospital. There was a dramatic picture on page one of Schultz on a hospital stretcher raising himself up to look at the dark bullet holes in his chest. The story described how Schultz and two of his henchmen had been killed by a hail of bullets in a Newark bar a few days before. At the same time, gunmen had shot two other men the police said were also mobsters in a Times Square barbershop.

Schultz was no stranger to the kids in the Neighborhood; names of well-known gangsters of those days were more familiar to us than those of the President's cabinet.

Half of Forty-sixth Street didn't know—or care—who was the vice-president or the chief justice, but everyone could tell you the story of how Owney Madden's hoods hired mailbags, mail trucks, and letter carrier uniforms to distribute their bootleg whiskey while federal agents saturated the West Side.

When I returned the paper, the old guard just shrugged.

"That's been in the wind for days, boy. Everybody in Harlem knew he was gonna get it one day."

"Why?"

"They's fightin' among themselves. Lots of gangsters with guns up in Harlem these days. They all wants to take over numbers."

"Is there a lot of money in numbers?" I said as I peered out of the door.

He gave me an incredulous look. "There's more money in numbers than they is in . . ."

As he searched for an apt comparison I prompted, "United States Steel?"

"That's right. Don't you laugh, boy. That's right."

"There's numbers in our Neighborhood. My aunt plays every day. Once she hit for ten dollars—"

The old guard chuckled. "Sure enough she hit. I know—she takes 'em from me."

I half listened as he rambled on.

"Numbers is a black man's game, boy. When I first came up from Georgia"—he rubbed a big bony hand around his black face—"let me see, that's more'n twenty-five years ago, Harlem was playin' numbers. That time King Chico he was the boss. Then his woman put a knife in him and a West Indian man with a hump on his back, he took over." He chuckled. "All Harlem just loved to touch that man's back. They rub his back, then they play a number. Folks said that little man's lungs just couldn't get enough air all bunched up in his humpback. So he died. Then Casper Holstein and Madam St. Clair took over. They was hot ones. The Kingfish, that was Holstein, he was a West Indian. On Easter he and the Madam would come sandin' down a Hundred Twenty-fifth Street, the Kingfish with his yeller shoes and honest silk vest and smilin' like he owned the world. The Madam would be wearin' her hat, big as a mule cart wheel!"

He added dolefully, "Ain't like that no more since the Dutchman took over . . ."

The name The Dutchman stuck like a spear in my mind.

"The Dutchman?" I asked.

He tapped the tabloid's headlines, "That's him, that's the man. That's the Dutchman."

I suddenly remembered the phone call, Valentino speaking low and intensely in Italian, and catching the name of the Dutchman.

But all thoughts of that evening at the Shadow Box, the dying gangster, Harlem, and the numbers vanished when I caught a glimpse of Chena. She was at the bottom of the steps, anxiously looking up and down the avenue and glancing at her wristwatch. I flew out the door and took the steps two at a time.

"Hiya, Chena," I called out.

She turned and waved, and my heart began pounding when I saw her face.

She had on a camel's hair coat with the collar turned up and wore her hair in braids under a jaunty black velvet beret. For the first time I noticed her dark hair had copperish glints that caught the strong sunlight. Her cheeks glowed with the cold and her dark eyes sparkled. I told myself she was as pretty as the morning.

"Oh, Frank, I'm late! I just couldn't find my notebook. I thought maybe you had gone home . . ."

"I'd wait until midnight," I said gallantly.

She smiled. "You're sweet."

"Well, let's get to work," I said offering her my hand. "I hope you have a lot of pencils."

We ran up the steps laughing. Inside, I introduced her to the old guard who gravely welcomed her while I checked our coats.

When I returned with the brass check the old man was showing her the tabloid's headlines. Only much later did I recall she seemed troubled as she listened to the old man's account.

"That's what I've been hearing for the past hour," I said as we walked to the elevator, "all about Schultz and the numbers racket in Harlem . . ."

She shuddered slightly. "I hate those stories and that picture of that gangster with those bullet holes in his body." She hugged my arm. "Please let's not talk about it."

"Fine with me," I said. "From now on it's King Cotton and the Southern slave aristocracy. Okay?"

132

"You sound like Sister Gerald," she said, giggling. She pursed her lips and stared down her nose; her voice became squeaky and high pitched. "I want every girl in this class to have their paper in by Monday with a precise bibliography. Not a lot of words!"

She was a wonderful mimic and I could instantly see the old nun, the kind that had been teaching me all my life, glowering down at her students. We laughed all the way to the third floor. On the way I made sure I nonchalantly answered the greeting of the old bearded gentleman who had charge of Rare Books and the captain of the guards stationed outside the Main Catalogue Room. I hoped Chena was impressed.

I gave her a quick tour of the top floor, pointing out the various departments and sliding out several trays in the card catalog. The Main Reading Room, with its solid row after row of varnished tables and countless small green lampshades that always reminded me of an army of Chinese dwarfs waiting for a command, made Chena gasp. With the air of an emperor of all the books in creation, I conducted her into the American History Room and sat her down at a table in the rear where I had piled the source books.

"I checked in for us," I whispered and pointed to the black number on the table. "We're Numbers 823 and 824. They're going to be our lucky numbers from now on."

"There's so much here," she whispered, "I don't know where to begin."

Down through the years I had watched the busy scholars and knew their technique. I took a pack of small white index cards and explained to Chena how we would work. She was all admiration and I ate it up.

We continued steadily through the morning until afternoon. She had a quick mind and an almost photographic memory for detail. When we had finished we had a mound of cards filled with her superb penmanship and my careless scrawls.

"Frank, I only need ten pages," she protested. "I have enough for a book!"

"I insist you know your subject thoroughly," I told her and squeezed her hand. "How about lunch? Then we can come back if you think you'll need more . . ."

"More?"

She glared down her nose. "Miss Valentino, you have too many notes. You have to eat what you don't use!"

"How about the Automat, it's just around the corner?"

"I love the Automat," she said linking her arm with mine.

The Automat was crowded with shoppers but we finally found a table in the corner.

"Frank, why don't you try for CCNY?" she said. "I hate to think of you way up in Vermont."

"I bet you wouldn't even write me a postcard."

"But I would!" she protested. "I'd write to you as often as you would want me to."

"Every day?"

She studied me for a moment, her dark eyes luminous and thoughtful.

"Would you want me to?"

Would I? I almost crushed her slender hand when I told her how much I would want her letters.

After lunch we walked up Fifth Avenue to the Plaza, then circled back. I was desperately wondering what else I could offer when my eye caught the street sign, Fifty-second.

"This is Fifty-second!" I said, stopping. "Your uncle's art gallery is just down the block on Madison, isn't it? Why don't we walk over and say hello?"

She hesitated. A shadow fell across her face.

"Would you want to?"

"Sure. We can just drop in."

At that time Pepe's art gallery was only a deep niche in the wall next to an empty store on the corner. The windows were tastefully decorated with two huge paintings set on easels covered with black velvet. One window held a dismal canvas of a medieval scene of hovering angels and a Madonna, but the other I will never forget; it depicted a band of hunters who seemed to me to have come riding out of the Arabian Nights, encircling a pair of lions. The magnificent colors, the savagery of the scene was unforgettable. It was so real I fancied I could hear the agonized roar of the wounded beasts.

"That's a Delacroix," Chena volunteered. "It's a print."

"Who's he?"

"A French painter. He's Pepe's favorite."

"How much would a painting like that cost?"

"The original? Oh, thousands and thousands, I guess."

I was aghast. "That much?"

She laughed. "Pepe sold a painting last month for a thousand dollars. He told me many times he was sorry he sold it. He's always insisting valuable paintings are as good as diamonds."

From the depths of the Neighborhood I said, "I never knew people paid that kind of money for paintings."

"Oh sure. He and another gallery owner once sold one for five thousand dollars to a museum. Wait until you see the Eakins Pepe has." She quickly answered the question she read in my face. "I love Eakins. He's an American painter and I always tell Pepe he's better than Delacroix. Does he get mad!"

"How did you get to know so much about art, Chena?"

"From Pepe. I've been coming over here since I was nine—"

"How does Pepe know so much? Is he an artist?"

She bit her lower lip. "After you and Joe left the Shadow Box, Nicky and I walked home alone." She smiled. "We talked quite a bit about you. I guess of all the kids in the school Nicky liked you the best—"

"Good old Nick."

"He said he told you about Pepe."

"About going to prison for something that happened in your father's place?"

"The speakeasy," she said smiling. "Everyone in the Neighborhood knew he was running one, Frank."

"Nicky said Pepe came in when two stickup men were beating up your father—"

"My mother finally told me what happened. She shuddered. "I used to have nightmares after I knew the story."

"Nick said there was some kind of a deal and Pepe had to go to prison for a while."

"I was only a little girl but I know he was gone for several years. I always thought he was in Italy. Later my mother told me my father had paid a lot of money to get Pepe released. When he came out he knew a lot about art. His cellmate had been a counterfeiter and an artist. I can remember when I was small Pepe would draw kittens and little animals for me when I did well in school. When he was on parole he worked for an art gallery. I guess art became his whole life. I was in grammar school when he went to Italy for a year. He came back with a lot of money, and he and my father opened the Shadow Box."

"From what your father said the other night, your grandmother helped him get a start."

"My father likes to tell that story," she said, "maybe it makes him feel more American. Horatio Alger, like Nicky calls him. It makes him furious. Oh, my grandmother gave him the money to start the speakeasy but my mother said it never amounted to anything. The truth is my father isn't much of a businessman. It's Pepe who's the real boss . . ."

"I bet I know his favorite."

"That's because I was the only one who would listen to him talk about art and artists," she said laughing. "Nicky always wanted to go to the movies and see cowboy pictures. Before I was ten, Pepe was taking me to all the museums and galleries."

"He must know a lot about art."

She rolled her eyes upward. "You'll find out when he bends our ears all afternoon. But it will be worth it because I'm sure he'll take us to Hicks' . . ."

"Hicks? Is that another gallery?"

She giggled. "It's an ice cream store just a few blocks away. Haven't you ever heard of it, Frank?"

I shook my head. "The only ice cream soda I ever had was in that candy store on Ninth Avenue."

She wrinkled her nose. "That dirty old place! Wait until you see Hicks'. "

When she opened the door an old-fashioned bell tinkled somewhere in the dim recesses. It was like walking down a dusty narrow canvas box: paintings hung on the wall, frame to frame; others were stacked in rows along the sides. And there was Pepe, meticulously dressed as always, his dark face beaming.

"Chena . . . and my young friend! What brings you over here?"

"I had to do a paper for school and Frank showed me how the library on Fifth Avenue works. Then we walked up Fifth Avenue and came over to see you."

"Wonderful. Wonderful. I can't take you young people to lunch?"

"No, but you can take us to Hicks'. Frank's never heard of it."

"You are in for a great discovery, my young friend," Pepe said. A wave of his hand took in his gallery. "How do you like my treasures?"

"I don't know anything about art," I said, "but I think the painting in the window is just great—"

Pepe's eyes glowed. "Ah, the Delacroix print."

"What's the name of that one, Pepe?" Chena asked. I sensed she already knew the title of the painting but did not want to appear superior to me.

136

" 'The Lion Hunt.' He painted that in the 1850s after his trip to Morocco," Pepe said almost lovingly.

"The colors are magnificent," I said, trying to sound intelligent.

"Color dreams, thinks, and speaks," Pepe said. He walked to the front of the gallery, pulled aside the drape, and carefully turned the easel so the large painting faced us. Close at hand it was breathtaking.

"What do you see in it, my young friend?" Pepe said suddenly.

"Man against beast. It's always been a struggle, hasn't it?"

He smiled. "Very good. Delacroix loved to paint battles or struggles but he never tells you who is right or who is wrong. It is not true, Chena?"

"Pepe doesn't like it when I say it," Chena said firmly, "but some of his paintings frighten me." She hesitated, then added, "There's always violence and killings. That's why I like Eakins . . ."

"You are a woman," Pepe said almost brusquely. "You don't know of such things."

"And I don't want to—ever."

Pepe put his arm around her. I sensed her stiffen almost involuntarily.

"Chena! Get married! *Fare tanto bambini!*" Then suddenly he slapped his hand to his forehead. "*Ecco!* I didn't show you the Constable!"

"Constable's an English painter," Chena whispered. "He bought it last week at an auction. That's the way he spends his money. My mother told him he would walk around like a guinea laborer if he could have paintings in his bedroom. Pepe just looked at her and said, "You are right, *amante!*"

We followed him into another room as cluttered as the first. He pulled aside a velvet sheet and there lay a vista of fleecy clouds and gently rolling acres of wheat, motionless in the still heat of a summer afternoon. In the foreground was a small herd of grazing cattle.

"An original Constable," Pepe said proudly. "It is one of his favorite scenes from the Stour River Valley. Is it not magnificent, Chena?"

"It is, Pepe," she said admiringly. "So calm and peaceful." She turned to me. "Do you like it, Frank?"

"It's beautiful."

"It is better than the horsemen, my young friend?" Pepe asked with a smile as he covered the canvas.

"They're both wonderful."

"Ah, my young friend walks in the middle of the road," Pepe said laughing.

"Maybe that's because I don't know anything about painting," I said, slightly nettled.

"Good!" Pepe said, "Then I will teach you!"

Chena groaned theatrically. "Frank! You don't know what you just did! Pepe will have us here all day!"

"Only a few minutes, Chena," Pepe protested. "A few books, then we will go!"

We went back into his office and for an hour or two he flipped through a series of huge art books and portfolios, displaying them on an easel and describing the background and the technique of each artist with scholarship and a familiarity with the subject that impressed me. During those lonely years in that cell Pepe had devoured everything he was taught by his forger-teacher. There were times when my mind wandered and I could almost see him—a short, powerfully built killer—listening closely to the brilliant thief.

Like any shrewd authority, Pepe knew when to stop. Delacroix was in the midst of his Moroccan tour when he paused, glanced at his watch, and closed the book.

"*Pòrco misèria!* It is time for Hicks', no, Chena?"

"Yes, Pepe," Chena said quickly. "We love your paintings but I think Frank and I would rather have a double banana split . . ."

Pepe held up three fingers. For the first time I noticed that they were stubby and powerful looking.

"Three banana splits, Chena. Your Uncle Pepe will have one . . ."

On the way out he stopped to peer into a small room that smelled of turpentine and glue. A slender man of uncertain age with beetling brows, black glittering eyes, and a mouth like a trap, had apparently just finished working on a framed painting which he was setting on an easel. A coil of framing wire hung over one shoulder.

Pepe put his finger to his lips. As we watched in silence the man carefully made a loop at one end of the wire, casually whirled the lasso over his head and tossed it high up on the wall across the room. When it caught on a peg, he flung the rest of the roll to hit the target like a quoit ringing a stake.

"Like a cowboy, Lorenzo!" Pepe cried as he entered the room. "This is Lorenzo. He is also an artist with the varnish and the wire, eh, Lorenzo?"

Lorenzo's dark eyes flickered over me but he smiled.

"He restores oil paintings," Chena explained when we went out. "Lots of people, even museums, bring Pepe their old paintings to be fixed by Lorenzo."

"He's as good as Tom Mix with that wire lasso," I said.

"He was a cowboy in Cuba," she said with a giggle.

"An Italian cowboy in Cuba!"

"I'm not making it up," she protested. "It does sound funny but he worked on a plantation in Cuba before he came here. The man who owned the plantation had a stable of horses and Lorenzo took care of them."

"What was he doing in Cuba?"

"I don't know the whole story. Pepe once told me he had to leave Italy over what he called a matter of honor, but my mother said Lorenzo was a *squadrista*, that's like a gangster over here. When Mussolini broke up the Mafia he fled to Cuba."

"Why Cuba?"

"My mother said the Sicilians have friends there."

"Is your mother Sicilian, Chena?"

"Sicilian! She would never talk to you again if she heard you say that. Her family's Neapolitan. My father and Pepe are Sicilian."

"You make it sound like there's no love lost between them."

"My mother said there was a war between the Castellammarese—they were the men from around Castellammare del Golfo—and the Neapolitan gangsters in New York several years ago. Two of her cousins were killed." She shuddered. "I can still remember going to the funeral parlor. They couldn't open the casket because they had been burned in a car."

"You mean they had an actual war right here in the city?"

"Many of the Italian families on Ninth Avenue"—she smiled—" Guinea Alley—had people killed. It was terrible."

"But how did Lorenzo finally get here?"

"Pepe got him in. I think he helped him to jump ship. Every time my father hears that the immigration agents are around he tells Pepe and Pepe sends Lorenzo out to Detroit. Then he keeps moving from city to city living

139

with Italian families until it's safe to come back." She said archly, "I just don't know why I'm telling you all our family's scandal, Frank Howell!"

"Maybe it's because you like me," I suggested.

She smiled and whispered, "I know that's why . . ."

I walked on air all the way to Hicks'.

As Pepe had predicted the ice cream parlor was a delightful experience. When the waiter placed a towering creation of ice cream topped by whirls of whipped cream and fresh fruit and syrup before me, Chena burst out laughing.

Before I had finished that enormous portion of ice cream, Pepe had learned a great deal about me through what appeared to be casual questioning.

Never once did he allude to the farewell party at the Shadow Box. When I mentioned Nick, Chena fell silent and Pepe casually told me he was probably getting ready to dissect the corpse of some peasant in the Bologna medical school.

It was almost six o'clock when we left. I gulped at the cashier's desk when Pepe took out his wallet—it was stuffed with bills.

When we said good-bye Pepe insisted that we return the following Saturday for lunch at what he called the best Italian restaurant in New York City, to be followed by a grand tour of the Metropolitan. I agreed. In the gathering fall twilight Chena and I walked, hand in hand, up Fifth Avenue to Fifty-seventh Street.

I said good-bye at her door, with the elevator man smirking over his shoulder. I knew what he meant and I wanted to kick him in the teeth. Then, with one final wave, the elevator door slid shut and she was gone.

Saturday after Saturday passed; each one was spent with Chena and Pepe. I sensed Chena's reluctance to see Pepe every week but she said nothing. But I did notice that Chena did not like to be touched by Pepe. If he put his arms around her waist or patted her cheek affectionately, her smile became strained, her eyes wary. As for myself, I eagerly let Pepe guide me into new and exciting worlds, far removed from the squalid Neighborhood. We explored not only the Metropolitan but many smaller art museums and galleries in the city. Every Saturday was different; a new showing, a new museum, or a private viewing.

Joe and I were born only days apart, and we had always celebrated together. This time Pepe and Chena toasted my eighteenth birthday.

When Pepe was requested by out-of-town galleries or clients to appraise paintings privately offered for sale, he would make his appointments for Saturday and we would accompany him in the magnificent Cord sedan. I can still see him, a barrel of a man, squatting on the jump seat, chuckling, smiling, and gesturing as he told us the background of each potential seller. He always wore his expensive dark Chesterfield with the velvet collar and a black soft hat with a wide brim, the type usually associated with artists of the thirties.

After several Saturdays I was sure he knew all there was to know about my life—past, present, and future. There was nothing distasteful about his probing, and he always managed to include the questions in a lively discussion.

I noticed too, as time went on, that Chena seemed uneasy at the growing intimacy between me and Pepe. Finally she began to make excuses, not to avoid seeing me but for us not to visit the gallery. She would suddenly remember an important errand, there would be work to do in the library on a paper, or a movie that she just had to see.

Chena was always sweet and apologetic to Pepe, but sweet or not, she was still a feline at heart and a Sicilian feline—a combination I learned had to be handled as gently as a phial of nitroglycerin.

I first learned that one Saturday on Fifth Avenue, when I started to walk to Pepe's Gallery.

"Where are we going, Frank?" she asked.

"To see Pepe. Didn't he say last week he wanted to take us out to dinner?"

"He did but I also told him we had something else to do."

"What did you tell him that for?"

"Because," she snapped.

"Why because?"

"I don't think we should see him that much." She stopped and faced me. "*Marrone!* Do you have to drag me over there every Saturday?"

"I never dragged you anywhere—"

"Every Saturday it's been Pepe this, Pepe that!" Her

voice was rising and I was conscious of grinning pedestrians. But I also could be stubborn. I took her arm.

"Come on, Chena. Let's stop arguing and walk over to—"

She almost pulled the arm out of its socket. Her large black eyes were blazing and brimming with tears.

"*Bossa Scattaria!* Go over to that *carognia!* Look at his paintings. Listen to his talk, talk, talk!" She mocked him, "Peppino! My little Peppino!"

Then she turned and ran down the avenue.

"Looks like you have a handful, kid," a man nearby said, shaking his head.

I didn't wait to answer him but took off after Chena.

After some broken field running across Fifth Avenue against the traffic, I finally caught up with her. I pulled her to one side and let her weep on my shoulder.

"I'm sorry," she sobbed, "I acted like a fool . . ."

"Let's forget Pepe, Chena. We'll never go back there again."

She shook her head. "We can't do that. After all, he has been nice to us—to you."

"But I thought you liked him, darling . . ."

"I don't know . . . I guess I'm just being stupid, but there are times when I'm afraid of Pepe."

"Did he ever do anything to you?" I asked.

"No, that's it—he's always been wonderful. I don't know, Frank, but I've had this feeling a long time—I never told anyone, even Nicky—I think Pepe is bad. I heard him tell my father things when they thought my mother and I were asleep—"

"What things, Chena?"

"Please—let's forget Pepe," she said hugging my arm. "What is more important—are you mad at me?"

"Of course not. I just don't understand, that's all."

"Oh, it's something to do with the family," she said vaguely.

"Did Pepe and your father have kind of a fight over something?"

"No. Sometimes I wish they had. It's"—she waved her hand and shook her head—"it's hard to explain, darling, when you're not Italian."

I never pressed her for an explanation, but the Fifth Avenue incident warned me that, while I had a beautiful, charming, stunning girl, she was also all Sicilian, and when she blew . . . *Marrone!*

142

We continued to see Pepe, however, while he probed into my life with his shrewd, beguiling questions. I was also putting together bits and pieces I overheard from his cryptic conversations with Lorenzo, or even over the telephone. I began to realize it was Pepe, not Gus Valentino, who was the real boss of the Shadow Box. The hard-faced men who came to the gallery to see him had the smell about them of something far outside the world of oil, canvas, and paint.

And then one day I caught a glimpse of what frightened Chena—the other Pepe, the Pepe without the smiling, affable manner, the Pepe whose face was suddenly hard as stone, his eyes cold and glittering as a snake's.

One Saturday I arrived at the gallery early; Chena was late and Pepe had not returned from an appointment. Lorenzo seemed glad to see me. He grunted something about delivering a painting by cab to Park Avenue and asked if I would listen for the phone and tell any customers he would be back shortly. Pepe, he said, would be back soon.

He ushered me into Pepe's office where I idly leafed through some of the many art books. I was lost in the beauty of the plates when the bell tinkled. I looked up and suddenly saw a snappily dressed young man who appeared startled to see me.

"Who are you, kid?" he asked nervously.

"I'm just waiting for someone. The man who works here will be right back."

"Lorenzo?"

"That's right."

"Okay. I'll wait."

I returned to the book. A few minutes later the bell tinkled again. Pepe, his back to me, was talking to the visitor, and I went back to the book. Suddenly I became conscious of someone pleading in a low, frantic voice. I peeked out of the office and saw Pepe glaring at the young man.

Pepe suddenly grabbed him by the jacket collar and slammed him against the wall with such ferocity that the paintings shook. At a terse order in Italian the man ran out of the gallery. When I saw the man's frightened, pale face and staring eyes I suddenly sensed what was troubling Chena—Pepe was a dangerous man.

Pepe came toward me holding his hands, palms upward in a gesture of futile despair.

"A thief," he said, "a young thief who would steal his mother's bread money." He shook his head. "There are so few to be trusted these days." With an arm over my shoulder he walked me back into his office. When he saw the open book he cried, "El Greco! 'View From Toledo'! Was it not magnificent at the Met, Peppino?" More and more he was using that expression of affection—Little Pepe. A few nights after that I picked up a discarded tabloid in the subway and was flipping the pages when my eyes caught a small photograph in the heart of a news story. Adjacent to it was a large picture of two cops studying a charred car they had found in a swamp. The caption said the car had contained the garroted, burned body of a man described as "a known waterfront hood." I was sure it was the frightened young man I had seen in Pepe's gallery. I intended to mention it to Chena but I never did. I was afraid she would know all about it.

10 SLAUGHTER ON FORTY-SIXTH STREET

If it is true as Voltaire claimed that in every man's life there is one day etched in acid, then mine must be that December day. It was a day when I knew it was no longer wise for anyone in the Neighborhood to hope.

I can recall it in minute detail, from the weather to the color of the housedress my aunt was wearing. It had dawned cold and clear. I was up early to help my aunt clean the dish closet. Every year as the holidays approached it was inevitable that she became a furious housecleaner. I remember as I dried the dishes and glasses how we began our annual ritual; the size of the tree for the front room and the question of Christmas gifts. I had to turn away to hide my grin when she started telling me there was no money for gifts this year. I had heard it every year; by taking store cheese sandwiches from home for lunch she always pinched pennies to buy me a present. This year it would be different. I had almost fifteen dollars saved from working at Fat Freddy's potato warehouse; ten for a present for Aunt Clara, and five for a bottle of perfume I had already selected for Chena. I even had a few dollars left for our date.

I was to meet her at noon at the library lions. First we'd have lunch at Hicks', and then go to Radio City. This time she had insisted there was to be no visit to the gallery to see Pepe. It would be my first time in Radio City but I had carefully checked the matinee price and I knew Hicks' menu. I had my finances down to the penny.

We finished a few minutes after ten and my aunt prepared to visit the Gunnar flat for her usual Saturday morning coffee and buns and "gossip hour," as she called it.

Inside the Gunnar flat Tom was good-naturedly badgering Joe to take his shoes to the shoemaker. Mrs. Gunnar appeared brisk and happy. Tom, she announced, had decided not to take a scholarship examination for some school out west but would continue at Fordham Law. It was the big news of the day.

Joe finally consented to go to the shoemaker; I agreed to go along and keep him company. As we came out on the stoop Tom called from the window: Mrs. Gunnar wanted a pound of onions for a stew, and Tom threw down a dime. Joe missed it and we ran after it as it rolled into the gutter.

I was just about to tell Joe about my date with Chena when, out of the corner of my eye, I saw a black sedan pull away from the curb. It passed us, then stopped. Two men jumped out. One was Hennessy, the other was smaller with pepper and salt hair that matched his tweed overcoat. He had a lean, bony face under his snap-brim hat.

Joe grunted and we stopped. "Hennessy."

"I want to talk to you kids," Hennessy said in his strange whispering voice. "You have to come to the precinct."

"We're not going to any goddam precinct and have you kick our heads in," Joe said.

"Take it easy, kid," the other cop said. He moved to one side of me to cut off all means of escape.

"What do you want us for?" I asked.

"A super of a Ninth Avenue loft was robbed by two kids who rapped a lead pipe over his head," the cop said.

"So what do you want from us?"

"He looked out the window and saw the two kids running away. The description fits you and your friend."

"What are you tryin' to do, Kidneyfeet—frame us again?"

"Come on, kid," the other cop said to me, "it's not a pinch. We only want you to come over to the precinct and let the guy take a look at both of you."

He reached out for my arm but I pulled away.

Joe moved back to the tenement stoop and I joined him.

Hennessy said softly, "Don't give us any trouble, Gunnar."

"We're not goin' to give you any trouble, because we're not goin' anywhere," Joe told him.

The usual chorus of the Neighborhood people began shouting at the cops. Heads started to appear in open windows. Above us an old hag, her arms resting on a pillow, was shouting curses down at Hennessy. Men were on stoops and coming out of basements. A group of little kids had started to chant:

"Kidneyfeet! Kidneyfeet! You big piece of meat!"

Hennessy's lime-colored eyes never flickered, but his lips tightened. He glanced over at his partner who casually took my arm. It was not as casual as he tried to make it appear. I was sure I would have a black and blue mark where his fingers gripped me.

"Come on, kid, get in the car," he said quietly. When I made a move to get into the car he bent down to open the door. As his grip relaxed I yanked free and jumped to Joe's side. For a moment we stood shoulder to shoulder facing the two cops. The smaller one looked over at Hennessy.

"Let's get 'em," Hennessy said and they came toward us.

I tried to run but the cop was wiry and agile. He slammed me against the pillar of the stoop, but I bounced back and rammed him in the stomach. He grunted and wrestled me to the steps of the stoop; he had handcuffs in his hand and was trying to get one cuff around my wrist.

The sight of the cuffs made me frantic. I fought savagely and the next thing I knew the clear morning exploded into a shower of stars. He had a billy in one hand, and I could feel the blood running down the side of my face from a blow that had split my ear. I was on a step above him and my fist caught him in the mouth. Then he really started to work me over with his billy.

A few feet away, Joe struggled desperately with Hennessy, but it was obvious the big cop was too strong for him. He had gotten one cuff on Joe's wrist when we heard someone shouting.

"Hey, what are you doing? He's my brother!"

It was Tom. He was wearing a washed-out basketball jersey and sneakers and looked as angry as I had ever seen him.

"We're police officers," Hennessy grunted. "They're under arrest."

The other cop started to drag me down the stoop and Tom saw my bloody face.

"What the hell are you beating them for?" he shouted.

"Get out of here," the cop snarled. "We're takin' 'em in."

"Goddammit! Do you have to beat them? They're only kids!"

Tom grabbed the back of Joe's jacket and tried to pull him free of Hennessy's embrace. For a few minutes they engaged in a weird ballet with Joe pulled back and forth between them. Then, suddenly, Joe broke loose and Tom, off balance, staggered backward a few feet. Joe started to run but the cop holding me put out his foot and sent him sprawling on the sidewalk. As he scrambled to his feet he was overpowered by Hennessy. I saw Tom swing. His blow caught Hennessy on the side of his face, but the detective just tightened his grip on Joe with one hand and lashed out at Tom with the other. Tom ducked. Then the grotesque ballet commenced.

Dizzy from the blows I let the cop drag me across the sidewalk to the unmarked car and cuff me to its steering wheel. Then he jumped out to join the pulling, tugging trio.

I heard Tom's muffled cry, "Joe! Get going!"

I strained against the cuffs and leaned as far as I could toward the window as Tom violently pushed the gray-haired cop back against the car. Joe was sprawled out on the stoop and Tom was frantically pulling him to his feet. As they started to run a gun appeared in Hennessy's hand, it jerked twice, the sharp crash of the sound filling the morning quiet. Tom staggered, then reached for the post of a stoop. He clutched it for a moment, then slowly crumpled to the sidewalk, rolled over, and lay still. Joe stared at him and slid to a step on the stoop.

A large pool of blood slowly formed on the worn,

147

washed-out basketball shirt. Tom lay on his back, his open eyes staring at the sky.

I knew he was dead.

In that moment the whole scene seemed frozen by time in a tableau; the old woman in the open window above us, wisps of gray hair hanging down her face; a peroxide blonde, curlers like little wheels wound tightly in her hair; a man on a stoop clutching his pipe as he stared down at us in disbelief; three kids in ragged sweaters and sneakers, their chant broken off as if by a hand at their throats; Schultz the butcher in his bloodstained apron and incongruous straw hat.

Hennessy shattered the tableau. He slowly put the revolver back in his shoulder holster.

"You all right, Dave?" he asked the other cop.

"Yeah, I'm okay," the cop said. "How is he?"

"I don't know." Hennessy walked, almost ponderously to where Tom lay. He knelt down and felt for a pulse. Then he stood up.

"They bolted," he said flatly. "I warned 'em." He added defensively, his voice rising as he looked around the street. "We identified ourselves as police officers."

I was watching Joe sitting on the stoop. He just looked down at his brother's body. He didn't protest or make a move when Hennessy reached over and cuffed him to the stoop railing.

"This your brother?" Hennessy asked taking out a notebook.

"Is he hurt?" Joe whispered. "Is he hurt? Call a doctor. Is he hurt?"

"They killed him, Joe," I screamed. "They shot him in the back!"

Hennessy turned and started toward me. It was the signal the Neighborhood seemed to be waiting for. Suddenly bricks, flowerpots, parts of chimneys, and ashcans rained down. The gray-haired cop took out his gun and ran around the side of the car, his revolver aimed toward the roofs. When an ashcan bounced near him, Hennessy lunged for the car. Before he could open the door a red brick, the kind the Neighborhood lovingly called "Red Murphy," caught him in the head. When he went down the other cop reached over me and shouted in the car's mike.

"Signal Thirty ... police officers need assistance ... there's been a shooting ..."

I tore at the cuffs until the blood ran down my wrists and onto the seat. Hennessy was on his knees, looking dazed as he clung to the car door.

"You killed him," I kept shouting at him. "You shot him in the back!"

Joe, who was staring down at Tom's body, looked over at me but he didn't make a sound.

Within minutes the street was filled with cops, enough cops to start a St. Patrick's Day Parade.

They ran into the tenements and up on the roofs. By the time they brought down a few struggling, cursing men and women and threw them into paddy wagons, the kids who sent down the shower of brickbats were blocks away. There were ambulances, radio cars, emergency squads, and police brass. In the rear mirror I could see an intern from Polyclinic treating Hennessy, who had a patch on the back of his head and was talking earnestly with three men in plainclothes who had gold badges pinned to the lapels of their overcoats.

"Dave was lucky," a cop called out to another. "Hennessy got a brick in the head."

No one seemed to give a damn about Tom. Two plainclothesmen outlined his body with chalk and a photographer impassively took pictures. By now a large pool of blood had trickled from under his body and flowed across the sidewalk to the edge of the curb. Several detectives and cops were gathered around Joe as he sat on the stoop. As he talked, Hennessy kept pointing to Joe and me.

Suddenly the crowd of cops opened, and through the human aisle came Mrs. Gunnar and my aunt escorted by a priest. Mrs. Gunnar stumbled as she walked; there was a frantic look on her face. She clutched a rosary and her lips moved silently with the prayers. My aunt looked stunned but she clung to Mrs. Gunnar's arm and whispered to her.

When they reached the body the priest said something to Schultz the butcher, and he silently took Mrs. Gunnar's arm as the priest put on his purple stole and knelt beside Tom. Several cops removed their hats. I heard the low monotone of the priest's voice and saw a small gold case in his hands as he anointed the body with the holy oils of Extreme Unction.

Joe's voice suddenly rose in the breathless silence, so clear and piercing that even the priest's voice broke off.

"They killed him, Mom! They shot him in the back!"

The ring of cops scattered and two appeared, dragging Joe between them. They pushed him into a car, started the engine, rolled up the street.

"No ... no ... please ..." Mrs. Gunnar cried as Schultz and my aunt held her. The priest's voice began again, low, insistent, relentless.

"They shot Tom in the back," I shouted. "Aunt Clara, they shot Tom in the back."

My aunt looked up. When she caught sight of me straining against the cuffs to lean out of the window, she screamed. A man with a gold badge on his lapel ran to the car.

"Shut up! Don't you have any respect?"

"You sons of bitches," I cried, "you killed him."

He beckoned to a young detective nearby. "Get him over to the precinct. Tell the desk sergeant we'll book both of 'em later. ..."

My mouth was as dry as sun-bleached bone but what little spittle I had sprayed his coat. For a moment I thought he was going to strike me but he glanced beyond the car to the silent, hostile crowd and impatiently waved the detective into the car.

"Get him out of here—fast."

The young detective jumped into the car, rolled up the windows, and within minutes we were speeding up Eighth Avenue, the siren wailing like a banshee squatting on the roof.

I slowly realized that within the brief expanse of time since Tom had been shot and killed I had changed, minute by minute into someone else. I could never return to my books, or the worn, clean flat, or Aunt Clara's innocence.

I was dizzy and trembling with the desire to put my fist through the window of the radio car, to kick out the dashboard, to tear at anything, like an infuriated animal while I screamed out at everyone, at the outside world that had always been so hostile—Now are you satisfied? Is this what you wanted? He's dead! Tom Gunnar's dead!

Tom Gunnar who defended the cops, who insisted they weren't all bad, all crooked, who had a dream of unionizing them for the good of the community, was shot in the back by a cop and now his shroud is a dirty newspaper! And all the time the cops who had killed him were marking up the sidewalk with chalk, like kids getting ready for a hopscotch game.

But they had me trussed like a dressed chicken so all I

could do was cry, the tears rolling down my cheeks as I sobbed:

"Tom . . . Tom . . . I'm sorry. . . ."

We were a one-day sensation in the newspapers. The *Daily Mirror* and the *News* both had pictures of Tom's body covered with newspapers and detectives questioning Joe as he sat on the stoop handcuffed to the railing. The dean at Fordham ripped into the police in a statement—as usual it was buried at the end of the sensationalized facts—and while the Fordham Jesuits put pressure on City Hall, the police commissioner issued a pious statement absolving Hennessy and his partner and pointed out that the shooting had been the result of our resisting arrest after a police officer had identified himself.

We were booked on so many charges they made my head spin; resisting arrest, felonious assault on an officer while he was performing his duty, inciting a riot, disorderly conduct—everything they could find in the statute books. I didn't see Joe until our arraignment and then only briefly. He stared straight ahead while the judge made some innocuous remarks about the police maintaining order in the streets of the city—he said, as I remember, "our great city"—just enough so the wire service reporters standing near the witness box would be forced to include his name in their roundup stories.

The Fordham dean had arranged for a lawyer to represent us. But the well-dressed, soft-spoken man who stood at our side was more familiar with civil courts than the grubby little details of West Side Court. The assistant district attorney also made sure he wouldn't be forgotten by the press.

After a bitter denunciation of us, he demanded we be held in $50,000 bail. The judge made it $10,000 but he might as well have made it a million. I had exactly five dollars and fifteen cents in my pocket which was to have financed the joyful afternoon with Chena.

I saw her as they led me out. She was in the front row leaning over the railing.

"Frank, Frank . . ." she whispered.

I was really surprised. "Chena!"

"I called Pepe and told him what happened to you."

"Pepe?"

"He knows a lot of people," she said. "He promised he would help you—"

151

A court attendant rushed over and ordered her back to a seat. She ignored him and blew me a kiss.

On the orders of the magistrate, they kept us in the Children's Shelter pending the grand jury action. Two detectives drove us over there, and when I started to talk to Joe one turned and said, "Shut up, punk!"

"Screw you," I said.

We were at a stop light and the detective turned and slapped me across the face. It wasn't much of a blow and I rolled with it.

"Just a couple of wise kids from that goddam Neighborhood," he told his partner.

Joe stared at him, a look of hate on his face.

King Kong was still at the Children's Shelter and I remembered what Muzzy Blaze had told me when we were there some months before; at the first opportunity I bought him a few packs of cigarettes.

He smiled as he swept them into the drawer of his desk.

"Thanks, kid." He glanced at a typewritten note. "The cops are gonna pick you and your buddy up at eight to take you to the funeral parlor. . . ."

It was a moment I dreaded. Outside the Ninth Avenue funeral parlor—the same one Tom had joked about two weeks before—one of the two detectives who had driven us from the Shelter produced a key and started to unlock the cuffs on Joe's wrists. But he pulled his hands back.

"Leave 'em on."

The startled cop looked at him. "You're goin' in to see your brother, kid. Your mother's there."

"Leave 'em on," Joe said flatly.

"Why?" the cop asked.

"If you take them off I'll run," Joe said. "Then you can shoot me in the back. It will be good practice."

"That goes for me too," I said.

"If that's the way they want it, Ralph, leave the cuffs on 'em," the other cop said. He added, "I wouldn't try to run if I were you, kid," he told Joe.

"Drop dead," Joe said and we walked inside the parlor. Just before we entered the room where Tom was laid out, the cops tried to drape their topcoats over the cuffs but we flipped them off.

The room was dim and crowded. There was a heavy smell of wilting greenhouse flowers and dripping wax. At the end of one room was the casket, a crucifix hanging

152

from the satin lining. The detectives marched us down the aisle. I saw the white blur of faces, then Aunt Clara was holding on to my arm and Mrs. Gunnar was clinging to Joe, her body shaking with sobs. Joe stared down at the cold, painted face of his brother, then turned away. He whispered to his mother while the detective looked to one side self-consciously.

"Are they treating you all right, Frank?" my aunt asked softly. "All the people in the Neighborhood are signing a petition. Some of them went to see the leader. He promised to call on the mayor. There was a photographer from the *Daily News* who took a picture of Tom's trophy."

She held a handkerchief to her face. "Frank ... Frank ... it's so terrible it's like a nightmare ... poor Mary ... poor Mrs. Gunnar ... oh, my God ..."

We sat for a while in the back of the room. Men and women came up to shake Joe's hand and when they found the cuffs they glared at the uneasy cops and some even muttered curses. I was glad when we left. The cops drove us back in silence and after they had checked us in with King Kong one of them said to Joe:

"I'm sorry, kid."

Joe just stared at him, carefully cleared his throat and spat.

Two days later, on a bleak, bitterly cold morning, handcuffed as before to the two detectives, we followed Tom's body from the church to the cemetery. At the grave, Father John came over to Joe and said something in a low voice but Joe ignored him.

One of the detectives said, "Can't you even be nice to a priest, kid?"

"Why?" Joe asked as we walked toward the detective's car.

"He's a man of the cloth ... He's offerin' sympathy for your family," the other cop said in an exasperated voice.

"Who needs sympathy from a stupid, ignorant Irishman?" Joe asked quietly.

The detective's face flushed and he exchanged a hard look with his partner. Then they pushed us into the car and we drove down the frozen road. Behind us Father John was gently leading Mrs. Gunnar to the limousine.

A week later King Kong pulled me out of the breakfast line.

"You're goin' downtown today, kid."

"What for?"

153

"Grand jury. You and your pal'll testify this afternoon."

When I told Joe he just shrugged.

"You don't believe they're gonna do anythin' to Hennessy, do you?"

"At least we'll have a chance to tell what happened."

"They won't believe us ... You heard what the cops said—we're just a couple of punks from that goddam Neighborhood ... they'll believe the cops. You don't think the cops will testify against their own?"

"There's other witnesses, Joe."

"What can they say? That Tom slugged Hennessy? It's no use—you can't beat 'em, Frank. You just can't."

"Who—the cops?"

He shook his head. "All of 'em. Cops. DA. The Father Johns. The grand juries. The newspapers. Has anyone called that son of a bitch Hennessy a murderer?"

"The dean at Fordham said there should be a grand jury investigation—"

"So there is. Now everythin' is nice and neat and accordin' to law. But what will happen? You'll see, nothin'! Not a damn thing! If you live in the Neighborhood, that's all you can expect. We're dirt, Frank. We don't mean anythin'. Why should anyone listen to us? Do you think those goddam politicians care? Hell no! The only time they know we're alive is the week before election. Then they learn how to smile and to shake hands. Once they get in you can be invisible as far as they're concerned. There's only one way to make anybody listen in this town—"

"What's that?"

He held up his fist.

"If you have that, Frank, they'll listen. If it's big enough the whole goddam country'll listen!"

"Yeah. But that's one thing we'll never have, so forget it."

"I'll give you odds we'll have it someday," he said. I started to laugh but his air of supreme confidence stopped me.

"You serious?"

"Sure I am. Do you know how we're gonna get that muscle?"

"No. You tell me."

"Tom's cops' union. The idea you and him talked about on the roof that night." He snapped his fingers. "Just like you said—we'll tell 'em to roll over and they'll roll over.

154

We tell 'em to sit up and beg and the bastards will do just that. That's it, Frank! If we get the cops into a union we can own 'em."

"Maybe . . . someday . . ."

The idea stayed with me. I kept thinking about it all morning when we were waiting to enter the grand jury room. It was fantasy of course but the irony intrigued me; two victims of police savagery establish a union of police and in this fashion completely control and manipulate the largest municipal law-enforcement body in the United States for their own advantage! And the genesis for it all came from a fine, idealistic young heart stilled forever by a cop's bullet.

What silver-footed irony and tiptoed malice that would be. As I sat in the silent, sunny witness room, a bored cop standing over me, I felt as if I had suddenly discovered a legacy of hate.

I vowed that Joe and I would start a cops' union. Someday.

We testified that afternoon, seated in the center of a large oval room that reminded me of pictures I had seen of a surgeon's amphitheatre.

The assistant district attorney's questions were abrupt and cold; it was obvious he was not hostile to the police. He went into great detail of the business at St. Barnabas, the theft of the pipes and the enormous damage that had resulted. When we came to the story of the shooting he leaned back in his chair, listened for a time, then yawned and began shuffling some papers on his desk. His indifference was not lost on the grand jurors. When I had finished he waved me away.

"That's all . . ."

There were no questions. When I walked out an elderly woman gave me an indignant look. I knew what Joe meant.

The next day I heard the news from King Kong: the grand jury had voted no bill against Hennessy.

"What did you expect?" Joe asked bitterly, "that they would indict a cop for murder? Now let's see what *we* get."

A few days after the grand jury had cleared Hennessy, it met again, this time to vote indictments against us on two counts of felonious assault, four for interfering with the actions of arresting officers, and one for intent to riot.

155

As King Kong said, they hit us with everythin' in the grand jury room except the stenographer's bench . . .

The next day we were both summoned to the visiting room. This was surprising. It was early in the morning and hours away from the regular visiting times.

We found a short, slender young man in a shiny blue suit impatiently walking up and down the room. His black hair was parted in the middle and combed straight back. He walked on the balls of his feet, occasionally stopping to rise up and down as he talked. He seemed impatient about everything.

"I'm Maxie Solomon, your counsel," he said shortly.

"Our lawyer?" I said. "We didn't hire any lawyer."

"You didn't but someone else did. You know about the grand jury's findings?"

"Pepe?"

"Maybe. What's the difference? That's not important!" Solomon snapped. "If this had been a few years ago you would have been out in a day. But this Dewey!" He jerked open his briefcase.

"What does Dewey have to do with us?" I asked. "We're not gangsters."

"You might as well be," the lawyer said grimly. "It's even a big deal to put in a fix for these two-bit charges."

"We won't need a fix," Joe said savagely. "They killed my brother and we're put in jail. What kind of goddam justice is that?"

"I know it, kid," Solomon said softly. "It was a tough break. But that's over with. Now we have to do something for both of you—"

"What can you do?" I asked.

"You're going to cop a plea," he said briskly. "Harrison's sitting next week. He comes from the Winnesucca Club and owes us a favor—"

"Who is us?" I put in.

He gave me a cold look. "Why do you guys ask so many damn questions? Now as I was saying, Harrison's sitting. He's promised to give you both twelve. Once you get out you can screw the probation. We'll take care of that."

"Twelve what?" I asked weakly.

"Months. What elese?" He asked surprised, "You don't think you're going to serve time, do you?"

"We have to plead guilty—for what?" Joe asked, his voice rising.

156

"Wait a minute, kid," Maxie said softly, "don't shout at me. We didn't get you into this jam. We're only trying to help you. The cops have a damn good case and can crucify you." He turned to me. "Did you slug Hennessy's partner?"

I nodded.

"And didn't you resist arrest, Gunnar?"

"Well," Joe said, "what I did was to—"

"Resist arrest," Solomon said wearily. "Didn't the officers identify themselves? No crap now."

"They said they were cops," I admitted, "but they already had Joe . . ."

Solomon read rapidly from a typewritten sheet. "The arresting officers have witnesses who will testify that first grade detectives Theodore Hennessy and David Winkle both identified themselves as police officers to your brother Thomas Gunnar and told him they were taking you both to the Sixteenth Precinct for identification only. It was then that your brother attacked them. Is that correct?"

"Attacked them! Tom only pulled at Joe's jacket," I said. "I saw him!"

"That's interfering with the actions of an arresting officer," he explained mildly.

"Do we have to plead guilty?" Joe asked.

"Definitely—if you don't want to serve time. Look at it this way. You, Howell, and your brother slugged a cop and interfered with officers of the law apprehending two suspects wanted for questioning in a felonious crime. That's you and Howell. Out of this came a justifiable homicide . . ."

"A justifiable homicide!" I shouted.

"Easy, pal. I'm only quoting you the law. I didn't write it."

"Well then you can shove the law up your ass," Joe said bitterly. "All I know is my brother first tried to talk to those two cops and when they wouldn't listen he only wanted to help us." His voice trembled and tears brimmed in his eyes. "That's all. He didn't have a gun. He didn't slug a cop. He only pushed him. Did they have to kill him for that? If that's how the law protects cops I say screw every one of 'em! If I didn't know it before, now I do. They're no good. None of 'em." He turned to me. "From now on, Frank, they're the goddam enemy."

Solomon held up his hand. "Okay. Okay. Don't tell me

157

about cops. I know all about them." He smiled grimly. "What slum kid doesn't? I was brought up on Hester Street. My old man owned a furniture store on Bleecker so I knew cops firsthand."

Hester Street. I suddenly remembered the morning in the Shelter and Muzzy Blaze.

"Do you know a kid named Muzzy Blaze?"

"Izzy Blaze's kid? Sure. For years his old man operated the single action numbers on the East Side. He and a dame were the only independents left. How do you like that—a woman in numbers!"

"The Duchess," I said.

"Oh, so you know about the Duchess? She's the smartest woman in policy. Even East Harlem won't move in on her."

"Muzzy says she has connections . . ."

Maxie shrugged. "It's only what I hear; she knows somebody big downtown. She's a great dame. I remember when Izzy was sick and couldn't run his territory she combined their banks so he wouldn't lose any money."

"Was Muzzy's old man in numbers a long time?"

"As long as I can remember. My old man always said he was the most honest guy on the East Side. How do you like that? A numbers boss more honest than anyone else on the street."

I pointed out, "You keep saying 'he was'—"

"Oh, didn't you know? Izzy died last month. How well do you know Muzzy?"

"We met him up at the Shelter."

"Muzzy's back up at the Proc finishing out the time he owes. After his old man died they were going to parole him but the kid hasn't anyone so they decided to keep him for a while."

"Who do we thank for this?" I asked. "You?"

"Not me, kid," he said shortly as he snapped his briefcase. "I don't have that kind of pull. Let's say your friends. Anything else on your minds?"

"Yeah. Pleadin' guilty to somethin' we're not guilty of," Joe said.

"Do you want to go to bat?" Maxie asked him quietly. He looked over at me. "Do you, Howell? I'll defend you. Hell, yes. There won't be any trouble on this fee." He carefully put his briefcase on the table and studied Joe. "But don't say I didn't warn you. When they get you on the stand those cops and the DA will tear you both apart.

158

Without Harrison you could get an indefinite. God knows when you'll get out. Say you get up before Delaney. Not many lawyers know it but his grandfather was a police inspector. I know. That's why I'm good—I take the trouble to find out such things. The old son of a bitch is a cops' judge. He loves them. After he heard their testimony he would probably hit you with the book." He leaned toward us. "Do you know where you could wind up? On the Island."

"The Island?"

"Rikers. Over there the fresh fish"—he gestured to us—"are turned over to the old cons—"

"So Muzzy told us," I said.

"Take anything Muzzy tells you about numbers and jails as gospel. His old man had him hustling numbers on the East River piers from the day he could walk, and he's been in every can from the Bronx to the Island. So—make up your minds."

"What choice do we have?" Joe asked.

"If you ask my opinion as your lawyer—none."

"Okay," I said. "We'll take the plea. Joe?"

"What the hell else can we do?" he said with a tight face. "What a lousy setup!"

"The three of us made only one mistake," Maxie said with a grin.

"What's that?" I asked him.

"We picked out the wrong place to be born." He walked to the door, then turned around. "Oh, by the way, Pepe has something in mind for both of you when you get out."

"Like what?" I asked.

"Like how should I know? I'm an attorney, remember? Not an Italian mind reader." He rapped on the door with a coin. "Gentlemen, I'll see you in court . . ."

A few weeks later we appeared before Justice Franklin R. Harrison, who had a furrowed face like a peanut shell and the air of a peevish choirmaster. He intoned about the need for citizens to respect the law and its officers, then lashed out at us for resisting arrest and interfering with the police in the performance of their sworn duty.

He ended in such a denunciation of us that I uneasily wondered if the fix had really been in. A side glance at Solomon, however, assured me that it had. The young lawyer appeared bored as he studied the painting of some forgotten justice that hung over the judge's bench.

Standing near us, Hennessy and Winkle looked smug. I almost whooped with laughter when I heard the judge's sentence: one year's probation. With a flourish he signed the sentencing papers, and Solomon walked with us to the door of the detention pen.

"I see you got friends, counselor," Hennessy murmured.

Solomon only came up to Hennessy's chest, but he stepped back and, with an elaborate air of contempt, looked Hennessy up and down. Then he put out his hand and Joe and I shook it. "I'll see you guys outside. Don't worry—from now on it will be peaches and cream." He nodded to Hennessy. "If you have any trouble with this character just let me know."

He waved and walked briskly across the courtroom.

"Just a little wise guy mocky," Hennessy said to his partner.

But it wasn't all peaches and cream as Maxie Solomon had promised; we came out to find Joe's mother weary, grief stricken, and ill. She insisted on accompanying my aunt to the six o'clock Mass every morning; one freezing, sleety morning was too much. In three days she was in Polyclinic with pneumonia. Then, late one night, there was a knock on our kitchen door. It was Joe; he had just come from the hospital. His mother was dead.

The Neighborhood paid tribute to her in the small funeral home on Ninth Avenue where Tom had been laid out only a few months before. The people who came, the dock workers, the housewives, the drunks, the storekeepers, were angry, bitter, and defeated. As an old man whispered to me:

"They might as well have put a gun to her head. The bastards!" Then he shrugged. "But what the hell can you do?"

They sent what flowers they could afford and Mass cards. Dominating the room was a huge floral piece, I am sure the largest and most expensive ever delivered to the old funeral home. The card simply said: Pepe, Chena, Gus, and Nicky.

Chena came every day and stayed until evening, when I walked her home. She virtually dragged Joe and me upstairs one night for a seemingly never-ending meal. I had insisted that my aunt, stunned with grief, should not prepare any meals and we had been existing on coffee, doughnuts, and hamburgers—and whiskey. The Gunnar flat was locked and Joe was sleeping in our kitchen on a cot.

When we returned to the funeral parlor, Chena and her mother made my aunt return to their apartment to eat and to rest. Joe and I were left alone, staring silently at the cold white face of the woman we both loved in the coffin across the room when, suddenly, I sensed someone standing near me. It was Pepe.

He walked across the room, looked down at the corpse, made a hasty sign of the cross, then came back to us.

"We talk downstairs, no?" he whispered.

We followed him to the combination smoking and men's room where he clasped Joe's hand.

"I am sorry, *giovinotto*."

"Thanks for comin', Pepe, and thanks a million for the flowers." Pepe dismissed it with a gesture. "The lawyer took care of you?"

"Thanks for that too," I said. "The judge gave us a year's probation just as Maxie promised."

"*Ecco!* Forget the probation," he said. "It will be taken care of. If the *bastardo* downtown sends you a card, throw it away."

"Maxie said we should be sure and see you when we got out," I said.

"*Si.*" He put his hands on our shoulders. "Wait awhile my young friends. I have something in mind for you but we will talk about it later." He shook his head. "The cops! Nothing happened to them?"

"The grand jury refused to indict them . . ."

Pepe shook his head slowly. "Incredible," he murmured. "The law—"

"The hell with the law!" Joe said angrily. "I'll take care of Hennessy if it's the last thing I do."

"Easy, *giovinotto*," Pepe said softly, "you hurt that *panzione* and it will only mean more trouble for you."

"I'd give my right arm to see that fat pig bleedin' on the sidewalk . . ."

"No, no, you must not do anything to that *figlio di butana*," Pepe said, shaking his head. "The whore on the bench will hit you in the head with the book." He held up his hands, palms out. "You are on probation for a year, no? They will send you to the pen until you are an old man."

"It will be worth every day to bury him," Joe said grimly.

The cold black eyes studied us for a long moment.

"Maybe somebody else does it for you, my young friends."

"Somebody else?" Joe said with a frown. "Like who?"

"His wife," Pepe said. He made a circling motion alongside his temple.

"She is a cuckoo, no?" He fashioned his thumb and forefinger into the shape of a pistol. "One day she tried to shoot him because he is playing with a woman cop." He shrugged. "Maybe some day she will catch him and the blonde whore." He smiled faintly. "The cuckoo does the job for you, *giovinotti!*"

Joe said roughly, "I'm not goin' to wait until his goddam wife finds him screwin' that dame—"

"I wonder where Hennessy lives," I said.

"Who cares?" Joe said.

"*Abbeia paziènza!* You must have patience," Pepe said. He shook Joe gently by his shoulder. "Now I must go ... later you and Peppino will see me. . . ."

We walked him to the front door. As he left he said casually, "Peppino, you asked where the pig lives?"

"Hennessy?"

"In Astoria," he said. "*Addio!* Go with God!"

He stepped into the Cord waiting at the curb, waved, and was gone.

On the following Monday we buried Mrs. Gunnar in a crowded Brooklyn cemetery where the headstones were back to back. The mourners consisted of a distant cousin, Joe, myself, Chena, my aunt, and Father John who said the funeral Mass.

After he had said the last prayers the priest silently put out his hand but Joe brushed past him. I gave him the same treatment.

Out of the corner of my eye as we followed the casket down the aisle of St. Barnabas, I caught a glimpse of Elliott sitting in the rear of the church. He stayed for the Mass and, when we came out, we stared at each other; as much as I wanted to hate him I couldn't—there was sympathy and understanding in his eyes.

In the cemetery Chena held my hand and my aunt's arm as an icy wind tore away the final words from Father John's lips. Just before we turned away Joe bent down and studied the inscription on the headstone:

ANDREW GUNNAR: BELOVED
HUSBAND AND FATHER

"He was a fool, a drunk, and a wife beater, and that should be on his goddam stone from the top to the bottom," he said as he turned away.

 11 *GUNNAR'S REVENGE*

Three days after we had buried his mother, Joe Gunnar told me he intended to kill Detective Teddy Hennessy. He had been gone since early morning and I finally spotted him walking down the block from Eighth Avenue.

"Where have you been all morning, Joe?"

"Out to Queens."

"What were you doing out there?"

"Lookin' things over." He took a deep breath. "I intend to kill Hennessy tonight."

He sounded as casual as if he had asked me to join him for an evening at Loew's Twenty-third Street.

I stopped and turned to face him. "You're going to do what?"

"Why so surprised? I told you I intended to get that fat bastard. You don't think I would let him get away with what he did?"

The note of determination in his voice shook me. I knew Joe Gunnar. This was no bluff or idle talk. A chill went up my back when I realized that by tomorrow Hennessy would be dead, killed by the kid who was staring at me, amused.

"You're nuts, Joe!"

"I don't think so. This bum killed my brother and my mother. If the law refuses to help me, then screw the law! I'll do it my way."

"I know he's a lousy rotten son of a bitch, Joe—but kill him?"

"He's just what Pepe called him, a pig. And by Christ this is a pig I want to see dead."

"But Joe, he's a cop—a detective. How will you kill him?"

"With a gun."

"How will you get a gun?"

He reached inside his coat and slid out something wrapped in oily rags. I saw the butt of a revolver.

"Spider's," he said shortly, "I kept it hid in the hole behind the boiler."

"So you'll walk right into the Sixteenth's squad room, find Hennessy, and kill him. Is that right?"

"Okay. Let's forget it."

"I don't want to forget it, dammit, I want an answer!"

"Do you really want to know?"

"Of course I do. Why do you think I'm asking?"

He took a slip of paper from his pocket.

"Okay, here it is. Do you remember Pepe tellin' us Hennessy lived in Astoria? Well, here's the number I got from information. I called yesterday and talked to his wife. I told her I was from Macy's and we were makin' a survey to see what the people in Queens thought about us buildin' a store out there. Just as Pepe said, she's a real nut. She complained about her neighbors sendin' in rays through the roof, the milkman tried to rape her, La Guardia and FDR were Communists, and the police were a bunch of crooks. When she started on the cops I couldn't stop her. I put in about five nickels." He laughed. "Get this! She says all the policewomen are whores for the cops. Then she started to quote the Bible. Finally I got what I wanted out of her. Hennessy is working the four-to-twelve tour tonight in Safe and Loft—"

"I could have told you that."

He stared at me. "What do you mean?"

"Today is Tuesday. On Tuesday and Thursday nights he visits that dame in Nick's building—"

"Dammit! That's right. I forgot about that."

"So what will you do now? Walk into her apartment and give it to him?"

"Don't be a wise guy. You may think this is all talk but it's not. I'll get him tonight! I've been out to where he lives and I know the setup. There's a row of hedges alongside his house. It will be early in the mornin' when he gets home, and he'll probably be woozy from that dame and booze. He'll never know what hit him. But

164

before I leave I'm gonna make sure the son of a bitch is as dead as a herring!"

"Joe, you're crazy. They'll find you."

"How will they know it's me?" he asked with a shrug. "I'll be back in the flat sleepin' like an angel if they come lookin' for me."

"Someone might see you . . . maybe a guy in the subway . . . this is murder, Joe."

"Sure it's murder and I'll have to take the chances that go with it."

I argued with him for the remainder of the afternoon. At first he flared up, then gradually he only shrugged off what I said or listened in a disinterested silence.

"You might as well save your breath, Frank," he said at last. "I intend to kill him tonight and nothin' you or anyone else can say will change my mind."

We ate a quiet supper, so quiet my aunt kept asking me if I felt a cold coming on. After reading the papers and listening to Jack Benny on the radio, we all went to bed. In a short time my aunt's gentle snores told me she was asleep. I quietly slipped into my clothes and stretched out on the bed, tense as a coiled spring, waiting for Joe to make his first move. I knew his plan was insane, but I also knew I had to go with him. We only had each other in our desolation.

Gradually the moon rose higher and from my bed I could see the golden light gleaming on the porcelain top of the kitchen table. I heard the cot creak and saw Joe's dim figure walk across the floor. I tiptoed out to him as he reached the door.

"This is no concern of yours, Frank—"

"The hell it isn't. I'm going with you."

"You'll only—"

My aunt muttered something and we both stood still as posts.

"Okay, I don't have time to argue . . ."

"Let's go."

We hurried down the stairs and up Forty-sixth Street, heading across town to Grand Central and the Astoria train. Suddenly I wished with all my heart that a radio car would appear with a cop demanding to know what we were doing. Then I remembered Joe's threat to kill the first cop who put a hand on him, and again my prayers rose to heaven that the law would never show. The streets were cold, windy, and deserted. We were crossing Sixth

Avenue when a blonde whore in a hallway called out a greeting.

"That looked like that dame Suzy Miller," I said. "The dame Hennessy is banging tonight."

"He better enjoy himself," Joe said grimly. "It's the last time for him . . ."

Suddenly we both slowed down and turned to stare at each other. It was as if we were characters in a comic strip and lights of recognition were exploding above our heads.

"Are you thinkin' what I'm thinkin', Frank?"

"You mean about his wife? What Pepe said the other day about how his wife would murder him if she ever found out?"

"Right!" Joe said excitedly. "That's what Pepe said, we don't have to kill the son of a bitch. Let his wife do it!"

"But how will she know?" I snapped my fingers. "Wait a minute—you have her number."

He punched me on the shoulder gleefully. "What else? We call her, tell her that her fat slob of a husband is in the sack with Suzy and makin' a damn fool of her. Didn't Nick say she was so crazy she tried to kill a policewoman with one of his service revolvers down at headquarters?"

"That's right. Pepe said that too."

"Well, what are we waitin' for? Let's go."

The blonde whore sauntered over. "Hey, boys, how about—"

"Get out of here before I ram my fist down your throat," Joe snarled. "C'mon, Frank, let's go."

On Eighth Avenue I looked down Fifty-seventh Street; the two restaurants had lights in their fronts, the bars were still open.

"You call his wife," I told Joe, "I have two other calls to make."

When he looked puzzled, I told him about the owners of the restaurants, the Frenchman and the Italian, who were also getting a piece of Suzy on different nights.

"Wow! Will we fix this cop!" he said. "Do you know that dame's last name?"

"Miller. Suzy Miller." I searched my memory for a moment. "Nick said she lived in Five B."

"Let's go, we have a lot of telephoning to do."

We changed a dollar in the Eighth Avenue Automat and took over the phone booth in the rear. Joe dialed the number, smiled to himself, then leaned closer to the mouthpiece.

"Hello, is this Mrs. Hennessy?" he asked softly. "Well, Mrs. Hennessy, this is a friend of yours. I'm sorry to be callin' at this hour. No, you don't know my name. I'm only callin' because I respect you as a fine, God-fearin' woman. Yes, ma'am, it's about your husband and what a terrible sinful thing he's doin' at this very moment to you and your marriage. Yes, ma'am, at this very moment . . ."

Joe's voice became indignant, then sorrowful as he went on in detail of what Theodore Hennessy, Detective First Grade, was doing to his wife and their marriage in the luxurious suite of one Suzy Miller, a common whore who lived in Apartment 5B in the Fifty-seventh Street apartment house. Joe turned to give me a triumphant grin. I could hear the shrill, hysterical voice asking him to repeat the address. While Joe talked, I went into another phone booth and looked up the numbers of the two restaurants.

"She's on her way," Joe said gleefully when he came out. "When I suggested she come prepared she screamed, 'Don't worry, I'll bring something with me!' I hope she don't mean an umbrella. Wait a minute—how about the elevator man?"

"It's the day man who knows what's going on. The night man won't give her any trouble."

"How about the guys who own the restaurants?"

"Let's wait until we see her, then we can call them."

We had a cup of coffee and a roll, then strolled down Fifty-seventh Street toward Ninth. My heart was in my throat with every step we took. I was sure we would be spotted by a cruising Mickey Mouse. But the street was deserted. Less than a half hour had passed when Joe nudged me.

"There's a cab slowin' up . . . I bet it's her." His voice rose triumphantly. "It's her! Let's call the other guys."

A tall, angular, obviously angry woman carrying a cloth knitting bag was getting out of the cab. She hastily paid the driver and rushed inside the building.

"Let's go," Joe said.

Back in the Automat I dialed the number of the Italian restaurant and identified myself to the gravelly voice that answered as a cousin of Suzy who was outraged at what was going on. There was a brief pause when I had finished giving details, a string of oaths in Italian, and the receiver was slammed down.

But the Frenchman's line was busy. I continued dialing and the nickel kept returning.

"What's the name of that restaurant?" Joe snapped. I thought he was going to try the other phone but when I told him he disappeared. I was still trying when he returned, panting, his face flushed.

"I ran down the street and told the owner. He's a little Frenchman with a moustache and he was just sittin' at the bar talkin' with a waiter . . ."

"What did you say?"

"I told him I was Suzy's nephew and the Italian down the street just came into her apartment with some other guys. I said they were strippin' and beatin' her when they threw me out. Christ! He was out of that chair like a shot."

"Joe. That guy could identify you."

"Who cares now!" he said, his eyes glowing with excitement, "let's do it up brown. Let's call headquarters and tell 'em one of the Finest is gettin' his ass shot off in Suzy's apartment."

"How about the FBI?" I added. "I'll tell them one of their agents is shooting it out with a Frenchman who's a bank robber."

"There's also the Emergency Squad," Joe said. "Isn't this an emergency, Frank?"

"And maybe a fire."

"And let's not forget the hospitals. They may need more than one . . ."

We used a dollar's worth of nickels: the FBI's New York City office, Police Headquarters, Bellevue, Polyclinic, St. Clare's, St. Vincent's, were also notified. On top of that the desk sergeants of the Forty-seventh, West Thirtieth, and Sixty-eighth Street precincts were informed that a cop had been shot. It's an old New York story; the shooting of a police officer never fails to electrify the city's cops. Word flashes from precinct to precinct and they move fast. Before our last call had been finished, Fifty-seventh Street from Eighth to Ninth Avenue was filled with police brass, ambulances, emergency squads, carloads of brisk young men who looked like movie FBI agents, and numerous radio cars whose sirens made the early morning quiet shiver with their wails. Firemen in helmets and raincoats ran out hoses and poured into the building, axes at the ready. Cops filled the elevator. Someone said there was a gas leak and the emergency men smashed in the cellar door.

But there was a genuine need for the ambulances and the interns. When we saw a white-coated intern and an attendant carrying in a stretcher, we joined the small crowd gathered around an old man dressed in the uniform of an elevator operator.

"I was up on the ninth floor readin' the scratches when I heard this bang, bang. Then a lot of screaming. I brought the car down to the fifth and I see this guy that owns the restaurant across the street. He's in the corridor shoutin' in a foreign language and pointin' to the door of her apartment. The door was opened. This great big guy, he's a cop down on Forty-seventh Street, is on the floor covered with blood.

"He's nekkid! There's another guy in the room, this Eyetalian who runs the spaghetti joint across the street. He's holdin' a gun. At first I thought he shot the cop but he didn't—it was this crazy woman, she shot the cop. When I asked why she did it she kept screamin' that his sin had finally found him out and a lot of other stuff like that . . ."

"Where did she plug him?" someone asked.

"There was a lot of blood all over his face and his arm. The Eyetalian said he was shot in the head." He shook his head. "That gun musta done a lot of damage to that guy . . . it looked as big as a cannon to me."

"Who was this crazy dame?" Joe asked innocently.

"His wife," the operator said triumphantly as though we all had failed to guess correctly, "his wife. She caught him in the sack with Suzy and bang! That's it."

"Who's Suzy?" someone asked.

"That blonde with the big knockers that's always carryin' a little dog. She's always walkin' up and down the street with the mutt and wantin' booze brought in . . ."

"Yeah. Yeah," someone said impatiently. "Then what happened?"

"The Eyetalian guy said I better call the cops." He looked bewildered. "But I didn't have to. Before I could get to my car they was all over the place. Cops. Firemen. FBI. Ambulances. You name it, they was there. The cops are sore as hell. They don't like it when everybody knows a cop was shot in a dame's bedroom. One cop told me someone called the whole city out. . . ."

A cop came out and motioned to the operator who

hurried to his elevator. A few minutes later it came down. As the door opened we surged forward with the crowd. The cops pushed us back to make a path for several other cops carrying a stretcher.

Hennessy was on it. There was a bloody bandage over one eye and another on his arm. He was moaning as they slid the stretcher into the ambulance.

"How do you like it, Kidneyfeet?" Joe whispered. "How do you like those apples?"

A few minutes later a policewoman and three plainclothesmen hurried out with Mrs. Hennessy. Under a coat thrown over her shoulders was a straitjacket. She was wild eyed and incoherent. Behind her came the two worried-looking restaurant owners.

Last came Suzy. Before she left the elevator, she posed for the newspaper photographers who had just arrived, then gave her poodle to the elevator operator. She was wearing a skirt and sweater with obviously little beneath.

"Hey, she's quite a piece," someone said admiringly.

With a queenly wave to her audience she stepped into a police car.

Joe grunted with satisfaction. "Well that takes care of that son of a bitch! I'm glad we remembered his crazy wife . . ."

"It wasn't our idea, Joe," I reminded him, "it was Pepe's."

"I don't care whose idea it was," he said with a shrug, "it worked. That's what counts."

"Well, there's nothing more around here, let's go home."

He hesitated. "I'm not goin' back, Frank."

I looked at him. "Well, then where are you going?"

"I don't know and, frankly, I don't care. I'm goin' over to the yards and grab a freight."

"Why the hell do you want to do that?"

"There's nothin' more around here for me, Frank. And besides, you were right, maybe that Frenchman could finger me for the cops—"

He broke off when he heard a soft, familiar whistle. Somehow, without turning, I knew the gleaming Cord with Pepe's face framed in its open window would be at the curb.

"Hey, there's Pepe," Joe said.

170

12 *PATSY'S*

For years the small Italian restaurant had been known to scores of politicians, newspapermen, cops, judges, federal courthouse employees, and even prosecutors simply as Patsy's. The dining room was long and narrow with scraped, worn floorboards, a few booths, tables with checkered tablecloths, a single clothes tree that always tipped when it became overloaded, a stout cashier who had a visible mustache and who seemingly had worn the same black dress for ages, and Patsy the owner, stooped and taciturn, who his customers insisted had not smiled since he opened his tiny place on Thompson Street shortly after World War I.

Pepe took us to Patsy's that night. After a sumptuous meal of fettucine, tender stuffed clams, and a piccata of veal—more food than I had ever eaten in my life—he explained he had been parked on Ninth Avenue. He had been on his way home from the Shadow Box when a police barrier on Fifty-seventh Street forced him to detour around the block. After his driver discovered what had happened, they decided to wait on Ninth Avenue until the crowd broke up outside his building. It was then that he had spotted us as we passed. Later, looking back, I could see how pat his explanation was. But that night Pepe, his cold-eyed driver, and the marvelous Cord sedan were comforting and welcome.

"Now tell me, young friend, why were you there?" he asked.

There seemed to be no point in not telling: he listened impassively to the details.

"The officer was wounded?"

"He's a cop with a hole in his head," Joe said savagely. "I'll settle for that."

"You are satisfied now, my young friends?"

171

"I would still like to see the bastard dead," Joe said savagely.

"You think like a Sicilian," Pepe told him. "Only blood can satisfy the honor."

"Every day I ask myself, why didn't they do anythin' about Hennessy?" Joe said. "Frank and I even went before the grand jury. They acted as if *we* were to blame for everythin' that happened. Then they let him go and indicted us. They said it was our fault. And my brother was dead!"

"The law is always against us," Pepe said.

"We know that now . . . "

"It is best you take care of justice yourself." He reached across the table and tapped my forehead. *"Cervèlli.* With brains. Am I right, Peppino?"

Joe raised his fist. "This is more important. You demand—you get—"

"Power is never built overnight, my young friend," Pepe said. "It must be done carefully, like putting together a house. A board here. A brick there. Then one day it is all finished."

"I don't want to wait that long," Joe said. "You don't have to build any houses if you have one of these . . ."

He took the .38 from inside his jacket.

"Put it away," Pepe said with a frown. "Do you know what would happen to you and to me if the police came in and found this?"

"They would never find it on me," Joe said with a chilling casualness. "They would never get the chance."

"Put away the gun," Pepe said, his voice tight with anger. "Stop acting like a stupid Irish gangster. Do you have to be like the cripple?"

"The Gimp? He's not doin' too badly. He has the waterfront knocked up. He owns all the numbers and crap games on the piers—"

"He has power because the people who fought him were stupid," Pepe said. "Soon things will change . . . "

"Who will change 'em Pepe—you?" Joe asked.

"Perhaps you, *giovinotto,"* Pepe said with a smile. "Continue to use your brains as you did tonight and you will build your house . . . "

Joe slid the gun back inside his jacket. "All we can do now is get ourselves arrested."

"You did good tonight," Pepe pointed out. "You made

172

a fool of the law. You satisfied your honor. You arranged for a crazy woman to shoot her husband. *Marrone!* What cops! I have never seen so many. Now we will help you . . . " He looked from Joe to me. "Nothing will happen to you."

"Why, Pepe?" I asked him.

"Because you have friends."

"Friends?" Joe said scornfully. "What friends do we have?"

Pepe pointed to himself. "I am your friend. Gus is your friend. Our friends are now your friends. We have many. In a few years we will have many more."

Joe slowly tore off a small piece of the crunchy Italian bread.

"Why help us, Pepe?"

"Perhaps someday you will do a service for us." He washed his hands with invisible water. *"Una mano lavare l'altra*—one hand washes the other. No?"

"Yes."

He leaned over and affectionately squeezed my arm. "Peppino—my young friend, some day we will work together. You, your friend Joe, Pepe, Gus, and all our friends."

"That suits us, Pepe—when do we start?" Joe asked quickly.

"Not now," Pepe said shortly.

"But you said in the funeral parlor you had something in mind for us," I protested.

"Si. But that was before you did this to the cop."

"Who will know it was us?" Joe put in.

"You said you went into the Frenchman's restaurant?" He waved his hand. "We whisper in the ear of Pagnucci who owns the spaghetti house and he becomes like a clam to the cops." He shrugged. "The Frenchman may take a little longer."

"I think I should hop a freight out of here tonight," Joe said.

"You would be a fool to do that, *giovinotto*," Pepe said bluntly. "Where would you go?"

"Chicago. Down south. Anywhere. What the hell's the difference?"

"The railroad bulls ride the trains these days, my young friend. You would be picked up by tomorrow."

"Railroad bulls? They're stupid. All they know is how to kick your ass off their train."

Pepe leaned across the table and pointed a finger at Joe.

"Never, never despise your enemy. Never believe you have more brains. Remember, there are many policemen in New York City—"

"I would like to get every one of them like we got Hennessy," Joe said fiercely. "They're all alike."

"Perhaps you will one day," Pepe said calmly. "Now you must wait. Five, ten years. You are young and impatient, and time goes slowly. It will be different when you get older. You look at the clock and the calendar and you say—*pòrco di avolio!* Where has the time gone? You desire revenge like a Sicilian. *Si.* Then you wait like a Sicilian. *Abbeia paziènza*—have patience."

"Maybe the cops would never connect us with what happened to Hennessy, Pepe?" I asked.

He replied with a shrug. "Why not? All the police are not like that animal. A police officer has been shot by his wife. The newspapers will make them all look like fools. That little *figlio di butana* La Guardia down at City Hall will scream into the ear of his police commissioner." He made a series of chopping movements with his hand. "The chief inspector. The inspector. Down. Down. Everyone gets mad. This is a bad time for them. Every day there is a new scandal. They will work hard to find all there is to know about this shooting. Don't you think they can"—he slowly brought his two fingers together—"do this?"

"Pepe means they'll find out about the calls," I said to Joe.

"*Cèrvelli.* Brains," Pepe said tapping his forehead. "Of course. They will ask themselves, who called the police? The hospitals? The fire department? They will question the elevator operator. He will say, I did not make the calls. That unfortunate woman—the cuckoo—will tell them a young voice called her and said her husband was with a woman on Fifty-seventh Street. She came with a gun. The Frenchman across the street. What will he say?"

His waving finger took in both of us. "*Pòrco misèria.* They will have you!"

I asked him, "What would you suggest, Pepe?"

"Do not worry," he said, now smiling, "your friends
174

will take care of everything. Tonight you and Joe stay here."

"Here—in the restaurant?"

"No. No. Upstairs. It has been arranged." He glanced at a thin gold expensive-looking wristwatch. "Madonna mia! Where has the time gone?"

He waved Patsy over and said something in Italian.

"Patsy will take care of you. I will be back tomorrow. I will tell Chena everything is all right, Peppino," he said softly as we shook hands.

When he had gone, we followed Patsy through the small steaming kitchen and up a flight of creaky stairs to the second floor. At the end of the hall, in startling contrast to the shabby building, was a large luxuriously furnished apartment. There was a huge bed with a blood red satin spread, thick rugs, mirrors in heavy gold frames. When the silent Patsy had left, Joe and I stared at each other in disbelief.

"Maybe he's keepin' a dame," Joe suggested. "What do you think, Frank?"

"I think he's right about the cops."

"Maybe. They still have to find us. I wonder what he has up his sleeve?"

"I don't know and frankly I don't care at this point. All I want is a few hours in this bed."

I stretched out on the soft spread while Joe prowled about the room.

"Hey, there's iron shutters on the windows. This place is like a fortress!" He came back to the bed. "You've been around Pepe, what's the score with that guy and his art gallery?"

"I'm sure he doesn't make a living selling paintings."

"And Gus Valentino's no painter . . . "

"They have something going for them," I said. "I don't know what it is, but don't let that smile get you off-center. Pepe's a nice guy, but sometimes when he looks at you—I don't know why—but he can send a chill up my back."

Then I told Joe the story of the frightened young man I had seen in the art gallery.

"And the picture of the guy you saw in the paper was the same one Pepe threw out of his gallery?"

"The same one. He looked as if he needed to change his underwear when Pepe was yelling at him in Italian."

"Did you ever mention it to Chena?"

"No."

"Why not?"

"She wouldn't know anything," I lied.

"Don't kid yourself," he said, stifling a yawn as he slid under the covers. "Wop dames know everythin' that goes on in their families. Nothin' gets past 'em . . . "

"Joe Gunnar, expert on wop dames."

"Don't say I didn't warn you, pal . . ."

The big bed was as soft as a pile of feathers. Joe was asleep in a few minutes but I lay awake. Every time I closed my eyes I saw Chena's worried face.

Pepe returned late the next afternoon. He was brusque and businesslike, and over a small cup of thick black coffee spiked with anisette he told us what had happened and revealed his plans.

"There is an alarm out for your arrest," he said bluntly. He shoved a piece of paper across the table and I read my description in a police alarm: Frank Howell, age eighteen, and Joseph Gunnar, also age eighteen, were wanted by the New York Police as fugitives charged with conspiracy to commit felonious assault, turning in a false alarm of fire, disorderly conduct, and giving false information to police, the fire department, Department of Hospitals, and allied law enforcement agencies.

"The bastards found out!" Joe said. "I didn't think they were that smart."

"As I told you, young friend, never underestimate your enemy," Pepe told him reprovingly. "We talked to Pagnucci, who owns the restaurant across the street and he was—very friendly. He told the police he was in the apartment because of his arrangement with the woman. At first the Frenchman was friendly to us. He told the cops he was only delivering food to the whore. They were very mad and they gave him much trouble. The Health Department sent inspectors and threatened to close him down. After the cops said he would lose his liquor license he told them about you, *giovinotto*."

He silently put two fingers together.

"Did they talk to his wife?" I asked him.

"*Si.* She is cuckoo but she told them about a call from a young man." He asked Joe, "You told her about a store?"

"Macy's. I said I was makin' a survey in Queens . . . "

"Now they know that. The police are very busy on this case."

"Why, Pepe?" I asked. "Why so much over a cop's wife who shot her husband over another dame?"

Pepe silently spread out the *Daily News* on the table. On page one was a picture of Suzy, younger, even more beautiful, obviously taken many years before, then another of her walking out of the building after the shooting. It was a profile shot and showed her startling bust to great advantage. The account was a typical sensational tabloid story, but the evening newspaper Pepe put alongside it had another story: City Hall was raising hell with the police commissioner over how a detective, supposedly on night duty, was shot by his wife in the bedroom of a former Polly Adler call girl, once a favorite of every notorious gangster in the city. Poor Suzy. Newspaper reporters in checking their files had dug up her lurid past.

"There goes Hennessy," Joe said gleefully.

"The hell with Kidneyfeet," I pointed out, "what about us?"

"I'll take ten years in the pen and still be satisfied," Joe said grimly. He looked across at Pepe. "This is what I mean—I want to see 'em disgraced. Smeared all over the newspapers. Let the public know what kind of no-good bastards they have for cops!"

Pepe held up his hand. "Easy, my young friend. You hate the police? Good. I don't like them. But to hurt one cop? *Una còsa di niènte!* It is a thing of nothing."

He held up one of his powerful hands and slowly closed the stubby fingers. "We must get them all in our hands so that they are ours! *Ai capito?*"

"That's what I would like to do—just have all the cops in the city in my power. Just once!"

"Maybe someday," Pepe said leaning back.

"Frank knows a way to do it," Joe said.

"Yes, Peppino?"

"A union," Joe said, "a cops' union! How do you like that, Pepe? We unionize the cops. From Coney Island to the Bronx they belong to us."

I expected Pepe to greet the idea with a shrug, a wave of his hand to dismiss such things as a boy's fantasy; I was surprised at his obvious interest.

"Ah, a union of cops! That is good. Why did you think of this, Peppino?"

"It's not my idea. It was Tom's. Joe's brother."

He gestured to the floor. "The one who was—"

"Yeah. The one the cops killed," Joe said shortly.

"He did not like cops?"

"He didn't hate them, Pepe. In fact he always insisted they weren't all bad."

"So they shot him," Joe said bitterly, "in the back."

"*Si, Si.*" Pepe said slowly. "He was a smart one, no?"

"He was brilliant," I said.

"And you, Peppino, were his friend?"

"Frank was closer to Tom than anyone in the Neighborhood," Joe said. He smiled. "Sometimes I think he was closer than me . . . "

"And you know all about this boy's idea?" Pepe asked.

"As much as there is. Maybe it's only a daydream, Pepe . . ."

"*Va! Va!* What is this daydream? It is good. Very good. We will talk about it. But not now—later. We have other things to do."

"What about us, Pepe?"

"The police brought your aunt to the station house this morning—"

"Aunt Clara?"

My God, I thought, what more can I do to hurt her?

"There was no charge," Pepe said soothingly. "She told the police she hadn't seen you. One of them drove her home." When he looked thoughtful, I said, "The cop Elliott?"

"Yes. The one who once worked in the Neighborhood."

"Supercop," Joe said. "He's always around helpin' old ladies."

"You have to admit he stopped Hennessy from beating our brains out that day, Joe," I reminded him.

"He still smells like the rest of 'em . . . "

"Did they question anyone else, Pepe?"

"They didn't have to go to my flat," Joe said, "they killed everyone who lived there . . . "

"Pepe, how did you find out all these things?" I asked him. "The police alarm, their investigation, how my aunt was questioned at Forty-seventh Street?"

"Friends, Pepinuccio," he said softly, "we have friends."

"What do we do now?"

"It is all arranged," Pepe said. He took a thick envelope from inside his pocket and spread its contents on the table, There were two neatly typed forms, tags with little strings,

178

and some money. He counted the bills into two piles and pushed one toward me, the other to Joe.

"Fifty dollars." Joe said after he had counted his pile.

"You will need money."

"Where are we going, Pepe?" I asked.

He glanced at the typewritten form, then gave me a broad grin.

"It says here, Peppino, you are going to St. Marie, Idaho . . . "

"Idaho! What's in Idaho?"

"A CCC camp. You are going into the CCCs."

"The CCCs?" Joe exploded. "What the hell for?"

"To get you both out of New York for a year," Pepe said calmly. "When you come back here things will be settled. Then we will talk. Perhaps you can be useful to us."

"Idaho?" Joe said to me. "Where the hell is that?"

"It's out west," I said feebly.

"I don't want to go to any CCC camp! Do you, Frank? Why don't we just hide out here, Pepe?"

"You can't," was the blunt reply. "You are not that important to us. Perhaps someday you will be. You could mean trouble if we try to hide you in the city. Today we can't risk anything, my friend; next year will be different.'"

He hesitated, then remained silent.

Joe gave him a puzzled look. "Why will next year be different?"

"This is not the time for explanation," Pepe said, sounding slightly nettled. "We have done much to help you both. Here are tags with your names." He glanced at his watch. "I will take you to Pennsylvania Station. You will go to track five and ask for a man named Santucci. He will give you each a bag with your clothes and a seat number in the train. Also innoculation forms. Santucci will leave the train in New Jersey and there will be army people from Fort Dix. There is nothing to worry about. Your applications are in order. You will go to St. Louis. There the train will be broken up. Santucci has arranged for you to be together on the train that will take you to—" he glanced at the application—"Camp Five near St. Marie, Idaho." He said to me. "Chena looked it up on a map. She says it is in the mountains and near a big river—the name is like a fish . . ." He paused, then said triumphantly, "The Salmon River."

He leaned back and looked at us. "So *giovinotti*, what do you think?"

"Idaho. Christ!" Joe murmured.

"You wanted to take a freight," I pointed out. "So now we ride in a train."

"One year," Pepe said. "Santucci said you will receive twenty-five dollars a month. Twenty of that is sent home. Peppino, your aunt will receive your money—"

"Who gets mine?" Joe asked.

"An old woman in Brooklyn," Pepe said. "We have arranged it. Every month she will bring it to the bank. When you come home I will give you the bankbook." He sighed and got to his feet. "Old people make quick decisions; the young think too much." He held up his cup. "I will get *una tazza caffè*. When I come back and you tell me what you want to do . . ."

"If we don't go?" Joe asked.

Pepe shrugged. "You are free to do as you want." He paused at the door. "If you do not go we will know that you do not want our friendship."

"A year, Frank," Joe said pacing up and down after Pepe had left. "A year!"

"It will be better than a couple of years in the can. So we'll be nineteen when we come back. As Pepe said, a year can take care of a lot of trouble."

He sat on the edge of the bed and stared ahead. "We never seem to have a choice, goddammit!"

"I don't care any more. I just want to get out of this town. Nothing's gone right with us since September."

"I guess I started our bad luck," Joe said in a forlorn voice. He studied me for a long minute. "You really want to go, Frank?"

"I told you I do."

"Okay. So do I. What difference does it make—I don't have anybody. Hey, what about Aunt Clara?"

"Maybe I can see her for a minute before we go."

But when Pepe returned he shook his head when I asked him.

"We won't have time, Peppino. But don't worry, we have told her everything. She packed both your bags. She is a good woman. When you have time you write to her." He slapped me on the back affectionately. "I am glad you are going. Santucci has done this before for us. He
180

says this will be a new camp and the inspectors won't be around for a year."

"One more thing, Pepe," Joe said.

"*Si.* What is that?"

"I just want to make sure I keep the flat."

"How much is the rent?"

"Eighteen bucks a month."

Pepe waved his hand. "I will see that it is paid . . . are we ready, my young friends?"

When the Cord sedan stopped at Penn Station, Pepe leaned out and shook our hands.

"Who is this guy Santucci?" Joe asked.

"A friend," was the terse answer.

I asked, "Will you let us know when to come back, Pepe?"

"It will be arranged."

"When will that be?" Joe asked.

"You will be told when it is the proper time," Pepe said flatly. He waved. "Go with God, young friends."

The Cord carefully slid out from the curb, joined the traffic, and disappeared.

We passed through the stately, grimy columns and walked down the long marble hall to look for the track and Santucci who had aranged everything.

BOOK 2

the unions

13   *RETURN OF THE NATIVES*

We found Santucci without too much trouble. He was a nervous little man who carried a clipboard with many papers and was surrounded at the entrance to the track by a crowd of kids, CCC officials, and weeping mothers, sisters, and sweethearts. We pushed our way to his side and several times tried to get his attention without any success. Then Joe, exasperated, learned over and whispered, "Pepe said to look you up."

I thought he was poleaxed. He ignored everyone else, put his arms around our shoulders and personally escorted us down the steps to the forward car where he let us select our seats. We had no idea where we could locate our baggage; Santucci not only found our bags but personally brought them to our seats. He left in the middle of the Jersey meadows after the army had taken over the train, begging us not to forget to mention to Don Vitone how well he had treated us.

It was the first time I had ever heard anyone give Pepe that title—The Great One . . .

Although I have crisscrossed this country many times, I

still consider the valley of the Salmon one of the most stunningly beautiful sections of the West. Camp Five was situated on a mountain fifteen miles from the small logging village of St. Marie on the Salmon. It was still frontier in those days, with some big lumber companies from Washington working the high timber.

Our camp was assigned to build a highway across the range and, as the rough road edged across the mountain, Joe and I would accompany the local surveyor and ranger on two- and three-day mapping trips to lay out the work for the forward teams. For two kids raised in the squalor of the Neighborhood, the beauty of a mountain fall, the enormous silence of midsummer's day, and the sweeping vista of the valley seen from a crag high on the face of the mountain were unforgettable.

Then there was our never-ending crap game. The camp director was an old topkick who had been called out of retirement. His entire army service had been under Pershing, "servin' under Blackjack on the Border, chasin' Villa and his goddam greasers, then shovin' it up the Kaiser's ass," as he boasted to us many times.

Before our troop train crossed the Pennsylvania line Joe had discovered he was a lush and a thief. At each stop we made sure he had a pint. When Joe suggested that we start a game "to keep the boys happy," the old guy tried his best to look shocked—until Joe agreed we would split down the middle.

Once the camp was established we opened the game—the split was still down the middle—and the loggers in the line camps became our best customers. In a few months we were operating a lucrative crap game.

We were left alone for months in this desolate camp, surpervised by an old drunk who came to lean on two street-wise eighteen-year-olds. It was the same as if we had been dumped on a desert island. The other kids were mostly from Midwestern farm or rural areas, so we made the rules and formed our own government. The strongest, the shrewdest, the toughest, survived. It was the Neighborhood all over again so it was only natural we should take over. The bent of the times seemed to go that way.

Everyone in camp eventually became a thief. For Joe and me it was second nature to assume that anything not nailed down was fair game. The innocents soon caught on.

The farm kids slipped out of camp with bundles of

rakes, bags of blasting powder, gallons of paint, and work shoes to sell to the villagers, but Joe and I gave it the Neighborhood's professional touch. As requisition clerk, I made sure that a portion of everything that came into camp went direct to Jap Jenny, the Japanese woman who owned the village store, who paid cash; the old sergeant wasn't bashful, he took his split down the middle.

Then a crouching winter leaped at us with a howling fury. The days were bitter and deep snowfalls isolated the camp from the outside world, even the logging camps. At times the tension in the barracks was so great it vibrated like static electricity. The old sergeant was completely helpless, and it was Joe who ruled the camp. He organized the work details and his fist was the law. He was liked and admired, and the boys followed him, even into the subzero early mornings to clear the roads.

It was a tough, healthy, and primitive life. When there was no paper work to be done, I would join Joe on the plow, or lead the shovel details; when the weather cleared, I felled trees and took my turn on the jackhammer when we blew a side of the mountain.

Lights were out early in the barracks, simply because there was nothing to do but sleep, gossip, or read. I read and reread the discarded library books my aunt sent me and, surprisingly, they made the rounds of the barracks many times. Would I ever forget a Kansas farm kid reading Carlyle on the mess table in kerosene light—after he complained there were no pictures?

Lying in my bunk, my eyes heavy from reading in the dim light, I did a great deal of daydreaming and planning. Chena occupied most of my thoughts; there were times when I wanted her so much it was almost painful. Then there were the memories of Tom and that brutal Saturday afternoon. In all those months, Joe never mentioned his brother or his mother but try as I could, I could not erase from my mind the trickle of blood running from under the faded sweatshirt and the light going out of those eyes.

Why? Why? Why?

I never found the answer but I did make a resolution: never again would I accept impotence as a way of life. Never again would I overestimate the power of "them," the ancient enemy I had inherited from the Neighborhood.

Them. The Law. Justice. The hostile world outside the Neighborhood. And cops. Cops more than anything, because they had taught me the most despairing lesson of my whole life: that to hope is useless.

Although Joe's hatred of cops was explosive, those lonely months in that camp refined mine and made it deeper, perhaps more dangerous. To me, their inhumanity and corruption represented a perverse power that crushed the helpless. I plotted ways in which we could defeat, brutalize, and humiliate them. I enjoyed romantic daydreams of returning as a powerful business baron with vast political connections and watching them jump for my dollars as I snapped my fingers.

But it was my dream of a police union that occupied most of my idle hours. In the camp office I learned to pick and hunt on the battered old typewriter. For my own amusement I would write page after page of how Joe and I would organize our imaginary union. But there were many times, particularly when we were alone in the forward surveying camp, when we seriously debated whether it was possible for anyone to organize the police into a huge striking force, capable of dominating the city's life.

The only news we heard from the outside world came from an occasional newspaper left by a logger or what we heard from the ranger or surveyor. Tom Dewey, it seemed, was really cleaning up New York City; he had sent a big-time mobster named Lucky Luciano to prison. But the news that stunned us was the indictment of Jimmy Hines, who controlled Tammany Hall. Compared to him, our ward leader was an insignificant tinhorn. Hines had always been the symbol of invincible political power; it was hard to believe he was on his way to prison.

"Pepe was right," I told Joe.

"In what way?"

"Remember the night in Patsy's? He said the town was reform crazy. It has to be to grab Jimmy Hines."

"Maxie Solomon said the same thing," Joe reminded me. "I wonder if we'll ever hear from that little wop?"

"Pepe? I have no doubt about it."

We were sprawled out on our bunks listening to a howling storm that shook the barracks.

"Do you really think so, Frank?" he asked, turning over and resting his head on his raised hand.

"I told you I have no doubt we'll hear from him."

"I hope so."

"I'd like to make a bet they're in numbers."

"Pepe and Gus? Why do you say that?"

"Remember the night we were in the Shadow Box saying good-bye to Nick and his old man was on the phone all the time?"

"He was talking in Italian . . ."

"That's right, but I heard him mention the name, the Dutchman. That was Schultz."

Joe slammed his fist on the blanket. "That's right. And the next day Schultz was knocked off in Newark! You think they took over, Frank?"

"Who knows? They're certainly in something. Pepe doesn't make his living from that art gallery."

"They must have dough to run that high class gin mill."

"Every time I saw his roll it was big enough to choke a horse."

"We just have to get in with them someway when we get back," Joe said fervently. "Christ! To get into numbers would be great. We can hustle the West Side. Maybe Harlem." He grinned. "Between pickin' up numbers we can change our luck . . ."

Pepe kept his word. One day the old sergeant summoned us to the camp's office to read a letter from the inspector general in Boise: we were to be driven to the nearest railroad station and given fare to St. Louis where we would pick up tickets to New York.

"Hey, who do you kids know?" the sergeant asked bewilderedly.

Joe gestured to me and, in a stage whisper, told him:

"Don't you know he's FDR's bastard son?"

After a rousing farewell party in the barracks we solemnly turned over our dice and ownership of the game to two kids from Brooklyn who had recently arrived in camp, then the chef-mechanic drove us to St. Francis, the nearest railhead, thirty miles downriver.

A milk train took us to St. Louis where we decided it would be foolish to spend the government's money for fares. We cashed in our tickets and continued east by thumb.

We were so electrified by our first glimpse of New York that we could have been returning from a year's exile on another planet. We let out a whoop and pounded each other's shoulder when we crossed the Jersey meadows and

187

saw the outline of the Manhattan skyline, like a cardboard cutout pasted against the smoky horizon.

"There it is, kids—the Big Apple!" the trucker said. "There's nothing like it."

And how we agreed with him.

We took the subway to Times Square and stood in the front car like two kids, watching the red and green signal lights flash by as the train roared through the dirty iron darkness. Compared to the pale, bored passengers we looked like two rugged cowhands. We were lean, hard, dark, and much older. We were also brimming over with newly discovered self-confidence.

Just after we left the subway a truck narrowly missed us as it screeched to a stop for a red light. The driver leaned out his cab and showered us with the usual truck driver's obscenities. We walked over to the truck and dropped our duffle bags.

"What did you call us?" Joe asked quietly.

The trucker studied us for a moment, then wilted.

"You kids can get killed crossin' a street like that," he protested.

"It's a good thing we're tired, buddy," Joe told him, "or we would kick your goddam brains in and then take your truck apart wheel by wheel . . . "

The trucker never answered: he just threw his truck into gear and took off up Seventh Avenue. Joe and I looked at each other and grinned.

"We're not takin' any shit from anybody," Joe said. "Right?"

"Right."

At the corner of Eighth Avenue and Forty-sixth we silently surveyed the Neighborhood. The street hadn't changed, but after a year in the majestic mountains of Idaho the poverty, the dinginess, the squalor, only seemed more pronounced. It was a mild day with a hint of rain. As always, the supers had put out their garbage cans early—the Neighborhood's traditional weather barometer—so they would not have to haul garbage to the curb in a downpour, and disturb any beer drinking while they listened to the serials on the radio. Cats were daintily feasting on bits of refuse. Debris littered the streets. An abandoned tenement had its windows broken, a bunch of little kids were methodically, senselessly, battering an old icebox to pieces with a two-by-four under the indifferent stare of a stout colored woman who sat on a stoop with a sleeping baby in her lap.

"Hey, there's niggers on the block!" Joe observed indignantly.

We ran up the steps of our tenement two at a time; when I approached the door of our flat my heart was racing. Joe never glanced across the hall where he had lived. I pounded on the door and it cautiously edged open.

For a moment my aunt and I stared at each other through the narrow crack, then she flung open the door with a wild cry.

"Frank! Joe! Where have you been? I told myself that if you weren't home by this weekend I was going to call Mr. Armondo . . ."

She fell into my arms and reached out for Joe. We held her for a few minutes as she wept and then, when she had regained control of herself, we went inside.

Joe gave me a puzzled glance. "Mr. Armondo? Who's that?"

For a moment the name escaped me, then I remembered—Sortino Armondo—Uncle Pepe.

"That's Pepe," I explained to Joe. "What did he want, Aunt Clara?"

"Oh, he's such a gentleman," she said enthusiastically. "He came—" She broke off, then said over her shoulder as she hurried into the bedroom, "I must give you these before I forget."

She returned with two bankbooks. The one she gave to me had almost two hundred and forty dollars in cash—the monthly deposits of twenty dollars sent to her by the government.

"When Mr. Armondo told me you were on your way home I drew everything out except twenty-five dollars so the account would still be active." She hugged me. "I knew that when you came back, son, you would need money."

"But that was for you, Aunt Clara."

"I didn't need it. We got a raise at the library, not much but enough for me to live on. Besides, Mr. Armondo left fifty dollars when he came here. I tried to make him take it back but he refused. He really became very indignant. He said you were wonderful boys who had not been treated right and that was the least he could do for you. He also gave me Joe's book. He said the deposits had been made by an old friend of his who was very honest." Joe glanced at the book that bulged with cash and handed it to me. It was made out to Mrs. Mary Ronnezzi of Hoyt Street, Brooklyn. The deposits were the same as mine, twenty dollars the first of the month.

"Mr. Armondo said he gave the lady in Brooklyn fifty dollars for her trouble. I told him I thought Joe would certainly give her that and more," Aunt Clara said.

"When did he drop by?"

"Let's see, it's almost two weeks now," she said pensively. "It was so strange. First this man knocked at the door. He was very polite and said Mr. Armondo was downstairs and would like to see me."

"Did you see Pepe before that, Aunt Clara?"

"Why yes, Frank," she said. "The day after the police brought me to the station house and Captain Elliott asked me if I had seen either of you two boys . . ." Tears welled in her eyes. "That was so terrible! They kept me sitting there . . ."

I gently interrupted her. "What did Pepe say when he came here a few weeks ago?"

"Well, after his driver went down he came up and told me you and Joe had left the camp and were on your way home. He said the government would arrange your train fare and it would only take a few days. That's why I became worried when you didn't arrive."

"We hitchhiked, Aunt Clara," Joe said. "We didn't see any use of spending Uncle Sam's money when we could get rides . . ."

"I hope you boys learned to save your money," she said firmly. "Things are beginning to loosen up but jobs are not hanging from the washlines yet." She said brightly, "I saw your friends Danny and that big boy—"

"Train?"

"The one that lives with his grandmother off Ninth. They were passing on the avenue and I told them you were on your way home. They said to tell you they would see you at Regan's. Do they allow boys that young in a saloon, Frank?"

"Only to shoot pool in the back room, Aunt Clara," I told her with a straight face. Poor dear Aunt Clara . . .

"There's one important thing Mr. Armondo told me to tell you boys—"

"What's that?"

"To be sure and see him as soon as you get home. He has a job waiting for both of you."

Joe gave me a quick glance. "Did he say doing what, Aunt Clara?"

She shook her head. "All he said was that he had jobs for both of you." She hugged us. "You look wonderful! So much bigger and older looking. Whatever it was you did out there it certainly helped to mature you boys," she said lightly.

I didn't look at Joe. "I guess there were some things that helped us grow up, Aunt Clara."

Aunt Clara insisted upon preparing for us an enormous breakfast of ham, eggs, toast, coffee. We finished every crumb.

"Have you heard anything, Aunt Clara?" I asked her when we sprawled out on the sagging old couch in the front room.

"About your case?" she said as delicately as she could.

"Were the cops around after they brought you to the precinct?" Joe asked.

"They never came back after Lieutenant Elliott sent me home in the radio car," she said. "One day he saw me on the street and asked about you—"

"You didn't tell him where we were?"

"Of course," she said.

"You told him where we were?"

"By all means. I told him you were in California staying at the home of some relatives and you were both in the movies with Clark Gable."

We whooped when she told us that.

"Did he ever come around here again?"

"Never. But someone else did . . ."

"Who was that?"

"Chena Valentino. My, she's a lovely girl. This one Sunday I went to late Mass at St. Barnabas. As I was coming out someone took my arm. It was Chena. I hadn't seen her since Mary Gunnar's wake. I couldn't believe this beautiful young lady was that little girl in pigtails who was always in the playground when you boys were playing basketball."

"She's a beauty, Aunt Clara," Joe said shyly.

"My, that she is, Joe," my aunt said. "She told me what marvelous times you had, Frank, going around the museums. And you never told me!"

"He was only intereted in art, Aunt Clara," Joe said solemnly.

My aunt peered at him over her glasses. "Joe Gunnar, are you pulling my leg?"

"Me, Aunt Clara?" he said innocently. "Didn't you know Frank was a regular patron of the arts?"

I dismissed him with a wave of my hand. "Did you see Chena again, Aunt Clara?"

"Once she dropped by the library when she was doing some work for school. We had lunch. . . . Frank, she's a lovely girl . . ."

"She sure is."

"I hope you intend to see her."

"Are you kiddin', Aunt Clara?" Joe said disgustedly. "He would be kickin' down her door now if I didn't drag him over to see you first."

"This guy is getting too frisky, Aunt Clara," I told her, "we better get over to the gallery and see Pepe about that job . . ."

Joe stood up and stretched. "Don't kid me, buddy boy, you just want to see your Italian beauty . . . right, Aunt Clara?"

He put his arm around her and she smiled. "Joe Gunnar, I don't know what I'm going to do with you."

Joe, now serious, said, "Has the rent been paid on the flat, Aunt Clara?"

"Yes it has. The super told me only last week the real estate man said a check comes every month, just like clockwork . . . Who took care of it, Joe?"

"Mr. Armondo," I put in. "You ready, Joe?"

The mention of the Gunnar flat was like a bucket of icy water flung into our faces. At the door my aunt silently hugged Joe.

"I go out to the cemetery every Sunday afternoon," she said softly. "I haven't missed one yet and I never will. Your mother was as dear to me as a sister." She bit her lower lip and her voice trembled. "Oh, God, when I think of Mary and Tom and what happened . . . and how it used to be . . ."

Almost automatically we crossed the street rather than pass the spot where Tom had been killed. Joe stared straight ahead.

"How do you like that little guy, Frank? He sends us

192

out to the CCCs in style, gets us released when he wants to, takes care of bankin' our dough, and now is gonna give us a job."

"I wonder what he has in mind?"

"I don't care if it's contractin' to shovel coal in hell. We have to start movin'. Now!"

"Fine with me."

"I just hope it's in numbers," he said fervently. "Forget anythin' legit. We'll never make a buck that way." He asked abruptly, "When are you gonna call Chena?"

"The first chance I get."

"You're gettin' serious, lover boy. You know what absence does?"

"You tell me."

"Makes the heart grow fonder for somebody else—like a wop lover from Ninth Avenue. Maybe you don't know it but in all wop families the old man picks out his son-in-law. You think Gus has his eye on you, a nice Irish boy?"

"I couldn't care less what Gus thinks."

He hummed softly, "Chena with the dark eyes ... Am I gonna be your best man, buddy?"

"Chena's going to college and I haven't got a job."

He put his arm around my shoulder with mock seriousness. "You marry Chena and we'll take over the Shadow Box and the old man's rackets—how about that?"

"You're full of ideas today."

"It's not bad, Frank," he said with a laugh. "Chena's a good-lookin' head and we'll join Pepe and dump Gus. How about that?"

We found Pepe's gallery no longer a niche in the wall. The windows of the adjacent store were now filled with framed prints and oils; one featured on a scarlet draped easel was an Eakins.

"That's an Eakins," I told Joe.

"What the hell's an Eakins?" he asked.

"An American painter. You know you're an illiterate bastard?"

The soft buzzer that had replaced the tiny bell almost miraculously produced Pepe. His gallery had changed but he hadn't. He was still the well-dressed, smiling little man with whom I had shared so many Saturdays.

"Peppino! And Joe!"

He pumped our hands, smiling and shaking his head in disbelief.

"Tisei falta grande!" He gently tested our muscles. "The muscles! *Marrone!* They are like iron." He waved up across the room. "Let us go into my office."

The aisle of paintings and statues seemed wider, deeper, but the small room Pepe stopped at was still cluttered with frames of all sizes and still smelled strongly of turpentine and varnish.

Pepe's office was not the cramped, cluttered pack-rat's nest I had known. The walls between the empty store and the gallery had been eliminated to form a large room with thick carpets. There was a wide and highly polished desk and leather chairs and a couch gleaming like polished onyx that imprisoned the soft mellow light of the lamps in its bottomless blackness. Art books no longer spilled out of corners; now they were stacked neatly, in floor-to-ceiling bookcases.

Pepe motioned to the couch and leaned back in his chair. His smile was broad as ever, but his dark eyes had guessed our secrets before we stretched our legs out under the coffee table that held copies of art journals in French and Italian and a silver box of cigarettes. Joe selected one, fumbled in his pocket for a wooden match, the kind we had used in Idaho, lit the cigarette, and then studied it as he slowly exhaled.

"They are from Paris," Pepe explained.

"Fag butts," Joe grunted.

Pepe's slight shrug dismissed Joe's boorishness.

"You look older, Peppino," he said, "and you too, Joe. The camp—was it good?"

"It was fine if you liked trees," Joe said.

"It was great but we're glad to be back, Pepe," I told him. "Has everything been straightened out?"

"An arrangement has been made," Pepe said. "You will plead guilty to a misdemeanor. You will be given thirty days suspended sentence and that will be the end of that business. It is all forgotten."

"Cops don't forget so easily," Joe pressed. "Have they been taken care of?"

"Why do you worry about the cops, *giovinotto?*" Pepe asked with a smile. "When we need the *pòrcos* we buy them. Maybe we put them in Peppino's union. No, Peppino?"

194

"You can kid about it but we have done a lot of thinkin' about that union," Joe said.

Pepe, suddenly serious, looked at me.

"Yes, Peppino? You have thought about the union?"

"Sure I thought about it," I told him, "but we kidded around a lot what we would have the cops do—"

"No. No. Peppino," he said, shaking his head. "This is no *divertimento*. We should talk about this union."

"You're serious about this, Pepe?" Joe asked.

He looked at us, his eyes cold as stones.

"*Sì*. I am serious," he said softly. "*Sangue della patata!* What a trick! We could own the city! Yes, my young friends, it is something we should talk about—but not now—later." He suddenly became brisk and all business. "First you see the lawyer—"

"That young guy—Maxie Solomon?" Joe asked.

"You can trust him," Pepe said. "We have used him many times."

I asked him, "Pepe, who's 'we'? Don't you think it's time you told us?"

"That's right," Joe said. "How about it?"

Pepe held up his hands in a gesture of feigned despair. "Questions. Always questions, Peppino?"

"We'd like to know who our friends are," Joe told him.

"It is better to know your enemies," Pepe told him firmly.

"We never seem to have any trouble on that score," Joe said dryly.

"Why do your friends go to this trouble, Pepe?" I asked. "We're only a couple of kids from the Neighborhood. What can we do for them?"

"Have we asked you to do anything?" Pepe asked mildly.

"No, but we—"

"Questions! Questions! Did you come here like little children?" he asked impatiently. "There will be time for talk. Now you see the lawyer." He scribbled something on a card and came around the desk. "He will make arrangements for the court. Then you will come back here and we will have dinner and we will see Gus."

"You told my aunt you had a job for us—"

"When you come back."

On the way out I asked him, "How is Chena, Pepe?"

He linked his arm with mine as we walked across the main gallery. "*Ecco!* She is like a cat! Jump! Jump! Always the telephone! Her mother says she eats nothing.

She listens only for the telephone to talk to you. So you call her, eh, Peppino?" He swung open the door. "Go with God, my young friends."

14 THE JOB

Even Maxie Solomon had changed. The shiny blue serge suit was gone. In its place was an expensive tweed, a tab collar shirt, and a maroon tie that looked to be silk. His thin wristwatch was obviously gold and expensive, and his office was a large suite with a receptionist and typist. I guess it was a mark of our importance that he came out personally to usher us inside.

"You guys look great," he said enviously. "You look like you could eat nails. Where were you—Wyoming?"

"Idaho," Joe said shortly.

"We understand everything's arranged," I said.

"I had dinner with the judge who will handle it," he said. "You'll be in and out." He shrugged. "What the hell, everybody's forgotten about it."

"Yeah. Except us," Joe said shortly.

"I didn't mean it that way," Maxie said.

"Forget it. What did it cost?"

Solomon rapped a letter opener on his desk blotter.

"You know, Gunnar, you're a great guy for questions. What the hell difference does it make? One, two, three and you're out. You plead to a misdemeanor and you'll get a suspended sentence. No probation. Nothing."

"I'm curious," I told him. "Why is Pepe going to so much trouble?"

"Pepe happens to like you."

"How about his friends?" Joe asked. "He keeps tellin' us his friends are our friends but that's all he'll tell us. I like to have someone I can shake hands with—do you know what I mean, Maxie?"

"Sure," Maxie said jovially, "but why ask me—ask Pepe."

In an offhand manner Joe asked, "How many numbers cases do you figger they give you a year?"

"Nice try, wise guy, let's forget it," Maxie said with a tight smile. He flipped the pages of a calendar. "I'll see you in court Monday the fifteenth. Ten A.M. Be there on time. The old guy on the bench is a stickler for defendants appearing on time."

"What court?"

"Washington Heights. That's where the judge is sitting. I also know I can take care of the bridge man."

"What's that?" Joe asked.

"The clerk who takes care of the yellow and blue jackets —the misdemeanors, felonies, and short affidavits. You take care of him and he pushes your case up front." He added with a short laugh, "Things they don't teach you in law school . . ."

"You really know your way around, Maxie," Joe said admiringly.

"You work West Side, Harlem, and Yorkville Magistrate courts and you get to know the ropes," Maxie said modestly. "It costs a few bucks but it's worth it. Like up in Washington Heights. I even paid the reporter that covers the courthouse—"

"A newspaper reporter?" I said, startled.

He held up one hand, fingers spread wide. "It cost me five."

"Why the hell do you have to pay a reporter?" Joe asked.

"These guys that cover the courts send out everything. Even the crappiest case. They have a file in their offices. The name comes up. Bang! There's the case! Remember, you guys were big news a year ago. I don't want anything in the papers—not even a paragraph. Let's keep it nice and quiet. No publicity. No trouble." He pushed his calendar pad across the desk. "Okay. Washington Heights. The fifteenth. Ten o'clock on the nose. Be there early. I want it one, two, three and out."

As we were leaving he called out: "I forgot to tell you about Hennessy—"

"What about him?" Joe asked.

"Do you know he was kicked out of the department?"

"That's good news."

"He also has a glass eye . . ."

"A glass eye?"

"Yeah. His wife plugged him in the head and they had to take out his eye."

"Kidneyfeet with a glass eye!" Joe said. "News like that can almost make you believe someone is handin' out justice around here . . ."

Before we returned to Pepe's gallery we bought some clothes and took a room at the Railroad YMCA near Grand Central. After the makeshift showers in camp and the icy cold mountain streams, we couldn't take squatting in the small iron sink of our flat. Soaking in that full-length hotel-room tub was an extraordinary experience. We ripped open the boxes of suits, shoes, underwear, and socks, dressed carefully, then paraded up and down in front of the bureau mirror like two kids in their first long-pants Easter suits.

Joe looked ruggedly handsome in his tweed suit—I guess unconsciously he had been impressed by Maxie Solomon's air of affluence—and sports shirts. The dark tan set off his icy blue eyes and shaggy blond hair. His powerful shoulders seemed ready to burst through the seams of his jacket. There was a sense of restless animal vitality about him as he prowled up and down.

"Wait until Chena gets a load of that," he said as I took my place in front of the mirror.

There was no doubt I had changed. My face, now the color of worn leather, had lost its adolescent boniness and acne. Deep-set brown eyes stared out at me coolly, confidently. No one had to tell me my body was supple and strong as steel wire. The result of countless felled trees, hours on the jackhammer, and swinging sledges were in those forearms. And if I caught a sense of cynicism that should not have belonged in that young face, there was always the Neighborhood, Hennessy, cops, and Justice Triumphs to blame . . .

"Let's go, Frank," Joe said impatiently. "Let Chena do the admiring. We have a date with a couple of wops."

"Shall we keep any of this stuff?"

"Are you nuts?" He rolled up our long johns, pants shirts, and work shoes.

"No more of this crap for us. Give it to the porter."

"The hell with the porter," I said and threw the clothes in a drawer. "How do we know what this guy is going to offer us?"

"Numbers! We're gonna hustle numbers," Joe said. "I

told you that's what Pepe and Gus are in—policy! Didn't you hear me con it out of Maxie? He's their lawyer."

"Maybe. We'll see . . ."

We left that little hotel room like conquering heroes. At the gallery Pepe nodded his approval.

"Buòno! Buòno! You both look much better."

The same Cord and driver took us downtown; instinctively I knew our destination would be Patsy's on Thompson Street. The restaurant's ancient owner guided us through the busy kitchen and up the stairs to the luxurious apartment where a table had been set with antipasto. There was no menu and no ordering. Patsy himself served us, assisted by an old woman in black. It was obvious from their reverential attitude that they considered Pepe to be a man of vast importance.

All through the elaborate meal Pepe chatted with me about art, the new Ingres at the Metropolitan, the exhibition of the Dutch painter Van Gogh they were all talking about, and the Constable he had tried to buy at an auction. Joe was plainly bored.

When the dishes had finally been cleared and small cups of black bitter coffee served, Patsy and the old woman vanished.

"Now we talk," Pepe said. "What do you plan to do?"

"We don't have any plans," Joe said. "We thought you might help us make some."

He shrugged. "What is it you want me to do?"

"You told my aunt you had something in mind for us, Pepe."

"Sì. But perhaps you will not be interested, Peppino."

"We'll take anything . . ."

"A waiter at the Shadow Box?" he suggested cautiously. "The tips are very good."

"A waiter!" Joe burst out. "Who the hell wants to be a waiter?"

"I am only making suggestions," Pepe said unruffled. "Perhaps in the garment center? There are friends in the union—"

"Oh balls," Joe said disgustedly.

"We thought you could do better than that, Pepe," I put in. "The last night we were here you told us you and your people have many interests—"

"So *giovinotto,* you want to work for Pepe—is that it?"

"That's right," Joe said bluntly. "Preferably in numbers."

199

Pepe looked at him. "Numbers?"

"Policy. We'll pick up, deliver, hustle—you name it and we'll do it."

Pepe held up his hands, palms out, almost beseechingly. "Numbers. Numbers. Why do you talk about numbers?"

"We thought that perhaps you and your associates had a financial interest in numbers," I said as delicately as I could put it, "or maybe you knew someone—"

Pepe dismissed me with a wave of his hand.

"Come on, Pepe—level with us," Joe said.

"*Si.* I'll level with you, my young friend," Pepe said earnestly. "I cannot help you with policy."

He could read the disappointment in our faces.

"I have other interests . . ."

"Like what?" Joe said impatiently.

"We will come to it soon," he said bluntly as he pushed aside the cup and leaned over the table.

"You speak of numbers, my young friend, what do you know of it?'

"Not much, except since we were this high"—Joe bent over and held out his hand about a foot from the floor—"everyone in the Neighborhood's been playin' numbers. Old ladies. Dock workers. You name it, they play."

"*Si.* The whole country plays," Pepe said, nodding. "You know of the politician Hines?"

"We heard about it on the radio out in Idaho. He was a big man in this town."

"He was a fool who became greedy and could no longer think straight," Pepe said coldly. "Now what he left behind must be made into a business. The colored will work in the streets but certain people will be in charge." He added disgustedly, "No more Irish gangsters and their machine guns."

"What about Dewey?" I reminded him. "Isn't he cleaning up the town?"

Pepe gave me a thin, cynical smile. "Peppino, someday you will learn that sin will always be a part of the cities. If you allow it to get big and ugly, it will scare the people and they will cry out for the reformers to come and hold their hand. Then a Dewey will appear. The people will cheer. He offers them an old fool like Hines. The conscience of the people becomes quiet." He ran his hand over the back of an imaginary cat. "It lays down and goes to sleep. The tiger becomes a kitten." He held up his hand and said softly, "That is when to work, my young friends.

A man here, a man there. A few dollars here, some more there." He leaned across the table. "The colored woman who plays a penny. The storekeeper who writes it down. The *pòrco* cop on the street who turns his head for a dollar. The politician"—he jumped up and raised his left hand solemnly as if taking an oath while his right hand was held behind his back, palm out—"gives the people promises and still takes the money."

He drew a circle on the tablecloth with his finger and jabbed its center.

"Someday they will all belong in here."

"One organization," Joe said.

"*Si.*" Pepe smiled slightly. "No competition."

Like the Dutchman, I told myself.

"How about protection, Pepe?" I asked.

He shrugged. "Cops, Peppino?"

"From what we read in the papers they're head busters in Harlem. They're knocking over all the big policy setups."

"*Si.*" He made a swift downward motion with his hand. "One goes down."

His other hand came up.

"And one comes up," Joe put in.

Pepe nodded silently.

"And someone takes care of the cops?" Even while they're busting in the places? That takes a lot of doing, Pepe," I said.

"Yeah. You seem to know a lot about it, Pepe," Joe said. "You said you can't help us with policy. Who does it belong to? Can't you get us a knockdown to the guys in charge?"

"*Sente figlio mi!*" Pepe said wearily. "Do I have to talk all night about numbers to children?"

"But as you said, Pepe," I pointed out, "after the reformers get tired of reforming, policy will be very big . . . Joe and I thought we should get in on the ground floor . . ."

"It is not for you, Peppino. What would you do—run down the streets with a paper bag for the coloreds?"

"We thought we could be in a store or something," Joe said lamely.

Pepe shook his head. "I have plans," he said shortly, "but it has nothing to do with policy. *Marrone!* That's all you talk about—numbers, numbers."

"We're interested in anything you have to offer, Pepe," I told him and gave Joe a warning look.

Joe said quickly, "Right, Frank. How about it, Pepe?"

Pepe remained silent, staring down at the circle he had made. Finally I said, "Do you have something in mind, Pepe?"

He looked up and nodded. "*Si*. The waterfront. Unions."

Joe and I echoed each other. "The waterfront!"

"*Si*."

"The shape?" Joe asked disgustedly. "Is that all you have to offer? Who the hell wants to freeze waiting for one of the Gimp's goons to toss him a brass check?"

"You are too impulsive, my young friend," Pepe said quietly. "I didn't mention the shape-up."

"You have something in mind, Pepe?" I asked.

Pepe shrugged. "Joe isn't interested in the waterfront, Peppino."

I nudged Joe under the table.

"I'm sorry, Pepe," he said quickly. "I should have kept my mouth shut."

"You should listen, *giovinotto*," Pepe said mildly, "you learn when you listen."

"I always thought Johnny the Gimp and his Pistoleers had the docks knocked up," I told Pepe. "Anyone who is put on must kick back to them. That's the way it has always been . . ."

Joe nodded. "The docks never change, Pepe. Half the guys in the Neighborhood who make the shape kick in. The Gimp even gets a piece of what they steal."

"Wilson? The cripple?" Pepe said with an edge to his voice. "*Ecco!* Don't worry about him. There will be no kickbacks for you to pay and no shape."

"Who do we work for?"

Pepe tapped his chest. "Me." He took out an expensive-looking card case and handed us each a card.

I read: Metropolitan Strapping and Binding Company; there was a telephone number but no address.

"What do you do on the waterfront, Pepe?" I asked.

"When a ship comes into port there are many boxes, bales, and barrels to be unloaded. Some get broken. The damaged cargo is taken to the end of the pier where old men repair it before it is removed. It is the law." He smiled when he saw the recognition in my face. "*Si*. My company repairs the damaged cargo."

"Who are the old men?"

He shrugged. "They are on every pier. Old men they call the coopers."

"Who do you work for, Pepe," Joe asked, "the shippers?"

Again the thin smile. "No. The government. It is the law. We help the law."

"You and Uncle Sam are partners!"

"He makes the law," Pepe said with a shrug. "Like good citizens we help him to enforce it. For a price."

"Is this just on one pier?" I asked.

"No. No." He ticked off on his fingers: "The West Side, downtown Pier A at the Battery. Then the East Side to Canal Street. All the Brooklyn piers. Also Bayonne. Hoboken. Weehawken and Port Newark." He leaned back. "Next year we will get the work on the Philadelphia and the Gulf ports. It is good, no?"

"How did Johnny the Gimp let you get away with that, Pepe?"

The black eyes were cold and steady. "Arrangements have been made. There will be no trouble."

"But the Gimp has been boss of the docks since my old man died," Joe said. Then he added something I had never heard him say before, "From what I heard since I was a kid maybe the Gimp had somethin' to do with his accident . . ."

"Perhaps," Pepe said. "Perhaps. Your father was on the waterfront for many years—"

"Since World War I."

"The people remember him."

Joe looked surprised. "They do? I wouldn't know. But maybe they should. He bought enough booze for them to float the *Leviathan*. Let's get this straight. If we work for you, Pepe, what do we do?"

"You deliver the supplies to the piers. Cooper wire. Sheet strapping. Nails. You help the old men fix a few boxes. It is nothing."

"You said something about a union," I pointed out.

He took two worn cards from his pocket. "You are members of their union."

The soiled card said that the undersigned was a member in good standing of the independent Brotherhood of Coopers, Strappers, and Cargo Binders. It was signed, "Frederick Kenton, Pres."

"Fat Freddy Kenton!" I exclaimed. "The guy who owns the potato warehouse on Thirty-eighth Street!"

"The old man with the red face," Pepe said. With his hands he shaped a large stomach. *"Panzione!* A big belly."

"We worked for that bum for fifty cents a day," Joe said. "I never knew he had this union."

"It is very small," Pepe said. "Only the old men on the piers."

"Why do you want to do business on the waterfront, Pepe?"

Pepe filled his small cup from the silver pot, dropped in a cube of sugar, stirred carefully, then took a delicate taste.

"When you were in the camp," he said, "I was in Europe—"

"Why did you go to Europe, Pepe?" Joe asked impatiently.

"Business. While I was there I could smell war in the air. It won't come today or tomorrow, perhaps not for a few years. But it will come. And when it does, that crazy Mussolini will side with the Germans. All you can see in the cities are soldiers. Mussolini has the Italian people believing they are warriors! *Guerrièri lètto!* Warriors! The Italian only wants his pasta, his vino, and his culo!"

The maneuvering of the armies across the ocean, the savage diplomatic wars raging those years from Downing Street to Berlin were as foreign to Joe, myself, and the rest of the Neighborhood as were the complexities of the Russian Revolution or the gold standard. There were headlines about Hitler, who was always in the newsreels, and Mussolini, a bald-headed guy with a jutting jaw who kept shouting in Italian from a balcony. To the Neighborhood they were only names, what they did overseas to one another was not our concern.

"When war comes," Pepe continued, "The waterfront will be very important. There will be ships and cargo and everyone will be working."

"And Johnny the Gimp and his Pistoleers will get rich," Joe said.

"Perhaps," Pepe said draining his cup. "Perhaps we will share it."

"The Gimp share anything?" Joe said scornfully. "He won't give you the sweat. Don't mess with him, Pepe."

"You are so sure about everything, my young friend—I will remember your advice," Pepe said solemnly.

"When do we start, Pepe?" I asked.

"Do you both drive?"

"We learned in camp but we don't have a New York State driver's license."

"Tomorrow you will call me. I will make the arrangements."

"First we have to get a permit—"

"Forget it. You call me. There will be no permit."

"We get the licenses and then what?"

"You will meet Lorenzo and he will show you the truck and the warehouse. Peppino, you will visit the piers to find out what they want."

"What about the carpenter work on the piers?"

He made a grimace. "You help the old men fix a box. You drive a couple of nails and put some of the iron strap around the barrels. *Una còsa di niènte*. It's a thing of nothing."

"How much a week?" Joe asked.

"Fifty dollars."

I looked over at Joe, his eyes were glistening. Fifty a week! A fortune!

"Perhaps someday you'll expand, Pepe?" Joe asked.

"There are plans."

"Maybe you'll include us in those plans?"

"Perhaps. We will see." He leaned over and shook my shoulder. "Are you happy, Peppino? Is it enough money?"

"It's fine, Pepe, and we're both very grateful. Right, Joe?"

"Oh sure, Pepe, thanks a lot."

Pepe rose. "Now we will drive uptown and see Gus."

On the way to the Shadow Box in the Cord Pepe enthusiastically described for me the Delacroix he had seen at the Louvre; Joe just stared out the window plotting, I was sure, how soon he could take over the waterfront.

The Shadow Box was more magnificent than I had remembered. The bar had been extended and the entire wall was now covered with framed, autographed pictures. Waiters bowed lower when Pepe passed and the bodyguard that was on duty looked older, more dangerous, and wasn't reading a scratch sheet.

When we entered his office, Gus Valentino hurried across the room and gripped both our shoulders. Gus had put on some weight, but his clothes were flawless, and he wore a large diamond ring on his pinkie.

"Hey, you kids look wonderful. Don't they, Pepe?"

"Marrone! They have arms like iron," Pepe told him.

"Did you tell 'em about the docks?" Gus asked.

"They will start working in a few days," Pepe said.

"We just got this contract," Gus said. "You're in luck." He asked Pepe, "Did you tell 'em fifty a week?"

Pepe nodded. "I told them the cripple will not bother them—there is an arrangement."

"How is Nick?" I asked.

Mascalzone! Don't talk about it," Gus burst out.

"They saw the lawyer, Duchino," Pepe put in quickly.

Gus, his face tight, stared down at his clenched fist, then nodded.

"Maxie says he has it fixed so you kids will cop a plea. Did he tell you that?"

"Yes. He told us when to be in court."

"Okay. So you'll be in and out. No problem. No nothin'. That old bum owes us his arms and his legs. He doesn't play ball, he's dead at the next election." He said fiercely to Pepe, "Did you tell Maxie to tell him that, Pepe?"

Pepe nodded silently.

"Well then, you're all set," Valentino said, getting up. It was obviously our dismissal.

"You gonna see Chena, kid?" he asked me as we walked to the door.

"I'm going to call her as soon as I leave here . . ."

"Christ, call her will you, kid? Since she's goin' to that goddam college in Jersey you can't talk to her. I told her mother what she needs is her behind kicked! I don't know why I sent her over there in the first place. I told her to get married. *Fare tanto bambini.* Have many kids. Be a good wife to some guy. That's what a woman's for—not haulin' her ass over to Jersey every mornin'. You know I had to buy her a car? That should be Nicky! Not his sister."

He stood at the doorway, his face flushed with anger and frustration.

"If I had that goddam kid here right now I'd kick his teeth in," he said and slammed the door.

As we walked down the carpeted stairway Joe whispered, "It looks like Nick's in a jam."

When we shook hands with Pepe in the lobby, I asked him: "Not so good with Nick, Pepe?"

He slowly shook his head. *"Sangue della patata!* He gives us trouble."

"What happened?"

He patted me on the shoulder. "Chena will tell you."

"How do you like that?" Joe asked as we walked down Eighth Avenue. "In a couple of days we'll be carpenters."

I corrected him, "Coopers."

"Carpenters, coopers, what's the difference? And in Freddy Kenton's union. So that's where fat ass gets his graft!"

"He must have those old guys buffaloed."

"Who cares?" Joe said. "All I know is we're gettin' fifty clams a week. For that I'd dance a jig in the lobby of the Paramount." He said musingly, "What do you think Pepe meant about havin' an arrangement with the Gimp?"

"Maybe the Gimp gets a cut."

"I don't think so. I have a feelin' Pepe can be one tough wop when he wants to be. Maybe the Gimp just doesn't want to tangle with him."

"The Gimp is afraid to buck—"

"What do you mean?"

"When he made that circle on the tablecloth. I smell a new mob in the making."

"A wop mob. Like Capone in Chicago?"

"Who knows?"

"And who cares," he said abruptly. "All we want is to be part of any combination that can pay us fifty a week for nailing together old boxes."

"Don't kid yourself, Joe. Pepe has something else in mind."

But Joe wasn't listening. Almost automatically we had stopped at the window of an Eighth Avenue pet shop to watch the antics of several pups. When I nudged Joe and tapped on the window to get the attention of a frisky black poodle, I discovered he was staring down at the pups but I knew he wasn't seeing them.

"Now what's on your mind?" I asked him when he started down the avenue.

"It adds up, Frank. Just what you said. A new organization with a lot of power. They must be smart—they're movin' in right behind Dewey!" He turned to me. "That Pepe must have a lot of moxie. Do you remember what he said about the niggers and numbers up in Harlem? Schultz was knocked off. Hines is on his way to the can and they take over. And just when the town's red hot!" He whistled softly, admiringly. "Those wops have somethin' big goin' for them, Frank. That's what we have to get someday!" He snapped his fingers as if he had suddenly remembered.

207

"Did you see how he went for that cops' union idea of yours?"

"I'm more interested in that fifty bucks a week."

"Sure. It's great but I'm with Pepe—we kept your idea on the shelf. When we're ready we'll take it down, look it over, and bingo! We'll organize the cops!"

"As easy as that? Stop daydreaming Joe."

We walked in silence for a few blocks. I knew that in his mind Joe already had the police of New York, Chicago, Philadelphia, and points west all carrying pocket signs and shouting their demands as they marched up and down outside the precincts. Of course we sat by in a gleaming Caddy, smoking cigars and issuing secret orders . . .

To return him to reality I said, "Gus looked mad as hell when you mentioned Nick."

"Yeah," he said, irritated at having his daydreams interrupted.

"I wonder what that crazy guy has done now?"

"Who knows?" He brooded for a moment, then gave me a sly look." I noticed that he seemed eager for you to call Chena." He grinned. "Remember what I told you, pal, about wops selectin' their son-in-law."

"Drop dead."

"Are you gonna call her? You've been itchin' all day."

"Soon as I ditch you."

"Oh well, I guess I'll have to let my old buddy go." He sang softly with a sad look, " 'Those weddin' bells are breakin' up that old gang of mine . . . There goes Frank . . .' "

I swung at him playfully but he ducked, waved goodbye, and moved down the avenue.

15 CHENA

As soon as Joe had disappeared, I headed for the nearest telephone. In the gleam of the phone booth I found myself trembling. I dropped the damn nickel twice before I could get her number.

"Hello . . ."

My mouth was so dry I could barely form the words. "This is Frank, Chena . . ."

There was a pause, then the joy and happiness in her voice electrified me.

"Frank! Frank! Where are you? I've been living by this telephone since Pepe told me you were home. Where are you?"

"I'm over at Times Square. I thought perhaps I could see you—"

"Of course. When?"

"How about now?"

"Oh, Frank. Where?"

"The library—in front of our lions?" I glanced out at a wall clock. "It's four now—how about four thirty?"

"I'll be there in fifteen minutes," she promised.

I practically ran up Forty-second Street to the library. When I arrived in front of our lions I saw Chena jump out of the cab. I made the street in a few leaps. She had just turned from paying the cabdriver when I grabbed her.

She never had a chance to say anything. I kissed her long and hard.

"Frank," she whispered, trying to get her breath, "the people on the bus stop?" We had a smiling audience.

"I couldn't care less," I told her.

She pushed me back to study me for a moment. "Frank, you're bigger! You look older—and you're so dark!" She hugged me and added softly, "And you're handsomer."

I tucked her arm under mine. "I want to go where we won't be disturbed."

"Central Park? All the housewives are gone now."

I whistled down a cab and in minutes we were in the park walking down one of the paths off Central Park South where we selected a bench on a small knoll.

The odor of her lightly fragrant perfume intoxicated me. When I reached for her, she flung her arms around my neck and held me so tightly I could barely breathe. I kissed her hair, her eyes, her cheeks, her eyelids. When I pressed my lips to hers, she responded with a passion that shook me. Her eyes welled with tears, and I could taste them on my tongue as they coursed down her face.

She gripped my fingers until they cracked, and moaned

under my kisses. I wanted her more than anything on God's earth; I knew I couldn't live without her.

"I thought you'd forget about me by now."

She pulled back to look up at me.

"You don't stop caring for someone just because he goes away . . ." She gently touched my cheek. "God, what they did to you."

"It's going to be all right. We saw Pepe's lawyer this morning. He says we can plead to some minor charge and that will be the end of it."

"I knew Pepe would take care of it," she said, smiling and wiping her eyes. "He kept telling me not to worry."

"Joe and I are going to work for him, Chena."

A slight shadow fell across her face.

"He told me last week he had something in mind for you and Joe on the waterfront."

"You sound like you don't like the idea."

"It's—it's the waterfront, Frank. All those gangsters . . ." Her voice trailed off. "I was hoping you would go back to school."

"Maybe later, but not now."

"Why not now?"

"I can't come back here and keep drifting, Chena. I just can't let events sweep me along. A year ago I did and look what happened—now I have to make something happen! I'm not going to let myself get pushed around anymore. I want my share." Unconsciously I found myself repeating what Joe had said one night in camp, "We came back to collect the markers they owe us. The Neighborhood. The cops. Everybody—"

"Frank, let's walk over to the Youth Administration office. They help kids get to college."

"No more schoolboy stuff, Chena. Now I have to make some dough," I told her with a grin. "We even asked Pepe to set us up in numbers."

She looked horrified. "Frank, you're not going into numbers?"

"Pepe wouldn't do it. That's how he offered us this waterfront deal . . ."

"I'm afraid of the waterfront, Frank," she whispered. "When we lived on Ninth Avenue I heard stories. Horrible stories. . . . I think there's a better way," she added firmly.

"Maybe I'll find one, but until I do it's the docks for me. You know, Chena, I did a lot of thinking in the woods—"

"What about, darling?"

"About what we want to make of our lives. What did I have to look forward to except return to that damn flat and spend the rest of my life cursing the outside world. It's hostile, Chena. I know that now. It's an enemy. It killed any chance I had to go to college, to live in an apartment that has a bathtub that isn't in the kitchen, to be an educated guy and not a shenango on the piers, or a rock buster or painter on some WPA project or stuck in some factory where I could break my back—for what? It's gone, Chena. Like Tom. Take him. What did he ever want? A million dollars? No. Just a nice apartment for his mother. No rats. No roaches. No drunken supers. A new icebox. An Atwater Kent radio with a cabinet built like a church. Nice china to replace those ugly white, flowered plates his mother and my aunt got at Dish Night. Some flowers. A window that looked out on a yard and not an air shaft . . ."

"Darling, you can get all those things. They're not impossible."

"How will I get them? I haven't got a gun."

She put her head on my shouder. "I hate it when you talk like that, Frank."

"I'm only reciting facts, Chena. You know they're facts. The worst thing in the world is to think you have a case. It can deform your whole existence."

"Oh, Frank if only it had never happened!"

"But it did, and we must face it. Why should I go back to school? Why should I travel all the way up to some jerkwater college near the Canadian border when I could have gone to Fordham? I had the scholarship wrapped up. You know it. Tom knew it. Even Father John knew it. That no-good—"

She touched her finger to my lips. "Don't curse a priest, Frank."

"He's a priest without honor. He buckled under to the cops and the insurance company. He knew we didn't have anything to do with the boiler explosion. He even admitted that to Tom."

The words poured out. For months they had been locked up inside of me, not even Joe had been able to release them. But Chena could. With her head on my shoulder, she listened in silence as I spewed out the pain, the despair, the helplessness. I don't know how long I talked, but when I had finished, the twilight was closing in over the park and the neon lights in the side streets were flickering on and off. I felt empty and exhausted, but relieved.

I tilted her chin up and kissed her. "I talked your ear off."

"Do you feel better?"

"Much better. It's funny but you're the only one I could talk to like this."

She smiled. "I feel complimented." Then she became serious.

"So your mind's made up—you will work for Pepe?"

"Darling. I can't understand why you're against it. The waterfront isn't all that bad!"

She looked down at her locked hands. "I promise not to say anything more to upset you, Frank. All I ever wanted was for you to be happy." She looked up. "But without hurting anyone else."

"Chena, can I ask you something? You don't have to answer if you don't want to."

"I never want any secrets between us," she said solemnly.

"It's about Pepe. . . . Is he in something with your father?"

She bit her lower lip in silence, then took a deep breath as if she had come to some difficult decision.

"Darling, you're not Italian . . . it's hard to explain . . ."

"I have an Italian girl friend, maybe I'll ask her—"

"Frank—this is serious! If you were Italian, you would know what I mean."

I searched for her hand and she squeezed mine.

"I'm sorry, Chena. I didn't mean to joke about it."

"You must realize, Frank, that for my father, Pepe, and the people they know, everything is different. They live in a private world all their own and that's all they want to know. It's been like that since I was a little girl. There are mothers, fathers, cousins. All together. At Easter, Christmas. Weddings. Even in funeral parlors they sit around whispering to one another . . ."

"Whispering isn't a crime, Chena."

"It's what they're whispering about, Frank," she said, stone faced. "Early one morning about a year ago I got up to go to school and my father and Pepe were in the living room discussing a newspaper clipping they had spread out on the table. I can still remember what Pepe said, *"Questo ca e una còsa nostra—"*

"And that means?"

"This is something for us. The next day, on the way to school, I bought a back issue and found the story. It was about some strike in a downtown wastepaper factory. At first it puzzled me but later I discovered that Pepe and my father were in the wastepaper business—"

"It appears to me they just went into a business, Chena."

"No, no, no," she said wearily, "they don't buy a business, they take it! They have friends. They are always making deals. I can hear Pepe saying to my father, 'How about him, We must reach him, Duchino! Is he a friend?' " She said softly, "You must realize, Frank, that in Italian families women are never to be seen and certainly never to be heard when the men get together. But it is surprising how much they know. I can tell you my father has bribed policemen and politicians. Even judges call my father and ask him for a favor."

"They are part of a . . ." She hesitated, then silently held up her cupped hands.

"You mean the Mafia, Chena? There are always pictures of them in the Sunday supplements, old guys in chains and in cages on trial in Italy."

She shook her head. "That's the old country. Over here there is *la famil*, families related to one another by blood or marriage. My mother calls it *còsa lóro*, their thing. Many of them are old bootleggers or people who operated speakeasies like my father and Pepe. After repeal they went into other things—"

"Like numbers?"

"God knows what. When I was in grammar school there were terrible fights between my mother and father. Now all she does is go to Mass and light a candle for his soul."

"But this company Pepe owns seems legitimate, Chena."

"Darling, anything Pepe touches will never be legitimate," she said fiercely. "Pepe always talks of the deals. He's dangerous, Frank. I knew it when I was a little girl. After my mother told me the story of how he had strangled those men, I dreaded to have him touch me." She shrugged. "Yet he has always been good to me." She slipped her arm under mine. "He likes you very much, Frank, and that makes me afraid."

"Why should that make you afraid?"

"I don't know but it does."

"It's a legitimate job, Chena. We're not going to be

carrying a gun or hitting people over the head." I held open my jacket. "Look—no guns!"

She smiled and clung to my arm. "Job or no job—promise me that you will think about going back to school. Please!"

"I'll think about it, darling, I really will. I promise. But I don't want you to worry about Pepe."

"If I know Pepe he has plans for you, Frank . . ."

"There's one thing I can't understand. Why me? I'm not Italian."

"He has always admired people who are smart and who use their heads," Chena said. "I heard him complain many times to my father that the young fellows they had working for them were stupid and couldn't be trusted. He knows you're smart and he feels he can trust you. To Pepe that's more important than money."

"But what can I do for him?"

"When Pepe talks about their thing, it is not for today, Frank. It is always for tomorrow. I can still remember him when I was little saying over and over to my father, 'Tomorrow, Duchino. We must think of tomorrow . . .'"

"Where would Joe and I fit in?"

She put her head back on my shoulder and said softly, "Wasn't Joe's father an important man on the waterfront many years ago?"

"Sure. He organized some unions and was a big deal on the docks."

"And don't they still remember him?"

"Of course they do. Everyone on the waterfront remembers Andy Gunnar—"

I broke off, suddenly remembering that I had heard Pepe say what Chena had just said.

"How do you know the piers still remember Andy Gunnar?"

She looked up. Then I knew. She had heard Pepe say it.

"My mother and I were in the kitchen when they were talking about the company," she said. "Pepe was telling my father about how everyone remembered"—she hesitated—*ubriáco*, the big drunk." She begged, "Don't repeat that to Joe, darling. Please!"

"He calls his father the same thing. . . . What do you think Pepe has in mind?"

"As my grandmother used to say, to try to find out what's on a Sicilian's mind is like taking a watch apart;

214

there are just too many springs." She sighed. "I wish Nicky was here."

"Why Nicky?"

"He and my father were always fighting over his music but there were times when they sat down and talked. I used to kid Nicky and tell him that if he didn't watch out he would be like our cousins, whispering and making deals." She bit her lip. "Poor Nicky . . ."

"Why do you say 'poor Nicky,' Chena? Is something wrong? Your father didn't seem to be too happy when I mentioned him down at the club."

"That's one of the reasons I wanted to see you, Frank," she said in a low voice.

"About Nick?"

"About Nick—" She looked up. "And going away."

I was stunned. "Going away? Where?"

"To Italy. My mother and I will leave in a few weeks, right after my finals."

"Why Italy?"

"It's a long story," she said. "One day, after you left, my father's cousin in Naples wrote to him. He was having trouble with Nick. Nick wasn't going to school regularly. My father wrote Nick a strong letter and even called him on the transatlantic telephone. But Nick was sick of medical school and gave him some double-talk. Then three weeks ago, my father received a cablegram from his cousin telling him Nicky had dropped out of school." She sighed. "What an explosion that night! He finally made arrangements for me and my mother to go to Naples and see Nicky."

"Will you have to stay long?" I asked in such a forlorn voice Chena laughed and kissed me.

"I'm afraid we'll have to stay the summer. You don't realize how many relatives we'll have to visit."

"Oh God, how I'll miss you!"

"I'd die if I thought you wouldn't . . ."

I kissed her and she slipped into my arms. "Chena, Chena, Chena," I whispered over and over. At that instant several small boys burst out of the underbrush and charged up the path, whooping, shouting, and brandishing pieces of wood. As they passed one slammed the bench with a stick and shouted, "Hey, looka the guy kissin' his girl!"

I cursed all kids in creation as Chena pulled away.

"An Indian attack," I said with an awkward laugh.

"It's getting late, Frank, I have to get home."

I stopped her as she started to get up.

"Would you like to know the main reason why I want this job with Pepe, Chena?"

"I wish it was to get back to school, darling."

"Forget school. I want it for something more important. I want to get married, Chena—to you. That's all I thought of in those damn woods."

She stared at me, her eyes big and luminous in the light of the street lamps that had just gone on.

"Do you want to?"

"I don't know what to say, Frank."

"There's only one thing to say, Yes. Or maybe it's No . . ."

"No. No. Oh, I don't mean that! Yes, darling."

This time I kissed her, fiercely and passionately, and I wouldn't have stopped for twenty Indian attacks.

"I have goose pimples," she said breathlessly when at last I let her go.

"What about your father? Will he object?"

"Object to you Frank? Why on earth should they?"

"I'm not Italian."

"Your friend Pepe will take care of that."

"Pepe? What does he have to do with your family?"

"He has a lot to say about my family, Frank," she said bitterly. "My father won't sneeze without telling Pepe. He's not the only one. All our cousins and uncles are the same way. They kiss his hand like the Pope."

"Don Vitone?"

"Yes," she said surprised, "that's what they call him. How did you know?"

"I heard someone call him that." I put my arm around her. "Let's forget Pepe, Chena. You're the only Italian I'm interested in—"

"I wish we could go away," she said in a small, wistful voice.

"Why do you say that?"

"I guess I'm foolish." She sighed. "But I'm afraid, darling."

"Of Pepe?"

"Pepe. The waterfront. Even the Neighborhood. It's a dead place, Frank, it's not for beginnings. Maybe we could go to Long Island . . ."

We sat there holding one another in silence as the soft purple light faded and the streetlights went on along

216

Central Park West. Then, almost automatically, we rose and moved, dreamlike, down the path, slowly, awkwardly, our arms around one another's waists.

Before we left the park I stopped and kissed her long and hard.

"I love you, Chena."

"I love you too, Frank," she said, her voice muffled against my chest.

16 THE COOPERS

In the office of his gallery Pepe made exactly one telephone call. When we arrived at the Motor Vehicle Bureau in the State Building, our names appeared to have a magical effect on the bored clerk who waved us out of line and turned us over to an inspector with whom he had a brief, whispered conversation. The inspector took us for one quick circle of the block, jotted down a few personal statistics, and we left with our license.

Early the next morning, Lorenzo, uncommunicative as always, took us to a warehouse on Cherry Street in downtown Manhattan near the wterfront. The long, cavernous interior was filled with bales of wastepaper and the floor was knee-deep in scraps. Several men were feeding paper into the mouth of a huge square machine. Like a monstrous Buddha it swallowed the paper with a mechanical gulp that shook the building. Then it shuddered and ejected a solid square of paper bound with wire. Nearby were several open trucks loaded with burlap bags of paper and a smaller panel pickup with a crudely painted sign on one side that read: Metropolitan Strapping Company.

I suddenly remembered what Chena had told me about the wastepaper company.

"Does Pepe own this place?" I asked Lorenzo.

He ignored me and swung open the doors of the truck. Inside were coils of flat strapping wire, stacks of half-inch pine boards, containers of nails, coils of copper wire, and a toolbox.

"Does Pepe own this place?" I asked again.

He shrugged, handed me a sheet of ruled paper with a list of pier numbers and names of boss checkers, then left.

"I wouldn't call him exactly talkative," Joe said. "What made you think this was Pepe's place?"

"Chena mentioned something about Pepe and her father owning a wastepaper factory . . ."

He grinned. "What did I tell you about wop dames knowing everything that goes on in their families."

"Okay, Italian expert, let's go."

Pier 70, one of the luxury sheds not far from our old banana pier, was to be our working base. When we arrived the shape was over, but as Joe swung into the pier a man in blue pants and a gray shirt ran out of a small office to hold up his hand.

"Where the hell do you think you're going?" he shouted. Now I could see a badge on his shirt.

"We're from Metropolitan Strapping," Joe told him. "We're supposed to deliver supplies for the coopers."

"Yeah? Who said so?"

"Here's our list of piers, buddy," Joe said and started to hand him the sheet of ruled paper. "We were told to—"

"You know what you can do with that paper, kid?" he said and banged the truck's fender with his fist.

Joe, hands on the wheel, stared at him.

"You want to get hurt, mister, you just stay where you are."

He yanked the gearshift into reverse and the truck jerked back a few feet, then he threw it into first and stepped on the gas. As the light truck leaped forward like a deer, Bigmouth made a wild leap to one side and Joe slammed on his brakes.

"What's the matter—you crazy?" the guy shouted. "You almost hit me!"

"Well then get your fat ass out of the way," Joe told him. We drove off leaving him sputtering curses.

"He looked like some kind of a guard or inspector," I told Joe.

"I don't care if he was Christ Almighty," he said quietly. "We've been suckers too long for every bastard that wore a badge. Now we're not going to take crap from anybody—particularly guys who wear badges. If he has a beef let him come down and talk about it."

218

A liner had docked that morning and we made our way past the longshoremen unloading the fishnets and stacking the cargo. We finally found the coopers' shed at the far end of the pier. Inside were two old men sipping at cardboard containers of coffee and munching crullers.

"We're from Metropolitan Strapping," Joe said.

One man nodded. He had a pleasant weather-beaten face and a close-cropped bush of thick gray hair.

"Oh yeah. We been waitin' for you. I'm Jack Bailey." He motioned to the other man who had a pale, freckled face, watery blue eyes, and a tonsure of fading reddish hair. "This is Jim Collins. We're the coopers. You fellows want some coffee?"

"No thanks," Joe told him. "What do you want us to do?"

Bailey asked, "You carpenters?"

I explained, "We just got out of the CCCs."

"What the hell, there's not much to it," Bailey explained. "When a piece of cargo's broken they have to bring it in here and we strap it." He looked at his companion. "Right, Jim?"

Collins finished his container. "That's about it."

Suddenly the small shed shook as something slammed into it.

"Coopers! Coopers!" someone shouted.

"Here's one now," Bailey said and hurried out. He returned pulling in a four-wheeler with a large wooden box, its top stove in.

Bailey pried up the broken boards with a crowbar and read aloud the stenciled address of a Danish silverware company which Collins wrote down on a form. Then both men expertly burrowed inside the tightly packed excelsior to uncover a beautiful polished chest. Collins snapped open its lid to reveal a collection of the finest silver I had ever seen. He grunted with satisfaction, then handed the chest to Collins who hid it under a tarpaulin.

"Okay, Jim, let's have the metal."

Collins selected a slab of iron from a pile on a table, thoughtfully weighed it in one hand, then gave it to Bailey who inserted it in the hole in the excelsior to replace the chest, while Collins sawed several lengths of boards. Within minutes they had nailed down the new top, stenciled the address, and begun their strapping—binding the box with lengths of the flat, flexible strap-iron strips. When they had finished, Bailey silently motioned to us, and we lifted the box back on the four-wheeler.

"Okay, Jim," Bailey said. "Take it away!"

Collins dragged the four-wheeler from the shed shouting, "Coopers Cargo! Coopers Cargo! Come and get it, you guys."

"That's all there is to it, fellows," Bailey said.

Joe pointed to the tarpaulin. "What about that?"

Bailey gave him a sharp look. "Look, kid, you know about those three monkeys? They don't hear anything, see anything, or say anything. Well, you and your friend be those monkeys. Okay?"

"Let's cut out the crap," Joe said roughly. "If we're gonna work here we want to know what's goin' on."

Bailey nervously crumpled the coffee container and threw it into a box filled with debris.

"Where are you kids from?"

"The Neighborhood," I said.

"Oh yeah? Me and Jim's from Chelsea. Whereabouts do you live?"

"Forty-sixth Street, between Eighth and Ninth. I'm Frank Howell. This is Joe Gunnar."

Bailey looked startled. "You Andy Gunnar's kid?"

"He was my father," Joe said flatly. He pointed to the tarpaulin. "What about that?"

Bailey lowered his voice. "That goes to Wilson. You know, the Gimp."

"Does he get everything?"

"Everything," Bailey said. With a grin he added, "That's worth stealin'."

"What about customs inspectors?" Joe asked. "I thought this was a government job."

"They work with us," Bailey said. Then he slapped Joe on the shoulder. "You fellows will know the ropes soon."

"But suppose you don't give everythin' to the Gimp?" Joe pressed him.

"Look, we don't want any trouble," Bailey said nervously. "The boss told us you were bringin' over the supplies and to give us a hand—"

"We're not going to make any trouble," I told him.

"I hope not. It's nice and easy here. Let's keep it that way. There ain't many jobs like this around."

"Who's your boss?" Joe asked him.

"Freddy—Freddy Kenton."

"Fat Freddy? You mean the boss of our union?"

"President Kenton," Collins said with a harsh laugh.

"You fellows got cards?" Bailey said.

"Sure. How good are they?"

"Without a card you can't work on the piers as a cooper. That's the way it should be—no card, no work."

"Bullshit," Collins said so abruptly I was startled.

"Come on, Jim, cut it out," Bailey said pleadingly, "I want to set these kids straight."

"Well then set us straight," Joe said, "don't try to hand us any crap. How many are in the union?"

"I don't know—maybe a couple of hundred," Bailey replied. "That about right, Jim?"

This time Collins ignored Bailey to study Joe for a moment. "Why do you want to know?"

"We belong to the damn union!" Joe said. "At least we should know somethin' about it."

"No matter what you know about it, it won't do you any good," Collins said.

"Why do you say that?"

"Because better men than you—and me—have tried to get answers about this union."

"They might have been better than you, mister, but not better than me," Joe said with an edge to his voice.

"Perhaps," Collins said, packing an old pipe.

"We have members all over," Bailey said hastily.

"How about Brooklyn?" I asked.

"Brooklyn too," he said proudly. "The union goes over there. Same as Newark, Hoboken, Port Newark—all of Jersey, even Boston and Philly."

"How long has this been goin' on?" Joe asked.

Bailey gave him an incredulous look. "You pullin' my leg, kid?"

Joe shook his head. "No. I just asked you a question."

"You're Andy Gunnar's kid and you don't know!"

"No. I don't know," Joe said impatiently. "How the hell would I?"

"This is the union your old man started," Bailey said. He slapped Collins on the shoulder. "How do you like that, Jim? He belongs to the union his old man started and he doesn't know it!"

Joe appeared stunned. "My father started this union?"

"Sure," Bailey said. "Right after world War I. We had our first meeting in the back room of Regan's saloon on Ninth Avenue. He started another one too, something

221

called the Independent Dock Workers Association, but the Gimp's local took that over after he was killed . . ."

"You remember how he was killed?" Joe asked him.

"They said it was an accident," Collins said carefully.

"Yeah, it was quite an accident," Joe said dryly. "They killed him with a truck."

"How about the supplies we brought over?" I broke in. "You want them now?"

"Yeah. Yeah," Bailey said. "Suppose you kids bring that stuff in. "We're almost all out of strapping."

He seemed happy to change the subject.

Joe was silent, thoughtful, as we unloaded the truck.

"Did you know your father started this union, Joe?" I asked him.

He slung a coil of strap iron on his shoulder. "How the hell would I know? All my mother ever said was that he was in some union business on the waterfront. It was Tom who told me he had some trouble on the docks and the shippers were too scared to back him up. Then he was killed." He slid the toolbox out of the truck. "How do you like that, Frank?" he asked with a short laugh. "A wop who owns an art gallery gets us into a union that my old man started before I was born!"

On our second trip, he rolled a coil of copper wire to the tailboard and sat down.

"How do you like Fat Freddy's setup?"

"You mean the union?"

"What else? He has these old guys scared to death so they don't even know how many members they have in their own union! And they're on every pier from New York to Philadelphia." He hoisted the coil up on my arm. "You know these old guys could close down the whole eastern seaport if they wanted to?"

"How?"

"Didn't Pepe tell us it was a government regulation that the cargo has to be repaired before it can be stacked and shipped out?"

"So?"

"Suppose these old guys were on strike? Nothing could move." He mimicked Bailey, "Right, Frank?"

"Right," I told him. "Let's get this crap in the shed . . ."

That first morning we stored the supplies and helped Collins and Bailey repair the damaged boxes, bales, and barrels that were delivered to the shed by the dockwallopers. The old men were expert carpenters, and there was little we could do except act as their helpers and deliver the repaired cargo to the boss checker. Thirty minutes for lunch was spent in a dirty waterfront saloon jammed with shouting, cursing, laughing dockwallopers who lined the bars three deep to buy boilermarkers. Both Collins and Bailey downed three in rapid succession.

"No more of this for me," I said. "I'll have my aunt make us sandwiches from now on."

Joe shook his head. "We have to eat in this gin mill, Frank."

"Why?"

"We have to get to know these guys."

"Who wants to know these slobs?"

"I do. I've been thinkin'—"

I groaned. "Christ, don't tell me we're going to take over the waterfront now!"

He looked at me. "Why not? If my old man could do it, I can do it."

"That was a different time, Joe."

"Nothing changes on the waterfront, Frank," he said solemnly. "It's a jungle and the guy with the longest and sharpest claws is the boss. That's why my old man never made it big—he was only a loudmouth drunk and the best he could do was kick my mother around the kitchen floor. He just didn't have it when the real tough guys came around."

We stood on the curb in silence watching the dockwallopers hurry across Twelfth Avenue and pour into the big pier. Trucks were entering and leaving, the air was filled with impatient honking, the whine of the hoists lowering the fishnets, the impatient whistles of the checkers, and the cries of the baggage-smashers as they waved down their cabs.

Back in the coopers' shed we found Bailey and Collins rosy and garrulous from their boilermakers.

When Joe asked Bailey when Kenton would appear he vaguely answered that he was somewhere on the pier.

"He's no more on this dock than your aunt is," Joe told me. "He has a no-show job. I bet he's back in his warehouse countin' his money and his potatoes ... just wait. He'll show just before the boss checker blows the whistle."

It happened as Joe had predicted. Minutes before the whistle blew ending the day's work, Fat Freddy appeared to turn in his brass check to be listed for a day's pay. Apparently he had just come from his warehouse; his pants, shirt, and arms were coated with that thin pale-brown dust. We watched him hurry up the pier in a peculiar lurching stride. As the veterans in the Neighborhood would say, Freddy was carrying a pocketful of nickels; it was evident he hadn't missed a bar all day.

"Well for Christ's sakes, look who's here," he said in a thick voice as he entered the coopers' shed. "What the hell are you kids doing here?"

"We're workin' here," Joe said. "Any objections?"

"We thought we'd try and get up in the world, Freddy," I said.

Kenton looked over at Bailey. "Did Metro send them over, Jack?"

Bailey nodded. "They came this morning in the truck with the supplies."

"Oh, you're the guys Buck said almost ran him down," Kenton said. "You're lucky he couldn't leave the gate—"

"Who's Buck?" Joe asked innocently.

"The inspector at the gate."

"You mean lard ass with the big mouth?" Joe said evenly. "The guy who didn't want to let us in?"

"He's a nice guy, Joe," Kenton said defensively. "He works with all of us—"

He looked over at Bailey.

"We know about the loot, Freddy," Joe said.

"Yeah. I'm glad you kids can make a few bucks," Kenton said quickly. "I heard you were in a jam with the cops last year."

"We were in trouble with the cops!" Joe exclaimed. "Who would ever tell you somethin' like that, Freddy?"

"Well, you weren't around the warehouse for a long time," Kenton said lamely. He came closer and lowered his voice that seemed to have been dipped in a vat of whiskey.

"The wop send you over?"

"Christ, Freddy, you must have been eatin' puddin' all day," Joe said.

"Yeah. I had a few," Freddy admitted. "He send you over?"

"Do you mean Pepe?" I asked.

"C'mon kid, you know who I mean," Kenton said impatiently. "We call him the wop."

"We call him Pepe."

"What kind of a deal do you have with him, Freddy?" Joe asked him.

Kenton seemed taken back by the blunt question. "Whaddaya mean, deal? Metropolitan supplies all the docks—"

I took a stab in the dark. "Since when?"

"Since—well a long time . . ."

"You're full of shit, Freddy," Joe told him calmly. "They only just started. They don't even have a real sign for the truck."

"What's the difference?" Kenton snapped. "Ya got a job, ain't ya? Whaddaya askin' questions for?"

"Dont get your balls in a uproar," Joe told him. "We just wanted to know who was the boss of our union—"

"Me." Freddy tapped his chest. "Me. I'm the boss." Then he added, "Where do you get that 'our union' stuff?"

"Just what I said, Frank and I have cards."

"That's right," I said. "Pepe gave them to us. So now you're our president, Freddy—"

"Oh yeah. I gave him two cards," Kenton mumbled. "You're in a good union, kid."

"I bet it is," Joe said heartily. "When do we hold meetin's, Freddy?"

Collins snickered and Freddy gave him a hard look.

"You'll be notified," Kenton said gruffly. "Don't worry about it."

"We're not worried about anythin'," Joe said. "Are we, Frank?"

"Not a thing."

"The old man tell you about the loot?" Kenton asked.

"Sure. Everything goes to the Gimp."

"You make sure of that."

"Does that mean *everythin'*?" Joe asked.

"Everything," Kenton said firmly. " 'Round the holidays you'll get a little somethin' for yourselves. Ask the old guys. Johnny takes care of everyone on the pier."

I asked, "Who picks it up?"

"Buck does that—"

"Here he is now, Freddy," Bailey said.

The inspector who had tried to stop us at the gate that morning entered the coopers' shed. When he saw us he shook an admonishing finger at Kenton.

"These guys work for you, Freddy?"

"Yeah, Buck," Kenton said with a great show of joviality. "They're two good kids."

"You better tell these punks not to be wise guys, Freddy."

"Aw, they didn't mean anythin', Buck."

Joe walked to the doorway to face the inspector and I joined him. He was middle-aged and going to fat from too much beer. The silver shield on his shirt identified him as inspector for the U.S. Bureau of Customs.

"Just who the hell are you callin' punks, lard ass?" Joe asked him.

Buck looked startled at the unexpected confrontation. It was plain he was more mouth than muscle.

Freddy grabbed Joe's arm and pulled him aside. "For crissakes, what's the matter with you guys? Take it easy. Buck didn't mean anythin'. He works with all of us!"

"I just want to get somethin' straight, Freddy," Joe said softly. "As long as we're workin' this pier nobody is going to call us punks." He looked at the guard. "And that includes the Gimp. You can tell him I said so."

The guard's eyes darted like a lizard's from Kenton to us.

"Who brought 'em in? Does Johnny know 'em?"

"Pepe—the guy Freddy calls the wop," Joe said. He looked at me. "Maybe we better go over and have a talk with Pepe, Frank . . ."

Pepe's name had an immediate impact on Kenton. He put his arm around Joe and slapped the guard on the back.

"C'mon, you guys! What's all the argument about?"

"I don't want any trouble, Freddy," the guard muttered. "Where's the stuff, Jack?" he asked Bailey.

Bailey threw aside the tarpaulin. By now the chest of silverware had been joined by several Polish canned hams, a case of Scotch, and two leather-bound shaving kits.

"How do you want us to take it out, Buck?" Bailey asked.

Buck motioned to the old man's tool chest. "Use your chests tonight. Put 'em in the Gimp's car. His boys will bring your stuff back tomorrow before the shape."

Kenton took his arm. "Let's go, Buck. I want to buy you a drink." He left with his arm around the inspector's shoulder, whispering earnestly in his ear.

"Can we give you a hand with this stuff?" I asked Collins.

"Don't worry about it," he said, with a trace of bitterness in his voice. "The thieves make sure it gets out. Don't tangle with those people, boys, they're dangerous. You'll only get hurt."

"Don't worry, we know how to take care of ourselves," Joe said. "But tell me one thing, Jim—does the Gimp have any part of the union?"

A slow smile appeared on Collins's face, then he burst out laughing.

"My God, isn't that as evident as Freddy's breath?"

"I don't think we should talk about the union on the pier, Jim," Bailey said, lowering his voice.

"Oh bullshit, Jack. Bullshit," Collins said disgustedly. He pointed to the loot. "Let's get this out of here . . ."

"I don't think the old man likes the union too much," I told Joe as we drove up Twelfth Avenue.

"No. He's just livin' with it," Joe said, "but Bailey's scared to death."

"What was the idea of putting on the strong arm act with that guy Buck?"

"I did it on purpose," he said with a grin. "How else can we meet the Gimp? Buck's probably tellin' him now about those two wise guy punks on the pier."

"Why the hell do you want to meet Wilson? I don't!"

"We want to meet him because he's the real boss of the whole goddam waterfront," Joe said intensely. "Not the shipper or Fat Freddy or any of those other bums. It's the Gimp, Frank! It's because I think I know what Pepe has in mind."

"The loot? You mean getting a piece of the loot?"

"Hell no," he said disgustedly, "that's peanuts compared to the real dough. I mean the unions. I bet Pepe's after the waterfront unions. Do you remember what he said about how the piers will be big money when the war comes? It's unions, Frank. I know it. I feel it in my bones."

"Suppose you're right. You don't think for one moment that Pepe has sent us down to take over the Gimp and his Pistoleers! Come on, Joe—you're smoking hop."

"I'm Andy Gunnar's son," he replied in a flat, hard voice. "Did you see Bailey's reaction when he found that out? A lot of people on the waterfront must remember my old man. Maybe Pepe's as dumb as a fox. Maybe he doesn't care how much of this damn strappin' we deliver to the piers. Maybe he plans to use me because of my old man's reputation. Maybe. And you know somethin', Frank?" he added softly. "It's one hell of an idea?"

17 *THE GIMP'S UNION*

Those first few weeks I toured the Manhattan and Brooklyn waterfronts, checking each pier to make a list of supplies needed by the coopers. I discovered that Pepe's new business was not as haphazard as it had first appeared. The invisible network of communication which links all the piers from waterfront to waterfront, Brooklyn, Manhattan, and Jersey, had alerted every boss checker and every cooper; they not only knew we were working for Metropolitan, but had the license plate number of Metro's truck. I was treated with respect, almost diffidence, by some of the roughest, toughest boss stevedores.

I also sensed why Pepe was using Joe on the waterfront. I was asked again and again if it was true I was working with Andy Gunnar's kid. I heard many distorted tales, exaggerated legends, and numerous lies about Andy Gunnar, but it was true: Andy Gunnar was remembered on the New York waterfront. . . .

I found the coopers to be elderly, friendly, and extremely garrulous semi-retired ship's carpenters or dockwallopers who had been incapacitated by old injuries. I also learned that the Gimp's influence was very strong on the West and East Side piers and even extended to some sections of Brooklyn. Old men's whispers told me he had working arrangements with other waterfront mobsters in Jersey and Philadelphia also.

All the coopers were stealing from the cargoes; from pier to pier it was only a question of how crooked the guards and inspectors were and how much could be removed each day. From my rough estimate, the loot turned over to the Gimp's mob must have reached into the hundreds and thousands of dollars.

It took a week before Johnny Wilson showed up at Pier 70 and summoned us as Joe hoped he would. He might have been there the morning after our arrival if he hadn't been picked up by Dewey's men and taken downtown to be questioned about a waterfront shylock racket. Everyone on the pier was laughing over the picture of the Gimp on the steps of the courthouse, after leaving Dewey's office following a writ of habeas corpus hearing. It was not his picture that was so amusing but what his attorney had told the reporters. In denouncing Dewey for what he termed the "harassment of my client," the lawyer described Wilson as an honest man "who just happens to make his living from the waterfront . . ."

But there was something far more interesting in the picture. I pointed to one of the two men who were walking alongside the Gimp.

"Recognize him?" I asked Joe.

Joe studied the picture for a moment, then whistled softly. "Supercop! Who's the other old guy with him?"

I read aloud: "Inspector Richard Daye Cornell, head of the elite squad of police attached to the office of Special Prosecutor Thomas E. Dewey and Captain Elliott of the same squad, bringing Wilson into Supreme Court where the waterfront racketeer was later ordered released . . ."

"Supercop's with Dewey," Joe said, "and he's a captain now!"

On the morning the Gimp returned to the waterfront, Bailey hurried out to where we were unloading the truck.

"Hey, you guys have to get up to the front office."

"What for?" Joe asked.

"Someone wants to see you," he whispered. "Buck said not to tell you, but it's the Gimp."

"Okay, we'll go up and see him," Joe said.

Wilson looked older than I recalled him. His black hair was streaked with gray and there were slight shadowy pouches beneath his eyes. One part of him is still vivid; his narrow, highly polished black shoes, one with a raised sole and heel.

When we entered, he was reading a tabloid and having his shoes shined. Sitting on the edge of a desk were two of his tough young Pistoleers. The inspector was near a window.

"Here are those kids, Johnny," Buck said.

Wilson lowered the paper and studied us for a moment.

"You're Gunnar," he said to Joe. He spoke softly, forming certain words with special precision.

"That's right," Joe replied.

"Andy Gunnar's kid." He looked at me. "Who are you?"

"Frank Howell."

"Where did you come from?"

"We're both from the Neighborhood," Joe said. "What's on your mind?"

Wilson shrugged. "Nothin'. Just wanted to say hello."

"Hello," I said.

He smiled. "I hope you're not a wise guy, kid."

"We're not wise guys, Johnny," Joe said. He jerked his head in the direction of the inspector. "I just told him not to call us punks. That's all."

"You work for the wop?"

"We work for Pepe," I put in.

"I didn't ask you," Wilson said quietly. He pointed to Joe. "I asked him."

"We work for a guy named Pepe," Joe told him.

"Fine," Wilson said. He bent over to inspect the shine. "Do a good job, kids."

"Bailey told 'em about the stuff, Johnny," the guard said quickly.

Wilson gave him an exaggerated look of surprise.

"These are good kids, Buck. They're from the Neighborhood—they know the ropes." He looked at Joe. "Right, Gunnar?"

Joe didn't say anything but only stared at Wilson who waved his hand, our dismissal.

That was the only time we spoke to Wilson. After he had been questioned by Dewey's men, security on the pier became stringent—not to protect the shippers and the government, but to protect the Gimp. The stealing continued, but only those who were completely trusted by the mob handled the loot.

Strangers, even other dock workers, were barred from the pier by Wilson's hoods. Once a government agent from some Washington bureau came down to the pier after a shipper had filed a complaint. The story that ran the length of the pier was that he was wined and dined by Buck the first night, then taken to a Harlem cathouse where appropriate pictures were taken. Needless to say, his report cleared the pier of any wrongdoing.

On the other hand, the cargoes of the complaining shipper were savagely attacked. Bales were ripped, boxes smashed under heavy loads of iron or steel, and whatever was worth stealing vanished. It all stopped after four of

230

the Gimp's Pistoleers were put on the shipper's payroll as special guards.

The Gimp controlled the shippers through archaic, corrupt unions like the longshoremen's locals and the coopers'. Meetings were never held, Collins told us, but the dues were collected by the hoods every week. Those who were slow to pay had the money removed from their pay envelopes. Several months before we arrived, a young Polack from Chelsea had beaten up one of the collectors after he had found his pay envelope opened and the dues removed. He left threatening to go to Dewey's office. A week later his battered, bruised body was found floating under the pier.

"What about your union?" Joe asked. "Why didn't you pull a strike and shut down the whole goddam pier?"

Bailey and Collins looked at each other and laughed.

The Gimp also controlled the extensive shylocking, policy, and bookmaking rackets and the floating crap games that were staged in the rear of every pier along the upper West Side waterfront. Chelsea was controlled by other union mobsters who had working agreements with the Gimp. It was obvious that even though Dewey was after the Gimp, the rackets continued to run smoothly and efficiently.

The principal reason was his police protection. While the only cop we ever saw was a mounted patrolman who was more concerned about the care of his horse than about crime, warnings would move down the waterfront like the rustle of a slight breeze in the trees.

"No play today . . . no play today . . ."

Numbers would stop for a few days. The policy bank would vanish and the big floating crap games would shift locations.

"The Gimp must have someone big on the pad," Bailey told us one day.

"The district leader?" Joe asked.

Bailey said with a laugh, "He gets his piece but the Gimp must have someone big in the cops. Real big."

"Do you have any idea who it is?"

"Me and Jim don't know a damn thing," Bailey said hastily, "and if we knew we wouldn't tell anyone. Not even in confesson. Right, Jim?"

Three weeks after we had started working for Pepe, we received word from Maxie Solomon to meet him in Washington Heights Court. The judge was a dignified ancient who wore pince-nez on a long black ribbon. When the attendant called our names and we faced the bench, he mumbled something to himself, tersely informed the court stenographer that he had reduced the felonious assault charge to simple assault, dismissed the others, and accepted our guilty plea. He fined us a hundred dollars and suspended the sentences. We were outside within fifteen minutes.

"Thanks, Maxie," Joe told him.

The little lawyer replied, "You know who to thank. I get paid for this one. By the way, what are you guys doing now?"

"We're workin' for Pepe's strapping company," Joe told him.

Maxie didn't seem surprised. "Well, keep your noses clean," he said as we shook hands.

We continued to work five days a week, on Saturdays and Sundays when the big liners came in. The work was comparatively easy. Bailey was talkative while Collins was taciturn, but the few things he did say were intelligent. I was surprised to learn from Bailey that Collins had attended Dublin University for two years.

One day while crossing Twelfth Avenue to the restaurant I casually asked him about his days in Dublin but he just shrugged.

"Jack talks a lot," was all he said.

It was on my first trip to the Staten Island piers that I met Elliott. I always loved the island's ferry ride and this day began with one of those perfectly exquisite mornings when, after a rainy night, the scrubbed city across the water, its tower windows squares of frozen sunlight, appeared almost mystical, unreal.

I was on the deserted upper deck lost in the beauty of the view and I never heard the steps behind me.

"Quite a sight, isn't it?"

I turned to look into the face of Elliott. He appeared thinner. His eyes were weary and there was just a touch of gray at his temples.

"Supercop!"

"God, I haven't heard that in a long time. What are you doing here?"

"I'm working. Is that a crime?"

"Oh, come on, Howell, get the chip off your shoulder. only asked you a civil question."

232

"As far as I'm concerned cops don't rate civil answers. It seems damn peculiar you should just happen to come up here and find me. Am I part of your job now?"

He gave me a weary sigh. "I live on the island. I come up here every morning and every evening—at least when I get home at a reasonable hour." He gave me a curious look. "Do you believe me?"

"What the hell difference does it make?"

We stood there in an awkward silence, staring out across the sparkling water.

"The city is unbelievably beautiful, isn't it?" he said.

"Not from where I see it."

"And where do you see it from?"

"A flat on Forty-sixth Street. The air shafts are unbelievably beautiful."

"For Christ's sake!" he exploded.

I gave him a curious look. "Something wrong, Captain?"

"You know, Howell, you people in the Neighborhood can give me one stiff pain in the ass! Since when have you had a monopoly on poverty? Where in the hell do you think I was born? Park Avenue?"

"I couldn't care less . . ."

"Well, goddammit, you don't have to care but you're going to listen," he said angrily. "That's all I heard when I had a beat there. How tough things were. Maybe it doesn't make any difference, but after my father died my mother and I lived in a basement flat in Chelsea." His voice dripped sarcasm. "The rich people like you and Gunnar lived in the flats upstairs. My mother washed the halls and did her best to keep the place clean despite the slobs that lived there. Once a drunken Irish bum took a leak in the hall she had just cleaned and she not only hit him with the pail of scrub water but made him and his wife clean it up! Rain or snow she kicked me out of bed every morning to work with a milkman, three hours before school. I didn't steal our milk, I worked for it!"

"What do you want, Captain? A goddam medal? Tom Gunnar did twice what you did and got a scholarship besides. And what happened?" I almost shouted the words. "The cops killed him! They shot him in the back." I could feel the rage mounting inside of me and I put my clenched fist in my pocket. "You bastards stink. Every one of you."

I started for the door that led to the lower deck. "I

don't want to talk to you or any other cop. As far as I'm concerned there's not one that's any good."

"There's eighteen thousand of us."

"You meet one cop, you meet them all."

"That's a stupid remark and you know it. If I thought I was like Hennessy and some of those other morons up at the Sixteenth, I would turn in my shield tonight. Give me credit for that."

He gestured to the deserted seats.

"If you insist you don't talk to me, that's okay. I understand how you feel. But at least I think you owe me the rest of the fifteen minutes it's going to take to reach the Battery . . ."

"I don't owe you anything."

"The hell you don't," he said warmly. "I spent a lot of weary months up in the ass end of the Bronx because of you two guys."

"Why us? What did we have to do about it?"

"Sit down and I'll tell you. . . . I'm with Dewey now you know."

"I saw it in the *News*—Captain Elliott. Do they have many Supercops down there?"

"One qualification the boss likes is if you've been railroaded by the brass to the sticks. We have quite a few guys who bucked the system."

"And of course you're one . . ."

"That's right." He turned to me with a smile. "I guess in a way I got to Dewey's office because of you and Gunnar."

"Why us?"

"I arrived on Forty-sixth Street just a few minutes after they drove you away."

"Did you like what you saw? A great kid killed. For nothing. For only trying to get two stupid bulls to listen to reason! You and your goddam law and order. Shit!"

He waited a few minutes while I sat there glowering out across the bay.

"Okay," he said quietly at last, "let's agree you have a good reason to hate every cop in the city."

"Not the city, Elliott. The whole country. The world. I even hate cops in Moscow. That's what your friends have done to me. I even hate guys I don't know, I'll never see. Only because they wear a cop's uniform."

"I realize all that. If it's any consolation to you I got into a lot of trouble that day. In a way it's something I'll

234

always be proud of. It wasn't much but it was all I had at the time to offer to Tom."

"Trouble?" I asked surprised. "What trouble?"

"When I got out of the car and saw what had happened I almost belted Hennessy and his stupid partner. I was really sounding off. When the Captain of Homicide West told me to get back to the house, I told him off. Then the borough commander came over and I told him what I thought of him and the whole police department."

"What happened?"

"I had some friends at court but I was still suspended without pay for sixty days and sent up to the Bronx—on the twelve to eight tour—and I live out here on the island. I don't have to tell you what it was in the winter. The first five minutes I was up there the captain called me in to tell me he was out to get me and the first thing I did wrong he would crawl all over me." He chuckled. "I can only agree with you, Frank, cops can be bastards."

"How did you get with Dewey?"

"I said I had some friends at court. Do you know who one was?"

When I shook my head, he went on. "The Dean of Fordham Law. How do you like that? The last time he was down at headquarters he was denouncing Hennessy and the cops for what they did to you kids up at the Sixteenth. Then he came down again to defend me at my departmental trial. Those graybeards at headquarters hated the sight of me. Fortunately, the dean has good connections with City Hall. That saved me. They were ready to heave me when he personally went to La Guardia. You have to give that little guy credit—he told the commissioner to go easy.

"When Dewey organized his office in the Woolworth Building he got to someone in the department who knew the score. No one will refuse his requests, so when he asked for me and a few others who were burned by those bastards at headquarters they transferred us to the special squad of city cops attached to his office. I made captain last year." He shrugged. "So that's the story."

"No matter what you or anyone else did, I still consider you the enemy, Elliott," I told him. "Not only was Tom Gunnar killed by a cop, but they also beat our brains in for something we didn't do. When they weren't content with that, they had to put the muscle on Father John." I turned to him and said bitterly, "You were sent to the

235

Bronx, but instead of college I went to the CCCs and learned how to cut down trees. That's why I'll always hate cops, Elliott. They not only kill people—they kill hope."

"You can't condemn a whole army for the actions of a few, Howell," he protested. "It's not only unfair—it's stupid. I don't care what comparisons you make—the army, the navy, a business corporation—even the priesthood! For every hero you'll find two, maybe three, cowards, thieves, sons of bitches who will kick their mothers downstairs, take the pennies off a dead man's eyes, rob the widow of her rent money, or even sell out the country. Christ, take five men and put them in a room guarding the chalice from the Last Supper. Don't you think one of them will be plotting to himself how to steal it? It's human nature!"

"You worked in the Neighborhood," I told him. "Didn't you realize we all hated not only you and Hennessy but every uniformed man who ever walked a beat there? It's the same in Harlem and the lower East Side. When Joe and I were up at the Shelter we talked to kids. You know as well as I do, Captain, that wherever there are poor people cops seem to swing their clubs just a bit harder."

He squirmed in his seat and I knew I was getting to him, but his voice remained quiet, persuasive.

"What about the cops who have fed families out of their own pockets? What about the cops who walk into a dark cellar to arrest the nut who just raped a kid and maybe has a gun or knife? Don't they count?"

"If he doesn't want to go into dark cellars looking for kid rapists, then he better work in a grocery store . . ."

He took his wallet from his inside pocket and flipped it open. Pinned to the inside flap was a small eight-star gold shield with the name Captain Francis D. Elliott, 18th Patrol District and the number 721.

"He was my grandfather," he said. "This shield's been in our family since 1859. My father carried it until he died in 1927, then I took it." Bitterness edged his voice. "He was one of the cops I was talking about. He walked into a dark cellar on Tenth Avenue after a maniac who had just strangled a little girl in a hallway. The nut still had his ax." He put the wallet back into his pocket. "I hope my son will carry it, and then his son. I have a brother who's a lieutenant and an uncle who's retired."

"A dynasty of cops."

236

"The department has several hundred men whose fathers and grandfathers were cops. They're our backbone . . ."

I laughed. "Three generations of head busters!"

"You know there is something I can't understand—"

"What's that?"

"Why you people in the Neighborhood always sneer at anything that is clean and decent."

"You should know the answer, Captain—it's simple. The Neighborhood makes sure you are born with a sneer."

A series of bells sounded. The lumbering ferry shuddered slightly, then slowed down.

"Looks like we're coming in," I said, pointing to the nearing slip. "Thanks for the history lesson. I have to get back to the truck."

I was about to get up but then the thought struck me.

"You're so good at cop history lessons, Captain, maybe you can settle an argument . . ."

"I'll try," he said with a smile.

"There was an argument in the gin mill the other night. One guy who goes down to that labor school at Xavier claimed that someday every guy who works for a living will be organized. Teachers. Garbage men. Even cops. I said he was nuts. What do you think?"

He looked thoughtful. "Well, we have police line organizations."

"What are they?"

"The PBA—Patrolmen's Benevolent Association, the SBA, the Sergeants' Benevolent Association, along with a superior officers' council that represents captains, lieutenants, inspectors, and detectives. There are also a number of fraternal organizations in the department. The Irish have their Emerald Society, one of the oldest in the department. That one has been around since before the Civil War. Jews belong to the Shomrim, and Protestants to the St. George Society."

"Which are the social groups?"

He ticked off on his fingers. "The Emerald, the Anchor Club, to name a few. But PBA is the big line organization—"

"What do you mean 'line'?"

"They represent the cop on the beat."

"Are they any good?"

He shrugged. "They're mostly coffee and cake outfits. They try to help the cops but no one pays much attention to them. They may become a real labor group someday."

237

"So in other words there isn't a real ball-bustin cops' union? One that would really go all out for the guys on the beat?"

He looked startled. "Do you mean a union that would use direct union tactics?"

"Like a strike," I said bluntly.

He shook his head vigorously. "It couldn't be. A strike of cops would be comparable to teachers striking and closing down the schools. Or even doctors calling a shutdown." He chuckled. "Or priests in a union. No, I think you win that one, Howell."

He got up and swung open the door to the lower deck. "Tell that guy he owes you a beer."

As I started to go down he said, "By the way where are you working?"

"Metropolitan Strapping," I said as casually as I could.

"The piers?"

"We work the piers with the coopers."

"Who owns it?"

"A friend of Joe's father." I was down a few steps and turned to look up at him. "Why all the questions?"

He slowly descended to the step I was on.

"I don't have to warn you about the waterfront, Howell. There's a lot going on. My advice to you and Gunnar is to keep your noses clean. Those racket guys can give you a lot of grief . . ."

"Maybe not as much as the cops can."

"It's your life. I only had one purpose in talking to you. I wanted you and Gunnar to know I will always be sorry about his brother and his mother. Tom was a great kid. I hope some of him rubbed off on Joe . . ."

"I'll tell Joe. I'm sure he will be touched."

We walked down the stairs in silence holding on to the banister as the boat banged off the sides of the slip. When we reached the main deck, Elliott gave me a brief nod.

"Good luck."

I didn't bother to answer him but pushed my way through the crowd of passengers gathered at the door to the outside deck, then down the open middle of the boat to where my truck was parked. The boat bumped into its slip, the deckhands spun the wheels to tighten the hawsers and the first cars started to move off. I turned on the ignition and slipped into gear. I had gone only a few feet off the boat and onto the pier when I felt the steady bump-bump. A passenger pointed to my wheels and shouted:

238

"Ya got a flat, buddy!"

I started to slow down and behind me rose a chorus of horns. I was wondering where to turn when suddenly someone was at the window of the driver's side. "Pull across the pier to the left. I'll give you a hand."

It was Elliott.

He jumped into the front seat, waved to an officious deckhand, who looked as if he was eager to blow the whistle he had between his teeth, and silently directed me to a far gate down the pier. He swung it open and directed me out into the street. I found myself off to one side of the ferry entrance and away from the bustling Battery and Governors Island ferry traffic.

"Where's your spare?" Elliott asked.

I got out the spare and the jack. After I jacked up the truck he spun off the lugs and slammed the spare on the rim. Elliott worked swiftly and competently.

"You know Chelsea?"

"Pretty good."

"Do you know that big garage on Twenty-eighth off Tenth? Farley's?"

"Sure. The one that's open all night."

"Right. I worked there at night when I was going to school. I started pumping gas and fixing flats. Then old man Farley broke me in as a mechanic. I even thought of opening my own place on the island."

"Why didn't you?"

"An Elliott not a cop? My family would have disowned me." He stood up. "You can tighten them. I have to get uptown. Make sure—"

"What are you doin', Captain—moonlightin'?"

I turned around and saw a cop about fifty, with white hair and a ruddy, weather-beaten face. The leather thong of his club was wrapped about his shield and hung down his side.

"Hello, Tom," Elliott said getting up. "How's the Battery?"

"It's always a madhouse with those goddam trucks from the market." He gave me a curious look.

"Frank, this is Patrolman Tom O'Hara from the Front Street Precinct. My old man broke him in in the West Thirtieth but then he got to be lace curtain Irish and moved out to Queens. Right, Tom?"

"After countin' trucks and cars all day I want a little

peace and quiet at night," Tom said. "I haven't seen you on the ferry before have I?"

"This was my first trip to the island . . ."

"I'm trying to talk him into ditching this lousy truck job and try for the department," Elliott said. "Maybe you can help me, Tom. He could be a good cop."

I turned to Elliott with a furious reply but he gave me a look of pure innocence. I bit my tongue. After all, he had helped me change that damn tire so I figured I'd go along with his perverted sense of humor.

"A good career for a young fellow," O'Hara said promptly. "When you're twenty years on the job you can get a pension. You won't get that driving a truck."

"Come off it, Tom," Elliott said scoffingly. "You've been on the force since you were two years old. They'll have to carry you off!"

"It has its points." He studied me for a moment. "You could do worse, young feller. The department is not all that bad . . ."

Elliott looked at me with a grin.

"Listen to an expert, Howell."

"Stop off and say hello when you're on the ferry line," O'Hara said. He groaned and looked out across the square. A large truck loaded with rolls of paper was blocking the flow of Battery traffic. The driver had swung down the street, a bill of lading in one hand.

"I bet he's lookin' for the Journal Building up on South Street," O'Hara grunted. "If I don't get him the hell out of there he'll have everythin' backed up to West Street. I'll be seein' you, Captain." And to me he added, "Stop and say hello, young fella."

He hurried across the wide street to where the truck driver was already trading insults with an angry cabdriver.

"You see we're not all Hennessys," Elliott said.

"The public will be very happy to know that."

"Oh don't be so goddam sarcastic, Howell. O'Hara's like me, he's from a family of cops." He said roughly, "Your dynasty of head busters. He has twin sons, a brother, and a nephew on the force. He had a cousin who was killed chasing a hit-and-run driver who had knocked over some people on the sidewalk. His neighbors are also career cops—"

"You guys eat alike. You dress alike. You think alike. You live next door to one another. Do you screw alike?"
240

For the first time I got to him. His eyes narrowed and his lips thinned.

He tossed me the lug wrench. "Have fun."

Elliott whistled down a cab and was gone within minutes. Across the street O'Hara had finished giving the truck driver directions to the Journal Building and was untangling the miniature traffic jam.

I tightened the lugs, threw the tools and flat into the truck, and drove up South Street. I should have gone over to the West Side Highway but I didn't want to pass O'Hara.

Tom Gunnar was still dead and I was driving a truck.

Later that night in Regan's I described for Joe my meeting with Elliott.

"He's on the up and up but he's still a cop," Joe said.

"I never knew he lived in Chelsea, or that his old man was a cop and was killed. Did you, Joe?"

"So what?" Joe said scornfully. "His old man was killed and his old lady had to take in floors. It only proves that cops are not only lead-plated bastards but also suckers."

18 ADDIO

I had been seeing Chena as much as possible—two, three, four times a week and twice on Sunday when I wasn't working during that beautiful spring and glorious early summer.

I couldn't wait to get home at night to see Chena. I dreaded the day when she would leave. One night, using an atlas, she showed me the places she and her mother would visit. First Naples to see Nicky and her father's cousin, under whose supervision he had been, then to Palermo and the villages in the north of Sicily where her grandmother had been born, and where their family still owned olive groves operated by relatives.

Finally that terrible day arrived when Chena had to

leave. Hours before the liner was scheduled to pull out, relatives from Long Island, East Harlem, upstate New York, and even Philadelphia jammed into their suite. I had never seen so much food, wine, whiskey, and champagne before in my life.

"My God, Chena, I never knew you were so popular," I told her as we pushed our way through the crowd to find an open deck.

"It's not me, Frank," she whispered, "it's my mother. She's carrying letters, even money, for their relatives. They all believe war will come soon and they won't have another opportunity."

"All these people? They represent a lot of letters! Will your mother deliver them all personally?"

"She wouldn't do otherwise. Did you see that linen bag my mother was holding?"

"That green bag? I thought it was her knitting."

"Porta fòglio del spòsalizo," Chena said giggling. "When a daughter gets married the guests put money in a bag like that, but now she's using it for the letters they give her. It's a mark of respect . . ."

We finally reached the top stern deck which happily was deserted; in a tiny alcove we clung to each other.

"This is the last time we're ever going to be separated," I told her fiercely. "I don't care what your father, mother, Pepe, or anybody says; the day you come back we'll name the day. Agreed?"

There were tears on her cheeks and I kissed them away.

"Do you want to, Frank?" she whispered. "Do you really want me?"

"Even without that damn—what do you call it—the money bag!"

Arms about each other we walked to the rail and looked out over the water to the stern gray Jersey cliffs. "I hate this waterfront," she said. "I'll be worrying about you every minute I'm over there."

"There's nothing to worry about, Chena. It's an easy job. Pepe pays us well and we don't even see him."

"He's been traveling," she said shortly. "He's always calling my father long distance."

"Where did he go?"

"Boston, Detroit, Chicago. My mother and my father had a big fight a few nights ago."

"Over Pepe?"

242

"It's always over Pepe," she said bitterly. "My father wanted her to deliver a letter to a man and she refused."

"What's so bad about delivering a letter to someone?"

"He's in Sicily—"

"Is that a long journey?"

Chena was silent for a moment. "It's not the traveling—it's the man who is to get the letter—he's the *Capo dei Capi*—"

"What's that?"

"The head of all the chiefs of the Mafia families in Sicily. Finally he made my mother take the letter and promise on a crucifix to deliver it."

"What do you think is in your father's letter that's so important?"

"The letter is not my father's, Frank—its Pepe's."

"But why should Pepe want to contact the boss of the Mafia in Italy?"

"God only knows. It must have something to do with their deals. My mother says he has been holding meetings with Italians all over the country. They're all bootleggers and gangsters—"

"About what?"

"*Còsa loro*—their organization, or whatever they call it. My mother begged my father to sell the Shadow Box and not have anything more to do with Pepe but he just laughed and called her a stupid old guinea. One night I tried to talk to him but he just shouted, *'Sposare chi volere . . . fare tanto bambini!'*"

"What's that?"

"Marry who you want and have plenty of children . . ."

"Well that's one thing he and I agree on."

She found my hand and held it tightly. "Oh, Frank," she said, exasperated, "you know Pepe has something in mind for you and Joe! That's the way he is! He's like the devil! I pray every night to the Blessed Mother that you will get some sense in that thick Irish head and go back to school."

"I promise you—"

Her face brightened. "You will go back to school?"

"Sure. After we're married.

"Oh, Frank."

I pulled her close and kissed her.

When the steward's gong rang, announcing all visitors ashore, we returned to the cabin.

243

I was the last one to leave. Chena's mother unexpectedly kissed me on the cheek and patted me on the shoulder.

"She knows we're going to get married," Chena said.

"Is it all right?" I asked.

"She said we should get married and give her many grandchildren," Chena said laughingly.

"*Si*," her mother said vigorously. "*Compare uno peffo di terra.*"

"Momma, neither Frank nor I know the first thing about running a farm," she told her mother. She explained to me with a sigh, "She wants us to go away and buy a piece of land for a farm."

"That would be great," I told her, "but the only cow I have ever seen was on an evaporated milk can."

A few minutes later I was on the stringpiece, surrounded by a small army of her wailing, weeping relatives,

"*Addio*," they cried, "Go with God."

"*Addio*," I echoed silently to the beautiful black-haired girl on the upper deck who waved a tiny square handkerchief, and whose tears were for me alone . . .

19 JOE'S ESTABLISHED BUSINESS

A few weeks after she left, Chena wrote from Naples that Nick had dropped out of medical school and was in Rome studying at a music conservatory, but when they reached Rome he was gone. Then, the following week, came a tearful letter: they had found Nick—he was in the Italian army! He had apparently gotten drunk one night with a cousin, and they had both enlisted. Chena wrote that they had notified the American consul in Rome to set the machinery in motion to get him released. I shuddered when I read the last, foreboding line; Chena's mother had vowed never to return to the United States unless her Nicky was released and accompanied them home.

During the summer the waterfront is traditionally lethargic; there are liners with tourists but cargo and freight, the lifeblood of the piers, dwindles to a trickle. But not in the summer of 1937. That summer everyone on the docks felt the stirring, the increased tempo. The cargoes were heavier—steel, tin, medical stores—then one day came the planes. The day they arrived the whole pier either watched or took part in loading them aboard the freighter. Even the Gimp came down from the front office to study the crated wings and fuselage. Of course everything went aboard intact; there was nothing to steal.

There was still no word from Pepe. After the meeting in the spring when he had hired us, we never saw or heard from him. At five o'clock every Friday night when we pulled the truck into the wastepaper factory on Cherry Street, one of the helpers silently handed us our pay envelopes. Like Lorenzo, he seemed to be a mute; when I asked about Pepe he just shrugged, smiled, and said, *"Non capito."*

Our social life, at least mine, was dull. Joe occasionally picked up a girl on Broadway and worried the usual nine days. I accompanied him once or twice, "hunting" as he called it, but the nights of cruising about the bars and streets had little appeal for me.

Whether a woman was married or single meant nothing to Joe. He would spot one at a bar or seated in the dim back room of a gin mill on the avenue and in a few minutes he would be buying her drinks or dancing cheek to cheek on the postage-stamp-size floor. Fistfights with outraged husbands or boyfriends became commonplace on Saturday night for Joe.

He still paid the rent for the Gunnar flat, but he had never spent a single night there after his mother's death. He lived a nomadic life, either staying with us, sleeping on a cot in the kitchen, renting a room for a few days at the Railroad Y, or sharing the apartment of some woman he had picked up on one of his Saturday night "hunting" sprees.

"Joe, you just can't keep paying rent on that flat and not living there," my aunt protested.

"I'm keepin' it, Aunt Clara," he said firmly. "Someday I'll use it."

"But why, Joe?"

He leaned over and kissed her and winked at me. "So I'll always be sure of livin' next to the finest woman in the world . . ."

I could almost see my aunt preen. When she left the room I told him, "You can really hand it out, pal!"

He only winked again.

During that summer we followed the same dull routine: eating, sleeping, working, and meeting in Regan's to swill beer and discuss a million and one inane subjects—a comparison of the batting records of the newly retired Lou Gehrig and Babe Ruth or what had gone wrong when the submarine *Squalus* sank off Portsmouth?

Then one night Joe abruptly swung off his stool.

"The hell with this," he said defiantly.

"What's the matter with you?"

His wave took in the smoky, crowded bar. "Who wants this every night? I'm going to walk to the Automat and get some coffee. How about it?"

I was as bored as he, but I left him on the corner; he walked to Eighth Avenue and I went home to dream of Chena.

The next day when he joined us for dinner, I noticed a change in him. He seemed more intense and preoccupied.

"What happened to you?" I asked.

"I met somethin' last night."

"A girl?"

"No chicken but plenty of class. As I came out of the Automat a cabbie was yellin' at this woman. She looked as if she was about to burst into tears, so I walked over. He was a real creep and I was just in the mood for one of those wise guys. I asked her what was wrong. She had this ten in her hand and said the cabbie had told her it was four fifty on the clock. He swung up the flag real fast and she thought it was too much. When I asked her where she had come from she said Grand Central."

"That's not even a buck!"

"Of course. I threw this son of a bitch half a buck and told him if he didn't scram I'd ram my fist down his throat. He started to talk tough and I yanked open his door. That did it! He took off."

"Who is she?"

"Her name is Helga Strom. She lives on East Seventy-fourth Street, off Park. Real class, Frank, I could smell the dough."

"Well, what did you do?"

"I brought her into the Automat, fed her some coffee and cake, and treated her as if she was the Queen of Camelot and I was her Golden Knight."

246

"Did you take her home?"

"Right to the door." He whistled softly. "Frank, you should see the brownstone!"

"What's next?"

"Tonight the Golden Knight takes her out. Maybe Radio City. A few drinks, then home. Right to the door." He smiled faintly. "When I walk in—she'll do the invitin'."

"How old is she?"

He shrugged. "Who cares? I told you I like an established business, didn't I?"

Helga Strom became Joe's new interest. He saw her two or three times a week; there were movies, the theatre, and dinners. Finally one Sunday afternoon when we were sprawled on the stoop he said simply, "I scored last night."

"Helga?"

"Who else?" He looked at me with a lazy smile. "She didn't want to go out, she insisted we have dinner at her place. She has this old German woman workin' for her and they did it up brown. Candles. Music. Wine. You name it—we had it. After dessert the old lady did the disappearin' act. I knew what Helga wanted. We had a few drinks, then I started on her. Ten minutes and her tongue was hangin' out. We went upstairs and by the time she had enough it was daylight." He stretched. "Dammit! I'm tired. I'm gonna knock off early tonight!"

"Now what?"

"I'm in," he said, surprised. "What else? I'm her Golden Knight. Now I have a nice steady piece—a little old maybe but still great—dinner with candlelight, music, and wine—whenever I want it. What else do I want—an egg in my beer?"

Joe's romance continued.

There had been a night at the opera, a gallery opening, a full-dress charity ball, a cocktail party for Irene Dunne and a special preview of her latest picture at Radio City. . . .

Joe was captivated, but I also knew he would soon become restless. Then one night he insisted I join them for dinner at a small exclusive East Side restaurant where the light is very bad and so are the food and the prices.

Helga turned out to be a petite, shy woman with black hair shot through with gray. With the arrogance of youth I judged her to be old—about forty. It was obvious she was cultured and eager to please me. Yet during the entire

247

evening I felt ill at ease, like having dinner with the mother of your best friend. After a sedate and polite evening I was glad to join Train and Spider at Regan's. Somehow there seemed to be more truth in that grimy, smoky bar than in East Side brownstones.

Spider and Train were still on WPA—Train was breaking rocks on the highway project, and Spider was painting his way through the county courthouses.

In one he had painted the office of the director of a small project that was photostating and putting on microfilm the ancient historic records of Kings and Queens counties. The director, a woman named Vera, turned out to be a plain but efficient former schoolteacher with excellent political connections. She was married to an older man, a chronic alcoholic. Like Joe, Spider never had any trouble with women; to his dying day he would look like a choirboy ready to sing the glorias of the Lord at High Mass. He boasted, too, he had captured Vera—the director—before he had finished applying the first coat of paint to her office, and before he reached the moldings, they had spent a wild afternoon in the Half Moon Hotel in Coney Island. As Spider put it, Vera hadn't been serviced by her husband for some time.

"When she popped off, she was yellin' so much I thought every goddam bellboy would be bangin' on the door."

At Vera's insistence Spider abandoned his paintbrush for her photostatic unit.

Curiously, Spider revealed a talent for photography and, judging from the photographs he showed us, evidently had developed into a skilled technician.

The hot nights we didn't walk over to Regan's we sat on the stoop of our tenement with my aunt, listening to the sounds of the Neighborhood. Sometimes above the tumult we could hear the crisp, doomsday voice of a broadcaster named Kaltenborn. He kept interpreting the news of Europe—I remember he called it "Yirrup"—and my aunt would inevitably mutter, half to herself, "There's bound to be trouble over there yet . . ." We couldn't have cared less.

Aunt Clara, however, became a regular war expert. When she heard of new names or places in Europe she would look them up in the library and then bend our ears about them. We knew all about the Spanish Civil War, the Republicans who were Communists, and Franco and the

Monarchists who were fighting to preserve Catholicism. Aunt Clara was certainly partisan.

Out of boredom I began taking an interest in world affairs, reading when I had the opportunity. I can still recall some of Orwell's splendid, vivid memories of the winter cold outside Monte Pocoro, the ragged uniforms of the militiamen, the oval Spanish faces, and the phrase that never left me, "The Morse code-like tapping of the machine guns . . ."

During the entire drab summer, I had only a few letters from Chena. The last one stunned me: she had written to her college dean requesting permission to skip a semester.

> I wish that I could come back, my darling [she wrote from Rome], but I can't leave my mother here alone . . . all she does is cry, visit the consulate two or three times a day. I don't feel they are getting anywhere. All we can find out is that Nicky joined the Italian army and was sent to the air force and then just disappeared. . . . I will come back as soon as I can—remember, darling—I love you more than anything—please be patient . . .

20 THE O'HARAS OF QUEENS

It was a desolate winter without Chena. Books became a bore, and more than one movie a week became wearisome. I was at loose ends until, one evening, while watching some kids play stickball, I began thinking of the police union and Pepe's admonition that I should never let it go.

The more I thought about it, the more enthusiastic I became. One night when my aunt was out, I sat at the kitchen table and, remembering what Tom had told me about people and unions, I made out a rough schedule:

Personality:
Who are they? What kind of people? What do they think of: family, job, country, city, politics, etc.

Physical structure:
How is the police department run? By whom? Philosophy? How many cops? How many precincts? How much does a cop get a week? What about pensions? Arrests?

I sat back and stared out the kitchen window at the junk-filled square of dirt that passed for a yard. Suddenly the ruddy, weather-beaten face and the white hair came to me. O'Hara, the cop Elliott had introduced to me and called a "dynasty cop." He and his family had a deep love affair going with the police department and he had invited me to drop by and say hello. I decided to start with O'Hara and pose as a dreamy-eyed kid who was dying to get on the cops.

A few days later I drove down to the Battery and parked in the ferry line. O'Hara, the majestic king of the traffic was casually directing cars and trucks, occasionally blowing a whistle and pointing an accusing finger. It never failed. The toughest truck driver instantly obeyed his silent hand signals.

"Good morning, Mr. O'Hara," I said with the manners of a Lord Fauntleroy.

"I spotted your truck crossin' Whitehall Street," he said with a grin. "I was wonderin' if you were goin' to say hello. How's the captain? Have you seen him lately?"

"I haven't seen him since that day we met you," I said. "He's a busy guy."

"That he is." He blew a sharp blast and pointed a warning finger at a Jersey driver trying to edge ahead of the ferry line.

"Those goddam Jersey drivers," he muttered. "Since they opened that Lincoln Tunnel there's no holdin' 'em." He added abruptly, "Have you made up your mind to try for the force, young feller?"

"I've been thinking about it," I said slowly, putting on a great show of appearing perplexed. "I thought maybe you could help me decide, Mr. O'Hara."

"The name's Tom. Sure I'll help. Any time."

"Maybe some day when I'm on my way back from the island I can buy you a cup of coffee?"

"You never get a minute here. I take a leak and there's a traffic jam. The sergeant comes by and wants to know what the hell is goin' on. What are you doin' Sunday?"

"Nothing special."

"Good. You want to come out to the house for dinner?"

"I don't want to be a nuisance—"

"It's not a nuisance. We have the family every Sunday. What the hell's one more plate." He said with a note of pride, "I have twins. They're both cops. One's out on the island, the other rides an emergency truck."

"Yes, I know. Captain Elliott told me."

He chuckled. "Elliott calls us 'dynasty cops.' I guess in a way he's right. Grandfather. Father. Sons. I also have a brother and a nephew in the department. He's a detective on the East Side." He shook his head. "The department's not without faults, mind you, but it has its good points. So it is Sunday?"

"Yes and thank you."

The O'Hara house wasn't hard to find. It was a two-family stucco in Astoria, one of fifteen in a row on a dead-end street. There was a small garden and a stoop with an iron flowerpot. Across the street were similar houses and a wooden church with the inevitable bingo sign. The street stopped at the edge of a wide lot with what appeared to be a baseball diamond with a homemade backstop where several kids were leisurely batting out flies.

O'Hara greeted me at the door. Somehow without his uniform he looked older, less of a cop. He introduced me to his wife, a small plump woman rosy from her cooking, then ushered me into the living room where four men, young and old, were sitting. Two were twins in their early twenties. Both were husky, bull necked, and wore identical sports shirts and gray pants. In an easy chair was a slender, wiry man with a cap of iron gray curls. He had a thin face with a sharp nose. The twins were obviously curious, but this man's smile was friendly. The fourth man sat on a straight-backed chair. He was older than the twins but younger than the man with the graying hair. He was almost flashily dressed, like a bookmaker, I thought,

251

in a sports shirt and sports jacket. There was something hard and forbidding, almost puritanical in his face and searching gray eyes.

No one had to tell me they were cops. My Neighborhood-developed instinct set off a clanging alarm in my head before I had taken two steps into that room. I could almost feel the hair rising on the back of my neck.

"Fellows, this is Frank Howell, Capt'n Elliott's friend, the youngster I told you about is thinkin' of tryin' for the department . . ."

He brought me from man to man; the twins were named Casey and Jim; Danny, the man with the gray curls, was O'Hara's brother a sergeant in Brooklyn. His nephew George Drummer, the hard-eyed guy, was a detective, second grade, in East Fifty-first Street. One of the twins brought in a chair from the dining room; the other handed me a cold can of beer.

"Tom says you come from the West Side," Danny said.

"Forty-sixth Street, between Eighth and Ninth."

"Did you hear that, Tom?" Danny shouted to Tom who was out in the kitchen. "The Neighborhood!" He shook his head. "Many a battle we had there."

"Oh Christ," one of the twins said, looking upward "here we go again, Case. All about the old days in Chelsea."

"Did you live there, Mr. O'Hara?" I asked.

"Danny, for God's sakes, lad. Sure we lived there, Tom and I. Twenty years in Chelsea. In the goddamnedest, coldest flat—"

"Danny! Watch your tongue!" Mrs. O'Hara called in.

"I'm sorry, Mary, but every time I think of the donkey that owned our tenement . . ." He turned to me. "He lived like a prince in Jersey. Butter wouldn't melt in his mouth when he came over to collect the rent but he counted the coal like it was gold nuggets."

"The man's been dead for thirty years, Danny," Mrs. O'Hara said, bringing in some dishes. "Let him rest in peace."

"Rest? I hope the bastard's busily occupied with a shovel," Danny murmured.

"So you're thinkin' of tryin' for the force?" Danny asked me.

"I was thinking about it," I said cautiously.

"Was anyone in your family a cop?" one son asked.

I shook my head. "My father worked on the ships."

Danny said, "I swung a hook on the piers while I was waitin' to be called from the list. That's rough work."

"There's tough guys on the piers," George Drummer put in. "Most of 'em have a yellow sheet as long as their arm."

"Good men swing a hook too over there, George," O'Hara admonished his nephew. "I know a lot of 'em. They break their backs for a few bucks. But it's honest sweat. By the way I see you and your partner made the papers." He explained to me. "George and his partner made a good pinch on Monday. They picked up an A & R bum ... "

"A & R?" I echoed.

"Assault and robbery," Drummer explained.

"What did he do, George?" Danny asked.

"He was workin' the Murphy game." He said to me, "That's a con man posin' as a pimp. He takes your money and blows. But this bum was greedy. He got this old guy—he's the mayor of some jerkwater town in the Midwest, who was here for a convention—and sold him a bill of goods he had some young dames ready for a good time. The old guy falls for it and follows this guy to the top landing of a tenement near Third Avenue. He beat the hell out of the old guy and when he tried to get away he threw him downstairs."

"Pop said he gave you some trouble, Uncle George," one of the twins said.

"Those animals," Drummer said scornfully. "I eat that kind up. We got this guy as he was gettin' into his car. He was workin' with this young hooker. He gave Mike—" he said to me, "that's my partner—the knee and Mike went down. That's all I wanted." He held up his fist. I swallowed hard. It looked like a rock. "I left his teeth on the street. He tried to get out a blade and I let him have my jack." He gave us a thin smile. "He didn't look too good when I brought him in."

The others were silently, eagerly drinking in the details. The eyes of the younger men were glowing, and Danny was solemnly nodding.

"That's all I have to hear," Mrs. O'Hara said as she carried in a plate of steaming potatoes. "My God, I'm on my knees every morning when they leave."

"Are there many police families in the department?" I asked.

"Oh, quite a number," Danny said. "We have five sons

and grandsons of cops in the precinct I work out of. George, you have some in your house, don't you?"

"Oh, quite a number," Drummer said. "If they're not in the cops, they're in the Fire Department."

"We even have an organization, so to speak—the Police Dynasty Club," Danny put in. "Nothin' as big as the Anchor Club, mind you, but we meet once or twice a year at a picnic. I don't want to bore you now—"

"No. I find it interesting."

"Maybe we ought to walk over later to Tony Contada's place," Danny said. "He's a nut on this police dynasty. He's collected a lot of old stuff. We call it our museum. I think one day he'll give it to the department. It's very interestin'. Old badges, pictures, guns—that sort of stuff. He goes around to the schools and shows the kids the stuff and talks up the department."

"He sounds Italian . . ."

Tom O'Hara looked surprised. "Tony's as Italian as spaghetti and meatballs! What the hell do you think we have in the department—only Irishmen? We have everything. Danny's partner is a squarehead. In our house we have a Polack whose father and uncle were the first mounted cops. They were in some kind of Polish cavalry and when the department was lookin' for guys who knew horses they joined up."

"We have a League of Nations: Irish, Germans, Polacks, Italians, Jews—what about Lenny Farber, Safe and Loft? Three generations—grandfather, father, and Lenny. What they didn't know about the garment center wasn't worth knowin'. Lenny knew every loft thief in the country!"

"Yeah," Drummer said grimly. "What about Lenny?"

There was a moment of stiff silence. Then Tom said we all needed a beer and sent Casey out to the kitchen.

"Soup's on!" Mrs. O'Hara called. "Come and get it."

It was a boisterous happy meal. Danny told me he drove a radio car and his partner was a nervous, henpecked German cop named Fritz. There was also a great deal of police gossip traded back and forth; who was transferred and why, the latest news of the "gumshoers"—the Police Commissioner's Confidential Squad, that, I gathered, was despised as deeply as the FBI—when the next meeting of the Emerald Society would be held, how La Guardia was keeping Valentine, his police commissioner, on the run to city hall every time he heard some "tinhorn gamblers" were on the loose in the city. They argued fiercely over subsections of the penal code, the best way to remove spots from a uniform, how to depress a man's tongue when he is having an epileptic fit, and how many feet must legally separate a picket line from the main entrance of a business.

It seemed to me Mrs. O'Hara's main task was cautioning them when their voices were raised too high, making sure every plate was filled, clearing the dishes, and serving dessert—homemade apple pie. Without a doubt it was the finest I have ever tasted.

As the dessert plates were being cleared away, I said to O'Hara, "I was in a gin mill the other night and I heard a couple of guys arguing about unions. This one fellow goes to a labor school at Xavier and he claimed someday everyone will be in unions. He mentioned cops. Is there such a thing?"

Danny O'Hara shrugged. "The PBA. We all belong to it. It's not much of a union but it's all we have."

"Every time the president begins talkin' back to headquarters they send him up to Twelfth Avenue directin' traffic at six in the mornin'," Tom grunted.

"So it really doesn't have too much muscle?" I ventured.

Drummer shook his head. "We have a couple of redhots in the house, but all they do is shoot their mouths off. Nothing ever happens."

"This fellow that was doing all the arguing claimed that some day there would not only be a teachers' strike but also a police strike . . ." I continued. It was like hitting them all over the head with a club. Even Drummer stared at me as if I had just blasphemed the Virgin Mary.

"A police strike? In New York City?" O'Hara said unbelievingly.

"Well, it was only an argument," I pointed out.

"Ridiculous," Drummer murmured. "Don't you think so, Uncle Tom?"

"I would say so," O'Hara blurted out.

"Now wait a minute," his brother said, shaking his head. "You're forgettin' Boston."

I was surprised. "Was there a police strike in Boston?"

"And a good one, I know something about it because I had a cousin who was a cop in Boston at the time." Danny said. "That strike helped to make Coolidge president."

255

"He was governor," Tom said, "and he broke it."

Well, I thought to myself, this is a morsel. So there had been a police strike!

"Suppose we walk over to Tony's museum?" Tom O'Hara suggested.

"We can go through the lot and see how the game's comin' out." He turned to me. "The kids in the neighborhood have a team. Casey and Jim are the coaches."

We walked across the lot at the end of the street and briefly watched a kids' baseball game. There was a small group of parents watching and cheering and, from the way they greeted them, it was evident the O'Haras were popular in the neighborhood.

"There's a lot of cops and firemen movin' out this way," O'Hara said when we left. "A couple of guys back there are clericals at headquarters. That's not for me. Sittin' at a desk would kill me. I got to be out in the open."

"Why do you like the job so much, Mr. O'Hara?" I asked.

We were slightly in front of the others and Tom turned to them.

"The lad wants to know why I like the job so much?"

"Well tell him," Danny said. "It's the bundles of money you get from the racket boys every week . . ."

Tom and Danny chuckled at this but George gave them an angry look.

"It's no laughin' matter, Uncle Dan. Lots of cops have their hands out these days. And you know it."

"There's them that takes and them that don't," Tom said grimly, "and we don't. And neither do our friends." He shrugged. "Sure there are cops with their hands out. Plenty, as George says. If they want to make it that way, it's up to them. I had a lieutenant once call me a fool because I wouldn't take from a truckin' company that wanted a special place to park. I told 'em if they did they'd get a ticket. The lieutenant got himself another boy."

We crossed the lot and followed a small path through a field that led to another dead-end street. The house we stopped at was similar to the O'Hara dwelling. The only difference was the front yard; a small stone niche, obviously homemade, held a statue of the Virgin Mary; it was evident someone had been working in the garden.

The man who answered the bell was well over six feet with thick black hair, swarthy skin, and a booming laugh.

Unlike George Drummer, when he laughed it came from the inside.

"Hey, Tom! Danny! George! *Come esta te?*"

"Hiya, Tony. We thought we'd drop in and say hello. This young fellow is Frank Howell, a friend of Captain Elliott's. He's thinkin' of tryin' for the department. We thought we'd bring him over and see your museum. Georgie hasn't seen it either."

"Sure. Sure. Come in. Come in," Tony said. "I just got off the phone with the squad."

I could almost see their ears stiffen like jackrabbits'.

"Oh? What's up?" Tom said.

"Aw, they found a couple of sticks of dynamite out in Jackson Heights. They thought they had something going. It turned out a couple of kids had broken into a construction shack and hid it."

Tony ushered us to a basement stair. "Come on, you want to see the great Contada cop museum? Go right down. I got some guinea relatives drinkin' my wine outside in the yard. I'll just give 'em another bottle . . ."

"I'm sorry, Tony," Tom O'Hara said. "I didn't know you had company . . ."

"What is this company?" Contada said. "You come at two o'clock in the morning to see my junk and I'll be very happy to show it to you. My wife keeps threatening to put it out cleanup week."

It was a small, finished basement. Along the walls were homemade wooden benches on which lay assorted badges, old revolvers, bits of scorched metal, battered books, ledgers, handcuffs, jimmies, police shields, and clubs. There were also rows of photographs on the walls of cops in old-fashioned uniforms, framed letters, documents, programs, and ancient, station-house rosters.

Contada joined us in a few minutes. "Okay, we start from the beginning. A lot of this stuff was collected by my father. He was the second wop on the original bomb squad. He said to me, "You ever hear the name Petrosino?" When I shook my head he looked at George. "You, Georgie?"

"Wasn't he on the bomb squad? I think he was shot . . ."

"Marrone!" Contada groaned. "What do you do, O'Hara? Only tell 'em about the Irishers?"

"Petrosino was the guy who started the bomb squad," Danny explained. "Tony's father was the second guy he

257

picked. That's when the Black Hand was big on the Lower East Side. They sent Petrosino to Italy. But they killed him there . . ."

Contada said grimly, "Four shots in the back. Right in the open. And they couldn't get a single son of a bitch to admit he saw it."

"They got Tony's father too," Danny said.

"They put it in a box of Italian pastries," Contada said. "My father should have known better but they forced a guy from the bakery to deliver it. I was out with my mother. My little sister was home with my father. We lived on Madison Street then. When it went off it blew out the whole first floor. The undertaker couldn't find enough to fill one casket."

"Didn't they get 'em, Tony?" Danny asked.

"Two of 'em. The others got away to Italy. Now I'm on the same squad with my kid brother. Did I tell you, Tom? My sister's kid is goin' to Delehanty's?"

"If you can get up the money, Frank, that's where you should go," Tom said to me.

"Now let me start with this," Contada said lifting a framed photograph which showed seven tough-looking moustached Italians in dark suits staring at the camera.

"Petrosino's original bomb squad," he said proudly. He pointed to a stocky man wearing a derby. "That's Lieutenant Petrosino. The guy next to him is my old man. Four of these guys were shot, and one guy was run over by a Model T by the Black Hand. But they were tough guineas." He shook his head. *"Marrone!* What they did to those Black Handers when they got 'em in Elizabeth Street!"

We went from item to item, each one lovingly detailed. Tom and Danny O'Hara had evidently seen it all many times before but they appeared as interested as if it was their first visit. It was twilight when we were finished. Contada's wife appeared with coffee, Italian pastries, and a bottle of wine, along with some of their relatives who had evidently finished a few bottles. One of them had a concertina and in a few minutes the basement was rocking with a medley of Italian songs. Tom and Danny O'Hara seemed to enjoy it but Drummer seemed restless.

"Do you want a ride back to the city, kid?" he asked me.

"That will be great."

"Okay. Let's get out of here now or we'll never get out. I know these Sunday afternoons in Queens when cops get together . . ."

Contada begged us to stay but Drummer insisted he had an appointment back in the city. My excuse was getting a ride back. I thanked the O'Haras profusely and Tom walked me to the front door.

"Any advice you want, lad, just give me a call. You know where we live now. Any O'Hara will be glad to help you. Remember what I said, the department's far from perfect but it's not all that bad. There's some bad guys but there are more good guys."

Drummer wasn't much of a talker. In fact he was almost monosyllabic. But I got some basic facts; he was in his late thirties, a bachelor who was "in the job," as he put it, for twelve years and a detective for seven.

I finally gave up on my questions and we crossed the bridge in silence. As we started across town he said suddenly:

"Look, you're a nice kid. My uncles mean right but they'll fill you to the ears with nonsense about the department if you listen. With them it's a romance and the broad always has stars in her eyes. I don't want to see you go wrong. You have to look at the other side of it."

"Like what?" I asked.

"Like the dirt you have to deal with every day. The bums. The hustlers. The pimps. The scum of the earth. Who do you meet? People in trouble. People trying to con you, trying to beat you. I listened to my Uncle Tom until it came out of my ears. Dynasty of cops. We have to keep the shield in the family. Bullshit! I was a kid learning to be a plumber. I piss on the day I quit."

He glowered and we rode in silence. When he turned into Eighth Avenue and Forty-sixth Street he said as he opened the door:

"Want to take a tour with me? I can get my ass in a sling if anyone finds out about it, but if you keep your mouth shut I'll bring you along for a night so you can see the other side of it. My partner's a good guy. He'll go along."

"Any time you say."

He thought for a moment. "Thursday night, eight o'clock. We'll pick you up outside Grand Central on the Forty-second Street side. Okay?"

"Fine with me."

"I'll see you then, kid. We'll give you a tour of our high-class garbage dump . . ."

21 THE HIGH-CLASS GARBAGE DUMP

The O'Haras had given me the opportunity to put my foot in the door; accompanying Drummer and his partner for a night's tour would be a step into the room. As Tom had said, the principal ingredient that separates a successful union leader from a routine hack is that one knows the people in his union, what makes them tick, while the other is all mouth, no heart, and has a liking for the good life.

I also decided to make dossiers on the cops I met, the good guys. I was sure that if I remained with Pepe I would get to know the bad guys eventually, but if this wild dream of a police union ever surfaced, it wouldn't be the bad guys I wanted to know—only the good guys. Bad guys can be bought; good guys give you trouble.

I was in front of Grand Central promptly at eight. I had just walked to the curb when a black sedan pulled up and the door opened. "Okay, kid, get in," Drummer said. I got into the back, Drummer drove off, and the other man in the front seat turned around and put out his hand. He looked like anything but a cop. Where Drummer was brutally hard, he was round and soft with an almost cherubic face.

"Hiya, kid. I'm Mike Boston, George's partner."

"Pleased to meet you. I'm Frank Howell."

"George said you live in the Neighborhood."

"Forty-sixth between Eighth and Ninth."

"When I was a kid I used to visit my grandmother on Ninth and Forty-fourth. Over Reilly's grocery."

"It's still there. His son has it now."

"No kiddin'? He was a nice old guy. He used to let the old lady chalk up a bill. Every week I had to come over and pay. We lived in Bensonhurst. Did you go to St. Barnabas?"

"I graduated from there."

"No college, eh?"

"No money."

"Yeah. That's the way it is. Got to have coin to go to college these days."

"College. Who needs it?" Drummer grunted. "This job'll teach you what they don't give you in college. Like how a Murphy man works."

It was a clear cold night. We had come up Madison and down Lexington above Fiftieth. Ahead of us a slender Negro jauntily dressed in a light tan polo coat and slapping a rolled-up newspaper against his thigh was strolling down the avenue, intently eyeing the passersby.

Mike said softly, "That's Jamaica John, George. He's lookin' to make a score."

"The best in the business," Drummer said. "At least he's not an A & R bastard. See those three kids on the corner. They're out for pussy. Watch him tag 'em."

The Negro stopped and chatted with the three youths. I saw an envelope pass. Then the Negro walked rapidly down the street, the trio hurrying behind him.

"He sold 'em a bill of goods he has three luscious broads just waitin' to clean their pipes," Drummer said. "He'll take 'em down to Forty-fifth Street, waltz 'em up to the roof landin', give 'em the part of a paper book of matches with somethin' scribbled on it, and blow. The kids will go upstairs and find the roof. Good-bye, dough—and they still have their tongues out."

"What's in the envelope?"

"That's why he uses the newspaper. He tells 'em the madam wants the money in an envelope so they put it in, he seals it, palms it for another in the paper that has only strips of paper, then gives that to 'em when they start for the roof."

It happened just as Drummer predicted. The Negro and the kids disappeared into a tenement. The Negro reappeared within a few minutes and quickly vanished at a loping gait. I noticed he was now wearing a black topcoat.

"He stashed the polo coat under the stairs so it will be hard to spot him," Mike explained. "He'll come back for it later."

We watched the three kids, cursing furiously, run out

into the street. They stayed there for a few minutes looking up and down, then walked away.

"We're not gonna make a pinch tonight," Drummer explained. "Tomorrow we're off. If I bring this bum in tonight that means I'll spend all day in court. I have other ideas."

"Besides, it's a good lesson for those kids," Mike put in. "There's more VD around here than in a Panama whorehouse."

"Mike was in the Marines in Panama," Drummer explained with a grin. "Anyway let's get Jamaica the hell out of our territory."

We cruised up into the sixties and parked near a bar. After about a half hour we saw the Negro, still in his black coat, jauntily walking up the street.

"Let's go," Drummer grunted.

The Negro stopped when he saw them.

"Come here, Jamaica," Drummer said.

"What's up?" the Negro protested. "Why you nailin' me, man? I didn't do nothin'."

He came forward cautiously. Drummer grabbed the front of his coat and slammed him against a car fender. I heard the air whoosh out of the black's lungs while Mike expertly ran his hands up and down his coat and pants legs.

"Okay, he's clean."

"I'm not going to take you in this time, creep," Drummer said in a low voice. He held that big fist in front of the apprehensive black face. "If I see you on our beat again I'm gonna ram this right down your throat and out your black ass. Understand?"

Jamaica nodded and Drummer moved back a pace. When he started to take off, Drummer gave him a kick in the rear that sent him stumbling ahead for several feet.

"That hurt. You got no call to do that," he said, rubbing his backside.

"On your way," Drummer snarled and started toward him. Jamaica John ran down the block.

We were cruising down Lexington Avenue again when Mike pointed to a crowd milling about the side entrance of Grand Central. Drummer slammed on the brakes and we jumped out. Three husky, well-dressed men, obviously drunk, were pummeling a street peddler while a crowd silently watched. A trayful of little dolls was scattered on
262

the street. He was begging the others to stop but they were kicking him in the sides and face.

Drummer shouted, "Police . . . we're police . . ." but one of the attackers with a curse pushed Drummer to one side. I swear Drummer smiled. His gesture to Mike plainly said, "Leave him to me." He spun the man around and that fist, hard as iron, went home. The man slammed against the bank of glass doors and crumpled. The other two, wide-eyed, held up their hands.

"Okay, okay. We don't want any trouble . . ."

Drummer's open hand sounded like a shot against one man's face. He backed away, sober and frightened. The smaller of the trio pushed himself into a doorway.

"I told you we were cops," Drummer shouted. "What do you want—our birth certificates? What's going on?"

"They said they gave me a tenner," the peddler said, getting to his feet. "The bums gave me a buck." He held out a sheaf of crumpled bills. "Here's all I got. All night, six bucks. They never gave me a ten."

"He gave you a ten," the guy said, holding one side of his face, now bright red. To Drummer he said, pointing to his groggy friend, "Why the hell did you hit him for?"

"Because he was a goddam wise guy, that's why." He said to the peddler, "Do you want to make a complaint?"

"Naw. Let it go," the peddler said.

"You owe him five bucks," Drummer said to the man rubbing his cheek.

"Five bucks? Why? We didn't even get a doll!"

Drummer picked up a broken doll.

"Okay. So now you got your doll. Give him a pound."

The other reluctantly handed over the five dollar bill to the peddler who took it, closed his tray and picked up his toys.

"Thanks, Officer."

"Get your ass out of here and get over to the Eighteenth's territory. Hear me?"

"Yes, sir. Yes, sir."

The other two assisted their groggy friend to his feet and hustled him into Grand Central, one still holding the dangling, broken doll.

"These guys from Scarsdale get a couple of drinks under their belts and they think they're Jack Dempsey," Mike said.

"Let's cruise."

We drove up and down the main avenues, in and out

side streets, only stopping for Mike to make their periodic check to the squad. As they explained to me, they worked in teams of quartets, or "blocks," with the other two men remaining in the precinct, answering phones, taking "walk in" complaints, and finishing their paper work.

"You arrest a Murphy man and you get four tons of paper to make out," Mike told me mournfully. "Right, George?"

"Four tons? More like six tons."

After one call to the squad, Mike hurried out of the drugstore.

"Trouble," he snapped. "Sixty-eighth and Second. Guy with a gun."

Drummer was a skillful driver. He weaved easily in and out of the traffic at high speed. When we arrived at the scene, he threw me his overcoat and told me to stay near the car. There were several radio cars, an ambulance, and an emergency truck with a searchlight framing a tenement window.

"It's a jumper with a gun," one cop shouted to Drummer. "He was on the ledge and when a cop tried to talk him in he shot the cop. He also plugged his wife and sister-in-law. He's a psycho!"

Using the parked cars as a shield, Drummer and Mike ran along the length of the building to join several policemen with rifles crouched in a cellar doorway. They pointed to the window. At first it sounded like a cap gun but they all ducked. Then it went off again. One of the cops cried out and held up his hand, covered with blood. Two other cops rushed him to the ambulance.

I suddenly realized there was a maniac in that window and he was shooting down at all of us. Especially the cops.

I saw Drummer, Mike, and two cops with rifles rush into the tenement. There was a long suspense-filled wait. Then, suddenly, Mike appeared at the window waving his hand. Below him the cops waved back and began returning to their radio cars. I was amazed at their casualness. The cold, white shaft of the searchlight suddenly snapped out.

Drummer, in his jacket, appeared on the stoop with Mike and two other cops. Between them they were dragging a wild-eyed, screaming old man, his hands cuffed behind him. They pulled him to the ambulance, pushed him inside, and slammed the doors. I could see the twisted

264

old face at the window, saliva dripping from his lips, as he pounded his head against the glass. The red light on the roof flashed and the siren wailed. In a moment it was gone.

Drummer and Mike conferred with the other cops, then walked back to the car. I got into the back seat.

"Psycho," he said shortly as he slid into his overcoat. "He shot two cops along with his wife and his sister-in-law. The women are dead. One cop's in rough shape, the other was only nicked. They say Valentine is on his way to the hospital."

"That's just dandy," Mike said. "Who wants to see the goddam police commissioner when you have a bullet in your gut? Man, I want to see a priest!"

"It will take the priest all night listenin' to you, Mike," Drummer said.

"How about you, pal? How's that little piece you have stashed away in the Lexington?"

"Day-off stuff," Drummer said shortly.

"How did you get him out?" I asked.

"The nut?" Drummer shrugged. "There's only one way to get 'em out, kid—go in after him."

"We busted in the door," Mike said. "George hit him with a chair." He said to his partner. "You know, George, you're almost as good as Lefty Gomez?"

"That reminds me," Drummer said. "I promised the twins I'll go out and see their team play next Sunday."

"Do you go out to Queens every Sunday?"

"He's either sponging on the O'Haras or on the Bostons," Mike said.

"Policemen seem to hang out together," I observed.

"You know that's true, George?" Mike said. "Who goes out with you to the track on our days off and gets my wife nuts? On our vacation who are my neighbors? Cops. Who are my kids' godfathers? Cops."

"Who signed your loan for National City?" Drummer said with a grin.

"Yeah. A cop. You."

"Why?" I asked.

They were both silent. Drummer studied me in the overhead mirror.

"It's a good question, kid. Maybe we don't have anything else to talk about with other people. Right, Mike?"

"It's an occupational hazard," Mike said. "Years ago when we were first married my wife asked me the same thing. 'Why always cops, Mike?' she said. 'Why don't we invite carpenters? Plumbers? Electricians? Why always cops?' "

"So what did you say?" Drummer said.

"Simple. They speak my language. What am I going to do all night? Talk to some guy about wiping a joint? Putting up a partition?"

They live together, they eat together. They speak the same language. It was something to remember . . .

We had a brief lunch in an all-night restaurant. After he had called the squad to give them the number of the restaurant's pay-telephone booth, Mike settled for a soft-boiled egg, milk, and a large white pill.

"Acid stomach," he explained. "Every time we have a little action it tastes like carbolic in the back of my throat . . ."

I was becoming quite an interrogator. I'd discovered that Drummer was a teetotaler, he loved the track, he was wary of marriage and he hated the "creeps," as he called them, who inhabited his night.

"The way I feel, kid, it's either them or me. They're the enemy and I'm being paid to fight 'em. So I fight 'em." He held up his fist. "I rather use this but they have a rod, then it has to be this—" He patted his shoulder holster.

"Have you shot anyone?" I asked.

He gave a thin smile. "Three. I'm not braggin', mind you."

"Three DOAs," Mike said shortly.

"The way I see it is this, they have a gun, you're their target. You have to get 'em first. No woundin' 'em. Kill 'em. Right between the goddam eyes! Do you think the other guy with the gun is worryin' about woundin' you?" He laughed harshly. "The only public mistake some cops have made is their obit. Not me . . ."

Drummer insisted it was a quiet night. There were only two more incidents: an elderly man had a heart attack on an IRT platform and both Drummer and Mike worked over him trying to keep him alive until the ambulance arrived. But it was no use. The old man died as they lifted him gently onto a stretcher. The other incident resulted from a call Mike had made to the squad.

"A guy's waiting on Third and Forty-ninth. He claims some dame lifted his wallet."

Drummer groaned, "Oh, Christ! What a way to end the night."

We found the victim, a man about fifty, well dressed

266

and obviously very nervous under his facade of an indignant, victimized taxpayer.

When he started to sputter his explanation Drummer asked wearily, "Let's cut out the crap, pal. Did you get laid?"

The man stiffened and his voice rose.

"Don't shout at me," Drummer bellowed, his voice echoing in the deserted street. "Did you go to bed with this woman?"

The man wet his lips, then nodded quickly.

"Okay," Drummer said, mollified, "don't lie to me. I only want to help you. I'm not your priest. I'm a cop. What did she look like?"

He listened impatiently to the man's description, then pointed across the street.

"Wait for us in that gin-mill over there."

"But I don't have any money," the man said almost tearfully, "I don't even have enough to get home . . ."

"Tell the bartender you're waitin' for Drummer," he said. "Let's go."

I followed them into an all-night Automat on Lexington Avenue, crowded with night postal workers. Drummer seemed to know exactly where he was going. In the rear, five women were seated about a table eating. They were in their twenties; all except one were nondescript. She was a striking, expensively dressed woman in her fifties.

She looked up as George approached and waved.

"Hey, sweetie . . . come on over and join us."

Drummer's cold eyes passed over the women, then settled on one who seemed younger than the others.

"Hand it over, sister."

The older woman, no longer smiling, asked, "What's up, George?"

"You should get a goddam Actor's Equity card, Annie," Mike said mildly. "We have a complainant. Cough it up or we'll pull you all in. Robbery. Assault. Procuring. Soliciting. Spittin' on the sidewalk. You name it, you'll get it."

"This is the last time I'm gonna ask," Drummer said softly. "In a minute I'm gonna take what's left of this beef stew and plant it right in your kisser, Annie. How many times do we have to warn you? Screw 'em all you want but don't heist 'em!"

"Give it back to the fellows, Chickie," Annie said.

Chickie looked indignant. "Give back what? The gentleman gave it to me."

Drummer reached for the plate of beef stew but Annie shrilled to the other girl, "Give it to 'em!"

The girl hastily reached into her bag and handed over a wallet.

"We're gonna make one more tour in fifteen minutes," Drummer said. "If I find you in here we'll lock you up."

He spun on his heel and walked out. Mike elaborately tipped his hat.

"I recommend their glacé cakes, ladies. They're very good. C'mon, kid."

I followed him past the staring diners and out to the car. In the barroom George nodded to the bartender and threw the wallet on the bar in front of the man.

"What does he owe you, Louie?" he asked the bartender.

"Just for two drinks, George."

"Pay up and buy Louie a drink for being so nice," Drummer said.

The man, with trembling hands, slid some bills out of the wallet, bought the drink, then looked over at us but Drummer silently shook his head.

"Don't offer us anything, pal. I might spit in your face."

Then he walked out. Mike leaned over and said to the man, "Did you go in bareback?"

The man looked embarrassed and shook his head.

"One word of advice, pal. If you did, drop off at a drugstore and get somethin' or you might discover a little surprise in nine days."

"That bastard will keep his zipper closed for a few days," he said, chuckling as we left.

We cruised until their tour ended in the early hours of the morning. Then, after a final check-in call to the squad, Mike came back to the car.

"Want to see Lenny now?" he asked Drummer.

Drummer nodded and turned about in his seat to face me.

"We're gonna show you somethin' now that my uncle would never mention. This is what every kid who wants to join the department should see. For all the crap you got from Uncle Tom, what you're gonna see now is the sum and substance of what every cop has to face every night, every mornin', every tour . . ."

"What is it?" I asked.

"Do you remember on Sunday in Queens when we were

268

talkin' about the dynasty cops and someone mentioned Lenny Farber, the Jewish cop in Safe and Loft whose old man was in the same squad?"

"They said something about him knowing every crook in the garment center . . ."

"Right. We're gonna pay Lenny a visit now."

He threw the car into gear and we moved up Lexington Avenue.

"We go over to say hello after every Thursday tour," Mike said. "The other fellows drop around during the week. In this way he'll always have someone . . ."

Farber lived in a flat in the Seventies off York Avenue. The woman who opened the door was slender, gray haired, and smiling. Beyond her a kitchen table was set with coffee cups and cake.

"Hello, Esther," Drummer said. "How's Lenny?"

"Fine, fine," she said eagerly. "He's waiting to say hello." She looked surprised when she saw me. "A rookie, George?"

"No. This is Frank Howell, Esther. He's thinkin' of joinin' the department, so Mike and I thought he should have a taste of it first with a tour."

"He should. They all should," she said. Her eyes brimmed with tears as she turned away.

There was a lamp on the table and in its soft light the man in the wheelchair could have been a mummy. He was wrapped in a blanket with another covering his knees. His face had shrunken. It was barely a skull, covered with skin so thin it looked like parchment that would split if the man opened his mouth. Only his eyes, brown and sparkling, were alive.

"Lenny! How are you?" Drummer said loudly as if the man was ready to spring up and grasp his hand. "You look like you're ready to come back to work. How is he, Esther?"

Mrs. Farber said eagerly, "Now he can move his right hand. Show George, Lenny."

The hand, emaciated to a claw, resting on the side of the chair moved slowly.

Drummer and Mike nodded approvingly.

"That's great, Lenny," Mike said. "Every day a little more. Next the legs, right, Esther?"

"Sure. Sure," she said and leaned over and kissed her husband.

We stayed in the warm, almost suffocating, flat for about an hour drinking coffee and eating cake. Mike and Drummer kept up a constant flow of conversation, all police gossip. Finally Mike glanced at his watch and stood up.

"Lucy will have my scalp if I'm not up when the kids go off to school," he said. "I think we have to go, Esther."

After elaborate good-byes and a promise to return on the following Thursday, we left.

In the car Drummer said, "Okay if I drop you off at Times Square, kid?"

"That will be fine."

We drove in silence for a few minutes, then Drummer said, "Lenny and his partner went into a loft on Seventh Avenue one night. They had a tip three guys were gonna knock it off. What they didn't know was that the watchman was paid off. They watched the truck back up and waited until they started to move out the stuff, silks and imported stuff, then they moved in. Two of the guys came out with their hands up. They were cuffin' 'em when the third guy and the watchman came out shootin'. Lenny's partner was killed in the first round but Lenny got the third guy and plugged the watchman. The other two guys took a powder. They found him more dead than alive. One of the bullets severed his spinal cord, another smashed his voice box. The only thing he has been able to move is that hand. Every week it's been that way. His wife makes it out to be a big deal. The doctors say it's only a matter of time. They had him in last month for his kidneys. They're gone . . ."

"When did this happen?" I asked.

"Four years next month," Mike said. "I can remember like it was yesterday. When my wife told me she had heard on the radio that a cop was shot I called the house."

"Every cop off duty went out lookin' for the two bums," Drummer said. "One guy got a squeal from a hustler. Two Safe and Loft guys got one of 'em in a farmhouse up in Westchester. The other out in Jamaica."

"George and I took the guy in Jamaica," Mike said quietly.

"Did he do time?" I asked.

Drummer glanced at me briefly in the overhead mirror.

"He had a gun and he was usin' it, kid," he said softly.

270

"He caught me in the shoulder," Mike said. "George got him."

"Right in the head," Drummer said savagely, "right in the goddam head! It could be me. It could be Mike. It could be any of us. That's one thing we never forget, kid; they hurt one of us, they hurt the whole squad. The whole department. If it happens you have to make sure you do two things: get the bastard that did it and never forget the cop that got hit. Or his wife. Or his kids. You have to bleed with every one or it's nothin'. Only outsiders can shrug it off."

I was startled at the word, Pepe's word, outsiders.

"What do you mean outsiders—people who aren't members of the department?"

"Exactly. In the department it has to be shoulder to shoulder. There are those that are in and those that are out. Those that are out"—he made a gesture—"they can't understand. We don't expect 'em to . . . we know we have to take care of our own . . . it's the rule. You don't hear of many guys breakin' it."

"How about Captain Elliott, you know him?" I asked.

Drummer grunted. "Everybody in the department knows Elliott. He has more guts than most."

"Crazy as a loon and straight as an arrow," Mike said with a chuckle. "Remember, George, when that kid was killed over on Forty-sixth Street and he blasted the brass?"

I froze.

"Yeah. You must remember that, kid. It happened in the Neighborhood."

"No. I was in the CCCs. But I heard about it."

"A nice kid," Mike went on. "Some jerk in the Sixteenth shot him. There was a big stink about it but it blew over . . ."

"They shot a kid and it blew over?" I said.

"Yeah. It was one of those things I guess."

"You can let me off here," I suddenly said.

Drummer said surprised, "It's only Fiftieth Street, kid."

"I'll walk. I feel like getting some air," I said. "Thanks for everything."

We shook hands.

"If you want a little more," Drummer said with a tight smile, "give us a call. And look, kid, if you can get anything else—dump the idea of the department. Forget my uncle's fairy tales."

"I'll think it over . . . thanks again. . . ."

They drove off and I looked after them, my fist clenched so tight it hurt.

22 *HELGA*

Despite the usual summer doldrums along the waterfront, Metropolitan's strapping business expanded almost daily. While Joe remained behind with the coopers, I continued to deliver supplies, not only to the East and West Side piers of Manhattan, but from St. George to the Jersey piers; several times I even made a run to Philadelphia. We still could never find Pepe in his gallery; Lorenzo always insisted he was out of town. All our business contacts were made through Maxie Solomon.

In midsummer I began to see more of Joe. He appeared to have become weary of Helga; when I mentioned her he just shrugged.

"If I don't come up she calls me at the pier or sends me notes. The stupid dame is even talkin' of wantin' to marry me!"

"Marry you! She's almost old enough to be your mother, Joe."

"Don't I know it?" he said roughly. "It was all right for a while but now she's becomin' a nuisance. The other night it was rainin' and I sneezed. She kept runnin' around with hot lemonade and aspirins. What the hell is she tryin' to be—my mother?" He gestured to the bartender for another drink. "When I see her again, her tongue will be hangin' to the floor . . ."

I was just as happy to see Joe. By now I had my fill of cops for a while. I hadn't heard from Chena in some time and I was getting restless. Every day that week, as Joe had predicted, Helga called him at the pier until he finally agreed to accept her dinner invitation, but only on one condition—I had to come along.

To satisfy my curiosity about her brownstone, I agreed.

Joe had not exaggerated. The house smelled of money. There were three floors and a tiny elevator. The first floor was a music room and a library with shelves of books that appeared to have been read. The dining room was on the second floor, a luxurious bedroom and bath on the top floor. There was a beautiful garden and even a patio on the roof.

We were served by an old German maid who chatted with Helga in German; I later found out she spoke not only German but French and Norwegian.

The amount of cutlery threw me but I knew enough to watch Helga só as to not make a fool of myself. She was a perfect hostess and immediately put me at ease. I was fascinated by her stories of Europe and of the people she had met—musicians, writers, statesmen. She was never condescending, only interesting.

Joe looked bored.

She was stunningly dressed in a long velvet skirt and flowered blouse. At our first meeting I had judged her to be in her forties—I later learned she was in her late fifties. It was obvious she had fallen for Joe; whenever possible she leaned over and gently squeezed his hand.

I took my clue from Joe and we said good night early, leaving behind a clearly frustrated and disappointed woman ...

This routine continued for the next three weekends. I could feel the tension mounting in the cozy library where we always started the evening with drinks, then gradually mounting at the dinner table. It was the first time I had ever seen Joe operate with a woman. I could almost smell his sensual, animal vitality in every move; it was easy to see he had her charmed dizzy. One night when we were leaving I went back into the library to get our jackets. There was a long mirror in the music room, and I could see Helga whispering desperately and clinging to Joe who just smiled coldly down at her. That settled me. I told Joe on the way home that he would have to go it alone; I didn't intend to hold the candle. He gave me a grin and promised that next weekend would be different.

The following Friday he didn't show at the pier. Later in the day he called to tell me he had stopped off at Helga's and asked me to come up; he promised a surprise.

When Helga ushered me into the library, I could see that Joe had been drinking. Surprisingly so had Helga. She seemed unusually tense, laughing too quickly and filling my glass too often.

"Hey, Helga, did I ever tell you Frank is my closest friend?" he said after I had lifted my first glass in a silent toast to her.

"Many times, darling."

"Do you like him?"

She gave me a nervous smile. "Very much."

"How much?"

"Very much."

"As much as me?" he said leaning toward her with a grin.

"I like Frank very much, Joe, but I love you," she said solemnly. "Very, very much, Joe."

"See that, Frank?" Joe said, leaning back and stretching out his legs like the lord of the manor. "She loves me so much she'll do anythin' I ask. Right. Helga? Anythin'?"

"Yes, Joe," she whispered.

I didn't like the smell of what was happening, but before I could say anything Helga announced that dinner was ready. This time there was no German maid, Helga served.

Before we reached dessert I knew I was getting drunk. We had reached the stage where we all laughed too loudly and kept dropping glasses or stumbling over furniture. Finally I found Joe standing in the middle of the room glaring at Helga.

"Let's cut the crap," he said roughly. "It's gettin' late. You know what you promised. Let's go!"

I was bewildered. "What's the matter, Joe?"

"Nothin's the matter with me—it's her! She promised to take care of you tonight!"

Helga looked straight ahead. Then she turned and walked to the elevator.

"If you will come up in a few minutes, Frank," she said evenly, "I will be ready."

The elevator noiselessly ascended. In the silence I could hear the gate slide back on the floor above.

"Are you nuts?" I told Joe. "This woman doesn't want to have anything to do with me."

He gave me an owlish, drunken look. "Oh, yes, she does—she's upstairs now, just waitin' for my pal Frank."

I started to put on my jacket but he jerked it away.

"Wait a minute," he said. "Your party is upstairs. I

mean it. Okay. She loves me so goddam much, now let her put out."

"For Christ's sake, Joe!"

"Why the hell do you think I've been playin' Chinese checkers and wastin' my time for the last month? I've been settin' her up, makin' her beg for it. I took care of her last night, now she does what I say." He gave me an elaborate wink. "When you get these old dames on the hook, buddy, they do anythin' you want."

"I don't want any part of this, Joe—"

"The hell you don't! You need it. You've been hangin' around with too many cops lately." He slipped into his jacket.

"I'm going with you . . ."

"Not tonight, you're not." He gave me a push and I landed back on the sofa. "Have fun, Frankie boy . . . just remember one thing—anythin' we have we split fifty-fifty. Broads, booze, dough. You and me. That's all we have left . . ."

He stumbled to the elevator and it slowly descended. Then I heard the front door slam.

In the silent house, the ticking of the grandfather clock in the corner seemed to get louder every minute. When Helga called quietly I took the elevator and went upstairs. Now there was another sound, the thumping of my heart. I didn't want to but I did . . .

I stepped into the large, beautiful bedroom. I can still recall the mellow light of the tiny lamp and the picture in the old-fashioned gold frame of Helga, her arm linked with that of a stern, dignified old man with a white moustache and a goatee. I told myself it was easy to see her husband had not been fun to live with . . .

She was standing in the middle of her room, her hands clasped in front of her. She had on a frilly negligee and under it I could see the full body of a mature woman.

"I feel terrible about this," she said in a low voice. "Please don't think badly about me."

"I'll go if you want me to, Helga . . ."

"No, No. Joe swore he'd never see me again unless . . ."

She came to me hesitantly. I was surprised to discover how soft and supple she was under the negligee. She stiffened when I touched her, then moaned softly and pressed against me.

I reached over to turn off the lamp but I was so nervous I almost tipped it over. She quickly snapped it out and for a moment we faced each other, two blurs in the warm darkness. Then I quickly slipped out of my clothes while she primly removed the spread, pulled back the covers, and slid in. I joined her.

It was callow, amateurish, and over in a minute. As I lay back she turned and kissed me on the cheek.

"There is the whole night . . . I promised Joe . . ."

The sun was high when I finally awoke to the smell of brewing coffee. I came to the breakfast table to face not a lustful Catherine of Russia but a wan, embarrassed middle-aged woman who kept urging me to have more scrambled eggs and toast.

The bright, cheerful warm morning was brutal after all the whiskey I had consumed and the feverish hours in the darkness. But the cups of coffee and plates of scrambled eggs and bacon helped to establish an intimacy between Helga and myself that had been lacking before. I found her to be a grimly realistic woman after four bitter lonely years following the death of her husband. Before that there had been more than a year of caring for a fretful, dying man.

Her husband had been a wealthy banker and twenty years her senior. Her family had made a fortune in Minnesota lumber in the last century and she had lived most of her life in a staid, Midwestern town. Her father had died many years before and after the death of her mother she had come to New York.

"I thought at first I would go to Paris but then I decided to stay in New York," she said sadly. "I thought it would be a glamorous life. Glamorous! What a joke. I lived for a year in one of the most expensive apartments on Fifth Avenue but up to the time I moved I didn't even know the names of the people on the same floor with me.

"I was dying of loneliness when I met my husband at a charity tea. It was all very stiff and formal. He was like that, inside and out. He had been a widower for many years and I guess it was a combination of loneliness and affection that led me to marry him. He was a kind man and quite worldly. We traveled to Europe every spring and in the winter we had a house in Nassau. Then he became sick . . . it was the most horrible year of my life."

She looked down and stirred her coffee. "For a year after his death I was in a daze. I went about doing things automatically. The few friends we had just drifted away.

Then it was like coming to the surface again. Oh, Frank, if you only knew how lonely I was—worse than before . . ."

She smiled and pointed across the room to a large, expensive-looking cathedral-style radio.

"Saturday night at ten o'clock one of the stations featured an hour of dance music from the Pennsylvania Hotel. It sounds crazy but every day, every hour of the week I would wait for Saturday night. I would have my hair done and put on my best dress as if I were going out; in fact, I even made up little stories for my hairdresser of my attractive escorts. Then, when the music started I would get up and dance around the room. I had a Persian cat and sometimes I would dance around with that stupid cat in my arms." She said with a harsh, short laugh, "Isn't that crazy, Frank? An eccentric old woman dancing about her dining room with a cat? But I guess if it hadn't been for the radio, the music—and even the cat—they could have taken me to Bellevue . . ."

She sighed and reached over and squeezed my hand.

"Please forgive me, Frank, if I ramble . . . I don't have anyone to talk to. . . . May I go on?"

"Of course. Please do."

"I've always had this fantasy about a young stranger who would some day appear and fall in love with me." She shook her head. "God, when I say it what an utterly foolish woman I seem to be! But when Joe showed up when that nasty cabdriver was yelling at me, I was at the end of my rope. I just stood there crying and letting that horrible man abuse me. Then Joe came over, put his fist in that man's face and told him he would have to settle with him if he didn't leave me alone. He was so handsome and brave and seemed such a gentleman—well, I was lost. I knew then I could have no shame. I had to invite him to dinner." She smiled weakly. "And I hoped he would accept my bed."

She said slowly, "I couldn't stand it if he didn't come to see me anymore, Frank. I have no pride when it comes to him."

"I feel terrible about this," I told her.

"Please don't. You're a fine boy and"—she hesitated— "I would do anything he would ask me to make him happy. What did Coleridge say about love being blind because his eyes are in his mind?"

She got up and walked to the window.

"Shame? At this point in my life what does it mean?

277

You're his friend, Frank. Do you think he would consider me . . .?"

What could I tell this lonely woman? Explode her pathetic daydreams?

"Please tell me the truth, what do you think?"

But I knew that the truth would only shatter her.

"Well, Helga, Joe's tied up in this business we're in . . ."

"Something to do with the waterfront, isn't it?"

"We operate a small company that supplies the coopers on the piers. They repair the broken boxes and barrels."

"Well then I'll buy the company for him," she said eagerly. "I can call my lawyers on Monday. I'm not stupid, I know business from my husband. My God, that's all I heard for years and years . . ." She hurried to the table and sat down, leaning toward me. "Frank, I know I'm much older than Joe, many years older, but it's not unusual for an older woman to marry a younger man. Believe me, it isn't. I know. I've traveled around the world. I've seen it—many times. He wouldn't have to be with me *every* minute. I just want to see him now and then, to talk to him, to have him put his arms around me. . ."

She was trying hard but tears rolled down her cheeks.

"Anything is better than dancing with a cat, Frank! You're young, you don't know what loneliness is . . . Oh God, how young you and Joe are . . ."

Saturday night I met Joe in Regan's. He was shooting pool with Train and when he saw me enter he slowly chalked his cue, ran off a few balls, and joined me at the bar.

"Okay?" he asked with a grin. "Did she take care of you?"

I cringed, not because of myself but for the shattered pride of that lonely woman in the palatial brownstone who was at this very minute, sitting, waiting for the telephone to ring. I had promised her Joe would call.

"I promised I'd get you to call her, Joe."

He yawned. "I'm layin' off. No more old ladies for a while."

"Listen, you bastard, I told her you would call. Now call her!"

His eyes widened in mock surprise.

"Hey, what is this? Did that old piece captivate my buddy?"

"C'mon, Joe, call her. It will only take five minutes."

278

"Maybe I will and then again maybe I won't."

I knew it was useless to push him.

"Okay. I'll see you around . . ."

"Hey, wait a minute. Where are you goin'?"

"You don't call her, I'm going to a show—by myself. Then I'm going to do a little hunting—by myself." I gestured to Train. "Have fun and get your baseball scores correct or Train will clobber you . . ."

"Okay, okay," he said with a grin. "You win. I'll call her."

"Now."

He flipped a quarter on the bar. "Give me five nickels, Pat, I have to make a charity call."

"Don't hurt her, Joe. She's a lady."

"And who wants a lady—particularly an old lady?" he asked as he walked to the phone booth.

When he came back he said, "Okay, she's happy now. She wants us to come up next Friday night . . ." He looked thoughtful. "That might be an idea." He smirked. "We'll drink her booze and give her a real party. She's got a big bed!"

"You go, Joe. No more for me."

At first he became angry. Then, during the week, he mocked and taunted me. Finally he lapsed into a sullen anger. When I tried to explain he flared up.

"You're the guy that kept tellin' me to call her. So I did. We can have somethin' real good goin' up there with a lot of laughs. I fix you up and now you want to play altar boy!"

Finally, he stopped asking me. I knew he went back to see her, but it wasn't the same. He returned complaining that Helga was trying to mother him.

One night he came into Regan's carrying more than his share of Helga's whiskey.

"That goddam stupid woman," he mumbled. "I got a little loaded and first thing I knew she's kneelin' down and takin' off my shoes! I felt like kickin' her in the teeth!"

"If you feel like that don't go there anymore," I told him.

"Look who's talkin'," he said, "Sir Lancelot. Goody Two Shoes, who I set up with some free old tail and now it's too good for him!"

I bit my tongue and walked away. It was the closest I had come to slugging Joe since the battles we had in the first grade. . . .

I recall very vividly that Labor Day weekend. For days Joe had been impossible. He was quick to start an argument, irritable, moody, and drinking more than I had ever seen him.

In Regan's he baited Train, cursing, mocking, and taunting the big moron. Train took it with a puzzled grin. Then, during a game of pool, Train missed a shot and Joe slugged him. He slammed back against the wall but only rubbed his jaw.

"Geez, Joe, you didn't have to do that!"

I jumped off the stool at the bar and spun Joe around.

"Listen, you son of a bitch, you've been aching for a fight all week. You say one more thing to Train and you and I will walk out into the alley? You got that?"

He glared at me. For a moment I had the eerie feeling he didn't know me. He tore his arm free and stalked out.

We didn't see him all weekend. On Tuesday he didn't show at the pier, no one had seen him. That evening, minutes after the boss checker blew his whistle to end the day, the phone rang in our office. When I picked it up there didn't seem to be anybody on the line. I was about to hang up when I heard a tiny, almost indistinct voice. It was Helga; she was begging me to come and see her.

As I walked up the steps of the brownstone something told me I would dread discovering what lay behind that heavy grilled door. I rang the bell but there was no answer. I finally knocked on the glass. I could hear the echo in the hallway but no hurrying footsteps. Then I tried the heavy brass knob and the door swung open. The house was as staid and quiet as a dentist's waiting room. In the library the ashtrays were clean, and the current magazines neatly piled on a table.

It was a different story on the second floor. A hall mirror was smashed, glass scattered on the rug.

"Helga!"

My voice sounded cracked, like an old man's frantic call. When there was no answer I walked into the dining room. It was a shambles. Broken dishes littered the floor, the fine china closet was tipped over. Food was congealed on plates. There were glasses filled with stagnant whiskey and spilled ashtrays.

In the third floor bedroom with the drapes half-drawn, the dim, filtered twilight outlined someone seated by the window, staring out. An enormous sense of relief flooded over me.

"Helga! What's wrong? Don't you feel well?"

As I approached her she turned. What I saw made me almost physically ill. In the dull light I could see a dark bruise under one eye, swollen cheeks, and a split lip. The nose was surely broken.

"My God, what happened?"

"Joe," she whispered. "He had been drinking when he came up. I tried to make him comfortable. All I did was try to take off his shoes. Then he started shouting and cursing me . . . the next thing . . ."

The sobs shook her. "He beat me, Frank, he beat me like a dog . . . then he ripped off my clothes and held me by the hair while he slapped me. . . . Oh, God, I thought he would never stop."

For one brief moment I had the weird feeling I was looking into the battered face of Mrs. Gunnar, I could almost hear the loud, rasping snores of her drunken husband as he sat there by the kitchen table, the whiskey bottle held tightly in one hand as she gently tried to take off his work shoes . . . so long ago.

"Let me call a doctor, Helga."

She lifted her tortured face to me. "Please! Please don't call a doctor! He would laugh at me. Helga Strom, an old fool bringing in a boy young enough to be her son. Please! Please! Don't tell anyone you saw me. Please!"

"You need food, Helga," I told her. "And what about the woman who works for you?"

"I called her and told her I was going out of town for a while," she whispered. "I'll be better in a few days." The smashed lips tried to form a smile. "I can always tell her I fell." She groped for my hand. "Please go, Frank. I don't like to have you see me like this. Please!"

"Can't I get you anything?"

"No. No. Please go. I'll be all right in a few days . . ."

I turned away reluctantly, wishing with my whole being that Joe had never met her. I wanted to reach out and hold her but I knew it would be a travesty.

"Good-bye, Frank," she whispered. "Please tell Joe good-bye. Maybe someday I'll see you both again . . ."

I searched all that night—from the pier to Regan's—without finding a trace of Joe. It was as though he had dropped out of sight through a hole in the earth.

In the early hours of the morning I reached our stoop. I was weary and heartsick. My initial rage had died out, leaving behind only bewilderment tinged by a fear I didn't understand. I sat on the steps and started to take out a cigarette when the picture of the day we had returned from the CCCs suddenly flashed across my mind: Joe standing in the hall, telling my aunt he would keep the old Gunnar flat . . .

At that moment I knew where I could find him.

The kitchen door of the flat opened to my touch. I smelled sweat and raw whiskey. A figure sat sullen, slouched in a chair by the window.

"Joe?" I whispered.

The figure moved. I struck a match and, in the feeble glow, Joe's agonized face emerged from the shadows.

"For God's sake, Joe, what are you doing here?"

He shook his head slowly. "I don't know . . . I don't know . . ."

"Well, goddammit, you should know after what you did to Helga!"

"Helga?"

His eyes were dull, his face slack.

"Joe—don't you remember what happened?"

"I don't even remember comin' here, Frank," he whispered. "I just came to sit here in the dark a little while before you walked in. . . . I must have really hung one on."

"Joe, listen to me. Listen very carefully."

I told him about Helga. He kept staring at me, shaking his head. "No! No! Why would I want to hurt her? Why? Somebody else must have come in and done that . . ." He went on, pleadingly, "I wouldn't hurt her for anythin', Frank. Sure, lots of times I said she was an old pain in the neck, but hurt her. Christ! Never." He hesitated. "I'm scared, Frank," he said. "I really am." He buried his face in his hands and rocked back and forth. "I swear I don't know what happened! She kept fillin' my glass and beggin' me to dance with her. Finally I did. Then I remember I was in a chair and she was kneeling' down takin' off my shoes. I kept yellin' at her to stop . . . that she was not my mother . . . and then I guess I passed out. . . . My God, I wouldn't hurt her for the world."

"Forget it," I said, "you just had too much booze . . ."

"There's somethin' more to it, Frank," he said slowly, "a hell of a lot more. . . . I can feel it . . . maybe I better see a doctor."

282

"Forget it," I told him and slapped him on the back. "Le's hit the hay."

"Do you know what we haven't got, Frank?" he asked quietly as I locked the kitchen door and we stood in the darkened hallway.

"What's that?"

"Someone to tell us what our next move should be."

How true, I told myself. What lay behind was a bitter unintelligible failure. Now the future, for all of Pepe's brisk, bright predictions, appeared as dismal as the shabby flat we had just left.

23   THE PLAN

We never saw or heard from Helga again, but that tragic affair seemed to bring us closer. The bond between us was cemented by the knowledge that we were alone, that together we had to screw the world to survive. This intimacy had brought me for the first time to the edge of the unknown, had given me a glimpse into Joe's inner being, where a river of violence ran still and deep. I have always blamed myself for the terrifying events that crouched in our future. But in those days our relationship was the only value in our shabby world, the only certainty that existed so I said nothing, did nothing, and thrust the fears from my mind. I chose, in a sense, my own doom when I chose Joe Gunnar.

That summer and fall I nourished my secret plans for a national police union. Then, one day, I was surprised to discover that Joe had his own private dream of a union—only coopers, not cops.

One unusually warm fall day, as we walked up Forty-sixth Street, Joe nodded to some longshoremen and their families sprawled about a stoop. They were big and sloppy and were wearing slippers and dirty undershirts. Kids fought on all sides of them while their wives gossiped, occasionally pausing to yell at an offspring who paid no heed. Containers of beer made the rounds among the men and their women.

"You know, Frank, that's what we're becomin'. It's a complete circle in this goddam Neighborhood. You work on the docks. You go to the gin mills. Every once in a while you get laid in one of those cathouses on Fifty-first Street. Then you meet a dame, get married, have kids, still work on the docks and you do this on a hot Sunday afternoon. In ten years that's you and me!"

"You'll never get Chena sitting on a stoop on Forty-sixth Street drinking beer."

"So you'll drink wine in some backyard in Astoria with her guinea relatives. I've had it. I don't intend endin' up on a stoop like those bums."

"Do you have something in mind?"

"Damn right I do."

He lit a cigarette, inhaled deeply, and let the smoke curl out between his lips. "I'm goin' to take over the union."

"The union? The coopers?"

He nodded. "Lock, stock, and barrel."

"Are you nuts? That's the Gimp's union. You make a move he doesn't like and you'll be killed."

"That's the chance I have to take."

"Now wait a minute, Joe, talk sense. You're twenty years old. You've been working on the pier for only a year and now you want to take over the union that's owned by a waterfront racketeer that even Dewey can't arrest?"

"According to the books, the union has three hundred and twenty-seven members," Joe said softly. "That's only on the Manhattan, Brooklyn, and State Island water-fronts. That's not countin' Jersey and Philly. It could be tripled if you count the coastal ports from Boston down."

"How do you know how many members they have?"

"I got it out of Bailey."

"Jack Bailey? How would he know?"

"He was secretary of the union for years until the Gimp kicked him out. To keep the old man happy he gave him the cooper's job."

"How about Collins?"

"From the way Bailey spoke, Collins was a bit of a troublemaker when the Gimp's mob first took over the union, but they paid him off by lettin' him work with Bailey. They're all scared to death of the Gimp; they know what happened to the Polack. This guy was grabbed after he told everyone he was goin' down to Dewey's office and finger the Gimp. They beat out his brains and threw him into the river."

"And these are the guys you want to screw out of their union racket!"

"We won't be as stupid as the Polack . . ."

"How did you get Bailey to talk?"

"Remember the week Collins was out with a bum back and I agreed to stay with Bailey while you were deliverin' to the piers every day?" When I nodded he went on. "That's the week I really got friendly with the old guy. Every lunchtime I fed him enough boilermakers to get five dockwallopers drunk. The bastard has a hollow leg, he just kept knockin' them off one after the other, but nothin' happened. Then one night I took him out and we hit every gin mill on the avenue. This time he was stoned and I took him home with a pint. He finished the pint and I got him to tell me about the books." He flipped his butt into the gutter. "Do you know what the Gimp steals every month, only from this union? Over six hundred bucks!"

"Where does it come from?"

"Dues!" Joe snapped. "Our dues! The shop steward just turns it all over to one of the Gimp's hoods."

"And this is the outfit you want to take over. Joe, are you nuts?"

"I have a plan. Bailey finally told me they have a secret office on Eighth Avenue. That's where the Gimp meets his shylocks and that's where he has all his records includin' the union books."

"Did he give you the address?"

"It's on the avenue just above Twenty-second Street. The office is on the second floor; it's listed as a jewelry company. There's a Greek restaurant in front and a paint store on the ground floor."

"And the Gimp has his records there just for the taking? He's not that dumb, Joe!"

"Of course not. There's a safe as big as a house in the office but he doesn't keep the books there."

"Well then where does he keep them?"

"Behind the safe in the wall. You remove the molding and there's a panel that just lifts out. The Gimp has it all planned to protect himself if Dewey ever gets a line on the office. He had some racket lawyers fix up a set of books and put them in the safe. The real stuff is in the wall."

285

"So . . ."

"Doesn't Spider copy those old records out in Queens?"

When I nodded he said softly, "Suppose we find the Gimp's books, bring them to Queens, and have them copied?"

"How about the safe? You just said it's as big as a house?"

"If Train can move a caboose he can move the safe."

"Okay. We move the safe, find the Gimp's records, and get them copied. What do we do with the copies? Blackmail him? The only thing we'll get out of him is a tire iron across the head!"

"Do you think I'm crazy enough to try and put the arm on him? Hell no! I have somethin' better in mind. Remember when you pointed out Supercop's picture in the paper? Didn't the story say Dewey had to let the Gimp go because the judge said he didn't have enough to hold him? Well, suppose Dewey had somethin' on the Gimp? Suppose . . ." He grinned and let his voice trail off. "Suppose someone sent the Gimp's records to Supercop! It's a perfect setup. Dewey can't do anythin' about the Gimp because he hasn't anythin' on him. Well, we'll give him somethin'—nice and neat and all wrapped up in a bundle. In fact, we're gonna put it right into his cop's hands!"

"It sounds too simple, Joe."

"Its so simple it will work."

"Why not just send the books to Elliott? Why go through the trouble of having them copied?"

"By the time they get the books and go over them, the Gimp may find them missin'. He'll be ready with his lawyers when they come around." He shook his head. "No sir. I want him surprised with a good kick in the head . . ."

"There's one other thing—"

"What's that?"

"How do we get into the Gimp's office?"

He reached into his pocket and held up a key. "I bought it from a locksmith on Ninth Avenue. He deals only with the best heist men. He guarantees it will open any lock. It cost me twenty-five bucks but it will be worth it."

"Joe, you're nuts!"

"Maybe. But I'll do it. Do you want to come along?"

When I hesitated he said quickly, "It will be okay with me if you pass this one up, Frank . . ."

"You know as well as I do I'll come along."

He smiled. "I know it."

"Someday you're going to get me killed."

"They'll have to kill me first."

"It will be a tight squeeze, Joe."

"We'll make it," he said with his usual air of unshakable confidence.

"Let's find Spider and the Train."

We had no problem with the Train, he would have gladly moved the Empire State Building at Joe's request, but Spider looked doubtful.

"Jeez! I'll have to get a key to the lab," he said. "Then I have to fix the old watchman."

"Will he take ten?" Joe asked.

"He'll take five," Spider said, "but we have to give him a story he'll buy."

"We can tell him I need stuff copied for an exam I have to take to get into college in September," I said. "I'll bring some books along to make it look legit."

"Good idea, Frank," Joe said. "Will he go for it?"

"He'll buy that," Spider said. "But I still have to get the key from Vera—"

"So? Jazz her and have some fun," Joe said. "What's the big deal about that?"

"I have to buy a fifth of booze so I can get her jerky husband drunk," Spider complained.

"So what's the problem? I'll buy the booze."

"That ain't it, Joe!" Spider said indignantly. "They only got two rooms out in Queens. How would you like to jazz a dame when her husband's snorin' next to you? It's hard to concentrate."

The following day, just as the whistle blew for quitting time, we received word from Pepe. It came by way of Fat Freddy Kenton who made an unexpected appearance at the coopers' shed.

"I have a message for you guys," he said belligerently. "The wop wants to see you."

"Okay, Freddy," Joe said, smiling, "we'll drop over on the way home." He pointed to the bulging tarpaulin, "You can tell Johnny we have a good collection for him tonight . . ."

Joe's friendly manner mollified Kenton. "Yeah. Okay. I'll tell Johnny." He added seriously, "You know all you guys have to do is keep your nose clean around here and you can make out."

"Sure—you boys can make out like bandits," Collins said.

Kenton glared at him and stalked out.

"Christ, do you have to needle that guy all the time, Jim?" Bailey said. "You know he tells everythin' to the Gimp."

Collins just shrugged.

"I want to keep that fat slob dumb and happy," Joe explained as we left the pier. "I wonder what Pepe has in mind?"

"I don't know, but I think we should level with him."

"You mean about takin' over the union and sendin' that stuff down to Dewey?"

"Everything."

Joe nodded. "Maybe you're right. Besides, we may need his help some day if the Gimp starts to get rough . . ."

24 THE WINEPRESS

When we arrived at the gallery, the door was swung open by an exuberant Pepe.

"Peppino! Joe! My young friends! How are you? Come in."

He swept us in and escorted us to his office.

"Please. A drink," he said. "What will it be—a little wine, scotch . . ."

We both had scotch. Pepe lifted his glass.

"Salute al mio giovani amice!"

"Anything special you want to see us about, Pepe?" I asked.

He threw up his hands. *"Marrone!* Can't I see my young friends? So tell me, Peppino, how is our cops' union?"

"I've done some work on it this summer," I said.

"Buòno! Buòno! What did you do?"

He listened intently when I told him.

"You must continue," he said. "It is for the future but we must be prepared."

"Prepared for what?" Joe asked.

"For the time when we want to organize them," Pepe said.

"And when will that time be?"

"Maybe when Peppino tells us," he said with a grin. "No, Peppino?"

"The hell with the cops now, Pepe," Joe put in. "We have somethin' that can't wait."

Pepe looked quickly from me to Joe.

"You have trouble with the strapping?"

"The cargo's no problem."

"The old men?"

"No. They're nice old guys."

"The union—it gives you trouble?"

Joe swirled the drink about in his glass.

"That's what we want to talk to you about, Pepe. Frank and I want to take over the coopers."

Pepe's eyebrows lifted slightly, and I caught a flashing glint of triumph in his dark eyes.

"Ah, the union . . ."

"The coopers," Joe explained. "Remember the cards you gave us?"

"*Sí*."

"Well, we want to take over—"

"You are only boys," Pepe said with a wave of his hand. "The cripple's *squadrista* will eat you up!"

"They might get indigestion."

"Why do you want this union?" Pepe asked. "What is to be gained?"

"A lot of things," Joe replied.

"It is money you want, my young friend?" Pepe asked quietly.

"Money—among other things," Joe said. "But more importantly, it will be a toehold in a union."

"You wish to go into unions?" Pepe said nodding. "You think that is good?"

"Very good. The Gimp is stealing over six hundred a month. We would like to have a taste of that. It will also give us some muscle."

He studied us for a moment, then said softly, "The children want power . . ."

"Don't fool yourself, Pepe," Joe said warmly, "we're no longer kids."

"Ah, so now you are men. Will you fight like men?"

"We'll fight anyone who gets in our way," Joe said

grimly. "We took it long enough—now it's somebody else's turn—"

"Fight with fists?" Pepe said contemptuously. "That's for boys in the street." He leaned across his desk. "Will you kill a man if he gets in your way? You, Joe? You, Peppino?"

A small cold lump formed in my stomach and my mouth went dry. I knew this wasn't just talk; Pepe meant every word. I looked over at Joe, he was staring at Pepe.

"You mean kill the Gimp?"

"Why not?" Pepe asked with a shrug. "He will only kill you and Peppino."

"We don't have to kill anybody," I put in. "Joe has a great plan. Tell him, Joe."

Joe leaned forward and explained in detail what we intended to do with the Gimp's books. To my surprise Pepe dismissed it with a wave of his hand.

"Va. Va," he said impatiently. "You are fools! Peppino, where are your brains? What will happen to you when the cripple gets out on bail?"

"He won't suspect us," Joe said.

"Marrone! You try to take away his union while he is in jail and it is nothing?"

"He'll be afraid to make a move," I said. "Dewey's men will be on his back."

"Dewey," Pepe sneered. "Can his people protect you for the rest of your life? Will they go with you to the toilet when you are old men?"

I dreaded to ask the question. "What would you do, Pepe?"

"What would I do, Peppino?" he echoed mockingly. He pressed his powerful stubby hand down on the glass-topped desk. We watched, fascinated, as the fingers spread slowly, the knuckles cracked and the tendons in his wrist and forearms became taut as cables.

"Like a grape in a winepress," he said softly. "It is the only way."

"We don't need any rough stuff, Pepe," I said hastily. "We'll stick with Joe's plan. If the Gimp gets out on bail we will force them to hold a meeting and sell Joe to the members . . ."

"What do you think, *figlio mio?*" Pepe asked Joe.

Joe was staring at the powerful, almost surgically clean hand on the glass.

"Suppose we need your help, Pepe?"

290

The hand turned over and a finger pointed to the telephone.

"We won't call," I said emphatically. "Never."

"Peppino whistles in the graveyard," Pepe told Joe. "You must kill the cripple or he will kill you. Would you want to wind up in the river with irons about your feet, Joe?"

"No, I guess not," Joe said slowly.

"I still think the idea of getting the goods on the Gimp and sending them to Elliott will work," I said.

Pepe gave me a wintry smile. "When the whore of a judge lets the cripple out on bail he will pat you on the head. 'Ah, friend Peppino, who took care of my union when I was in jail.'" The smile vanished and the cold eyes glittered as he ran his finger across his throat. "He will slice your throat like a pig in a pen!"

"We'll have to take that chance."

"I will bury you, Peppino," Pepe said sorrowfully, "and buy your Masses for a year."

"We can handle him," Joe said.

Pepe tapped the edge of his desk and stood up. "We shall see."

At the door to the gallery he lifted an imaginary receiver to his ear.

"Suppose we called you, Pepe?" Joe asked. "What would happen?"

"Many things, my young friend," Pepe replied. "Many things."

"Your way," I said.

"Pepe's way, Peppino," he said in his soft, merciless voice.

The following Sunday afternoon we cased the Gimp's headquarters, a one-flight walkup from Eighth Avenue. At the top of the stairs was a typical Eighth Avenue Greek social club. Through the half-open door we could see a small group of men standing around a card game, intent on the players. We tiptoed past and down the long dark hall. At the end was a door with the name "Starlight Jewelry Company." Joe pressed his ear against the door, then took out the skeleton key, carefully inserted it into the lock, and turned it. There was a loud click. The door opened and we moved inside to find ourselves in a two-room suite that smelled of stale cigar smoke. The larger room was sparsely furnished with a battered desk, a closet, a few chairs, and a letter file that contained back issues of racing forms and the *Morning Telegraph* with entries circled in ink. The smaller room had a deep niche filled with racks of coats, another desk and chair, a Bunsen burner, jeweler's glass, rows of chemicals, and boxes of watch parts and ring settings.

There was no safe.

"Maybe the old man was just drunk and lying," I whispered hopefully to Joe. But he shook his head and reached into a scrap basket. He came up holding several crumpled brown envelopes—pier pay envelopes.

"Our president was making sure we paid our dues," he said softly.

I had come to the conclusion that the Gimp was either smarter than we had thought or had removed or destroyed the records. Then for the tenth time I examined the deep clothes closet on the far side of the big room. Suddenly the thought struck me: It was summer, why were so many obviously old worn overcoats hanging in there? I walked back into the closet and, behind the coats, discovered the heavy oak door. Joe's key opened it and we walked into the adjacent room, dimly lit and smelling strongly of paint and turpentine. It was filled with scaffolding, tarpaulins, and stacks of paint cans. In a corner, under a pile of ladders and covered with canvas drops, was the safe. It was a huge old-fashioned two-door affair that clearly weighed a ton. Train, I told myself, was going to have one hell of a job budging it. Fortunately, it rested on iron casters.

Something about the room puzzled me: the wallpaper. In contrast to the dust and grime, the paper appeared expensive and luxurious with clusters of roses every few feet.

We carefully replaced the canvas and ladders and closed the closet door. The hallway was deserted and we tiptoed past the Greek cardplayers. In a few minutes we were walking back uptown along Eighth Avenue.

I was bathed in sweat and my heart was pounding against the walls of my chest. When I looked at Joe he was grinning. Sweat beaded his forehead and his upper lip, while his dark blue polo shirt had black patches under his arms and on his back.

"We better bring towels when we come back here," he said laughing.

I was in no mood for laughing; all I could think of was the Gimp and his Pistoleers walking in on us. . . .

25 *THE LONGEST NIGHT*

We made our plans that week as though we were going to rob the Chase National Bank. I went to the library and took out some books on chemistry, biology, and math. Spider made a date with his ladylove on Friday night and took the fifth of Golden Wedding provided by Joe.

On Sunday morning Spider rang my bell. Joe and I rushed down to the shop where Spider silently held up the key to the microfilm and photostating lab.

"How did it go?" Joe asked with a grin.

Spider looked disgusted. "No more. I swear. That's the last time. Job or no job. The bastard drank most of the fifth but didn't conk off. Vera had to go out and buy another pint before he flopped into bed. There was this jerk snorin' like a buzzsaw alongside of me and I'm tryin' to jazz his wife!"

"Business with pleasure, Spider!"

"The hell with that. What do I get out of this?"

"If we ever take over this union you'll be part of it."

Spider studied him. "You kiddin' me, Joe?"

"It's a promise," Joe said solemnly. "I had it in mind all the time. I'm goin' to be president and Frank's vice-president. We have to use those two old guys we work with, but you and Train will be in the union . . ."

"Train?" I said.

"Who will argue with Train?"

"The guys from the Neighborhood take over," Spider said delightedly.

"I want people I can trust."

"Okay, boss," Spider said, "I got you the key—what else?"

"I want to move tonight," Joe said. "Get Train and bring him over."

"I won't be able to raise him with a derrick. He was at Regan's all night guzzlin' beer—"

"Frank, go over with Spider and get that big bastard out of bed," Joe said in exasperation. "I want to examine this thing in detail so there won't be any slip-ups."

"Where will we meet?"

"On the pier," he said without any hesitation. "We won't be disturbed over there."

After persuading Train's grandmother, a vague, deaf old lady, to wake him up, he came into the kitchen, a stumbling giant in a dirty undershirt and work pants.

"Phew! You stink like Regan's cellar," Spider said with a grimace.

"What the hell do you guys want?" Train growled.

"Joe's waitin' for you," I said. "We're goin' out to Queens tonight. We want to go over it."

"Now! It's Sunday mornin', Frank," Train protested. "I ain't even been to church."

"Church," Spider snickered. "You big bastard. You haven't been inside one since grammar school."

Train yawned. "Okay. Where's Joe?"

"He's over on the river waiting. Let's go."

After vigorously ducking Train into the river to clear his head, we sat on the end of the pier in a circle and listened to Joe tell us what he had in mind.

"Frank and I have been down there. There's only a couple of Greeks playin' cards in the front. The Gimp's place is in the rear. There's a door from the closet that leads into the office." He looked over at Train. "Train, you'll have to move a safe that's as big as a house."

"Don't worry about it," Train growled.

"You said the stuff is in the wall?" Spider asked. "Did you and Frank see it?"

"We couldn't move the safe," Joe explained. "But I know it's there."

"What about the Gimp, Joe?" Spider said anxiously. "If he and some of his hoods drop in, we're dead."

"These bums don't work on Sunday night. There won't be any trouble."

"What time?"

"As soon as it gets dark. Is the watchman set?"

"I gave the old man a fin," Spider said, "and told him that crap that Frank gave us about copyin' some stuff for an exam. Don't forget to bring some books," he said to me. "We have to make it look good."

Aunt Clara insisted on making us sandwiches and iced tea, then we set out for what I told her was an evening at

Loew's Twenty-third Street, I warned her I might be late. When we reached Eighth Avenue the lights were on in the Greek Club. As before, there were several players grouped around a card table. I made sure the coast was clear, then waved the others down the hall. The key worked perfectly, and in minutes we were in the stale-smelling darkness. We followed Joe's flashlight through the clothes closet and into the room where it played up and down the huge safe.

"There's the baby you have to move, Train," he whispered.

Train stared in silence at the safe, then nodded. "I'll move it, Joe," he promised quietly.

I can still see his tortured face in the faint glow of the yellow beam—teeth bared, the cords swelling in his neck, all of us holding our breath. Then Spider whispering excitedly, "She's movin'! Train, you big bastard you did it!"

He leaned against the huge iron box, his lungs greedily sucking in air, the sweat rolling down his big face and onto his rust-smeared polo shirt.

"You owe me a new shirt, Joe," he said panting.

"I'll buy you a box of 'em, Train," Joe said and affectionately hugged him.

Train grinned and gave me a look of triumph. "I told ya I could do it."

We watched intently as Joe's flashlight examined the wall. Suddenly he grunted and with a screwdriver carefully eased out four pieces of molding and slid free a square of wallpapered plaster. The flowers on the paper had been so carefully matched that not a petal was out of line.

"Mr. Painter downstairs did a swell job," Joe whispered.

"The books!" Spider exlaimed as the beam of light moved across a mound of ledgers and small memorandum books.

"Remind me to buy Bailey a quart of boilermakers," Joe grunted as he lifted the books from their hiding place.

"Holy Christ! Look at this," Joe said. "It's a list of the Gimp's shylock customers."

There were names, amounts, dates—the delinquents in red—scrawled IOUs, a package of car ownerships, house deeds, pawn tickets, all collateral for the Gimp.

Joe said triumphantly, "This is it, Frank—this will hang him!"

There were pages of union dues payments, our names

included, the names of the officers of the union and the amounts paid to them.

"Fat Freddy! That son of a bitch!" Joe burst out pointing to an entry on the page. "He got three thousand dollars last year!" He snapped shut the ledger. "Let's move. We have a lot of work to do."

We piled in Spider's heap and headed for Queens. Spider's car was ancient. It rattled, creaked, and shook with backfires as we crossed the Queensboro Bridge. Joe kept demanding speed, but Spider warned him that his tires were bald and his carburetor faulty. It was a nervous, exhausted quartet of conspirators that finally reached the old schoolhouse that housed the historical project.

Then there was more trouble; the watchman couldn't be found. While Joe fumed, Spider visited the neighborhood gin mills and finally returned with the old man who complained that Spider had interrupted what he called his "lunch hour." He was a crotchety complaining old man who was obviously trying to hold us up.

"Here you are, sir," Joe said, one arm around the old man's shoulder, the other slipped a five dollar bill into his jacket pocket. "We apologize for interruptin' your lunch hour but my friend here has to pass his college entrance exams next week and he's tryin' to get his stuff copied." He turned to me. "Show him the books, Frank."

I silently held up the pile of books I had been carrying under my arm.

The old thief put his hand in his jacket pocket and felt the bill.

"Well, I certainly want to help you young fellows," he said expansively. "There's nothing like an education ... you know I used to be a plumber and had my own business before twenty-nine?"

Joe, nodding sympathetically and, with his arm still around the old man's shoulder, walked him across the schoolyard and disappeared into the darkness.

We ran down the long marble corridor to the basement. Spider cautioned us not to put on the ceiling light.

"A Mickey Mouse from the Queens Precinct makes a midnight check; if they see the lights they'll come in."

Joe appeared in a few minutes. "I bought the old man a beer in the gin mill down the street," he told us. "He's good for a couple of hours. Let's go."

I was amazed at Spider's technical knowledge. Once in the lab he was no longer the smooth, lying little thief I had known all my life but a cool, effortlessly proficient expert. While we watched in silent admiration Spider carefully set up each page, photostated it, then went to the next. As the hours passed, the heat in that small windowless room became almost unbearable.

"Christ, there must be three hundred pages!" Spider said, running his forearm across his brow. "Maybe I won't have enough stock, Joe."

"Do all you can, Spider," Joe said. "We can—"

He broke when he heard banging at the basement door, the sound of voices, and approaching footsteps. I yanked the ledger from the metal clasp, threw it under the table, and had just replaced it with a chemistry book when the lab door swung open.

It was filled by two big cops. Between them was the old watchman, so drunk he could barely stand.

"What are you guys doin' here?" one cop asked.

"We're just copyin' some schoolwork for my friend's college exam, Officer," Joe said coolly.

"I work in the lab, Officer," Spider said and showed him a WPA identification card in his wallet.

"Yeah, but what's this?" the cop said pointing to the book.

"Crosson's *Chemistry Problems*," I said. "I'm trying to get into CCNY in September and I need this stuff for the entrance exam. I got the books out of the library." I took the book from the rack and showed him the N.Y. Public Library card.

"Why be a college boy?" the older cop said as they both examined the book. "Why don't you get a job and help your parents?"

"I wanted to make the cops but I couldn't pass the physical," I said. "Hernia."

"Hell, that's nothin'," the older cop said. "Get it fixed, kid."

"I'm goin' to Delehanty's after my project winds up," Joe said fervently.

"You all on WPA?" the younger cop asked.

"We're breakin' our hump on the roads up in Westchester," Joe said.

"Yeah. Leanin' on a shovel," the younger cop said dryly.

I laughed loudly. The others took the cue and joined in. The cops looked pleased.

"They're all right," the watchman said. "Okay. Okay."

"Suppose we take care of him, Officer?" Joe said. "We'll be finished here shortly and we'll drive him home. Okay, Pop?"

"Okay, okay," the old man said.

The older cop turned to me seriously. "Get that hernia fixed, kid, and try again. Forget that stupid college. Get on the cops. You can't beat that pension."

The other one winked, "And that's not the only fringe benefit, fellas!"

We held our breath until we heard the outside door close, then all of us whistled softly in relief.

"That was close!" Joe said. "Thank God you moved, Frank." He nodded to the book. "Let's wind this up."

We put the old watchman on a pile of newspapers in the corner and worked feverishly until the stock of paper was exhausted.

"Christ, Vera's gonna blow her top," Spider said. "We used two weeks' supply!"

"Tell her she's only doin' her civic duty," Joe said. He held up one of the negatives to the light.

"There's enough here to hang the Gimp twice over. Let's get out of here."

We dumped the old man unceremoniously on his doorstep, then headed west toward Manhattan. But our troubles weren't over. We had two flats, and the car conked out on Third Avenue. The sky was graying in the east when we jumped out of a cab and ran up the stairs to the Gimp's offices. The ledgers were returned to their hiding place, the plasterboard carefully replaced, petal matching petal, and the molding restored with the same nails. Then came the big job of getting the safe back to its exact spot, the iron wheels in the same worn groves. There was a barely perceptible incline in the old uneven wooden floor but it stopped Train. The big safe refused to budge.

"Train, it's gettin' late! You have to move it!" Joe said desperately.

Train nodded. The dead-white freckled face was streaked with dust and sweat, the shaggy hair damp and matted. The long hours at Regan's bar and the gallons of beer he had swilled were exacting their payment.

Train glared at the safe, angry enough, I thought, to club it with his fist.

Joe nudged me and nodded. His lips formed the words—needle him . . .

298

"We better help him, Joe," I said, "he can't do it alone—"

"Whaddaya mean? Whaddya mean?" Train said fiercely. "I'll do it, goddammit! Get out of the way!"

He got on his knees like a lineman, fitted his shoulder to the edge of the safe, then pushed. We held our breath and watched the iron wheels. Slowly, the rear ones moved up the rough floor board, then over, followed by the front wheels.

"Got it, Train!" Joe exclaimed.

Train sank to one knee. He looked up at Joe, a huge exhausted bull.

"I did it—didn't I, Joe? Didn't I?"

Joe slapped him on the shoulder. "Sure you did, Train. You were great!" He looked at me. "Wasn't he great, Frank? What the hell would we have done without this guy?"

"No one else could have done it, Joe," I said.

"I told ya all along. Frank, I could do it," Train said, lumbering to his feet. "Just ask me, that's all."

We left the building as the sun was coming up and the first-shift workers were hurrying toward the subway. We took a cab, dropped Train and Spider off at their flats, then headed home. But there was no sleep for us. We brewed some coffee and had a dish of the usual corn flakes while we excitedly discussed our next move. Joe readily agreed with my plan of putting together a dummy package of the same weight and size of the bundle of photostats to get the proper postage.

"Elliott's no dope," I explained. "If we mail it from a branch station, he'll be there talking to those postal guys ten minutes after he knows what he has. They'll remember us sure as hell and Supercop will be knocking at our door before noon."

That afternoon, after we had delivered the truck to the Cherry Street wastepaper plant, we bought heavy wrapping paper and labels and made up a dummy package. Then at a branch station we got postage. Joe packed the photostats between cardboard and I printed a crude note, listing the address of the Gimp's headquarters and the location of the books in the wall behind the safe. Just before the main post office on Thirty-third Street closed, we joined the long line of nondescript messengers and garment workers all loaded down with bales and boxes and slid our carefully stamped

299

package across to the clerk who never looked up as he automaticaly stamped it and threw it into a bin.

All we could do was wait . . .

26 A VISIT FROM DOWNTOWN

For weeks all we did was read newspapers. There was plenty about a nut named John Ward who stood on a ledge of the Gotham Hotel all day and night before he took a dive, and about the killer hurricane that was ripping up along the coast, but nothing about the Gimp.

He seemed as unconcerned as ever as he toured the waterfront with his entourage of hoods like a visiting potentate. The two-year contract with the shippers would be up the following spring. But already there was some grumbling on the piers about the usual sellout. Yet there was no tangible opposition. The mobsters and the crooked politicians could quail before the mention of Dewey's name, but not the Gimp. He seemed untouchable.

"Don't worry about the Gimp," Bailey told us, "he's got big connections downtown. They can't hurt him, not even Dewey."

"Maybe he's right," Joe said in disgust one night after we skimmed through the first edition of the News, "the bastard must know someone real big downtown . . . I guess we better think of somethin' else . . . "

"Like what?"

He shrugged. "Suppose I start movin' around the piers with you for a couple of days a week."

"What do you have in mind?"

"I want to talk to some of these old guys. What the hell, you're always tellin' me how they bullshit about my old man. If this thing with Dewey doesn't work out we'll push for a meetin'."

"The Gimp will never hold an election, you know that, Joe."

300

"It's better than just sittin' on this goddam stoop doin' nothin'," he said fiercely.

"Okay. Don't get excited. We can start tomorrow over in Brooklyn."

The next week Joe accompanied me when I delivered supplies to the piers. At each stop I elaborately introduced him to the old men I knew. Joe really surprised me—he had ease, patience, and joviality. He listened to all the old stories—most of them lies or exaggerations—they told him about his father: the fights, brawls, drinking bouts, the confrontation with the shippers in those long dead days after the First World War, the dances in the hall behind Regan's saloon, and the wild electioneering when the men on the waterfront put Tammany's candidates into office at a nod from Big Andy Gunnar.

Joe listened to them all—slapped many backs, bought many boilermakers, accepted many drinks which he didn't finish, and agreed that the Commies had to be driven from the waterfront. Then, almost casually, he would bring up the question of the union and how he was interested in "putting it on its feet again" as he called it.

In the beginning, I could see the fear in their rheumy old eyes. But as the days passed, to my amazement, they began to listen to Joe, agreeing with him, slamming their gnarled, work-worn hands down on the bars as they cursed the hoods who had robbed them without any protest down through the years.

"They're startin' to listen to me," Joe said excitedly one night after we left a Brooklyn bar where he had an attentive if slightly drunk audience. "Maybe we won't need Dewey—"

"Don't worry, we'll need him. It's one thing for these old guys to shoot their mouths off in a bar, but it's another thing to tell off the Gimp's Pistoleers . . ."

"Okay, maybe they won't stand up to the Gimp now—but at least they're listenin' to me," he said doggedly. "It's a start, isn't it?"

Gradually I noticed a change in Joe. When he had three or four old-timers about him he cultivated a delivery composed of a mixture of demagoguery, lies, personality, camaraderie, and false promises. But it worked, and the more Joe saw it worked, the better he became. He had a naturally deep voice, and I could see it hypnotized them.

I began to experiment with writing pieces for him, stories I had heard of the old days on the piers—there was

301

nothing better to attract their attention than reciting the old lies and legends—and sprinkling it with subtle denunciation of the union's leadership. Wilson was never named outright, it was always "the thieves who have sold us out to the shippers."

Finally, I insisted that we spend a few hours each evening practicing his delivery of the pieces I had written. One night when he had finished, the sweat was pouring off his face, his fist was extended, and his eyes were filled with an intensity I had never seen before. For one brief moment he was transfixed.

From behind, my aunt said, "My goodness, Joe Gunnar, you sounded like an actor! My arms are all goose pimples. What are you reading?"

Joe pointed to me.

"Frank, did you write that?" she asked. "It was very good. Now come on into the kitchen, I have some sandwiches for you boys . . ."

When she left we just stared at each other.

"Buddy, I think we have somethin' goin' for us," Joe said. "You write it and I'll say it, okay?"

We shook hands.

Then one day it happened. We were crossing Twelfth Avenue returning from lunch when suddenly the street was blocked off by several unmarked cars. From everywhere on the pier men who had been lounging about, eating hot dogs by the stand, or sitting on the tailboards of trucks were suddenly galvanized into action and rushed into the pier. As we ran up a big man in dungarees stopped us.

"You work on this pier?" he snapped.

"We work with the coopers," I said.

"Where's your check?"

He examined our brass checks and waved us to one side of the entrance where we joined a group of dock wallopers.

"What's up?" Joe asked one.

"Dewey," one whispered. "We just got word they hit three piers on the East Side. They even found the bank for the numbers. They got the Gimp in the office."

A few minutes later they led the Gimp out in handcuffs. Behind him came four of his hoods and Buck, the inspector, who was indignantly demanding to know why he had been arrested. But he received no answers from the stone-faced man who hustled him into a police van with the

Gimp and the others. Then the big man in dungarees who had stopped us called out to the boss checker.

"Okay. It's all over. Send the men back to work."

We were just starting to drift back into the pier when someone tapped me on the shoulder.

"What are you fellows doing here?"

We turned and looked into the face of Supercop. He was thinner, and his eyes were weary. With him was a distinguished-looking man with white hair and a white moustache who looked like a banker but smelled cop. I wondered where I had seen this man before.

"Supercop," Joe said.

"Who are these people?" the white-haired man asked Elliott.

"They're two kids I know from Forty-sixth Street, Inspector," Elliott said.

"Bring them in if you think they can tell us anything."

"I don't think so, sir—"

"Well, I'm on my way downtown to talk to the boss—" He nodded abruptly and got into a car.

"Wasn't he the guy who was with you in that picture in the *News?*" I asked Elliott.

"Inspector Cornell," he said.

"We must be important, Frank, all the brass came up to say hello to us," Joe said.

"I haven't seen you in a long time, Gunnar," Elliott said. "It's been a couple of years, hasn't it?"

"Do you mean since the time the cops at the Sixteenth used us for a punching bag?"

"Did Frank tell you I met him on the Staten Island ferry?"

"Yeah, he told me. So what?"

"Did he tell you how I felt about what happened?"

"He told me. But do you want to know something . . ."

"Don't tell me," Elliott said wearily. "Let me guess."

"I hope you guess right," Joe said harshly. "I hope you guess I think you and the whole police department should be wrapped up in a big bag and dropped in the river off Hellgate. With all your goddam guns and clubs wrapped around your necks."

"It looks like Gunnar hasn't changed," Elliott said when Joe walked back into the pier.

"*We* haven't changed," I told him.

"Okay, hard guy," he said cheerfully. "How's your aunt?"

303

"Fine. So you finally got the Gimp?"

"It's no secret. You'll read it in the afternoon papers. They've been indicted on ninety counts of extortion, larceny, assault, and usury. We have them this time."

"The bookies were giving odds Dewey would never get the Gimp."

"No use arresting anyone unless you can send them to jail. We never had the goods on him. I guess you can say now we do."

"You must have gotten a lucky break," I said with an altar boy's innocence.

"You can say that again."

I tried but I laughed out loud.

"What's the joke?"

"The look on the Gimp's face when you put the cuffs on him," I said quickly. "I bet he didn't even have a chance to get a shine."

"As a matter of fact," he said with a smile, "we grabbed him as he sat down for the kid to shine his shoes. How well do you know him?"

"I only said hello to him once."

"I guess you wouldn't know that bum has been milking you guys in the unions for years, would you?"

I gave him a look of exaggerated surprise. "Mr. Wilson! Robbing the unions?"

"Okay, I'm sorry," he said with a resigned air. "I should have known better." He nodded to the pier. "How's the job?"

"No squawks."

He tried to be casual but the question was fast and blunt.

"Do you have a friend in that wastepaper company that owns Metropolitan?"

Obviously he had checked Metropolitan's ownership but he didn't catch me napping.

"Yeah. I told you—remember? An old guy who worked for Joe's father got us the job. We work. They pay us. Any other questions?"

"Do you know Gunnar's old man started the coopers' union?"

"Somebody mentioned it."

"A few of the old cops on the squad remember Andy Gunnar. He was a big man on the waterfront in his day."

"You sound like you've done some checking . . ."

"You have to do your homework to stay in Dewey's office."

"Well, now that we talked about Metropolitan, the coopers, and Joe's old man, is there anything else on your mind, Captain?"

"Tom O'Hara said to say hello if I saw you."

"Tell him hello. They're nice people. For cops."

"Tell me something, Howell. Why did you go out there?"

"Curiosity."

"Is that all?"

"That's all. I guess I just wanted to see how a cop lives."

"And what did you think?"

"Like I told you, the O'Haras are nice people. But for every O'Hara you have fifty Hennessys."

"Come off it, Howell—"

I gestured to the circle of longshoremen who were silently watching us.

"It looks like the guys I work with are worried about the company I'm keeping."

"Okay, tough guy," he said, "good luck."

That night we couldn't wait until we got the *News*. Page one had headlines about the arrest and indictment of the Gimp, his hoods, and the government inspector. There was a picture of Wilson snarling at photographers as he was led handcuffed into the Criminal Courts Building. In the glare of the streetlight I ran through the story.

Sources close to the investigation of Wilson's waterfront underworld empire revealed that for over a year Dewey's aides had desperately sought the books of the various unions, rackets, and businesses controlled by the Gimp and his hoods.

The same source in the Special Prosecutor's Office disclosed that a few weeks ago there was a dramatic and unexpected break in the investigation when one of Dewey's aides received a package from an anonymous informant. It contained not only the address of the Gimp's secret union headquarters, where he also conducted his extensive shylock operations, but also photographic copies of the books. The source said Dewey's accountants and his assistants described the records as "explosive." Bench warrants were issued by Supreme Court Justice Cook and a raid on the secret headquarters on Eighth Avenue and Twenty-

305

second Street took place simultaneously with the arrest of Wilson, three men later identified as his enforcers, all with extensive police records, and the government inspector for the pier. When the source was asked who he thought had sent in the copies of the union, shylocking, and racketeering records, he smiled and said, "I wouldn't call him a friend of the Gimp's, would you?"

27 *THE MEETING IN REGAN'S HALL*

The arrest of Wilson and his gang caused both chaos and jubilation on the waterfront. The morning after his arrest there were detectives and government agents all over the piers, security was unbelievably tight. The Gimp's enforcers were gone and his boss checkers were frightened and confused. There was a growing sense of revolt, resentment, and anger among the dock workers. They never had the courage to speak out before, but as they milled about waiting for the shape, they were loud and voluble. Joe knew his chance had come.

Before I knew it, Joe had scrambled on the top of a box and was haranguing the dockwallopers. That young, clear, fervent voice whiplashed them—and they loved it.

"These bastards have stolen money from your pockets, from your table, from your kids' mouths!" he shouted. "They sold you out to the shippers every spring! Where did the money go? Not in your pockets but in the Gimp's! I say strike! Let's walk out! Let's show all of 'em we're through lettin' them rub our noses in the dirt!" He pointed his finger at them. "You! You! You! They can't move a piece of cargo without you." He shot his finger at the liner that had arrived the day before. "I say let her rot at the pier! Frank Howell and Joe Gunnar are on strike right now! How many of you have the guts to join us?"

A roar went up, and Joe jumped down from the box and grabbed my arm.

"Get an American flag somewhere, Frank! We're goin' to march!"

"March! Where to?"

"Fat Freddy's warehouse! Now is the time to get him to call a meetin'."

We gathered outside on Twelfth Avenue. Word flew along the waterfront with the speed of a grass fire in a high wind, and other piers emptied. There was a carnival air. The gin mills did a brisk business and the hot dog stands were cleaned out within minutes.

It was one of the weirdest demonstrations in the history of the waterfront. I carried the flag, flanked by Joe and Collins and followed by a small army of coopers and dockwallopers, some drunk or feeling no pain. We crossed Twelfth Avenue and started up Forty-sixth Street. The mounted cop who covered the area looked confused and started to tell us we couldn't march without a permit but Collins just pointed to the shouting, angry, drunken mob and said quietly: "Do you want to stop 'em, Officer?"

The cop thought twice and phoned for reinforcements. Three Mickey Mouses arrived with an inspector who was wise enough not to interfere; instead he had his men lead us across town.

The Neighborhood greeted us with cheers. Traffic stopped and heads leaned out the windows of a Ninth Avenue el train. Photographers appeared and reporters interviewed Joe as we marched down Eighth Avenue.

When we arrived at the potato warehouse, the inspector agreed to allow a delegation of two—Joe and myself—to go in and see Freddy. As we entered the dusty old place, Joe whispered to Collins, "When Frank appears at the window start 'em shoutin'."

Freddy had apparently been tipped off about our arrival, and he tried to greet us with a hearty smile and a handshake. But Joe brushed his hand aside.

"We're here for one thing, Freddy. We want a meetin' called—"

"Sure, sure, Joe," Kenton said. "We'll call it for next week. Okay?"

"Bullshit!" Joe said. "We want it called now. In Regan's Hall on Ninth Avenue!"

"I got to see some guys first—"

"Don't wait for the Gimp," Joe told him, "he's in the can."

"You're the president," I told him, "you call the meeting."

"I gotta get the books . . . they're in a bank."

"Bullshit they're in a bank!" Joe snapped. "The *News* says they're in Dewey's office!"

Joe gave me the eye, and I walked over to the window and leaned on the sill. Suddenly there was a roar from the mob.

"Okay. If he won't hold a meetin' maybe Freddy wants to talk to the members," Joe called out.

"Are you nuts?" Freddy cried. "Those guys are loaded!"

I walked menacingly over to the warehouse door.

"Wait a minute," Freddy shouted. He rubbed his stubbled cheeks nervously. "Okay. Okay. I'll call a meetin' tomorrow night at Regan's."

"Eight o'clock on the nose," Joe told him. "We'll put the notice on the piers."

"Yeah. Yeah. Now get those guys out of here, willya?"

Outside Joe told the crowd, "The coopers will hold a meetin' tomorrow night at Regan's Hall. You guys in the other locals better get together and decide what you want to do . . ."

A roar went up from the crowd.

"Okay, get your officers and tell 'em," Joe cried, "like we just told Fat Freddy. We're in the driver's seat now!" He pointed to the waterfront. "Now everybody back to work!" In a whisper he said to me, "Start marchin' with that flag, Frank. We have to get 'em back before there's trouble."

When I started down the street with the flag Joe shouted, his voice as reverent as a bishop's, "Follow the flag, fellas, follow the flag!" Yelling, laughing, and hooting, they ran after me and we marched back to the pier.

"Now that we have a meeting set what will we do with it?" I asked Joe as we walked back to the coopers' shed.

"What the hell do you think we're goin' to do?" he replied. "You and I will elect ourselves president and vice-president of the Brotherhood Coopers, Strappers, and Cargo Binders Union."

Back in the shed we found a worried Bailey and a jubilant Collins.

"Boys, I would never have believed it," Collins kept saying. "It's too good to be true . . ."

"We're gonna hold an election tomorrow night, Jim," Joe said. "Will you help us?"

"Sure. Do you have a slate?"

"What would you say if I ran for president and Frank for vice-president," Joe said, humility just dripping from every word.

"Why not?" Collins said promptly.

"They're kids!" Bailey snorted. "What the hell do they know about runnin' a union?"

"They know enough to get Kenton to call a meetin'," Collins said warmly. "I'd vote for my grandmother if she could do that." To us he added, "You boys have my support."

"I'll run for president, Frank will run for vice-president, and you'll run for treasurer, Jim," Joe said. "We'll nominate Jack for secretary—"

"Not me," Bailey said holding up his hand. "You're not gonna get me. I don't want any part of it."

"What are you afraid of?" I asked Bailey.

"The Gimp," he said promptly. "He'll be out of the box yet. The papers said he'll be arraigned this mornin'. I don't care what bail they set, he'll make it and get out. You wait and see."

"So what?" Joe said. "If he gets tough, Dewey will throw him back in the can and forget where he put the key."

We tore up several cardboard boxes, painted crude signs announcing the meeting, and then Joe and I toured the waterfront, tacking them up on the piers. While the news of the Gimp's arrest had shaken everyone, the racket boys were far from dead; an old carpenter who had urged his fellow coopers to attend the meeting was found in the men's room with a fractured skull and two broken arms. No one objected when our sign was ripped down and tossed in the river.

On our pier, after the first shock waves had died down, the Gimp's Pistoleers passed the word that anyone who attended the meeting would be in trouble. One, a tough young black-haired Hi-Lo driver named Mick tried to run Joe down and when I went for him there were three guys with baling hooks waiting. It was a question of a valorous retreat.

It was also happening on the other piers. When we walked down a string-piece we could smell the old musty fear. We spent all that day and most of the next touring the waterfront, bolstering up the courage of frightened, wavering old men with pleas, promises, and a great many lies. We saw to it a million times during those forty-eight hours that the ghost of Andy Gunnar was summoned up and canonized; a humble, powerful spirit of the past—their friend, their protector, their saint, their myth.

Although we had only a day and a half to electioneer, we reached every cooper's shed: East Side, West Side, and all of Brooklyn. Joe talked until he was hoarse, and the money we spent on booze made a sizable dent in the funds we had brought back from the CCCs. By late afternoon of the second day we were exhausted, exuberant, and superbly confident. We glowed from the handshakes, pats on the back, and promises. We were even interviewed by the labor reporter from the *Tribune*, while the *News* took our picture as we held high a handmade placard. We were invincible.

We decided to get to Regan's at seven, an hour early. As an added precaution, we pooled what money we had left to buy votes if necessary and to give liquid courage to the coopers if any of the Gimp's supporters made an appearance.

When we entered Regan's, Pat, the big bog-jumper of a bartender who usually greeted us with a shout and a quip, was strangely silent. All we got was a nod. The bar was empty.

"Somethin's up," Joe said softly. "Watch yourself." He called out to the bartender, "Any of the boys here yet, Pat?"

Pat, who looked like a witness for a hanging, nodded to the rear where the hall was located. As we passed, he silently pushed his ice bat and ice pick across the bar. Joe slid the bat inside his pants, and I put the ice pick up my sleeve.

In the rear room tables with checkered tablecloths held piles of dirty dishes, several kegs, numerous glasses, and a wicker basket of empty whiskey bottles. Several coopers, some of whom I recognized from other piers, sat stupefied at smaller tables, others were stretched out between chairs; one barely able to stand, sang "The Wearin' of the Green" in a cracked weary voice. On the small raised platform at the end of the hall an orchestra was packing up. Seated at a table near the entrance, as though they were waiting for us were the Gimp and several of his hoods. He pointed indignantly at us as we entered.

310

"How do you like that?" he said loudly, turning around to his grinning hoods. "Here are the guys who kept beggin' us to hold a union meetin', and they show up after it's all over!" He feigned a show of sternness. "You young fellas are not gonna get far in this labor racket if you don't show up for your own meetin's." He shook his head and made a clucking noise with his lips. "We've been waitin' for you guys for hours. Where the hell have you been?"

Collins, who was seated at one of the tables, came over to us.

"The Gimp got out on bail and they called the meeting for four o'clock after you left," he said quietly. "It was all you could eat and drink. Freddy and their slate was reelected. They even told us what the terms will be for the next contract—" Wilson joined us.

"A raise for all you old bastards," Wilson said.

"It's a sellout like before," Collins said.

"Why the hell didn't someone tell us?" Joe said angrily. "You know where Frank lives."

"It would have been worth anyone's life to try to tip you off, Joe," Collins said. He added bitterly. "They herded us like sheep from the piers and brought us here."

"Why didn't you tell that to the goddam dick from Dewey's office who was on my tail all afternoon?" Wilson demanded.

"Not me, Johnny," Collins said shaking his head. "You heard what I told him; this was a duly run union election and Mr. Kenton was elected president by acclamation." To us he said wearily, "One of Dewey's men was up here, but Wilson's attorney had a writ to keep him out of the hall until the election was over." He shrugged. "They elected Kenton and that's what we told him."

"Listen to the way a good union man talks," Wilson said with a sneer, "always supportin' his union."

We stood there stunned as if we had been hit by a two-by-four.

"So all you old sons of bitches sold out?" Joe said bitterly. "You got down and kissed his ass!"

Collins nodded. "One by one, Joe. There's no denyin' it."

"Now it's your turn, bigmouth," Wilson said. He stood up and fumbled with the buckle of his belt. "A nice little kiss on each cheek and we'll be friends again . . ."

"I'll see you in hell first, Gimpy," Joe said.

Wilson's face hardened. "Break their legs if they won't kneel down," he told his Pistoleers.

When they started around the table Joe slipped the bat from inside his pants and I held the pick, needle tip out like a good street fighter.

"At least we'll get one of you bastards," Joe told him. "Maybe you can explain to Dewey what happened . . ."

Wilson hesitated, then waved back his goons. He understood this logic.

"Okay, wise guys. Just don't walk under any ladders."

It had all come about as Pepe had predicted. The Gimp had raised his $75,000 bail and engaged the best criminal lawyer in the city who insisted that Wilson made his living from a waterfront trucking business and had a legitimate reason to be on the piers. At one of his court appearances Dewey's assistant tried to get the court to forbid Wilson to appear on the piers. But after his attorneys produced books, records, and affidavits from prominent shippers showing the need for Wilson's cooperation to move the vital cargo now pouring overseas, permission was granted.

The Gimp's victory wasn't lost on the waterfront. Joe and I began to feel like lepers ringing their bells; I barely got a decent hello when I delivered the supplies. Only Collins remained friendly. Bailey told us bluntly that the less he saw of us the safer he felt.

Fat Freddy Kenton was intolerable. He never failed to swagger into the coopers' shed before the quitting whistle to tell us to keep our noses clean.

"Somehow we'll take care of that slob," Joe promised.

As the days passed, Pepe's strategy became evident to me: he was waiting for our phone call, he knew it was only a question of time.

28 THE ACCIDENT

Joe refused to acknowledge defeat. After the meeting, he insisted on switching with me and delivering the supplies for a few weeks so he could continue to harangue the coopers. I thought it curious at the time that the West Side and East Side piers, traditionally Irish, were frightened of, even hostile, to Joe, while the dockwallopers on the Brooklyn waterfront dominated by the Italians were friendly and even protective.

"Every time I go over there two guys are always walkin' behind me," Joe told me, a puzzled look on his face. "When I asked them what they were doin', they just gave me a shrug."

"Maybe Pepe sent word over."

"Maybe. Maybe he wants to make sure nothin' happens to his truck."

A few days later when we arrived at the wastepaper factory to collect the truck, we discovered we were indeed under Pepe's protective wing. The young paper handler who usually gave us our pay envelope on Friday night silently pointed to two hard-faced men dressed rather formally in blue suits.

"You guys are gonna deliver to Brooklyn today," one told us.

"Why Brooklyn?" Joe asked. "We finished those deliveries yesterday. This week we work our own pier and down to Chelsea."

The man just shook his head. "Brooklyn this week, kid. Get goin'."

"Who said so?" I asked.

The hard dark face turned to me. "The guy you work for. Now get goin'."

We stayed in Brooklyn all that week, moving aimlessly from pier to pier until quitting time, then driving back to Cherry Street. When we finally returned to our pier on the West Side, we could taste the tension in the coopers' shed.

"Where were you last week?" Collins asked.

"Workin' Brooklyn," Joe replied. "Why?"

"It was just as well you were out of here. Two guys we had never seen before were working the hoists. One of the coopers from Chelsea sent us word they were a couple of outlaws the Gimp used as muscle men. This cooper said two years ago they killed a checker that was givin' the Gimp a hard time."

I asked, "How did they do that?"

Collins looked worried. "On the waterfront you can always say, 'I'm sorry . . . please boys—watch out.' "

Even Bailey went out of his way to warn us.

"I don't want to see anyone get hurt, especially some-one workin' in my shed," he told me, "but your friend has a big loud mouth and he's made a lot of people mad at him."

The black-haired Mick on the Hi-Lo seemed to take delight in swooping down on us, the twin forks of his machine pointed like charging spears, then to spin away at the last moment. But whenever we moved toward him there was the silent trio of dockwallopers with their curved baling hooks, waiting.

"I'll get that black Irish bastard if it's the last thing I do," Joe raged.

I had all I could do to stop him from taking all three. As Collins told me, that was what they were hoping for . . .

Then it happened. One morning we got into a shouting argument with the Mick and his three protectors and it took Collins and the nervous boss checker to break it up.

"For crissakes, will you guys take a ride to Brooklyn?" the checker whispered. "Johnny's back there takin' it all in."

Standing in front of the office were Wilson and his henchmen. Joe turned away, stopped for a moment as if debating with himself, then spun about. He made a funnel of his hands around his mouth and, before I could stop him, he had shouted:

"Next time, Gimpy, we'll shove those books."

"Joe! Are you nuts?" I told him. "What are you doing?"

"I'm sick and tired of waitin'," he said grimly, "now it's his move."

It took Wilson four days. During that time he vanished from the pier and even Mick stayed away from us. There was a tense air of expectancy about the stringpiece; every-one seemed to be holding his breath, waiting. Then, early one morning after a liner had tied up, fishnets dipped in and out emptying the holds. When Mick dropped two crates at the door of the shed and yelled for us to bring the four-wheeler to get some more, I thought nothing of it. I joined Joe and together we pushed the cumbersome wagon down the pier.

"Hey, we got company this time," Joe exclaimed. I looked around and was surprised to see Collins trotting behind.

"Want a ride, Jim?" I shouted, "hop on," but he waved a refusal.

As we came to the unloading spot, an emptied fishnet

swung up revealing two smashed barrels. We lifted both onto the four-wheeler and started back to the coopers' shed when someone whistled. It was the Mick. He was pointing to two smaller broken crates at the base of a wall of heavy cargo waiting to be loaded on the barges for the Jersey terminals. Joe automatically swung the wagon around and headed for them, and I followed. The Hi-Lo jockey watched us approach, made a sharp U-turn, and vanished behind the crates and boxes. The Mick's unexpected disappearance made me apprehensive. I glanced qiuckly around the pier, and then scanned the towering wall of crates and boxes. I could see that the top level was askew.

"Hey Jim," I called out to Collins who was ahead of me and just behind Joe, "we better get away from those crates."

Collins was quicker, smarter, and more experienced with the deadly ways of the waterfront than I was. He glanced up and yelled at Joe who stopped, dropped the handle of the four-wheeler, and looked around in surprise just as something smashed into the rear of the wall. It was like slow motion. First the top crates swayed forward, then the whole wall was falling. Collins, who was only a few feet from Joe, plunged forward, both arms thrust out. He hit Joe and pushed him to one side, but the momentum kept Collins lurching forward. He slipped and recovered his stride, but it was too late. I could only catch a glimpse of his pale, freckled face and tonsure of faded reddish hair as the barrels came down. He was looking up and his face was calm.

He knew what hit him.

There was a roar, and the pier trembled as the wall tumbled down, became a large mound of scattered boxes and crates that had held plumbing supplies. When the dust started to rise, the pier still echoed with the sounds of the dull rumble as every dockwalloper on the stringpiece began clawing away at the debris. Checkers' whistles frantically summoned Hi-Los and hoists.

I wish we hadn't found him. The only recognizable parts were the brown work shirt and pants. Someone quickly threw a tarpaulin over him while another yelled to get a priest from St. Barnabas. The waterfront is realistic about these things; anyone in that condition needs a priest, not an ambulance.

"Jim! Jim! Is he all right?" Bailey shouted as he ran up.

As I pulled him away, I saw Joe out of the corner of my eye grab a pinch bar and scramble over the broken boxes. His target was Mick who was still seated on his Hi-Lo, explaining what had happened to the shouting boss checker and a group of milling longshoremen. When he saw Joe, he leaped down from his machine and ran toward the front of the pier. Joe's first blow caught him across the back; you could hear the grunt of pain the length of the pier. He staggered but kept going. Joe stayed at his heels, raising the iron club for a blow that would have shattered his skull. Before Joe could swing, I caught him by his shirt collar, spun him around, and wrestled him to the ground as Mick staggered up to the office where he fell at the feet of his three protectors who waited with their baling hooks.

"Joe! Don't be a fool," I shouted in his ear. "That's what they're waiting for. They'll rip us apart!"

"Okay," he said, panting. "We'll take care of them some other time." He thrust his hand in his dungarees and came out with a handful of change.

"What are you doing?"

"Lookin' for a nickel. I have to make a phone call."

29 PEPE'S WAY

How do you plan to commit a murder? In the Neighborhood you hone a blade, buy a cheap revolver in the Eighth Avenue pawnshop or know your enemy's daily routine so well that the falling chimney finds it target. But Pepe's way was different. Joe spoke to him for only a few seconds. He listened, said he understood, and hung up. We just had to wait.

The death of Jim Collins produced a brief flurry of official action. After the precinct cops had left and the morgue wagon attendants had shoveled the remains into a body bag, Captain Elliott appeared.

"How did it really happen?" he asked Joe.

316

"There's no mystery," Joe replied. "Some crates fell, a guy was passin', and he was hit."

"Where was Wilson when all this happened?"

"The Gimp?" How would we know?" Joe said with a great show of indignation. "We haven't seen that bum in weeks."

"His lawyers raised hell with the court to get him back to the pier," Elliott pointed out. "He's here every day, but he's not around when Collins is killed. Doesn't that mean anything to you?"

"Why should it? We're not cops."

"Collins worked with both of you . . ."

"A lot of people work with us," Joe said blandly.

"Don't give me any of that waterfront crap, Gunnar," Elliott said roughly. "He was with you and Howell when you marched the longshoremen over to Kenton's warehouse . . ."

"What are you trying to prove?" I asked him.

"Anything that will help me get Wilson's bail revoked," Elliott said grimly. "Will you help me?"

Joe gave him a look of contempt. "Drop dead, cop."

Following the waterfront tradition, the pier closed down the morning of the funeral and the beer container of contributions was given to a niece from Bensonhurst. In a week Collins was forgotten.

Some of the dockwallopers accepted the Hi-Lo driver's story of a tragic accident; those that didn't, kept their mouths shut, they had no choice. All the firm resolutions and the promises to fight the Gimp's rule had vanished the moment those crates had fallen on Collins. The Gimp didn't have to say a word or make a threat. He toured the piers as confidently as before; shippers, checkers, coopers, and longshoremen continued to view him as the undisputed boss of New York's waterfront.

When we left in the afternoon the Gimp was always in the doorway of the pier's front office. He never failed to call out for the amusement of the circle of his young hoods: "Let us know where to get in touch with you fellows—we want to make sure you're on time for the next meeting!"

It was a cat and mouse game; he knew it, we knew it, the pier knew it.

"I wish you guys would move over to Brooklyn," Bailey said one day. "You're makin' me nervous."

"How are we making you nervous?" I demanded. "We're doing our job."

"That you are but I don't want my sister collectin' my life insurance!"

Joe dropped the hammer he was using. "What do you mean by that, Jack?"

"Just what I said," he said nervously. "Everybody knows the Gimp is after you and Frank and sooner or later he'll get you—just like he got Jim. I just don't want to be around when it happens." He said pleadingly, "Look, go over to Brooklyn or Staten Island, why don't you? Work out of a pier over there . . ."

"We're stayin' here," Joe said bluntly.

"I wish I had never seen you," he said bitterly. "You've been nothin' but trouble from the day you started."

When we went out on the pier, we kept an eye on the Hi-Lo driver but he avoided us; the Gimp's boys with the baling hooks were never far from his machine.

Once, when we were passing, Joe turned to him.

"Someday I'm comin' lookin' for you," he told Mick who put his fingers to his mouth like a trumpet to give us a Bronx cheer. His three protectors thought it was very funny.

"Did you see that Irish bastard spit in my face?" Joe raged. "Did you see him? Do you know why he did it? Because we're nothin' that's why—we're just dirt under his feet. But if we had the muscle he'd be on his knees, tippin' his hat when we passed. Crissakes, don't give me any more of that crap about Pepe ownin' us! So what if he owns us? Let him take care of the Gimp and we're home! Then leave that Mick to me."

After two weeks had passed and nothing had happened I was relieved. But Joe became a raging fury under the banter of the Gimp, the sneers of the Hi-Lo driver, and the apprehensive looks of the dockwallopers on the stringpiece.

Especially after the second "accident."

He was pushing a four-wheeler up to a loaded patten to pick up some damaged cargo when the fishnet's hawser slipped. Anyone who has worked the docks knows the warning—the whirring noise of missing gears in the hoist's big drum—so Joe had plenty of time to jump clear before the fishnet crashed. The operator was a stranger. It took the boss checker and some of the stevedores to keep Joe from rushing the operator who just sat there, chewing thoughtfully on the stub of a cigar. He was big, built of pig iron, and would have crippled Joe if he laid his hands on him.

"Still carryin' around your hoseshoe, kid?" Wilson called out as he drove by. This time Joe didn't bother to answer.

"I'm givin' Pepe until the end of this week," he told me.

"Then what?"

"I'll take care of that bum myself," he said. "It's a question of him or us . . ."

Joe only had to wait until the next day. When we arrived in the morning to pick up the truck the two hard-faced men in blue suits were waiting.

"Be here at eight o'clock tonight," one told us.

"What's up?" Joe asked.

"There's a meeting."

When we arrived that evening Pepe and the Blue Suiters were waiting in the factory's tiny office. The third man was a surprise—Lorenzo. He only nodded when we said hello.

The room was dirty. The floor was covered with scraps of paper, and the walls were decorated with ancient rotogravure pictures of girls in bathing suits. Around the wall telephone were numerous numbers scrawled in pencil and crayon. There was a large window that looked out on the open floor, but its panes were coated with dust and grime. A sagging couch and an old-fashioned kerosene stove completed the room's furnishings. Pepe silently waved us to the couch; this time there were no amenities.

"The cripple and the fat pig will soon be here."

"Fat Freddy?" I asked.

"*Si.* I have spoken to them."

Joe gave me a bewildered look. "Why would they come here?"

"There is an arrangement to be made."

"For the pier?"

"*Si.* When we first took over the contract from the government, we told the cripple he would be our partner. He wants more money." He looked almost sorrowful. "It is not good to have a partner who puts a gun to your head . . ."

"So what will you tell him?" Joe asked.

"We are no longer partners," Pepe said blandly. "Last night he sent his gangsters to the club and they saw Gus—"

He made a pistol of his thumb and forefinger and pointed it to his temple.

"They showed the gun and made many foolish threats."

"What about that guy outside Gus's office?" Joe said.

Pepe looked thoughtful. "The cripple paid him."

"What did you do—fire him?" Joe asked.

Pepe looked up at him with a faint smile.

"*Si*. He is no longer with us."

The two Blue Suiters guffawed; even Lorenzo smiled.

Pepe put up his hand.

"But there is something else the cripple wants . . ."

"What is that, Pepe?"

"Another arrangement," he said carefully.

"For the pier? I thought you said—"

"No. No. The pier is finished. The arrangement is for you, Joe." Pepe glanced over at me. "And Peppino. You are trouble to the cripple. He wants you killed."

The easy nonchalant manner with which he said it startled me.

"The Gimp wants us killed?"

"Tomorrow when you come here for the truck—poof! You and Joe are dead." He said in his soft, ominous voice, "The cripple"—he motioned with his hand to the giant paper baler outside the door—"suggests that."

"Why would the Gimp believe you would have us killed?" Joe asked, trying to keep his voice from trembling.

"You work for us. You make trouble for him. We are partners. Who else would he go to?"

I managed a weak smile. "What do you intend to do, Pepe—have us killed?"

"Why do you make jokes, Peppino?" he said sternly. "It is no time for jokes."

"You still haven't told us what you intend to do," Joe pointed out.

Pepe gave him a look of surprise. *Ecco!* What is there to do, my young friend? We will do what you asked us to do—kill the cripple, the fat one, and their people. *Marrone!* What would you have me do—kiss that *pòrco diavolo!*" He turned to me with a sigh. "Peppino, did I not tell you this would happen?"

"The bastard's been tryin' to get us on the pier," Joe said.

Pepe gave him a pitying look.

"Do you think the cripple is a *stùpido?* He was playing

with you. He laughed when he told us, 'Every night I make the kids change their underwear'." He muttered something in Italian to Lorenzo who left with one of the Blue Suiters.

"Tonight you will see that Lorenzo is a master," Pepe said proudly.

"A master at what?" I asked.

"You will see," he said quietly. He started out but stopped at the doorway. "Ah, Peppino. Did I tell you about the Delacroix sketch?"

When I shook my head like a mute, he rubbed his hands together.

"The owner is a fool who has sold his soul to the horses. I have spoken to the shylocks and an arrangement has been made." He shrugged. "It is only an oil sketch but it is still a Delacroix. No, Peppino?"

Then he went out with the Blue Suiter.

Joe and I stared dumbly at each other.

"Holy Christ," Joe whispered. "He's goin' to kill somebody and he talks about buyin' a paintin'! What kind of a guy is he, Frank?"

I couldn't begin to offer him a description; what I had just heard was incomprehensible. All I wanted to do was run.

"They're really going to kill the Gimp and Freddy, Joe."

"It looks like that . . ."

"I don't want any part of it—I'm getting out of here."

"What are you going to do—just walk out?"

"You're damn right I am! You coming?"

He hesitated. "No."

I stared at him. "Do you want to watch them kill those guys?"

"The Gimp needs killin'," he said savagely. "It's either him or us. Do you think he'd come down to this hole if it wasn't to take care of us? Didn't you hear what Pepe said—we're trouble to that guy. We have to go."

"But Freddy's only a big fat slob, Joe."

"Yeah. But a fat slob comin' down with his boss to make sure we're knocked off." He added softly, "Look at it this way, Frank—if Pepe takes care of the Gimp and Freddy that leaves no one else but us! Those old guys will be so scared they'll wet their pants if we look cross-eyed at 'em." He leaned over and gripped my arm. "This is our chance, Frank, to take over their crappy union. Then we can move into another one and then another—"

I shook off his hand. "If they do this for us—they'll own us. I told you I don't want—"

Blue Suiter was standing in the doorway glowering at us.

"What you guys yellin' for? Shut up and sit down."

I'll never know how long we sat on the battered couch. It could have been fifteen minutes or an hour. I had lost all sense of time. Every part of me was alert for the first sound, the first familiar slamming of the tin-sheathed door, the first footsteps, the first sound of voices. There was only the silence. Then it began raining, and we could hear the gurgling of a broken rainpipe in the alley and could feel the cool wet night air that came through the broken window overhead.

Even though we were expecting it, the slamming of the heavy street door sounded like a bomb in the cavernous building. Both of us jumped.

"That's the Gimp," Joe said. I could hear him cautiously answer Pepe's loud and jovial greeting. Joe made a circle in the grimy pane, stared out, then silently made room for me.

The Gimp, two of his young hoods from the pier, and Freddy Kenton were standing in the center of the large room, their raincoats glistening in the stark white light of the naked bulb that dangled overhead. A smiling, immaculately dressed Pepe faced them. Wilson, who seemed angry, was doing most of the talking in a low voice. Finally Pepe turned and waved to Blue Suit at the door.

"The boss wants you," he told us.

We followed him outside to stand alongside Pepe. Wilson looked tense and angry. Kenton, obviously frightened, smiled uncertainly at us and rubbed the stubble on his chin. The two bodyguards who kept their hands in their pockets were plainly apprehensive. They kept glancing from Pepe to the two Blue Suits. For the first time I noticed Lorenzo had disappeared.

Wilson angrily demanded, "Why did you bring 'em here for?"

Pepe put on a good show of looking stunned.

"My friend, you wanted to talk about the arrangement—no?"

"I changed my mind," Wilson said quickly. "We can talk about it tomorrow. I'll see you on the pier."

Pepe gestured to us. "What about these bad boys?" he asked, almost jovially.

Wilson was obviously uneasy and impatient to leave. He kept looking from Pepe to one of the Blue Suiters who sat on a bale, plucking at ribbons of colored paper that dangled between his legs.

"You do what you want, wop. Anything is okay with me."

He turned to go but Pepe raised his voice. "No wine? No talk?"

"No. No. I don't want any wine. I'll be seein' ya."

"*Animale!* You refuse my wine?" Pepe called out.

"Shove the wine up your ass," Wilson exploded. "I told you I don't want any."

"The boss wants to know whaddaya want us to do about these two guys," Blue Suit on the paper bale called out. His unexpected rasping voice made me jump.

Wilson said over his shoulder, "Let him do what he wants." In an undertone, he said to Freddy and his hoods, "Let's get out of here."

"Aw, what the hell, Johnny, they're only kids," Freddy protested, but Wilson swung around and slapped him across the face with the back of his hand. "Shut up!"

"So, cripple, you don't want to talk?" Pepe called out as Wilson limped toward the door. The Gimp's two young Pistoleers, smelling the danger, kept their eyes on Blue Suit who was studiously rolling the paper ribbons into tiny balls between his palms.

"My people don't want you as a partner anymore, cripple," Pepe told him.

Wilson turned and looked at Pepe. "That's all right with me, wop. You go your way—I'll go mine . . ."

He broke off as Pepe started to remove his jacket.

We all watched, hypnotized by the careful attention he gave to the garment. He held it up, folded it, and placed it across a paper bale. Then he removed his heavy gold cuff links and rolled back the starched cuffs, revealing powerful hairy wrists.

Wilson's hoods looked questioningly at their boss. The dangerous incongruity of the whole scene apparently had reached Wilson. His pouched eyes were now only slits in his strained face. He muttered something to his two hoods and slid a gun from his raincoat pocket.

"You try anything and there'll be a wop goin' to hell without a High Mass," he said.

"Why do you show me a gun?" Pepe cried. "Do we give you trouble? You ask for more money and we said to come and talk about the arrangement."

Sorrowfully, almost melancholy, Pepe approached Wilson, his hands outstretched.

"My friend—we offer you wine and you curse us."

"We're gettin' out of here," Wilson snapped. Now he seemed more confident. "We don't want to talk, wop. Okay? Maybe some other time."

"You want to go—you go," Pepe said and motioned to the door.

"That's just what we're gonna do," Wilson said and slid the gun back into his pocket. Followed by Freddy and the two worried-looking hoods, he headed toward the overhead door that led to Cherry Street.

"Wait! I will press the button," Pepe called out and hurried across the room to the large black button on the wall that electrically raised the heavy door used by the trucks.

There was a rumbling noise. The corrugated door shook, then slowly started to rise. Almost automatically, the four men looked up.

Then came a series of sharp coughing sounds from overhead. One of the bodyguards staggered against the door and slowly slid to the floor. The other whirled around and pulled his gun out of his coat pocket. Then, suddenly, he jerked over, held his stomach, and tried to make his way along a row of paper-filled burlap bags. There were two more coughing sounds and he staggered and fell. Wilson had his gun out, frantically looking for a target when another cough made him drop it, scream, and clutch his arm. Freddy, one hand still rubbing his doughy, sweaty face, kept backing away from Wilson until he was stopped by a wall. He stood there, on the verge of hysteria.

A figure that had been sprawled across the top of a huge pile of bales rose to one knee. It was Lorenzo, unscrewing a silencer from the barrel of a gun. Wilson, his thick shoe making a weird, clopping sound on the concrete floor, ran across the room to a smaller door that also led to the street. From behind one of the bales came the second Blue Suiter who stood in his path. When Wilson awkwardly tried to dodge, he lashed out with his foot. The kick caught Wilson in the side and he fell. The enforcer contemptuously dragged him to his feet and pushed him toward Pepe. The Gimp clutched his arm to his side and I could see the blood running down his fingers and onto his raincoat.

"Wait a minute, wop," he said hoarsely, "we can—"

Pepe's hand on his throat shut off the words. Wilson clawed at the fingers and tried to walk back, his head arched high, his eyes staring, his mouth opening and closing like a beached fish.

From his perch on top of the bales Lorenzo studied the frightening tableau for a few moments, then slid down and vanished.

The stubby fingers were now buried in the soft flesh of the Gimp's neck. His eyes, filled with terror and staring down at the smaller Pepe, looked ready to pop out of his skull. His face first flushed, then slowly turned a deep red, finally purplish, as foam bubbled from between his lips.

Pepe turned his head. "Peppino! Joe! See what I have for you!" he cried, his eyes glowing like coals in a grate. He stepped aside and gently shook the Gimp as if to admonish the lifeless figure.

"So now the cripple is quiet," he said finally and let go.

The dead man crumpled like a pile of clothes, his head crashing to the floor like a dropped melon.

I kept swallowing desperately but the bile came up with a rush and arched from my mouth across the floor. I clung to a post, my stomach heaving until my throat was raw. When I looked up, Joe was still standing there, his fists clenched at his side, his chalk-white face shining with a sheen of sweat as he stared down at the Gimp. There was a sickening smell of excrement as a trickle ran from the Gimp's fly.

"*Figlio di butana!* You wet your pants, cripple," Pepe said mockingly. When he saw me he cried, "Peppino! You are sick!"

He gave an order to one of the Blue Suiters who went into the office and returned with a shot glass of what I thought was water.

"Drink it, kid," Blue Suit said with a laugh. "It will take the shit out of your blood."

It was water laced with fire. It exploded in the pit of my stomach and sent tendrils of flame along my blood-stream, making my eyes water. But it did make me feel better; at least it stopped the heaving of my stomach.

"Grappa," Blue Suit explained. "A real wop drink." He said to Joe, "Want some, kid?"

Joe just shook his head.

A wail, so filled with terror that it raised the hair on the back of my head, suddenly rose in the still warehouse. There I saw Freddy Kenton, now on his knees in the center of the room, his hands clasped in front of him, slowly rocking back and forth.

"Oh, my God," he kept screaming. "Oh, my God!"

Pepe who had slipped into his jacket was finishing snapping the cuff links back into his cuffs.

"No, no," he said soothingly as he walked toward Freddy. "There is nothing to worry about, my friend."

He smiled and held out both his hands, muttering solicitously as if to help the terrorized man to his feet. Freddy, a hesitant smile on his tear-streaked face, eagerly reached up. As Pepe grabbed the pudgy hands Lorenzo, a lasso of thick picture wire in one hand, tiptoed from behind the bales. The wire whispered through the air, the noose settling neatly around Freddy's fat neck. As Pepe jerked Freddy to him, Lorenzo slammed his foot into the helpless man's back and pulled his deadly lasso taut. Pepe, still smiling and whispering softly, put his knee on Freddy's chest and using it as a lever, pulled the big man to him as Lorenzo, his saturnine olive face impassive, unemotionally bulldogged Freddy to death.

As the wire quickly vanished into the thick fleshy folds the whole ghastly scene was reenacted again; the purplish face, the pleading bulging eyes, the swollen tongue like a cylinder of freshly ground meat stuck between the lips.

Freddy died quickly. Pepe let go and the body slumped over, Lorenzo still holding to his deadly lasso.

"Like a cowboy in the movies, Lorenzo," Pepe cried. "Is he not a master, Peppino?"

There was a series of loud rubbery noises and one of the Blue Shirts called out:

"Hey Dom! Fat ass is fartin' in hell."

They both laughed uproariously.

When one of the Blue Shirts walked over to the body of the Gimp and threw a chain around one leg, Pepe called out sharply:

"Prima di aversi fatte ossa . . ."

The hood dropped the chain. "The boss says you gotta make your bones . . ." He jerked his thumb at the door of the baler. "You're gonna help these guys be part of next week's funny papers . . ."

He said to Joe, "You too . . ."

"No," I whispered, "No . . ."

"Peppino," Pepe ordered in that soft deadly voice, "make your bones."

"Come on, Frank," Joe said hoarsely. "We have to do it."

He walked over to Wilson's body and picked up the chain attached to the leg. I forced myself to grab one end of the raincoat. We pulled the body to the baler, leaving behind a trail of blood. The enforcer named Dom swung open the heavy door.

"Okay, in with the bastard."

We pushed the dead man into the machine's gaping mouth. It slid gently into the shredded paper leaving one neat black shoe, now smeared with grease and dust, sticking up like a marker. Both Blue Suiters dragged over burlap bags of paper and kept stuffing them into the machine until it overflowed.

"Now he becomes part of the 'Katzenjammer Kids,'" Dom shouted as he slammed the door and threw the switch. The iron monster came to life, its insides heaving and clanking. I closed my eyes and told myself it couldn't be true.

The machine slowly ground to a halt. It shuddered once and then spewed out a large compressed crimson-flecked bale of paper bound with copper wire. I swallowed hard when I saw the strips of a tan raincoat.

Dom turned and pointed to Freddy. "Okay, get that fat pig in here," and threw us a chain.

I closed my eyes to avoid looking into the swollen, purplish face and glazed staring eyes as we dragged the dead weight to the machine. His body was too big for the opening and Dom impatiently jammed it with an iron rod, like a furnace tender, until it vanished into the paper. It was too much for me and I vomited again, the raw grappa making me gasp. When I looked up this time, Joe was leaning against the baler, sweat glistening like a handful of water flung into his dead-white face.

Burlap bags of paper were forced into the machine and again it came to life, savagely clanking and churning until, with a gulp, it cast off its wirebound bale.

Wilson's two gunmen came next. Then the four bales were lifted by a block and tackle into a truck that was loaded with scrap paper. A tarpaulin was flung across the top and tied down.

Pepe silently beckoned and we followed him into the office. I was so weak and trembling I almost fell down on the couch. He filled two glasses with grappa and pushed them toward us. When I shook my head he briskly ordered: "Drink. Drink. You're not little boys anymore!"

I forced down the fiery liquor, so strong it made me shudder.

Pepe looked from me to Joe.

"So. Now the cripple and his fat pig are gone. Are you glad, my young friends?"

I found it difficult to talk, my voice was hoarse and the words were slurred.

"We were crazy to come here . . ."

"How did you think it would be, Peppino?" he asked mildly. "It was necessary to kill them or else they would have killed you."

"But Holy Christ, Pepe!" Joe whispered. "To put them in that . . ."

Pepe answered with a shrug. "A few hours in the vats and they will be gone."

"The funny papers, Don Vitone," Dom said with a giggle.

Pepe ignored him and continued to study us.

"You called and asked for help. Did I not answer you?" He looked over at me. "Is this not true, Peppino? Did you not ask Pepe for justice?"

When I remained silent he leaned across the table and his voice rose slightly. "Yes, Peppino?"

"Yes," I said with an effort.

"What are friends for?" he said expansively, "if not to help one another?"

"Did you have to bring us here to watch it? Why couldn't you have . . ." Joe began but his words died off when Pepe glared at him.

"You said you were men and you would fight like men. Now you act like women. You see pigs killed and you want to run away and hide!" His voice was as rough as a saw cutting through ice. "Like men you must kill your enemy before he kills you. *Stùpido!* Do you want to run around the pier while they drop crates on your head? Would you rather be in the machine? Would you rather have Lorenzo's wire around your neck? This is what brought the cripple here. You, Peppino! You, Joe! *Marrone!* You can thank us he did not squash you like bugs."

328

"We know that and we're grateful, Pepe," Joe said, "but Freddy—he was just a slob—"

"*Si*, a slob," Pepe said coldly. "But if Lorenzo did not play with him like a cowboy he would be babbling to the cops tomorrow." He waved his hand. "He was more dangerous to us than the cripple . . ."

"What do we do now?" Joe asked.

Pepe looked startled. "Joe, you are a fool. The union belongs to you and Peppino!"

"We take it over, just like that?"

"Don't worry, kid, when these two bums don't show up with their shooters tomorrow the Gimp's boys will know what happened," Dom said with a chuckle. "All you have to do is—"

"*Silenzio!*" Pepe snapped. "You have a tongue like an old woman."

The tough, cold-blooded hood became flustered, almost frightened, as he mumbled apologies under Pepe's hard stare.

I said quickly, "So we just walk in and take over?"

"It is how you wanted it, Peppino," Pepe said quietly. "Now it is your union and the old men belong to you and Joe."

I repeated his favorite: "One hand washes the other, Pepe. What do we have to do for you?"

"Perhaps someday we will call upon you and Joe to do us a service, Peppino," he said casually. "A year? Two years?" He shrugged. "That day may never come." He added contemptuously, "Do we hold a gun to your head like the cripple's gangsters? No. No. We are your friends."

"Friends we don't even know . . ."

Pepe answered softly, "Tonight they helped you have your justice, Pepino. Not the kind you got from the cops. Not the words of the old whores in their black robes who kiss the behinds of the politicians." He pointed at me and Joe. "You and Joe. You were the law. I, a friend of your friends, helped you. That is all." He pushed back the chair, stretched and yawned. "Now we go home."

He snapped the orders to Dom: "Take care of the floor then take Joe home," and to the other hood, "You will drive me and Peppino."

When Pepe and I left, Dom was using a hose to wash the pools of blood across the dirty cement floor while the other hood swept the red-stained water into a drain. Both were whistling. When Pepe grunted impatiently the hood with the broom dropped it and ran across the room and opened the door that led to the street. Outside he vanished in a nearby alley to reappear driving the Cord. He swung into the curb and, like a royal chauffeur, jumped out to open the door and stand at ramrod attention. I slid down on the leather seat almost automatically. My brain was numb; it held only one picture—the truck and its tarpaulin cover.

I believe that I have never felt more helpless, hopeless, and pathetic than I did at that moment. Swaggering talk of murder was one thing; to have been part of it was impossible . . .

We rode uptown in the Cord. It was in the early hours of the morning and the rain had stopped and had left the streets glistening ribbons of tar. Pepe ordered us dropped off on Lexington near Seventieth. At the corner newsstand he bought the morning papers, joking in immigrant English with the dealer. He could have been a jovial well-dressed waiter on his way home after a tip-filled night. I followed him down the quiet street to a brownstone; he didn't have to ring the bell, Lorenzo silently opened the heavy grilled door as we mounted the steps.

"Lorenzo! Look who is here?" Pepe said enthusiastically. "Our friend Peppino."

I stepped into a deep hall that had a bronze Peter Pan playing on pipes, mounted on a pedestal.

Pepe said briskly, "it is a thing of nothing. The English are not good in bronze." He ran his hand over the statue. "Look, Peppino. No detail! No feeling! Even the Americans are better. *Marrone!* You could buy it in a five and ten cent store." He stepped back, studied the statue for a moment, then handed the newspapers to the silent Lorenzo and waved me upstairs.

The room we entered on the second floor appeared to be a combination gallery and office. There were several paintings on the wall, one the Eakins fight scene I had seen on my first visit to the gallery.

Lorenzo served us a tray with trimmed sandwiches of spiced Neapolitan ham, a silver pot of coffee, and goblets of brandy, the first I had ever tasted.

"Hold it like this, Peppino," he said grasping the glass in two hands. "Let the blood warm the brandy."

I hastily took a taste. It was a thousand times more delicate than the harsh, almost savage, grappa, but it had as much potency. I could feel the sweat beading my
330

forehead. Pepe grabbed a sandwich and waved me to eat. I told myself I would never again be able to swallow, but surprisingly after the first bite I discovered I was ravenously hungry. We ate and drank in silence until Pepe had filled our tiny cups with espresso laced with anisette.

"So, Peppino," he said with a smile. "What do you say to Pepe?"

"My God," I blurted out. "What kind of rules do you people play?"

"Rules?" He gave me a cold smile. "Why do you talk of rules like a little boy? There's only one rule in this game, Peppino," he said quietly. "Whoever is the strongest wins."

"Did it have to be this way?"

"Do you think we are priests who balance right and wrong?" He went on relentlessly, "Do you think I want to kill people in front of the loudmouths I pay a hundred dollars a week"—he laughed harshly—"to protect me? Could I not have had them killed in the street?"

"Then why did you bring us down there?"

"To show you our justice, Peppino," he said coolly, "and so you could make your bones."

"Christ Almighty!" I cried. "Do we have to dip our hands in blood for you?"

"*Si*," was the quiet answer, "that is the way."

We studied each other for a long moment, then he said: "There is a price for everything, Peppino." He held up his hands palms out. "It is the world."

"It makes us the same, the same as you."

"Not yet, Peppino," he said grimly. "Not yet."

He leaned back in his chair and clasped his hands across his belt. "Tomorrow your enemies will be part of the funny papers."

"Killing people doesn't seem to worry you, Pepe."

"We were brought up differently, Peppino. In our world there were never any good Samaritans. I was taught to keep oneself strictly to oneself. Never hear the shot fired at night. Never see who runs down the alley. Turn away from the body in the gutter. When your enemy seeks to kill you, keep your own counsel, but get him first." He finished his coffee and delicately wiped his lips. "There is one thing you must never forget—only have witnesses you can trust with your life . . ."

"You have it all thought out for us, haven't you?"

"A long time ago, when I first met you with Nicky, I told myself you would fit our mold, Peppino. Also your

331

friend Joe. You are not important to us today—perhaps tomorrow you will be. I think many times of your police union idea, Peppino, many times."

"Perhaps it's only a wild dream, Pepe."

"So? How many wild dreams have men turned into reality? Me and you, Peppino—someday we will make it come true. No? You must never forget the police." He leaned across the table. "You have seen an ant, Peppino? He takes away a crumb. Then another and another. When you look down you say, *Marrone!* that little ant has taken all the bread! That's the way it should be. Every day, every month, you get a little something from the cops. Maybe names. Good cops. Bad cops. Someday we will need them . . ."

"I have been doing that for a long time."

"Buòno! Buòno!" he said delighted, "you are like an ant, no?"

At the moment the police, the union, weren't important —only the scene in the warehouse still crowding my brain.

"Pepe, a little while ago you said you must never have witnesses."

"Si."

"What about Joe and me?"

He said softly, "I trust you."

"Your two men in the blue suits . . ."

He shrugged silently.

For a moment I didn't realize what he was telling me; then I suddenly knew.

"My God, Pepe, you don't intend to kill them too?"

"Easy, Peppino. They are only a nuisance that can grow into danger."

"But they are your men! They work for you!"

Another shrug. "They take risks . . . if not now perhaps later." He yawned. "That is the price they pay; to live good, to have many women and feasts and money and not to break their backs like a guinea in the subways—"

"What's to prevent the same thing from happening to us someday?"

"While I watch over you, Peppino?" He shook his head. "Never."

I gulped down the thick fragrant coffee. My mind was staggering from fatigue, bewilderment, and horror.

"Vicaria, malalia e' nicisitati, si vidi lu cori di l'a icu." He solemnly translated, "In prison, in sickness, and in want, one discovers the heart of a friend."

He pushed his cup under the silver pot and we silently watched the steaming tarry liquid rise to the rim.

"I'm afraid, Pepe. Suppose the cops lean on us? How can you be sure we won't talk?"

He gave me a quizzical look. "You and Joe who talk about putting cops into a union someday like cattle in a pen? No, Peppino," he said firmly, "you will never talk. The hate of the cops has been beaten into you and Joe. You are not like the others. You have the hate but you also have it up here." He tapped his temple. *"Cèrvelli—* brains. You once had hope, my young friend, but they stole it from you. The cops can steal a man's home, his mule, his cow, even his money—and perhaps he will forgive them. But never if they steal his hope. Never. Until we appeared you no longer had any hope. You were frightened. You were like a little boy crying for his mamma. There was only darkness and a locked door. Then we held out our hands to you." His voice was soft, almost caressing. "Is that not true, Peppino?"

I answered as if hypnotized, "Yes, yes. I guess it is . . ."

"Tomorrow when you and Joe walk on the pier they will jump to kiss your behinds. You will say to yourself— could this have happened to me?" He pointed his finger at me. "I promise you this—someday your wild dream will become as real as . . ." He hesitated, then lifted his executioner's hand. "As real as this hand . . ." He raised his cup. *"Salute,* Peppino! Salute to our dream! Someday we will whistle and the cops will jump. New York. Los Angeles. Detroit. Pittsburgh." He added savagely, "We will shake this goddam country, my young friend, like a dog with a rabbit!" He leaned across the table and spoke slowly, deliberately, intensely. "I know this, Peppino! You and Joe and I, as friends of our friends, will do many things together. This I swear to you on my mother's grave . . ."

"Friends, Pepe? You keep calling these other people our friends. Who are they?"

"What are names?" he said indifferently.

I said boldly, "Is it the Mafia?"

His smile was cold. "That is a name used by the outsiders."

"You said we are outsiders?"

"Si. You are not Italian. You can never be proposed. Not even I can do that."

"Proposed to what? You talk in riddles."

He waved his hand. *"Va. Va."*

"Don't wave me away, Pepe," I said, my voice rising.

"Tonight you said I made my bones, whatever the hell that means, and you keep telling me to act like a man. Okay. So now I think it's time to stop this hocus-pocus crap and talk straight. What the hell are you and Gus into? Who are these friends you're always talking about?"

"Easy, Peppino, you'll know all there is to know in good time."

"Is it a new mob that's taking over. Is that it?"

"A mob?" he said contemptuously. "It is men of honor not Irish gangsters!"

"That may be true but—"

"What I told you is enough," he said with mounting irritation.

It was clear there was no point in pressing the issue; Pepe—at least this time—had no intention of revealing to me any details of his mysterious and terrifying association of "honorable men" and, besides, his patience was wearing thin.

But someday, I vowed, I would find out . . .

"You told us to take over. How do we do it?"

"You must be strong. Show no mercy. You know the driver of the Hi-Lo?"

"The one who pushed over the crates?"

"*Si*. He is no good. He deserves to die."

"For God's sakes—no more killing!"

Pepe looked bored. "If you don't kill him, break his legs. Make him fear you or someday he will harm you. Then the boss checker. He worked for the cripple but he's soft like a woman." He made a slapping motion with his hand. "That's all he needs and he will kiss your hand. The others are like sheep. They will follow you. Call a meeting at once of the old men. Did you not plan to make Joe the president and you vice-president, Peppino?"

I was surprised he knew all the details. When I told him, he only smiled.

"There will be no trouble this time at the meeting." He held up both hands. "Now it is your union. Do with it as you wish."

"What about the racket guys who have the locals on the other piers? They own most of Chelsea!"

"They won't harm you. I give you my word."

"The way we understand it, the Gimp had a deal with them. He kept out of their territory and they kept out of his."

"An arrangement will be made."

"Fat Freddy ran the union but the Gimp got a piece of it and all the loot . . ."

The insinuation was not lost on Pepe who looked sincerely hurt.

"Have we asked you for anything, Peppino?"

"Why not?"

"*Illbraccio destro*—someday perhaps you will become my right arm," he said wearily. "Questions, questions. Must you always be a *sbirro*, Peppino? A detective who sniffs about like a hunting dog? Now enough of this foolishness. When will you marry Chena?"

I was startled by his question. "How do you know I intend to marry her?"

"Am I blind?" he cried. "Am I a fool? You asked her, no?"

"We talked about it."

"Talk! Talk!" he said disgustedly. "You sound like a banker. Get married and you will have the finest wedding in the city . . ."

"How the hell can I even think of getting married when you sent Chena and her mother to Italy?" I protested. "Why?"

"It is of no concern of yours," he said coldly. "Chena is a good girl. She obeys her mother."

"And that goddam Nicky had to join the Italian army—"

"Our friends in Palermo know where he is," Pepe said casually. "His mother and Chena are going to him."

I could only stare at him unbelievingly. "You knew this all the while and didn't tell me?"

Suddenly his fist, hard as a chunk of iron, slammed down on the desk almost cracking the thick glass.

"*Marrone!* Will you stop acting like a little boy! That young fool has been found in a hospital. His babbling mother swears she will not leave until she can take him home. *Sangue della patata!* What are we—nursemaids for this young fool? Do I have to sit down and hold your hand and tell you all these things? You are a man. Act like one."

His savagery shook me. All I could think of was those powerful hands on my throat. But his fury quickly died away and he smiled.

"Forgive me, Peppino— I upset you. Our friends are afraid of this woman's safety. When she was told Nicky had been found and they would get him across the border she became hysterical and insisted on going to where he is—"

335

"Where is he?"

"In an army hospital—"

"My God, what is he doing there?"

Pepe took a deep breath "He went to Spain to fight. Why I do not know." He shrugged. "He was wounded. It is war, Peppino, people get wounded in wars."

"But Spain! I don't understand—"

"Nicky is crazy," Pepe said impatiently. "What can we do?"

"What about Chena? Is she with her mother?"

"Sì." He sighed. "Chena is good to her *parenti*. She will stay with her mother."

"Did Gus talk to them?"

He shook his head.

"If he didn't talk to them, how do you know all this?"

"Our friends over there," was his blunt answer.

"God knows when she'll be back . . ."

"Easy, Peppino," Pepe said soothingly. "Chena will come back and you will be married." He leaned over and held out his hand. I silently took it. "This I promise you."

"But suppose Italy sides with Germany? You said yourself Mussolini will go with Hitler . . ."

"Sì. That bald-headed pig will bring in the Germans—"

"Then they'll never get out of Italy," I said desperately. "How the hell can you promise—"

"Peppino," he said roughly, "I have promised you. No?"

"Yes," I said, "you did."

"Remember always. I will never break my promise to you." He glanced at his wristwatch and got up from behind the desk. With his arm around my shoulder, he walked me to the door.

"Tonight you are a man," he said quietly. "Never forget—always act like one." The door closed on his farewell. *"Addìo.* Go with God . . ."

On the first floor Lorenzo, silent as a shadow, emerged from the rear of the dim hall.

"Good night, Peppino," he said softly.

THE TAKEOVER

Aunt Clara happily blamed a night in Regan's and our "carousing," as she called it, for my ravaged face and trembling hands. She was coldly indignant as she served my breakfast. But this morning her silent martyr's role was too much to take; I hit the street as fast as I could.

A few minutes before the shapeup whistle, Joe joined me outside the gin mill. I was surprised to see him looking so fresh and clear eyed.

"Christ! You look like you're going to a party."

He grinned. "I can't say the same thing for you, buddy boy. Where did he take you?"

"Pepe? We drove back to his house. He lives in a brownstone in the seventies. Where did you go?"

"I got some busthead whiskey from the night man at Regan's and waited for you on the stoop. When you didn't show, I drank your share."

"Is that all? I didn't see you."

He gave me a lazy smile. "That you didn't. I was getting laid."

"Laid! Joe! For Christ's sake. We saw—"

"Forget it, Frank," he snapped. "Forget it. That's what I did. It all happened for the best. Pepe did us a hell of a favor." He shrugged. "If somebody had to get hurt, let it be the Gimp and Freddy—"

"But Freddy was only a poor slob, Joe."

"Yeah. A slob that came down to see us knocked off." He waved his hand. "Let's talk about somethin' else. Like the dame I banged last night."

"How did you make out?"

He gave me a big grin. "There was nothin' on the avenue so I went into this coffeepot on Columbus Circle. That's where I picked her up. She was a dame from Westchester—"

"Westchester!"

"She had a fight with her husband," he explained impatiently, "and was barhoppin' all night." He gingerly flexed his fingers. "We had quite a time. She was just drunk enough."

"What's wrong with your hand?"

He shrugged. "Nothin'. The lady from Westchester wanted to drink, and I wanted to screw. She finally got the message."

"Where did you leave her?"

"In a fleabag on the avenue. She's all right."

"One of these days, Joe," I began but he waved me away.

"Forget it," he snapped.

"Did you hit the pier yet?"

"No, I was waiting for you. We're not goin' in until we pick up Train and Spider."

"Why?"

"Because we made promises—remember?"

"About giving them jobs in the union when we take over?"

"Exactly."

"How the hell can we promise them anything, Joe? We don't know what's going to happen."

"I do. We're goin' in there this mornin' and take over that goddam union, lock, stock, and barrel. Just like Pepe said we should."

We got Train out of bed, but it took a gallon of black coffee before we could get it through his thick skull that he was through busting rocks on the highways for the WPA.

"You're in the union with me and Frank now, Train," Joe told him.

"You're kiddin', Joe!" he said. "What the hell do I know about wirin' up busted boxes?"

"You don't have to know a thing," I told him. "Just do what we tell you to do. There may be a little rough stuff this morning."

Spider was more reluctant. Like a true native of the Neighborhood he refused to believe anything that he couldn't see.

"Okay, I'll take a day off and we'll see what happens," he said, "but I ain't quittin' any job until I see the gelt." He said pleadingly, "I'm not sayin' it's not so, Joe, but I gotta pay the rent. Okay?"

"As soon as I'm elected president and Frank vice-president I'll make you guys somethin' in the union even if we have to invent it."

338

"Why all the action today?" Spider asked. "Somethin' happen?"

"We heard the Gimp blew and they can't find Freddy," Joe said abruptly. "So this is a good time to move in."

Spider studied him. "You're not kiddin' me, Joe—the Gimp won't show and stick a gun up my ass?"

"I guarantee it, Spider," he said softly.

The moment the four of us walked onto the stringpiece I had the feeling that every stevedore, checker, winch driver, and even the shenango and gofer, had been awaiting our appearance. Voices were muted, heads turned too quickly, fishnets lay too long on the floor while the hoist operators studied us, hoping for a clue as to what was going to happen. I wondered whether the failure of the Gimp, his Pistoleers, and Fat Freddy to make their casual appearance informed the waterfront of what had happened just as clearly as if the news had been flashed on the Times Building?

Whatever the source—they knew.

Joe seized that moment to do a bit of stage acting. He stopped in the middle of the pier and slowly looked around. Hoists ground to a halt. Men stopped what they were doing to watch. Joe slowly walked to where the Mick sat on his Hi-Lo, frantically looking to his three bodyguards who carefully stepped aside.

The king is dead, I told myself, long live the king . . .

He jammed down the accelerator, but the little machine stalled. As he scrambled off his seat Joe picked up a length of chain.

"Get him, Train," he shouted.

Train was quick on his feet. He cut off the Mick who darted to one side, only to see Spider, an angel's grin on his face and a switchblade in his hand. Then we all moved in on him. Train's first blow almost tore off his head. From then on it was like hitting a punching bag while the men on the pier watched in silence. When the Mick was a battered, bleeding hulk, Joe ordered Train to drag him across the pier to the river side.

"Open it up," he shouted.

One of the dockwallopers quickly pushed the button that raised the heavy corrugated iron cargo door. Joe put his foot into the Mick's back to send him hurtling into the river. In seconds he surfaced, paddling feebly about.

"Go in and get him, Train," Joe ordered.

Train kicked off his shoes and dove in as the Mick was going down. Someone threw him a hawser which he tied

339

around the half-conscious man's waist, and they pulled him in.

"Get off this pier," Joe told him. "If I ever see your kisser around here I'll throw you in again, only the next time you'll have an anchor around your goddam neck . . ."

Next Joe walked across the pier to where the boss checker was standing near the loading pallet. Almost casually he grabbed the whistle that hung around the checker's neck and gave it a yank that snapped the string.

He blew one shrilling blast.

"Okay," he shouted, "everybody back to work."

Then he tossed the whistle back to the checker.

"We'll be in the office," he said, and walked off with the three of us in his wake.

"Okay, okay, the show's over," the checker was shouting, "Back to work."

That was our entrance into American Labor. . . .

I have always asked myself as I look back on that morning, why did it work? How could a quartet of kids cow a pierload of tough dockwallopers? I guess the answer was twofold: the threat of violence and murder that always hung over the waterfront and its unions; age meant nothing, it was how many guns you had and how willing you were to use them.

One firm invisible motto that hung on every pier was: Why be a hero?

More sinister was the emerging power of Pepe. At the time he was only a shadow, a whispered name of "The Sicilian," who represented a vague but deadly organization of "greaseballs" whose influence was starting to show in all the rackets. The old-time established mobsters from Prohibition, who for years had ruthlessly eliminated all opposition, now suddenly found their best shooters charred and unrecognizable in burned-out cars in swamps, in the gutters, or in the river. That summer the establishment of organized crime was caught between two forces: one they could see and fight, like Dewey and an aroused public's demand for reform, and the invisible savagery of Pepe and what Chena had told me was *còsa loro*—"their thing."

Indefinable fear is communicable and it had seeped down the ranks to prove to be more formidable for us than any army of the Gimp's Pistoleers.

When we had lunch that afternoon in the gin mill across from the piers, we could see that Joe had started his campaign. He spent money freely, slapped many backs, and made many promises.

Before the quitting whistle blew, I had ordered signs printed announcing the meeting at Regan's Hall; the next day we toured the waterfronts of Manhattan, Brooklyn, and Staten Island putting them up.

Train made a formidable appearance; this time no one beat up our old members or tore down our signs.

In one area, however, there was a noticeable coolness toward us and that was among the leaders of the racket longshoremen's local who controlled most of the West Side piers from Chelsea to the Battery. For years the Gimp had had a friendly relationship with them; each carefully respected the other's piers, shylocking interests, numbers, and floating crap games.

Now the Gimp was gone, and two fresh-faced punks from the Neighborhood were about to take over the coopers ...

"Stay uptown, boys, and don't go near Chelsea," Bailey told us, "and everything will be all right."

"Maybe we don't want to stay uptown," Joe said thoughtfully. "Maybe we might want to go downtown someday. What then?"

"We can't fight the whole waterfront, Joe," I pointed out. "Besides most of them are in with the shippers."

"Maybe you're right," he said. "Anyway, we have too much to do now as it is. Let Pepe take care of the opposition."

Joe refused to accept victory before it was reality; as he admitted to me, he would never forget the lesson the Gimp had taught us. We planned our strategy carefully, cultivating old men who now eagerly accepted our drinks and handshakes. Joe even insisted we invite Elliott to the election.

"We'll go down and see him in Dewey's office," Joe said. "What the hell, we have nothin' to hide." He grinned. "It's all in the funny papers."

When we finally saw Elliott he was sincerely surprised.

"What's the matter, Gunnar—change your mind about us cops?" he asked.

"I will never see anythin' that will help me change it," Joe told him coldly. "We just came down to invite you to attend the meetin' of our union next Wednesday night at Regan's Hall—"

"Why invite me?"

"Because Frank and I are runnin' for president and vice-president of the coopers."

"Rather young, aren't you? Most of your members will never see sixty again."

"Maybe they need young blood," Joe said dryly.

"I still don't know why you came down and told me."

"Because if we didn't and one of your stoolies told you, you'd have your goddam cops tryin' to get some old guy drunk to find out what happened in the hall. Isn't that right?"

"As a matter of fact we already know about your meeting," Elliott said. He slid open his drawer and held up one of our placards. "It's a better printing job than the last time."

"We have a printer's bill," I told him.

"I'm sure you have. By the way aren't you fellows somewhat presumptuous?"

"How do you mean?"

"Suppose Mr. Kenton, your president, shows up? In the company of Mr. Wilson?"

Joe gave him a look of sweet innocence.

"I am sure the union members would be very happy."

"Of course you don't have any idea of where they are?"

"Of course."

"You don't think for one moment the Gimp tells us his plans, do you, Captain?" I asked.

"Waterfront unions make strange bedfellows," he said softly. "Very strange."

"We're careful who we sleep with," I told him as we stood up.

"Well anyway, thanks for the invitation, fellows," he said. "I'll pass it along. Come on, I'll show you out . . ."

Waiting at the elevator was a white-haired man in a pepper and salt suit. When he turned toward us I remembered him; it was Inspector Cornell, the man who had been in charge of the raiding party the morning the Gimp was arrested.

"What do we have here, Captain?" he asked, "friends or enemies?"

"I guess we can call this a friendly mission, Inspector," Elliott said. "This is Joe Gunnar and Frank Howell. They're heading the slate for Wilson's union—"

"Slightly premature, aren't you?" Cornell asked. "Suppose Wilson pops up again?"

"The whole waterfront would stand up and cheer," Joe said solemnly.

342

Cornell gave us a thin smile. "I doubt that."

On the trip down to the lobby Cornell stared straight ahead without speaking. In the lobby he told Elliott: "If anyone wants me I'll be at headquarters."

"Yes sir."

His eyes slid over us, then he nodded to Elliott and went out.

"That guy sounds important," Joe observed.

Elliott's reply was a short, "He is."

When we arrived home Aunt Clara was cooking, one ear glued to the radio.

"It's terrible what they're doing in Spain," she cried. "Mr. Kaltenborn said they just ripped that beautiful city of Barcelona apart with bombs! Can you imagine that? Can you imagine—the churches and everything? He said hundreds of planes just kept flying over dropping bombs. What is this world coming to?"

She returned to her pots. "It's just around the corner, boys. There's a war coming. I hope to God you're not in it!" She turned around. "You know there even may be a draft?"

"A draft?" we echoed.

"They pick the names out of a fishbowl," she explained. "Then they set up draft boards . . ."

"And what do the draft boards do?"

"They decide who goes into the army or the navy."

"And who is on these boards?" Joe asked.

"Your neighbors," Aunt Clara said. "People in the Neighborhood."

"You mean like Schultz, the butcher? Or Dago Frank who runs the shoe store down the corner?" Joe asked indignantly.

"I don't think you can get out of it," Aunt Clara said. "In the last war only the slackers stayed behind."

"Let's look up what the slackers did to get out of it, Frank," Joe said with a grin.

"Joe—you wouldn't be a slacker, would you?" Aunt Clara said, all rosy with the heat of the stove and patriotism.

"You're damn right, Aunt Clara," Joe said grimly. "The way I see it, if there's a war, there will be lots of money to be made. Not over there. Right here. And that's where Frank and I will be—where the money is."

"Oh, Joe," Aunt Clara said horrified.

Joe put his arm around my shoulder, thrust his hand

343

inside the front of his jacket, and adopted an elaborate Civil War pose.

"Aunt Clara, meet two of the best slackers in the Neighborhood . . ."

"That's not nice," Aunt Clara said. "After all—it's your country!"

When she turned back to the stove Joe's lips silently told the world what they could do with his country.

And so the election took place: a hundred or more old men streamed into Regan's Hall to be greeted by us with a pat on the back, a cheery welcome, and a wave to the kegs, the bottles, the roast beef and cold cuts, all part of the ancient waterfront election ritual.

The election was the most honest in the history of the coopers' union. On Joe's orders the door to the hall remained wide open and representatives of the Honest Ballot Association—we hired them—counted the ballots.

As they said in Paddy's Market, it was all sliced, cleaned, and ready to be delivered; there was no need to cheat or use threats. The old men had been on the piers long enough to develop an instinct as fine as any electronic device. And that instinct warned them a new force was emerging in the waterfront unions and we were part of it . . .

BOOK 3

the outsiders

31 DAYS OF THE COOPERS

In the beginning it was chaotic. The books Gimp and Freddy Kenton had kept for appearances were full of lies and the ledgers they had hidden in the wall told only how much they had stolen. There was no head or tail to the union; we didn't know whether we had five members or five thousand.

Then, suddenly, Maxie Solomon appeared to inform us he was our lawyer.

"We didn't contact you, Maxie," I told him when he called.

"I know that," was his quiet answer.

"Well, who did?"

"Get all the union's ledgers, books, accounts, bills and bank statements up to my office as soon as possible," he said ignoring my question. "I'll have my accountants go over them. Give me a few weeks and I'll call you. Don't do anything until then."

A few weeks after we turned over our records to Maxie, he called us into his office. He summed up very quickly the findings of his accountants. The detailed examination of the books—legal and illegal—revealed that the Gimp and Freddy Kenton had steadily milked the union and its treasury for years; there wasn't enough left even to maintain a small office.

"What you guys have now is a union charter and a busted treasury. There were a number of large withdrawals lately from the accounts," Maxie explained, "probably to help pay the Gimp's bail money and for his lawyers." He pushed across a typed sheet of names and addresses. "I think some of the names of your members are phony. Just for the hell of it I had someone in the office make a spot check with the phone book. The first two we called died some time ago."

"What do we do now, Maxie?" Joe asked.

"First look into your membership and your locals around the city, over in Jersey, in Philly, and the coast ports," he said briskly. "Find out exactly how many members you really have . . ."

"In other words, start from scratch," I said.

"Exactly. In the meantime, I'll wipe out the old accounts and set up new ones. You'll have to have an office and at least a secretary . . ."

"Christ," Joe said angrily. "Where the hell will we get money for office rent and to pay a secretary?"

"I'm setting up an account with a thousand in both your names," Maxie said easily. "That will help you get a start . . ."

"Who put up the dough, Maxie?" I asked. "Pepe?"

He gave me a cold stare. "When are you guys going to learn to stop asking questions? It's dough and it's in your name! Maybe it came from my fairy godmother—who cares?"

"Thank God for fairy godmothers," Joe murmured.

Maxie went on. "You'll both have to live on starvation wages along with those other two guys you hired until the shekels come in. One of my clients owns an office building on Sixth Avenue. He's starving, so he'll be glad to let you have a small office for peanuts." He looked thoughtful. "We have an old dame here who's good on steno. I can let you have her for—"

"Let's skip the secretary, Maxie," Joe said abruptly. "We'll answer the phone ourselves."

"Don't be a jerk, Joe," Maxie said sharply. "Who's going to type your letters?"

346

"If we have any typing we can get it done in a hotel by a public stenographer."

"Don't you boys trust me?" Maxie asked with a grin.

"Let's say what you don't know won't hurt you," I told him.

He chuckled and waved his hand. "Okay. Anything you say is fine with me." He added seriously, "Any graft you guys get will be done legally. We'll have our own board. Raise the dues. Declare assessments. When the real dough starts to come in we'll buy some mortgages—"

"Mortgages?" Joe asked puzzled.

"Sure," Maxie said. "Use the union funds for mortgages. We can set up a mortgage company. As president of the union, Joe will channel all funds through us to be used for mortgage loans. We'll split the commission three ways. Once you guys get going there will be a million ways to make a buck with this crappy union."

"And Pepe doesn't want a cut, Maxie?" I asked.

"Has anyone asked for anything?"

"No. But you can't make me believe in fairy godmothers, Maxie."

"I guess for the time being you'll just have to, my friend," was his quiet answer. He suddenly became businesslike. "There's one thing both of you will have to do—and do right—"

"What's that?" I asked.

"Get off your ass and check that membership list and your locals. Make sure every name is legitimate, then sign them up again so there is no question. You'll have to reissue new charters for the locals. Make a careful list. What piers are they working? How many members do you have on a pier? What lines use the stringpiece?"

"Christ, that seems like a hell of a lot of work," Joe said slowly.

"You'll have to drink beer and eat pretzels before you can have champagne and caviar with this union, my friends."

Joe gave a short bitter laugh. "And I thought we would be ridin' around in Cadillacs . . ."

"Sure you will—someday," Maxie said cheerfully. "There's another reason why I want you boys to put in a lot of work on this crappy outfit—"

"What's that?"

"Elliott. We know he has stoolies on the piers. With the Gimp and Kenton"—he gave us a cold smile—"failing to

347

make an appearance as we lawyers say, Elliott will be watching you."

"We saw him down in Dewey's office," Joe said.

Maxie looked startled. "What the hell for?"

"We told him we knew he would be interested in the union's election so we invited him to come up and count the votes."

"Good. Very good," Maxie said with a satisfied nod. "But don't press your luck. If he wants to talk to you or asks you to come down, contact me immediately.

"That's why I want a legit list of members and locals," he went on, "it's something to shove in Elliott's face if he starts with questions. It will prove what I will tell him—that you are both honest, dedicated young unionists!" He stood up. "Okay, I guess that's it."

At the door we shook hands.

"You'll find it's going to be a lot of work," he said solemnly, "but it will pay off big—real big."

In the months that followed, we worked hard at rebuilding the coopers' union. Joe and I tramped the New York and Jersey waterfronts while Spider and Train visited Philly, Boston, and the other coastal ports.

The early reports from Train and Spider and what we found out in the city were anything but encouraging. They made it apparent that our days of champagne and caviar were a long way off.

Some locals had been inactive for so many years that their members had never bothered to notify Freddy or the Gimp when their officers died, retired, or left the waterfront. Yet, year after year, they had faithfully sent in their dues and assessments; if they failed to do so or fell behind, a pair of Pistoleers would pay them a visit. Someone would be shot or roughed up in an alley, and the flow of dues would continue as always.

We discovered cases where coopers had been dead for years but boss checkers had received their "disability" claims, forged their names, cashed them through pier shylocks, deducted a "fee," and turned the balance over to the Gimp's collectors. We carefully noted the name of each checker and collector; they would receive a visit from us when Train and Spider returned.

Whipping the union into shape again was a bone-weary, exhausting task. There was no easy way to do it. You simply had to visit every stringpiece and personally locate the members to establish their legitimacy. We climbed a million stairs in flats and tenements in Brooklyn, the Lower East Side, Harlem, and Flatbush and spoke to a million frightened, fawning, creaking old men. The routine bored and frustrated me but, curiously, Joe loved every minute of it. He loved the sound of his voice and loved performing for the old men. Joe was a brilliant amateur. It didn't matter if there were five or twenty, Joe hypnotized them all. Within minutes he had them eating out of his hand. When he promised that someday they would own the waterfront, they cheered him and really believed him. I guess there were nights I half believed him myself.

Summer, fall, and winter we kept up the dull, plodding task of seeking out every old cooper, carpenter, and baler along the coastal ports from New England to the South.

Our routine was grindingly monotonous. After a weary day on the piers we would meet in the Sixth Avenue hole-in-the-wall office to go over the applications we had gathered or the ones Spider and Train had sent in from out of town, we'd walk over to my flat, shovel down supper, then fall into bed.

Even the weather was against us. For every clear, sparkling fall day there were five rainy ones. The whistling wind on the waterfront seemed to drive the cold rain right through my skin and into the marrow of my bones. Dry socks became a luxury. I was never so damp, exhausted, or miserable in my whole life as I was during those fall and winter months of 1938–1939.

But you couldn't hold Joe down. He was full of dreams.

"We'll have the Caddy when we do the cops," he said one night.

"What do you mean when we do the cops?"

He gave me a look of surprise. "The cops? When we put them into that union. What do you think I mean?"

"Joe, for God's sakes stop dreaming! Look at the trouble we're having just getting these old bastards together. What the hell would it be trying to sign up the cops?"

"It will be different," he said doggedly. "We won't be walkin' on our uppers then. Believe me, Frank—we won't! They'll listen."

I just sighed, burrowed down deeper in my saggy easy chair, and let the heat of the old coal stove thaw out my ice-cold feet.

"I'm sorry I ever mentioned that stupid idea to you and Pepe."

"Well I'm not," he said emphatically. "Someday we'll pull it off with Pepe—and"—he held up a cup of steaming tea—"our friends. You'll see . . ."

"Forget it," I murmured, half asleep.

Maxie's hunch that Captain Elliott was keeping his eye on us proved to be correct. One morning, two of his investigators appeared with a subpoena and removed our files; at the same time Maxie was subpoenaed to turn over the union's bank accounts and ledgers.

We were surprised when Maxie didn't fight the subpoena in Supreme Court and waved away our protests.

"Of course I'm not going to court," he told us. "Why should I? I want them to have the books. What do they show? Only that you guys have been killing yourselves for a few lousy bucks a week. Remember what I told you? They only can convince Dewey's office that of all the unions on the waterfront yours is the cleanest."

"Suppose he wants us down?" I asked.

"Fine. You'll go down with me, and we'll answer every question he throws at you."

"What will we tell him?"

"The truth, fellows!" Maxie said warmly. "The truth. You haven't stolen a dime." He grinned. "Not that you're not going to when there's something to steal." He went on. "There's another reason why I want you down there. Publicity. I know a couple of reporters who cover Dewey's office. I think I can sell them a story on you two guys. You know, two young guys from the Neighborhood fighting single-handedly for a clean union, working day and night—that crap. It will be good for you."

"You mean when we pull a strike?" Joe said suddenly. Maxie gave him a thoughtful smile. "You catch on fast, Joe."

Captain Elliott held our books for a week, then sent for us. His questioning was perfunctory and he was impressed by our sincerity. This time we even shook hands.

Maxie was good at his word. Before we left Dewey's offices in the Woolworth Building he guided us into the press room where we were interviewed by some reporters. Later that day the *World-Telegram* sent a photographer up to our office. He posed us all over the place and then made us tour the Neighborhood with him.

Despite our growing success, there was one constant heartache I had in those days: Chena. A few weeks after

Pepe had told me about Nick, I received a letter from her confirming the details. But Chena revealed what Pepe had not:

It was not our government who helped us, but the Mafia. There is no truth to the story that Mussolini destroyed them, they are still everywhere. In the village we visited, our cousins took me and my mother to the village square to see an old man with a big stomach who was sitting on a stool in the sun. I thought at first he was a peddler but everyone was kissing his hand. He just sat there smiling like the Pope. I was told he was the *Capo dei Capi*, the man who is the head of the Mafia in Sicily. It was the man to whom my mother delivered Pepe's letter. After he read it he became very friendly and told my cousins that if there was any "service," as he put it, that could be done we should let him know at once.

Everywhere you turn there is talk of war. I kept begging my mother to return to Rome and see the consul, but she refused. I didn't know it at the time but she had our cousins ask this little man to help us find Nicky. When I heard about it I was furious to think we were waiting in a dirty village until this fat little man sent for us. But my cousins told me I was wrong, that Don Carlo, as they call him, was a man of great respect, and if anyone could find Nicky he could.

One day a messenger came for my mother to take her to see this man. When she came back she was hysterical. The whole house was crazy with women wailing and crying. Finally my cousin came in from the vineyards and told me Don Carlo had found out that Nicky had been badly wounded and was in an army hospital in the north, near the border. As soon as she heard this my mother insisted on going there.

I refused to believe it and asked my cousin how this man who sits on a chair in the sun outside his house could find out what the American government couldn't find out. He looked at me as if I were crazy; the information, he said, came from Don Carlo—he acted as if it had come from God. Well, I wasn't impressed so I insisted that my cousin take me over to the square in the village where I went up to this little man and asked him how we could be sure we

351

wouldn't be making a wild-goose chase traveling all the way to the north to an army hospital.

My cousin, who was shaking so much I thought he had a fever, kept apologizing that I was an American and didn't have "respect," as he put it, but the little man just kept smiling and eating grapes.

That was the whole interview. Then one day a man came up to me in the street in the village, very politely handed me an old black wallet, and said it came from Don Carlo. I amost fainted; it was Nicky's. Inside was a small picture he had had taken in one of those snapshot machines in a drugstore on Eighth Avenue. There was also his dogtags and a letter my mother had written him a year ago. When I looked around the man was gone. I ran home and showed the wallet to my mother and of course there were more hysterics. But I was satisfied that the story about Nicky was true and we had to go north and find him. Poor, poor Nicky! Oh, Frank, it seems that everything is against us!

I love you, my darling, I love you more than anything else in this world and I promise that I will return as soon as possible.

There is no doubt, darling, from what my cousins say, that this man Don Carlo thinks a great deal of Pepe. What was in that letter my mother delivered I don't know. All the time she carried it pinned to her corset! I am sure now it has to do with what my father and Pepe and what Pepe calls "this thing of ours."

Please, please, my darling, beware of Pepe!

Love,
CHENA

Chena's letter depressed me and left me with an aching sense of hopelessness. I wasn't satisfied until I had confronted Pepe. But it wasn't easy to find him. Every time I dropped by the Madison Avenue gallery Lorenzo said he was out of town.

Then, one night, I found him. He was obviously weary and in no mood to listen to a star-crossed lover. When I told him that Chena and her mother were on their way north he sighed.

"Did I not tell you this, Peppino?"

"It's true, you did, Pepe, but what I want to know is,
352

when will she come back? Italy may declare war, then what?"

"Her mother is a crazy woman," Pepe said harshly. "What can we do? She won't even listen to her husband! Our friends told her they would get Nicky out and across the border but she insisted on going there. What would you have us do—tie her up? Chena is a good girl, so she goes with her mother." He reproached me, "You should be glad she is like that, Peppino . . ."

"I'd rather have her back here."

"Sente, figilio mio!" He threw up his hands. "Did I not promise I would bring her back to you?"

"If there's a war, Pepe . . ."

"Sangue della patata!" he shouted. "If there is a war I will bring her back. Now go back to your old men. You are becoming a nuisance."

This was no time to test our friendship so I left hurriedly. There wasn't much I could do except trust his promise. Somehow, deep inside, I knew he would keep it. How, I didn't know.

As Pepe suggested, I returned to our old men boring as they were. Slowly, ever so slowly, the results began to show. The secondhand file cabinets we had bought on Canal Street now bulged with the names of our members. There were over five hundred, representing every stringpiece on the metropolitan waterfront and along the coast from New England to Florida. We obtained a free gasoline map and tacked it on the wall with red dots showing our strength. We kept a bottle of Golden Wedding in the file and, every time I added a new dot, we toasted the map with a shot in paper cups before we left for the evening.

On the wall and in the files our union looked damn impressive, and we began to get cocky. Cash in dues began to trickle into the treasury and the entries in the bank balances mounted even after we repaid Maxie his thousand-dollar loan. That summer, when we talked of a strike and how our union could tie up the waterfront, Maxie just looked disgusted.

"When is your contract up?"

"Next spring."

"Why the hell are you talking about a strike now?"

"With all that stuff about war over in Europe, cargo is startin' to come in," Joe pointed out.

"So wait for the war," Maxie said. He pointed to a

newspaper with the blaring headlines on his desk. "The way things are going over there you won't have to do much waiting."

"What about the pistol locals, Maxie?" I asked.

"So what about them?"

"If we do pull a strike, will they honor our picket lines?"

"They better."

"Why should they? Who are we?"

"Let's just say they will. Don't worry about them. The members are more important. How do they stack up?"

When we showed him a copy of our master list, he appeared satisfied.

"Okay. Keep it up. The more you get, the stronger you will be and the better bargaining position you will have with the shippers. Now, the next thing we're going to do is form our executive board. Do you have an old guy you can trust?"

"Jack Bailey. He's a cooper on the pier," Joe said. "We can trust him. Why?"

"The board is going to be made up of you, Frank, me, and that Bailey."

Maxie wrote it down. "Okay. Get him over here next week and we'll form the board. I'll have some papers for all of you to sign."

"When do we start stealin', Maxie?" Joe asked.

"Pretty soon," was Maxie's candid reply. "But it's going to be done legitimately. I don't want any trouble with those guys down in Dewey's office. He's going to run for DA, and that means he could be around for a long time."

The next week we formed the union's executive board. Our first act was to vote salary increases for me, Joe, Train, and Spider with a healthy fee for Maxie. We took care of Bailey at twenty-five a week, which pleased him. He was scared to death of us anyway and the extra loot made him more of a stooge. And a watchdog; we didn't have to spell it out—if there were any rumblings of discontent on the pier it was his job to let us know.

The knowledge that our work was starting to pay off infused us both with new enthusiasm. Every morning of that rainy spring and sultry summer of 1939 found us on the docks. The second trial of Jimmy Hines was the big news—at least in the Neighborhood—and we read every line of the testimony. I wondered at the irony: Pepe's sinister faceless friends had disposed of Dutch Schultz and now—while the trial of his protector was going on, they were taking over the Dutchman's policy empire. No siege. No shots. Just fear. Our friends.

When August panted to its soggy end, the Nazi-Soviet Pact was signed, the Spanish Civil War had ended with one last strangled cry from within Madrid, and I discovered what Franco meant by his Fifth Column. One hot night on the stoop, while Joe was daydreaming out loud about the police union and the cop strike, I jokingly pointed out what we should establish was a Fifth Column in the police department.

"What do you mean Fifth Column?" he demanded. "What the hell is that?"

I told him about the story I had read in which Franco had watched the bombing of Madrid. When an aide informed him four columns were converging on the city, he said the Fifth Column, already inside, was stronger than the other four.

Joe thought it over for a moment.

"Not a bad idea," he said. "Let's remember that . . ."

That fall Train, who had fought his way into a packed Yankee Stadium to watch Lou Gehrig say good-bye to the Yankees, recounted the details of that sad tableau in Regan's. It was the Big Subject of the season.

But the only two guys in the neighborhood who could not have cared less about Gehrig were Joe and I. What really impressed us was FDR's cash-and-carry Neutrality Bill that lifted the arms embargo. We did not have to be international experts to realize this legislation gave Europe access to the war markets of the United States. The gathering storms of war in Europe meant only one thing to us: the return of prosperity to the waterfront.

Then one morning in September, Aunt Clara woke us up shouting, "Frank! Joe! Mr. Kaltenborn's just announced that war has been declared in Europe!"

"Send 'em some bullets, Aunt Clara," Joe mumbled. "Tell 'em they're from the slackers . . ."

Then he rolled over to the disgust of Aunt Clara, and I am sure Mr. Kaltenborn. . . .

To the waterfront, war in Europe was a gift from heaven. For the first time since the boom days of the 1920s there was a second shift, then a third, and finally a fourth. Some dockwallopers worked round robins from dawn to dawn for time and a half. Cargo crowded the West Side stringpieces, and camouflaged freighters, the first we had ever seen, began to wait their turn in the harbor to be loaded for a convoy makeup.

We were destiny's children: the right guys at the right time. Coopers, carpenters, balers came out of retirement to work the docks and, before they could pick up a hammer, they had to sign up with us and get a union card.

That fall and winter passed quickly. On one bitterly cold night in December, after we had signed up some coopers on a Lower East Side pier, we decided to stop off at a waterfront gin mill for some dinner. We were both ravenous.

The bar was typical: one large room with a floor of old-fashioned tiles covered with sawdust. There was a long mahogany bar. Wooden latticework in the rear separated the "family" section from the open bar; the menu was printed on a piece of cardboard pasted to the mirror. Several battered tables and chairs lined the wall under the windows. We selected one after giving our order to an old waiter who appeared pickled in alcohol. The bar was three deep, the noise of a jukebox in the corner competed with the bedlam produced by a crowd of dockwallopers around a pool table.

The food was savory and delicious. I had just wiped my bowl clean with a chunk of thick Italian bread when I heard someone shout above the tumult:

"Joe! Frank! My old buddies."

Standing in the open archway of the latticework partition was Muzzy Blaze, a little older, a little heavier, and quite drunk. He also looked prosperous. A custom-made suit replaced his ragged bell-bottom sailor pants. He staggered over and pumped our hands.

"Where've you guys been?" he demanded. Without waiting for our reply he shouted to the old waiter, "Hey, Sparky, bring some drinks over here."

"We've just eaten, Muzzy," Joe protested.

"So it will help you digest," Muzzy said. To the waiter, "Tell Tommy I want Bell's Twelve Year Old. Tell him no check for these guys."

"Hey, what goes on? Do you own this joint?" Joe asked.

Muzzy looked disgusted. "Are you kiddin', Joe? Who wants to own a dump like this? I'm in numbers since my old man died. I've been workin' with the Duchess. Remember that dame I told you about? Sort of partners. But what happened to you guys? Every day up at the Proc, I looked for you. You guys never showed. . . . No Joe . . . no Frank. . . . Then someone said the Bulls was lookin' for you guys. Is that right?"

"It's a long story, Muzzy," I told him. "We never went up to the Proc. We had a little dispute with a cop and left town."

"We were in the CCCs for a year," Joe said with a grin. "Out west cuttin' down trees."

"You're kiddin'!" Muzzy said.

"No we're not," I said.

"What are you guys doin' around here? You need any work? How would you like to pick up for us?" Muzzy said rapidly.

"No thanks," I said. "We have something going in a union."

"You guys in a union!" Muzzy said unbelievingly. "What kind of a union?"

"Coopers."

He snapped his fingers. "Yeah. I know. The old guys on the piers who fix up the broken cargo." He leaned over and said with a great deal of drunken caution. "Hey, watch out for those piers. The racket guys don't like guys from the outside comin' in . . . you know what I mean, fellas?"

"Don't worry about us, Muzzy," Joe said easily. "We won't have any trouble, we don't hurt them, they don't hurt us."

Muzzy poked me hard in the ribs.

"Hey, Frank! We got a big man here. They won't hurt us. Hey, Joe, those guys'll kill ya. I swear it. I know 'em, I grew up with them bums."

"I guess we just have to take our chances, Muzzy," I told him.

"How's the numbers goin' Muzzy?" Joe asked.

"Great! I think I told you—my old man and the Duchess were the last big independents—the wops didn't take over after they knocked off the Dutchman. Now they run everythin' from East Harlem. They have it set up so the niggers can't even cross Fifth Avenue. A guy comes over from the East Side and picks up the day's ribbon— you know, the addin' machine tape—for the bank. Then they bring back the dough for the hits. No more free lance. A few guys tried single action on the avenue and— bango! They were found in a hallway. You can't buck those wops."

"Well then why do they let you and the Duchess operate, Muzzy?" I asked him.

He gave me an elaborate, drunken wink.

"We got an ace up our sleeve, Frankie boy."

"Who—the Duchess?" Joe asked casually.

Muzzy's eyes widened. "Hey, what do you guys know about the Duchess? Who told ya?"

"An old friend of yours, Muzzy—Maxie Soloman—"

"Maxie! You know Maxie?"

"He's our lawyer."

"All the numbers guys go to him," Muzzy said. "He works for the wops."

"We don't care who he works for. He takes care of our union."

"What's this with the Duchess?" Joe asked in a puzzled way. "What does she do—pay off big?"

"She pays—we all pay—but it's more than that . . ."

He waited until the drinks were set down, then we all solemnly touched glasses. Joe gave me the eye and we sat in silence for a long moment.

"Know what it is?" Muzzy asked suddenly.

"We don't want to know any of your business, Muzzy," Joe protested. "You don't have—"

Muzzy leaned over, put his arms around our shoulders, and pulled us toward him.

"Look, you guys are my friends, right? Ya gotta trust

your friends, right?" He lowered his voice. "She has a connection downtown."

"City Hall?" I asked.

"Naw! In the cops. She's got someone down there who's real big—she's the only one who can make a single deal—"

"What do you mean a single deal, Muzzy?" Joe asked "I don't get it."

"A single deal," he said firmly. "Only one guy gets paid. The wops have to pay everybody—the precinct commander, the sergeants, the dicks, the Mickey Mouse guys—you name it—they pay. Not us. We pay one guy. The Duchess whispers in his ear and that's it!"

"Don't you have to pay?" I asked.

"Sure we do," Muzzy said. "But we pay half what those jokers shell out uptown. One guy gets it, he takes care of everybody. That's all. If the commissioner's confidential squad starts actin' up we know about it before they leave headquarters. If the precinct gives us any trouble, the Duchess makes one call and they get off our back. We have it made."

"And the wops—"

"They pay. And pay and pay," Muzzy said gleefully. "In the last couple of months we hear the precincts are fightin' each other over the loot. The wops would give their right arm for our connection. That's why they don't fool around with us. They know the Duchess has it made and they don't want any trouble." He started to lift his glass then stopped. "Hey! You guys should know the Gimp! He had a nice deal."

"Johnny Wilson? From the docks?" Joe asked. "Sure we know him. He was a good friend of ours."

Muzzy whispered dramatically, "They dumped him."

I forced myself to ask, "Who dumped him?"

"We hear it was the wops,'" Muzzy said. "They had some kinda argument over the piers. When he dropped outa sight, the wops took over his shylocks, bookies, and numbers runners. They're gettin' bigger every day."

"Who's gettin' bigger?" Joe asked.

"The wops!" Muzzy said indignantly. He finished his drink in a gulp and looked around for the ancient watier.

"Do you think they're taking over?" I asked.

Muzzy made a circling motion with his hand to the waiter that took in our glasses.

"Someday they'll own this town." He poked his chest with his thumb. "Remember what Muzzy told you guys. A year. Two years, they'll own every racket." He grinned. "The only thing they don't have is Mr. Big down at headquarters."

"And he belongs to the Duchess," Joe said softly.

"Right."

"What about the Gimp?" I asked.

Muzzy looked bewildered. "The Gimp? I told ya, Frank—they knocked him off!"

"You were saying something about him and a deal . . ."

He put his glass down. "Oh yeah. Who do you think was the Gimp's connection?" He turned to Joe. "Take a guess, Joe."

Joe shrugged. "I haven't the faintest idea, Muzzy. Do you, Frank?"

"The wops?" I suggested.

Muzzy looked disgusted. "Naw. He hated the wops. From what we hear they reneged on a deal he had with them. Somethin' to do with the docks." He leaned toward us and whispered triumphantly. "The Duchess! That was his contact. Louie—that's her husband that was killed by a truck—and the Gimp ran beer together for Owney Madden. They were real good friends. When the Duchess took over Louie's numbers she made this connection, downtown. If the Gimp wanted anything to be okayed, he would come over and see the Duchess. He paid, but the Duchess saw that the money got to the right guy."

"What about Dewey?" I pointed out. "He finally got the Gimp. It was in all the papers."

"Dewey?" he sneered. "He only got the Gimp because some stoolie sold him out."

"Someone in his own mob?" Joe asked with a choirboy's look.

"Sure," Muzzy said with an exaggerated gesture. "Who else? Nobody could help him once Dewey got his books." He carefully lit a cigarette and let the smoke curl up around his face. "Me and the Duchess, we're not complainin'. We have the territory around here and the piers. We're doin' real good. When they dumped the Gimp and took over his stuff, I told the Duchess, let 'em choke on it, someday they'll get too greedy. Just like Schultz. He kept wantin' more and more so they knocked him off. Never be greedy, my old man always said, there's enough for everyone . . ." He gave us a wink. "Enough for everyone."

"Is there real dough in numbers, Muzzy?" Joe asked.

"Why do you think the wops put the muscle on the

niggers? There's a couple of million a year up there! Do you think they're gonna let that kind of dough hang around in the street for some niggers to play with? Hell no!"

"A couple of million a year!" I exclaimed.

"That's right, Frank, and the wops got it all. Niggers, spicks, the single-action guys. Harlem, the west Side, Downtown. We hear they're ready to take over the Baker Brothers in Brooklyn. Bang! Bang! and the Baker Brothers will have big holes in their heads. Who's gonna fight 'em? Not me!"

"But you're doin' okay," Joe said.

"Just great! We got runners good for three, four hundred a day. We got a damn good comptroller—Ally Fox, he's been around for a long time. We give him thirty percent of the daily gross."

"Isn't that high?"

"Sure. But he's good."

"What do you do, Muzzy?"

"I take over the bank. You know me with figures," he said proudly. "I'm better'n the addin' machines. They don't try any funny business with me."

"How much is paid out to the cops?" Joe asked.

"Three grand a week."

"Three grand a week," Joe gasped. "Just to this one guy?"

"He's gotta take care of his people," Muzzy explained. "Hell, there may be more than fifteen locations in one precinct. Candy stores, tailor shops, restaurants, you name it, they're pickin' up for us. To pay off each cop would cost you a fortune. That's what's hurtin' the wops! Pay. Pay. Pay!"

"What would you say an average daily take in your bank is, Muzzy?" I asked.

"Take today's play," he said. "It's not too much, because it's near Christamas. But it was thirty thousand dollars. We only work a five-day week. We let some single-action guys take the weekend."

Joe looked stunned. "Thirty thousand! One hundred and fifty thousand a week, Muzzy? What the hell are you doin' with your money?"

"Stashin' it away," Muzzy said with a grin. "I'm not gonna be like my old man, supportin' every goddam relative from here to Minsk! Not this baby."

"And tax free," I pointed out to Joe.

"That's right, Frank," Muzzy said. "Uncle doesn't get a dime. Me and the Duchess. We combined. The wops won't touch us because we have that little ace up our sleeves. They would give their nuts to get it."

"Who are the wops, Muzzy? Do you know? We've been hearin' about them on the docks."

Muzzy shrugged. "Nobody knows, Joe. All I can tell ya is this—if you ain't in it you're out of the big time." He threw up his hands. "It's a new combination."

I pressed. "But who runs it? Who's behind it? Are they only in numbers?"

"They're in everythin' that can make a buck," Muzzy said fiercely. "Now we hear the bastards are bringin' in junk. Drugs. Real hard stuff like heroin. That's bad. Once ya get hooked on that stuff yer dead. The Duchess really hates that stuff. When the guys from East Harlem come down to talk business the Duchess always screams at 'em for dealin' in that stuff. They don't care. They just laugh at her."

"Does she know who runs the wops?" Joe asked.

"Nobody knows, Frank."

"Do you know who the Duchess's connection is?" I asked casually.

"His name? Hell no! I know the Duchess since I was this high—" He held his hand about a foot from the floor—"and she trusts me with her life. I swear it. But tell me that guy's name . . ." He added fiercely, "I wouldn't even ask her—do you know that?"

"Why not?" Joe asked. "You're her partner."

"Yeah but that contact is her personal business," Muzzy said firmly. "All I care about is the okay. She gets it, that's good enough for me."

Joe asked suddenly. "Is she here, Muzzy?"

Muzzy finished his drink and tried to focus his eyes on us. "Who?"

"The Duchess."

"Naw. She's gone home. We've been workin' in that damn bank all day . . ."

"I'd like to meet her," Joe said. "Wouldn't you, Frank?"

"She sounds like a great dame."

"A swell dame, Frank," Muzzy said fervently. "A real swell woman. No bullshit about her. Real swell. Hey, I tell you what!" He put his arms about our shoulders. "What are you guys doin' Christmas Eve?"

"Nothing much. What do you have in mind?"

"We're gonna have a party here—right here. We call it the Numbers Christmas party. All the collectors, the runners, and the ribbon men are invited. Drinks on the house. Why don't you guys come down and I'll introduce you."

"Will the Duchess be here, Muzzy?" I asked.

"Be here? It's her party! She gives it every year for the boys."

"We'll try to make it, Muzzy," Joe said. "I think we better blow now." He caught the bartender's eye and held up a hand.

"No check," Muzzy said indignantly. "I told you, no check. How about another drink?"

"We'll take a rain check for Christmas Eve," I told him.

He walked us to the door, his arms linked in ours.

"Don't forget Christmas Eve."

"We'll be there," Joe called out.

The wind coming off the water was dank and frigid. We bent to it and almost ran to the subway.

"What a break. I can't believe it," Joe said as we went uptown.

"What do you mean—the Duchess?"

"Of course. Now we know who was the Gimp's rabbi! How do you like that? The Duchess has a contact down at headquarters and not even East Harlem can touch her!"

"So now you're going to get close to the Duchess . . ."

He grinned. "What else? Don't you see what's happenin,' Frank?" he went on. His voice tightened with excitement. "It's just as Muzzy says, Pepe and his combination are movin' in all over town. Now they control all the numbers combination, except Muzzy's and the Duchess's and those guys in Brooklyn. It will only be a matter of time before they knock over the Brooklyn mob. But they can't take over Muzzy and the Duchess."

"But East Harlem pays off, Joe."

"Of course it does—and big. And that's the rub! They don't have a system. They're forced to pay off every cop who puts out his hand. There's no central payoff. Everyone from the precinct commander down to the cops in the Mickey Mouse gets his handout. That's why the wops let Muzzy and the Duchess operate. They're lightin' candles every day, prayin' they'll find out who their contact is so they can take over. I believe Muzzy when he said they would give their eyeteeth to know what she knows. They need a central payoff."

"Like the Duchess has."

"Exactly. In a few years Pepe and his mob will own everything in this town. Unions, numbers, bookies, waterfront—you name it and they'll control it. But they will also need protection to survive."

Now I could see his plan.

"That's it, Frank!" he said thumping my back as he read it in my face. "One guy, one payoff."

"And we'll be the payoff men through Mr. Big downtown . . ."

"The outsiders payin' off the insiders," he said. "This is just the thing we need to get some real muscle in this town. What we have now will be peanuts compared to what we can get. This is big money, Frank. But there is somethin' more important in it for you!"

"Why me?"

He put his arm around my shoulder and hugged me. "The cops, Frank! How better could you get to the real inside of the cops? Suppose we really set up a central payoff for Pepe with the cops? You could find out what you wanted—precinct by precinct. The good guys—the bad guys! The creeps! The guys that could give you a hard time! It's an open door to the whole goddam department, Frank."

He thought for a moment, then snapped his fingers.

"Hey! Remember that night last summer when we were sittin' on the stoop and you and Aunt Clara were talkin' about Madrid? Somethin' about a column in the city."

"The Fifth Column."

He snapped his finger again. "That's it! A Fifth Column in the police department. It's perfect for what you want."

"Trying to form a union is not a war, Joe."

"The hell it isn't! Any time I'm dealin' with cops it's a war as far as I'm concerned. And it should be for you too." He added thoughtfully, "Speakin' of cops, there is somethin' you should do."

"I hate to ask what it is."

"Read up on the cops. Get to know everythin' you can about the department. How it's organized. What the chains of command are. Who runs the precinct. What territory it takes in. All that stuff."

"In other words you want me to become a cop expert?"

"You and that library! I bet you can find plenty of

books on cops over there, Frank. What the hell, someone must have written a book on cops."

"All this and you haven't even met this dame."

He shrugged. "So what? I'll get to her if it takes me five years." He punched his fist into the palm of his hand. "This is what I've been lookin' for, Frank. Not only a way to get some real muscle but an inside track into the cops, what makes that department tick."

"You're forgetting one thing, Joe."

"What's that?"

"The name of this guy downtown. Do you think for one moment the Duchess is going to roll over and give it to you? Just like that? Because she likes the way your hair is parted? C'mon, Joe, stop dreaming. Muzzy is her partner. He's been around her since he was a kid and he doesn't know who her contact is. You're smoking hop!"

"Christ! Don't compare me with Muzzy. Please!"

"Forget Muzzy. Don't you think there are plenty of young guys working with her? If she wants a little nooky they are always available. Why you?"

"Don't worry," he said quietly. "There won't be a problem with the Duchess. Do you know why?"

"I'm dying to hear it, Valentino."

"Because I'm different. Muzzy says the Duchess has been around since he was a kid, that means she's no chicken. I'll charm her ass off and make her believe she's Queen of the Nile. I'll make a bet those jerks over there don't even light her cigarette. Old dames go for things like that. I don't care who they are, in policy or on Park Avenue, when they get to a certain age the night seems awful long and lonely . . ." He punched me playfully on the shoulder. "Wait until Christmas Eve, Frankie boy, and watch me move!"

Confidence? That's one thing Joe Gunnar never lacked— especially with women.

Older women.

33 THE DUCHESS AND HER
CHRISTMAS EVE
POLICY PARTY

That first wartime Christmas season was extremely lucrative for us. The holiday cargoes included everything
from hams to chests of Danish silverware and casks of
Irish whiskey. Each load that left our stringpiece contained a choice piece of scrap iron or a chunk of concrete. The daily loot was impressive and the fences were
overwhelmed. At first the new customs inspector was an
untouchable, but Joe soon discovered his weakness; he
liked the horses. Arrangements were made through Pepe
to let him have unlimited credit from the bookie who
covered our pier. One day he was presented with several
hundred dollars in markers. Joe went to great lengths to
get the bookie off his back. The inspector was exceedingly
grateful—and cooperative. We never had any trouble
after that.

We were learning and fast.

We also made sure the checkers, the hoist men, the
Hi-Lo boys, the guys working the stringpiece, even the
go-fers, all got a taste of the good life. When Bailey
notified us that a case of scotch was under the tarpaulin in
the coopers' shed, Joe would pass the word to the boss
checker to get paper cups, break it open, and take care of
the boys.

In the Neighborhood, tradition was religiously followed.
Christmas Eve meant a small tree in our front parlor and
gifts piled on the little rosewood table that one of my
aunt's uncles had made for her when she was a kid. Then
there was the traditional Christmas Eve meal of scalloped
oysters that Aunt Clara lovingly served. Later that evening
we dropped in at Regan's for a fast one with Spider and
Train, then left for the Duchess's Christmas policy party.

When we pulled up in a cab the waterfront gin mill was
really jumping. They had a combo—not good but loud—I
imagined that if I reached out and touched the building I

366

could have actually felt its timbers quivering from the vibration of the blaring music.

We were hit by a wave of sound solid as a fist. The place was packed with white, black, yellow men and women, even little kids who crowded about the tables that lined the walls. Waiters balancing drinks and pitchers of beer pushed their way through the crowd that had made a makeshift dance floor in the open space before the bar. The pool table, now covered with red and green paper tablecloths, was used as a buffet that held steaming plates of spaghetti, meatballs, sausages, shrimp, oysters, sandwiches, fried rice and pork, pigs' knuckles, chitterlings and greens, chunks of cheese and bologna, and onion, beet, and potato salads. In the center was a large Santa Claus. Twisted ribbons of red and green fringed crepe paper crisscrossed the room and behind the bar was a small decorated tree trimmed with miniature bottles of liquor.

Written in soap on the bar mirror was: "Today's hit 792."

At the far end of the room on a platform made of planks and horses was a three-piece band. When we entered, the trumpeter, his face dripping sweat, was pointing his horn to the ceiling finishing the final bars of "Sleepy Time Gal." Below him the shoulder-to-shoulder dancers swayed slowly from side to side with the rhythm—it was impossible to dance—while some mournfully howled the words, a rapturous look on their drunken, glistening faces.

For a moment we stood bewildered to one side of the door. Then suddenly through the smoky haze there was Muzzy pushing through the crowd and waving his hands. He was wearing another expensive suit only this time he had a white carnation in his buttonhole. He wasn't as loaded as when we had last seen him.

"Joe! Frank! Christ, I'm glad you could make it. Let me have your coats."

He piled our coats on his arm and guided us through the singing, howling, swaying dancers to the room beyond the latticework. At what was evidently the kitchen turned into a checkroom he laid down our coats at the door and stuck his head inside.

"Hey, Jennie! Take care of these, will ya? They're friends of mine. Don't let any bastard steal 'em, willya? ... Jennie'll take care of 'em," he assured us. "She's a good kid. C'mon, I want you to meet the Duchess. I've been tellin' her all about you guys."

367

As Muzzy led us through the crowd toward a booth, Joe stopped so suddenly I bumped into him.

"What's wrong?" I asked.

He was staring at someone across the room.

"She's a nigger!" he whispered. "The Duchess is a shine!"

I looked over his shoulder at the woman seated behind the table in the booth. She was new fall honey poured into an orange dress, stacked not with young, milk-and-cream softness but stolid, settled. She was probably forty.

"Well, Joey boy," I asked softly, "are we going to see you move?"

He shrugged. "I don't care if she's a cannibal. Let's go."

When we sat down I was conscious of a sensuous, clinging perfume.

Before Muzzy could introduce us, Joe said with a smile: "You know that perfume matches you?"

Cool black eyes above high cheekbones studied him for a moment.

"Why do you say that?"

"It's exciting and I like excitement. Don't you?"

She smiled haughtily. "It all depends."

"On what?"

"Oh, lots of things, young man," she said with a faintly amused air as she took a cigarette from her pack and tapped it on the table. Joe had already held out his lighter before she could reach for the matches. She accepted it with a smile and studied him across the tiny flame.

"This is Joe Gunnar and Frank Howell, Duchess, the guys I've been tellin' you about," Muzzy said with a wave of his hand toward us. He looked up as a bald-headed gnome of a man with a pasty face unceremoniously squeezed past us and sat down at the side of the Duchess. He slid a drink toward her, then turned to eye us with the cold, unblinking stare of a lizard viewing an ant.

"This is Ally Fox, fellows," Muzzy said with a great deal of unconvincing geniality, as if he wanted to cover up the hostility in the other man's face. "Like I told ya, he's our comptroller. He's been around for a long time. What he don't know about numbers ain't worth knowin'. How long has it been, Al?"

"You weren't born when I started," Fox told him. He had a voice like a rusty file.

"I was tellin' the Duchess how we met up at the Proc," Muzzy said.

368

"What did you kids do—rob the five and ten?" Fox rasped.

Joe looked over at him with a smile. "No. We knocked off the Chase Bank but they made us give it all back."

Muzzy and the Duchess chuckled but the gnome just glared.

"You in numbers?" he grunted at me.

"No. A union."

"What union?"

"The coopers."

"You mean those old guys on the docks?"

"Don't laugh at them, buddy," Joe said warmly. "They carry a lot of weight on the piers."

"Aw, they're only crummy old guys," Fox grunted. He explained to the Duchess. "They fix up broken barrels and stuff like that and these guys say they carry muscle on the piers! How do you like that?"

Joe shrugged. "Okay. You don't think so. Forget it."

"They're nothin'," Al said bluntly. "They're dirt."

"Take it easy, Al," Muzzy said with a nervous laugh. "These guys are friends of mine."

"So they're friends of yours," Al said. "What do you want me to do?"

"Be polite," the Duchess said softly. She turned to us with a smile. "Will you boys have a drink?"

"By all means," Joe said.

Muzzy asked, "Scotch?"

When we nodded he put two fingers in his mouth and whistled shrilly. In seconds a waiter appeared and Muzzy gave him our order.

"Is it a big union?" the Duchess asked politely.

"It's getting there," I said.

"A couple of crummy old guys," Fox said. "You kiddin'?"

"You seem to know a lot about our union," Joe told him.

"I know the docks, kid," Fox said. "I was hustlin' numbers on 'em when you were stealin' fruit from the peddlers."

"It's a different time, Pop," Joe said easily.

Fox bristled. "They're still crummy old bastards who can't go to the toilet unless the checker says it's okay."

"Those old guys can close down your waterfront, mister," I told him.

He gave me a look of disgust. "You're playin' with

yourself, kid. Your goddam union can't get itself arrested. Close down the waterfront? Are you nuts?"

Joe gave him a cool, even look.

"When we do, Pop, we'll be sure and send you a special delivery letter. Okay?"

The Duchess giggled. "I guess that told you, Al."

Then the waiter appeared with our drinks and this helped to break the tension.

The Duchess lifted her glass. "Here's to you and your old men, Joe."

"It's quite a party," I observed trying to keep our table on an even keel.

Muzzy said, "The Duchess throws it every year."

"It's something my husband started a long time ago," she explained. "It's for the people who work for us." As if struck by a sudden thought she turned to Al, "Al, did you take care of the envelope?"

"Do I ever forget?" he said fiercely. "If there wasn't an envelope they'd be ringin' your doorbell."

Joe inquired softly, "Cops?"

Her face hardened and she nodded.

"In policy they're a fact of life."

Then she said abruptly, "Muzzy said you knew Johnny Wilson."

"Johnny? Oh sure," Joe said warmly. We're from the Neighborhood. He and my father were real good friends . . ."

"Oh, was your father on the waterfront?"

"A long time ago. Long before your time, Duchess . . ."

"Thank you," she said laughing, "but maybe it wasn't."

Suddenly Fox pushed his glass away. "I gotta be goin'."

"So soon, Al?" the Duchess asked.

"Yeah. I gotta see someone . . ."

We got up and let him squeeze out from behind the table. Without a good-bye he pushed his way through the dancers.

"Al isn't very friendly," Joe observed.

"You'll have to forgive him," the Duchess said, "he's an old, old friend of my husband's. I guess he would be suspicious of his own mother."

Muzzy nodded. "Yeah, but he gets things done, Duchess. He's the best comptroller in the business."

"Sort of like an office manager?" I suggested.

Muzzy ticked off on his fingers: "Runners. Collectors. Ribbon men, and the comptroller in the bank. You get a bad one and he can ruin ya. Al's the best. The wops offered him all kinds of dough but he won't leave. He says Harlem makes him nervous . . ."

"Whatever happened to Johnny?" the Duchess asked suddenly. "Did you boys hear anything?"

"Nothin'," Joe said. "We had coffee with Johnny the day after Dewey grabbed him but then he just disappeared." He looked from Muzzy to the Duchess. "What did you hear?"

"The wops dumped him," Muzzy said. "I'm sure of it. What do you think, Duchess?"

"East Harlem," she said in a tight voice, "they want to own the world."

"Hey, this is Christmas Eve," Joe reminded her. "We're supposed to be havin' a good time. Remember?"

"Yeah," Muzzy said. "Let's forget that crap."

"Come on, Duchess," Joe said. "Let's go!" He reached across the table and gently squeezed her hand.

"What we need is another drink," Muzzy said.

The Duchess turned around and called out an order in Spanish. One of the waiters hurried over with a tray of drinks.

"She can speak Spanish as good as any spick," Muzzy said admiringly.

"That's all part of being a good business woman," she said with a laugh.

"Let's try to dance," Joe said.

"You call that dancing?" she said, pointing to the swaying crowd on the dance floor. "It's more like Times Square on New Year's Eve . . ."

"Baby with you in my arms even Times Square on New Year's Eve would be heaven."

We all groaned.

"Wow, what a line," she said to me. "Is he always like this?"

"Watch out for him, Duchess," I warned her. "He's dangerous."

"Are you dangerous, Joe?" she said laughing up at him.

He leaned down and whispered, "Why don't you try me?"

He reached out for her hand and guided her carefully, as if she were the only woman in the world, past a shouting, singing group who had their arms locked around each other's shoulders like a football huddle. On the fringe of the dance floor he made a slight bow and held out his

371

arms in an exaggerated gesture. She smiled and they began to dance.

"Hey, Frank, she likes him!" Muzzy said.

"How can you tell?"

"I can just tell," he said. "She usually doesn't dance. She's afraid she'll have to say no to the niggers."

"Why? She's black herself for crissakes!"

"I know. She's funny like that. Maybe it's because she is almost white." He shrugged. "What the hell, in the summer she looks like she just has a nice tan."

"Who is that guy Fox?" I demanded. "What's wrong with him?"

"Aw, don't mind Al. He's always had a yen for the Duchess. Maybe it's because she's nice to him." He said in wonderment, "He's so ugly, even the whores on Canal Street don't like to bang him."

"Has he been around for a long time?"

"A long as I can remember. He started in with Louie— that's the Duchess's husband who was killed by a truck. My old man usta say that if the Duchess told him to jump off the Municipal Building he'd do it. I guess if a guy's hot for a woman he'll do anything for her." He shook his head. "Not me. Love 'em 'n' leave 'em. That's what I do, Frank. Just love 'em 'n' leave 'em.'

"Al's an old guy, Muzzy."

He turned to me with a grin. "The Duchess ain't exactly a chicken . . ."

"How old would you say she is?"

"Who knows? It's hard to tell with niggers—"

"About thirty?"

He gave me a look of disgust. "She'll never see thirty again! Are you kiddin'?"

"Forty?"

"Could be. All I know she's been around since I was a little kid."

"What about her husband, was he white?"

"Louie? As white as you and me. Only his hair. It was kinda kinky. She's a nigger but she's a great dame," Muzzy said fervently, "a real great dame." He stood up. "Let's go."

"Where are we going?"

"To fix you up. I got a Polack broad for you. She'll break yer back. Name's Sonia. She's even went to business school. She runs the addin' machines in our bank. My

372

dame's with her. Her name's Fay. She's a great dame." He added indignantly, "But she wants to get married!"

Fay and Sonia were sitting with a noisy group of collectors and runners who greeted us with loud cheers and an invitation to join their table. They were both blonde. Fay's came out of a bottle but Sonia's was natural, thick and light as corn silk. She had magnificent breasts and a voice that could have won any hog callers' contest. I will always agree with Muzzy's description of her: "Sonia's a good kid. Maybe she has a hollow leg and a voice like a foghorn but she also has a terrific pair of knockers and a heart as big as all outdoors."

"What about Joe?" I asked Muzzy.

"Let Joe take care of himself, f'r crissakes," Muzzy said. "We'll catch up to 'em before the night's over."

But we never did. The band became louder, if that was possible, and the whiskey never stopped flowing. It seemed as if my glass was always filled. Sonia had an exciting shape which she allowed me to explore freely as the evening progressed, but she also possessed an almost compulsive desire to sing every number the orchestra played. In addition she loved the onion salad they served and was always begging Muzzy to order another bowl. That powerful, vibrant voice became weighed so heavily with onions, beets, and pigs' knuckles it almost removed the crease from my new suit. As the evening passed the more whiskey Sonia consumed, the more she sang until Muzzy exploded.

"For crissakes, Sonia, willya shut up and lay off the onions! Every time you open yer yap I get a whiff that'd choke a horse."

Then Sonia wept and said she was insulted so she and Fay denounced Muzzy and left us to go to the bar where we later pried them loose from two powerfully built guys who looked as if they could shave every hour and still have a beard. Fortunately they were old friends of Muzzy; he identified them as Sanitation men who collected the numbers on the piers where the garbage scows tied up. I had the orchestra play "A Tisket-A-Tasket," which Sonia led us in singing while I nibbled at her neck. Then when the door prize was raffled off—it turned out to be the tiny Christmas tree decorated with miniature bottles of whiskey—two giant black numbers runners got into a fight over who held the winning ticket. They tipped over a table and began slugging to the cheers of the spectators who climbed on chairs and made bets as to the outcome. All this time Sonia was singing the endless bars of that idiotic tune and I was studiously concentrating on her neck and breasts, while Muzzy had bent Fay back on the seat of the booth almost in a rape position and she kept screaming that he was spoiling her new hairdo. The rest of our party paid no attention to us; they were either cheering on the fighters, making fervent love overtures, or hotly debating who had failed to turn in what they called the holdover numbers from the play of the previous night.

Waiters finally broke up the fight, then the bloody but unbowed winner insisted upon giving his battered opponent the tree to the cheers of the crowd. That meant more drinks. By this time I found things out of focus. Once I fought my way to the men's room and on my way back tried to find Joe, but the booth we had occupied was now filled with two drunken Chinamen and an enormous peroxide blonde who kept shouting, "Joe? There's no Joe here, buddy, only one Hung Lo!" And she screamed with laughter.

I dimly remember standing with my coat on at the bar, my arm around Sonia, the other tenderly caressing her while Muzzy passionately soul-kissed Fay who was so drunk she could barely sit on the stool. Sonia had finally agreed to go but she first insisted on singing "Silent Night" with the band. I guess as a reward for waiting she kissed me, her tongue expertly moving in and out of my mouth, a promise of Christmases yet to come.

It was the onions she had been eating all night that did it. They were powerful, so powerful they killed any plans I had of taking her to bed. They also must have cleared my head somewhat, because after Sonia staggered over to the orchestra I can recall staring at myself in the mirror behind the bar and asking: What the hell am I doing here?

I mumbled something about thanking them all for a nice evening, then fought my way through the mob to the door. The clean frigid air burned like a torch in my lungs and made me so dizzy I had to hold on to a post. Cabs were lined up at the curb and I staggered over to one and slid in the back seat. I had the cabbie leave me off at an all-night coffeepot on Eighth Avenue and there I consumed several cups of black coffee to sober me up so I could at least make the stairs.

Happily Aunt Clara was asleep. On the kitchen table

were two small packages, one addressed to me, the other to Joe. Inside was a gold pen with my initials.

I tried to hold them back but the tears came and they weren't from the booze. They were for things that I knew now had been lost forever. . . .

I didn't see Joe for several days after the party. As usual in the holiday period, the docks were slow. For the first time in months I had time on my hands, and I began thinking about the police union. One night I took out my shoe boxes of material on the police that I had gathered while visiting the O'Haras and the dynasty cops in Queens and reread my notes and queries. Before the night had ended I felt my interest stirring again.

The next day I left Spider in charge and walked over to the library, determined to find out all I could about the Boston Police Strike. The O'Haras had insisted that during the strike the city was taken over by the underworld, but I had always figured that their story was just another cop myth.

I was startled, however, to discover an impressive number of books, pamphlets, and magazine articles on America's police organizations in the library's main catalog. Much of the material was melodramatic, eighteenth century accounts of notorious criminals and outstanding cops. But Costello's standard history of the department gave a primitive, yet fascinating account of the growth of the New York police. I discovered in my reading that two dominant and paradoxical characteristics existed in the New York City Police Department: dedication and corruption.

I also began to understand the pride of Elliott and the O'Haras in what they called the "dynasty" police. But I also began to see more clearly the accuracy of Joe's instinct: through corruption, it was possible to control important segments of the New York City police.

When I exhausted the New York Public Library, I transferred my research to the Municipal Library, where I read volumes of police trials and numerous Seabury reports. It appeared that small cliques of police, with perhaps a high-ranking officer as their protector, had periodically been accused of corruption, but no proof had been found of a smoothly operated central payoff system for the distribution of bribes. The more I read the more excited I became at the possibilities Joe had outlined; a

375

new era in corruption faced the New York City Police Department with bribery shuttling from precinct to precinct on an assembly line basis.

I also discovered that, throughout history, when the city administration had turned down increases for police, the line organizations had been impotent and ineffective, leaving the department restless and embittered.

The crime-busting fervor of the Seabury and Dewey crusades was dying away, and the corrupters would soon be leaving their storm shelters and doing business again. As one report warned: "During the next decade the business-as-usual signs will again be hanging outside the 'blue chip' precinct doors unless the department abolishes its archaic management programs and introduces a firm method of inner control. . . ."

But I knew that proposals for reform had no chance of becoming reality. As I had suspected after my days in the company of the O'Haras and the other dynasty cops, the ruling police clique had successfully resisted all reform movements. Power rested within the hands of a small group of ancients. Commissioners arrived and departed, but few saw their great expectations fulfilled. Before their regime ended they had either been frustrated and defeated by the department's vast bureaucratic system, or had been compromised so much by ancient loyalties and traditions that their new programs were ineffectual or without strength.

I could sense the outrage and frustration experienced by the authors of some of the reports. As one young Seabury crusader wrote:

"The investigator is lost in a maze of interlocking departments, ancient customs, much cordiality, numerous smiles, a profusion of goodwill mixed with an incredible number of shrugs and blank looks. Before one realizes it, he has been escorted from the building with a gentle pat on the shoulder and is walking down Spring Street, outwitted, outsmiled, and with the task undone . . ."

One afternoon, after I had been through almost all of the police material, I came across a doctoral dissertation written in the early thirties by a forgotten graduate student on the structure of the New York City Police Department, including organizational diagrams of various departments and a breakdown on the precinct level. I immediately had it photostated.

The dissertation included a fascinating account of the
376

1919 Boston Police Strike, its causes and effects. One page leaped out at me:

The actions of Coolidge (then Governor of Massachusetts) of course broke the strike and historians of law enforcement in this country have insisted that such a thing could never happen again. However, Langly's study of municipal law enforcement agencies, civil and criminal, disputes this. As he states:

"A strike by a police department in a major American city cannot be dismissed as improbable. In the winter of 1933–34 police in at least three large cities, two in the midwest and one on the eastern seaboard, held secret meetings debating the advisability of leaving their posts. One department had suffered three deaths in a riot following a sitdown strike in a Works Progress Administration Center which the local press and the county prosecutor charged had been instigated by radical elements from a nearby community. At the police meetings which were reported many weeks later in the community's daily morning and afternoon newspapers, it was stated that 'cooler heads prevailed and the talk of strike died away.'

'It is significant that in 1910–1912, following the bombings of industrial buildings and the homes of prominent citizens, particularly those connected with western mining interests, and the shooting of four policemen in a northwest city (all attributed to the IWW), the small force of ten policemen, a sergeant and a lieutenant, left their posts for two days, refusing to return until the leaders of the community publicly stated their support of the police and the county government and in an emergency meeting allocated a three thousand dollar reward for the arrest and conviction of the perpetrators of the bombings and the shooting of the police.

"A survey of the newspapers of the time reveals a state of panic existed in the policeless community following the daylight robbery of a small local brush factory, extensive vandalism by schoolboys who the local press charged 'acted like savages' and the fatal shooting of a prominent citizen by his neighbor who said he thought the man was an intruder. Local accounts reveal extensive public display of firearms with one man armed with a shotgun pictured on the

377

porch of his home. His wife and three young sons who surrounded him were all similarly armed."

If this could happen to a small, policeless community, I thought, what would take place in New York City if the cops went out on strike? Or Buffalo? Or Albany? Or Philadelphia? Or Detroit? Or Los Angeles?

Or a string of American cities—if their police all walked out at the same time?

It was no longer a New York City police union I was contemplating—now it was a national organization with every large city in the nation linked by one union of police!

On the day after New Year's shortly before the shapeup whistle blew, Joe walked into the pier office, nonchalantly hanging up his coat as if he had just returned from the diner across the street. He was as dark as an Indian.

I finally managed to blurt out, "Where the hell have you been?"

"Miami," he said flopping down in the chair across the desk from me. "Believe it or not it hit ninety the day before yesterday."

"What were you doing down there?"

He stretched and yawned. "I was down there with the Duchess."

"The Duchess!"

"Sure. We took off at the party. She said it was too damn noisy and was givin' her a headache so I suggested we go somewhere where it would be quiet."

"Joe! You went down there with a colored dame?"

He shrugged. "You get used to it after a while. I just had to—there wasn't any way of gettin' out of it."

"Why did you have to?"

"I knew she was settin' up a situation to test me—to see if I was just talkin' or if I meant what I said. She wants to be seen with a white guy, especially a young white guy . . ."

"What line did you hand her?"

"The usual crap—that I had never met a woman who so excited me, who had all the things I wanted—she was intelligent, she was attractive, she knew how to wear clothes, and above all she wasn't some jerky young dame who only cared about lindy hoppin', boozin,' and roughin' it up in the hallway. I told her I wanted an established business. She liked that."

"And she swallowed all that stuff, Joe?"

"At her age they're all hungry." He added with a grin, "You know the old ones, Frank: 'they don't yell, they don't swell, and they're grateful as hell . . .' If that's for whites . . . what is it for colored?"

"But didn't you feel funny walkin' around with a colored dame in a hotel?"

"We didn't go to a hotel. She has her own place right on the beach." He shook his head. "You wouldn't believe it, Frank, it's like one of those places in a magazine. You sink down in the furniture and there's slidin' glass doors that lead right out on the sand. Palm trees. Sun all the time. The ocean right there"—he laughed—"a little different from the pier."

"But didn't you go out?"

"Every mornin' we made plans to go out that night and do a little gamblin'. But at the last minute she would cop out. I'll lay a bet she's afraid of whites. She doesn't like niggers but she can't do without them."

"What did you do, just walk around with her on your arm?"

"We ate. We drank. We went to bed." He said blithely, "How does that sound? Food. Drink. Bed. The perfect vacation."

"Did you get what you went after?"

"The name of the big cop?" He shook his head. "I wouldn't have listened if she had wanted to tell me. Every time she started to talk about numbers I told her to forget it."

"I thought that was the whole idea."

"It was and still is."

"I think you missed a chance of a lifetime, Joe . . ."

"You're wrong, Frank," he said firmly. "When she spills her guts to me she's gonna beg me to listen. You know, one way of not getting' a woman to tell you her secrets is to let her know you're dyin' to hear them. If they think you don't give a damn they'll bust a gut to tell ya. This is their big thing and you couldn't care less? It eats them . . ." He put his feet up on the desk and gingerly leaned back in the old swivel chair.

"Then do you know what they do? They start—a little bit at a time—throwin' out pieces of information. But only to lead you on. If you bite, that's it. You won't get any more until they're ready to give. Then out goes another piece. Remember when we were kids, Frank, and we would

379

go down to the pier and fish for tommycods with pieces of bread? Remember how in the beginnin' when we didn't know any better, every time we got a nibble we would jerk the line and lose the bait? Well, that's the way it is with women and their secrets, especially older dames." He looked thoughtful for a moment. "When the Duchess gives, it will be everythin'. I want to know who and when, how much and—most important—why? That will be part one of my campaign. When I get it, then comes part two . . ."

"What's part two, Joe?"

He let his feet go down with a bang, then stood up and stretched effortlessly like a cat.

"You'll see. But let's talk about somethin' important. Did you do any work on the cops?"

"Oh, I spent a few hours in the library," I told him as casually as I could.

"Yeah? What did you find out?"

"I probably know more than Elliott about the history of the cops."

"The hell with the history, what else did you find out?"

"There's been a few police strikes—"

He suddenly came alive.

"C'mon, baby, tell me, what did you find out?"

I talked for more than an hour. He didn't say a word, only listened. When I shoved the photostats of the dissertation toward him he read and reread the pages. Then he leaned back and whistled softly.

"Frank! You did one hell of a job!" He tapped the pages. "We got it. Right here. If it can be done in Boston it can be done right here in New York. In L.A. In Detroit. Christ! We could pull a nationwide strike of cops! Do you know what that would mean?"

"Take it easy, Joe, I admit the idea isn't as crazy as it seemed but it's still only an idea. It would take a fantastic amount of money and work even to make a dent in the New York cops . . ."

"We can do it."

"Not at this time. First we need a tremendous amount of union experience. Then money. More important, I don't think the timing is right—"

He slapped his hand down on the photostats.

"This says right here the cops in New York were only recently turned down for a raise and they're mad as hell . . ."

"It's universal, Joe. Nobody has money. It would be different if everybody had money and the cops were refused a pay raise. We have to wait . . ."

He slid the sheets into his desk. "Okay, if you say so. But we're not goin' to forget it!"

"We won't."

"There's another guy who won't—Pepe. He's real hot for this one, Frank."

He jumped up and grabbed an old lumber jacket hanging from a nail on the wall. "Let's take a walk around and see what's happenin'."

On the way out I asked him: "How long do you think it will take to pull off part one of the campaign?"

"With the Duchess? Maybe a year. Maybe less, maybe more."

"A year! You intend to screw around with this dame for a year?"

"Don't knock it, Frank. She's no chicken but she knows a lots of tricks." He grinned. "Like one night when we got loaded . . ."

34 STRIKE

In the beginning, only after we had taken over the coopers and reorganized the union did I finally realize I could make people do as I wanted. It was intoxicating for a young man, even though in those early years my influence, compared to other labor leaders, was infinitesimal. I was not an official of a major seaport union but only vice-president of a small, untested organization of decrepit old men. If we made threats only they trembled; if we made promises only they were pleased.

As the winter of 1939–40 passed into history, however, with the whole world seemingly balanced on the Maginot Line, I discovered in our tiny barony that power, no matter how limited, produces rewards that can shape a man's life. I noticed this first in Joe, then myself. We talked differently, walked differently, even looked differently. Harder. Older. Suspicious. Knowing. Cynical.

It was catching; Train finally abandoned his eternally raveling sweater and baggy pants and bought a suit. Spider rented an apartment off Central Park West and replaced his sex-starved ex-schoolteacher, her alcoholic husband, and their two-room apartment in Queens for a series of flashy showgirls. He became an enthusiastic photographer and an avid buyer of gimmicks that promised to improve his prints—sometimes pornographic. Joe and I agreed many times we would move to a beautifully furnished apartment somewhere on Central Park West, but somehow we kept delaying the move. I always remembered Tom Gunnar's explanation of why the Gimp had constantly returned to the Neighborhood; he needed identity. . . .

We purchased a secondhand Dodge, and Train became our chauffeur. He loved the car and spent hours washing and polishing it.

That winter we had more old men for friends than I had ever wanted. When we came onto the piers, they greeted us with shouts and waves; even shippers on a rare visit to our stringpiece went out of their way to give us a jovial hello and a look full of curiosity. I suppose in their view we were freaks, curiosities, and the savage, established world of the racketeering unions on the waterfront would take care of us in the months to come.

Joe and I had also acquired more enemies than we had ever wanted. The Gimp's Pistoleers who had lost their no-show jobs were ready to cut our throats, while the tough old hoodlums who ran the racket locals on the Chelsea piers would have been only too happy to hear we had been found in the river. They had lived with the Gimp for years; for them it was a question of one crook working with another—we were merely pawns backed by shadowy forces. We half expected that one day a disgruntled Pistoleer or a hood working for one of the racket piers would peg a shot at us. But at that time they seemed content to sit back and see what would happen.

I soon learned to accept the fawning old men and take the hard looks and whispers as part of the game, but not Joe. He adopted Machiavelli's favorite philosophy: that a leader should try to be both loved and feared; if not both, then it is safer to be feared. He tested the philosophy only once, but it worked.

It was a few months after the Duchess's Christmas

party when we received a call at our pier office from Polyclinic; Spider had been admitted to the emergency ward.

We rushed over to find him badly battered. Two of the Gimp's Pistoleers who were working as enforcers for the shylocks on the Chelsea piers had followed Spider into Regan's. They worked him over with a pinch bar, and it took fifty stitches to close the lacerations in his scalp and face. It took all of Joe's influence over Train to prevent the big moron from roaring down there in the Dodge and taking on all of Chelsea by himself.

"They must be taught a lesson, that if they hit one of us they hit all of us," Joe said. "If we don't, then someday they'll walk in and everythin' we have will go down the drain. You could be next, Frank, then me. And Train . . ."

"Well, what do you want to do? Go down there and let Train take care of them?"

"No. Not us. Someone will talk—and Supercop will have us downtown. I'll make a call . . ."

"Pepe?"

"Who else?"

"Joe, Pepe will only own more of us."

"What the hell, he's payin' high rent for the property . . ."

Joe made two calls, one to Pepe, the other to the boss checker of the racket local's pier to inform him that the two hoods would be found in the river very shortly. All he got was a Bronx cheer that even I could hear outside the phone booth.

A week later the harbor cops fished them out. When we received word that a Mickey Mouse was on the pier waiting for the harbor squad to drag the bodies out of the river, Joe insisted we tour the waterfront as a show of strength. With Train driving we visited pier after pier, greeting the coopers, carpenters, and balers in their sheds like visiting game wardens.

On the Chelsea pier, Joe casually walked to the end of the stringpiece where the cops were still standing, alongside the covered bodies, surrounded by a group of morbidly curious longshoremen.

"An accident, officer?" Joe innocently asked a radio car cop who was leaning against the bulkhead. Below us the harbor tug was just moving out.

"A couple of floaters," the cop said. "The guys around here say they worked the pier. Want to take a look? Maybe you know 'em. We gotta make an ID down at the morgue . . ." He made a face. "Whew! When that breeze hits you!"

"There they are," Spider muttered as we walked back down the stringpiece.

"Don't start anything, Train," Joe said softly. "Just keep walking."

The racket guys gathered in a small knot at the door of their office, turning to stare at us as we approached.

As we passed them Joe called out, "I see some of your boys had an accident. What were they doing, diving for a pinch bar?"

Western Union did not have to deliver the message. If they had not known it before, they knew it now.

Lay off.

During the winter of 1940 we devoted all our energies to the strike we planned to call in the spring when our contract ran out. Day after day, the grisly revelations of Murder Incorporated in Brooklyn shook us up; we were sure Pepe and his combination had something to do with it.

But there was never a mention of Pepe, Gus, or even East Harlem in the newspaper accounts. One day when we were talking to Pepe, I impulsively threw an evening newspaper on his desk.

"Did you see what's happening in Brooklyn, Pepe?" I asked.

He smiled and pushed the paper aside. "Bums, Peppino," he said softly, "bums."

Gradually the headlines grew smaller. Then one day Abe Reles slipped out of the window in the Half Moon Hotel, Lepke went to the chair, and the stories were pushed out of the papers by news of a new movement of Hitler's armies.

As the Nazi armies kept marching across Europe, we were making plans for our own surprise attack—the dock strike.

In every meeting we had with Maxie, he solemnly promised that the racket locals would respect our picket lines. As the spring neared, Joe and I began to believe him. Dead men were being found in alleys, hallways. Shylocks, enforcers, and even one or two of the old-time Prohibition-era racket boys had been dumped quietly in the drink after being beaten or tortured. Dewey had been elected DA and, according to the newspaper stories, Captain

Elliott had taken over the police unit formerly attached to the Special Prosecutor's office. Inspector Cornell had returned to the police department in some big job. You could tell times were changing.

We set up a strike fund, leased coffee wagons, had placards printed, and ordered a free lunch in the rear of Regan's Hall for every day the strike lasted. We also made our maximum demands ridiculously high. This was not only for bargaining, Maxie explained, but for the under-the-counter deal we could make with the lines. Of course, we had every intention of selling the old guys out.

I had a brief twinge of conscience which I rationalized by pointing out that they would be getting much more than they would have gotten under the Gimp's rule. Besides, I figured, it was about time someone paid us for all the time we put in on that bitterly cold waterfront.

Maxie also told us that there would be another part of the deal—a secret agreement with the shippers to use our trucks.

"What trucks?" I asked him. "We don't own any trucks."

"We will. Our company will lease them out to the shippers . . ."

"I guess this is stupid question number ten, but where is the company and where are the trucks?"

"We'll have more trucks than we'll know what to do with," Maxie said. "First let's make the deal . . ."

The shippers were totally unprepared for the strike. United States Customs was formally notified that damaged cargo would have to remain on the stringpieces indefinitely; under federal law shipments could not be cleared until they were repaired and restored to their original loading pallet.

I notified the newspapers and the Fox Movietone News that an unusual strike would be taking place. I had also prepared a small contingent of ancients—one had a long white beard and looked like Santa Claus—to line up behind Joe as he marched our membership up Eighth Avenue to St. Malachy's, the Actors' Church, where the strikers were to be blessed by one of the priests. I had conned the good Father into doing this by pointing out that ninety-nine percent of the coopers were really jobless actors and stagehands working the docks to survive!

Somewhere in the flat I had found an old St. Barnabas letter sweater and forced Joe to wear it. Even cynical

Maxie agreed it made a fascinating picture—handsome, young Joe, looking like a male Joan of Arc, leading his parade of trembling, creaking old men. I insisted that they kneel in the street for the blessing; this of course stopped traffic and brought the Times Square cops on the run. I slipped them each a ten and suggested they take off their hats. It certainly added a solemn touch.

Despite the ever-increasing amount of war news, we obtained a respectable amount of newspaper space. The radio newscasts gave us prominent mention and the *News* ran a story with the headline: Methuselah, Inc. Joe Gunnar (22) Pres.

As Pepe and Maxie had predicted, the racket locals respected our pickets and the waterfronts slowly but determinedly ground to a complete halt. The Brooklyn piers were closing one by one and Staten Island was shut down. Then came calls from Jersey that longshore gangs in Hoboken and Jersey City were refusing to cross our lines. A few truck drivers who tried to drive onto the stringpiece were clobbered. It was a complete victory. A blitzkrieg. But I wasn't naive enough to think that Pepe's gunpower hadn't helped.

The shippers caught on fast. By the afternoon of the first day we were in a paneled conference room on top of a building near the Battery, listening to Maxie carefully spell out our demands to their spokesman.

The shipper was a tough, rasping-voiced guy who had come up from the waterfront himself.

"Don't give me any crap, counselor," he snapped. "What do you want?"

"A contract for our lighters," Joe said suddenly.

Both Maxie and I stared at him.

The shipper carefully lit a cigar. "What do you mean, Gunnar?"

"Maybe we shouldn't be here," Joe snapped to Maxie.

"Wait a minute," the shipper said hastily. "Do you *have* lighters?"

"We have lighters. You need them. We supply them. A simple business deal," Joe explained.

The shipper gave him a knowing smile. "Okay, kid, you have a deal." He held out his hand. "You and your partner want to shake on it?"

Joe and I shook his hand.

"Now let's get down to this goddam union of yours," the shipper said. "What's the best you will take?"

We settled for a few pennies more an hour and a host of insignificant concessions. When we spoke of a pension fund the shipper just laughed.

"You have as much chance of gettin' that one, counselor, as a snowball has in hell."

"Maybe so," Maxie replied, "but you are still going to give us a letter of intention that at the next reopening of the contract you will agree to talk about it . . ."

"Are you crazy?" the shipper shouted. "The boys would never stand for a pension for those old bastards! Nobody gets that on the waterfront!"

"I didn't say we *wanted* the pension," Maxie said quietly, "I said we wanted the letter of intention. I don't want any DA coming around to tell us we sold the old guys out."

"In other words you want somethin' to tell 'em?"

"Exactly. I also want a wage reopener clause for next spring—"

"A reopener? The association always turned that one down!"

"You mean they did before today, but they're going to do it now," Maxie snapped. "Let's not bullshit each other—these piers are loaded with war cargo. If we get into this thing you won't have enough piers to handle the stuff. The shippers are making a mint. Remember when those Commies pulled that wildcat last spring? It cost you guys a big piece of change. We don't want that and neither do you. So let's keep everybody happy. Okay?"

The shipper gave him a tight smile.

"Okay, counselor, you got it. A letter of intention on the pension and a reopener clause."

"And you're goin' to pay 'em for the time they walked out," Joe said, "plus a week's pay as bonus."

The shipper laughed. "Okay, Jesse James. Let's have a drink on it."

We closed the so-called contract negotiations with what the shipper claimed was the best scotch money could buy.

Outside Maxie asked Joe, "Where the hell did you get that lighter idea? I thought we were going to sell him trucks?"

"Forget trucks," Joe said. "There's too many pissant truckers now. Lighters are bigger. They mean more dough. Now where the hell do we get 'em?"

"Don't worry about it," Maxie said wearily. "I'll set up
387

the deal. But for crissakes next time let me know about these ideas beforehand, willya?"

That night in a packed Regan's Hall Joe gave our members the news of their "victory" he shrewdly pointed out they had lost only a day's work but this would be paid for by the shippers along with a bonus of a week's pay. In other words, they not only received a raise but a week and a day's vacation. It was the old idea of screwing "them" and they loved it. Joe also described in glowing terms the pension plan the shippers had agreed to discuss at the next contract.

Our friend Captain Elliott, however, wasn't impressed with our efforts.

"Not much of a contract, boys," he said a few days later as he strolled into the stringpiece.

"It was a solid victory," I told him. "It was the first time the coopers had an honest election and got a square deal from the shippers."

"Well, you had an honest election," he said softly, "but a square deal?" He shook his head. "You had the waterfront shut down tight. You could have gotten twice as much. Why not?"

"We have to walk before we can run," Joe said. He turned to me. "What the hell are we talkin' to this cop for, Frank? We don't have to discuss our union business with cops!"

"That's true, you don't have to discuss anything with me," Elliott replied. "I'll see you boys around."

Joe stared after Elliott. "I have a funny feeling that son of a bitch is gonna be on our backs for a long time . . ."

We organized a lighter-leasing company with an office on Tenth Avenue, bought several ancient lighters, and signed a contract with the shippers. Aunt Clara, bewildered but excited, was our president, at fifty a week. All she had to do was sign the checks and the documents we put in front of her.

With the strike settled, Maxie showed us the ropes. When the cash flow of dues, assessments, and payoffs for side deals began to flow in, Maxie set up a mortgage company through which Joe, as president of the union, channeled funds to be used in mortgage loans; the fees we received were split three ways. After the payments had substantially reduced the value of the mortgages, we would buy them for the union. We had taken the original purchase at the par value but sold them to the coopers at the reduced value. We also established a "Coopers' Public Relations Department Account," which sounded innocent enough but was, in reality, a revolving fund in which we deposited union funds, and then withdrew them in cash to be forwarded to a safety deposit box that Joe and I maintained in a small bank not far from the Jersey waterfront.

The success of the coopers won us a great deal of publicity. We were young, imaginative, outwardly as honest and brave as King Arthur's Knights, and we caught the imagination of the public in a time when capital and the bosses were the villains. It was the time of Reuther and his men fighting the giant Ford, of John L. Lewis and his golden voice crying out to the country to take his grimy-faced miners into their hearts, of the new sit-ins and picket lines marching everywhere. War in Europe was easing the Depression, the economy was rising, and the guy in the street had his hand out.

When I saw what publicity could do I made sure Joe championed the cause of the police at every opportunity. He didn't need much coaching, in fact I was surprised at how much at ease he was with reporters.

Once when a young labor reporter for the *Tribune* sought us out, we gave him a tour of the waterfront, pointing out the obscure, virtually unknown workers who desperately needed union representation.

"We're interested only in Nobodies," Joe told him, giving me the eye, "the guys everyone takes for granted but if he's not around everythin' falls apart. . . ." He pointed to a traffic cop. "Now take that ordinary cop on the beat . . . every mornin' he kisses his wife good-bye but she doesn't know whether or not she will have to go to a morgue to identify him before five o'clock. Does the city give a damn? Hell no! But suppose this cop wasn't around? Can you imagine the traffic jam on this street! And how about the cops who have been shot up? The guys still in wheelchairs . . ."

I was mistaken if I thought Joe had forgotten the things I told him about the O'Haras, Drummer, and the crippled detective Lenny Farber. . . . I was to learn he absorbed information like a sponge, wringing it out whenever he needed it . . .

That was the first time Joe mentioned the plight of the forgotten policeman and how badly he was treated by the public and his city. The young reporter, apparently impressed, gave us quite a write-up including a picture of

Joe, standing on a sidewalk thoughtfully studying an obviously harassed cop directing traffic.

We received an amazing amount of mail on that, mostly from wives of cops. The police magazine, *Spring* 7-3100, reprinted the entire *Trib* article with a glowing editorial. But it didn't set too well with the police line organizations and they blasted us in public statements, yet the cop on the beat remembered what Joe had said for a long time.

The war continued in Europe. First Hitler's armies blitzed their way along the Western Front, tore Rotterdam apart with bombs, and bypassed the Maginot Line to sweep on to the English Channel. On the waterfront it was impossible to ignore the war; it was thrust into our faces almost daily. As the Battle of the Atlantic mounted, stretchers started to come down the gangplanks to the waiting ambulances lined up on the stringpiece.

As the war moved into 1941, and we turned twenty-three, we did some recruiting among stock clerks and helpers in the city's big warehouses and organized a small union that played hell with the manufacturers when we pulled them out for a week. The timing was perfect. Shipments were coming so fast that when we threatened to call out the coopers in sympathy—which would have tied up all the overseas cargoes—they gave in. This time Maxie got his way and we went into the trucking business. On a loan from the coopers we bought a fleet of trucks and contracted to haul for the same warehouses with which we had signed. It was a cozy deal.

We now had two small but very profitable unions and two rapidly expanding businesses, lighterage and trucking.

"You only have to remember two things," Maxie warned us. "Don't be greedy, and when Pepe says dance—dance. Okay?"

Okay.

35 *MR. BIG*

It wasn't all work and no play. Every free night found Joe with the Duchess in Harlem which was the thing to do in those days; there was more music, more excitement, more exotic sin north of 110th Street than in all the city.

Sonia and I drifted into a casual affair. She was always available, friendly as a kitten, was marvelously funny when she was drunk, had an exciting body and a head as empty as a gourd. I even got to endure her singing that idiotic melody "Hutsut Song."

In the beginning I felt as if I had betrayed Chena but as the months, then the years began to slip by without a letter or a note, what hope I had that I would ever see her again began to waver.

Yet Pepe insisted that one day he would surprise me and bring her back. Nicky, he explained, was recovering from wounds that had almost killed him and his mother was adamant in her refusal to leave until she could bring him back home. Chena had no choice, she had to stay in that tiny, remote village. The mail, he said, was almost nonexistent but he swore that she was alive and well.

How did he know? Pepe would only answer with a smile and one word: friends.

I wanted to believe him; I still loved Chena more than anything else in the world. Yet life and time were moving fast. I had more money now than I had ever dreamed of owning. My closet was filled with Kolmer-Marcus suits. Joe and I had each bought a car. We were virtual dictators of a pier and ruled the lives of men three times as old as we were. We were confident, cocky, and growing arrogant with power.

Then there was that cozy little apartment off Union Square with the lights low, the music soft, the glasses never empty, and a statuesque Polack eager and ready for bed.

Only a monk would have refused and I wouldn't give you odds on a monk . . .

Our weekends usually began with a great deal of wild enthusiasm and ended—at least for me—with much regret and firm resolutions at the first whir of the six o'clock alarm on Monday morning.

We would meet Friday night at the Duchess's where we tried to outdrink and outshout each other over the boogie-woogie records until everyone was hungry. Dinner was usually at Mr. A's, which I always considered offered the finest Italian food in the city—outside of Patsy's. Next came Small's Paradise or the Cotton Club, then on to the Savoy where young black bodies whirled, twisted, writhed, and were flung over heads and down between legs in a froth of swirling skirts as the lindy hoppers leaped into action to win the weekly Friday Night Silver Cup.

We usually ended in an after-hours club. Our favorite was Papa Joe's on 118th Street which was simply an old colored guy's apartment in a shabby brownstone where booze, beer, and sandwiches were served after the regular bars had closed. It was the hangout for musicians and the numbers guys; after the clubs had shut down that place really jived and jumped. You could hear the greatest horns or the wildest drums and one unforgettable morning Lady Day sang until dawn.

Here in her court where smoke banked like a fog, the Duchess was blood royal. Runners, collectors, shylocks, musicians sought her out to tell her their troubles, ambitions, problems, and I guess even dreams.

As 1941 flowed by, I got to know the Duchess. She was a devoted hedonist, the softest touch in Harlem, a shrewd businesswoman, a superb organizer, and a fervent gambler. Running her numbers operations—and keeping it independent—were the joys of her life—and then there was Joe.

As Muzzy had told us at the Christmas Eve party, the Duchess secretly despised her dark skin and was contemptuous of black men whom she viewed as spineless, without ambition, and content to let their women take over as head of the family. I heard a lot of this from the Duchess, especially when she was loaded. She was enthralled when Joe told her I had read more books than any five guys he knew. Perhaps that was why the Duchess confided in me; I was also a good listener. But Joe was different. When he

392

began to nod automatically to everything you said, you knew gears were meshing.

Yet while the Duchess scorned her blackness, it was only among the "coloreds," as Pepe called them, that she relaxed or felt at ease. Like the Gimp who always returned to the Neighborhood, she desperately needed to retain her sense of identity. North of Ninetieth Street she was somebody.

I believe the extremes she saw in Joe—ruthlessness, aggressiveness, and, parodoxically, compassion and tenderness—attracted her.

"When that boy wants to be nice," she would tell me, "he's a dream."

Then with a shake of her head, "But when he's not he's a bastard—"

In the beginning, Joe had been something of a novelty for the Duchess; a handsome young white guy to show off in the Cotton Club, the Savoy, or in Papa Joe's afterhours club, where she regally ruled her black and white courtiers.

Gradually I noticed a change. I could see in the way she looked at Joe that the Duchess had fallen in love with him. Fox saw it too. One day he told Muzzy he was leaving to work for the wops in East Harlem.

"You see the bums that hang around her, Frank?" Joe said when I told him about Fox. "As I told you, I'm different. When she's with me she's not black, she's as white as Aunt Clara and bein' treated as the most beautiful, most respected woman in the world. Of course she's fallin' for me! What the hell competition do I have? Muzzy?"

"She's going to be hard to dump, Joe."

"When I get what I want she'll play ball," he said.

"And if she refuses?"

"She won't refuse—that I guarantee!"

In Harlem we also saw hard drugs for the first time. Whiskey had been the scourge of the Neighborhood, but in Harlem it was heroin and cocaine.

One night when we were coming out of the Cotton Club, the Duchess left us abruptly and walked over to a young girl standing in a doorway. She spoke to her earnestly for a few minutes, then slipped something into her hand. The girl quickly disappeared.

"What was that all about?" Joe asked.

"The kid's a junkie," the Duchess said bitterly, "and she's mainlining . . ."

Muzzy jabbed his finger into his arm.

"Right in the arm with the needle."

"She's only a kid!"

"She's sixteen," the Duchess said. "I know her mother. She picked up for us in a laundry on Spring Street. She did everything for that kid. She even brought her down to the laundry so she could keep an eye on her."

"Looks like she didn't have enough eyes," Joe said.

"You know, you're a bastard, Joe?" the Duchess said indignantly. "A real bastard?"

"What happened with the kid, Duchess?" I asked.

"Who knows?" she said with a shrug. "One day her mother came in and said she couldn't pick up anymore, she had to get a job closer to home. When we came up here last month, I met her in the ladies' room at the club—"

"In the Cotton Club!" Muzzy said. "What the hell was she doin' there?"

"She was the matron in the ladies' room," the Duchess said. "She told me how her daughter was a junkie and hustling. Her mother's working inside and that damn kid's trying for two-dollar tricks with the white guys that come up here . . ."

"Hey, honey, I wouldn't touch her with a ten-foot pole," Joe protested.

She turned around and kissed him.

"I don't mean you, baby—"

"The boys say the wops on the East Side are startin' to bring that stuff into Harlem," Muzzy said.

"Is there more money in drugs than in numbers?" I asked Muzzy.

"Money!" he cried. "There's millions more than in numbers! Why do you think the wops are goin' into it?"

"Who needs that kind of money?" the Duchess said angrily. "Did you see that kid? How can you have any luck dealing with stuff like that?"

Joe pointed out, "Nobody twists their arm to take it, honey."

She answered softly, "Sometimes, baby, for the kids up here, there's nothing else. . . ."

The docks were never so busy. The war in Europe was spreading day after day and, in the metropolitan area, we were gradually entering a wartime economy. Business was on the move.

Spring, then summer, arrived and Joe never mentioned his "campaign" with the Duchess and I never asked him. Then one day he said, "The Duchess is about ready to give, Frank."

"Mr. Big?"

"A couple of times when she was loaded she started to talk about him. She dropped his first name a few times—Dick. I let it pass. In fact I told her I wasn't interested in her"—he snickered—"extracurricular activities. That really burned her." He added. "She wants me to marry her."

"What did you tell her?"

"I didn't say yes and I didn't say no."

"Joe! Are you nuts? She's colored and at least forty!"

"You would never know it in bed, buddy."

"Be serious! You're not thinking of it, are you?"

"Don't be a jerk! In a couple of weeks I'll know everythin' I want to know."

"Then what?"

"We'll take it from there—"

"I still don't get it, Joe. Why would a guy with a top spot in the cops mix it with a colored dame? And an *old* colored dame at that?"

"Maybe he likes to change his luck. Who knows? But we'll find out."

It took Joe longer than he had estimated, but by the start of the fall he had what he wanted. One morning he came into the office and carefully shut the door.

"Spider around?"

"He's out on the pier."

"Tell him to take over. You and I have a lot of talkin' to do." As we walked to the banana shed, Joe burst out, "I got it. Everything. The guy's name, how he operates, his cut—everything."

"Why?" I asked.

"He likes—little girls. Black!"

"How little?"

"Very little. Ten, twelve, fourteen—no more. But get this—nothin' happens! That's the deal. He sits there—"

"What does he do?"

"The Duchess says each kid comes in, takes off her clothes, and walks around in front of him like a model. He doesn't say a word. After it's over, he gives her a hundred bucks to whack up among them and that's it."

395

"That sounds crazy!"

Joe threw up his hands. "Of course! Who's denyin' it?"

"But who is the guy and how—"

Joe held up a protesting hand. "Better get back from the edge, Frank, you'll fall right into the river. Mr. Big is the guy Elliott worked with when he was in Dewey's office—Inspector Richard Daye Cornell!"

"That white-haired guy we met by the elevators?"

"The same. Listen to this." He read from hastily written notes. "As soon as I got out of her place, I put this stuff down so I wouldn't forget it. Cornell has been in the department most of his life and is supposed to have fantastic connections with politicians. From what the Duchess said, he satisfies all of them—Democrats and Republicans. He's a friend of whomever gets elected. The guy does a million favors for the right people. He knows everybody, and he's supposed to have a tight little clique down at headquarters.

"And get this: he's been promised the job of Supervising Chief Inspector. That means he will be in charge of the Commissioner's Confidential Squad and all gambling investigations! The Duchess swears that some day he'll be appointed Commissioner."

"How did a guy like that ever meet the Duchess?"

"Do you remember Muzzy tellin' us her husband Louie, was killed by a truck? Well him and the Gimp got to know Cornell when he was a cop on the West Side and they were runnin' beer for Owney Madden. When he became a sergeant, Louie went to Owney and persuaded him to put Cornell on the pad. Even then he was a con merchant, kissin' the ass of any politician he thought could help him. The Duchess said she never met Cornell while her husband was livin'. She only knew what he told her, and that wasn't much. After he was killed, the Gimp came over to see her and spilled the whole story—"

"About how queer this guy is?"

"No. I don't think the Gimp ever knew that. He only told the Duchess how her husband had been payin' off Cornell for protection and she should continue operatin' the policy bank. Only this time he wanted to be included in the deal. He set up a meetin' with the Duchess and Cornell and the deal was made, but Cornell didn't want any part of the Gimp. Everything had to go through the Duchess."

"So he protected the Duchess's policy racket and whatever the Gimp had going on the piers?"

"Right. But the Gimp paid the Duchess and she took care of Cornell."

"What was the pad? It must have been a big one."

"It wasn't. And that puzzled the Duchess at first. Then he hits her with this little kid bit. She said she was floored when he came up with that—"

"But she went for it?"

"What could she do? She got a couple of kids and promised them a fin apiece to take off their clothes and just walk around. She said the first time her heart was in her throat; these little black kids walkin' around her apartment with the lights turned low and this guy sittin' there without any clothes on. When it was over he thanked her and gave her some dough for the kids."

"And she's been doing that all these years?"

"Every few months she gets a call that he's comin' so she goes up to Harlem and gets the kids. The Duchess says she can get all the kids she wants, half of them are sleepin' in cellars anyway . . ."

I felt a sickening in the pit of my stomach.

"That son of a bitch! Acting like he was God Almighty when we saw him!"

"Don't knock him, Frank, that guy can be valuable to us."

"But there's one thing I still don't understand. What made the Duchess so upset she talked?"

"She saw him Friday night and he wanted his usual party. She told him she could get a couple of dames— white, black, or yellow—who would do anythin' he wants, but he walked out. She realizes that no more parties means no more protection. If that happens the wops will move in and she and Muzzy will be out on their ass . . ."

"Is she going to get the kids?"

"I told her to stall him for a while—"

"Why stall him?"

"It's all included in Part Two of Gunnar's Campaign, buddy," he said cheerfully.

It didn't take long before Part Two went into effect.

Joe didn't show up for the Friday night dates. When he did show, he was cool to the Duchess, vague, even irritable. It went on like that for weeks. It was clear the Duchess was getting edgy. Then one day Muzzy asked me:

"Frank, what's wrong with Joe?"

I managed to look surprised.

"Joe? Nothing as far as I know. Why?"

"Somethin' 's not right between him and the Duchess."

"Oh. Did they have an argument?"

Muzzy shook his head. "Not that I know of. But somethin' 's wrong. The Duchess just mopes around. I know she has called Joe a lot of times but she can't get him." There was a puzzled look on his face. "She called me the other night—"

"What was up?"

"You got me. It was late. I was in bed when the phone rang. The way she was babblin' I thought the cops had hit our bank. I got dressed and rushed over to her place."

"What was wrong?"

"Frank, ya got me. All she did was lap up booze and talk about Joe. What the hell's wrong?"

When I told this to Joe he snapped his fingers in triumph.

"Great! Now comes Part Three!"

Part Three was to be the reconciliation scene; Joe repentant and loving, the Duchess rejoicing that her prodigal had returned.

Then, a week later, came the crusher.

"I laid it on the line," Joe explained, "I told her she had to set up the kids as always with this joker. But this time they would have their pictures taken."

"Pictures?"

"Spider has invested a fortune in all that photographic crap he has. I've been goin' through some of his catalogs. For three hundred bucks we can buy a tiny camera and set it up in the apartment—"

"Joe! You're not going to take pictures of those little kids and that queer!"

"What else?" Joe asked calmly. "The kids won't know it and Cornell will be the only one to see the prints. Nice big glossy prints of naked little kids walkin' up and down in front of him."

He carefully lit a cigarette and blew out a puff.

"He will be told that if he doesn't play ball a set of prints will be sent to the mayor, the police commissioner, the newspapers, and every police official at headquarters. I'm sure the son of a bitch has some enemies who will be only too happy to see that the prints get into the right hands. How do you like that idea?"

"I feel like throwing up."

"Go outside on the pier if you have to," he said, "but that's what we will do with Inspector Cornell. What do you think Supercop would say if we sent him a set of these prints?"

"What about the Duchess?"

"What about her?"

"Didn't she ask you why you're doing this? There's no reason for her to squeeze Cornell."

"I sold her a story of how the cops were givin' us trouble on the waterfront and how we needed a connection. I also had some ideas about branchin' out, and I couldn't make a move unless I could get an okay from downtown. I needed one guy who I could pay for everythin'; for our setup and for the Duchess's. She wouldn't have to do a thing."

"What did she say to that?"

"Naturally she put up a howl. Cornell was her boy and she didn't want anyone else to touch him. Then I gave it to her short and sweet; I was desperate to get this guy in our corner. If she didn't come through, she could whistle 'Dixie.' I told her that if she really loved me as she kept sayin' she did she'd do what I wanted. And no questions asked."

"And if she didn't?"

"She would never see me again." He smiled. "I even stayed away a few days until her tongue was hanging down to the floor. She came around."

"Joe, you're a no good son of a bitch! You know that, don't you?"

"Sure I do," he admitted cheerfully. "How the hell can you get anywhere without being one?"

He started to walk away but turned around.

"Nice guys finish last, Frank."

I didn't have anything to do with the arrangements; Joe and Spider took care of wiring the apartment and setting up the camera. The Duchess sat with me, watching them.

"He knows I'll do anything," she told me bitterly. "I couldn't bear it if he went away." She shook her head. "I'm wound up like I've never been wound up before over this whitey with the big smile and the blond hair. Tell me I'm nuts, will you, Frank?" She brooded for a moment, then added, "You know you have one son of a bitch for a friend?"

There was a short silence, then the Duchess went on in a voice that was both curious and thoughtful.

"When it comes to Joe you don't argue much, do you, Frank?" She paused, then became querulous like an irritated child. "Don't you ever think he's a son of a bitch, Frank? Don't you?"

"I've told him that many times."

The Duchess finished her drink and, with a smile, added, "And the thing is we both know it and it doesn't mean a damn—does it, Frank?"

We got the pictures. I don't know why, but I felt pity for this pathetic white-haired man who sat in the easy chair, both hands on the arms, obscenely naked, staring intently as the giggling young girls walked up and down in front of him.

"Now for the meetin' with Cornell," Joe said.

"I hope you know this is blackmail. If the guy blows the whistle we're dead!"

"Do you think for one minute this old bastard will squawk?" Joe asked coldly. "We can ruin him in an hour." He motioned to the prints. "This isn't all we have. Don't forget, the Duchess has had him on the pad for years!"

"But he knows the Duchess will never blow the whistle, Joe."

"Will you stop worryin'!"

We were sitting in the Duchess's apartment with the prints spread out on the carpet. There was only Joe, the Duchess, and myself. Muzzy had been excluded at her request; I think she was ashamed. This was one of her "brandy days," as she called them, and she had been drinking steadily all afternoon.

"What happens to me?" she said staring into her glass.

"Nothing, baby," Joe said cheerfully, "I intend to take a load off your shoulders, that's all."

"If you take off that load, honey," she said looking up at him, "the wops may decide they don't need me anymore . . ."

"We'll take care of 'em."

"What will you do, fight 'em?" she said scornfully.

Joe gave her an exasperated look.

"Why don't you knock off that booze?"

"Because I don't want to, that's why," she said defiantly. "How the hell I ever let you talk me into this I'll never know."

36 *THE DEAL*

Joe's blackmailing scheme worked out as Joe had predicted. We found out where Cornell lived in Queens and early one morning, before his driver arrived, we rang his bell. He opened the door, but started to close it quickly when he saw us. Joe thrust a print in front of him.

"We just want to talk about your queer tastes, Inspector," he said softly.

Cornell looked stunned for a moment.

"You will have to wait a few minutes," he said at last. "I will call my driver—"

"We don't have the negatives, Inspector," Joe said with a smile. "I thought you should now."

"I understand completely," Cornell said grimly.

During the few minutes we stood on the steps of his Tudor-style home I sweated blood. I was sure we would soon hear the wail of a police car. But we didn't. He came out dressed like the president of the Chase National and asked where we had parked.

We had our first meeting with Cornell in a small, half-deserted, highway restaurant. It was early and the commuters rush hadn't started, so we had a booth and complete privacy. As soon as we sat down, Joe silently spread the best prints in front of Cornell. Cornell ignored them.

"Is this the Duchess's idea?"

Joe slid the prints back into an envelope. "Let's say it's our idea."

"This is obviously a shakedown. What is it you want?"

"Don't get us wrong, Inspector," Joe told him. "We're not shakin' you down for a dime. All we want to do is help you make a better business arrangement."

"Oh? In what way?"

"We know the whole setup. It's old fashioned. It needs some fixin'—"

"And you want to do the fixing I suppose?"

"Exactly. What we want is to set up a central payoff for everything—East Side, West Side, Harlem, Brooklyn. Someone pays us, we pay you—"

"What am I supposed to do?" Cornell asked, "take care of everyone down the line?"

"You take care of the people that you think should be taken care of . . ."

"Who do you represent?"

"Don't worry, it's someone big."

"Why play games?" Cornell said. "If you represent some—"

"East Harlem. Does that satisfy you?"

"I would like a name."

Joe hesitated. "The Sicilian. That's as far as we can go."

Cornell carefully buttered a piece of toast.

"You're crazy if you think I'm going to sit here and discuss this with you two! I don't even know who you are."

"Who we are, what we are, doesn't mean a goddam thing to you," Joe snapped. "This does," he said, patting the envelope. "If you don't make a deal with us right now, a set of prints will go to the mayor, the commisioner, Dewey, and anyone else we can think of. Today. By special delivery. Now do we stop the bullshit and talk?"

The only outward sign of agitation he showed was a slight twitch in his cheek and the bunching of the muscles along his jaw.

"You can't make such an arrangement offhand," he protested. "You have to talk to people. The right people."

"Fine. I'm sure you can do it," Joe said heartily. "Let's talk money. Five thousand a month for everything. Horses, shylocks, numbers. That's a hell of a lot more than you're gettin' now from the Duchess. There will be an extra five hundred bonus every time we get a call that the Commissioner's Confidential Squad is plannin' to pay us a visit."

Cornell sipped at his coffee. "It's not enough. Do you realize how many precincts, how many commanders this could entail? With every precinct the risks double." He hesitated. "It should be at least seventy-five hundred."

"Seven thousand and no bonus," Joe said.

Cornell calmly continued eating.

"Let's not dicker as if we were on Orchard Street."

402

"What do you think of the idea?" I asked him.

"Actually, something like this has been in the back of my head for a long time. That is why I have an idea of how much it would take. Perhaps I should talk to someone older and more experienced—"

"Okay," Joe said. "Seventy-five hundred. That's tops."

"With the bonus," Cornell reminded him.

Joe said in a tense, low voice, "I heard you the first time. Now what's the next step?"

Cornell held out his hand. "The negatives."

"You must think we're simple," Joe said grimly. He pushed the prints toward him. "We hold the negatives. Let's call it life insurance."

"How do I know someone else won't make another set of prints and come knocking at my door?"

"You don't. And we don't know if you'll keep your end of the bargain," Joe said cheerfully. "That will help to make us both honest. I guess we just have to trust each other."

"If such a plan has been on your mind, Inspector, why haven't you done something about it before this?" I asked.

"Simply because there was no one to talk to on your side of the fence."

"What was wrong with the Duchess?"

"The people you say you represent would never go for that. Women are not dependable." He tapped the envelope of prints. "I guess this proves a point." He sighed. "I suppose I knew that this would happen someday. But I am curious, why did the Duchess allow this—"

"You can be curious all you want, Inspector, but that's none of your business," Joe told him.

"You're a couple of new faces in this sort of thing," Cornell said to me. "You haven't been in policy, have you?"

"No. And I wouldn't advise asking Elliott about us."

Cornell looked startled. "Elliott! God no! The only reason I bring up your age," he said, "is that if you are only looking to make a fast buck, I would advise you to forget it. The people in East Harlem would not like that. We could all get hurt—you more than me."

"We have no desire to wind up in the river, Inspector," I told him.

He snuffed out his cigarette. "I don't have to tell you I can't promise the whole city. No one can. We have some

403

very idealistic young men, like Elliott, who would indict his brother if he caught his hand in the public till."

"We knew Elliott when he was a cop in the Neighborhood," Joe explained. "By the way, Inspector—there's one thing *I'm* curious about . . ."

"Oh? And what is that?"

"As I understand it, the Gimp paid you through the Duchess. Why wasn't he tipped off?"

"That was unfortunate but unavoidable," Cornell said. "I was in Florida a few days and I came back to find the office in an uproar. Someone had sent Elliott enough to hang Wilson several times over. It would have been too risky for me to tip him off. That's one thing you must all understand—there is just so much I can do."

"We understand," I told him. "Who sent the stuff to Elliott?"

"A stoolie perhaps," Cornell said with a shrug.

"Is Elliott going places?" I asked.

"Yes, I would suppose so," Cornell said. "Dewey likes him and, if the boss makes governor, it certainly won't hurt."

"How about you, Inspector?"

"I've had all the glory I want. When I retire"—he flashed a cold smile—"it will be with appropriate funds. I guess there is only so much idealism in a man's life." He asked abruptly, "Do you fellows have a yellow sheet?"

"Nothing important," Joe told him.

Cornell nodded, but I knew he would be looking up our records as soon as he got to headquarters.

"Can I tell our people we have a deal, Inspector?" Joe asked.

"Let's say the basics have been settled," Cornell said. "Many details must be ironed out. You realize, of course, you will have to supply accommodation arrests?"

"That's part of the deal," Joe said. "If a bust has to be made we will supply the setup."

"I'll meet you again in a week," Cornell said, consulting a small black memorandum book. "Let's say a week from today. Do you boys know New Jersey?"

"After Hoboken we're lost."

"Take Route One to a village named Glover's Mills. You'll find it on a road map. It's about an hour's drive from the city. On the edge of the village is an inn called the Continental Soldier. You can't miss it. There's a large white sign with the figure of a Revolutionary soldier in front of the place. Elderly people who live along the shore during the summer use it in the winter months. Ask for John Daye. That will be me." He patted his lips with a napkin. "There's one more, very important detail—"

"What's that?"

"You will have to tell your people I insist on a liaison man"—the smile—"a bagman if you please. Once we have made our agreement, you will not exist as far as I am concerned. Is that understood?"

"You pick the bagman?" Joe asked.

"Definitely. Someone I can trust."

"Who will it be? Do you have an idea?"

"As a matter of fact—yes. He's in Florida now but wants to return to New York. He was highly recommended to me last winter when I was down there."

"Who made the recommendation?"

"Tell your people they don't have to worry. The recommendation was made to me by an official in the Miami Police Department who, like me, will retire in a few years—with the appropriate funds."

"There's one thing we have to get settled right in the beginning, Inspector," I said.

He studied me. "What's that?"

"You can select your own bagman, that's fine with us, but I want to make a tour with him. I want to know everybody we're paying."

"I don't know if he'll go for that."

"He'll have to go for it."

"What's the difference? You're paying him. He takes care of the others."

"Little gears make a watch run, Inspector," Joe said. "We want to know exactly who we're doin' business with."

Cornell shrugged. "I guess it can be arranged—if you insist."

"We insist."

He nodded, picked up the envelope of prints, and slid out of the booth.

"Gentlemen, you will have to excuse me. I must get a cab downtown."

"By the way, Inspector," Joe said quietly, "I think you should know the negatives are in a lawyer's office. Just in case."

405

Cornell gave us a bleak look and hurried out of the restaurant. When he had gone I sank back in my seat in relief.

An hour after we left Cornell, we picked up the negatives we had hidden in my flat and went to see Pepe in his Madison Avenue gallery. He listened intently to our story from the Duchess's Christmas Eve party to our meeting with Cornell. Then he carefully studied the negatives with the aid of a lamp.

"This colored—do you trust her?" he asked.

"The Duchess? Why not?" Joe said. "I'm sleepin' with her."

Pepe looked disgusted. "Coloreds can make you sick—"

"Not this one, Pepe," Joe said with a grin. "She wants to marry me."

"*Ecco!*" Pepe cried. "Get rid of her!"

"We can't. She's too important."

"She is a stupid woman," Pepe growled.

"You sound like you know something about her, Pepe," I said.

"*Mascalzóne!* We know about her!" he said grimly. "She gave our friends much trouble. When the old man died and the kid took over—"

"Muzzy?"

"He is young—about your age, Peppino. He and the colored got together. Our friends offered a great deal of money for their business—"

"And her connections," Joe put in.

Pepe shrugged. "To peddle numbers is a thing of nothing, but the protection"—he threw up his hands—"it is everything."

"She will never sell out," Joe said. "It will take more than money."

Pepe threw the negatives on the desk. "So now you have her—"

Joe added softly, "And Cornell."

"*Marrone!*" Pepe said disgustedly. "This is a thing our friends have been talking about!"

"For East Harlem?" I asked quickly.

"*Si.* We are *stùpido,* Peppino!"

I suddenly realized that this was the first time Pepe had directly linked "our friends" to the shadowy, powerful force expanding out of East Harlem, the wops who Muzzy had predicted would some day own the city.

"Stùpido!" he repeated, slamming his fist on the desk. "We are *stùpido!* I will tell Harlem"—he held one cupped hand to his lips—"they talk, talk, talk and they pay, pay, pay, to the cops. I ask, 'Why do you pay so much?' and they say, 'The cops are like vultures. If we don't pay, they bust us.'" He threw up his hands. "Now the little Outsiders come and lay it on my desk."

"It's not only policy, Pepe," I told him. "There's something else."

"Ah," he said.

"The cops. We told him I had to make a tour with the bagman. This way we—"

I didn't have to finish. He leaned over and shook my shoulder.

"Bravo, Peppino!" he cried. "It will be better than a thousand little ants! You will see them—you will talk to them, no?"

"Of course. It will be an excellent opportunity to find out who are the good guys and who are the bad guys."

"Buòno! Buòno!" He looked up with a smile. "Now my young friends, you have done good work—what do you want?"

"You said that someday you may ask a service of us, Pepe," I volunteered. "Let this be it."

He shook his head. "This is no service, Peppino, this is business." He dramatically stabbed his chest with a finger. "One comes from the heart." He reached inside his jacket and slid out a wallet. "The other comes from this."

"Let's leave our cut up to"—Joe emphasized the words—"our friends."

"Have they disappointed you before?" Pepe asked mildly. "An arrangement will be made. Now you must see Maxie."

"Maxie? Why Maxie?" I asked.

"He is handling our interests," Pepe said. "Questions. Questions. Peppino! All the time questions! Like a *sbirro!* a detective!"

"With something this big I think we should have the answers to a lot of questions," I told him.

He patted me on the shoulder. "See Maxie, Peppino—and talk. I will call him."

There was open admiration in Maxie Solomon's face a few days later when he carefully closed the door to his office.

"Is it true what Pepe tells me? You have the Duchess's connection in a corner?"

Joe silently opened an envelope and threw him the negatives.

"Son of a bitch!" Maxie said admiringly. "That's what the wops have been talking about for months! It's getting ridiculous up there—they move across the street and they have to pay." He tapped his letter opener on the desk. "Who's going to dish out the dough?"

"We are," Joe said firmly. "Not you, not Pepe. Only Frank and me—and Cornell's bagman."

"Who will that be?"

"That's up to Cornell. We won't have anythin' to do with that."

"It's a hell of a lot of responsibility," Maxie said. "Suppose Cornell dies, or retires, or has an accident?"

"In a year we won't need Cornell," Joe said.

"You're kidding," Maxie said. "How do you figure that?"

"Once we have the system workin' it will be like perpetual motion," Joe explained. "The only problem is to start that money flowin' into the hands of the cops. Take a sergeant whose palm has been well greased for six months. No competition. No worry. Just money in his kick week after week without fail. To him it's clean bucks. Within a few months he'll depend on his graft as he depends on his salary. He'll get used to it. His wife will get used to it. Even his kids. The car payments will get easier to make. The wife will get a new coat. Multiply this sergeant by all the others we will have on the pad. After six months do you think they will give a damn who's on top? Believe me, they won't. In a year, two years, our graft will become as important a part of the job as their goddam uniforms and shields. Cornell will no longer be important—only the system."

Maxie gave him a thoughtful look.

"You know he's right, Frank?" he told me. "After a while the cops will scream if they miss one payday . . ."

"We won't miss it if our friends don't," I pointed out.

"Don't worry—they won't," he said warmly. "Seventy-five hundred is peanuts compared to what the numbers bring in." He leaned over and said softly, "Millions! That's what policy means to them—millions!"

He walked across the room and pushed aside a picture

which hid a small wall safe. He spun the dial, opened the safe, and returned with an index book.

"You had better take some notes," he said, "and for crissakes don't lose them!"

"Notes of what?" I asked.

"You have to know the policy drops and the banks, don't you?" he asked. "How will Cornell know what to protect?"

37 WHERE THE HELL IS PEARL HARBOR?

During the fall and early winter we met Inspector Cornell several times in that jerkwater village in New Jersey. I had to admire his caution. He had selected as a meeting place a summer resort that became a winter ghost town. The only persons we saw were elderly residents sitting in the lobby staring into space or going into the dining room. Cornell never registered. After someone else signed in, he slipped into the room which was paid for by cash in advance.

Each time we met him, it was apparent that he trusted us only as far as he could see us; I am sure he was aware that we shared the same opinion of him.

Among the setups we established for the payoff system was a phony midtown business office and a branch across town—both were monitored twenty-four hours a day by one of Pepe's men. The tipoffs, in code, were turned into the main office, then relayed to the branch office. The branch office then tipped off the drop, shylock, or crap game. The main office was also used as an emergency clearinghouse for cops who wanted a fast check on any guy in our setup.

"You'll have to guarantee that number as clean," Cornell said. "The DA's office is starting to go in for taps in a big way."

"You can depend on our guarantee," Joe told him. "We'll have the wire checked three times a day."

"Let's not forget every inch of the way, Gunnar, and you too, Howell, that it is your necks as well as mine."

"Dealin' with you, Inspector, how can we forget it?" was Joe's answer.

At our last meeting in November I finally brought up the subject that had been on the tip of my tongue for weeks—the police union. Over our final cup of coffee I asked Cornell:

"We would like to get your advice on something, Inspector."

"My advice?" Cornell asked coldly. "About what?"

"A police matter. What chance do you think a police union would have?"

"A police union?" Cornell said with an air of offended surprise. "With picket signs, striking, and that sort of thing?"

"What's wrong with that? Cops work for a living, don't they?"

"My God, man!" Cornell cried "you can't put police in a union like plumbers or carpenters. The public would never stand for it."

"We're not interested in what the public thinks," Joe said.

"You have to be!" Cornell snapped. "City Hall couldn't stand the pressure from the public and the politicians."

"But would the cops go for it?" I asked.

"Not at this time, they wouldn't."

"Would they ever consider such a thing?"

"It's an interesting question." He looked thoughtfully out across the winter-ravaged gardens and deserted highway. "But your timing is off. There is too much international turmoil right now. Who knows, we may be in the war by next year? If your crazy idea ever becomes a reality it will take place in a time of some great domestic strife when conditions in this country are so unsettled that the police will be viewed as villains and their lot becomes unbearable either because of political creeds or a violent change of their status in the community. Do you know of the Boston Police Strike?"

"I've read about it."

"Well then you know about the conditions in that city at the time. Those same kind of conditions would have to become compounded and nationwide."

He gave us an amused smile. "Don't tell me you fel-

410

lows are contemplating organizing the New York City Police Department?"

"We have been talkin' about it," Joe said.

"Don't waste your time or your talents," Cornell told him in a voice edged with contempt. "Stick to your crooked unions, numbers, and corrupting police. You're very good at it."

I shot back, "You're our best example, Inspector."

He nodded. "Touché."

Joe ignored the exchange. "What about the line organizations? Would they fight such a plan?"

"Obviously. You would be taking away their membership, dues, and power."

"From what we understand they haven't done a hell of a lot for the cops."

Cornell said, "How can they get anything done? They are regarded by City Hall as a nuisance and downtown we don't pay too much attention to them. They are mostly coffee and cake fraternal groups."

"Thanks for the advice. Now when do we get the name of your contact, and when do we meet him?" I asked.

"Next Sunday. Right here. Ask for Daye's room as usual. I'll leave a note for you in the mailbox. It will have his name. He'll be waiting."

"Why don't you give it to us now?" I asked.

"He will come up from Florida next Friday," Cornell explained. "I will meet him halfway and outline the final details. Let's say I intend to be perfectly sure before you meet him."

"Does he know anything about his? Have you spoken to him yet?"

"Of course. I have reported to him after every one of our meetings. He has already been in touch with certain friends of his in the department."

"What is he—a bookie?" Joe asked.

Cornell shook his head.

"A cop?"

Cornell held up a protesting hand.

"Wait until you meet him. He'll tell you anything you want to know. I am sure you will find his background very interesting."

"Suppose we want to get in touch with you?" Joe asked him.

"You can't," he said tersely. "I want it understood that
411

everything will be done through the man you will meet next Sunday. As I told you, once I leave this room you don't exist as far as I am concerned."

The following week was agony; Sunday seemed never to come. When we finally returned to the inn in New Jersey to meet the bagman, the hotel clerk handed Joe a small envelope that had been in the mailbox. We walked to one side of the lobby and tore it open. On a sheet of cheap paper was printed one word: Hennessy.

We looked blankly at each other. I could almost hear Cornell's triumphant chuckle loud in my ears. He had known all along what Hennessy meant to us.

Joe slowly tore the note into tiny bits and let them fall into a waste basket.

"How do you like that? Hennessy!"

"There's nothing we can do, Joe—we have to go up and see him."

"Of course. That big slob never frightened me before and he's not goin' to now. Let's go!"

The carpet was gritty and there was a feathery fringe of sand along the wall. A child's forgotten pail and shovel were in a corner. When we entered he was staring out at the waste of gray winter sky, a large sandy lot and a stretch of uneven sidewalk with thin marsh grass flourishing in the cracks.

He was seated on a stately red velvet couch stamped with a pseudo seal of the Republic in gold and silver thread, looking like a cold, monstrous bullfrog. He had gained a great deal of weight, and his huge belly stretched tight the gaily flowered short-sleeved shirt he was wearing.

There was a scar over one eyelid, the skin appeared shriveled, the eye lifeless and dead as marble. The other eye—a tiny lime buried in mounds of tanned flesh—scrutinized us relentlessly.

Next to the couch a sports jacket hung over the back of a chair, from one arm dangled a shoulder holster with a police .38.

"Take a chair," he said, without emotion.

A chill ran up my back at that familiar soft, deadly voice.

He motioned to a bottle of scotch and some glasses on a table.

"Have a drink?"

412

When we both shook our heads, he said, "Don't like to drink with cops, heh?"

"We hate cops," I told him.

He shrugged. "What the hell, it's a living."

"You're not a cop," Joe said. "You're a goddam book-maker—"

"Bagman," Hennessy corrected him. "Nothing moved in Miami unless I paid off. We had a good thing going down there."

"Why didn't you stay there?"

"I had enough of that goddam sun and those old women sitting in the street," he grumbled. "There's only one town—New York."

He saw me studying the gun and holster and chuckled.

"What's the matter, kid—think I'm gonna plug you and your friend?"

"Not that we don't think you would like to . . ."

He waved a beefy hand at me. "Don't be stupid. I don't want any trouble with you or anyone else. I have too much riding on this one. Maybe you kids did me a favor. They kicked me out of the department so I went down south and made a lot of money. And best of all, I got rid of that nut. A crazy woman. Carryig a Bible around and reading it to store clerks! She's better off where she is." He poured three fingers of scotch into a glass and silently toasted us.

"I don't suppose you kids heard what happened to Suzy, did you?"

"No," I said. "You put us out of touch. Remember?"

"Oh yeah. You were up at the shelter for a while. What the hell, that was a vacation. How did you kids ever get close to Cornell?"

"Some day we'll tell you the story of our life," Joe said. "Let's get down to business. We want to get out of this jerkwater town."

"Okay by me," Hennessy said. He paused and lit a cigar. "Well, where do you want to begin?"

Without waiting for an answer he began to chuckle. It resonated as though it was coming up from the bottom of a well.

"Two goddam kids from the Neighborhood and a cop that made them all crap in their pants when he walked down Ninth Avenue! We're gonna play the tune and the wops are gonna dance—how do you like that?"

413

"Let's cut the comedy, Hennessy," Joe told him, "and get to work."

"Fine with me." He shifted his big bulk about on the sofa. "Where do you want to begin?"

"Did Cornell tell you I insisted on making a tour with you?" I asked him.

He looked uncomfortable. "He did but I told him *I* didn't like it. My contacts might get buck fever."

"It's not a question of what *you* like or *they* like, it's what *we* like. Got that?" Joe asked him grimly.

"Okay. Okay. I don't want any arguments," Hennessy said quickly. I'll do my best. I'll talk to 'em. Who do you want to see?"

"The people we're doing business with. The guys we have on the pad."

"When do you want to start?"

"As soon as possible."

"Give me a few weeks to set it up."

"Fine. No longer," Joe said. He pushed aside the bottle and glasses and spread out our map of the city.

"You have a copy of the code we made up with Cornell?"

Hennessy reached inside his holster and took out a small notebook.

"Right here, kid." He chuckled. "I keep it in a good place."

"Let's begin a rundown, precinct by precinct."

We spent all morning with Hennessy at the inn. When we left, we had established the organizational framework of the central payoff system of the New York City Police Department. Included in this plan was the famous "Sergeants' Club" by which monies were turned over to desk sergeants and distributed to those on our pad in the precincts. Although this framework was flexible and would expand, it would never fundamentally change. For a certain segment of the police, it would become as familiar as their blue uniforms and silver shields.

"Honest Bucks" was the ironical tag name given to the payoff. During periodic investigations by headline-hunting politicians and police commissioners who were trying to play Teddy Roosevelt, brief suspensions took place. But once the dust had settled, the organization never failed to slip back into gear without a clink or a miss, like the works of a perfectly tooled machine.

The strange loyalty the cops felt—and still feel—for the system has always fascinated me. Although they were found with payoff books and threatened with long jail sentences, not one turned informer. As Pepe always said, our side never had to silence a talking cop; the cops would do it themselves.

As we left the room in the early afternoon, Joe turned to me. "Do you trust him, Frank?"

"Strangely enough I do. He knows this isn't a five and dime operation and he wouldn't last five minutes if he pulled a double cross or played footsie with the DA. That's one advantage of working with crooked cops—they have lived on both sides of the fence."

"Well, I don't trust him," Joe said roughly. "The minute I saw him I felt like grabbin' that .38, shovin' it down his throat, and pullin' the trigger! That son of a bitch!"

"Easy, Joe. It's either working with Hennessy or forgetting the whole thing. You know what Cornell said, he picks his own bagman . . ."

"I know. I know. But someday we won't need that big slob. And even if it's a hundred years from now, I promise you I'll take care of him!"

"There's nothing we can . . ."

I broke off, when the desk clerk inside his little cubicle suddenly began shouting. Then he rushed into the lobby, excitement blazing on the tips of his cheekbones like spots of rouge.

"Pearl Harbor! The Japs have bombed Pearl Harbor! It's just come over the radio!"

"Pearl Harbor?" Joe asked the clerk. "Where the hell is Pearl Harbor?"

"It's a big base in the Pacific," he cried. "This means war!"

"Now watch those docks boom," Joe said, his eyes gleaming. "We can—" He stopped to stare at me. "What's wrong, Frank? You're as white as a sheet?"

My feet were frozen to the floor; the words of the clerk had seemed to physically stab me.

"Chena!" I blurted out. "She will never get out of there now!"

We rushed back to New York on a highway that was almost deserted. The only reaction we found to the momentous news was from a kid pumping gas at a station where we stopped. He grumbled that the football game over WOR was being interrupted by news bulletins.

It looked as if the whole Pacific fleet had been sunk.

When Lorenzo ushered us into Pepe's office we found him studying an art catalog.

"Peppino! Joe! Lorenzo, get them some coffee!"

"Did you hear the news?" I asked him.

He shrugged and held up his hands, palms out.

"Did I not tell you the bald-headed pig would go with the Germans?"

"This means we will be at war with Italy, Pepe! Chena could be killed!"

"*Va! Va!* She won't be hurt, Peppino—this I promise you."

"How the hell can you be so sure?" I cried. "She's in a village halfway around the world in the middle of a war and you tell me not to worry!"

"Take it easy, Frank."

"Goddammit, I don't want to take it easy! I want to know exactly how—"

"Did I not tell you she is safe with Nicky and that crazy woman her mother?" Pepe went on. "Why do you doubt me, Peppino? We have many friends over there. When the time comes you will see your Chena. This I have promised you on the grave of my mother!"

He spread out the glossy pages of the catalog. "Look what this *figlio di butana* is asking for his picture!" He chuckled. "Doesn't he know there's a war on?"

"Pepe, we saw Cornell's contact this mornin'," Joe interjected.

He looked up, now all business.

"Ah, who is it?"

"Hennessy."

Pepe slowly closed the catalog.

"*Pòrco diavolo!* The *animale* who beat you in the station house? The one with the wife who is . . ."

He made a circling motion with his finger by his temple.

"The same one we took care of that night. He's back and he's Cornell's bagman."

"You talked with him?"

"All morning and most of the afternoon," Joe told him. "Here's the setup . . ."

He spread the map out on the table. Pepe studied it for
416

a long time, then began snapping questions at us, tapping the map for emphasis.

"This Sergeants' Club—they will pay out the money to the cops on the beat?"

"All the cops we need," Joe told him.

"Will they tip us off?"

"Any time there's any action in their house we'll know about it."

"What about the Commissioner's men? The Confidential Squad? The *bastardi?*"

"The precincts won't know about them. That's Cornell's job. He'll make one call to this setup we'll have in midtown and give them a code number. Your telephone man will relay the information to another phone and the second one will get word to the drop. Close up. No play."

"The shylocks?"

"That's in the detective division. We won't be able to protect everyone but we'll take care of most of 'em. Once we get tipped by Hennessy the shylock will have to move fast—get out of the bar or wherever he's hangin' out."

Pepe looked at me. "We have a lot of crap games, Peppino . . ."

I told him, "You'll have to keep moving them around but we'll be tipped off when the hammer and crowbar guys go out on a job."

He put both hands on the map and leaned toward us.

"We are buying peace, no? One bundle of money for all?"

"A central payoff . . ." Joe said. "No more eager beavers puttin' out their hot little hands."

"And if they do?"

"Cornell promised he would chop it off. By the way we worked out accommodation arrests so the brass can't squawk—"

"*Buòno! Buòno!*" Pepe said, nodding. "We will use stand-ins."

"Stand-ins? What's that?" I asked.

"I have told our people in Harlem," Pepe explained, "get the bums on the street, wash them up. Give the *zìngara* a haircut and send them to court. Let them plead guilty. If the judge sends them to the island we will pay fifty dollars for every week they spend in jail." He threw up his hands in disgust. "Every day the good runners, the good ribbon men—they go to jail. Now we use the bums. What do you say, *giovinotti*—Do you like it?"

"That's a great idea," Joe said. "The cops don't care who they get in court. All they want are bodies."

"Did you make the arrangements, Peppino, to go with that *animale* to see the cops?"

"He agreed to give me a tour. Before I'm finished I'll know all there is to know."

He made a motion of writing with a pen.

"You write it all down, Peppino?"

"I'll put everything on paper."

"Why do you want it on paper, Pepe?" Joe asked.

Pepe gave him an enigmatic smile.

"Questions, questions, *giovinotto* ... tell me, are you still seeing the colored?"

"Now who's askin' the questions?" Joe said with a grin.

"Shall we see Maxie now, Pepe?" I asked.

"*Si.* Make a copy of this"—he gestured to the map— "for him."

"Do you want a copy?"

He tapped his head. "I keep it here, Peppino." He turned to Joe and this time he was serious.

"The colored—do you trust her?"

"I have her eatin' out of my hand," Joe told him.

"Does she know about this?"

"The setup? Hell, no. She thinks we're only payin' off for her and Muzzy's operations. Don't worry, Pepe, nothin's gonna happen with the Duchess . . ."

He toyed with the catalog for a moment.

"Maybe we should take care of her."

Joe looked stunned.

"What do you mean, Pepe?"

Pepe only stared at him. We knew what he meant.

"No, Pepe," I said quickly. "She's fine. Leave her alone. Joe can handle her."

"Yeah. Sure I can," Joe interjected. "Don't worry about it, Pepe . . ."

He looked from me to Joe. "You are responsible, *giovinotto* . . ."

"Sure, sure, Pepe, you don't have a thing to worry about."

He went back to studying the print of the oil. Finally, after a few minutes he murmured half to himself, "*Marrone!* What colors! It is so genuine . . ."

Joe looked at me and shrugged. I nodded and we got up.

418

"We'll see you, Pepe," he said.

Pepe lifted his hand in farewell but did not raise his eyes. When we went out he was still studying the print.

That was our Pearl Harbor Day.

38 THE GOOD GUYS AND THE BAD GUYS

Three weeks after we had made our deal with Cornell I went on my first tour with Hennessy. I despised that monstrous toad of a man but I forced myself to spend more days and nights with him than I care to remember. I can still vividly recall the stale cigar smoke smell in his car, the grunting, groaning, and rumbling deep inside of his big body as he carefully edged himself behind the wheel, the antacid tablets he constantly munched until, by the end of the afternoon or evening, there was a white powdery circle about his lips.

I despised him but I came to respect him. I soon discovered there were few police precincts about the five boroughs where he couldn't enter and address the desk sergeant by his first name.

It was a nerve-racking, delicate, and probing business. As Hennessy explained, most of the cops and superior officers we met were part of the payoff system and could be trusted. But some were undecided and, as he said very bluntly, could even be informers.

"In every house there are cops who are poison to us. First there's the ambitious cop. He wants only one thing—to get ahead in the department. He wants it so bad he can taste it, and to get it he is willin' to step on a lot of bodies, including' the guys he works with. Sure they're on the take, but it's only *honest* bucks!"

"That isn't the way he thinks! No sir! When he gets a smell of money being passed he figgers here is a chance to be picked for the Shoofly Squad, so he plays detective, then he goes downtown with what he has found out.

"Before you know it, the Commissioner's Confidential

419

Squad walks in, takes you into a room, and starts throwin'
questions. It's only then you realize there's been a squeal
in the house.

"Then there's the other guy, the holier-than-thou guy.
This damn fool really means it! He gets so mad if you offer
him some dough he's liable to drag you in for offerin' him
a bribe. Those are the guys we have to watch out for."

"Those are also the guys I want to know something
about, Hennessy."

"Sure. That's no problem. They're all over—Manhattan,
Brooklyn, Queens. Even in Harlem—all of 'em ready to
make it hard for a guy to make a few extra dollars . . ."

I met my first cop on the take in the rear of a Harlem
bar late one night. He was a stocky, middle-aged lieutenant who was openly suspicious in the beginning.

"He thinks you're too young, Frank," Hennessy told
me.

"What the hell does age have to do with the color of
my money?" I asked the lieutenant.

He pointed to Hennessy. "I trust him because I know he
knows that if I go down he comes with me."

"That's the way it has to be," Hennessy said solemnly.
"We all hang together."

"I've never seen you around before tonight," the lieutenant said, almost peevishly.

"And you have never been paid before what we are
going to pay you," I told him, "so let's cut the social talk.
Did Hennessy explain the setup?"

"Yeah. It sounds fine to me but why this meet?"

"We want to know who we do business with. We don't
like paying out big money to blank faces. Until I sat down
here an hour ago how did I know that he"—this time I
pointed to Hennessy—"knew you? He told us he can do
business with the brass up here—well we want proof."

"Okay. Now you have proof. What do you want to
know?"

"What about the borough commander?"

"He doesn't want any trouble. He has enough headaches
as it is. The way he sees it, what he doesn't know won't
hurt him."

"You have the list of drops?"

"Every one is nailed down. The word is out."

"How about the good guys in your house?"

He shook his head. "I'm not gonna tell you they can't be
trouble—they can."

"Who are they?"

He listed on his fingers two superior officers and several cops. I wrote down their names.

"Don't try to reach 'em," he warned me, "they'll blow the whistle on us. We keep out of their way."

"How many in your house?"

"Nearly two hundred. The roll call's big, but don't forget it's a slum precinct."

I looked over at Hennessy. "Then actually most of the cops are not on the pad."

"How many do you need?" Hennessy said with a shrug. "Who wants a traffic man or a clerical guy?"

"The ones who are with us are important," the lieutenant explained. He said admiringly of Hennessy, "This guy knows his business."

"I'm beginning to agree with you. How about another round?"

I made sure he was well oiled; Hennessy saw what I was up to and kept pushing the drinks. By the time we drove the cop home to the Bronx I had gone over the complete roster, not only his precinct but two other neighboring houses, to get a list of the good and bad.

The biggest contact I made on our tour was with an inspector. It took weeks of negotiations by Hennessy to get him even to meet me, and even then our first meeting was very formal: dinner, a few drinks, and general conversation. Two more followed. Then, finally, the inspector cautiously answered my questions. I knew the general structure of the department but he filled in many details of day-to-day operations, especially the activities of the Commissioner's Confidential Squad.

"It's a good time now for you to go into business," he explained, "a lot of the young guys have been drafted and they're shorthanded as hell downtown."

"Where do they get their recruits?"

"Anywhere. Sometimes they even take a rookie right out of class if he shows any promise."

"How do they work?"

"Let me give you a typical example of how those guys operate," he said. "About four years ago they had a squeal from the wife of a ribbon man. He was shacking up with another dame and she got mad. She sent this letter downtown and it got to the commissioner's office. He passed it to the first deputy, who gave it to the guy who ran the squad.

421

"It was an all-black neighborhood so they couldn't risk sending in any of the regulars. So they grabbed this black rookie, an eager beaver kid, and sent him up there to live on the block and get in with the combination. They gave him a whole new background, just in case he made contact and was checked out by the boys in the precinct . . ."

"The Commissioner's Squad knows there's cops on the take?"

"Of course. They're not dumb. Even an idiot would figure that the numbers wouldn't work if somewhere along the line cops weren't on the pad!"

"But what do they do about it?"

He gave me a tight smile. "They keep looking, kid. If they catch your hand in the till they slam shut the drawer and you're out."

"But no one hears about it . . ."

"Only if a DA gets into the act. Then his press agents tell the reporters down in the Criminal Courts pressroom that they have uncovered another scandal—it's always as big as the Tweed Ring."

"But it's not?"

"Of course not! Even Dewey didn't make a big score with police corruption."

"But Seabury did."

"Granted. But only because there was one Seabury and a lot of cops became greedy. And when cops get too greedy, they get stupid. Right, Teddy?"

Hennessy nodded and waved the stub of his cigar.

"That's what I told 'em in Miami—one of these days it will blow up. The cops are askin' for too much. Every week they want a raise. Some day there'll be a squeal and—bingo—there it goes!"

"What about that rookie? Did he get anything?"

The inspector smiled. "Almost. The black bastard was this close"—he held up his thumb and forefinger and let them barely touch—"but they made one mistake downtown." He chuckled, "I caught it and saved not only my hide but the whole setup."

Hennessy nudged me. "Listen to this."

"One day two Navy Intelligence guys came into the precinct to see me. They were up to check on a Jap cook. Now there are lots of guys in Navy Intelligence who are real pros but there are also a lot of young lawyers, smalltown cops, even newspaper reporters. Happily for us, those two guys were anything but pros. One guy had been a cop upstate, the other an insurance investigator. But they were both gung ho and when the nosy landlady tipped them off that a guy on the third floor had a gun they played Dick Tracy, kicked in the door, and found the gun under the pillow."

"The rookie's," Hennessy said and nudged me again.

"Right. But no rookie," the inspector said smugly. "They came over to me with the gun, a cop's .38 Special. Of course I thanked them and praised them to the skies. They loved that. Now at this time I didn't know it was the rookie's gun—it could have been lifted by some guy in a heist. But something made me suspicious. You get that way up here. You can almost smell a plant. So I sent one of our boys down to the flat and he went through it until he found what we wanted. The stupid kid had hidden his shield in a shoe. That's all we needed. He put the gun back, gave the landlady some cock-and-bull story, and in ten minutes I had the whole operation up there shut down. They blew their cork downtown. The shooflies came up with their crowbars and busted up some of the drops but they didn't find a thing—not even a slip!"

"Yeah, but tell him how near that kid was, inspector!" Hennessy said.

"They needed help so they had taken this kid on, checked him out and let him pick up. He was intelligent and a hard worker and they thought they had a jewel." He shook his head. "In another week they were planning to give the kid the ribbon and let him deliver it across Fifth Avenue . . ."

"He would have led 'em right to the bank!" Hennessy grunted. "Can you imagine those wops if they were hit?"

"They would have caught the day's ribbons, all the dough and the biggest bank in the east," the inspector said smugly.

"That's why we want this new setup," I said.

"One man, one payoff," Hennessy said. "What do you think, Inspector?"

"Good," the inspector said. "There's too much cut-throating going on now. This way everything will be nice and businesslike. You handling the dough, Teddy?"

"Only me." He nodded to me. "Our friend here has it sent over on the first Monday of every month and the bucks go out that same day."

"It sounds good. I'm sure it will work."

There were more drinks. The inspector was not as

thirsty as the other cop but his tongue loosened as the evening passed and my list of names grew longer.

I spent the next few weeks with Hennessy, meeting cops in the rear of bars and in cars parked on deserted side streets—and once in a Queens attic where I met an extraordinarily careful sergeant who informed me he didn't trust me, Hennessy, or anybody.

"I want the dough in a plain envelope dropped on the floor in the back of my car," he said. "The next time my wife uses the car she will find it—then finders keepers."

"Christ, you're careful!" Hennessy said.

"I intend to put twenty years in the job, then pull out for Arizona," the sergeant said quietly. "The way I see it, you have to protect that pension at any cost. I just can't be too cautious. I won't even trust my brother—and he's a cop!"

By the end of a month I had several boxes filled with dossiers on the cops I had met, from ordinary patrolmen to the superior officers—good and bad. We had cultivated a tightly knit core of dishonest cops who obviously would sell themselves for a buck. But only "honest bucks," as they called it. Only a few failed to insist self-righteously that they would never take "dirty money," revenue from prostitution or drugs.

My desire to tour with Hennessy ended when he threw a newspaper to me one night after I had gotten into his car.

"Another cop got it," he said. I was surprised at the savagery in his voice. "You give 'em a break and the next time they kill you! You have to get 'em the first time . . ."

"You sound like a cop again, Hennessy."

"When you've been a cop for as long as I was, kid, and you read about how some guy got it, you just can't forget all the time you put in the job. You can't help but remember how it was when you kicked down a door and went in like Frank Merriwell, hoping your goddam partner was backin' you up." He handed me the tabloid. "This guy went in once too often . . ."

The name jumped out from the first paragraph, Second Grade Detective George Drummer, shot and killed on a Second Avenue roof by a man suspected of dealing in black market and stolen tires.

I remembered Drummer's fierce, hawk-eyed face and cold eyes as he was telling me, "I eat up those bums, kid

424

... it's either me or them ... the only public mistake a cop makes is his obit ..."

In the tabloid's centerfold was a layout of pictures of the scene on the roof. One picture showed Mike Boston, Drummer's partner, a stricken, agonized look on his face, standing next to the body.

Three days later, another story appeared. This time the picture on page one showed only a man's legs sprawled on the sidewalk, the rest of the body was draped over the steps leading to a basement apartment. It was the second gunman. Standing nearby was a grim-faced Mike Boston talking to reporters.

"Detectives from the East 51st Street precinct working on their own time had trailed the suspect to the basement apartment of his girlfriend. Detective Second Grade Michael Boston, Drummer's partner, killed the gunman in an exchange of shots that shattered windows of nearby shops and scattered pedestrians ..."

Hennessy chuckled, "Never kill a cop."

I had all I could do to keep from spitting in his face. I felt like shouting—they protect their own but what about the innocent—like Tom Gunnar?—who you killed! One shot. Right in the heart.

39 THE SERVICE

As the war continued, the docks boomed. The amount of tonnage passing through the waterfront soon surpassed all World War I records.

Gasoline and food stamps were a nuisance until we found out how to buy them in blocks for our trucks through a waterfront contact in Jersey. As shortages developed in day-to-day living, we went into the black market in meat, sugar, and gas. Transactions were fast and money changed hands in hours. For example, stamps for the equal

425

of 100,000 gallons of gasoline gave us a profit of over $1,500. But Pepe put us in big time: OPA offices were tin cans to experienced burglars, it seemed they had no one to go to except Pepe and our friends. I am sure we sold millions of what we called "black gas" in those days for impressive profits.

One of our best distributors was Hennessy, who sold the gas stamps he bought from us to the cops. It was a real patriotic round robin.

Pepe even developed a new gimmick when it became evident that our supply could not match the demand. When ration stamps were turned in by stations and garages, they were supposed to be burned. Pepe simply put several of his own men in the incinerator centers to reclaim them.

"The government is crazy," he told us. "We must put these stamps back into circulation!"

Our only danger was the draft but we beat that—with Pepe's help.

A few weeks before we were scheduled to take our physicals he sent us to a doctor in the mid-Sixties. We arrived late at night and the doctor himself ushered us into his office. As I recall it, he was a distinguished-looking man with a gruff manner. He studied us for a moment then dialed a number and took the phone into the next room where we could hear him speaking softly.

"I can't risk any mistakes," he explained. "I have to make sure the right party sent you. When was the last time you men had physicals?"

Joe looked at me. "I guess when we were little kids."

"Get undressed. I want to examine you."

"That suits us, doc," Joe said. "What do we do?"

After a thorough physical he gave us each a small box of pills; mine was to produce a heart irregularity, Joe's was to induce temporary high blood pressure. He also wrote out a phony medical case history for each of us, testifying he had been treating Joe for years for chronic high blood pressure, while I had been under his care since infancy with a congenital heart defect.

We took our draft physicals at Grand Central. By nightfall we were 4-F.

Some months later Spider and Train both proved they were hardship cases; Train's was legitimate, he was the sole support of his aged and feeble grandmother. But the only dependent Spider had was a young Broadway showgirl he was keeping. He had four brothers, only two were in the

Marines, and the others were living home and working. But somehow he conned the draft board his mother would starve without him. I guess Spider's saintly smile was still working.

The war years passed swiftly. Before we knew it 1943 had arrived. Money continued to flow in from all directions, from the coopers' treasury, our mortgage investments, our trucking and lighterage business, the warehouse workers' union sweetheart contracts, and our share of the numbers arrangements. Weekends became longer, and our parties less inhibited. It was an unusual Monday morning when I did not arrive at the pier still tasting the raw scotch that lay in the pit of my stomach and had to drink a couple of bottles of ice cold Coke to put out the fire. Every week was the same; the foggy, smoky places, the shrill intense laughter, the endless flow of whiskey, the debates on the war, Hitler, Churchill, Ike, FDR, and why Patton should not only have slapped these two kids but kicked their asses back to the front. . . .

We saw a great deal of Maxie Solomon in those days. One fall day in 1943 I wasn't surprised to hear him on the phone.

"Pepe wants to see you and Joe, tonight at gallery," he said. "No excuse. This is a must."

I was surprised at his brusque, businesslike tone.

"What's up, Maxie?"

"I wouldn't know," he said shortly and hung up.

Hanging in the back of my mind like a sword on a thread was the knowledge that someday we would have to fulfill our "service" to Pepe. Something told me this was Collection Day.

We found Pepe jovial as ever in his gallery. He insisted upon showing me an Eakins portrait he had bought from a dealer.

"Daumier, Peppino!" he cried. "Look at that face."

We stood in a respectful silence, then Joe said, "What do you intend to do with all these paintings, Pepe? Sell 'em?"

Pepe stared at Joe as if he had flung a flatiron at his face.

"*Marrone!* Sell them? Are you crazy?"

Then he went on from painting to painting, savoring

427

their beauty like a miser letting gold pieces slip one by one through his fingers.

Joe just looked bored.

When he waved us into the Cord I instinctively knew we were going to Patsy's. On the West Side Highway Pepe gleefully gave us the details of how he had flimflammed the gallery owner into selling the Eakins. After he had made an offer, Lorenzo, posing as a wealthy Italian banker who had fled from Mussolini's wrath, paid a visit to the gallery, ostensibly fell in love with the Eakins, and made a higher offer. The gallery politely informed Pepe that a mistake had been made, the painting had been promised to another collector.

Then Lorenzo returned and sadly informed the gallery that his villa had been destroyed by the retreating Germans and he could not risk purchasing a painting at this time.

As Pepe had predicted, the chastened gallery called him. This time, with a great deal of indignation, Pepe forced their price down.

Joe found the passing piers more interesting.

Patsy's had not changed. There was still sawdust on the uneven floors, checkered tablecloths, heavy glass beakers of wine, breadsticks, the rich aroma of spices and cheese, and the stout cashier with the heavy moustache and severe black dress. As before, Patsy greeted us and the old crone left her pots to kiss Pepe's hand as he passed through the kitchen to the rear stairs.

The second floor apartment was as richly decorated as I recalled it, with a table prepared, antipasto on the plates, and a small rolling bar.

Only this time there was one difference: Gus.

He was sitting in an easy chair by the heavy red velvet drapes that hid the shuttered windows. When we entered he waved the breadstick he was chewing.

"Hey! *Como esta te?* How are you kids? Okay?"

"Fine," I said.

"Good. What will you have to drink?"

When we told him, Patsy silently served and left.

"No talk now, Duchino," Pepe said briskly, "we must eat!"

"I can't stand this goddam food anymore," Gus grumbled. As he got up from the chair he staggered slightly. "Tonight I'll be living on Pepto-Bismol." As he sat down

428

he grunted, "How do you like that? A wop can't eat marinara sauce without belching like a pig all night!"

"You drink too much, Duchino," Pepe said. I looked at him, surprised at the lack of joviality in his voice. His face was impassive, his eyes coldly studying Gus.

"Yeah. Maybe you're right, Pepe." He explained to me, "I got all the headaches of that goddam club! Taking care of the cops. Hustling the meat out of those bastards down at the market. Making sure the big shots are happy. Last night we had a general in the club. The son of a bitch got drunk and tried to rape the kid in the hatcheck. He was a big bastard. What a time we had with him. We couldn't slug him. We had to try and talk to him!"

Close up I could see a change in Gus; his face was pudgy and there were threads of red veins in the corners of his eyes.

"Wine!" Pepe said ignoring him, "a glass of wine, Peppino?"

It was a marvelous dinner, one of the finest I had ever eaten. I love Italian cooking, and Patsy's offered the best in New York but this time I didn't taste half the food—I was waiting for what I knew would come after the tiny cups were filled with espresso.

Finally Pepe smiled and patted his stomach.

"It was good, Peppino? Joe? You liked it?"

"It was great, Pepe," I said. "What's up?"

Pepe filled a tiny fragile glass with anisette, and silently offered us the bottle. When we shook our heads he sipped the liqueur, then nodded as if satisfied.

"Perhaps you can do us a service, Peppino—and Joe."

"What kind of service" I asked quickly.

"Something on the docks," Gus put in, but after a glance at Pepe he said, "Pepe will tell you what it is."

"In a week, on the sixteenth, a freighter named the *Carabello* will dock at your pier, my young friends," Pepe said briskly. "It will have a cargo of flowers—"

"Flowers?" Joe repeated incredulously.

"That's us," Gus said. "We're in flowers now. Imitation flowers."

"You and Pepe in flowers! Since when?"

Gus shrugged. "It's a new business with us."

"You're getting a cargo of flowers?" I asked Pepe.

"Let me explain, Peppino," he said patiently. "Before the war we had done business with a man in Marseilles—"

"An inventor—a goddam good one," Gus put in.

429

"Please! Duchino," Pepe said, plainly exasperated.

"Okay. I'm sorry. Let Pepe tell you," Gus said.

"This Frenchman puts the flowers in wax," Pepe went on.

"In wax?" Joe asked.

"To keep them fresh," Pepe said. *"Marrone!* It looks like you took them from the garden. Wait! I will show you."

He hurried across the room, broke open a small box and held up a magnificent lily.

"It looks nice," Joe pointed out, "but what do you do with it?"

"For decorations," Pepe explained. "For festivals! Parties for big shots—"

"You know who we have a contract with?" Gus said from across the room. "Uncle Sam! When FDR's elected again we supply the flowers for the ball! How do you guys like that?"

"What do you want us to do?" I asked.

Pepe carefully put the flower back into the box.

"You must make sure we get the cargo, Peppino," he said in a soft voice.

"It looks like an ordinary cargo," I said as casually as I could. "Why can't anyone take care of it?"

"Don't play the fox with me, Peppino," Pepe said harshly. "If we talk like this we will be here all night!"

Joe said, "Why don't you guys level with us?"

"A service for a service," Pepe said coldly. "Equally."

Joe looked over at me; this was no ordinary cargo of wax flowers.

"We have to get the stuff off that pier without any trouble," Gus said fiercely, banging on the arm of the chair. "We have to!"

"Duchino," Pepe warned.

"Christ! Tell these kids, Pepe," Gus said, almost frantically. Then to us: "Look, anything you asked you got, right?"

"Right," I said.

"Then take care of this one. That's all we ask."

"There seems to be a lot of problems just for a shipment of wax flowers, Pepe," I pointed out. "I think you should level with us. What's in the crates?"

"I think so too," Joe put in. "If we're grabbed it's our necks not yours."

430

"Christ! Don't talk about being grabbed," Gus said wiping his face.

"No," Pepe said harshly. "It is no concern of yours what is in the crates. Did we ask you questions when you came to us for justice? Now we ask you for this service—will you do it or will you refuse?"

The question clanged like a hammer on an anvil in the silence.

"We promised, Frank," Joe said.

"I know," I said slowly, fearfully, "We'll do it, Pepe."

"Buòno! Buòno!"

"Do we have to carry a gun?" Joe asked bluntly.

I said quickly, "We won't need any gun."

Pepe shrugged. "Do what you must do."

"Tell 'em how many crates, Pepe," Gus said impatiently. "Show 'em the stamp."

"There will be thirty crates," Pepe said briskly. "Ten will have this stamp." He made a fist, stamped the back of his hand, and showed us the sketch of a top-hatted Frenchman bending down to smell a flower. Under it were the words, "Liroux's Flowers of the World."

"What about the other crates?"

"They will be delivered. You have no interest in them."

"What do we do with the cargo after we get it off the pier?" Joe asked him. "Where do we take it?"

Pepe went over to a small table and came back with a Manhattan telephone directory. He quickly flipped the yellow pages, then pointed to a small advertisement that read:

ALBERTI FUNERAL HOME   147 Madison Street,
New York City, N.Y.
SERVING THIS AREA SINCE 1892

"A funeral home?"

"What the hell, you're deliverin' flowers!" Gus said. "Stiffs 'n' flowers go together, right?"

"Who will be there?"

"I will be there with Lorenzo," Pepe said solemnly. "We will be mourning a friend."

"Do we ask for you?"

"Lorenzo will be at the door."

The *Carabello,* a rust-bucket from the Far East, came

431

in on schedule. She had scurried her way from India to Naples, then joined a convoy in London. She was stuffed to the hatches with an exotic-smelling cargo of spices, oils, and raw medical material and was captained by a Greek who would have scared Peter Lorre. Before the hatches were opened, he sought us out in our office to inform us that a special cargo of fragile flowers was in the lower hold and to ask for the address of the nearest whorehouse.

It was a nerve-twisting morning watching the holds empty. When the last fishnet had dipped in and out, Joe casually walked about the pier.

"I found the crates," he told me in a low voice when he returned. "I had a gang put them in the rear of the shed."

"Are they heavy? Do we need Spider and Train?"

"No. We'll do this one ourselves."

"What do you think it is, Joe?"

"Maybe they're smugglin' diamonds. I don't care. I only want it off this pier and down in that goddam funeral home!"

"Joe—no gun."

"Let me worry about that."

"Count me out if you carry a gun—"

"You'll come, Frank," he said, "whether I carry a gun or not. You can't get out of this and neither can I."

It was a blinding truth. I was only giving lip service to the thin, dying voice of what was left of my battered conscience. I knew Joe would carry a gun—in fact if he didn't, I would. Nothing could stop us from fulfilling this contract that had been written in blood in a dingy waste-paper factory a long time ago . . .

"We'll have to hire a truck," he mused.

"How about the guard?"

"He won't be any trouble. I'll get him to go to the can for ten minutes when we pull out—"

"What will you tell him we have?"

"The usual—a load of scotch. It will only cost us a couple of quarts and a pound note . . . there won't be any problems."

But there were problems. The next morning when we drove our rented truck up to the pier a strange young customs guard stopped us at the gate. He was very formal and very gung-ho. He not only went into the van but inspected the truck's undercarriage with a flashlight.

432

"We have eight German spies in the radiator," Joe told him.

But the guard didn't crack a smile. He just waved us on.

"We're not goin' out this way, Frank," Joe grunted as we drove down the pier to the coopers' shed. "I wonder what's up?"

When we got to the shed, Bailey told us: during the night customs guards on every West Side pier had been replaced. Customs inspectors, accompanied by details of treasury agents, plainclothesmen, and Army and Navy MPs under Captain Elliott, had been reported on the Chelsea waterfront. One pier had been closed after the shape, and all personnel ordered to remain while the cargo and all vehicles were inspected.

"Somethin's up," the old man said shaking his head. "The boys down in Chelsea say there's a crackdown. Maybe the shippers been squawkin' about the pilferage. Oh, by the way, Joe, someone called you just before the shape . . ."

"Who was it?" he asked quickly.

"You got me. All he said was to be sure and wait for his call. He had a little voice, soft like a woman's."

"We have to get those crates off and fast, Joe," I told him after Bailey had left.

"Don't you think I know that?" He slammed his fist into the palm of one hand. "Now we can't use the goddam truck!"

"If we can get them up to the banana shed—"

He snapped his fingers. "That's an idea! There's a float under the pier that we use for the lighters. Tonight when the third shift comes on, we can transfer the crates to the float."

"You mean pull that damn float up to the banana pier, Joe? We'll have to go into the river to do that!"

"Do you have any other suggestions?" he asked impatiently. "Let's face it—we're stuck with those goddam crates! Get Spider and Train and send them down to Chelsea to see if they can find out what the hell is goin' on."

The news they called back to us was disquieting; one pier had been shut down all morning and piles of cargo were being inspected, crate by crate.

"Nobody can get anywhere near the stringpiece," Spider reported. "One of the shop stewards raised a fuss and they busted him and took him downtown. Remember Supercop? He's in charge. He has an army of bulls on the pier with some Army Intelligence guys . . ."

A few minutes after Spider called, the phone rang again. Joe picked it up, listened for a few seconds, then hung up.

"Hennessy," he said. "He just whispered, 'If you have any hot cargo—dump it.' "

Fortunately Elliott's raiders remained in Chelsea. He apparently didn't find what he wanted, but he shook down half a dozen piers, busting anyone who had numbers slips, phony ID cards, or a record.

Late that afternoon we parked our truck outside the banana shed. When we returned in the evening to our pier there was another guard at the gate. He was older and wasn't impressed when Joe told him who we were. He simply examined our waterfront ID cards before waving us through.

The gangs were working at top speed. The rust-bucket was being loaded while another freighter waited in midstream; it was plainly a convoy makeup. The night checker, an old boozer, wasn't too happy to see us, but after Joe explained we had a great deal of union paper work to finish and gave him some dough for several containers of beer we became blood brothers.

The crates had been moved to the far side of the shed, next to the door that led to the end of the stringpiece. We were hidden from the working gangs by a wall of cargo. We found the marked crates, each weighing about fifty pounds. While I moved them to the outside, Joe stripped to his shorts, slid down a hawser, and vanished into the water under the pier with a splash and a whispered groan that the river was ice cold.

The scene is still vivid in my mind; the whir of the hoist drums, the creaking of the booms like old giants bending down; the Hi-Los racing about the pier with the sound of mechanical bugs nibbling at cargo after cargo, the muffled shouts and laughter of the dockwallopers. Below me rollers from a passing ferryboat hit the bulkhead, the thin spray reaching up to one hand.

Suddenly Joe appeared, his body glistening in the gloom as he scrambled up the hawser, the float rope tied around his waist.

"Okay, let's go," he whispered, his teeth chattering uncontrollably. "Damn! Is that river cold!"

I picked up his pants and shirt and handed them to him.

I stripped, went down the hawser, and stacked the crates on the bobbing float as Joe lowered them with a line. With the last one was our clothes, a pinch bar, rope, and a pint of whiskey. Then we went over the side and started hauling and pushing that heavy, cumbersome raft upstream, past several piers, to the banana shed.

It was brute labor but we had two things in our favor: the tide was coming in fast and the brownout on the waterfront prevented anyone on the piers from seeing us. At each bulkhead we tied up to get our breath before casting off again.

Finally, the familiar scent of coffee and bananas told us we had reached the shed. For one frantic moment we thought the old hawser was gone but it was still there, the part in the water slippery as an eel from the river slime and the upper section like sandpaper from years of encrusted salt.

We tied up the float, climbed to the open end of the pier, and lay panting on the splintery old planks. We shook as though we were suffering violent attacks of malaria. One of the convoy's liners, anchored like a giant ghost ship in the middle of the channel, had emptied its oil tanks in the river and we were coated with oil. When we caught our breath we rubbed ourselves dry with our shirts and polished off a good part of the pint.

Then we unloaded. Joe stayed on the float while I pulled the crates up onto the pier. When we had finished we checked outside—our truck was there and the street was deserted. I was about to lift one of the crates when Joe stopped me.

"Let's take a look, Frank. Let's see what's so important about their goddamn flowers!"

We carefully removed the strapping and the heavy wooden cover with the pinch bar. Joe gingerly pulled aside the thick layers of excelsior to lay bare trays of tissue-wrapped, long-stemmed lilies. He took one out and carefully removed the paper. In the pencil gleam of the flashlight it was as fragile and beautiful as if it had been picked a few minutes before in a spring garden. There was even a delicate scent.

Joe ran his hand down the stem.

"It's wax but"—he sniffed—"it still smells."

As he held out the flower to me one curved end of the petal caught in the buttons of his work shirt and snapped. A trickle of white powder poured into Joe's open hand.

"Drugs! The bastards are bringin' in drugs!" Joe whispered as he pinched shut the waxed end of the petal.

Now that we knew what the crates contained we couldn't get rid of them fast enough. We ran up and down the old shed, stumbling and falling, cursing, loading the crates on the truck.

When we finished we hid the pinch bar and flashlight, wrapped what was left of the whiskey in our clothes and made the trip back to our pier, leaving behind the heavy float and hauling our bundles between us on the top of a small crate we found in the water. When we reached the pier I was exhausted and chilled to the bone.

Inside the pier we moved along the rows of stacked cargo until we found a small hill of boxes and barrels topped with burlap bags. From this vantage point we had a clear view of the entire pier. We had been settled on the bag for a short time when Joe nudged me and pointed; the Customs Guard was sauntering up the pier.

"When he gets near let's start down so he'll see us." Joe said.

When the guard was several feet away Joe scrambled down.

"Oh, so that's where you were," the guard said. "I dropped by your office a few times to see how things were going. Nobody knew where to find you."

"We got tired of workin' so we had a few and decided to grab a couple of winks." Joe yelled, "Hey, Frank, it's gettin' late . . ."

I slid down, rubbing my eyes.

"Let's have one fast one, then we'll go home," he said. He waved to the guard. "See you around, pal."

The guard escorted us to the gate, in fact he started after us as we crossed the wide avenue. We made a pretense of looking into the darkened window of the nearby waterfront bar, banged on the door a few times, then walked off.

"That ought to convince him," Joe said. When we looked back the guard was walking inside the pier.

"Let's go," Joe said. We made a circle of about a block, then crossed back to the waterfront side of the avenue to where our truck was parked in the deep shadows. We sped up the Forty-first Street entrance of the West Side Highway and in a few minutes were headed downtown.

We left the highway's Chambers Street exit to enter the noisy crowded world of Washington Market; it was something we had not expected. The narrow streets were packed curb to curb with unloading food trucks. Butchers in bloodstained white coats and straw hats mounted slabs of beef on hooks. Black and white helpers flung crates of vegetables from trucks to platforms, flames of bonfires in oil drums licked at the crisp morning air filled with shouts, laughter, curses, food quotations, blaring radio news reports of the war, and the stink of rotting potatoes and lettuce.

We inched up the street. Joe's knuckles were white as he gripped the wheel. I just sat there and let the sweat run down my face. I could taste the bile in the back of my throat when a mounted cop holding a jug of steaming coffee came out of a lunchroom and silently watched Joe maneuver the truck through a narrow lane. We crossed Broadway and Lafayette, went under the Municipal Building arch, then down New Chambers and up Madison Street, trembling at every traffic light. Almost in the shadows of Manhattan Bridge, Joe nudged me and pointed to the sign; Alberti Funeral Home.

We parked the truck on the deserted street and rang the bell. At the first muted chime Lorenzo swung open the door to beckon us inside. We followed him down a corridor smelling of dead flowers and dust to a room with a coffin banked with flowers and candles at one end. The corpse was that of an old woman. There were rows of chairs, all empty but one. There sat Pepe.

He held both our hands but never asked the question.

I answered it.

"We have your cargo of flowers."

He only nodded to Lorenzo who hurriedly went back down the corridor. In a few minutes the truck's motor was started, a garage door rolled up, the truck crawled inside, and the door slid shut. As I watched in amazement, several men dressed in black hurried into the room with armloads of the wax flowers which they carefully placed about the corpse of the old woman. The casket was unceremoniously flipped closed and bolted. Another crew appeared wheeling a pinewood box with the name of a Midwestern funeral home stenciled on one side. They joined the others and lifted the coffin into the box. Again clamps and bolts were tightened. Then the box was rolled out of the room.

"Come, we have a lot of work to do before it gets light," Pepe said shortly.

We hurried after him and Lorenzo, entered a gleaming funeral car parked behind a hearse, and took off. Pepe, leaning over, pulled down the gray shades and stared ahead. I decided it was useless to ask questions—I guess Joe had come to the same conclusions—so we sat in silence as the cortege purred its sorrowful way along the East River Drive to Harlem.

The scene in the second funeral parlor was a repeat performance of what had taken place in the first one—with only one grisly difference: three corpses instead of one were quickly covered with the wax flowers. One by one they vanished in wooden boxes that all bore stenciled out-of-town addresses. When the last box had disappeared some tough-looking young hoods brought in piles of cardboard boxes, all with names of different Harlem florists. The wax flowers were wrapped in tissue paper and carefully placed in the boxes. Then each hood, with one or two under his arm, left the funeral home.

Before the first gray light appeared we had visited ten funeral homes in the Bronx, Queens, and Brooklyn. Then we accompanied the last casket to Grand Central where we helped Lorenzo and two other men, who looked like undertakers' assistants, carry it into the station's railway express mail room.

I almost laughed out loud at the sympathetic old man who made out the receipt.

"Somebody you know?" he asked Joe.

"My uncle," Joe said soberly. He glanced down at the stenciled address. "He wouldn't rest if he wasn't buried on the old Illinois farm . . ."

"Well, we all gotta go someday," the clerk said solemnly.

All across the nation, dead men and women were now delivering Pepe's cargo of the devil's own flowers . . .

"Cèrvelli," Lorenzo whispered to me as he tapped his head. "Sortino is a smart man; no, Peppino?"

Yes, Lorenzo.

The tension and the tough, chilling swim had left me so fatigued I was staggering when I came out of Grand Central. The limousine and the hearse were gone, but Lorenzo guided us to another car in which Pepe was seated in the back.

"Would you like breakfast, giovinotti?" he asked us. "Perhaps we can stop somewhere.

438

"Not me," Joe murmured. "I just want to crawl into bed."

"I'm with you," I said.

"*Marrone!* You look tired, Peppino."

"Christ, we had to swim a goddam float up the river for ten piers so we could get the cargo on the truck," Joe said.

"Ah, they changed the guard at the gate . . ." Pepe said.

I was stunned. "How did you know that?"

"There was a traitor among our friends overseas," he blandly explained. "When he was discovered it was too late—the ship had sailed. But when it arrived in London certain people transferred the cargo to the *Carabello*—"

"Who was tipped? Army Intelligence?" Joe asked. "They were on the docks all day with the cops."

Pepe shrugged. "Before he was silenced the informer was seen going into the army office. We were lucky. In London the police searched the ship after our cargo was removed."

"So all they knew is that it was somewhere in the convoy?"

Pepe nodded. "We were lucky, my friends."

"All this for wax flowers?" I asked bitterly.

Pepe stared ahead, not answering.

"But why did the cops and the army hit Chelsea and not the Upper West Side piers?" Joe asked.

"A prisoner in the West Side House of Detention became a friend of the government and told them all about the shipment—"

"Including the wrong ship and the wrong pier," Joe added admiringly. "What happens to him now?"

"To the government he is an informer, to us he is a friend. His family will be taken care of."

"That still left us in one hell of a spot, Pepe," I told him. "Suppose Elliott got hot under the collar when he couldn't find anything in Chelsea and started a sweep up the piers? We could have been nabbed! Can't you understand that?"

"Don't get excited, Peppino," he said calmly. "You didn't get caught."

"Dammit! But we could have! What I want to know is why you let us take that chance?"

"The cargo, Peppino, is more important than even you," Pepe said sternly. "Now let us stop this foolish talk. As you and Joe will discover we are not ungrateful."

"Pepe! For love of Christ, listen to me. We could have

439

been sent to prison for a long time if they had hit our pier. For what—wax flowers?" I was almost shouting now. "You and I know what the hell was in those flowers. I hope it's worth it to you!"

"Emozianato, Peppino," he said quietly, "You are tired. You will sleep and things will not be so bad when you wake up." The car had turned into Forty-sixth Street and stopped at our tenement. "I will never forget what you and Joe did for us tonight." He patted me on the shoulder. "Be content. Do not ask questions. Soon you will see Chena, this I have promised you on my mother's grave. You will be married and you will be happy. You have done us a great service. Once we had talk and I told you the returns will be great—now you will see. What more can I say, *mio figlio?* Go with God . . ."

A few weeks later our "friends" showed their gratitude. We were notified by an impressed Maxie Solomon that we were to be appointed to the Joint Board of Waterfront Unions.

"What does that mean?" Joe asked him.

"It means you're coming up in the world," Maxie explained. "What the hell did you guys ever do to deserve this? Marry one of the wops daughters?"

"They carry a lot of muscle, don't they, Maxie?"

"Somebody on the waterfront must think so. After you're elected I want you guys to issue a lot of charters for locals."

"Why?"

"More votes. Maybe someday you may even take over the whole waterfront. Who knows?"

"Oh, didn't you know we plan to do that, Maxie?" Joe asked innocently.

Not only were we elected to the Board, but a few months later the two old-time Prohibition hoodlums who for years had ruled the biggest local in the longshoremen's union and the Chelsea piers mysteriously vanished. We were advised by Maxie to launch a campaign immediately to consolidate the coopers with the local, run Joe for the presidency and me as business agent.

"Are you nuts, Maxie?" Joe replied. "We wouldn't stand a chance!"

"Try it," Maxie said. "What have you got to lose? Maybe you'll both be surprised."

We went through the routine of papering the three piers

controlled by the local with our propaganda and Joe made some fiery speeches to the dockwallopers before the shape, at the lunchtime break, and after the quitting whistle blew. We noticed in every group there were some tough-looking hoods who gave Joe a big hand and made sure those around them joined in.

Then one day we were summoned to Maxie's office to learn that the members of the local had "unanimously" voted to join the coopers and had elected us into office.

"Unanimously?" I asked weakly. "We didn't even know there was a meeting."

He threw a mimeographed card across his desk. On it was a brief message that at an "emergency" meeting of the "new" local a "new" slate of officers had been elected; Joe was president and I was its business agent.

"How did this happen?" I asked.

"Ninety percent of the members received this card the day after the meeting was held."

"Did any squawk?"

"Wartime mail. What can you do?"

"What about the other ten percent?"

"They love you guys," Maxie said sarcastically. "They think you did such a terrific job with the coopers that they want you to take over their local."

"Let's cut out the crap, Maxie," Joe said. "Who is this ten percent?"

"Let's call them friends. Guys who have jobs they want to keep."

"Maybe the other members won't take it."

"That's to be expected. Some of them will pull a wild-cat and get off steam, but they'll come back. Go down and talk to them, Joe. Tell them all about the coopers and how you and Frank and those old guys shut down the waterfront." He leaned across his desk and said seriously, "Always remember one thing about the guys on the docks, they're physical people. They respect power. They're brute labor but they love their work. And above all, they respect people with iron balls. They don't want to play with people like that—"

Joe asked softly, "You mean us, Maxie?"

"I don't have to spell it out for you guys anymore," Maxie said bluntly. "You know who we are working for—so do the guys on the docks. They can smell power down there, and when you show up they'll take your bullshit, Joe. In a few months any one of them will kiss your ass in

441

Macy's window. That's what happens when you're a god-dam human mule . . ."

As Maxie predicted, some angry members of the local pulled a wildcat strike to protest the election, but Joe went down and talked to them. He was impressive and he sounded sincere. They listened and finally went back to work. Deep down they knew there wasn't anything else they could do—it was either return to the stringpiece or face a going-over with a baseball bat from the hoods who stood on the fringes of the crowd applauding everything Joe said.

Leadership of this local now gave us control of the biggest sheds on the West Side. We had a loud voice during the negotiations with the shippers, only this time we didn't sell out for a truck or a lighterage contract. We gained an impressive increase for our members. In fact, our stand was so tough that one day the old shipper with whom we had negotiated for the coopers warned us:

"Watch out for those guns you have behind you—someday they might blow a hole in your head!"

We notified Hennessy that our areas of shylocking, bookmaking, numbers, crap games, and bookies had to be expanded to include the new piers. Then we raised our salaries and funneled some of the local's treasury into our mortgage company. As we had done with the coopers, we first skimmed off the cream, then sold the mortgages to the local for their decreased value. We had to rent another safety deposit box in the bank in order to hold our stacks of cash. Pepe was fulfilling his promise to take care of the devil's own.

 THE BIG NUMBERS WALKOUT

It was shortly after the cargo of drugs had been delivered that Captain Elliott dropped by the pier. When I saw him step into our office my throat dried up and I wondered if he could hear the thumping of my heart. Joe put on an excellent show of nonchalance; he called out, "Supercop's here, Frank," leaned back in his chair, put his feet on the desk, and stared at him.

"Somethin' on your mind, Elliott?"

"Oh, come off with that tough guy role, Gunnar," Elliott said wearily, "I only dropped by to say hello and give Frank a bit of news." He looked over at me. "Casey was killed in the Pacific."

"I'm sorry," I said and I really meant it.

"Who's Casey?" Joe asked.

"One of the O'Hara boys Frank met out in Queens."

"He was a cop," I said.

"And a good one," Elliott added. "Tom and Mrs. O'Hara are really broken up. You know Tom retired last year. There will be a Mass at St. Bridget's on Wednesday if you're interested."

"You goin'?" Joe asked when he left.

"Maybe I will. . . . He was a nice guy . . ."

"Could be. I wouldn't know and frankly I couldn't care less. There's a lot of good kids from the waterfront who're dyin'. Cops don't have a monopoly on dyin' in this war, buddy . . ."

"But we don't have to worry about that."

He looked at me, amused. "I'm no goddam patriot. The hell with 'em! I pick my own enemies—cops, not Japs!"

At first I told myself that Casey O'Hara's funeral was no affair of mine, but I couldn't stay away. That Wednesday morning I went to Queens and sat in the rear of the church in the shadow of a pillar. The church filled slowly, but, by the time the priest appeared, the crowd had spilled out on the steps. There was no doubt the dynasty cops were paying tribute to their own. Older cops looked like faded copies of their sons who sat behind them; kneeling in some pews were grandfathers and grandsons.

When the sad Mass ended, I left by a side door. I was congratulating myself on slipping past all of them when a car horn honked. It was Elliott.

"I'll give you a ride back to the city," he called out as he swung open the door.

It would have been foolish to refuse; after all, it was only a fifteen-minute ride.

"Quite a sad morning for them. First George, then Casey." He said. "The Red Cross tried to get Jim back but he's out in the boondocks somewhere."

"In the Pacific?"

"He's with the Marine Raiders. He was wounded in the Tulagi landing but went back."

"That was quite a turnout . . ."

He gave me a grim smile. "Do you mean your dynasty of head busters, Howell?"

"You have a long memory, Captain."

"I try to remember things that are important. Like a cargo of narcotics we never found on the piers."

He said it casually but it was like a thunderclap on a beautiful clear day. I stared straight ahead, hoping my face did not show the turmoil I was feeling.

"Yeah. We heard you were knocking off some of the piers a few weeks ago," I forced myself to say.

"Somehow they got the load in," he said. "The Treasury people say it's starting to show up in Harlem." He shook his head. "I wonder if those bastards who bring that stuff in have ever seen a kid hooked." He asked abruptly, "Have you?"

"No and I don't want to."

"Sometimes I think it would be better if they put a gun to their heads. . . . I hope after the war it doesn't get worse."

"Why should it get worse?"

"Drugs mean money. Big money. That's all the mob wants. Money." He quickly switched the subject. "How's the union?"

"Fine. Anytime you want to look at our books give our attorney a call. Want his number?"

"Maxie Solomon? One of these days we'll be getting around to him. Is Gunnar going to run for president again?"

"Any objections?"

He shrugged. "Not for now. If I ever have any he'll know about them."

We drove in a tight silence, then, finally, he said, "The guard on your gate said you and Gunnar have been working late at night. What's up? Expanding the coopers?"

"We had a lot of paper work to do," I said as nonchalantly as I could.

"He said one night he couldn't find you for a long time, then he came across both of you sleeping on some cargo . . ."

"Let's cut out the crap, Elliott," I said. "If you want to talk about any cargo of drugs, call our lawyer."

"I'm only asking a few friendly questions."

"And I gave you a few friendly answers. Thanks for the ride. I'll get out here."

He swung over to the curb. When I got out he said:

"Thanks for coming. I'll tell Tom you were there."

I walked away without answering him.

When I told Joe he just shrugged. "I think you were a jerk for goin' out there in the first place."

"We're not talking about me going out there."

"Well, if you didn't go out there you wouldn't have seen the bastard." He yawned. "I wouldn't worry about him. He's all mouth. If he had anythin' on us he'd yank us down to Dewey's office so fast we wouldn't know what hit us. Relax."

Elliott paid us a few more visits, all casual and with a great show of friendliness. The last time, Joe warned him he would inform our attorney to obtain legal protection from what he called police harassment.

I almost laughed at Elliott's reaction. "Harassment?" he said in his best aggrieved voice. "I'm only stopping off to say hello."

"We don't want any cops droppin' by to say hello," Joe told him. "It gives us a bad reputation."

"Of course if you don't want me to—"

"We don't. The less we see of cops, the better we like it."

"You carry a long grudge, Gunnar."

"Someday you'll be surprised how long."

The menace of Elliott and the cops was suddenly forgotten, however, when without warning came trouble from a completely unexpected source—the Duchess.

The payoff system had been working perfectly; the cops were content and so was East Harlem. If anything it had developed into a mutual aid society; the police, from the brass down to the man on the beat, were now assured of weekly, tax-free "clean bucks" while the numbers racket flourished and expanded. The success of our system was underscored by queries from other precincts—as far as Queens—seeking to get into the combination. Hennessy, if anything, was a model of efficiency. He not only took care of the money but screened other precincts that wanted in and arranged the necessary accommodation arrests. We had no reason not to trust him, but Joe remained dubious.

It was typical of Joe that once he got what he wanted from a woman she no longer interested him. I could see this happening with the Duchess after we had made the deal with Inspector Cornell. Our parties and dates were not the same. Joe was no longer the joking, laughing, hard-drinking escort he had been in the beginning, and he didn't try to hide his boredom.

"I'm sick of goin' up to Harlem every weekend and hanging around with a lot of goddam jigs, Frank," he said one night. "And frankly, the Duchess is startin' to give me a royal pain in the ass! Christ, the way she hangs on me! I want to throw up every time she talks of us gettin' married."

"I'm warning you, Joe, don't ditch her too fast. She could mean trouble."

"What trouble could she give us? She's lucky East Harlem lets her operate . . ."

"You know there's one thing I agree with the Duchess about," I told him.

"What's that?"

"There are times when you can be a no-good bastard!"

"All my girls tell me that," he said with a grin. "Do you want to know somethin'—they love it!"

"Maybe you've forgotten—there is another reason why we can't lose the Duchess."

"What's that?"

"Who would get Cornell his little black girls?"

"I told you a long time ago, we won't have to worry about Cornell. Once our system gets goin' it will never stop—Cornell or no Cornell."

"We'll still need someone at headquarters."

"That won't be too hard to find. Down there you will always find someone who smells money. But don't worry about Cornell—he won't leave the setup until he retires—little black girls or no little black girls. Remember what he told us? He wants to retire with 'appropriate funds' . . ."

"That may be true, but I feel a lot more comfortable with the Duchess around. Don't dump her, Joe."

"I'll think about it, old buddy," he said, stretching and yawning. "Maybe I had better ring you in and change your luck—"

"Count me out on this one."

"She's an old dame but she knows a lot of tricks." He threw up his hands in a playacting gesture. "I'm even pimpin' for you! What more can I do for my pal and buddy?"

"Just take it easy on the Duchess . . ."

Joe apparently listened to me. Once again he became

her devoted swain, wining and dining her almost every night.

Then, without warning, it became the Duchess's turn to act vague, disturbed, and irritable. Joe was mystified; he wooed her even more fervently until he discovered the reason for the strange change in her behavior.

"It's that shipment of drugs," he said. "They're floodin' Harlem. Look at this . . ." He spread out two issues of the *Amsterdam News* in front of me. The headlines told of a drug epidemic that was sweeping through the community. I couldn't read it. I pushed the papers aside.

"When I read this I want to jump in the river."

"Christ! The smell of goodness around here! If *we* didn't unload the crates, someone else would have. And if this cargo had been dumped, there would be another one in a few months. If Pepe and his friends—whoever the hell they might be—are in drugs, that's their business, not ours. There's money—big money to be made."

"Maybe. But what did the Duchess say?"

"She's all upset. She says the wops are destroyin' the kids in Harlem. She got mad as hell when I said, 'What do you care, baby? You don't even live up there.'"

" 'It's my people,' she kept shoutin'. How do you like that? The bitch won't even dance with one but now they are all *her* people. When you understand niggers let me know."

"What is she going to do?"

"I don't know," he replied with a gesture of disgust. "She has some kind of a meetin' this Sunday."

Early Monday morning Joe got me out of bed. He was sober and looked concerned.

"This crazy dame! I took her up to this meetin'. All the policy guys in Harlem—ribbon men, runners, collectors, comptrollers—you name 'em and they were there. Do you know what they did? They called a strike! A goddam policy strike! This crazy bitch got them all worked up and sold 'em the idea."

"A strike? What for?"

"To force the wops in East Harlem to stop sellin' drugs! She's wacky! Nuts! Who the hell ever heard of a policy strike?"

"Frankly I think it's a hell of an idea. If they don't pick up, that's the end of policy in Harlem. Nobody can play."

He stared at me, outraged.

"For crissakes, Frank, use your head. If those jigs and

447

spicks go through with this crazy strike, it can mean trouble for us. What about the cops?"

"What about them?"

"East Harlem will still have to pay off. But there won't be any policy to protect. Who do you think Pepe will blame? Not the Duchess. You and me!" His eyes became cold and his hands curled into a fist. "I should have clobbered that dame and kicked her ass out. I should never have listened to you!"

"Like Helga?"

"Yes, like Helga! That's what she needs to keep her in line. There's someone else I should have taken care of, too—that ugly little Ally Fox—"

"What did he do?"

"He's been eggin' her on and she's been listenin' to him."

"Why would he do that? He's working for East Harlem."

"No more. He quit last week. Muzzy told me he has an idea of settin' up an independent operation with some niggers . . ."

"He won't last a day. They'll kill him and anyone else that's in with him. You know that."

"Don't you get it, Frank? If this strike goes through and he sets up a combination with the niggers, East Harlem will be forced to deal with him. Policy players don't care who is backin' the game—all they want to do is put down their nickels and dimes and get paid off if they win!"

"Where are you going now?" I asked as he got up.

"I'm goin' back up there," he said wearily, "and make her believe she's the Queen of May. It's gettin' so now I want to throw up every time I see her."

Joe didn't show at the pier Monday or Tuesday. On Wednesday he had Train drop off copies of the *Amsterdam News* which told the whole incredible story of what was to be known in Harlem as the Big Numbers walkout. Early Monday morning hundreds of thousands of numbers players in Harlem, the garment center, the downtown financial district, Broadway office buildings, and even the Criminal Courts Building discovered that they could not play their numbers; the collectors refused to take their slips or their money.

Panic spread throughout the city as the hours passed and the first race neared. Lines formed in front of policy drops but the doors remained shut. Word of the strike spread from the cop on the beat to the precinct house. The police

448

were so stunned by the news that some captains personally visited the drops to find out whether what they had heard was true. It was.

As the strike spread, the community's leaders jumped on the bandwagon to praise it and denounce East Harlem for its drug traffic.

On Wednesday, Joe and Muzzy picked me up and we joined the Duchess in her apartment. In one corner, nursing a drink, was Ally Fox. The Duchess was exuberant, flitting about filling glasses, offering snacks, and chain-smoking as she described the success of the strike.

"The wops are going crazy," she cried. "Tell Joe and Frank what happened today, Ally."

"They got two of the collectors over to East Harlem and put a gun to their heads. They told 'em that if they didn't open up for tomorrow's play they should make sure their life insurance was paid up."

"They might kill some of those guys," I pointed out.

"They won't dare," the Duchess said fiercely. "We sent word over—if one of our people is hurt we'll never go back." She gave a long, throaty laugh. "We have another surprise for them, don't we, Ally? A real good one!"

"What's that, baby?" Joe asked quickly.

"Wait a minute, Duchess," Fox snapped. "I don't think we should talk too much in front of these guys. They're not in with us—"

"What do you mean we're not in with you?" Joe asked him calmly. "Didn't we arrange the payoff setup for your combination?"

"And who the hell needed it?" Fox snarled. "We were doin' damn good before you showed up."

"C'mon, Al," Muzzy protested. "Let's knock it off . . ."

"There's a strike meetin' uptown," Joe said to me. "We'll drive the Duchess. . . . I want to find out what that surprise is," he whispered as we went out.

I have lost count of the strike meetings I attended in my life, but none was as weird as the scene in the Casbah Hall. The heart—or at least the main cogs—of the policy racket in the city were present: blacks, Cubans, Puerto Ricans, a smattering of Chinese who picked up numbers from the Chinese laundries in Harlem, and whites.

They held up the signs they were using to picket the drops:

"BOLITA YES—DRUGS NO!" . . . "NUMBERS IS

Some of the runners were drunk and kept chanting slogans as they marched around the hall. Others, in the balcony, tossed down confetti made of numbers cards and the daily ribbons, adding machine tapes.

There was no doubt that the Duchess was their leader. She gave a fiery speech to the unruly mob, then switched into Spanish. She was cheered wildly when she mentioned the name of the Sicilian and warned him to stay out of East Harlem. The hall was packed, and the crowd outside got the news of what she was saying through a series of translators who called out from one to another like a bucket brigade, passing words and phrases over the heads of the listeners.

When the crowd began to get out of control, a radio car drove up and two cops began pushing and shoving their way into the hall. The crowd beat them mercilessly, stole their guns, and sent them fleeing up Lenox Avenue. Then the radio car was turned over and set afire. After the meeting, the hall emptied and angry mobs roamed the streets, gutting policy drops, and tossing adding machines, typewriters, and streamers of ribbon tapes into the streets. As one veteran policy runner observed: "The Commissioner's Squad couldn't have done a better job."

The Duchess insisted we tour Harlem with her. Whenever she saw a small group of looters, she made Joe stop while she got out and told them to destroy anything that belonged to East Harlem.

"They will take her apart inch by inch," Joe said angrily as we drove home. "Can you imagine that stupid bitch cutting off the hand that feeds her? She's nuts, I tell you. She's nuts."

We drove in silence for a while, and then I said, "She's right, Joe. East Harlem is destroying a whole community. Do you know how much junk must have been in those flowers? Millions' worth! And we brought it in! Every time I think of it—"

"Please—no preachin'," he said with a groan. "We brought the stuff in because we had to."

"We didn't have to do anything. We could have told them to drop dead."

"Stop kiddin' yourself, Frank. You wouldn't have said no and neither would I. We like what we have too much. We've been drinkin' our coffee with cream too long to drink it black anymore . . ."

As we drove down Forty-sixth Street, Spider, who was waiting in the doorway, rushed down the stoop to meet us.

"Where the hell have you guys been?" he asked, sticking his head into the car. "Train's been lookin' all over the waterfront for you."

"What's up?" Joe asked.

"Maxie, the lawyer, has been callin' you all day. He sounds like he has a bug up his ass. You guys better go over and see him."

Maxie certainly had a bug; he almost dragged us into his office.

"Chirst!" he said, "what's happening up there?"

"A policy strike," I told him. "Haven't you heard?"

"I heard but I didn't believe it! A policy strike? It's crazy!"

"Maxie, that's all we have been hearin'," Joe told him wearily, "for crissakes don't repeat it."

"What about the Duchess? Can't you control her? She has all those spicks and niggers crazy. They've busted every adding machine in West Harlem!"

"We'll take care of her. This thing will end in a few days."

"A few days!" he cried. "Joe—it can't last that long. The cops are screaming up there. The newspapers are eating it up. Even the *Times* has it."

"I warned you guys," Maxie added, "it's sweet dough but you have all the headaches . . ."

"Don't worry, we'll take care of everything."

"Maxie said, "You better see Pepe right away. I pity you guys . . . that little wop is looking to tear someone apart."

When we met Pepe at the Gallery he looked like a madman.

"*La tutto a minchia!*" he shouted. "So you can control the colored! You sleep with her. You tell her what to do. *Fesso!* Look what she has done to our friends."

He walked up and down alongside his desk pausing only to slam down his fist and curse.

"The cops—they call us. What the hell's going on, they ask? What are you going to do about it, Peppino? *Cèrvelli!* Where were your brains?"

Joe looked shaken but he tried to keep his voice calm.

"Take it easy, Pepe. Don't get excited. We'll have her under control—"

"Figlio di butana! I will cut off her head and feed it to the birds." He held out his hands imploringly. "There is no policy. Our people sit up there—there is nothing. The cops—what can we tell them? The coloreds—they run around the street breaking our windows, throwing our machines in the gutter."

He smashed his fist down on his desk again so hard I thought the heavy glass would crack.

"Peppino! You Joe! The colored belong to you."

"What do you want us to do?" Joe asked.

Pepe slowly turned to stare at us, an incredulous look on his face.

"What is there to do? You ask me that?"

"Wait a minute—" Joe began but Pepe stopped him with a roar.

"No wait a minute! You are not children—you are men. Act like men. Did I not tell you that when a bug troubles you"—he held up his clenched fist—"squash it!"

"Christ! We can't do that, Pepe," Joe cried. "She's a woman."

"You kill when you must kill," was the cold answer. "Use the hands. If she doesn't die it will be a *disgraziato* for me."

"We're not going to kill any woman, Pepe," I told him, "not for you or anybody . . ."

He studied me for a moment, then shrugged. "Call her. Get her some place and Lorenzo will do it for you." Now he spoke softly. "Peppino—that black whore must go. Understand?"

Then he impatiently waved us out of his office.

We drove over to the small park near the East River Drive and sat in the car staring out at the lights of Brooklyn and a tug fighting its way upstream.

"He wants us to set her up," I told Joe. "I can't do it."

"If we don't he may set us up instead. Let's face it, Frank, I don't want to take the place of a goddam jig. Do you?"

I forced the words through my lips. "No."

"There is nothin' else we can do. She has to go."

"But God, Joe! Setting up a woman. And the Duchess!"

"We won't have to do it . . ."

"It will be like holding her throat for someone to use the knife," I said bitterly.

452

He looked at me. "Any other ideas?"

"Let's talk to her—"

"The hell with that. If I couldn't do it no one else can. She's playin' Harlem's Joan of Arc and she loves it."

"What about Muzzy? Maybe he can talk some sense into her."

"You know Muzzy, Frank—he's a nice guy but he's a jerk. All he cares about is the policy racket, gettin' drunk on Friday night, and bangin' that dame of his."

"It sounds as if you were talking about the both of us, Joe."

"It could be. But no more. The Duchess, Muzzy, Fox— they don't mean that much to me that I want to put my head in a noose for them." He gave a short, harsh laugh. "I found out somethin' else that will send those wops sky-high."

"What's that?"

"Do you remember when the Duchess said she had a surprise for the East Side and that bastard Fox jumped in and started the argument? Well, I found out what it was . . ."

"What is it?"

"None of the drops turned in last weekend's work or money. Every son of a bitch and his mother in Harlem is screamin' they have a hit number. No one knows who won because that crazy Duchess told them to destroy the ribbons. And get this—they also kept back the cash."

"How much is it?"

"All the drops have been bringin' their money to the Duchess. She told me she has over a hundred grand. Fox wants her to use it to start another combination."

I whistled.

"And the dough is still comin' in," he added. "Can you imagine those guys in East Harlem when they hear this? They'll climb the walls!"

And so did we. Every newspaper and radio station picked up the story. Then the mayor got into the act. The police commissioner rushed to City Hall for a conference after a citizens' group in Harlem publicly charged wholesale police corruption was allowing policy racketeers to take over the community.

When the Young Communist League began papering Harlem with mimeographed propaganda, it was evident the strike was fast becoming a *cause célèbre* with racial overtones. Less than a year had passed since Detroit and

453

then Harlem had had race riots, and jittery cops sent word to Hennessy—end it and fast!

Then, to add to the confusion, the Duchess dropped out of sight.

41 ANOTHER RAINY NIGHT ON CHERRY STREET

We searched among the Lower East Side policy drops, along the waterfront from Fourteenth Street down to the African lines on Catherine Slip, without finding a trace of her. The collectors we knew—old women in candy stores, janitors in shabby, smelly basement apartments, decrepit elevator operators—just shrugged when we inquired about her. It was as though a conspiracy of silence had settled about the area. Ally Fox had done a good job.

We finally found Muzzy and Fox in the Duchess's apartment.

"Where have you guys been?" Joe asked.

"Around," Fox replied laconically.

Joe ignored him. "Where is she, Muzzy?"

"We're not tellin' you or anybody who's not in the combination," Fox replied.

"Someday, you little son of a bitch, I will throw you right out this window," Joe told him quietly. Then to Muzzy. "Come on give—where is she?"

"I'm sorry, Joe, I can't tell ya," Muzzy said, looking uncomfortable. "Ally got word the wops will knock her off if they can find her. We all agreed not to tell anyone." He turned to Fox. "Why can't we tell Joe and Frank, Ally? They're with us."

"They're not in the combination," Fox said. "You know what everybody agreed on—only those in the combination until the strike's over!"

"What does this jerk know?" Joe said. "He can't find his way out of a paper bag."

"I know enough not to trust you two guys," Fox snapped. "Maybe you and the wops are real close . . ."

454

For a moment I could only stare at him, goose pimples traveling up my arms.

"Why do you say that?" I asked.

He gave me a crooked smile. "I got my reasons."

"Why don't you drop dead?" Joe said. Muzzy, do me a favor—tell the Duchess I want to see her."

"Over my dead body she will," Fox said.

"Maybe that's not a bad idea," Joe told him.

We didn't hear anything for two days. Hennessy sent the monthly envelopes uptown but he received some disquieting news in return; if the strike didn't end within twenty-four hours the cops were planning to set up their own combination!

"How do you like that?" Joe said. "You can't trust the bastards even when you're payin' them."

On the afternoon of the second day the phone in the pier office rang. It was Muzzy telling Joe the Duchess wanted to see him, but not on the Lower East Side—in the Village or in Harlem.

"Tell her Frank and I are buyin' into a wastepaper factory down on Cherry Street," Joe told him. "We have to go down there tonight about eight to look over the place. We have the keys, there won't be anyone around. Tell her to get in a cab and come downtown ... sure, the address is ..."

When he hung up he looked at me. "That's funny."

"What's so funny?"

"Muzzy. He sounded mad. He kept sayin', 'The Duchess wants to see you but I want to see you and Frank twice as bad.' What's wrong with him?"

"I don't know and I don't give a good goddam about Muzzy. I'm just thinking of the Duchess ..."

"What else could I say?" he demanded harshly. "What else is there?"

Why does murder always bring rain? I asked myself as we drove down the East River Drive, the methodical swish and groan of the wipers keeping a rhythmic cadence. The downpour hadn't started until we reached the Drive, but then it came down in torrents like water from a shattered bucket. The streets, baked for days by the August heat, steamed after the storm's first fury. Lightning flickered over the river and thunder muttered sullenly in the distance. It was an evil night.

We turned into one of the wide slips, passed through

455

the damp caverns of the Williamsburg Bridge that echoed with metallic tappings as cars drove over the loose plates in the roadway, went down Water Street to Cherry Street and the wastepaper factory.

As if by silent consent we ignored the switch that illuminated the open truck area—neither of us could have taken the sight of that iron monster, mouth open, waiting for its next load.

We fumbled our way through the darkness to the office where Joe turned on the naked light bulb. We stood there in silence for a moment, listening to the rainwater gurgling from the broken gutter in the alley. With the suddenness of a hand thrust into my face I remembered the grim details of that other rainy night. . . .

A short time after we arrived a car pulled up, the front door slammed, and Lorenzo walked into the office. He carefully hung up his raincoat and sat down on the sagging couch.

"Marrone! What weather!" He indicated our soggy jackets. "What's the matter—no raincoats? You get sick like that."

"It didn't start rainin' until we reached the Drive," Joe explained.

Lorenzo just sat there staring into space, the harsh light revealing the lines and furrows in his olive face. For the first time I noticed his hair was sparse but carefully combed from one side of his head to the other in an attempt to cover the baldness.

"The guy on the radio said it will rain all night," he said at last. He could have been a weary tie salesman exchanging chitchat with two customers as they waited for the rain to stop.

This was the first time Lorenzo had said more than four words to us: murder, I told myself, must make him loquacious.

"Good for flowers," he said at last. "Everything grows." He added, looking from me to Joe:

"You see her first?"

"I guess she will have to see us," Joe said. His face was white and drawn and he kept licking his lips nervously.

"You talk for a minute, then you go," Lorenzo said. "Make some excuse like you have to go to the toilet—"

"I'll tell Frank to wait in the car. . . . I'll make an excuse to go out and talk to him . . ."

"Buòno! Buòno!" Lorenzo said. He studied his fingernails

for a moment, then looked up, listening to the gurgling of the broken gutter.

We sat in silence staring out through the open door into the gloom. Lorenzo was the first to hear the car. He was on his feet in a moment, then he turned, nodded to us, and vanished outside among the towering bales of shredded paper.

I crossed the dark area and opened the street door to look into the grim face of Muzzy under a dripping umbrella.

"Muzzy! What are you doing down here?"

"I drove the Duchess," he said shortly.

It was evident from the way he glared at me that something was wrong.

"What's up—you look like you want to take a swing at me."

"Maybe that will come later," he said. "Joe here?"

"He's waiting in the office."

"Okay. I'll get the Duchess. She's in the car across the street."

"You didn't have to come down, Muzzy—Joe told her to take a cab . . ."

Over his shoulder he replied, "Where in the hell are you gonna get a cab on a night like this? Besides, I want to talk to you guys."

When he crossed the street I ran back to the office.

"Joe! Muzzy's here. He drove her down."

"Muzzy! Get rid of him. Tell him anything . . ."

"It's not going to be that easy. He wants to talk to us. You were right—something is eating him."

"What do you think it is?"

"I don't know but I'm sure we're going to find out very shortly."

When I arrived back at the front door, Muzzy, his umbrella held high, was escorting the Duchess across the street. As she came close I could smell the perfume. For one wild moment I almost pushed them back out into the street, shouting for them to go, to run, to get out of our lives. But then Joe broke the spell. He was standing in the doorway of the office.

"Duchess? Is that you Duchess?"

"That's me, honey. I'm coming!" she cried, shaking out her raincoat.

She ran toward him.

"Baby, I never thought we would find it . . . even the cabbie wasn't sure. . . . What are you doing down here?"

"We were offered a deal on this place," Joe said. "This is the only night we could see it."

She threw herself at him. They clung to each other, then went inside.

"Why don't we leave them alone?" I told Muzzy. "How about giving me a ride uptown?"

"No dice," Muzzy said tersely. "I have some things I want to talk over with you guys. Important things."

"Like what? Come on, Muzzy, you can talk to me."

He hesitated for a moment, then nodded. "Okay. I'll tell ya what's on my mind. Ally knows a guy in East Harlem. They grew up together in numbers. He met him again when he went to work up there. They got cozy and this guy tells Ally East Harlem now gets the same protection we usta get—only now one guy dishes out the coin to the cops. When I heard this, Ally and I went to see the Duchess and I squawked. Hell, I told her, your boy downtown gave us the double-cross. Now the wops can move in and take us over anytime they want. Why? Because they have our guy on their pad—they don't need us anymore. She was crocked that night and she began cryin', all about Joe and what he had done to her.

"At first it came out in little pieces, then she told us everything. How you guys framed that queer Cornell and how ya put the arm on him with those pictures! Now this guy Cornell is takin' care of everyone—and that sets us up for a takeover by East Harlem. The Duchess didn't know that until Ally told her. In fact that's the only reason she came down to this—" He looked over the damp, gloomy cave with contempt. "This goddam joint." His voice started to rise. "You and Joe screwed us, Frank! Ya gave us the old rinky dink right up the ass."

"Nobody is trying to screw you or the Duchess, Muzzy," I said. I reached out to put my arm on his shoulder but he shrugged it off.

"You're not gonna bullshit me anymore, buddy! It's yer friend in there I want to talk to." He hurried toward the office.

As soon as he was gone I heard a rustle and Lorenzo was standing next to a bale.

"Who's the loudmouth?"

"Wait here," I told him. "Don't do anything until we tell you—"

When I entered the office the Duchess had her raincoat draped over her shoulder and was nervously puffing at a cigarette as she sat on the edge of the couch. Joe was perched on the corner of the desk studying a very angry Muzzy.

"Joe, I think you and I had better talk," I started to say but he held up his hand.

"I think so too," he said slowly. "Muzzy is just tellin' me that he, Ally, and the Duchess are settin' up a new combination—"

"I told Ally and Muzzy I want you and Joe to come in with us," the Duchess said swiftly. "We can really make it big, Frank—"

"Wait a minute, Duchess," Muzzy snapped. "There ain't gonna be any invitations until I get the whole goddam story of what these guys have been up to."

"I told you I didn't want any arguments," she said firmly. "What's done is done. Like I told you and Ally, from now on it's a clean slate—"

"I still want to . . ."

Her voice fractured the stillness of the factory.

"It's a clean slate, Muzzy! I told you and Ally that."

"Let me and Frank go outside for a minute and have a little conference," Joe said. "I think we can come back with somethin' that will satisfy everybody. Okay?"

"Talk! You can talk until tomorrow but I want some answers," Muzzy said. "This time Ally got it straight. I believe him. I want to know what the hell is goin' on around here."

"Okay, Muzzy," Joe said, "give us a minute."

"That's the ball game," Joe whispered as we hurried across the room. "Where the hell is—"

"Right here," I said as Lorenzo came from behind the bale.

"They both go," Joe told him.

From inside the office I could hear Muzzy shouting and the Duchess soothing him. Lorenzo moved along the edge of the bales like a menacing shadow. He paused for a moment on the fringe of light that poured through the open door. He was holding that familiar silencer and a coil of wire.

As we opened the street door, we heard a snapping behind us, a sound like a man breaking a dry stick across his knee, then a wild cry. We slammed the door, ran
459

through the rain to our car, and headed for the East River Drive.

We pulled off at Forty-second Street with a huge bow wave as the car plunged through a big puddle.

"I'm goin' to stop off at my place for a minute," Joe said. I jumped, startled. It was the first time he had spoken since we had left Cherry Street.

"What for?"

"To get my gun."

"Spider's .38? What the hell do you want a gun for now?"

"I'm goin' to get Fox. I could never live with myself knowin' that ugly son of a bitch was still around and Muzzy and the Duchess had to go."

"Christ, you sound like God's ordained executioner—"

"With Fox I will be," he said grimly. "You don't have to come, Frank. I'll see you tomorrow mornin' . . ."

"Why do you always say that?" I said wearily. "You know I'll come along. I always do."

We stalked Fox from the Lower East Side to West Harlem. Just before dawn we finally found him in Papa Joe's, the after-hours place. The place was jumping and jiving, fortunately the lights were low. There were several couples standing in the middle of the floor, so Fox didn't see us. He came out with a bunch of policy runners and left them at the subway.

We got him as he stopped to light a cigarette. I will never forget the look on his face when he saw us. He started to run but the first bullet staggered him; the second and third killed him.

Harlem is like the Neighborhood when it comes to gunshots. No one comes running out, witnesses are not available, shades are pulled down, curtains are drawn. A milkman who had started to come down the street made a sharp U-turn and disappeared.

"Let's get him in the car," Joe said.

"What do we want to put him in the car for? Let's get out of here!"

"They have to know we mean business," he snarled. "If they don't, then all we did tonight doesn't mean a god-dam!"

I lined the back of the car with cardboard and we flung Fox's body in. Then we drove to 118th Street where the largest policy drop had been located. It was an old store with the usual flyspecked candy bars, small toys, and water-stained crepe paper in the window.

The ash can that had shattered the windows when the strikers went looting was still there surrounded by jagged blades of glass like a Dali sculpture. The street was littered with torn cut cards and old ribbons. The adding machines and the typewriters had been snatched up the moment they hit the sidewalks, but two neatly sharpened pencils still lay in the gutter. We heaved the body into the window and it hung there, feet dangling, blood dripping.

"Pepe should like this," Joe grunted.

He did. A few days after the strike collapsed Pepe called to invite us—I guess order would be more correct—to a barbecue in New Jersey. We were finally going to meet our friends. ... And I was to bring all my material on the police union idea.

42 OUR FRIENDS

Spy Town, New Jersey, was a tiny community located in the heart of the rugged Bear Paw Mountains in the northern part of the state. It had two commodities which it sold to tourists: Spy Town hand-carved rockers which had been made in the town since before the Revolution, and the "hanging tree," an enormous gnarled oak which Mad Anthony Wayne had used to execute Tory spies from New York who tried to encourage the mutinous Continentals during that fateful winter of 1781.

At first we had considered driving out to Jersey but Pepe told us to pick up a hired limousine at Ninth and Fortieth near the entrance to the Lincoln Tunnel. As it pulled into the curb we were surprised to find we had a fellow passenger —Maxie Solomon.

Since the Neighborhood had always considered territory more than an hour from Times Square to be unexplored frontier, Joe and I dressed for a day in the country, slacks and sports jackets. But Maxie was formally attired from starched shirt to highly polished shoes.

In the beginning Maxie was tense and tried to avoid answering our questions. But as time passed he relaxed and revealed that Pepe had ordered him to accompany us to the barbecue to discuss a business proposition.

"What kind of business do you think he has in mind?" Joe asked.

"Maybe it has something—" Maxie began but Joe cut him off.

"Wait a minute," he said. Then he leaned over to the driver and said softly, "Hey, buddy, how about some privacy?"

The driver gave him a quick glance in the overhead mirror, then reached over and pressed a button. The glass partition between the front and back rose slowly.

"That guy was all ears. As you were sayin', Maxie . . ."

The lawyer gave him a thin smile.

"Joe, you're learning."

"Yeah. What were you sayin' about Pepe?"

"I think he wants to talk about gambling. Maybe unions."

"I thought you only handled the court end," I said.

"I guess I can tell you this—when you and Joe were setting up the payoffs for the cops I was doing a lot of traveling for Pepe. Detroit, Boston, Rhode Island, upstate. It had to do with gambling. In Chicago I made a deal with Pepe's contacts to lease us a wire for results. After Pepe made some calls I met two upstate politicians and got the okay to build a trotters' track. Then he found some guy in Boston who had steel." He said wryly, "And you tell me who has steel these days! After that he had me go up to Canada—"

"Canada!" Joe exclaimed.

"That's right, Canada. Pepe's guy up there owns the biggest club in Montreal. He wants to get into the flats. Pepe has a deal going for a track down south—"

"How do you like that little son of a bitch?" Joe asked me. "He's buyin' up the United States!"

"Why do you think he selected us?" I asked Maxie.

"Let me put it this way. Every time they sent us to bat we hit home runs. I never fell down when they gave me a contract." A note of pride entered his voice. "Pepe likes the way I set up deals. I guess I proved I know how to get

462

things done. No trouble. No fuss. Everything nice, clean, and quiet."

"That takes care of you, how about us?"

"You know better than I do."

"Come off it, Maxie. You have your ear to the ground."

"Okay. Maybe I do hear something now and then. I know this, they liked how you handled the Duchess . . ."

He broke off and stared straight ahead.

"You took care of her, right?" he asked softly.

"Didn't the strike end?" Joe asked roughly.

"It did."

"Then that's your answer. Now who's askin' questions, Counselor?'

"I'm sorry. Asking questions is not one of my weaknesses."

When he seemed to hesitate, I prompted.

"Is that all they like?"

"No. They've gone hook, line, and sinker for your cop idea."

"The cops' union?" Joe put in. "I guess that's why they want to see Frank's stuff."

He raised his hand. "Now for crissakes don't quote me, but I think Pepe told them about it."

"Who are these others—the ones he keeps calling our friends, Maxie?" I asked. "Have you any idea?"

"I don't," he said cautiously.

"Oh come off it, Maxie. Let's stop dancing with each other. You know as well as I do the three of us are in something big."

"I agree," he said earnestly, "but exactly what I don't know. And that's the truth. It's a society, organization, syndicate, combination—you name it. Pepe and Gus are the big wheels, but I think Pepe more than Gus. It's not only in New York but Chicago, Detroit, Rhode Island, Boston, even the West Coast. After I went upstate for Pepe and met those two guys I went to a hotel and just lay on the bed—thinking. I asked myself if I wanted to be another Dixie Davis."

He turned to us. "Do you know who I mean? Dixie Davis, Schultz's lawyer who testified against Hines?" When we nodded he went on. "A guy I went to law school with knows a dame whose brother-in-law works for the DA's office. He says they promised to buy Dixie a gas station somewhere out in the west. I said to myself, 'That may be okay for Dixie Davis but not for Maxie Solomon.' What the hell is the DA going to do—assign a cop to stay with him for the rest of his life? In a gas station?"

He brooded about this for a moment as he stared out of the window.

"We're not interested in the history of a two-bit mob lawyer who blew the whistle on Hines," Joe said impatiently. "All we want to know is—who are the guys we're supposed to meet today?"

"Look, in this business you have to study all the angles. Anything can happen."

"Do you think it's the Mafia?" Joe asked.

"You mean with all that hocus-pocus stuff like in the Sunday Supplement?" Maxie said with a shrug. "I don't think so. Maybe it's the American brand. Who knows? Who cares? And you can bet they're not going to tell you what it is."

"You said you thought it over in a hotel room, Maxie," I said. "What did you come up with?"

He gave me a sad smile.

"I'm here."

"Pesonally I don't care who they are," Joe was saying. "They have more muscle than anyone else in this town and that I like. Before we met Pepe we were nothin'. Just punchin' bags for cops. Now we got everythin' we want."

"Everything? Nobody has everything."

"Well, almost everythin'. There's a few things left."

We rode in silence for a while, then Maxie added softly: "As I said, I don't like to ask questions. But what about Muzzy?"

"Maybe he ran into a fan," Joe said coldly. "Like you told us, you ask too goddam many questions."

Maxie held up both hands.

"Forget I asked it! I can tell you this, Tony Cupid thought that guy in the window of the drop was terrific. He told Pepe that brought the niggers into line."

"Who is Tony Cupid?" I asked.

"Antonio Capido," Maxie explained. "He's big in gambling. He's in all the papers. A big good-looking guy who is always with dames. Dewey tried to nail him but he couldn't. He's not like those other Moustache Petes you —can talk to him."

"How did you get to know him, Maxie?"

"Years ago when I was working out of a telephone booth in the lobby of West Side Court I met Pepe after he had been picked up on an eight ninety-two, that's dis con. He had only six months to go on parole and the cops were bleeding him and Gus white. That's when they owned that little wop speak on the West Side. But this arresting officer happened to be a straight arrow cop who wouldn't take a dime, so I had to go to bat. I got Pepe off. From that time on he always threw me something. I have to hand it to that little guy, he never forgets . . ."

"You were going to tell us about Cupid?"

"Well, one day Pepe drops around my office." He laughed shortly. "Office! I was still in the lobby hustling for the big ones, like whores or drunken Irishmen who beat up their wives on the weekend, when Pepe introduces me to this big guy who is Tony Cupid and explains he was busted on a Sullivan rap and wants me to represent him. Tony has quite a record from larceny to five-to-fifteen for manslaughter and believe me this one wasn't easy. But I got him off. The arresting officer was a bit of a jerk. Since then Pepe has always been my rabbi." He grunted. "Like you guys. Before I met him, everything I had was in my hat and booth five. Now I'm on Easy Street. A big office on Madison Avenue. No partners. A staff. Easy cases, and some fine crooks for clients—like you two guys."

"Let's face it, Maxie," I told him, "you've forgotten more than we know now."

"But you're learning," he said quietly.

That we were.

We had held our breath since the body of Ally Fox had been found and the Duchess and Muzzy had disappeared, but there was no intensive police investigation.

As Hennessy reported to us. "The boys up at One Hundred Twenty-third Street consider it just another nigger knockoff. They're not even carryin' the Duchess or that other guy. Like they said: 'If it isn't reported, it isn't a crime.' "

As the drive grew longer, and the three of us ran out of conversation, we settled back, each occupied with his own thoughts. After Pompton Lakes we started to climb along twisting, blacktop WPA roads. It was a hot steamy afternoon but the air became cooler as the country grew more isolated.

"Do you get out to the country much?" Joe asked Maxie.

"For a guy born on Hester Street, Queens is the country," he replied.

Suddenly we passed a deserted gas station with a cardboard sign hanging from the pump that said: "Gone to war." Then down a steep grade to a crossroad and a strikingly beautiful little village surrounded by large farmhouses, broad fields, and orchards with baskets of fruit under the trees.

"Spy Town," I said.

"How do you know?" Maxie asked indignantly.

I pointed to a small sign that read: "Home of Spy Town's Famous Rockers and the Hanging Tree of the American Revolution. A Community where the Glorious Past Meets the Exciting Future."

Maxie rapped on the glass partition and it silently rolled down.

"It's supposed to be just outside the village, driver," he said nervously. "Maybe you had better ask someone."

The driver ignored him and cautiously moved through the one-street village and continued back on the upgrade along a road rougher than before, until the blacktop became dirt. We continued on the dirt road for about half a mile. Then the trees ended and revealed a large lawn with tables set and a number of men walking around in pairs or groups, talking, listening, and holding drinks. Across the lawn in a cleared space in front of a garage that was as big as a small house were numerous cars, all new and expensive, mostly Cadillacs.

Then Pepe hurried toward us with a broad smile, his hands held up in an extravagant gesture of welcome.

Pepe led us around the grounds like a medieval baron showing off his castle, introducing us to everyone he saw. The introductions were elaborate and in the Sicilian dialect. The men—I judged there were about a hundred— were middle-aged or, what I considered with the arrogance of my youth, very old. Obviously, they were all Italian—some were dark as Arabs, while others were fair, even blue eyed. There were no names, only smiles, nods, handshakes, or cold, assessing stares.

My instinct told me we were on view as Pepe's special exhibits. I could almost hear the unspoken: "In whom I am well pleased . . ."

Pepe was in great demand. Someone was always calling him over to throw their arms about his shoulders, shake his hand, or clutch him in a tight embrace. Our host turned out to be smiling, affable Gus, the owner of Grand Vista.

"How do you kids like this, eh?" he asked, his proud wave taking in the lawn and the sprawling brick house. "C'mon, I want to show you something."

He led us past the barbecue that cast off waves of heat like a blast furnace, to a high hurricane fence in a clump of trees. The view was breathtaking; the valley below stretched for miles to another mountain chain. A sultry, gray vapor hung over the countryside, its mists slowly forming and re-forming, then reluctantly breaking. On the green carpet a cattle pond glowed like a slab of frozen light. The only sound was a distant automobile horn.

"I can tell you kids this is not like Guinea Alley," Gus said fervently.

"It's really beautiful," I said. "How long have you had it?"

"Only a couple of months. I was goin' crazy in that club. Too damn much." He pointed down to the valley. "I own half the mountain. There's even a little lake back here where you can go fishing. I told the agent I get all the fish I want from Socks Lanza down in the market. Who the hell wants to sit in the sun all day with a little pole?" He shook his head in disbelief. "One hundred and sixty acres! I wish my old man was still around. To a wop a piece of land means everything. Out here he could have grown a million tomatoes!"

We obediently studied the pastoral scene.

"Gus—have you heard anything about Chena or Nicky?" I asked.

I received an impatient grunt for my response.

"Yeah. We heard somethin' last week. Ask Pepe."

"Is she—"

"Pepe will fill you in," he said shortly. "I gotta go back. You kids want anything, just ask."

As he turned away Joe asked hastily, "Can you tell us why we're here, Gus?"

"*Abbeia paziènza!* Have patience! You'll find out."

We followed him back to the lawn where he hurried off to join Pepe who was welcoming some late arrivals.

Maxie looked relieved when we returned.

"I go over to the bar to get a drink and you guys drop out of sight! Where did you go? I've been looking all over for you."

"Gus was showing us the view," I told him. "Anything new?"

"I've been visiting—I know some of those guys."

"Like who?"

"See those two guys getting a drink? The big guy in a sports jacket?"

"What about him?"

"That's Tony Cupid. The other guy is Charlie Victory, the biggest whoremaster in the country. But don't let him hear you use that word. He'll break your arms and legs. I don't know the whole story, but a couple of years ago . . ."

What he told us that afternoon proved to me Maxie Solomon did his homework. His profiles of the guests at the barbecue were excellent; the head of Dewey's investigative staff would have drooled had he heard him. In his travels for Pepe, Maxie had done thorough research on the people he was visiting. As he said many times, "I like to know something about the people I'm dealing with."

The first man he pointed out, Antonio Capido, better known to newspaper readers as Tony Cupid, claimed New Jersey as his barony. Cupid was then an extraordinarily handsome man, tall, slender, and poised, with an attractive smile and a lifeguard's tan that showed off his even teeth to a fine advantage. He was carefully and expensively dressed.

But for all of his country club look, Cupid had been born on Madison Street in Little Italy and had served time in a reformatory before he was sixteen for stealing packages from a truck. He developed a flair for gambling in his teens, and, in his early twenties, was running a floating crap game in East Brooklyn. He had a love for the tracks and bought two racehorses, but within a year the Jockey Club barred him for life after he had been convicted of bribing a jockey and financing a band of race track "ringers" who were so clever they sold their dyed crowbait as champion breed to the best stables before they were exposed.

To avoid a grand jury subpoena he bought a luxurious home on the Palisades, spent a small fortune to bribe enough politicians to insure protection for himself and his crap games, which attracted players from as far as Philadelphia, then set up a company to deliver new cars. Before the war his Interstate Auto Delivery Service received ten percent of the wholesale price for every car that left New Jersey. The automobile companies at first scoffed at his percentage, but after several trailers of new cars were reduced to hulks by sledgehammers and several more drivers ended up in the hospital, it was decided Capido's price was reasonable after all.

Capido was gradually becoming a café society figure; pictures of him and a well-known movie star dancing and drinking were becoming commonplace in the tabloids. But, as Maxie explained, it was only for publicity—he owned the club through a front for the liquor license and the star was a Lesbian.

The other man with Capido was Calegero Villalba, known as Charlie Victory. In contrast to Tony Cupid, he was short, squat, with thick iron gray eyebrows and cold, searching eyes. He was wearing a wrinkled sports shirt and had a heart tattooed on one arm with the words: Love to Mother.

Victory's closeness to Cupid was through blood; their fathers were cousins and had immigrated from the same village in Sicily to Philadelphia, where they opened a store dealing in cheese and olive oil. After Capido's father sold out and left for New York, Charlie Victory carried on his father's business, which later included gambling, prostitution, and nightclubs. I noticed that Capido appeared to be the only one in the group who drank with Victory. This, as Maxie explained, was because the others contemptuously called him "the whoremaster" behind his back because of his traffic in prostitutes. Since the war started, Victory had almost tripled the number of his whorehouses until it was claimed that he put on as many whores as there were shifts in the navy yard.

Among the late arrivals, Maxie pointed out Salvatore Grossi, or Sally G, whose territory took in the upstate cities including Buffalo, Syracuse, and Utica. White-haired and dignified, he appeared to be readying himself for a portrait session. He greeted the others with a formal handshake but he embraced Pepe and whispered in his ear.

As Maxie dryly explained, there was a reason for the enthusiastic welcome. "Pepe had me meet the two upstate politicians to help this guy get his okay to build the trotters' track. I not only paid them off for a guarantee that the local tinhorns wouldn't cause any trouble, but I also laid out the campaign for a referendum in November. He thought he would have to wait until after the war to build the track, but Pepe found the guy in Boston who has the steel, and now the track can be finished by spring. Not only will Grossi's construction companies do the job, but he'll be president and he'll put in his own unions! By the time the war is over he'll be a millionaire twice over."

"What does Pepe get out of it?" I asked.

"Oh, he's getting a piece, but I don't think he's doing it only for money . . ."

"What then?"

"He's leaving markers with those guys. Like politicians when they're running for a big office. They go out of their state to help a guy—but later, when they need a favor, they collect."

"Do you mean in this organization or whatever it is?" Joe asked.

Maxie nodded. "I think—and now I'm only guessing—that some day Pepe wants to own it . . ."

"Who's the other guy with Grossi?" Joe asked.

Maxie looked across the lawn and studied the stocky man in the brown suit who was loudly greeting some of the other guests.

"Buster D'Agostino. He controls the Boston trucking locals with the Irish mobs. He's rough when he gets drunk. Last month he almost killed his brother-in-law. I don't think the guys like him."

"Why do you say that?"

"When I was in Boston talking to Pepe's contact about the steel, I heard D'Agostino was in trouble over the beating. His father-in-law is the boss in Rhode Island and from what I heard they sat this guy down and told him to lay off the booze."

"And if he doesn't?" Joe asked.

"I don't think he'll celebrate Armistice Day . . ."

"Who told you all this, Maxie?" I asked him. "You sound as if you were reading their mail."

"You don't have to. After you have been with them for a while you sense certain things. Look at the fuss Pepe made over Sally G—that means something to them. And how he only shook hands with D'Agostino. That means something else. They're tough and primitive, but the more I see of them the more I understand them."

"And you understand them, so that's why you're here?"

He smiled. "I can't help but think the three of us are like that guy in the circus with the whip and the chair who walks into the cage with the lions."

"Don't worry, we'll tame 'em," Joe said impatiently, "Who's the little guy gettin' out of the car?"

470

"That's Little Nino—Nino Verga. He's Mr. East Harlem. The niggers turn white when they hear his name."

"He looks like he owns a fruit stand on Ninth Avenue," Joe observed.

Verga was slightly under five feet tall with tiny hands and feet and the frame of a young boy. At that time he was in his sixties. As I learned later, his wan, sad smile and slovenly dress—he carried his jacket over one arm and wore old-fashioned suspenders over a drab sports shirt—were typical affectations.

"Don't let that getup fool you," Maxie warned. "He's a tough little guy. He thinks both of you are great . . ."

"Why should he think that?" Joe asked. "We never met him!"

"You ended the strike in his territory, didn't you? And that guy in the window made the jigs think twice. He also likes your setup with the cops. Before that, he had to pay everybody. Tony Cupid and Nino are very close. Their mothers are cousins or something like that."

Years later I heard from Pepe the rather revealing story of how Verga had fled Sicily when he was nineteen after murdering a family with an ax in a vendetta over the killing of an uncle who was a *gabèllòtto*—a tax collector. Someone asked him if he could turn back the clock would he repeat his monstrous crime? Nino gently admonished the questioner by his answer.

"Did I have a choice? I had to drink the blood of the man who killed my uncle. Honor is honor and a vendetta is a vendetta. You might say that the priest of the devil took me by the hand and hung me on the hook."

As Pepe said in agreement: that was the way it was.

Little Nino, Maxie told us, was known among them as *"Il Buonanima*—The Good Soul."

As soon as the guests had spotted Nino, many of them rushed across the lawn to greet the little man. He smiled, shook their hands, accepted their salutations with a brief nod, then slowly looked about the groups. When he saw Pepe he raised his hand and called out. Then they hurried toward each other to embrace.

"See what I mean?" Maxie said softly.

These were the men to whom we were introduced by Pepe. I later became aware they were the blood royal; we never met the lesser figures of the court, and never the peasants.

We didn't sit at the long table where the conversation was mostly in Italian, but at a smaller table nearby. Pepe was constantly jumping up from his seat at the main table to come over and urge us to eat. Yet, all through the meal, I was aware of the fact that we were not at the main table. I remembered Pepe's word: outsiders.

The meal was long, almost ritualistic. Even before espresso was served some of the guests had started to leave while others drifted toward the house. Finally we found ourselves alone.

When the last group had disappeared, Pepe sat down at our table.

"Peppino! How do you like the country?" he said, squeezing my shoulder in his powerful grip.

"It's certainly not Ninth Avenue."

"Ecco!" he cried. "It is too quiet. I told Gus run a subway out here and I'll feel better!"

We laughed politely and waited.

"Only a little while and we will talk to you, young man," he said seriously. He pointed to the screened summerhouse. "You will wait there. I told Lorenzo to put whiskey, coffee, and cakes on the table for you. If you want anything, call him!"

"Lorenzo? Where is he?" I asked Pepe. "I haven't seen him all day."

"Your eyes, Peppino," Pepe admonished me and pointed across the lawn. Seated in a chair near the rear door of the house was Lorenzo. When he saw us looking over, he raised his cup of espresso.

"What is this all about, Pepe? Can you tell us?" Joe asked.

"We wish to talk to the three of you," he replied. "Cannot friends talk together?"

"About what?" I asked.

He shrugged. "Maybe we can tell the generals how to end the war—no, Peppino?"

He slapped me jovially on the back and hurried off to the house.

"It's a Table," Maxie said as we walked to the summerhouse.

"What the hell's a Table?" Joe asked.

"A meeting held to make an important decision." He laughed nervously. "Like when they want a guy knocked off—they hold a Table and agree who will make the hit . . ."

472

"They wouldn't bring us all the way out to Jersey, feed us, and then decide to kill us?" I said.

"Oh, it's nothing like that. Like I said, it's some kind of a business proposition."

"Are you sure you don't know, Maxie?" I asked.

"I swear I don't."

"But in the car you said it would be something to do with gambling and unions."

"It was only a guess."

"But somethin' must have made you come to that conclusion," Joe said doggedly.

"It's the way I feel. As I told you, the more you are with these guys the more you can sense things. Take the ones he introduced us to—they all control gambling." He shook his head and said slowly, "I think they're moving into something big."

"And they want us to be part of it?" Joe asked.

"Your guess is as good as mine, Joe," was Maxie's answer.

43 THE TABLE

When the sun went down, cool, damp air crept up from the valley and across the mountain. The monotonous orchestration of night insects was accompanied by hard-shelled bugs hurling themselves against the screen with the sound of hidden small boys spitting peas at us with a peashooter. Once we heard cars moving cautiously down the narrow lane to the main road and saw the flicker of headlights through the trees.

Finally Lorenzo appeared and beckoned to Maxie. When we started to get up he shook his head.

"Only the lawyer."

"Don't they want to see us?" I asked.

"After the lawyer, Peppino."

When they had left Joe said, "What do you make of that?"

"It's just as well," I said. "I don't think Maxie should know all our business."

"Like what?"

"Like the cargo of flowers. He didn't make any mention of it coming out so they probably haven't told him . . ."

We waited for about an hour. Then Lorenzo appeared again and smilingly waved us across the lawn to the house. I had an immediate sense of exquisite luxury; crystal chandeliers, a sunken living room with deep red carpet, ornate mirrors, and a fieldstone fireplace. Then we entered a room that looked like the typical boardroom of a financial house. It was paneled with oak, the only decorations a few hunting prints. In the soft light the faces of the men seated about the table were shadowy and indistinct. There were several, but I had expected to see more. This handful, I told myself, are the leaders, the others were subordinates.

They were smoking and sipping at cups of espresso or glasses of cold drinks. The ashtrays in front of them were empty and the air in the room, despite their cigarettes and cigars, was clean and fresh. There was no sign of the lawyer; we were the main attraction.

Seated behind each man was a younger man who I later discovered was the *consiglièro* who gave advice. Gus sat at the head of the table; on his right was Pepe, who waved us to chairs. There was a clearing of throats and a shifting of seats as some of the men turned to study us.

Pepe was obviously the spokesman. He smiled as if to put us at ease, then began.

"First of all we wish to thank you, Peppino and Joe, for coming," he said in a quiet relaxed way. "We apologize for keeping you waiting but there has been a great deal of important business discussed here—some of it had to do with you." He leaned forward and clasped his hands in front of him on the table. "We will come to that in a minute." He addressed me directly. "These are your friends, Peppino. You have asked to see them many times— now how do you like them?" He explained to the others, "All the time Peppino says, 'Pepe, when do we meet our friends?' *Pòrco diavolo!* I told him, '*sempre* questions, Peppino? You are like a *sbirro!*' Now he is here!" He turned to Joe. "Joe! How do you like your friends?"

Joe said tersely, "Fine. Fine. They're okay, Pepe."

When he came back to me I said, "Perhaps it is not us

who should be asked the question, Pepe, but our friends—what do they think of us?"

A murmur went round the table and some of the men looked at Pepe.

"That is why you are here, Peppino," Pepe said gently.

Somehow I felt he was glad I had asked the question.

"As you will find out, we are a gathering of honorable men," he went on.

"Our interests are many but we have our own way of doing things. We have no time for strangers that are not of our world. Even you two—we had a great deal of discussion about you—shall we speak to you like this or shall we discontinue our relationship?"

He probably saw the surprise in our faces because he held up his hand to cut off any questions.

"We feel we have to come to a point where we must either speak to you as men or shake your hands and tell you, *addio*—go with God!

"Some among us argued that we should pay you a good price for your operations, letting you go your own way. But there are others who pointed out that such an act would be unworthy of us as men of honor. There are no written contracts among us. No lawyers' words, perhaps a word or a handshake. Above all, we are loyal to our friends. We defend and protect them—as they do for us. In our language there is a saying—*una mano lava l'altra*—one hand washes the other."

He paused and Lorenzo was at his side with a glass of water. He sipped at it, then continued.

"We were impressed with you, *giovinotti,* you have shown us that you know when there is a time for"—he patted his arm—"*muscolo* and"—this time he tapped his temple—"*cèrvelli.*"

"What you have done with the payoffs is very good. Some of us could only talk, talk, talk like crows in the field while we greased the palm of every cop who walked down the street."

"They acted like we had turnstiles in the drops," Nino grunted.

"But no more cowboying, my young friends," Pepe went on. "You see the pictures in the newspapers! *Marrone!* You should hear the cops squeal." He made a gesture as if listening on the telephone. "The mayor. The police commissioner. They all call the precincts. It makes a lot of trouble . . . Once is enough—no?"

"It certainly brought the jigaboos into line," Cupid said. "Did you see the picture on page one of the *News* with that guy's ass hanging out the window?"

There was a chuckling around the table.

"Buòno! Buòno!" Nino said smiling at us. "No more trouble with the coloreds."

"Si," Pepe said. "It is settled. The cops are satisfied. The people are quiet. Let us light a candle that Dewey stays in Albany. We are at peace. For us there is no more *squadrista*. No more mattress war where we kill each other." His voice became hard and cold. *"Castellammarese!* Let us not forget it, my friends."

Sober faces nodded. Later when I learned from Lorenzo about *Castellammarese,* the so-called Mattress War, I understood the momentary pall that had settled over the room . . .

"Castellammarese is in the past, Sortino," Nino said. "It is best forgotten."

"It is good to remember the bad things, my friend," Pepe gently admonished him. "It helps to avoid making foolish mistakes."

He turned to Gus. "Duchino, you wished to talk?"

"We must know about the cops," Gus said. "Will the payoffs work if they are not around?"

Pepe looked at us.

"Peppino? Joe?"

For a moment the wild idea raced across my brain—they are going to kill us . . .

"There is no problem as long as the bagman gets the dough," Joe said cautiously. "Why? What's up? Don't you like the way we have been handlin' it?"

"No. No," Gus said. "Your way is fine."

"Just as long as you get the money to the cops; lost paydays make them nervous."

"Si," Little Nino said. "They get like old women."

"Anybody can do it?" Gus asked.

"That's it. The system is runnin' like a clock."

"Are you sure?"

"We can guarantee it. But we would like to know what is going on."

The words slipped out before I knew it.

"If it's more flowers, Pepe, I can tell you now—count me out."

Pepe looked surprised.

"No more flowers, Peppino!"

476

"We had a lot of trouble with that last one," Joe said.

"Things like that happen," Gus said.

"Maybe they do. But we don't want them to happen to us anymore," I said.

"Speak your mind, kid—that's why we're here . . ."

"That's all . . . maybe Joe thinks differently . . ."

"No I don't," Joe said firmly. "No more flowers."

"It was a great service to us," Pepe said. There were grunts of approval as he looked about the table.

"You asked us and we did it," Joe said.

"We know that," Pepe replied. "We *all* know that." He went on almost apologetically. "It was unfortunate that our friends overseas had a traitor among them. What is important they took care of him—"

"*Páglia!*" Nino snorted. "They put him in the *casséta* for a few days. *Carnazza successe!*"

"*Si.*" Pepe grinned. "As Nino says he was only good for the slaughterhouse. But this is no concern of yours, my young friends. We like what you have done with the cops, with the old men and the unions on the piers, and the warehouse men. Perhaps in a little way we have helped you. You know you cannot be one of us," he went on, "this I have explained. You are *stranieri*—outsiders. Yet you will always be close to us as if we were of the same blood . . ."

He stared down at us for a moment in silence.

"You understand this, Peppino? And Joe?"

"We understand," I said.

"I must speak of all these things so the air will be clear. Now I come to our proposition."

There was a clearing of throats, some tasted their coffee or drinks, chewed on their cigars, stared at the ceiling or at Pepe.

"Our friends overseas have told us that the Germans are licked. That is not to say there will be no more fighting. We are not generals! We must believe what we have been told by men of honor. Every day in Italy the underground grows stronger. More Germans are killed. More trains wrecked, and in many towns they hang the Nazi flag in their toilets." He smiled grimly. "Now they're warriors . . ."

"Your friends must know Eisenhower, Pepe," Joe put in.

"In an invaded country the peasants know more than the generals," Pepe said mildly. "But we are not stupid. We don't expect the war to be over tomorrow or the next day. Perhaps a year. Perhaps two years. But the war does not concern us, what happens after does. We must have plans. This is only common sense." He shrugged. "We are businessmen. If our business is gambling, the unions, the waterfront, then we must think ahead. No?"

Heads nodded and there was some whispering but it broke off when he continued.

"We have many interests in New York, New Jersey, Philadelphia, Florida,—even in the West. Up to now the police have been busy with other things but we must not fool ourselves. Gambling means nothing today. Everyone is making money in the war so there is plenty of gambling. But what of tomorrow? New governments are elected. New mayors. New cops. New politicians who dream of the White House so they chase the gamblers and get their pictures in the newspapers. This is bad business. You are forced to pay the lawyers and buy the whores on the bench. So we have decided to look to other places . . ."

He paused, studied his clasped hands, then looked up.

"And that place, my young friends, is Havana."

There was some whispering as I traded glances with Joe.

"Perhaps you are saying to yourself—what is on that miserable island that is good for all of us? There are only whores and dirty pictures and men who play with themselves for the tourists." He paused. "And politicians. *Marrone!* What politicians! They would sell their mothers' beads for a dollar. But that is good for us, my young friends. Nobody cares in Havana. When the Americans go there they"—he tapped his head *"—andato matto—"* they go crazy—out of their heads like little boys in the classroom when the teacher goes to the bathroom. They want whiskey and women—and gambling. The first two the Cubans will take care of. The last . . ."

He slowly made a gesture as if shaking dice and throwing them on the table.

"We will give them all they want."

"But don't they have gambling, Pepe?" Joe asked.

"*Si.* We will come to that."

He turned slightly and gestured to Lorenzo who stood behind him in the shadows.

"Before he came to us, Lorenzo lived there as a *vaccaro*—with a big hat like a cowboy in the movies—heh, Lorenzo? We have sent him back several times. What he reports sounds good to our ears. The Americans have built
478

a large airbase and there are many ships. But the Cubans are becoming restless. They whisper among themselves that the gringos are making all the money. 'Cuba for Cubans,' they tell each other ... 'the new government is no good ...' "

He looked to Tony Cupid.

"Batista, who was the president, refused to run," Cupid explained, "so this guy, Dr. San Martín was elected. He was okay in the beginning but now we hear the Commies are moving in ..."

"The Commies always make trouble," Gus observed, "I don't see why we have to have the sons of bitches as allies."

Pepe said impatiently, "For us the peso is more important than the Communist, Duchino. It is worth nothing outside of Cuba. I have found this out: every importer is forced to buy American dollars for his imports and every exporter wants American dollars. The politicians will do anything for our money!"

He turned again to us.

"All this we have discussed among us. What is important to you is this: before the war began, some Englishmen paid a lot of money to the government to build a hotel. It was almost finished when the war broke out. Lorenzo says it will be the biggest and the most beautiful in the Caribbean." He returned to his chair. "No, Lorenzo?"

Lorenzo silently nodded.

"It will be called the Columbia-International. There will be a casino bigger than all the others with a roof that slides back and champagne in the fountains instead of water. The Englishmen are here in New York. We have spoken to them and they have agreed to lease us this casino. Already they are making plans to finish it. There is only one problem—the man in the government who must turn his head when the casino opens wants money"—he grunted—"a great deal of money."

"How much?" I asked.

"Three hundred thousand dollars," Pepe replied.

"And the lease is five hundred grand," Gus added.

I gasped and Joe looked stunned.

"That's a lot of grease, Pepe. Are you going to pay it?"

He shrugged. "What is there to do? If we don't pay this *figlio di butana* he will send his soldiers to raid the casino the night we open."

"Is gambling legal in Cuba?" I asked.

"There is a law," Pepe explained with a grimace, "but everybody pays, so there is no trouble. We have been promised that the governemnt will legalize gambling after this *pòrco misèria* is kicked out of office."

Then Grossi spoke for the first time. He elaborately cleared his throat and drummed his manicured fingers on the table; the others paid close attention. Pepe looked bored.

"What we are hoping for is that Colonel Batista regains power," he said in a careful, stilted voice. "We have been in touch with some of his people and we know he would like casinos in Havana. The reason is simple: their tobacco industry has fallen apart and their sugar exports can leave Cuba only under convoy. After the war they'll need money . . ."

Nino made a zigzag movement with his hand.

"The submarines—they shoot and the ships go boom!"

Grossi frowned and continued.

"Since the war there is no more work on the waterfront, now for the first time in Cuba's history there are taxes. We feel sure that if the Communists continue to move in on the government, Batista will return to power. Then there will be legalized gambling in Cuba. By that time we will be all set up."

He turned his hands over, palms up.

"No more grease . . ."

A murmur spread around the table.

"True, my friend," Pepe said coldly. "But that is in the future. Let us discuss what is on the Table."

I asked, "How can we help?"

Pepe's answer was sharp and blunt.

"Go with the lawyer to Havana, deliver the money, and stay there to protect our interests until the war is over."

"With Maxie?"

"Si. He will arrange the lease."

"But, Pepe, we don't know anything about running a gambling casino!"

"You don't have to worry about the operations," Tony Cupid put in, "We'll have people down there to work the tables. But we can't make a move until we get that dough down there . . ."

"We trust the three of you, Peppino," Pepe said shortly. "That is important to us."

"Three hundred thousand bucks' worth of importance," Cupid said solemnly.

"Sortino said you should go," Nino said. "We have agreed."

"Sortino is Pepe," I whispered to Joe.

"What the hell, Havana is only an hour from Mexico City," Cupid said. "It's a hot town. You'll like it."

"I'm sure it is," Joe said. "Why don't you go?"

"I wouldn't be asking you if I could," Cupid replied coolly. "The feds would pick me up in a minute."

"I'm afraid that goes for all of us, young man," Grossi said. "Word gets around. It is as Sortino says, none of us can afford to have agents sniffing about our business. It would be too dangerous."

"Peppino," Pepe said, "what we ask can only be done by outsiders we trust. Who else can we get to deliver our money? A boy from the street? A bookmaker? The *umbriaccone* who sleeps with a whore and gets robbed? It would be *un disastro!* What could be better for us than our lawyer and our young friends?"

"Did you ask Maxie?"

Pepe nodded.

"What did he say?"

"He is waiting for you in the summerhouse. You will all talk together."

"Before you see Maxie let's get one thing straight," Cupid said. "Are you sure about the cops? The bagman doesn't care who brings the dough?"

"We'll talk to him," Joe said, "but there won't be any trouble. The system will run smoothly as long as the cops are greedy. It will only break down if the money fails to show."

"It's very simple," I explained. "Letters from drops, code numbers for desk sergeants and precinct commanders."

"Good," Cupid said nodding approvingly. "Any questions of identification, let 'em call." He looked over at Nino. "What does our *pòzzo di novanta* say about this?"

The little man shrugged and gestured to Pepe.

"If Sortino says it will work—it will work, Antonio."

"Okay," Cupid said. He explained to us, "I don't want any trouble with those thieves after you're gone. That business up there last time with the jigs wasn't good. By the way, do you guys have to contact the big man downtown?"

"We promised never to contact him," Joe said. "As far as he is concerned we don't exist. He gets his slice, the others get theirs and everybody is happy. No problems."

481

"Good. As Pepe said, that's the way we like it ... no problems."

"There is one thing we haven't told you kids," Gus said. "This is not for nothin'. How about it, Pepe?"

Without turning, Pepe put out his hand and Lorenzo placed a square package in it. Pepe slapped it down hard on the table.

"Fifty thousand dollars, my young friends," he said jovially. "Is it not a good price?"

"It's a long run for a short slide," Joe said.

"All you have to do is deliver the dough," Tony Cupid said.

"It sounds too easy."

In the silence I could hear a grandfather clock ticking in the far corner. In the dim light I saw the measured movement of the brass pendulum.

"Let's talk to Maxie," Joe said.

"We will have caffè while you talk," Pepe said.

We started to rise but he waved us down.

"There is something else we wish to discuss with you," Pepe said.

He studied the glass between his hands for a moment, then said:

"Tell us about your police union, Peppino."

I could see the interest in their faces as they twisted in their chairs to study me.

"I have done some work on the idea," I told him, "reading technical pamphlets, Seabury reports, articles—anything that had to do with the police."

"Seabury!" Nino murmured. *"Bastardo!"*

"We like what Pepe has told us," Tony Cupid said. "Can you fill us in with some more information?"

I showed them a chart detailing the structure of the New York City Police Department, the various precincts in the five boroughs and the chain of command. Colored dots indicated the areas where we had cops on the pad. Using the chart I explained how the department worked and how I thought we could unionize it. Then I gave a graphic description of the Boston Police Strike and passed around photostats I had made of the faded news pictures which had appeared in the New England and New York newspapers at the time.

They listened intently and carefully studied the photostated newspaper clippings and pages from various publications.

Before I had finished my presentation, Pepe waved his hand for silence.

"*Buòno! Buòno,* Peppino," he said smiling. "You have done well. Now tell me, how long would it take to form this union?"

"I don't have any exact idea, but it won't take place overnight. For one thing, you'll have to fight the line organizations. They have been around for years, they are not going to fold so easy."

"What would we need to take them over?"

"Muscle, money, and power. Lots of it. You must demonstrate to the cop on the beat that you have it and that you are willing to use it to get the gains he wants."

"But, Peppino, if we get all the cops—would they go out on strike?"

"Today? Never."

"Why?"

The others leaned forward, intent on the two of us.

I briefly consulted my notes. "Well, look at the Boston strike. Consider the climate of the country in that period. A year after World War I was a time of rising costs—there were also a great many strikes and riots. The Boston cops had been working seventy-three hours a week for a maximum of sixteen hundred dollars a year."

"*Marrone!* Sixteen hundred!" Little Nino murmured. "My bankers make that in a month!"

"Was it only the money, Peppino?"

"There was a great deal of unrest and dissatisfaction in the department, as I get it, because of filthy police stations, rats, roaches, and things like that."

"The bastards should have lived in the Neighborhood," Gus grunted.

"They were so mad they wanted to join the AFL, no?" Pepe pressed me.

"Three-quarters of the cops belonged to some social club and they voted to join the AFL. A month later the police commissioner suspended the leaders."

"Then boom!" Pepe said, slapping his hands together. "The cops walk out."

"That's right. Only three hundred stayed on the job."

"How many cops did Boston have?" Tony Cupid asked.

"About fifteen hundred."

"Wait, Antonio," Pepe said. "Peppino, tell us what happened when the cops went on strike."

I flipped through the photostats and read one aloud:

"The morning after the police strike, daylight robbery and looting began and the voluntary police were assaulted by mobs . . . then as the word spread, big-time crooks from all over the country hurried to Boston . . ."

Pepe looked about at the others triumphantly.

"They could have taken the city—like plucking a grape . . ." He turned back to me. "How did it end, Peppino?"

"Coolidge, who was then governor of Massachusetts, broke the strike by bringing in troops. They machinegunned the mobs and seven were killed."

"But there were other police strikes," Pepe told the others. He looked at me for confirmation.

"Before Boston there were police strikes in Europe. Liverpool and London had some very bad times in 1919 . . ."

"Someday, Peppino, it will be the right time," Pepe said grimly.

"What I want to know is—when?" Cupid put in.

"As I said, it's something no one can predict. It's timing. It may be years."

"I say we go ahead with the union," Pepe said. "Peppino says we wait for action, we wait. But in the meantime we build and build and build . . . like the ant, no, Peppino?"

"You can't do this thing overnight," Joe said. "It will take plenty of dough."

"How much?" Cupid asked.

"Hundreds of thousands," I told them.

"Hundreds of thousands?" Sally G gasped. "To form a union?"

I took a deep breath. "I am not thinking simply of one New York police union—I am thinking of a national police union. Every city in the country would be linked by the same organization."

There was a silence so profound it froze the Table in a tableau.

"A national police union," Pepe said slowly. He looked around at the others, their eyes were glittering. Little Nino was moving his head from side to side.

"Sortino! Can you see it?"

Pepe smiled. "I can see it, Nino. *Marrone!* Can I see it! We must do it. Peppino must start."

"We'd be crazy if we didn't," Tony Cupid said.

"A couple of hundred thousand is a lot of gelt," Grossi protested.

"You're talkin' about payin' three hundred thousand plus another five Gs to run a casino in Cuba," Joe pointed out. "We're talkin' about a cops' union clear across the country. When we pull out New York the other cities will follow. It will be so bad here they'll have to walk over the tops of trucks to get from Fifth to Eighth avenues. We could come up with the biggest, strongest union in the United States."

"Buòno! Buòno!" Little Nino crowed. "Listen to Sortino. We can wring this country's neck like a chicken."

"I still don't see it," Grossi said doggedly. "Why would cops strike against the communities they serve? They take our money but it would be different asking them to walk off their beats." He shook his head. "It's a crazy idea, Pepe."

Cupid leaned across the table.

"The hell it is, Sal. I'm with Pepe. This is a sweetheart! Just as Joe says, in the garment center they'll be walking over the tops of the trucks to get to Fifth Avenue. We can scare the bejesus out of the country and make a hell of a lot of shekels doing it. It's so big it scares me."

"Si," Nino said. "It is crazy but we should examine it."

"Maybe we should talk," Victory put in.

"What do we have to talk about?" Cupid shot back. "Either we want it or we don't."

"Lower the flame, Antonio, or you'll bust the pipe," Nino cautioned him.

Cupid grinned. *"Emozionato!* Okay. So I'm excited. I haven't heard anything this good since Prohibition. I bet if Chicago got wind of it they would go out buying cops like candy bars."

"But cops with picket signs?" Grossi said half to himself. "I find it hard to believe!"

"On the way out here Maxie was telling us about the teachers organizing in New York," I told him. "They're talking strike after the war . . ."

"See that, Sal" Cupid called out. "Your kid's teacher with a picket sign! No classes today because teacher is out on strike. Does that sound any crazier than cops pulling a strike in New York?"

"Perhaps there's somethin' to it," Grossi murmured.

"Last week in the newsreel I saw dames with rivet guns and workin' as plumbers," Gus said. "Everybody's going nuts!" He looked at Pepe. "What do you think, Pepe?"

"Fari vagnari a pizzu," Pepe said softly. "We should wet our beaks in this."

Cupid nodded approvingly.

"Ah, you're so right, Pepe."

"But not today, my friends. This is for tomorrow. Now we must deal with the casinos." He looked down at us with a smile. "Let the *giovinetti* talk together . . ."

I felt that Pepe had deliberately allowed the discussion to continue to reveal the defenders and opponents of my idea.

"Peppino," he called out, "come back with your answer."

Some heated discussions were beginning as we left the room. Before the door closed I looked back and saw the *consiglieri* hastily emptying the ashtrays, drawing back the blinds, filling water glasses, and leaning over to whisper to the older men.

Tony Cupid, his arm around Pepe's shoulder, was talking to him earnestly in a low tone.

Outside on the lawn I looked up at the clustered stars in amazement. I had never seen so many. Across the valley the brass doorknob of a moon was delicately balanced on the rim of the far-off mountain chain. The night seemed far too beautiful and peaceful for conspiracies.

"Well, what do you want to do, Frank?" Joe asked me.

"It sounds too easy. Three hundred thousand dollars is a hell of a lot of money to carry around . . ."

"Let's see what Maxie says."

The air was damp and the grass felt soggy. Across the lawn in the summerhouse we could see the shadow of Maxie pressed against the screen.

"Hello, Joe? Frank?" he called out.

"It's us," Joe replied. Then to me, "Did you see how they went for that cops' union idea?"

"That Grossi guy didn't think too much of it."

"But the others were for it. Especially Tony Cupid. He's a smart cookie, Frank . . ."

Maxie yanked open the screen door as we approached.

"I've been on pins and needles waiting for you guys! What do you think of their proposition?"

"We told them we wanted to talk to you," Joe said.

"Who is this guy we're supposed to pay?" I asked.

"His name is Gregorio Kaganovitch," Maxie said. "He's a Russian who has been in Havana for years."

"Is he the payoff man for the government?"

"You got me. All I know is what Pepe told me. He smuggles anything from Chinks to drugs into Florida. But he's supposed to run the cops in Havana."

"We don't know anything about Havana—do you, Maxie?"

He shook his head. "I don't—but I will." He added: "I'm beginning to get a smell of what they may have in mind."

"What's that?"

"Pay off some of the big politicians after the war, get them to legalize gambling, and then build their own hotel and casino."

"Pepe said they want you to make all the arrangements."

He smiled. "I told you they liked the way I do things."

"Well, what are we goin' to do?" Joe asked. "How about you, Frank?"

I had decided to go before we left the room. I had to get away from the city, away from the daily knowledge that we were profiting from the brute labor on the piers. And I wanted to leave the drab, squalid Neighborhood, to escape from the empty-headed arguments, the whiskey, the smoky gin mills, and the boobs who set my teeth on edge.

But that was only part of it; I was really trying to run away from the ghosts of decency gone, a failed self, the self that might have been.

"Sure, why not?" I told Joe. "When do we leave?"

"How about you, Maxie?"

He looked thoughtful.

"It will mean giving up my practice for a while . . ."

"Oh, come off it," Joe said impatiently. "Doesn't most of your work come from Pepe anyway?"

Maxie looked wounded.

"I have other clients," he said stiffly.

"Get off your high horse. I was only askin'."

"And I'm telling you! What about the cops? Who will take care of them?"

"They asked about that."

"Jesus Christ! I hope they did! What did you tell them?"

"The same as we are telling you—no problems. The setup is working smoothly—Tinkers to Evers to Chance."

"Will you see Hennessy and explain it?"

"Of course."

"What about Cornell? Will he squawk?"

"We promised never to contact him. To him we don't exist. As long as he gets his dough . . ."

"I want to make sure I warn Pepe never to talk to Hennessy, only to deliver an unmarked envelope, and to use a different messenger every month."

"Why?"

"Wiretaps! Tails! Christ, the DA would give both arms and a leg to get a smell of this."

"It's such a pleasure to talk to you, Maxie."

"You have to watch every angle in this business, Joe," I murmured.

"Frank's right, Joe," Maxie protested. "Who knows what will happen five, ten, fifteen years from now? Everytime you take one step forward you should take five back to make sure you haven't forgotten anything."

"Did Pepe tell you what they are offering?" I asked him.

He sniffed. "We would be crazy to take only fifty grand—"

"*Only* fifty grand!" Joe and I echoed.

He gave us an arch look.

"Don't forget, it will be a three-way split. Why take peanuts when you can get bananas? They come in bunches. Fifty grand could be a drop in a bucket compared to a percentage."

"In other words ask for a slice of the action?"

"Why not? They can skim it off the nightly gross."

"Will they go for it?"

"We can ask. They'll go for anything if they are hot enough to get that dough down there."

"Do you believe their reasons for asking us?"

"I do. Last month for the first time since the war started they had a big bust. The Border Patrol caught two of their guys with a phony trunk bottom."

"Drugs?"

"Lots of it. The story was in the newspapers and on the radio. Lowell Thomas said it was the biggest seizure in twenty years."

"How do you know about it?"

"Pepe asked me to hire a lawyer in Texas."

"Then they must have been Pepe's boys."

"I doubt it. First of all, Pepe wouldn't have used that cornball trunk trick. And when I called the Texas lawyer he said one of the guys had asked him to send a wire to Charlie Victory. I also had the lawyer mail me their yellow sheets; both were Philly hoods. It was accidental. A customs dick happened to spot one in Tijuana and alerted the border patrol. I think it hurt them. Again, I'm not sure but I believe they all put in shares for a big shipment." He made a grimace. "I told Pepe a long time ago—count me out on drugs. Saints are not my dish but I will never touch anything to do with drugs. Gambling. Policy. Unions. Even shylocking, yes. But drugs?" He shook his head. "No, sir!"

"And you think that is why they don't want to take a chance themselves?"

"They can't. I don't blame them. They're a combination—call it what you will—but no law enforcement group has put them together—yet. Police headquarters and Washington don't have the manpower, but after the war it could be a different story. You can bet they're not asleep. Somewhere, some eager beaver may be putting pieces together. Just like those two Philly hoods being arrested. Now Treasury knows Charlie Victory's in dope. It's always been whores. In a couple of years they could get a hint of what is going on with," he said sardonically, "all our friends. I can see their reasoning, why start something?"

"And we won't be suspicious?" Joe asked.

"While I was waiting for you guys I made some plans," Maxie said. "Nino has an old exporting company that used to deal in cheese and olive oil. We'll turn it around and make it sugar and tobacco. I'll set up an office in Miami and phony up enough paper deals so we look like experts—"

"What about passports and that stuff?"

"That's no trouble—Pepe has some great connections in Washington."

"We don't know anyone in Cuba," I pointed out. "How will we move around with all that dough?"

"Maybe they didn't tell you," Maxie said. "Lorenzo will be with us. He lived down there for years and has a connection with a senator who was close to Batista."

"Where do these guys get all their connections?" Joe asked.

"Money," Maxie said flatly. "Money buys anything—from integrity to passports."

"What about our unions?" Joe asked. "Those goddam coopers come up for a new contract next spring—and then there's the warehousemen."

"I wouldn't worry about them," Maxie said. "Let's face it. You have everything cut and dried. The shippers and the warehouse owners know they will get a good deal while the war is on. Strikes are not popular now. After the war will be another thing. So we'll arrange to get them a little more money next year. The shippers won't care. We'll put up a couple of stooges as front. Take those two guys who work with you. We'll make them business agents for the unions. Who will squawk? I farm out work in Criminal Courts to a guy downtown. He's hungry so I'll toss him the union work. I can talk to him. He knows the score. He'll work with your two guys."

"You seem real anxious to get down there, Maxie," I said. "Why?"

"I would be a schnook to give up a good New York law practice to spend a year or two on some spick island if I didn't think there was a bundle to be made. Not this baby! Did Pepe tell you he talked to the two Englishmen who built the Columbia-International?"

"He said, 'We talked to them.' "

"I have found out 'we' usually means Pepe. Before he met the Englishmen he had me look them up. I did a hell of a lot more than a Dun and Bradstreet on those two guys. It cost a good piece of change but I found out what I wanted. They own most of the United Railways that operates the trains in Cuba and the Havana Electric Company that runs the trolley cars in Havana and Marianao. Both of them are very close to Batista. In fact, I was told they put up a small fortune when he ran the first time."

"Wasn't Batista the last president of Cuba?"

"He didn't want to run again so this guy San Martín was elected."

"Tony Cupid said the Commies are moving in down there."

"Now all of a sudden they're international experts!" Maxie snorted. "I'm the one who told them that. The English syndicates with money in the United Railways, Havana Electric, and the Compañía Cubana de Electricidad—that's the Con Edison of Cuba—are getting uneasy about the Commies but they can't do anything while the war is going on. There is no doubt in my mind that after the war they will talk Batista into running again. So far he doesn't want any part of it but he will be back. There will be too much pressure for him to refuse . . ."

"And if he gets in?"

"If he runs he'll get in. Batista is very popular and has the army behind him. We know from several sources he's promised to legalize gambling. Sally G wants to build a luxury hotel down there and have their own casino." He shook his head. "But Pepe is against it. He only wants a lease. That's the big reason for this Table—"

"Why is Pepe against it?" Joe asked. "It sounds like a good idea to me."

"Pepe insists Cubans are as bad as Italians with governments. They change like the wind. In that I agree with him."

Joe asked, "So you really think there's a lot of bucks to be made down there, Maxie?"

"Believe me, fellows," Maxie said enthusiastically, "this is an opportunity for a big roll. Don't pass it up. We can make these casinos as big as U.S. Steel! I mean it."

He looked from me to Joe.

"Well, what do you say, fellows? Let's make up our minds."

"I'm ready," I said. "How about you, Joe?"

"Will you ask for a percentage?" Joe asked Maxie.

"You bet I will," he waved an admonishing finger at him. "But that's not saying they will give us what we want. Okay?"

"We'll grab what we can get. Let's go in and talk to them."

On the way back to the house I told Maxie about the reaction to my police union idea.

"Didn't I tell you they were hot for it?" he said triumphantly. "What did you tell them?"

"I told them the timing is off. Grossi agreed with me."

"What about Pepe? He's the one who counts?"

"He likes it. He wants to start on it right away. So does Tony Cupid."

"Stay with Tony and Pepe," Maxie said shortly. "Listen to Grossi—he's smart—but watch out for him."

"Why do you say that, Maxie?" Joe asked.

"Grossi would like to take over," the lawyer said. "Two years ago the Chamber of Commerce in that jerkwater city where he lives made him head of their war bond drive. He shook down everybody in town and they hit a big score. Then they named him as their Man of the Year. Sally G's so goddam civic minded he had an ordinance passed so only his cabs could park in front of the hotels and at the airport! All the other cabs have to park two blocks away. When a couple of old cabbies protested, Grossi's hoods put sugar in their gas tanks. Man of the Year! Bastard of the Year! Tony doesn't like him and neither does Pepe. He swings a big stick upstate but stay away from him—take my advice . . ."

"I couldn't care less about their affairs," I told him.

"Maybe someday you'll be forced to care," Maxie said.

"The hell I will . . ."

"So you think that cops' union is a good idea, Maxie?" Joe asked.

"Very much so," Maxie said promptly. "But that doesn't mean I want to play around with it now."

"Agreed," Joe said. "It's somethin' for us after the war."

"First things first," Maxie said briskly. "Let's get Havana squared away . . . when the time comes for the cops' union they'll put up the dough. Especially if we pull off Havana. They go for past performances. That's why we are here—the three of us. They said among themselves, why fight success? Give these guys the ball and let them run with it. . . . That's what they'll do with the cops' union . . . You'll see . . . I haven't given you a wrong steer yet."

They were waiting for us when we entered the big boardroom.

"Have you decided, Peppino?" Pepe asked me.

"We will go," I said. "But we have a proposition. Maxie will explain it."

"Instead of the fifty thousand we would like a percentage of the nightly gross," Maxie said. "You can skim it off the top."

"How much of a cut?" Tony Cupid asked.

"Ten percent. That includes all tables, of course. We'll make the count every night in my office—your man and me. Or Joe and Frank if they are around."

"The casino can't be opened until after the war," Cupid pointed out. "Do you want to wait that long?"

"We'll take our chances on what your friends overseas tell you," Maxie said with a smile.

"Ten percent and it's a three-way split?" Cupid said. "And for that you'll deliver the dough, arrange the lease, and stay down there until things get started?"

"Right," Maxie said. "But let's agree on the lease. I'll work out the details here in New York before we leave but you will have to make the financial arrangements. Three hundred thousand is enough to be carrying down there!"

"No problem. You'll work out the lease, we'll make the payment here. Now when can you get started?"

Maxie looked at us.

"Two weeks?"

We nodded.

"It's two weeks then. Someone will have to give us the rundown on Havana."

Cupid gestured to Pepe.

"You be in my office at the gallery at three o'clock," Pepe said. He turned to the others. "Now we talk."

Again we waited outside until Lorenzo opened the door and we went back in.

"We have decided, my young friends, to offer you seven percent," Pepe said.

"And expenses?" Maxie asked.

Pepe gave him a thin smile, edged I thought with contempt.

"We will give you your expenses."

Maxie looked from Joe to me; we both nodded.

"Seven percent can mean a hell of a lot of dough," Cupid said. "The tables will get a big play from those construction guys down there who have made a fortune. After the war you won't be able to hold the tourists."

"Okay. Seven percent," Maxie said.

"Good," Pepe said. "Let's have a drink on it."

It had sounded too easy. There was much more to it than they had told us as we heard from a worried Maxie the next day.

The Russian smuggler Gregorio Kaganovitch was indeed waiting for us and the three hundred thousand dollar bribe. He was the only man who could persuade the colonel in charge of the police to turn his head if a casino opened. As they said in Havana, for every pair of dice that rolled he got a cut.

"The son of a bitch has his hand in everything down there," Maxie told us. "Drugs. Whores. Army equipment. Unions. You name it, he runs it."

"He sounds like the guy we need," Joe said. "What's the problem?"

"Getting the money to him," Maxie said. "He pulled this before with the Englishmen. They sent a guy down a few years ago with a hundred grand. On the way to meet the Russian he was held up and robbed. When the Englishmen went back to Kaganovitch he just threw up his hands. No money, no okay. The second time there was no trouble. It was just double the rate."

"How did you find this out?" I asked.

"I told you I had done some digging for Pepe on those Englishmen. Most of my information came from a guy in a Fifth Avenue firm who represents them."

"Why would he tell you all this? Is he an old friend?"

"I saw him three times in my life. But our friend had some influence with him. It seems they have traded favors in the past. You know how lawyers are."

"Does Pepe know all this?"

"Are you kidding? He's not the kind of a guy you keep anything back from."

"And he still wants us to go down there? That doesn't make sense, Maxie. We could lose their three hundred thousand dollars."

"The way I see it they have decided to take the long odds. My friend the lawyer told me a Canadian syndicate and a Midwest group want the Columbia-International lease. It's the question of who gets the money first to Kaganovitch. That bastard is just rubbing his hands together. He thinks he's going to rob everyone who comes down with dough."

"But what chance do we have to beat this guy?"

"If I know Pepe he has an ace up his sleeve," Maxie said.

Pepe did; the ace was Lorenzo.

"Spick shooters!" Pepe said scornfully after Maxie told him about the Russian. "You afraid of them, lawyer?"

"It's not a question of being afraid of them, Pepe," I pointed out. "We don't like the idea of losing three hundred thousand to some thieves. Your money, not ours!"

He said smilingly, "Lorenzo will take care of everything. The Russian? Va! Pòrco misèria!"

"What does Lorenzo have that will help us, Pepe?"

"Connections!" Pepe cried. "He is not unknown there. The Russian knows Lorenzo."

"Yeah but—" Maxie blurted out, but Pepe stood up and impatiently walked around his desk.

"Lawyer, don't worry. We trust you. Lorenzo will take care of everything . . ."

As he escorted us to the front door of the gallery he
494

suddenly stopped and hit his forehead with the palm of one hand.

"Peppino! I never told you about the Cassatt! You saw the print?"

"You showed it to us the last time we were here."

"In two weeks I will have it," he said, his black eyes glittering with excitement, "*magnificenza!* You must see it."

"I will see it when I get back," I told him, "if I ever do . . ."

He squeezed my shoulder.

"Why talk like that, Peppino? In a few weeks you will say, 'That Pepe! He is like my *nònno!* I will raise my glass to him.' You will be as happy as"—he searched for the proper analogy—"as an angel," he cried triumphantly.

He solemnly raised his right hand.

"Peppino—on my mother's grave I swear it!"

BOOK 4

Cuba

44 HAVANA

Our preparations for Cuba began immediately after the gathering at Gus's New Jersey house, what we now called "the Table." For the next two weeks Joe, Maxie, and I were swept up in a whirlwind of details concerning our union and business affairs. We had numerous conferences with Spider, Train, and the very shrewd and completely unprincipled young attorney Maxie had hired to assist them in running our affairs.

Joe and I agreed that we had to level with Hennessy, so this time we personally delivered the monthly envelope and explained, without much detail, where we were going.

"What about the envelope?"

"No problem," Joe told him. "It will be brought over the same as always."

"Maybe I better tell the inspector."

"What for? You'll only make him nervous. Nothin' will change. All those greedy bastards want is their dough."

"Suppose there's trouble?"

Joe tossed him a scrap of paper with a number written on it.

"That's only in case of trouble—real bad trouble."

"There's one other thing that's very important," I told him.

"What's that, Frank?"

"We'll be coming back from time to time. Every time we do I'll stop by and say hello. Make sure I'm updated on everything."

"The good guys and the bad guys," Hennessy said with a grin. "Who died? Who retired? Who got caught? Who are the latest goody-goodies?"

"Exactly."

"Don't worry, I'll have it when you come in."

"I know we don't have any choice," Joe said when we left, "but every time I see that son of a bitch I want to kill him. I have all I can do to keep myself from goin' at him! You know, Frank, I made a promise to myself."

"What's that?"

"Comes the day we don't need that bum—" He snapped his fingers. "That's one service Pepe owes me."

"What do you mean, Joe?"

He looked at me surprised. "I want him knocked off! If Pepe won't do it—I'll do it myself. You don't think for a minute I will ever forget what he did? He killed Tom. Shot him in the back. You were there, Frank. He might as well have shot my mother while he was at it. And I'm goin' to forget that? Not in a million years I won't!" We walked in silence for a moment. "And if Pepe's shooters do it down in Cherry Street I'll even help stuff his fat ass in that baler! The son of a bitch should bring three hundred pounds of wastepaper."

The way he said it chilled me.

"Let's forget it now."

"Forget it?" He shook his head. "Never, Frank. Never . . ."

By noon the next day we had said our last good-byes, received Aunt Clara's final tearful hugs, and were in Spider's car on the way to the airport. But Pepe was very cautious. He insisted we take an out-of-the-way route, traveling across country to the West Coast, south to Mexico City, and from there to Cuba. As he explained, although Lorenzo was only an obscure Italian fugitive from Immigration, wartime customs in New York might include one veteran agent alert enough to recognize him . . .

"It is the little thing you overlook that makes the big plans go wrong, Peppino," he told me.

Pepe's influence followed us across the country. As Maxie had predicted, our passports and tickets were promptly issued. On the plane to L.A. we were among the few not bumped for passengers with higher priority. I saw salesmen, technicians, engineers—even one furious old guy who insisted he was a tank expert—collect their baggage and leave. But not us. We received nothing but red carpet treatment.

In L.A. we caught a plane for Mexico City where we had to wait overnight.

At Lorenzo's suggestion we had divided the money between us, each of us carrying an attachè case containing $100,000 in bills of large denominations. I don't think I guarded anything more closely in my entire life; poor Maxie took his to the bathroom.

We left for Havana the next day aboard a creaky, ancient plane. Every seat was taken and I ended up with Lorenzo. To keep my mind off the bouncing, creaking plane I began to talk to him.

"Tell me about yourself, Lorenzo."

"What do you want to know?"

"Where do you come from? How did you ever wind up in Cuba?"

At first it was only a trickle, accompanied by a shrug, a gesture. Then the words flowed more freely. As he talked about his past life, the years he had spent in Cuba and what faced us there, I sensed an intensity behind that impassive, furrowed face; he was like a man returning home from a long journey.

As he put it, he had left Sicily over "a matter of honor. There was this stone fence . . . my old man was always fighting with the other farmer who had the place next to ours . . . It was only a piece of land but then one day they had a big fight and this guy shot my old man and my uncle. My uncle croaked but my old man just got a bum arm from it. I was the *picciòtto*, you know the boy in the family, so they gave me the *lupara*—"

"What's a *lupara?*"

"A sawed-off shotgun . . . every family in Sicily has one. That's what they use in the vendettas. I gave this guy the spur and everybody on our side of the fence was happy. But then the other side hired a *sicário*, that's like a torpedo over here, and I had to run. I jumped ship in

Brooklyn and got a job in the subway. That's where I met Gus's old man. When they opened the speak on Forty-fourth Street, I quit the subway and became their bartender. Then there was some trouble and Sortino went up for a while. But Gus was payin' the cops so we stayed in business . . ."

"How did you ever get to Cuba?"

He brooded about this question for a long time.

"*Ècco!* It is not good to speak of the dead," he said at last.

Surprised I asked, "Who is dead, Lorenzo?"

"My wife. One day I came home from the speak early and she had this kid with her." He shrugged. "I worked her over and she died. Gus dished it out to the cops and the judge so I copped a manslaughter plea and got ten to fifteen. But I never served a day. They turned me over to Immigration and the government gave me a free ride back to Sicily."

He shook his head.

"Who's gonna stay in a dirty little wop village after New York? Not me. I lasted only three months then I got a job as a waiter on a ship. I jumped it in Cuba and hooked up with this old *guajiro* selling mules and horses in the provinces. Believe me it was a good life, young man, plenty of wine, women, and dancin'. Only the stink of the mules was bad.

"Then one day we came to this senator's ranch in Mantanzas. He was a real big shot, a member of the Directorio Estundiantil and one of the guys who helped to kick out Machado. He was in with the army and a friend of Batista when he was only a sergeant. Later I learned the senator—his name was Manuel Alvarez—graduated from West Point. How do you like that? A spick goin' to West Point!"

I prompted him, "What happened when you went to his ranch?"

"Oh, yeah. The old man sold him some mules so we're unloadin' them from this truck. Suddenly I hear someone fall. I turned around and I see the old man in the road."

He tapped his chest.

"Those mules are as hard to push as a stalled truck. I guess the old man's ticker gave out. I'm tryin' to help the old man when this guy drives up. He's dressed like a gentleman *colono*, like a cane planter. It's the senator. He looks at the old man in the dirt and says to me:

500

" 'Hey, *amigo*, you speak English?' "

"English, Spanish, and Italian," I tell him.

" 'You want to work for me?' " he says.

"Sure," I said, "but what about the old man?"

" 'We bury him,' he says. Then he has me drive him up to his house. It's the biggest I've ever seen."

"What about the old man?"

"We buried him," he said simply.

"And did you work for the senator?"

"Seven years. He had a big polo field and I took care of the horses." He said proudly, "I got good with the lasso, just as good as Tom Mix. Twice a month when the Congress was in session in the Capitolio I drove the senator to Havana. That's how I know that crazy city."

"Pepe says you know Kaganovitch."

He grunted. "I knew the lousy bastard. He'd cut off his mother's fingers for a dollar."

"Who brought you back to the States?"

"Sortino, my gombah. When I heard from my friends in New York he was out of prison I wrote to him. He sent back a letter tellin' me to sit tight."

He picked off the years on his fingers.

"Four years I sit tight. Then he sends me my ticket and tells me to come back right away and help in the trouble ..." He sighed. "It was just as well. The senator was married to a wonderful woman but he was always chasin' dames. In Havana he had one lined up for every night. *Marrone!* Did that spick like to screw! Then he started to play around with the wife of a major in the police. One night this guy walked into the restaurant where the senator was eatin' with the woman and shot him right through the head."

"In the city!"

He shook his head. "He was shackin' up with her in Trinidad, halfway down the coast. This piece had him so crazy he didn't know they had set him up—"

"Who? His political enemies?"

"You have to understand these Cubans, Peppino. To them politics is like the Madonna to an old Italian woman; nothin' is more important. *Ai capito?* The senator was like that; when he organized the opposition to Machado the army supported him. But then he joined another bunch the army didn't like. So someone decided Machado had to go. Like always, they had the Russians do their dirty work. That *figlio di butana* has a charmed life,

501

Peppino! He started under Machado, then Batista. Now he's a big man under this new presidente. He's a cat who will never use up his nine lives! *Stùpido Spagnuolo!* Who knows what they're gonna do next?"

He sighed.

"Like I told you, I knew my way around Havana so I got next to some guy who could put the squeeze on the newspapers. I paid a bundle but I kept that dame's name out of the story. They said it was the result of a political fight and down here that's okay, no *obbròbrio*. The senora never forgot that—she would do anything I asked."

He sighed again.

"Then I went lookin' for the guy . . ."

"The man who killed the senator?"

"Si. There was a place called the Salon H Café where I knew all *parristas* hung out. He was there every night tellin' how he plugged the senator. One night he was drunk, really drunk, and when he came out I drove up in a cab. *Ècco!* Did I take care of that *maiale!* To make it look nice I put him in the trunk of one of the police cars. They found him after they smelled him. But I made a mistake. *Stupido!* I left my rope behind. The ends were whipped with linen thread, a trick only a *guajiro* would use. The Russian grabbed a kid from the ranch and twisted his balls until he told 'em I was in Havana. Then the Russian came lookin' for me."

"You said you had known him before?"

"A few times. The senator hated his guts. Whenever we came to Havana, the Russian had his *parristas* around us like flies in honey. It got to be a big joke. One night there were so many on our tail the senator made me stop and he bought all of 'em a drink. That's the kind of a guy he was."

"Were you arrested?"

"What is this arrested?" he said contemptuously. "In Havana they don't arrest you, Peppino. They take you to the station house and cut your throat! I heard the Russian was lookin' for me, so when he came out to the ranch I told the señora to stall him for a while. When he drove away he found me with the gun to the back of his head."

He chuckled and slapped his knee.

"Peppino, you should have seen the face of that *bastanza!*" He added admiringly, "He has moxie, that I will grant him. I kicked out his driver and we had a little talk.

502

He said he didn't like the guy in the trunk anyway but that I had better leave Havana. I was only too glad to. He even drove me to the plane in one of the police cars!"

"And that's the last you saw of him?"

"I saw him again when Sortino sent me back. That *mascalzóne* smells money, so I was safe as a priest in Rome."

"What did Pepe mean when he asked you to come back and help him in the trouble?"

"*Castellemmarese*—the Mattress War," he said with the zest of a Union veteran recalling Gettysburg.

"Is that what Pepe meant at the meeting?"

"*Sì.* It was very bad. It was started by a *pózzo di novanta*, a big shot named Joe Mosseria from Brooklyn who wanted all the Sicilians killed. It was a long time ago. You were still a bambino. Most of us come from the Gulf of Castellemmare in Sicily and we didn't want to be killed. So we went to the mattress."

When he saw the puzzled expression on my face he grinned.

"I will explain, Peppino. During the trouble we all took mattresses with us when we moved from apartment to apartment. Sometimes you would get a phone call and you had to jump. So you needed a mattress to sleep on."

"It was very bad," he said, solemn at the memory. "They killed a lot of us before the trouble ended."

"How about Pepe? What did he do?"

"Ah, that Sortino!" he said chuckling. "When the others heard his name they ran like chickens."

Then I took a shot in the dark.

"This combination, Lorenzo, those who were at Gus's house in Jersey—what would you call them?"

His smile faded.

"*E prohibito parla de questa còsa,*" he said coldly. "It is not allowed to speak of such things."

I quickly switched the subject back to Kaganovitch.

For years Kaganovitch had a mysterious but deadly connection with the old Machado regime, Lorenzo said, shaking his head in bewilderment. But after the dictator fled from the island, the Russian disappeared, only to show up again a few weeks later in his office at police headquarters. Now he was a fiery revolutionist leading the very students he had helped to torture in the dungeons of El Morro. He had also inherited Machado's *parristas*, a band of young hired killers who murdered for fifty dollars or broke bones for five.

"Marrone! They are evil people!" Lorenzo murmured.

With Don Quixote, I wondered what to say when the pot calls the kettle black . . .

"Pepe told us you have connections down here, Lorenzo. How will they help us?"

"The Russian will look for the new birds in the nest of the last. But we will fool him," he said.

"How are you going to avoid this guy's stickup artists? Do you have someone who will tip us off?"

He hesitated, then said shortly, "A woman."

"A woman! A girl friend?"

"My wife. I have a son." He put out his hand to show me how tall. "Sortino has promised to bring them to the States after the war. . . . It will be a service for a service."

"How can your wife help us?"

He leaned back, closed his eyes and smiled to himself.

"She works in the household of the Russian . . ."

I will always associate Havana with the blinding glare of the tropical sun, narrow twisting streets, glimpses of small green patios through open doorways, the smell of burning coffee, the cries of newsboys and peddlers who sold everything from combs to dishes like the cart men in Paddy's Market on Eighth Avenue, and the beautiful Prado lined with royal palms which Lorenzo told us were regarded by the peasants in the back country as the souls of soldiers marching into eternity.

Gay and friendly, it had nothing of the seriousness of a wartime allied capital. There was no drabness or sense that countless thousands were dying overseas. It was a city that seemed bereft of any seriousness; except for an occasional American sailor or airman stationed at San Antonio de los Banos, the airfield from which our planes patrolled the Caribbean, the war didn't seem to exist. It was evident to me that Havana's daily life was devoted to daily survival, physical or political.

On the way out of the airport lobby Lorenzo gestured to two mulattoes lounging near the doorway of a coffee shop.

"Parristas!" he said softly. "They will follow us wherever we go."

As we walked toward the taxi stand both men hurried to a car.

"Did you see the bulge at their belts?" Joe said. "They're carryin' guns!"

"So what?" Lorenzo said with a grin. "To carry a gun in Havana is like eatin' fried bananas."

"Let's try to lose them," Joe suggested.

"Not now," Lorenzo said. "They are part of a *chequeo* . . ."

"What the hell is that?"

As Lorenzo explained, *chequeo* was an old Cuban police system. *Parristas*, working shifts for forty-eight hours, pinpointed every moment of their subject, checking and rechecking his daily routine until a minute-by-minute schedule is completed. In times of political crisis, a suggested spot for assassination is included with the final report. In our case it would be robbery.

"That's just great," Maxie said nervously. "What do we do? Wait to be robbed?"

Lorenzo didn't appear disturbed. "We will let them play at their *chequeo* . . . then we will make the payment to the Russian."

"If we ever get there," Maxie muttered as he wiped his face. "Christ, it's hot . . ."

We registered at the Hotel Inglatera overlooking Central Park and across from the Manzana Building, the headquarters of Cuban-based American firms.

After the bellboy left, Lorenzo combed the room, inspecting lamps, peering behind mirrors and feeling along the woodwork.

"Anything wrong?" Maxie said. "It looks like a nice room."

"I'm lookin' for police wiretaps," Lorenzo said. "The Russian always does that."

"You're a very careful guy," Joe observed.

Lorenzo gave him a morose look.

"That's why I have lived so long, my friend."

"We better take care of this money," Joe said. "Where will we put it, Lorenzo?"

The three attaché cases lay on the bed like ticking bombs.

"How about the hotel safe?" Joe asked.

"*Ecco!* They would have it in a minute!" Lorenzo said. "The manager would give it to them! No guns. They would walk in and say, 'Hey, amigo, give us the Yankees' money.' What does the manager care? He wants to see his wife and kids. So he gives them the money."

"Havana is beginning to sound like a rough place." Maxie said with a nervous smile.

Lorenzo said indignantly, "Crazy spick shooters! Someone sneezes, it starts a riot against the government. The cops are no different. You grease 'em and they smile. We will stay in the room until they get tired of playing *chequeo*, then we will give the money to my woman."

"What do you mean *your* woman?" Joe asked.

"His wife," I said. "But get this—she works in the Russian's house—"

"In the Russian's house!" Joe exploded. "Are you nuts?"

"No, no," Lorenzo said waving his hand. "It will be safe. My son will sleep on the money."

We looked at each other.

We followed Lorenzo's plan and stayed in our room for the next few days. To establish a pattern for the teams of police agents, Lorenzo would take one of us on a taxi trip to the American consulate; El Capitolio, Cuba's stunning capitol building; the Swift & Co. plant; or the Cia. Cubana de Electricidad Building. We would wander about the buildings, sometimes only visiting the men's room, then hurry back to the hotel.

The agents who tailed us were usually youths with caffè cón leche complexions and baby faces. Their wrinkled white suits and worn panama hats appeared to have come from the same mold. Lorenzo explained they were members Pro Ley y Justicia (Law and Justice), the student militia that had helped to overthrow the Machado regime several years before.

"If there is a revolution after the war it will come from these *bastardis*," he predicted.

On the afternoon of the third day he made several telephone calls speaking softly in Spanish, then he opened the three attaché cases and dumped the packages of bills on the bed. From the closet he took a straw shopping bag used by tourists and poured in the money.

"Like we have come from the *bodegas* with bananas," he said with a grin. "Today we fool the *parristas* . . ."

The plan he outlined was simple: the gunmen would expect only two men to leave the hotel. These would be Maxie and Joe, each with a telephone book in his attaché case. They would take a taxi to the Columbia-International and make a show of inspecting the hotel.

"And what will you and Frank do?" Joe asked.

"Deliver the money to my woman," Lorenzo said. "We will go out the back way."

"When do we meet this guy Kaganovitch?" Maxie asked. "Let's give him the money as soon as we can ..."

"Soon," Lorenzo replied.

After the plan had been explained, Joe and Maxie left with their load of telephone books; two *parristas* sped after them. Lorenzo and I took the elevator to the second floor and walked down to the basement. At the far end was a tiled tunnel. The lattice gate was locked but Lorenzo had a key. The short tunnel opened into a lush garden with beautiful marble fountains surrounded by clusters of lights. Before the war, he explained, the arches of colored water were among the city's important tourist attractions. But now the fountains were grimy and filled with rotting coconuts and dried flowers. Beyond the empty pool was a coconut grove and another lattice gate which Lorenzo opened and carefully locked behind us. Finally, we came out into a deserted side street where a taxicab, motor running, waited at the curb. As soon as we appeared, the driver's brown-skinned hand reached out to open the door. In seconds we were speeding down the street.

The cab dropped us off on a wide street lined with palatial homes and estates in what Lorenzo called the Volado district. The sight of an old Ford parked nearby made him tremble and mutter to himself. He threw our driver a few bills, handed me the straw bag of money, and, waving his hands wildly, ran toward the car.

A woman and a small boy jumped out. Lorenzo feverishly kissed the woman, then picked up the boy and held them close for a few minutes whispering to the woman who kept nodding as they walked toward me.

"Peppino, this is my woman, Marta, and my son Felipe."

The woman was plain and slightly dumpy, the boy about seven, shy and clinging to his mother's skirt. She kept smiling and holding onto Lorenzo's arm.

"I told her what to do with the money, it will be safe."

Then he gave the straw bag to his wife and spoke rapidly in Spanish. She asked him a question, searching his face for the answer. Tears came into her eyes when he shook his head.

"She wants me to go to her cousin's house for the night with her and the boy," Lorenzo explained. "I told her it

507

was impossible. There are things I must do tonight for Sortino. She is a good woman, she understands."

He kissed her, then swung up his son.

"Falta grande! My son you have grown!" he cried as Felipe wiggled excitedly in his grasp. He kissed the boy and returned him to his mother.

"Now we go," he said briskly.

Without a word his wife took her son's hand and walked back to the car, Felipe pulling and protesting. As the car pulled away the little boy waved frantically from the rear window.

"After we pay that Russian pig it will be different," he said firmly. *"Ècco!* How I missed that kid."

I was startled to see tears in his eyes. After those nightmarish nights in the wastepaper factory I would have laughed at the suggestion that Lorenzo was anything but all evil, that sentimentality or human warmth was entirely alien to his almost mechanical malignity that served only one master—Pepe.

"Will you stay down here with us, Lorenzo?"

"It is up to Sortino," he replied with a shrug.

"Jeez! It seems we all jump when Pepe whistles."

"Sortino is my *goombah,* Peppino," he said disapprovingly. "I will always do what he asks me."

"What the hell service do you have to do tonight?" I said with a forced laugh. "Who does he want killed now?"

He ignored the stupid remark.

"I have to go out to the ranch," he said mildly.

"The ranch? Where you worked for the senator? Why do you have to go out there?"

"It is the service for Sortino," he said with a slow smile. "Nobody's going to get killed, Peppino."

"I don't see what the hell's so funny," I told him. "I don't like the idea of being left alone in that goddam hotel. Suppose someone calls for you? Suppose it's the Russian? What do we tell him?"

"There won't be any calls, Peppino."

"How do you know? How can you be so sure?"

"Because we're goin' to see the Russian today . . ."

"Today! You didn't say anything about this before now."

"I myself only knew it a few minutes ago . . ."

"How did you find out?"

"My wife." He chuckled and made ears with his fingers. "The Sicilian donkey . . ."

"When will he call?"

"In a few hours." He nudged me playfully. "Peppino, don't worry so much. Before you know it you will be as happy as—"

"I know," I said wearily, "as an angel . . ."

"*Sangue del la patata!* How you will be happy, my young friend!"

"Why will I be happy? Why me?"

"*Abbeia paziènza*—have patience. You will find out."

"You mean because we are going to pay the Russian today? How can we? Your wife has the money!"

"No pay today for the Russian," he said. He held up one hand, his fingers opening, closing like a bird's beak. "Only talk. Talk. Talk."

When we arrived at the hotel, Maxie and Joe were waiting for us in the room.

They were wildly enthusiastic about the Columbia-International. Landscaping had been started and both the pool and casino were near completion. All major work would be finished within six months, the foreman had told them. After an additional three months of minor alterations and repairs, furnishing could be installed.

"That means a year at the most and we can open," Joe said rubbing his hands.

But the Columbia-International was forgotten when I described the meeting on the street, Lorenzo's prediction that the Russian would summon us within a few hours for our first meeting, and that he intended to leave us alone that evening.

"What will we do if some of those guys following us decided to come up and say hello?" Maxie asked, desperation in his voice.

"There will be no calls and no one will come up here," Lorenzo said almost wearily. "You worry too much, *avvocato.*"

"Why the hell do you have to go way out to that ranch?" Maxie asked.

"It is for Sortino, lawyer. The Russian will call." He glanced at his watch. "In one hour. He will take us to lunch. He will talk, talk, talk. His people from all over the city will come and look at us . . ."

"It will be like we're in a lineup," Joe said. "Do we have to go?"

"*Si.* We do what he wants. Okay?" He made a quick upward thrust of his arm. "Then—*pirapa nel cula!*"

"Holy Christ," Maxie said with a groan. "This is crazy! Real crazy!"

We sat there hypnotized waiting by the old-fashioned upright telephone on the table between the beds. Maxie paced the floor and made frequent trips to the bathroom. Joe and I halfheartedly played seven-up. Lorenzo dozed in a chair.

The first ring transfixed us into stone. Lorenzo got up, yawned, stretched, and answered the phone. He listened, spoke briefly in Spanish and hung up.

"Now we see the Russian," he said.

45 *THE RUSSIAN*

Newspaper photographs of Kaganovitch published in *Life* when Castro's secret police called him Batista's *carnicero*, or butcher of Havana, revealed how little he had changed since the first time we met him in Havana's police headquarters, two blocks from our hotel. He was a Russian bear. His large head was topped by a tangled iron gray mop, his arms were thick as posts and covered with coarse hair, his nails were neatly trimmed and polished, and traces of talcum powder could be seen in the dark stubble on his jaws. A shoulder holster held an army automatic.

Two of our young shadows guarded his office and made no move to stop us when we opened the door. Kaganovitch was seated behind a desk in a luxurious office overlooking the Prado. He jumped up to embrace Lorenzo, then turned to study us. Above his fixed smile, his eyes were startlingly blue.

"Welcome to Havana," he said in perfect English after Lorenzo mumbled introductions. "But to come at such a sad time, my friends! Only last week the Germans sank two of our ships. Many Cuban sailors died. One of your warships brought them to Havana. Lorenzo! You should have seen it. The coffins were placed in the Capitolio for

510

the people to see. All night they passed. Then the next day they were carried to Colón to be buried. Everyone wept and cursed the Germans. Then the presidente promised that a memorial would be built to their memory. It was very beautiful."

He put his arm around Lorenzo's shoulders.

"And now you bring your friends to Havana at such a sad time, Lorenzo."

He called out sharply, "Papo."

One of the young agents hurried into the room.

"Get the car," the Russian ordered. "We will go to the restaurant—"

Lorenzo looked at us and shrugged slightly.

"*Almuerzo*," the Russian said slapping his hands together. "Do you know what it is, my Yankee friends? Lunch! Eggs. Rice. Black beans. Soup. Fried bananas. That's all these people eat. For a good piece of meat you have to go out into the country." He hugged Lorenzo. "Out to the ranch, eh, Lorenzo? How is the señora? Have you seen her?"

"I hear she is well," Lorenzo said quietly.

"A saint. She is a saint," the Russian said firmly. He asked us, "Do you know the senator's widow?"

"No," Joe said. "We haven't been doin' much sightseein' . . ."

"No La Parisienne?" the Russian said with a look of disbelief. "Lorenzo, what the hell have you been doing?"

Lorenzo, with a faint smile, explained, "La Parisienne is the whorehouse."

"A whorehouse!" Kaganovitch said with mock severity, "a place of worship, Lorenzo."

He considered that very funny and we all politely joined in.

Kaganovitch threw on a wrinkled white jacket and insisted on giving us a tour of police headquarters. The colonel in charge of Havana's National Police and his two assistants were introduced to us. I didn't need Lorenzo to tell me we had been set up for them to take a good look at us.

Then the Russian took us to the Cosmopolita Restaurant almost directly across the park from our hotel, where we had, as he had predicted, a fine meal of eggs, black soup, meat, and fried bananas.

He was an energetic, entertaining man with an encyclopedic mind and a vast disregard for facts.

We stayed over three hours in the restaurant listening to his endless flow of trivia about Cuba and Cuban history, each fact or anecdote accompanied by a bottle of Tropical Beer. It was amusing to watch his plainclothesmen come in, order a cold drink, and study us intently in an overhead mirror.

Finally he jumped up, waved casually to the glum-looking cashier who knew better than to write out a check, and led us to his limousine. He ignored our protest, and gave us a tour of the city that lasted until dark. At our hotel we shook hands. He invited us to the christening of his new son, embraced Lorenzo, and drove off. Not once during the entire afternoon had he mentioned the hotel, the money, or the casino.

"What was that all about?" Joe asked as he sprawled on the bed.

"He was setting us up. All his *polizia* know us by now," Lorenzo said.

"That's for sure," Maxie said. "There was cop written all over them."

"Did you get that cornball business of lookin' us over in the mirror?" Joe said disgustedly.

"Don't laugh at them, *giovinetto*," Lorenzo said warmly. "They still know how to cut your throat."

"What do we do now?" I asked him.

"We wait for the demonstration . . ."

"What demonstration?"

"*Pro Ley y Justicia* . . . they are used by the Russian to create incidents . . . Perhaps tomorrow they will begin . . ."

"What will they demonstrate against?" Joe wanted to know. "What has a gamblin' casino got to do with politics?"

Lorenzo gave him a bland look.

"The hotel. Perhaps they will say it is being built by imperialistic Yankees."

"But Englishmen are building the Columbia-International," Maxie cried.

Lorenzo held up his hands in a gesture of helplessness.

"*Si*. They are crazy. *Ecco!* In this city the *umbriaccone* shouts in the streets and he starts a riot. What do you want from me? They will demonstrate for the Russian. This I know!"

The following afternoon Lorenzo received another telephone call.

"Pro Ley y Justicia," he said. "Now you will see what I mean."

We took a cab to the Columbia-International. Adjacent to the hotel the large area that one day would be a parking lot was filled with a shouting, jeering mob of students. Lorenzo translated the signs which read: "Casinos for Cubans. No Yankees!" A man in a white suit was addressing the mob. When he turned and dramatically pointed to the hotel, the crowd roared and bricks flew through the air. The glass-sheathed bottom of the hotel collapsed into splinters. Then the mob rushed for the front doors. In a few minutes, lumber, electrical fixtures, workmen's supplies, even wheelbarrows, crashed to the pavement while men with lead pipes went from floor to floor systematically smashing windows. Then almost on a signal they jumped into trucks and cars and vanished. It took less than fifteen minutes.

"It is our present from the Russian," Lorenzo said. "Now tonight we will get a call to meet him."

The call came about ten o'clock.

"We will deliver the money tomorrow night," Lorenzo said after he hung up.

"Where?"

"In the Tenth Police Station in Marianao."

"Where is that?"

"Across the Almendares River. The people call it the Russian's barbershop. During the revolution it is said the Russian killed seven Machadistas in the police station by cutting their throats with a razor."

"That's just great," Maxie said in a strained voice. "What's next on this idiot agenda?"

Lorenzo opened his valise and took a snub-nosed revolver from a leather shaving case. He inspected it carefully, then slid it back. Next he zipped open what I thought was a cloth-covered set of brushes; the familiar silencer was among the brushes.

"We will let the *parristas* rob us," he said. "We will give them the money."

Joe gave him a stunned look.

"We will do what?"

Lorenzo held up his hand and went to the closet. He returned with the same straw bag in which we had delivered the money to his wife and dumped the contents on the bed.

"Christ! I thought this was our dough," Joe said wonderingly as he held up a package of green notes.

"*Si*. It looks like money," Lorenzo explained. "We will do this." He took several crisp new thousand dollar bills from his wallet and carefully inserted them on the top and bottom of each package. Then he filled an attaché case with some of the bundles and proudly held it up for our inspection.

"It looks like money, no?"

"Where did you get this stuff, Lorenzo?" I asked.

"My wife," he said proudly. "She got the paper and measured the bills." His fingers imitated a pair of scissors. "She said it was like cutting out paper toys for the boy."

"She was cuttin' out this stuff in the Russian's house?" Joe asked.

"*Si*. Everybody was asleep." His scissors cut through the air. "She cut, cut, cut all night."

"How did she get it here?" I asked.

"Her cousin is a maid in the hotel," Lorenzo said. "While we were out with the Russian she put it in the closet. My wife is a very smart woman—no, Peppino?"

"Yes," I said. "Very smart."

"We'll still be giving those bastards about ten thousand dollars," Maxie said grudgingly.

"You would kick in clover, Maxie," Joe said disgustedly. "It's cheap at half the price!"

"We pay nothing," Lorenzo said. "The bills are queer."

"Counterfeit," Joe cried. "How did you work that?"

"Sortino made the plan." He held out one of the notes. "Feel 'em. Just like the real thing."

"How do you like that guy Pepe, Frank?" Joe said admiringly. "He thinks of everything." He pointed to the attaché cases.

"Will they fall for it, Lorenzo?"

"*Si*. It will be dark in the cab. They will put guns to our face . . ."

I swallowed hard as he cocked an imaginary pistol.

". . . and ask for the money." He held up his hands. "We will be good fellows and give it to 'em . . . what the hell, it's not our money . . . like the guys the Englishmen sent down—what did they care? Did they want to get a bullet in the head? *Ecco!* Let the bosses get up some more dough! That's what these bastardos think . . ."

"But then how do we actually pay the Russian?" Maxie asked.

514

"We will pay that *pòrco misèria*," Lorenzo said grimly. "Tomorrow night there will be a big fiesta at his house to celebrate his child's christening. He's invited us, no? We will go and we will pay him."

"The money is still there? In his house?"

"My son has been sleepin' on it," Lorenzo said chuckling. "Every day, ten, fifteen times the Russian passes the room. It is better than ten banks . . ."

"What's to prevent the Russian from saying he never got the money?" I asked.

Joe turned to Lorenzo.

"What about it, Lorenzo?"

Lorenzo only winked. Then he slid his pistol into his belt and said, "I am leaving now. Go to bed. I will wake you when I return tomorrow morning."

"Tomorrow morning! Where the hell are you going—Florida?"

"It is a long ride to Mantanzas," Lorenzo said patiently. Then he left, locking the door behind him. In a few minutes we heard the elevator door slam and he was gone.

It felt like I had been sleeping only a few minutes when someone gently nudged me. I awoke with a start and discovered Lorenzo standing over me. It was dawn.

"I just wanted to tell you I'm back, Peppino," he whispered.

He looked drawn and tired and his cheeks were covered with a stubble.

"Did you drive all night?"

"*Si*." He patted me on the shoulder. "Go back to sleep."

"Did everything come out all right?"

He gave me a strange smile and nodded. Then he shut the blinds and, without undressing, threw himself across the bed.

We stayed in the hotel room all that day. It was about eight o'clock that night when Lorenzo stuck the revolver and silencer in his belt and we left in a cab for Havana's Tenth Police Precinct in Marianao. The city's nightly blackout was typical Cuban: only four blocks along the waterfront were completely dark; the rest of Havana glowed with lights.

The police station guarded the bridge across the Almendares River. As we approached it, the cab slowed down. Lorenzo spoke sharply in Spanish to the driver who ignored him. Suddenly the cab was surrounded by several men in white suits. One shouted an order to the driver who jammed on the brakes so hard we almost slid out of our seats. A flashlight blinded us, but I could see the glint of guns.

Someone said in broken English, "Give us the money."

The attché cases were yanked out of our hands and snapped open. In a moment they had slipped away in the darkness. It was all done as neatly and efficiently as any West Side Friday afternoon payroll robbery.

Lorenzo moved quickly. The butt of his gun crunched on the driver's head. Lorenzo slid behind the wheel, opened the door, and pushed out the unconscious man. Then he gunned the engine and we sped across the bridge, past the precinct glowing with lights, and into a side street on two wheels.

We were several miles outside the city when Lorenzo swerved into a wide street and slowed down.

"The Russian's house," he said shortly.

As I would learn in Havana you never ask the location of a fiesta, you hear it. Cubans love to dance and as we moved down the street the sensuous throbbing of the rumba filled the night. Cars were parked on the street and in the circled driveway. A dance floor erected on the lawn was crowded. On the wide veranda under strings of Japanese lanterns couples strolled about or chattered in groups.

"Grab a drink, act simpatico," Lorenzo said tersely.

"What the hell's simpatico?" Joe asked.

"Be nice. Just keep bowin' and smilin' like you're havin' a good time . . ."

"Where are we going?" Maxie asked. "You're not going to leave us now, are you?"

"Only for a few minutes," Lorenzo said quickly. "I must find my woman . . ."

After Lorenzo left, we accepted drinks from a passing waiter and did our best to look simpatico. It seemed an eternity before Lorenzo returned. He put on an excellent show of spotting us accidentally.

He said softly, "Keep smilin' and follow me into the house."

"Where's the Russian?" Joe asked.

"Showin' off his son. He has a private office on the second floor. The money is there."

With Lorenzo in the lead, we pushed our way through

the crowd on the veranda and into the house, where another orchestra was playing in a large dining room filled with rumba dancers. Maxie and I had followed him up the first steps of a wide marble stairway. Within minutes we were up the stairway and hurrying down a hallway. At the far end Lorenzo led us into a room that appeared to be a study. It was dimly lit and furnished with wicker furniture. On the wall hung a fine lithograph of a church with an onion-shaped dome. Lorenzo searched under the desk and triumphantly held up the straw basket of money.

"Where's the Russian?" Maxie whispered but Lorenzo put a finger to his lips. At the sound of footsteps in the hall he slipped the gun out of his belt and stepped to one side of the door. In a moment it opened and Kaganovitch walked in. When he saw us he whirled around but Lorenzo slammed the door.

The Russian said something angrily in Spanish but Lorenzo waved his gun impatiently.

"Speak English . . ."

"Why do you come with a gun?" Kaganovitch snapped. "Didn't I invite you?"

"Some of your friends paid us a visit before we got here," Joe said. "They weren't very friendly."

When Lorenzo nodded to me I picked up the straw bag and dumped the money on the desk. The Russian didn't blink; he simply walked over to the pile, flipped over one package of the bills, and smiled.

"We'll wait if you want to count it," Joe said.

"I trust you, Yanqui."

"No more demonstrations?" I asked.

He shrugged. "Who can control those crazy students?"

"That's not the way we hear it," Joe said. "The people who put up this dough don't want any trouble. From now on let's have it nice and easy."

"When will the Englishmen like to open?" he asked as he selected a thin black cigar from a humidor.

"Sometime next year."

"You will stay in Havana?"

"We intend to be your neighbors for a while," I told him.

"*Buen*," he said briskly. "Tell your people there will be no more trouble. You have an arrangement. Now will you let me show you my son?"

"Open the safe, Russian," Lorenzo said harshly. "We want a souvenir."

Kaganovitch's face tightened and he lowered his head, glaring at Lorenzo. For a moment I thought he would lunge at him.

"There is no safe," he growled.

Lorenzo pointed with his gun to the lithograph.

"Open it, Russian, or I'll blow a goddam hole in your guts . . ."

Kaganovitch was an old hand at murder; he knew Lorenzo would have no qualms about pulling the trigger.

"Is this the way you do business, Yanqui?" he asked Joe.

". . . two . . ." Lorenzo called out.

Without a word Kaganovitch walked across the room, pushed the lithograph aside, and spun the dial of the safe. When it opened Lorenzo gestured him away and reached inside. He knew what he was looking for: a folder of official documents bound together by rubber bands and packages of money were tossed on the desk. Then he grunted and held up a small indexed book.

"Maybe we'll give it to the Autenticos, hey, Russian?"

Kaganovitch's face was stone.

"Let's get out of here," Maxie pleaded.

"He will show us to the door," Lorenzo said. Then he jammed his gun into the Russian's belly. "Stay alive, my friend, your son needs a father . . ."

As our cab drove off, Lorenzo called out, "Good night, Russian, *Felicitazione!*"

Kaganovitch spoke for the first time since we had left his study.

"Perhaps someday I will remember your loud music, Italiano . . ."

Then he turned and walked up the driveway to his house.

"God, I'm glad that's over!" Maxie said as he slumped back on the seat.

"That wasn't too bad," Joe said happily. "What's in that book, Lorenzo?"

"He splits his take with the colonel in charge of the Police Bureau of Investigations and a couple of other guys in the government," Lorenzo said. "It's all in the book."

"You said something about turning it over to—who?" Maxie asked.

"Directorio Revolucianario—the revolutionary party. The people call 'em Autenticos," Lorenzo explained. "Every time the Russian gets one you can hear him scream
518

down to Santa Clara. *Stùpido!* He made a list! The Autenticos would give their *cauzionos* to get this book!"

"How did you know where it was?" I asked.

"My woman," he said. "One morning after the police colonel had left she brought the Russian some caffè cón leche. She came up the stairs when the door was still half open and saw him put the book into the safe. I put two and two together. He and this other guy were splitting the loot, right? That book must have something to do with their graft . . ."

"We couldn't have done anything if it hadn't been for your wife, Lorenzo," I told him.

"She is a good woman," he said warmly.

"How can we say thanks?"

He thought about this for a few minutes, then said hesitantly: "She lights a candle every day so she and the kid can get to the States. . . . Sortino has promised to bring 'em in." He added softly, "It will be a service for a service. . . ."

"What you just did—is that the service?" Maxie asked.

"Oh no, lawyer," Lorenzo replied. "This is business."

"Well, what's the service?"

"You will see," was his quiet reply.

He swung the car into the curb in front of an old Packard. Obviously someone had given it loving care. Unlike most of the cars in Havana it hadn't nicked paint, and the chrome glistened from constant polishing.

"Aren't we going back to the hotel?" Maxie asked.

"No," Lorenzo said shortly. "We are goin' to the ranch . . ."

"The ranch! What the hell are we going to the ranch for?"

Lorenzo ignored him and opened the door of the Packard.

"Whose car is this?" Maxie demanded.

"This is the one I drove for the senator," Lorenzo said wearily. *"Pòrco diavolo!* Will you get in, lawyer?"

"Why do we have to go out to the ranch, Lorenzo?" Joe asked as we got in. "Do you think the Russian will try anythin' tonight?"

"We don't have to worry about the Russian," Lorenzo replied shaking his head. "This is something I promised Sortino I would do . . ."

"What the hell is this big secret?" I asked.

He only smiled as the car pulled away from the curb and sped down the street.

"Maybe he's gonna take us to La Parisienne," Joe said. He slid down in his seat. "Wake me up when the dames show up."

"Jeez!" Maxie said angrily. "First we have all this stuff with the Russian. Now this guy insists we take a joyride out to a horse ranch." He leaned forward. "Goddammit, Lorenzo! Just where the hell are you taking us?"

"La Bello."

"What the hell's La Bello?"

"The ranch of Señora Alvarez."

"Dammit, that's no answer. Why don't we just go back to the hotel?"

"We must attend a wedding," Lorenzo said solemnly. "I promised Sortino you would all attend."

"Things down here are getting more screwy every minute," Maxie cried. "Who's getting married that it's so important we be there?"

"Your friend, lawyer," Lorenzo said and winked at me.

"A friend of mine?" Maxie said, startled. He looked at me. "Who can that be, Frank?"

"Do I know him, Lorenzo?"

"*Si.* You are such good friends, Peppino . . ."

Joe's voice was muffled from inside his arm as he coiled up on the back seat.

"Then I must know him."

"*Si.* You are also a very good friend, Joe. You all like him very much."

Then he started to whistle the wedding march.

"Is this a gag?" I asked him.

"What gag?" he replied indignantly. "What do you think I do—drive all the way out to Mantanzas for a joke?"

It was obvious he cherished his secret; we kept guessing but each time Lorenzo shook his head. Finally we all gave up and settled back to doze.

46 *LA BELLO*

We drove for hours along the Central Highway, up and down hills covered with royal palms and finally into the Yumuri Valley, one of the most beautiful sections of Cuba. Once when I awoke I discovered we were entering a town with a magnificent harbor. I caught a glimpse of iron shutters, alleys, and a streetlight glinting on the damp cobblestones of an ancient square. The Central Plaza of Mantanzas, Lorenzo said, yawning.

We left the town and continued on the highway, our tires finally crunching on a gravel drive. We were approaching a beautiful white building screened by palms. The air was heavy with the perfume of flowers and newly cut grass.

"La Bello, Peppino!" Lorenzo cried, his voice taut with excitement. "La Bello!"

"Christ, it looks like something out of the movies," Joe said as he sat up. "Is this the ranch, Lorenzo?"

"*Si*. Senora Alvarez is waiting for us . . ."

As we stepped out of the car, a soft voice called, "Lorenzo."

A woman stood on the veranda—she was Spanish, about sixty, with a jeweled comb in her gray hair. She had an air of old-world dignity.

"Welcome to La Bello," she said to me with a smile.

"This is Senora Alvarez," Lorenzo said. He tapped me on the shoulder. "This is Peppino, Senora—"

"Ah," she said, 'Señor Howell . . ."

"And this is Señor Gunnar and Señor Solomon . . ."

She shook hands with each of us.

"This is beautiful, ma'am," Joe said softly, "just beautiful."

"We are happy to have you," she said.

"It doesn't look as if any other guests have arrived," Maxie said as we followed Lorenzo into the house.

"There won't be any other guests," Lorenzo said.

"No other guests for a weddin'?" Joe asked, looking at me.

"No," Lorenzo answered with a grin. "Just us. It's a sort of private wedding."

We entered a magnificent room, typical of the Cuban estates outside Havana; floors of tiles set in cunning designs, thick rugs, old carved mahogany, high beamed ceilings, and a fireplace that could accommodate a truckload of wood. Later I would learn that La Bello was built by the Spanish hidalgos. On the wall was a crossed pair of swords and an oil painting of a handsome man in his early forties.

"That's the senator," Lorenzo whispered. "See those swords? They were his dueling swords."

"Señora Alvarez must think a lot of you, Lorenzo," I pointed out, "to invite you and some strangers to her home for a wedding . . ."

"She knew I always did my best to take care of the senator," he said. "She never forgot how I paid those newspaper *bastardi* to forget that dame's name when he was knocked off." He looked up at the portrait. "Yeah. He was a great guy. The only bad thing was he wanted to screw everythin' in sight. He acted like he thought it was his duty."

Lorenzo led us past a dining room, its long table set with a beautiful lace tablecloth, candles, sparkling cutlery, and delicate wineglasses to a veranda.

"Well, at least we're going to eat," Maxie glumly observed.

From the veranda, the gardens and the graceful palms were incredibly beautiful in the moonlight. In the distance I could hear the measured booming of surf.

"How do you like it, Peppino?" Lorenzo asked.

"It's beautiful."

"Nice for a honeymoon, eh?" He nudged me and laughed. "Maybe some day, Peppino . . . who knows . . ."

To my surprise before we left the veranda he carefully inspected me, even brushed off my jacket. "Now we go."

We followed him downstairs. With a mysterious smile, Señora Alvarez gestured to the hall. We walked to its end where Lorenzo swung open a shuttered door. Joe was about to enter but Lorenzo tugged at his sleeve.

"No, Joe—not you. First Peppino . . ."

He pulled me forward and gently pushed me into a

large patio with a tiny waterfall. There were marble benches and, behind a small hedge, a pool with lily pads glittered in the light of the lamps. Across the patio a stairway led down from an overhead balcony.

The door clicked behind me. When I turned there was no one there.

For a moment I thought it was a joke. Then, suddenly, a door on the balcony opened. A girl came out and began descending the stairs, slowly, one hand on the iron rail. It was dim at the far side and her face was a white blur. The only sound was the tinkling of the waterfall.

"Frank . . ."

It was a whisper.

"Frank . . . Frank, darling . . ."

"Chena! Chena!" I shouted. "Chena!"

I cleared the marble bench like Jesse Owens but I didn't quite make the hedge. A thin wire ran through the bushes and, as I soared over it, it caught my heel. I executed a miserable belly whop into the shallow pool and came up entangled in lily pads.

Chena ran to me and knelt down at the edge of the pool. For a moment we just looked at each other. If anything, she was more beautiful than before.

Then I took her, lily pads and all.

"Oh, Frank," she whispered. "Oh, Frank . . ."

We were married at 3:00 A.M., September 14, 1944, in the private chapel of Señora Alvarez at La Bello by a grumpy old Franciscan who smelled of wine, wore a tonsure, and had on a cassock pocked with food stains.

Joe was my best man and the señora was Chena's matron of honor. Maxie and Lorenzo were my ushers— only there wasn't anyone to usher, just three thieves and a savage murderer.

After the last toast had been made, the señora informed us we were to spend our honeymoon at what she called their summer house on the beach near Casilda, on the Caribbean Sea. Lorenzo gave me the keys to the old Packard and drew an elaborate map to show me where to get off the Central Highway to reach the summer house. Then he drew me aside.

"In a few hours I will be leavin' for New York, Peppino—"

"Leaving for New York! What about Joe and Maxie?"

"Don't worry about them. Nothing will happen. I will return within a week."

"But why now, Lorenzo? The deal has been made. You say there is no danger from the Russian—"

"There is no danger," he said firmly, "Not now anyway." He shrugged. "I must deliver something to Sortino. It is very important." He held out a small white envelope. "He told me to give you this after the marriage."

The envelope contained a check for five thousand dollars and these words scrawled on a scrap of paper:

"*Una mano lava l'altra . . .*"

"It is good to remember this, Peppino," he said solemnly. "One hand washes the other . . ."

They all came out on the veranda to say good-bye. Maxie, who was half-gassed, kept shaking my hand. When I opened the car door I felt Joe's hand on my shoulder.

"You know somethin', Frank? This is the first time since we were two years old that we haven't gone home together." He gripped my hand. "Good luck." Then he bent down and looked into the car.

"I don't know what he has, Chena," he told her, "but whatever it is I better get some of it if I want a bride as pretty as the one I saw tonight . . ."

Then he kissed her.

With a final honk we moved down the driveway and out to the highway.

"Frank," Chena whispered.

"What, darling?"

"I'm so happy I could cry . . ."

"Well then, cry."

She did.

47 *CHENA'S STORY*

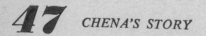

Señora Alvarez's summer house was a smaller replica of La Bello.

There was a table with cold sliced meats, fruit, a pot of

caffè cón leche with a small spirit lamp to keep it hot and several bottles of champagne in a bucket filled with chunks of ice wrapped in thick towels. I silently blessed Señora Alvarez.

Hand in hand we walked into the bedroom that faced the sea. There was a veranda, and we stood out there for a minute feeling the growing heat of the sun and tasting the heavy salt in the fresh dawn breeze. Then we went inside. I closed the shutters and Chena came to me.

This was a Chena I had never known. I had never seen her that she didn't have on a dress, skirt and blouse or sweater. I hadn't even seen her in a bathing suit. Our physical encounters—with the exception of that one exciting moment in the park when I returned from the CCCs—had been a series of sweaty thigh-to-thigh embraces in the deep doorway of the empty store on Eighth Avenue—to Chena it had always been "our store" like "our lions" in front of the library.

Now the last piece of silk was gone, I was undressed and she was standing in front of me, shafts of sunlight coming through the shutters bathing her silky skin with a soft, golden glow. She had left a delightful, pretty teenager; now she was a woman, full breasted, perfect in every line and plane of her body. She was so beautiful it hurt.

I stretched out my hand and with a smile she took it. I was sitting on the bed and drew her toward me. She bent down and kissed me. Then she was in my arms.

In that fantastic room by the sea we made love unhurriedly. When I finally took her for the first time she met me with an intense eagerness and a passion that both surprised and delighted me.

At one point of that lovely morning when we were half-dozing in each other's arms, one of those intervals when the world beyond the shutters and walls was completely forgotten, Chena suddenly started to giggle.

"If this had happened in that damn guinea village I was in," she whispered, "the old women would have demanded the sheets ..."

We stayed at the beach house for seven days. We saw no one except an old man with a face seamed like a walnut who appeared each morning silently pointing to the ancient Packard, and his ancient wife who delivered our meals. He was our driver. When I shook my head he would bow, obviously disappointed, put on his straw hat, and walk back down the road to Casilda. Every morning there was a bowl of fresh fruit.

We got up when we liked and went to bed after hours of feverish lovemaking. I couldn't get enough of Chena, often it was dawn before we both fell into an exhausted sleep. Years on the piers had turned me into an early riser and sometimes, before Chena awoke, I would slip out on the veranda to watch the dawn explode over the sea.

For the first few days we explored the beach and went on picnics with a lunch basket prepared by the old man's wife.

There was a distance of seven long years between us but I never pressed Chena to fill them in: I knew when she was ready she would tell me. One morning, after we had discovered the wreck of an old ship, we played like kids in the surf until we were water-soaked. Chena wouldn't let me touch her until she had dried her hair, but I wrestled her to the blanket and we made love with a passion that shook us both.

She was lying on my arm playing with the St. Christopher medal and chain I had worn since I was a kid, when suddenly she leaned over to gently kiss me.

"Where do you want me to begin, darling?"

"Wherever you want to."

She sighed. "There's so much—so very much." She pressed her face against my chest. "Oh, Frank, if you could have seen Nicky . . ."

I touched her cheek and felt the tears.

"Do you want to save it for some other time . . .?"

"No," she said firmly. "I want to tell you now. The whole story. Did you ever get the letter I sent from the village?"

"The one where the guy was waiting with the car to take you to see Nicky?"

"That's the one. It took us two days to get there. He was in an Italian hospital that had the worst cases from Spain—the glorious volunteers as Mussolini called them. Most of them were from the Air Force—"

"Was Nicky a pilot?"

"Poor Nicky," she whispered. "He joined up when they were looking for anyone who could speak English, Italian, or Spanish. Do you remember how good he was in Spanish, Frank?"

"Sure. President of the Spanish Club."

"After he enlisted they made him sergeant and attached

him to a group of pilots Mussolini's son took to Spain to join the Germans for the big push against Madrid. Nicky really didn't care; he said anything was better than cutting up cadavers in Bologna. He never saw the war, Frank, never heard a shot fired! He was in Spain only a few months when some government guerrillas raided the airstrip. It was crazy, stupid. They never had a chance, but two managed to reach the hangar and throw in some phosphorus grenades. Before the guards killed them Nicky was badly wounded."

She buried her head in her arms.

"Oh, Frank, it was horrible! Most of the time he was like a mummy, only slits for his eyes and mouth, and moaning, always moaning. There wasn't anything they could do for him, he had lost an arm and a leg. Every day I prayed to the Blessed Mother that God would take him.

"Month after month it went on like that in the hospital. His wounds became infected and they had to operate. Then something happened to the stump of his leg and they had to remove more bone." She shuddered. "I couldn't believe this was happening to Nicky! I couldn't pray any more. I cursed God. There were times at night when I thought I could hear him screaming. When I tried to talk to the doctors they only shrugged. Wait until the war is over, they said. Then one day I forced a young doctor to let me stay in the room when they removed the dressings from his face."

Her hand gripped mine.

"Oh God, Frank, it was horrible! I will never forget it."

She tried to hold back the tears but they rolled down her cheeks.

"After the Eastern Front opened, the Germans took over the hospital. The wounded came in truckloads. They had no time for Nicky or the other Italian soldiers—only the Germans. They moved him into the corner of a ward." She closed her eyes and shuddered. "It was for the hopeless cases waiting to die. It was looking into a corner of hell every morning . . ."

"Wasn't there anyone who could help you, Chena?"

"Only one," she said. "Don Carlo, the *Capo dei Capi*, the old man who sat in the sun and ate grapes. My cousin finally found him in Villalba where the flour mills were located, about fifty miles from the hosiptal. He arranged with the local *gabèllòtto*—who acted as the intermediary between the peasants and the millowners—to drive us to Villalba to see Don Carlo. It was as if I had left him only a few hours before; he was still old and fat and sitting on a little stool in the sun eating grapes.

"This time I had respect," she went on in a tense, low voice. "I would have crawled on my knees to the old devil! I begged him to get Nicky into some hospital where plastic surgery was being done. He kept eating grapes, delicately spitting the pits into his hand like an old woman without saying a word. I only knew the interview was ended when my cousin kept tugging at my sleeve."

She took my hand, kissed it, and hugged it against her cheek.

"I'm sorry, darling. This is a terrible time to tell you all this! But you're the only one I can talk to . . ."

She slipped into my arms and I held her close.

"Did the old man help?"

"Our cousin, who was with the Partisans in the mountains, came to us one night and said Don Carlo had arranged for Nicky to be transferred to another hospital, this one was near Milano far to the north. We were frantic. It was a terribly long journey and we had no friends or relatives there. I was half out of my mind. I didn't know what to do, but my cousin kept saying over and over, 'Have faith in Don Carlo. He has a long arm.' There was nothing we could do but go north. Everything was arranged; we went from village to village, sometimes by truck, by car, or by train."

"What sort of hospital was it?"

"We found it was only for burn cases that were supposed to be hopeless. The doctor in charge was a Nazi colonel. How I hated him in the beginning! He walked around like he was God. He cared for nothing but his knife. Once I heard him say how happy he was with the war because now he faced a different challenge with every patient."

"Did he help Nicky?"

"He was a fanatic but a genius, darling," she said. "For two years he worked on Nicky along with some other severe cases; German, Italian, French, British, Canadian— he didn't care who they were. The more hopeless the case, the better. He rebuilt Nicky's face with cartilage and bone from his ribs, skin from his thighs. He even made him ears!"

"And did Nicky finally . . ."

"You would never recognize him, Frank," she whis-

528

pered. "But at least he has a face. He has to wear a cap because his hair had been burned off, but the doctor even made him eyebrows from my hair . . ."

She closed her eyes.

"What finally happened? Is Nicky still in that hospital?"

"No, he's in Switzerland with my mother."

"In Switzerland! How did the three of you ever get out of Italy? How did Nicky—"

"One night my cousin slipped through the German lines into the city to tell us that Don Carlo, because of his respect for someone in the United States, had arranged for the three of us to be smuggled across the border into Switzerland, where Nicky would be admitted into a hospital in Zurich. I tried to tell my cousin that Nicky wasn't well enough to make that kind of a journey but he kept shaking his head."

" ' If you do not obey *Zu Tanu's* orders I will no longer be responsible for you . . .' was all he would say.

"I believe he spoke privately to my mother because the next morning she couldn't wait to leave. Late that night a German army ambulance left the hospital and we followed in my cousin's car to a small village. We hid all day, then continued the journey at night. Later my cousin told me why he had insisted we leave so quickly; a German troop train was derailed outside Milano and a large number killed. In retaliation the Germans destroyed several villages in the district. In Milano many men were shot and the Gestapo sent all the women and children they could find to labor battalions in Germany."

"Thank God for Don Carlo," I said fervently.

We silently watched a gull suddenly bank and fall like a stone to the sea. The bird hit the water with a shower of spray and soared upward, a struggling fish in its mouth.

"Finally we reached an area near the border which my cousin told us was controlled by the partisans and even German patrols were afraid to use the roads. The only difficulty was getting Nicky across the pass.

"He still had bandages on his face but a doctor among the partisans said the danger was pneumonia. Two men carried him on a stretcher until we reached a shepherd's hut. We stayed there until the sun came up, then we continued on to Switzerland."

"My God, Chena, did your mother make this journey?"

"No. Don Carlo arranged with someone in Rome who gave her papers and took her into Switzerland. Ten days after we left the village Nicky was admitted into a hospital in Zurich. I cabled my father, and of course there is no problem about Nicky getting the best of care."

"Darling, I can't believe all this happened to you . . ."

"I can't either, Frank," she said wearily. "As I said before it's all so unreal."

"How is Nicky now?"

"The doctors told us there must be four more operations and lots of therapy . . ."

"God! That poor guy. I can't believe it, Chena."

"He's like an old stranger sitting in a chair. Oh, Frank, he's so brave! In all the hospitals after all the operations he never complained. He only kept saying it was all his stupid mistake and he had to make the best of what happened . . ." She smiled sadly. "When I left I told him I was coming back to you. He said it was the greatest news he had heard since they told him he was in Switzerland. He said, 'Tell Frank I bet him a buck I could walk down Guinea Alley and he'd never recognize me!' "

"Will they come back after the war, Chena?"

She shook her head vigorously.

"Never. My mother wrote to my father and told him this. She hates him for what he did to Nicky. If only he had let him go to Juilliard! But no, he had this crazy guinea pride! He had to have a doctor or a lawyer for a son."

She said softly, bitterly:

"Now he has a son with a new face and one arm and one leg! *Chi sputo a cièlo da fàccia venuta . . .!* That's what my mother says, 'Who spits in the sky gets it in the face . . .' and someday he will . . . I never want to see or speak to him ever again!"

She put her head on my shoulder and wept softly.

"Please, darling, put your arms around me and hold me very close. Please let us forget everything. Please don't let us think of tomorrow—only today. Please just hold your arms very tight and love me very much because I have had such an ache in my heart for so long . . . so very long . . ."

This time I let her cry. When she finally brushed away the tears. I helped her to her feet and pointed to the sea. She nodded and hand in hand we went in. We got beyond the surf and slowly, effortlessly, swam out quite a distance. Then we rolled on our backs, floated for a while, and returned to the beach. I dried her on the blanket and for a long time she lay in my arms.

"Is it my turn now?" I whispered.

"No! Please, darling," she said fiercely, "don't tell me. Don't ever tell me! I don't want to know." She smiled up at me. "I want to be a nice Italian wife—give my husband lots of babies and keep my nose out of his affairs."

"One thing, Chena—when the old *capo* Don Carlo told your cousin he was doing a favor for someone he respected back in the States, who did he mean?"

She looked at me.

"Pepe?" I prompted.

She nodded. "Always Pepe. You won't believe it but when my cousin spoke of him he took off his hat! *Capo dei Capi*, he called him—the boss in the United States . . ."

I gripped her hand very tight.

"I've had to do things for him, darling—me, Joe, Maxie. *Una mano lava l'altra . . .*"

She closed her eyes.

"I know," she said in a strained voice, "one hand washes the other. So have I . . ."

I was stunned.

"You, Chena? How? In what way?"

"The day I was to leave Zurich my cousin met me outside the hospital. With him was a man I thought I recognized. Then I remembered he was the man who had said he was from Don Carlo. It seems they had a very important letter for Pepe and as a mark of our friendship Don Carlo wanted me to deliver it."

"Why didn't they just mail it?"

"When I asked him that he only smiled. 'Letters have a way of getting lost or read by eyes of strangers, signora,' he said. Do you remember how I wrote and told you my mother had kept Pepe's letter to Don Carlo pinned to her corset? Well I didn't have any corset but I kept it in my bra going through customs in Switzerland and Lisbon."

"Where is it now?"

"It was the first thing Lorenzo asked for when he met me."

"So that's the reason he's going back to New York! He's taking the letter. What do you think is in it that's so important?"

"I can only guess. One day before we left Italy I

531

overheard my cousin telling another man how to hide some trucks. That night several American army trucks drove through the village where we were staying. Later American MPs came to the village with the mayor asking about the trucks.

"It was like asking the people if they had seen St. Anthony. They looked surprised, then shrugged. But when the women in the village began talking among themselves my mother told me the trucks were loaded with boxes of penicillin. There were thousands of boxes for the hospitals—"

"Penicillin? What's that?"

"It's a new miracle drug. Only the army hospitals have it. People over there will sell their soul for a few tablets. The Nazi colonel once told me the only Englishman worth saving was the doctor who invented penicillin. Those truckloads must have been worth millions."

"So Don Carlo stole the penicillin and now they're smuggling it into New York. That letter must give Pepe the details."

" 'I couldn't refuse,' the man kept saying. 'It is for the *éminence grise*, signora . . . a service for a service.' "

"Do you know what this thing is, Chena? Is it the Mafia?"

"The Mafia? *Madre nobile*—the noble mother—the peasants call it." She shook her head. "It's not the Mafia, darling."

"What is it then?"

"What Pepe called it that day I overhead him and my father talking in the kitchen, 'Còsa Loro' . . . Their Thing. . . ."

She turned and kissed me passionately.

"Who cares what it is, darling. They own us both but I don't care! They found Nicky. They gave him a new face and an artificial arm and leg. But most important of all they brought me back to you! And for that I would have delivered a letter to the devil!"

Our week passed all too quickly. We clung to every hour, to every minute.

Pepe. Don Carlo. Nicky. The Duchess. The wastepaper factory on Cherry Street. Joe. New York. I never gave them a second thought. . . .

Then one day it was over. We took a last look at the house, the beach, the sea, waved good-bye to the old man and his woman, bumped over the cobblestones of the plaza, and headed north toward Havana.

And all of our tomorrows together.

48 CASINOS IN THE SUN

In March 1946, seven months after the war ended, the Columbia-International Hotel opened. From its very beginning our casino was a success. Then, in the late 1940s, came a period of revolutionary unrest in which all the predictions of Tony Cupid came true. It began with Communist mobs stoning our embassy roaring, "Fuera Yanquis!" and ended with the government taking over the British-owned United Railways of Havana. Batista returned to Cuba, and in the spring of 1950 we met him at his beautiful country estate called Kuquine, to receive his promise that should he be reelected president gambling would be legalized in Cuba.

Maxie and Lorenzo returned to New York to report to the Table. They returned with an attaché case filled with money, this time real, for Batista's campaign. In the event he was elected, Maxie told us, we were to make preparations to build a new luxury hotel to hold the largest gambling casino in the Caribbean. Maxie told us the debates had been heated with Pepe warning the others it would be foolhardy to invest so many millions in a country of uncertain politics. Grossi's counterargument was that Batista had the support of the army and would probably die in office. He urged the council to build a luxury hotel and create a gambling monopoly.

Then came the order to us from Pepe to find out if there were pension or retirement funds belonging to groups of Cuban workers. Maxie and I did the research and came up with three major retirement funds of Cuban unions all in American banks but controlled under law by the administration in power.

Maxie reported to a hastily called Table. This time
533

Pepe presented his plan—build the biggest and most luxurious hotel and casino in the Caribbean—but financed by one of the funds.

It was a master stroke and was enthusiastically endorsed by the entire Table although a disgruntled Sally G—Grossi—insisted we would never be able to swing the deal.

Then without warning came the military coup of March 1952 when Batista, supported by high-ranking officers, seized Camp Columbia, the army center, while his followers took over Cababas Fortress and the interior military posts. In two hours Batista had made himself ruler of Cuba. Business and industry quickly supported him. And Batista kept his promise—he legalized gambling.

Those early years of Batista's regime confirmed Pepe's shrewd instinct for picking the right men for the right jobs: Maxie was a superb organizer who carefully built the world's most powerful gambling organization. His system is still followed in the casinos of London, the Grand Bahamas, Haiti—wherever American dice are rolled or a wheel is spun.

To eliminate competition he wrote a law which was forced through the Congress by Batista's senatorial bloc permitting casinos only in hotels or nightclubs that had an investment of a million dollars or more. The same law had provisions to permit dealers, stickmen, and pit bosses to be listed as "technicians" so they could be issued two-year visas. He had all import duties waived on building material and even had the Cuban tax laws altered or provisions added for the benefit of what we called "the new industry."

All this took time but Maxie was in no hurry. We operated the Columbia-International, then went on to build the Condor-Caribbean, an unbelievable luxury hotel with a magnificent gambling casino. It cost a staggering fourteen million dollars—but ninety percent was financed by the Retirement Fund of the Cuban Railway Workers—which was Pepe's brilliant idea. In turn the hotel and casino were leased to the Caribbean Amusement Enterprises, Inc., a paper corporation consisting of me, Maxie, and Joe. In the first three months of operation, the casino cleared two million dollars.

Lorenzo's description of Kaganovitch as a cat with nine lives was underscored in the early days of Batista's regime when, one day, he marched into our office and announced he had been appointed director of Batista's newly organized Department of Havana Propriedad Horizontal (co-operative apartment houses) and Hotel Enterprises.

We put the Russian on our payroll—along with several other government thieves—for half of what he had demanded. He blustered and made threats, but Joe and I paid a brief visit to his attractive office in Havana's police headquarters and informed him that if he didn't quiet down and return to his hole, the entry book we had taken from his safe would be turned over to the Autenticos. The Russian, like the Gimp, had a self-destructive habit of listing his crimes.

To be on the safe side, Kaganovitch was forced to accept our offer. But Lorenzo warned us that the Russian was known for his vindictiveness; he would wait a lifetime to get his revenge.

Cuba prospered under Batista. Year after year the country's sugar crop, the taproot of the Cuban economy, was sold for record rates. The government poured millions into industry through its various banking institutions, and a real estate boom began.

Joe and Maxie took over a large suite in the new hotel, but Chena and I built a small beach house in Casilda, almost a replica of one in which we had spent our honeymoon. From Thursday until Sunday we lived there, usually alone, but sometimes with Joe or Maxie and their current girl friends.

In a few years we were established members of the English-speaking colony in Havana made up of Americans, British, and Canadians, known to the Cubans as the "ABC Colony." Because of Cuba's strict labor laws, most of the colony were executives not classified officially as "workers."

Everyone knew we ran the casinos, but in polite circles we were delicately referred to as the "American hotelmen."

For my part, in those days I chose to ignore the odorous villainy in which I was engaged. I was well aware that the profits from the casinos were going into many and varied criminal enterprises in the States, but I never attempted to find out what they were. My attitude was, what I didn't know wouldn't hurt me. If it was good enough for Krupp it was good enough for me . . .

Chena and I kept that secret between us. As we had promised each other we lived day to day; every morning was a gift, every night a delightful surprise. All we cared about was the stability of our own lives.

Chena asked no questions and we both came to accept our feverish, fantasy world. Evil is a subtle seducer and we were both willing victims. . . .

After the war, Pepe paid his service to Lorenzo; he brought his wife and son to the States, but Lorenzo remained as our courier. A special account was opened in the Caribbean Coastal Bank in Miami, and every month Lorenzo carried out sums ranging from $500,000 to a million in cash and checks. It was Lorenzo who delivered vital messages and instructions from Pepe, along with our annual summons to attend a Table.

We were still the Outsiders, trusted strangers, but nothing more. When the Table convened, I always came alone or with Joe and Maxie. Chena steadfastly refused to see her father. I felt sorry for Gus. There was always the hearty greetings and "What's this, Peppino? No bambino? Maybe I better go down and talk to my daughter, no?" But he never came down. I guess he knew how Chena felt.

Pepe remained ageless, the carefully polished Cord had been replaced by a carefully polished Cadillac. He was always smiling, always eager for news of Chena, and always promising to come down to Havana for a visit. Like Gus, he never came; but unlike Gus, he had reasons.

At every Table we sensed that a power struggle was going on. Gus was still the head, but Pepe kept the members in line. Changes gradually took place. Old faces like Charlie Victory disappeared from the Table to be replaced by new members—"from the Families," as Lorenzo put it. When Little Nino died right after the end of the war, I could almost feel the violent lurch in the organization; the Table lasted three days and ended in a defeat for Gus and Pepe when a member of Grossi's upstate territory was voted to replace Nino. Even Lorenzo was disturbed.

"Bad," he said shaking his head, "very bad. Sortino!" He threw up his hands. "Vulcánico!"

There was one thing that never varied at every Table; a discussion of the national cops' union. It became as much of a ritual as the espresso and anisette or the flowery praise they heaped on us for making the casinos a success.

The study of police structure and municipal law enforcement became an intense hobby with me. I subscribed to about every police journal or publication published, not only in the States but in Europe. Friends in the various consulates provided me with free translation service. I also became a choice customer of Americana bookdealers who had standing orders to send me histories of American police departments, especially New York City's.

This interest brought me closer to Hennessy. I despised the man but I could not ignore the splendid contacts he had in the department which were necessary to update my knowledge of the force and to keep in touch with the current gossip, inner politics, feuds, and transfers. My dossiers obviously changed because of deaths, retirements, and transfers, and it was only through Hennessy that I kept them current.

We were in Havana when Hennessy sent us the clipping from the *Times* obituary page; Chief Inspector Cornell had died of a heart attack while at work in his office at police headquarters. There was a distinguished photograph and many glowing tributes from dignitaries. I was surprised to learn he had four sons, two doctors, a lawyer who had graduated from Harvard Law, and an engineer.

One paragraph in the article especially disturbed us: Elliott had been appointed chief inspector.

It was Joe, not the Russian, who endangered all of us.

I should have recognized the early warnings: the moody periods, the flashes of irritability, the hard drinking, the pugnacity and dissatisfaction.

"What's wrong with this guy?" Maxie said after a heated argument with Joe. "If he keeps fighting with the croupiers they'll all walk out!"

When I protested Joe would only shrug.

"Tell Maxie to drop dead. I'm not takin' any crap from him or his goddam croupiers. They're all thieves! Every one of 'em!"

My role became peacemaker until even I was sick of the endless squabbles.

Chena put her finger on it.

"Is almost seems as if there is a tiny volcano inside him bubbling with hate every day, getting ready to explode . . . "

"Who does he have to hate down here, for God's sakes?"

"I don't think even Joe knows, Frank."

He certainly didn't have a scarcity of women, they fell

over him. He and I kept in excellent physical condition with endless games of handball at the Community Center with the other ABC athletes, while Chena and I swam endless miles every weekend. He was the color of old saddle leather, and while Maxie and I anxiously counted the strands in our combs, Joe's hair remained thick, yellow, and wavy as ever.

He had several casual affairs; one, the beautiful daughter of a French consul Chena and I agreed would be the real thing. Womanlike she was making all kinds of wedding plans when Joe abruptly went on a wild carouse ending up at La Parisienne with a two-dollar whore who had picked him up on the street.

It didn't make sense. When I tried to talk to him he yawned and suggested I save my lectures for the Masonic Lodge . . .

Christmas Eve our new rival, the Havana Riviera, opened with a glittering party; every member of the ABC Colony was there. Chena was absolutely stunning in a Paris gown and I was determined to have a good time despite the rumors of revolution that hung over all of us. I guess in a way we were the Caribbean version of the aristocrats in Paris when the mobs were building the tumbrels in the cellars.

The party had only started when I noticed a striking gray-haired woman I thought was absolutely exquisite. I judged she was in her early fifties with the figure of a young girl and the natural dignity of a queen. She was a new face, and Chena told me she was the widow of a Cuban ambassador to a South American country.

Later in the evening I was surprised to see Joe dancing with her. From where I stood I could see them, her head was back and she was looking up into his face and laughing. In that warm, luxurious room filled with an intense gaiety I felt a sudden chill. In one blinding second I was again in that waterfront hovel of a bar and Joe was holding the Duchess in his arms and she was looking up into his face and laughing at what he had just said . . .

After that night he changed; now even the croupiers greeted him with a smile.

He became the constant companion of this woman—no purpose would be served by using her real name, let me call her Sarita—and the entire ABC Colony was impatiently making bets on the date. She had an estate in Volando and a home in Paris. She was a recognized, if

538

aging, beauty—gracious, intelligent, and as the months passed I could see she was hopelessly in love with Joe.

I was not only pessimistic, I was fearful, so much so that one night Chena berated me. Her Sicilian temper exploded and I had to take a long walk along the Prado to cool off.

It happened a year to the day they had met, Christmas Eve. There had been a round of parties all that week and Joe had done more than his share of drinking. Despite the rumors of war the tourist trade boomed, there were few empty rooms, and action never stopped in the casinos. While Maxie and I were busy with a thousand and one details, Joe dropped out of sight; he never showed up for the big Christmas Eve party. For the tourists it was a wild, gay night but for Maxie and me it was anything but gay; Lorenzo had appeared with disturbing news of movements by Fidel Castro's troops in the Escambray Mountains in Los Villas Province. And with Joe gone . . .

After a miserable, gloomy night the phone rang as Chena and I were getting ready for bed. It was Lorenzo and he was whispering he had just received a call from a friend, a police sergeant in an outlying precinct—Joe was in serious trouble.

We found him unconscious and handcuffed to a bench in the rear of the small precinct. Fortunately Lorenzo's friend the sergeant had been the only cop on Christmas duty when the call had come in from Sarita's frantic maid. He arrived at her estate to find Joe, raging drunk, smashing crystal chandeliers, mirrors, dishes and glasses with the leg of a chair. Joe had rushed at the sergeant but a twisted rug tripped him. He fell against the corner of a table and was knocked out. It was fortunate, the sergeant told Lorenzo; he was preparing to kill Joe had he advanced a few more steps.

The sergeant, a little old guy in a natty green uniform, had probably survived countless informers, investigations, the secret police of many regimes by never getting excited and knowing exactly what to do. I could see he was aware of what he had, and the price would be high.

He wasn't in any hurry and insisted we both have coffee. Lorenzo gave me the eye and I knew we would have to go along with the old man's play. Over the coffee cups he gave us a vivid picture of how he had found Sarita savagely beaten in the shambles of her bedroom.

He made a point to murmur his appreciation of her

539

figure which he said was exquisite for a woman of her age. After he had described in detail the damage Joe's fists had done, he told us that on his own he had hired his cousin to drive the young maid back to her parents in Camagüey. When she was admitted to the hospital, Sarita had insisted on a private room and her own physician. But the sergeant hinted we should talk to the intern on duty who had revived her.

Lorenzo spent most of the night paying off the sergeant, the intern and the nurse who had been on duty when Sarita was admitted. He also drove to Camagüey and succeeded in persuading the maid to take a vacation at a relative's house in the interior—well paid, of course.

It was the familiar story when Joe came around: he had suffered a complete blackout, he wasn't aware of what he had done. He was shaking with both remorse and a hangover when I put him and Lorenzo on a plane for Miami.

All that sergeant could do, even for a staggering price, was delay sending his report to Havana Police Headquarters. I knew that once it reached the Russian's desk anything could happen.

I deliberately booked a reservation in Joe's name on a Pan American jet leaving the Havana airport for Mexico City, then used all my connections in the ABC Colony to hire a small private plane and an oil company's pilot to fly them out from Mantanzas.

I had Maxie at the airport and, as I suspected, the Russian and his plainclothesmen twice searched the Pan American plane before he allowed it to depart. He was in a foul mood when he stormed into our office at the hotel and it didn't ease our relationship when I informed him Joe was back in the States but he had turned over to me for safekeeping a certain little black book.

He left, shouting at me his favorite expression, something about never forgetting our loud music . . .

For the next few days Maxie and I sat back and held our breath; we had been in the islands too long not to know that no matter how much you pay, some Latin tongue will wag.

And it did. We almost heard the explosion in the Capitolio; it was louder than the morning Batista was informed some thief had stolen the famous diamond embedded in the lobby floor. For a time it appeared we might lose our casino license. Friendship or bribery didn't count with our Spanish cavaliers where a woman's honor was concerned.

No one could beat up a Castilian aristocrat and go unpunished—especially a Yankee.

Sarita saved us. A proud woman, she personally informed Batista no more was to be said about the matter, it had to be dropped at once. In a few weeks she slipped out of Cuba for Paris. We never heard from her again.

I believe that despite Sarita's intervention they would have lifted our license had they not been so concerned with Castro and his Rebels. In looking back, my first instinct is to curse Castro with a vengeance. If he had not appeared and we had been kicked out of Cuba, perhaps the future terrifying events would never have happened. Yet, even in hindsight, I must admit Castro wasn't to blame; it would have taken a hell of a lot more than a banana revolution to change our fates . . .

The affair stunned Chena, she couldn't believe it. What could I do, tell her it was true, that it had happened before? That I knew a dark stain of violence flowed deep in Joe? That while I knew it would happen again I was powerless to do anything about it? . . .

A few months later, Lorenzo returned to Havana with orders for me from the Table to return to New York: Maxie was to supervise the casinos with Lorenzo as his courier.

Chena and I spent a last bittersweet weekend at Mantanzas, racing each other on the deserted beach, wrestling in the surf, and doing a wild conga in the village bar to the concertina of our old driver. I only knew the last night how Chena felt. Just before dawn I wroke up to find her sitting at the window. I didn't know she had been crying until I kissed her.

"In the beginning I wanted to tell you, Chena, I didn't think we'd have much hope together."

"I wouldn't have listened, darling."

"It will be different back in the States."

"I don't care as long as I'm with you." She slipped into my arms. "What will you be doing?"

"I'm sure it will be the police union. Pepe's eager to get it going. Thank God, we'll see the last of the dice tables."

She shuddered lightly. "I don't know why but that police union frightens me."

"There's nothing to be frightened of, Chena. It's only

another union. Instead of coopers, this time it will be cops. What I hope to do is—"

"Look, darling!" she said softly, "our last sunrise here."

Within minutes the brilliant golden platter edged up over the rim of the sea to hang in the startling blue sky. A cool breeze softly toyed with the curtains, and the coiffured heads of the royal palms outside our window nodded sleepily. In a few hours we would close this house forever. . . .

On an impluse before we had left Havana, I slipped the Russian's notbook into my bag. After I packed our car, I returned to the beach house and taped the book behind a framed landscape that hung over the fireplace.

I smiled to myself as I locked the door for the last time; it appeared I had learned how to obey Maxie's warning always to keep something for insurance and to examine every angle.

It was a wrench to leave Maxie, but beyond him our friendships had been temporary; the big companies had always viewed Havana's ABC colony as a temporary assignment.

Waiting to board the Pan Am flight I found myself looking forward to New York; snow and spring, no more croupiers' bored voices over the clicking of roulette wheels, tumbling dice, or the hungry, disappointed faces of the tourists . . .

But I knew that something more important than snow and spring awaited me back in New York—cops.

I had told Chena it was just another union but I couldn't lie to myself. To organize America's policeman in one national union for ulterior motives was to carry a phial of nitroglycerin on a roller-coaster ride. . . .

BOOK 5

the blue messiah

49 THE FIST OF THE WATERFRONT

Among the first things I did after coming back to the city was to make a nostalgic tour of the Neighborhood with Joe. It hadn't changed physically, but its people had. Mixed with white faces were brown and black; along with the familiar Ninth Avenue New Yorkese were Puerto Rican, Cuban, and the softer Castilian accents.

As Pat, Regan's eternal bartender, summed up:

"It ain't the same, boys, too many foreigners."

"And every one on welfare," an old-timer added bitterly.

But Aunt Clara said it differently.

"The Neighborhood will always be the same, Frank, it will always be the place for poor people, white, black, brown, or yellow."

I had given up trying to persuade my aunt to leave the Neighborhood. She had retired from the library only because it was mandatory but two days later she triumphantly phoned Chena with the news she was now working for the government—librarian in the Veterans Hospital, three days a week. When we returned from

543

Cuba I discovered she not only drove but owned a second-hand car.

Our tenement also held a strange, disturbing surprise for me. That first day, after we had left Aunt Clara, Joe walked across the hall to his old flat, put the key in the lock, and swung open the door.

"How about some cocoa and buns, Frank?" he asked with a grin as he waved me in.

It was eerie walking through the rooms again. A chill ran up my back when I turned around in the kitchen to the old porcelain-top table and the chair by the window where Tom Gunnar used to sit. I half expected to see him there—young, smiling, vibrant, and full of promise. . . .

"Why this, Joe? Why do you still keep it? You have an apartment big as a barn on Central Park West that a hell of a lot of New Yorkers would give their eyeteeth to have."

"I don't know why—maybe sentimental reasons. It's always someplace to come to get out of the rat race . . ."

"I begged him to give up that flat, Frank," my aunt told me later. "You can't come back here, Joe. I told him again and again. You don't belong here anymore."

"What did he say to that?"

"He just put his arm around me and said, 'I'll always belong to the Neighborhood, Aunt Clara.' "

She paused, a worried look on her face. "Joe hasn't been the same boy since he came back from Cuba, Frank."

"What do you mean, Aunt Clara?"

"It's different things."

"Like what?"

"Well, one night I got up to go to the bathroom and I saw a light in the Gunnar kitchen. I couldn't for the life of me figure out who could be in there that time of the morning. It was Joe, sitting by the window, mumbling and cursing to himself . . ."

As my aunt spoke, a scene flashed across my mind; again as a child I was edging open the kitchen door of the Gunnar flat to find Joe, his face bruised and battered, staring with horrified fascination at his mother's nude body as his father beat and kicked her in a drunken fury.

"Was he drunk, Aunt Clara?"

"There was an empty whiskey bottle on the table. I helped him to the bed but there was one thing that kept me awake all night, Frank . . ."

"What was that?"

"He thought I was Mary—his mother."

"What about the next day? What did he say?"

"Nothing. When he came in I made him breakfast and we talked about the Neighborhood. When I asked him if he felt all right, he actually seemed surprised that I had asked the question!"

Soon after my return to the States, Joe, at contract time, persuaded the other locals—I am sure they were aware of the shadow of the gunmen at his back—to join him in a brutal, agonizing strike, the longest in the history of the national waterfronts. For weeks not a stick of cargo moved. When the Gulf and West Coast unions walked out in sympathy, the shippers were brought to their knees.

Typically, once Joe gained control of the waterfront he became bored and restless—he looked for new worlds to conquer. This time it was communications and computers. He proposed to organize a new union in these twin fields and, after winning approval from the Table, plunged into the new venture with wild enthusiasm and unsurpassed energy. He was constantly moving from state to state, absorbing every detail, and urging me to read books, pamphlets, and financial and government reports.

Joe had shrewdly forecast the American Age of Computers, and as companies mushroomed across the nation so did the union, until it was a dominating force in the industry.

I have before me a news magazine of that time with a stern picture of Joe and a column of quotes giving his views on the future of American labor. I must smile at one paragraph:

"The old-line trade and craft unions will have to wake up and get with it," the ruggedly handsome young labor leader said emphatically, "there are new voices in American labor calling out today—not the usual demands of plumbers, carpenters, electricians, longshoremen. If you listen closely you will hear the voices of teachers, firemen, policemen, sanitation workers, municipal employees—the gallant, forgotten nobodies, who have been taken for granted so long by both the public and the cigar-smoking fatcats in the AFL and CIO. It's these new voices that interest me . . . brother, when these people pull a strike your town will wake up! That's when you will realize you must give 'em more than a cigar or an apple for Christmas . . ."

Was he talking about a police strike? Gunnar only winked.

Maxie sent me a clipping of the article from Havana with a note: "How do you like this, Frank? Joe sounds like John L. Lewis and Samuel Gompers rolled into one! That's good stuff about the cops!"

It should be, I told myself. When we heard the news magazine had assigned a researcher to Joe, I wrote out the quotes. . . .

Following the success of the waterfront strike and through the power of the Table, Joe was appointed head of the Joint Board of Waterfront Unions; his power on the East Coast became unquestionable. The men idolized him and the hierarchy of the AFL and CIO feared but respected him. He was Mr. Big in American Labor—The Fist of the Waterfront, someone called him. Jimmy Hoffa, who was then making his own way in the teamsters, said, "Joe Gunnar speaks my language." As I told Joe, I didn't know whether that was good or bad.

By now the central payoff system had become an integral part of certain important segments of the police department. Even the death of Inspector Cornell had failed to produce any major disruption. After Hennessy informed me of who in each precinct was on the pad, we held a meeting to select the likeliest member of the brass as a candidate to replace Cornell. A new contact, as cold, greedy, and cynical as Cornell, was easily found.

Only one man threatened the stability of our system—Elliott. As chief inspector he formed a Special Rackets Investigative Unit and successfully persuaded the FBI—whom the New York police traditionally regarded as a goody-good competitor—Treasury Enforcement, and police departments across the nation, to join what the newspapers called "Elliott's crime cooperative." The group distributed to its members pooled information on organized crime. Unfortunately, the New York County DA's office was honest and efficient. Teamed with Elliott's squad, they presented a formidable menace.

I had been back in the city only a short time when Elliott publicly announced that the policy racket in Harlem, the South Bronx, and Bedford Stuyvesant could exist only with the connivance of crooked police, and he intended to break up that alliance. He inaugurated a crash program of recruiting more black policemen and assigning them to Harlem.

We were uneasy at first, but Hennessy laughed off our fears. "What are you worryin' about, for crissakes?!" he asked me with a rumbling laugh. "Sure they're black but let 'em put on that uniform and they'll be white in a week."

Elliott doggedly continued to fight. He made some dents in the system, but Pepe's organizational genius aided by Hennessy and our network of crooked cops not only defeated him but allowed us to expand.

It was an unfair war; we had two advantages, we knew the enemy and we selected our weapons and our battle-grounds. Elliott, angry and frustrated, fought blindly against a foe that was shadowy.

He caught a few cops with their hands in the till and insisted that the evidence against them be turned over to the DA's office for grand jury investigation. It was a new weapon and the cops didn't like it. But they scrupulously observed their own code of silence and even accepted prison terms rather than talk.

When the tempo of Elliott's raids increased, Pepe criss-crossed the areas of the drops with lookouts equipped with walkie-talkies, all linked to a central post in a tenement. The instant Hennessy flashed word of a raid, the flat was alerted. Within seconds the lookouts hurried up and down the streets waving a rolled newspaper, the signal to the guards at the windows of the drops.

"No play ... no play" was whispered from stoop to stoop. When Elliott's raiders appeared, the store where the drop had been located would be selling candy.

When the black numbers syndicates organized and kid-napped one of our best ribbon men in an attempt to intimidate the East Harlem banks for a piece of the action, Pepe's answer was swift and savage.

Two of the black leaders immediately disappeared; their tortured, mutilated bodies were later flung into the bar-room where they had made their headquarters. Then the next day Pepe quietly called the blacks together and offered them a generous slice of the territory which they quickly accepted.

"First it was the Irish gangsters, Peppino," he explained to me, "then the Jews, then the Italians. It will only be a

547

question of time before the coloreds get a taste of the numbers." His voice hardened. "But not with the gun! When they do that we first shove it up their black *cula*, then we sit and talk." He shrugged. "This way they still know who's boss. But it is not wise to be greedy. We give them something and instead of enemies they become our friends—*chi sputo a cièlo da fáccia venuta*—who spits in the sky gets it in the face . . . *ai capito*, Peppino?"

Another of Pepe's innovations in the numbers racket is used to this day. He ordered the large, unwieldy policy territories broken down into smaller areas and set up so they could vanish in a matter of minutes and re-form just as quickly. Most of the operations were transferred to hideouts in middle cellars of blocks of tenements where holes were made in the walls to provide a cellar network for escape. When the lookout stationed in the hall above was alerted by the walkie-talkie-equipped runner in the street that raiders were on their way, he whistled a warning. The operation in the cellar was quickly shaken down, equipment such as adding machines, ledgers, and boxes of plays divided among the staff, which promptly scattered, to regroup again in another cellar a few blocks away. Here the "counters," responsible for the amount of money played on each number, resumed work. In this fashion the precious ribbon, the record of the day's play, could be turned over to East Harlem's ribbon man and taken to the bank in time for the first number.

Pepe was also aware that the community's economic life depended in a large part on the numbers racket, so he wisely ordered the East Harlem bank to set aside a small portion of each day's play to be loaned to any Harlem businessman who found himself in temporary financial straits.

"Who knows, Peppino?" Pepe said. "Someday we may need those coloreds. We lend them a little money and they pay us back. Maybe they whisper in our ear at the right time, no?"

His shrewdness soon paid off. One restaurant owner who was saved from bankruptcy by numbers money had a brother-in-law who worked in the DA's office. His whisper allowed one of Pepe's favorite bankers to take a vacation to Italy before a grand jury subpoena could be served.

Pepe also made sure our rackets elected the right politicians—even congressmen. In one election, a candidate who kept crying reform in Harlem was defeated overwhelmingly. He and his followers were stunned, and political analysts bewildered. They could never understand the reason for their man's defeat: it was all because of a brilliant stroke by Pepe.

After Hennessy told me that the candidate was promising reform groups a congressional investigation of the numbers racket and official corruption, I warned Pepe that it could be disastrous if the man won. . . .

We were sitting in his gallery office. He was studying an art catalog and, for a moment, I thought he hadn't understood the impact of my information. Then, without lifting his head, he said:

"We will give the coloreds a free play, Peppino." He held up a finger. "One dollar. No cut numbers . . ."

"For doing what, Pepe?"

He looked at me in mock amazement. "For registering and voting against that *figlio di butana! Sangue della patata!* We cannot let him win!"

On Election Day runners well known in the neighborhoods drove voters to the polls; each drop provided babysitters. The candidate the cops wanted defeated was defeated. His supporters never knew what hit them, and Harlem never told its secret.

One day, shortly after my return and just before a Table was to be held. I had a conference with Pepe at the gallery, now regarded as one of the finest in the city. I was shocked when he casually informed me that secret strategy meetings were now held by the various groups before every Table, and that he was having Grossi, his protégé, and even Tony Cupid tailed day and night before it convened.

"You look surprised, Peppino," he said with a faint smile.

"My God, why? I thought these people were your old friends."

"*Va!* What friends? That's the world, *giovinotto!* Who can you trust in our business?"

I asked him bluntly. "Me—do you still trust me?"

"I will always trust you, Peppino," he said quickly. "You. Joe. The lawyer."

"Why trust us and not the others?"

"*Marrone!*" he said in mock anger and immigrant English, "Pepe, he makea da mistake—" Then he suddenly reached over and gripped my hand. "Peppino, *tu sei un*

549

mio figlio ... you are a son to me. ... I will always trust you."

"Gus is not good," he added abruptly. "I must protect our interests."

I was surprised. "Gus? What's wrong with him?"

He held an imaginary glass to his lips.

"*Umbriaccone*. He drinks like a fish and plays around with the show girls." He sighed. "That bastardo downtown—"

"Elliott?"

"Si. *Malvágio!* Very bad. He likes to smell around. *Ai capito?*"

"Is Elliott or the DA after Gus?" I asked him.

He took a folder of clippings from a desk drawer and silently handed them to me. There were several not particularly explosive stories about Gus and the Shadow Box, mostly feature interviews by a well-known Broadway columnist on the early days of Prohibition and how the mobs had operated on the West Side.

"This is history, Pepe," I told him. "I bet it's half lies."

"*Si*. The old days. But if he talks like this to that *figilo di butana* who writes for the newspaper what will happen if they get him before a grand jury?" He slowly closed the folder and put it back into the desk drawer. "He drinks. Maybe he can't help it, but the others are beginning to talk. 'Duchino,' I told him, "throw away the bottle . . . kick those whores out of your office . . . be a man.' "

"What did he say?"

He shrugged. "He still has the bottle and the whores." He asked abruptly, "Does he see Chena, Peppino?"

"No. She won't even talk to him on the phone."

"Maybe it would be good if she would see him."

"I can't force her, Pepe."

. . "*Ecco!* Be an Italian husband!" He cried, "The woman, they do what you say—" He slapped his raised arm. "*Pirapa nel cula!*"

As I rose to leave, he insisted on escorting me to the door. It was clear there was something else on his mind.

"It is very bad, Peppino," he said softly.

"What is bad, Pepe?"

"Gus! He endangers us all. No? Something must be done. . . ."

Before I could reply he smiled, his face brightened, and he hugged me around the shoulders.

550

"Addio! Go with God, *figlio mio!"*

When I left Pepe I was disturbed. Had he summoned me to the gallery to tell me that Gus had to go, had to be killed? The thought stunned me.

On the way home that afternoon I impulsively stopped off at the Shadow Box. While it was still a fine-looking club, I sensed a kind of tawdriness that had not been there before. The silverware seemed less shiny, the tablecloths appeared wrinkled, the flowers plastic and dusty, the waiters arrogant or indifferent.

I had not seen Gus in over a year. From the moment I entered his office it was evident he had been drinking heavily: he had put on a great deal of weight, his eyes were bloodshot, his hands trembled. When we shook hands I could smell the whiskey on his breath.

I didn't stay long. We joked about my failure to produce some grandchildren for him. He elaborately praised the Cuban operation. Then, almost as an afterthought, he asked about Chena.

"How's that crazy kid of mine? Okay?"

"Chena's fine, Gus. She put on quite a show the other day—she discovered a gray hair . . ."

"How do you like that?" he said slowly. "Maybe some night you bring her over to the club for dinner? We have a great show, kid."

"Sure, Gus. I'll give you a call."

"She okay?"

"Chena? She's as healthy as a horse."

"Buòno! Buòno! You tell her I was askin' for her . . ."

We were shaking hands when I asked him. "Have you heard from Nicky, Gus?"

He dropped my hand and looked down at his desk as he fumbled with some papers.

"Yeah. I hear from time to time through our friends over there. He's doin' okay."

That night I asked Chena if she wanted to accept her father's invitation.

"A long time ago, darling, I made myself a promise never to see or speak to him again," she said softly. "Never."

That was the last time I mentioned her father's name to her.

In the early 1950s we kept an eye on Kefauver and discovered paradoxically the value of communism and patriotism. As Joe said, wave the flag hard enough and you can steal city hall.

When Pepe was tipped by a contact in Washington that Kefauver was prepared to come into the city with his entourage of TV cameras, feverish investigators, and sheafs of subpoenas, the Table decided a diversion was needed. Joe found it in a Russian freighter that had arrived at a West Side pier. He tied up the waterfront by ordering the coopers not to handle the Russian's cargo. He made a marvelous speech in a TV news interview about Americanism and the unending struggle against the threat of communism. From somewhere I recalled Washington's famous order, "Put only Americans on guard tonight," and that became the rallying cry on the waterfront.

Joe McCarthy's committee was in session when the strike was called so, naturally, the senator invited Joe to come to Washington to testify. Joe couldn't get down there fast enough.

To show his gratitude, McCarthy was our guest speaker at a mass waterfront Americanization rally attended by every nut that we could find who owned a flag. We presented the senator with an enormous plaque, a sizable check for his next campaign, and an impressive chunk of publicity.

In return, he canonized us and our crooked unions for a gallant fight against the infiltration of foreign agents into the American labor movement and made a bangup speech on the floor of the House; copies of the *Congressional Record* were sent to us. I had Spider and Train run off thousands. Each union member received one: his sprig of laurel to commemorate the role he played in the fierce campaign to save his country from the Red Menace.

Kefauver had all the trappings but we could only view him and his committee with contempt. Costello's hands, an assortment of small-time politicians with their fingers caught in the public till, and a gallery of colorful but insignificant hoods took the rap for all of us.

There were a great many fervent promises "to smash the back" of organized crime syndicates—how many times did you read this phrase in the 1950s?—yet there was never a hint of the Table, its power, or the extent of its operations.

In that period, money was no problem. We had plenty and more came in every day from the unions, the companies we owned, and the weekly payoff we skimmed from the cream we fed the police. When the Table voted to raise the pad, we shared the benefits.

While in Cuba, we had discovered a way to beat the IRS. Maxie set up a system by which we funneled our cash out of the island into the States and across to Europe. Accounts were opened in a private Miami bank. Then each month, after we had made a deposit, the bank issued its own draft for the amount which they sent to Zurich to be deposited in our numbered account.

Joe's foresight had also fattened our bank accounts. As the communications industry and our union prospered, he suggested we buy out a small Westchester County communications and computer supply company. With the boom in national computerization the company's revenues doubled, then tripled.

When we were not traveling, Chena and I found it difficult to adjust to the city's harsh, gray life. After a short time in a series of hotel suites, we played the New Yorker's favorite game: apartment roulette. Finally we discovered a charming and very expensive duplex near the Museum of Modern Art. Our first blistering summer in the city sent us hunting for a summer place. We found it on Fishers Island in the Sound off New London.

Lonely Isabella Beach, with its miles of sand and rugged cliffs, reminded us so much of Mantanzas we fell in love with it and bought a stunning ranch house.

On the day of the closing we stood on the patio, the real estate agent by our side, looking out to sea. I noticed an old-fashioned, sun-bleached clapboard house with many turrets and verandas rising out of the marsh grass and asked the agent who lived there.

"Oh, that belongs to one of the Du Ponts," she replied in her best finishing-school accent. "They're very nice."

Well, that's Democracy for you, I thought. Mr. and Mrs. Frank Howell, late of the Neighborhood and the gambling casinos of Cuba, meet the awfully nice people, the Du Ponts.

50 THE GROUNDWORK

With Joe deep in his waterfront and communications unions, I concentrated on the preliminary steps for the formation of a national police union. At the first Table held on my return, the project was formalized and $250,-000 approved—over Sally G's groans—for initial expenses.

I was instructed to do a pilot study and report back in a year with my findings. Every member of the Table was to supply contacts—corrupt police, politicians, labor leaders, businessmen—anyone who could open a door and let me probe their police departments.

I decided to start in the East and move West. I first selected a city that would be representative of the large upstate communities. This was Grossi's territory and, as I told Pepe, I hesitated to approach this stiff, prim man who lived so successfully in two worlds—a banker, almost Victorian in his lifestyle but a man who could match Pepe for cunning and ferocity when it came to self-survival. Yet, like all of them, I found him a coldly realistic man. He had fought vigorously against the idea of a national police union. But once the plan had been approved, he informed Pepe he would do everything in his power to help me prepare an objective analysis. At a brief meeting in the gallery it was decided that Utica would be our pivotal city in the East.

"I'm telling you, Sortino," he said waving a finger at Pepe, "I will do everythin' to help but if I see that it endangers us all I will speak up."

"Speak up. Speak up, my friend!" Pepe exclaimed.

"*Va! Va!*" Grossi said, pointing to one ear, then the other, "it goes in here and comes out the other side."

However, on the train ride up the Hudson he proved to be a pleasant companion who even made the historical trivia he had collected on points of interest along the route sound interesting.

554

When I told him I knew nothing about Utica, he began a lengthy description of how the Table dominated the community through corrupt police, businessmen, and politicians.

"Three years ago we had little smell of reform in the city. I didn't think it was anythin' serious so I made a mistake, I let it go. The day after Election Day I woke up to find the reformers had elected a young eager beaver for DA. He started in like a whirlwind, bustin' up all our games and raisin' hell. Then one of our cops tipped me this guy had put a bug on my bank phone. So I called Sortino who sent up a guy who checked my phone. Sure enough, there was the bug. So what do I do? I go over to his office and put it up to him.

" 'What the hell is this? I ask him. 'I own the biggest bank upstate. I got millions out in loans to businessmen in this community. I go to church every Sunday. When there's a Holy Name parade—who do you see in front with the monsignor? Sally Grossi! What about you, Mr. DA? What the hell have you ever done for this community?' " He smiled at the memory. "The bastardo just sat there, his mouth openin' and closin' like a dyin' fish."

" 'Who told you I had a bug on your phone, Mr. Grossi?' he said. 'My friends down in Albany,' I told him. 'Maybe the same friends that's gonna make you state senator next year. But only if I say so.' Then I walked out."

"I waited until the next day, then I had Sortino's boy give my line another check. The bug was gone."

"What happened with the DA?"

He arched his eyebrows. "He's our state senator. A good boy."

"How about the cops?"

"No trouble," he said. "Tomorrow I show you how it works up here."

He insisted I stay as his overnight guest. His house was old and set back behind towering hedges and surrounded on all sides by majestic elms. I felt as if I was entering a carefully dusted museum; there were hideous bronze maids with flower baskets and Arabs on rearing horses. An enormous rosewood grand piano dominated what he called the "music room," along with more bronzes and a bric-a-brac cabinet. A fading angel painted on one side of the wall reached out to give us benediction. But it was obvious his "library" was his pride. A floor to ceiling bookcase held collections of expensively tooled leather-bound volumes of Dickens, Hardy, Defoe, Gibbon. I slid one out only to discover that there were no pages, only a book spine and its hard covers.

"I got a friend who owns a book bindery," he explained. "Every year he sends up a new batch. Looks good, doesn't it? Like my sister says, you can get worms in books. Too much paper."

Grossi was a widower and his sister, elderly, morose and silent, was his housekeeper. We had a sedate drink in the "library" and then, while Grossi phoned his bank officials, I walked about the neighborhood. All the houses were similar; big, old, rambling, and surrounded by lawns and ancient trees.

The next morning a black Cadillac appeared promptly at eight; the driver was Grossi's stooge.

"We're goin' to a funeral," Grossi announced as we settled back.

"A funeral?"

He looked pleased that he had me perplexed. "I want you to meet our police chief. He's providin' an escort for someone."

"Oh, someone prominent in town died?"

His driver laughed and slapped the wheel. "How do you like that, Sally?"

Grossi ignored him. "Have you ever heard of Albert Anastasia?"

"The mobster? Only what I've read. Wasn't he in that Brooklyn Murder, Inc., setup?"

"Albert is in a lot of things," Grossi explained. "We have occasion to use his talents sometime. Not too often, mind you—"

"Al's nuts, Sally!" his driver blurted out. "He's crazy! He's makin' a lot of trouble. I told Pepe only yesterday—"

Grossi said shortly, "Don't worry about it. Sortino and I have discussed Albert." He turned to me. "He'll be with our police chief . . . it's as good a place to meet him as any."

"The police chief with Anastasia in a cemetery?"

"Let me explain. A member of Albert's family who has lived here for a long time died a few days ago and he came up to attend the funeral—"

"But what has the police chief got to do with it?"

"Sortino was advised that some Brooklyn shooters were following Albert up to Utica to make sure he joined his relative in the grave." He said firmly, "We don't want any of that up here. It would give us all a bad name." He added with a thin smile, "Sortino has promised to take care of Albert. But all in good time."

We entered the cemetery through a rear entrance and drove along winding roads until we came to the base of a small hill. I followed Grossi up a graveled path to a clump of trees on the hill's peak. Below us stretched out a green sea of the dead with shoals of marble shafts, square granite slabs, and stone mausoleums. A funeral procession was entering the main gate.

"He's on time," Grossi murmured. He said to his stooge, "Go down and tell the chief we'll see him up here."

The driver hurried to the Cadillac. In a few minutes, it emerged on the road below us and joined the procession of cars that finally halted alongside a fresh grave under a canopy that billowed and rippled in the crisp fall breeze.

"Watch this," Grossi commanded.

From the lead funeral car attendants escorted an elderly weeping woman to the canopy.

"The *madre*," Grossi said sympathetically, "a wonderful woman. She came over with my mother from the other side." He paused, then nudged me. Two men in plainclothes had jumped from one of the cars to stand guard at the entrance to the canopy. Then several others surrounded a stocky man in a pearl gray hat and topcoat who stepped out of a limousine. He paused, looked up and down, and said something to one of the men. In a tight circle they all walked to the gravesite. When the brief service was finished, the circle of men slowly moved back to the car.

"Well, that's that," Grossi said, plainly relieved.

"That was Anastasia?"

"The same Albert," he said grimly. "That crazy *bastanza!*"

"And those guards?"

"Cops! The best on our force." He slapped me on the shoulder. "You asked me about our cops—well, this is how we own 'em . . ."

"And the police chief?"

"His name is Cole—Elmer Cole. He tries to make you believe he's a farmer." He shook his head. "He fools a lot of people around here but he never fooled me. *Animale! Béstia!* He'd cut your throat for a dollar!"

"Can he be trusted?"

"Only as far as you can see him. But don't worry, we pay him good. As long as he gets the dinero he'll do whatever we ask him to do." He shrugged. "Use him any way you want . . ." He looked around at the sound of an approaching car. "Here he comes now."

The Cadillac was followed by a battered old Buick. When it stopped, the driver, a stout man in his fifties, jumped out and hurried toward us.

"Mr. Grossi! I dropped by the bank yesterday but you were out."

I judged Chief Cole to be in his sixties. He had shrewd, cold gunmetal eyes, but a mound of graying curls and a round, weather-beaten face made him look like a friendly old farmer.

"I was out to the farm over the weekend," he explained, "and I brought you a basket of apples. Good crop this year." He studied me with open curiosity. "Who do we have here, Mr. Grossi?"

"This is a friend of mine," Grossi said coldly, "a *particular* friend of mine from New York City. I want you to help him in any way possible."

"Sure. Sure. Any special area?"

"The police department."

The gunmetal eyes studied me. "Oh? And what in the police department, may I ask?"

I didn't see any reason for pussyfooting with this character.

"The good guys and the bad guys—and the in-between guys," I told him. "I want to know those who jump when we tell them and those who don't."

"Well now, that won't be too hard," he said carefully, packing a corncob pipe and shielding the flame of the wooden match from the wind. "When do you want to start?"

"Now," Grossi said.

"Fine." He looked at Grossi. "Was what you saw okay, Mr. Grossi?"

Grossi gestured to his driver. "The envelope will be dropped off tonight at your back door the same as usual."

"Good. The fellow we just left—"

"Albert?"

"That's the one. He took care of the boys." He gave Sally a sharp look.

"You look unhappy, Mr. Grossi."

"I heard what happened Saturday night from one of my people," Grossi said coldly. "You're a goddam fool, Chief, if you don't crack down on those idiots. Do you want to get the town up around our ears?"

Cole looked worried. "I know. I know. I talked to 'em real good yesterday. I told 'em, once more and they're out."

"Once more and they're out," Grossi mocked him in disgust. Turning to me he explained, "Some bums downtown have been runnin' a penny ante game and they won't kick in. So you know what these goddam cops did? Two of 'em shot the operator—from a police car! *Marrone!* How stupid can you be?" He shook his head in despair. "Fortunately there were only two witnesses; one was a whore we hustled out of town, the other owns a saloon, so he knows if he doesn't keep his mouth shut we'll lift his liquor license. But suppose one of those law and order guys saw it? What then?"

"Okay, Mr. Grossi, I see your point," Cole said hastily, "I really see it. I'll talk hard to those boys—"

"Talk hard! You tell 'em if they get out of line someone from Manhattan will pay 'em a visit." He nodded to me. "Make sure you give my friend everythin' he wants. Everythin'. Understand?"

"I will . . . I sure will, Mr. Grossi."

"I suggest it might be better if you stay at the hotel from now on," Grossi said to me, "if you want anything just call the bank and say Mr. Lawrence is callin'. Here's my private number."

He scribbled a number on a scrap of paper, shook hands with me, nodded coldly to the chief, and walked to the Cadillac with his stooge hurrying before him to open the door. In a few minutes they were gone.

"Whew!" Cole said tapping out his pipe. "Sally can be tough when he wants to!"

"What the hell made those stupid cops do a thing like that?"

"They were drunk. They were at Fanny's all night, and they got tanked up."

"Did they kill anyone?"

"Naw!" He looked disgusted. "That's the least they could have done. But they were so drunk they only nicked him in the leg. I had to go down and talk to the son of a bitch to make sure he told the troopers he didn't see who it was." He added confidentially, "It took some talkin'. I had to promise we wouldn't touch him for the next year. That really galls me—sure as hell the other guys who are payin' will put up a beef . . ."

"What does he operate?"

"He has a game goin' on now for a year. But look, young feller, this ain't what you came up to our fair city for, is it? What do you want to know about our cops?"

"As Mr. Grossi said, I would like to know everything."

"Suppose we sit in my car . . . this damn wind . . ."

We talked for hours. When the sun came up and warmed the morning, we left the car to wander about the tombstones, with Cole interrupting his descriptions of his crooked police by pointing out ancient graves and reciting the history of each old family. He told me proudly that his ancestors had been among the earliest frontier settlers; one had been captured by the Senecas during the Revolution but escaped to return to fight in the bloody Mohawk Valley.

I made a complete list of the crooked and honest cops in his department. When I asked him whether they would go out on strike if they were ordered to, he stared at me.

"Go out on strike? Cops?"

"With picket signs—the whole bit."

"I guess if we told 'em to, they'd walk out." He chuckled. "If we told 'em to jump in the lake they would do it—if the price was right."

"Don't worry about the price, it will be right."

He smiled, but the gunmetal eyes were cold and knowing.

"I'm sure it will be, mister."

After we had dissected the Utica police department among the tombstones, Cole drove me into the city for lunch.

"Suppose we have a drink first at Fanny's?"

I accepted.

Fanny's, a clapboard, two-family house on a side street, turned out to be the largest whorehouse in town. Fanny, the madam, was a gay peroxide blonde who served us a drink from a bar in the front room and broke off exchanging dirty jokes with the chief only to answer the doorbell and escort her customers upstairs.

"Fanny's been up here ten . . . no more'n fifteen years," he explained. "She runs a good place." He nudged me and
560

laughed. "Some of our best citizens come up on Saturday nights to look over the new arrivals!"

"You never have any trouble?"

"Well, the church people get their backs up every once in a while, so we just call Fanny and tell her to take a vacation. When it blows over we tell her to come back . . ."

"How's the rake-off?"

"Can't complain," he said. "Fanny's generous, I can say that."

"I understand you have a good layoff setup here . . ."

He chuckled. "Up here in Utica we have over a hundred and fifty industries, but I always maintain the best one's gamblin'. We have lots of folks comin' here for a quiet game. We don't have any crooked games. If I heard of any"—he made a violent gesture with one hand—"out they go!"

I stared at him, speechless. If I hadn't heard it, I would not have believed what he said.

"No trouble with the games I guess?" I managed to ask.

"Only once, a few years ago," was his grim answer. "The gateman at one of the games tipped off a couple of heist men from out of town. They hit the game and slapped one of the boys around." He was silent for a moment. "The local people took care of the gateman and the stickup artists never got a chance to spend their dough." He shook his head and sighed. "It takes all kinds, have you found that out yet, young feller?"

"It certainly does," I said fervently, "it certainly does."

I stayed in Utica for a week, completely fascinated by Cole's unabashed account of the Utica police department and its relationship to the community. I came to one obvious conclusion: the Table owned the city, the cops, the whores, the gambling, and even the people.

My stay was so successful Grossi suggested I visit several other upstate cities—all of which were under his control. The pervasiveness of corruption and criminality amazed me. I saw how the Table operated unions in these cities; charters for locals were granted by one man—who reported to Grossi every Monday morning. Law enforcement was laughable. Our contact in one police department said they gave the gambling spots "at least" one hour to shut down before a raid.

"We have a few goody-goodies," the captain said, "and when we get word they're goin' out to bust up a place we just call and they shut down. We have a citizens' group that screams, usually before election. When they do, the boys take a vacation to Miami or Vegas. Before you know it, it's business as usual again. How long can an ordinary guy afford to be indignant? Who wants to listen to the same goddam sermon Sunday after Sunday? And besides, half the guys who are listenin' are bettors!"

When I returned to New York I met with Joe and Pepe in the gallery and spent an evening going over the material I had collected.

"*Marrone!*" Pepe said. "They are bigger thieves than we are."

It was Pepe's suggestion that I visit a midwestern city to see if I could strike a balance. We selected the city of Loraine in western Illinois. After Pepe had made some contacts with a Teamsters' local, I spent a week out there.

Driving the car that met me at the airport was the Teamster delegate and the city's commissioner of finance, who made Chief Cole look like an unsophisticated rural crook. Loraine's gambling operations—horse rooms, policy, crap and card games—brought in millions every year to the Table. When I asked how well they controlled the police, the commissioner only laughed and left the room. He returned with a manila envelope filled with betting sheets and policy ribbons.

"This is the state's evidence against one of our big operators," he said, grinning. "The night before his trial last month, one of the boys slipped into the chief's office, opened his safe, and removed the evidence. So what was the result? Our lawyers screamed when the state couldn't produce the evidence and the judge had to throw out the indictment."

"Tell him about Joey Grapes," the Teamster delegate suggested.

"Joey Grapes is the nickname of a Greek who runs our biggest game in the south ward. He's good. Take Joey Grapes away and we're dead. Last year they voted in this reform group who hired a new police chief—some guy who headed a crime committee in the East. This new guy busted Joey on aiding and abetting a lottery. We couldn't reach the jury and they came in with a guilty verdict. Joe got a year and a half."

He held up three fingers. "He went to the pen for three days, then we got him out on a writ."

"We found Joey's rights had been violated," the delegate said with a straight face.

"Yeah. A phony search warrant," the commissioner added, "based on hearsay evidence. When the hearing took place, the state's assistant Attorney General got up and said he had to agree with the defense."

"It was a toss-out," the Teamster said gleefully, "right out the window."

"Yeah. It was a hell of a toss for us—twenty grand!" the commissioner said.

"You reached the assistant A G?"

"Who else?" the delegate asked.

"What about your cops?"

"You know the guy who I said slipped the evidence out of the chief's office? He's a lieutenant. You'll meet him tomorrow—right here," the commissioner said.

The next day I met the police lieutenant. Once the commissioner assured him he could talk freely, he spent most of the day detailing for me the Loraine police department. With a few exceptions it was for sale, and we had a ninety-nine-year lease.

"Do you know we're gonna have a new police chief next month?" the commissioner asked me.

When I shook my head he went on. "This bum who's been bustin' up the games for the past year finally kept bustin' until he got what he wanted—a seventy-five-thousand-dollar home in Miami, a cruiser, and the city council to vote him a pension of three-quarters disability pay. Next month he's suddenly gonna have a heart attack. After about three weeks he'll resign. Poor health. How do you like that?"

The Teamster said solemnly, "Wanna know somethin'? You can't trust anyone these days."

When I explored Loraine I found it to be a middle-sized city with flourishing industry, wealth, and culture and yet a city controlled and manipulated by the Table. It had a university with almost ten thousand students, its own symphony orchestra, a nationally known art museum, and an underworld empire that brought in over six million dollars a year in gambling.

Its main industry was a mill which supplied the major Midwestern steel companies. Loraine's population of 250,-000 was easily doubled, as a proud spokesman for the local Chamber of Commerce told me, in peak holiday shopping seasons.

Ironically, it was also known as the safest city in the United States. Outside of the city hall was a towering traffic barometer. When a red light indicated a highway death, the entire community was plunged into mourning. Yet there had been twenty-two unsolved gangland murders in the last two years alone.

"When we came in here we had to swing our weight around," the delegate later told me. "What the hell, the city doesn't care. 'Let 'em knock off each other' is all they say . . ."

Numbers were as big in Loraine as in Harlem, Brownsville, or Bedford Stuyvesant because the conditions were the same: a large ghetto area comprised not only of blacks but of Hungarians, Poles, and Russians who had immigrated in waves to the mills after World War II.

The geographical layout of Loraine was important in case of a police strike: the city was midway on all the major turnpikes, and was less than a hundred miles from major Midwestern cities.

When I asked the lieutenant what would happen if a delegate from our police union started recruiting, he shrugged and asked:

"Do you want 'em to join?"

"That's why I'm here."

"Then they'll join," he said promptly. "Not everyone, but we can get a good hunk of the department to sign up."

"What happens if they were told to walk out—strike?"

He whistled through his teeth. "Strike? A police strike in Loraine?" He shook his head. "If those hunkies down in the south ward get drunk and start lookin' for blacks, they'll be in trouble!" He whistled again. "We work with the turnpikes—they'll have to shut down. No truck deliveries. The mill will close. The city will be shut tighter'n a drum! But if that's the way you want it . . ."

"That's the way we want it," I told him.

In New York I opened a small office on lower Broadway, where Hennessy could meet me periodically and update my material on the New York City police department. Instinctively I was afraid of Elliott. It was simple logic: if I could sense the potentially explosive situation among the nation's police, so could he. I would have been a blind fool to ignore the simple facts: he was in a better position than I not only to gauge the temper of his New York police but of departments across the nation. Police were his business and he was damn good at it.

I explained all this to Hennessy. I insisted he concentrate on developing a leak in the headquarters' high command, not the member of the brass we had on our pad, but someone close to Elliott. The man was incredible; it took him less than a month before he appeared in our tiny office grinning triumphantly.

"I think I got what you want."

"A leak?"

"Right in his goddam office! A young captain who has too many kids and a big mortgage."

"How did you get to him?"

"The guy down at headquarters who's working with us. He heard this captain had problems, so they went out a few times. He finally came around. It cost me five Gs for openers but it will be worth it. I even got a little somethin' to sweeten the milk."

He pushed a folded sheaf of papers across the desk: a confidential order from Elliott to an inspector selecting his precinct as a pivotal subject for a special riot control study. The orders were specific; they detailed men and equipment.

"How can we check this out?" I said. "Let's make sure it's not a phony."

He looked pained. "Do you think I'm a jerk? I did that already."

"How?"

"I got to the inspector's driver. We met last night. He showed me the original of the order and said the project started last week."

"Will this captain continue to feed us?"

"Every few weeks—as long as we pay him." He raised his hamlike hand. "Now this guy can't come up with somethin' new every week."

"I understand. Let him give us anything he can get."

Hennessy's contact next informed us of Elliott's countermoves against corruption in the department. After a whispered call from Hennessy, we were reading a detailed confidential order to all precinct commanders in ghetto areas ordering them to establish a neighborhood civilian complaint bureau—a "Mini Bitching Bureau," in the street cops' contemptuous term.

I should have smelled something. While Hennessy's contact had supplied him with all the details, they were the same details that appeared in a *Times* story a few days

later, taken from the department's publicity release ...
what if we had it first?

I can see now I was too preoccupied with the national
scene. My surveys of the larger city departments were
beginning to give me an insight into the plus and minus of
the tremendous task that faced us. As the months passed I
continued to select communities of varied population
growths in the Deep South and Far West—all in the
domain of members of the Table—to complete my pivotal
study.

At the end of the year I reported to the Table that
corruption appeared to be a way of life among some
segments of police personnel in major American cities and
I was sure this weakness in national law enforcement
could be a vital help to our plans.

My findings were favorably received. At Pepe's urging,
the Table approved a proposal that I devote all of my
time to the national police union. Only Grossi remained
dubious.

"I don't know," he said slowly as we left the meeting
room, "I still say it has a hell of a lot of dangers and
headaches ..."

In the beginning I simply did missionary work, seeking
out the contacts supplied to me by the members of the
Table. For the next few years Chena and I traveled about
the country, visiting almost every large city where I conferred with politicians, corrupt police, and crooked labor
officials—after a contact had first been made by the Table's member who controlled the territory I was visiting.

Chena and I explored the country, north, south, east,
and west. We loved traveling, we were alone—with the
exception of the shabby depressing meetings I had—and
we found the experience exhilarating.

After I had talked to about every crooked, evil contact
the Table maintained, I divided the country into blocks of
four states, twelve in all, and selected a block as our
target for each year. During that year Chena and I leisurely traveled through each of the four states, while I
cultivated, analyzed, and gleaned information from police
in rural and urban areas. There was no hard sell; my role
was simply a doctoral candidate researching his dissertation on the police forces in the United States.

I had with me at all times an attaché case filled with
photostats of police reports, documents, law enforcement
566

studies, and the newspaper accounts of the Boston Police Strike of 1919. The British Museum had also furnished me with stats of the press accounts of the earlier London and Liverpool police strikes. This material not only authenticated my purpose but proved to be far more effective than any phony credentials.

I was constantly amazed at the ignorance, not only of the police I met but public officials and labor leaders; few if any had ever heard of the police strikes; my glib knowledge and mass of photostats never failed to impress them. It loosened their tongues much more than they realized.

There is little use of detailing the years that followed. When Chena grew weary of traveling, I would take along Spider and Train, grooming them for what I knew would eventually be roles in our police unionization movement.

At least once a year I reported to the Table on what I had accomplished. They never seemed to be bored with my charts and statistics. When I finished Pepe would always ask quietly:

"Is it time yet, Peppino?"

When I insisted it would be premature to announce the formation of a union, they accepted my decision without protest.

In the winter of 1958-59 Batista's army began to crumple. Maxie warned us the end was nearing for the casinos and notified Pepe to expect the worst. We dismissed most of our croupiers and shipped our equipment to another island for storage. While there was nothing to do but wait, the Table quickly selected Locado Island, another fast-blooming tourist resort, as Maxie's next assignment.

Castro and his bearded Rebels entered the city on January 8, 1959. Maxie's name had appeared twice in *Hoy*, the Communist daily Batista had tried to suppress, as an imperialistic Yankee gambler who should be sentenced to death by the People's Court.

Castro made his triumphant journey along the Avenida del Puerto with the mobs shouting "Viva Fidel!" and showering him and his troops with confetti and flowers as the Fidelistas waved the black and red "26th of July" flag.

A few days later Maxie was paying off the last of our employees when the luckiest son of a bitch in the whole Caribbean walked in—the Russian. Once again he had landed on all four feet. As he triumphantly took Maxie into custody, he informed him he was now a member of the "People's Government."

Of course Maxie was only held for two days. He was immediately released after our embassy made a protest. But Lorenzo had disappeared.

Castro's government announced—and our frightened and apprehensive embassy confirmed—that Lorenzo was not an American but a fugitive Italian gangster. The Italian consul filed a routine protest that was as effective as spitting into the wind.

A few days later, Maxie phoned to relate what had happened. He was packing when Lorenzo's body was discovered stuffed into a large steel calypso drum that had been delivered to the hotel and placed in the deserted casino. A porter notified him when he saw blood leaking from it. Lorenzo had been brutally tortured, then shot. The Russian had not forgotten how Lorenzo had outfoxed him.

Lorenzo's death shook me. I had always accepted Lorenzo as my shield of invulnerability; he stood between me and violence like a stone wall. Yet I should have realized that from the first time I met Lorenzo in Pepe's gallery on Madison Avenue there had hovered over him—with his predatory instinct, his dreadful loyalty to Pepe, his desolate and cold-blooded commitment to murder—an unmistakable air of execution. As a final tribute to his memory I played God and gave Lorenzo one last roll of dice. In my last phone call to Maxie, just before the government took over all the island's communications, I told him where I had hidden the Russian's book listing the numerous bribes he had received and split with the police and the names of the "Rebels" he had questioned and tortured during Batista's regime. I suggested that he make use of it. I can still recall the pause over the crackling telephone wire, then Maxie's grim, "I got you, Frank . . ."

He found the book and passed it on to the head of Castro's secret police. It was diabolically effective. When Maxie returned to New York, he gave me a copy of *Hoy*. Page one featured a picture of the Russian sagging against the wall under the bullets of the execution squad.

On the same page, *Hoy* had another picture: our Columbia-International Hotel was decorated with flags and a two-story-high portrait of Castro. It was now

568

"Workers Dormitory Number Five" in Castro's program of reforms which he insisted to the world would change Cuba's political, economic, and social life.

But no more casinos.

As the 1960s began, government and local investigations began seriously to probe organized crime with competent staffs. While there had been no public hints as to our identity or details or our operation, we were, as Tony Cupid put it, "Like some guys in a fort with the Indians ridin' 'round and 'round outside."

Informers surfaced and some of our lesser members were sent to jail or became fugitives, but the hierarchy of the Table still remained aloof, anonymous, and intact, protected by the fierce and primitive faith that surrounded the group, the faith in the Sicilian *omerta*—"manliness"— that is sustained even in the face of death or long jail sentences. That together with Pepe's shrewdness in organizing the hierarchy of the Table into a series of conferences, with final, irrevocable decisions made by a secret conclave of the ruling members, kept the organization together and alive.

The Table now consisted of six *capa famiglia*, each representing a section of the country in which his people controlled vice, gambling, narcotics, labor racketeering, and politicians. Gus presided but Pepe had the power: he was the real *Capo dei Capi* and the others still viewed him with enough respect and fear to accept his decisions.

There was also Tony Cupid, graying, still handsome, and receiving congratulations on his recent acquittal on federal bribery charges; Sally Grossi, stiff and disapproving, dressed in a banker's starched shirt, French cuffs, and a gray tie held flat by an old-fashioned stickpin. His upstate protégé who walked in his shadow filled little Nino's chair. The Table's newest member was Serafino ("Finny") DeLucca, a deeply tanned elderly man with a pair of light blue eyes that relieved the heaviness of his oval face. He toyed constantly with a diamond pinkie ring and had a habit of arching his neck as he pondered a question. From what I had heard, he was a soft-spoken killer who had made a bundle in a bloody strike that organized the plantation workers of Hawaii.

The Table was no longer a collection of ruthless, efficient, sometimes brilliant criminal opportunists; it almost seemed a retribution of some sort that it now resembled a petty Borgia court, riven with deadly intrigue, malice, greed, and jealousy.

51 THE NATIONAL POLICE UNION

A few days before the April 1965 Table was held, I asked for a secret meeting with Pepe, Joe, and Tony Cupid. I had finally come to the conclusion that the national climate had changed rapidly, so unexpectedly, in fact, that I was ready to announce publicly the formation of our national police union and to begin its organization.

The magic of Camelot had died with Kennedy in Dallas. Disillusionment, anger, and bitterness were stirring the youth; the enemy was the cop. It would only be a matter of time, I thought, before the cop also became embittered and struck out blindly, violently, and desperately.

I had just returned from a final sweep across midwestern and southwestern towns and cities where I could sense the bitterness and bewilderment of the police, particularly in rural areas when they encountered confrontations with angry young people. I described the changing social mores, the steady demoralization of the police, and their desperate desire to achieve understanding and sympathy. Then I tore open an envelope I had picked up at my office on my way to the gallery.

"What's that, Frank?" Joe asked as a stack of newspaper clippings slid across the polished desktop.

"For the last several months I've had a clipping service send me every news story or article on cops being beaten, shot, stabbed, or killed. We don't realize it, but these radical groups are gunning for the cops."

I glanced quickly at some clips.

"Here's one from the Midwest: two cops shot by a sniper. Here's another: a cop had his skull fractured in a demonstration. He may be paralyzed for life."

After they had carefully read the clippings Pepe asked.

570

"The public, Peppino—what does it think?"

"A good part of it thinks cops are bastards. The cops know this and they're mad."

"You have facts to back all this up?" Cupid asked.

"I'm finishing some charts today—"

"Good. Bring everything, Peppino," Pepe said, rubbing his hands. "At this Table we go for the union."

At Pepe's suggestion the April Table consisted of a series of meetings between lesser representatives in motels, private dining rooms, restaurants, hotel suites, and boat clubs in various parts of New York City, Long Island, Westchester, and northern New Jersey. I don't think there was any irony intended on Pepe's part when he convened the main Table in the apartment above Patsy's restaurant. It had to be coincidence; if one of us had opened an iron shutter and flicked a cigarette it would have landed in the lobby of Manhattan's police headquarters.

It was a fitting spot formally to organize the name The National Brotherhood of Police Communications Workers, Foot Patrolmen, and Superior Officers.

Joe and Maxie had been excused. Maxie had a delicate meeting on a yacht off Lacado with the island's governor; the subject—how much did he want for a guaranteed monopoly of the island's casinos? Joe was upstate, successfully ending a bitter strike against one of the nation's largest manufacturers of communications and computer supplies. I was to make the presentation to the Table on the police project.

I came with two attaché cases filled with charts and literature which, I had learned, never failed to impress the members. I mounted my charts on an easel and in the best boardroom manner, set out to convince them that this was the proper time to launch the police union. I read them newspaper clippings, copies of government studies, articles on police and law enforcement, and confidential reports—all underscoring the deepening unrest among policemen which was leading them to fight publicly for better working conditions and take a more active role in local politics. The information I had culled from talks with Hennessy—gossip, complaints, and rumors he had heard—strengthened my argument.

I told them of the startling decline in the public's estimation of the policeman. Bewildered by conditions in the streets, shot at, spat upon, and made a political scapegoat, the cop found himself held in contempt by the public he served. He was now ready to do something about it.

This, more than anything else, I told the Table, made him vulnerable for national unionization. He was desperate to fight back for his honor and his self-esteem.

To support this theory I read the most recent results of a national poll I had commissioned for the past four years to keep our fingers on the public's pulse. For the first time in four years, the man in the street's opinion of the cop on the beat had declined.

My survey recorded the following estimates of law enforcement officials.

—By 40-33 percent local police received poor marks for not doing their jobs.

—By 40-20 percent local cops were denounced as brutally sadistic in making arrests, especially of the young.

—By a shocking 73-12 percent the majority of those polled insisted the police should not get a pay increase.

When asked to characterize most law enforcement officers, the public had singled out such highly unfavorable words to describe them as:

"Thieves" (50%);

"Sadistic" (60%);

"Not Interested In Their Fellow Man" (58%).

The survey also revealed that, for the first time nationally, whites had begun to echo the black's negativism toward police. Young people, black and white, were almost unanimous in their denunciation and contempt of the police.

DeLucca questioned me closely on the problem of police unionization and I answered each question honestly and truthfully. It was evident he was no novice in labor.

"Great possibilities," he murmured, "fantastic." He looked about at the others. "*Ecco!* Do you know what this could mean? A private army! A police strike in Los Angeles!" He closed his eyes and shook his head. "You could steal the Freeways."

"We are not unaware of that, my friend," Tony Cupid said with a grin. "What do you think Frank has been doin' all these years? You want to steal, come here. We'll give you the Empire State Building!"

Grossi broke in, "I still say we should write off what we spent and forget it. It's too much like that thing on TV—what do you call it?"

He turned to his *consigliero* who whispered in his ear.

"*Si.* 'The Twilight Zone.' My kids eat up that crap. But it's for children not grown men. I say we stay with the waterfront. The trucks. The numbers. Computers and communication are the big thing—we're even gettin' a smell of Wall Street. Why don't we stay with them? Cops to me . . ." He threw up his hands.

"Who said we're not gonna stay with them?" Cupid shot back. "Don't we own their unions? When somethin' is ready to grab in Wall Street, we'll do the grabbin.' What more can we do? Do you want to build a factory like that goddam idea you had of the hotel in Havana? Suppose we went along with you on that, Sal? What would it be now with Castro? We would have our hands up our *cula!* No? Am I lyin'?"

"We all made money out of Cuba," Grossi said stiffly. "Lots of money."

"Sure we did—and the price was right. The spicks built the hotel and we took the cream. Just as we'll do in Lacado when Maxie gets goin'. Now we go into cops. I say it's the next big thing. We give Frank and Joe a million and let 'em play with it—"

Grossi looked startled.

"A million!"

"I warned you before," I told him, "it will take a great deal of money to set up a national cops' union. It's an enormous job . . ."

"How long will it take, Frank?" Cupid asked.

"At least three years of state-by-state recruiting. And that's only because I have spent so much time establishing contacts. If you are looking for instant success—forget this one."

"What's your plan?" DeLucca asked. "Organize the big cities?"

"No. Start in the smaller communities, towns, even villages where the departments are small. Lately their problems have been multiplied by bankrupt administrations, high taxes, school bonds, that sort of thing. We'll keep away from the coastal cities until the union is operating."

"Will you go for an AFL-CIO charter?"

"No. I suggest we keep it independent. In that way we can maintain control. I also think we should make it an affiliate of Joe's International Communications and Computer Workers Union. Joe will be president, I'll be vice-president. We'll fill the treasurer's and business agent's spots with people we trust."

"We agreed on the name, right?" Cupid said. "It will still be the National Brotherhood of Police Communications Workers, Foot Patrolmen, and Superior Officers."

"*Buòno! Buòno!*" DeLucca said. "Be sure to include everyone except the janitor."

"And with the communications workers you can tie up the biggest city in the world with a strike," Cupid said. "*Marrone!*"

"That's why it must be affiliated with Joe's union," I said. "We can call sympathy walkouts."

"Tie 'em together," DeLucca said slowly, "and you can have any city in the United States by the balls."

"You're makin' it too simple," Grossi protested. "All cops are not like the *stùpidos* we know. Do you think the honest ones will let outsiders come in and take over the works?"

"Who wants to take over their works, Sal?" Cupid asked mildly. "All we ask 'em to do is walk off their jobs. They're workin' for a livin', right?"

"They have their own organizations. Who are we that they should listen to us?" Grossi replied with a contemptuous wave of his hand. "Crazy. That's all it is—crazy."

"Not so crazy," I told him. "We have money and clout. That's all cops talk about when you mention unionization. They want to know what other unions you can make deals with to support them and how much do you have in your treasury."

"We're goin' in as a legitimate labor organization, Sally," Tony Cupid said. "Look at it this way. You're an honest cop. But they're beatin' your brains in. People spit at you. Your neighbors' kids tell your kids their old man is a thief. How do you feel when you come home at night and your wife tells you that? You want to put your hand right through the wall, right? Then the next day some long-haired kid kicks you in the balls. Why? Because maybe you asked him to stop shoutin' in some old lady's ear. Just as Frank says, when you get a guy in that mood he wants to do one thing—hit back! He wants to show those bastards who have been kickin' him around he has clout. He wants to sit back so when some guy gets mugged he can yell, 'Hey, maybe you want a pig now?' "

After Cupid finished they were all silent for a moment,

then DeLucca said slowly, "Tony's right, Sally. If we're gonna go—now is the time."

"Yeah. Let's go with Finny," Gus put in.

Pepe nodded coldly to Grossi and his stooge, then looked about the Table.

"Okay? Any more questions?"

I put in, "I would like to add one more thing."

"Go ahead," Tony Cupid said. "We want to know everythin'."

I turned to DeLucca.

"Last month didn't a group of cops on the West Coast publicly suggest they join Hoffa's Teamsters?"

"Yeah. I saw that," DeLucca said, nodding. "The police commissioner blew his top. You know, when I was readin' that article the thought came to me, why in the hell do we let Jimmy Hoffa pick up all the plums?"

"Marrone!" Gus said. "That guy Hoffa owns everythin' . . ."

"Not the cops, they belong to us!" Pepe snapped. "We screw that *figlio di butana!* What we do is—"

"I still think we should table this," Grossi said doggedly, "The whole damn thing—"

"Ècco! What do you want us to do—talk, talk, talk?" Pepe shouted banging his fist on the table. "Are we old women? We put one thing here, another thing there, but no action! If it is up to you, *amico*, we will buy a few more trucks, bust a few more heads, kick some owners in the ass and make a new contract. *Sangue della patata!* I am sick of this old man's talk. I say we go with the cops. No more talk. No!"

"Let's put it to a vote," Tony Cupid said quietly.

Pepe won, of course. Under his cold, hard stare, even Grossi voted for the cops' union and a million-dollar budget to be spent over three years.

I immediately opened an impressive but conservative office on lower Broadway overlooking City Hall Park and organized a national tour for myself, Train, and Spider, with the goal of contacting a modest section of the nation's forty thousand police departments to sign up delegates for our first convention to be held in Custer City, Nebraska, in the summer of 1968.

I had to laugh at the expression on Joe's face.

"Custer City, Nebraska? Why the hell do you want to hold it out there, Frank?"

"We're not hitting the big cities yet, Joe," I explained.

575

"Those are small town western cops, very conservative. They still go to cowboy and Indian pictures, for God's sakes. Get them out of their backyards and they would not only be uncomfortable but suspicious."

"When do we hit the New York cops? They're the babies I want."

"Not for a long time, Joe. First comes the job of setting up the union. We have to take one step at a time. That is if you still want to own the cops."

He stared out the window across busy City Hall Plaza.

"I hate the bastards today as I did thirty years ago. Maybe more now because I know what they really did to us."

He fell silent for a moment.

"Do you know, Frank, I still can't walk on the sidewalk where they killed Tom? I'm afraid. I always think that if I do I will look down and see the bloodstains . . ."

His hatred of police was undeniable. For thirty years it had been masked by frustration, greed, and ambition. But now it was time for action. At last he had his weapon of destruction.

I could still spit when I heard the word cop but I no longer left the kind of hatred Joe did. Chena and those happy years had dried up a whole sea of bitterness inside me. Now, instead of as enemies to the death, I viewed cops objectively. They were no longer individuals but groups like truck drivers, coopers, warehousemen, and longshoremen who had to be pushed, flattered, cajoled, wheedled, coaxed, and, when necessary, deceived and cheated.

The national unionization of police had always been my great challenge. But I was not unaware of the awesome power I had as the architect of such an organization. Obviously, this same idea had occurred to every member of the Table. The very idea that a small group could control hundreds of thousands of policemen, coast to coast, was staggering.

There were moments when I idly speculated as to how our lives might have been changed had we not gone to the St. Barnabas Dance that fatal Saturday night so long ago. Would I have won the scholarship to Fordham? Then gone on to law to spend a mundane life as an insignificant West Side lawyer? Would Tom have lived? And what of Joe? What of the war? Would we have been killed, wounded? The possibilities were infinite.

We were a strange pair those days, eaten inside by different poisons: Joe consumed by his unquenchable hate, me fascinated by the mechanics of labor organization. Motivations aside, together we were effective as hell.

It was the same old Neighborhood quartet, changed only by time. Spider, still slender as a reed, jet black hair flicked with gray at the temples, and the face of a ravaged choirboy, was paying alimony to two former wives, both show girls.

"No more show dames for me," he said disgustedly, "all they do is hustle your money and screw everything from the janitor to your lawyer."

He took a small color print from his wallet.

"How do you like this broad?" he said proudly. "A knockout, right? That's Gloria. She's a hell of a cook. Christ, what a difference it will be eatin' at home and not goin' to some crummy restaurant every night with a dame who took five hours to paint her face!"

Train, fifty pounds heavier and no brighter than he was in the eighth grade, still lived in the Neighborhood. When he wasn't traveling with Spider, his world was bounded on the east by Broadway movie houses, Regan's on the west, south by the apartment of a nurse he had been "goin' out with" for twenty years, and Madison Square Garden on the north, where Spider insisted Train saw every sports event from fights to pro or college basketball games.

"I even found the big bastard goin' to an ice show over there!" Spider said indignantly. "If it runs, fights, moves, skates, or plays with a ball Train will be there."

For three years Spider, Train, and I toured the country in a recruiting drive for delegates. During that time I discovered hicks don't live in the sticks but in the cities. Once you cross the Mississippi, the citizens may appear slower but they're a hell of a lot sharper.

Unlike the big city forces, cops in the small towns didn't need a Ph.D. from Harvard to tell them a crisis, almost as grave as the one in the pre-Civil War years, was rapidly mounting in this country with two lifestyles, two philosophies, two opposing forces moving toward each other like express trains on the same track.

After establishing central headquarters in Chicago I organized teams of researchers to make a telephonic check of all police departments in the western section of the United States, from the Canadian to the Mexican borders, and list every policeman killed, shot, or seriously beaten in ambushes, assaults, sniping attacks, demonstrations, bombings, riots, or group assaults.

The results were shocking: from 1965 to 1968 the three years of our recruiting drive, ten policemen had been killed in western and midwestern states and hundreds more assaulted or injured. In addition, there had been numerous attacks on police stations; one had been bombed.

"Holy Christ!" Spider said in awe. "It's sure open season on cops out here."

I had the same researching team do a state-by-state survey of policemen's wages in comparison to plumbers', carpenters', pipe fitters', and construction workers'. When we finished the chart, I asked myself why a guy would want to become a cop and starve when he could become a plumber and live a princely life? After all, you don't get shot at installing a new faucet.

The comparisons gave me another idea. Some police wages were so low that I had Spider and Train check the local welfare requirements and discovered, as I had suspected, that cops were eligible for welfare assistance. It took much talking and persuasion, but I finally got a dozen or more to apply for relief. I also composed a case history of each cop from the first day he joined the force, analyzing every aspect of his daily life, down to his family's menus. While I was prepared to do some faking, I found the facts more startling: few cops, if any, were eating roast beef every Sunday.

In late August 1968, the National Brotherhood of Police Communications Workers, Foot Patrolmen, and Superior Officers held its first national convention in Custer City Civic Auditorium. We had one hundred delegates representing eighty-two police departments in villages, cities, towns, and small cities, all west of Pittsburgh.

In the early summer, Joe joined us in Chicago. To make sure we controlled key delegates, we paid each one a visit so Joe could wine, dine, and feed them enough pie in the sky to make their heads reel. It was the early days of the coopers all over again; I wrote the keynote speech for Joe and we rehearsed it until we knew every phrase, comma, and dramatic pause.

I was well aware of the power of publicity. When, years before, Joe, for the first time praised the cops as "gallant, forgotten nobodies," we received coverage from the New

York City newspapers. Even the AP picked it up. I was no professional newspaperman or press agent, but I realized that sort of rhetoric wouldn't work in the sixties. Any worthwhile news coming out of our convention had to be topical and real, not a gimmick.

I decided to titillate the press, to tease the insatiable curiosity of most newspapermen. *The Editor and Publisher's Annual* and *The Broadcaster's Guide* supplied me with the names of the daily, weekly, and Sunday newspapers and television stations in every state where we had a delegate. Each one received a continuous flow of press releases. I tried to be as professional as possible, supplying information rather than propaganda.

Several days before the convention opened I sent all of them a carefully worded telegram, hinting at a sensational news story which might emerge in Joe's keynote speech.

I was proud of the results. Our Chicago hotel phone rang constantly. Reporters tried to wheedle and cajole us into giving them the story; they even offered deals of extensive coverage in exchange for the exclusive story. The more we dangled the bait, the more frustrated they became—and the more advance stories about the convention appeared. Before long, we were included in the early and late TV news programs.

When the convention opened, our two press sections, newspapers and TV, were filled. Joe was interviewed extensively, but I made sure he was always in the company of one of the delegates we controlled. I hired a cameraman to duplicate every news shot and send a print to the delegate's family and local newspaper. Even cops have egos.

We subtly but firmly controlled the convention through our delegates. When it came to making vital decisions—like voting down opposition to the strike clause—we had our way. Some delegates were disturbed by the section in the union's constitution which gave any local the right to take what action it deemed necessary to gain economic security—after the said local had received permission from the National Board of Directors which, of course, consisted of Joe, me, Train, Spider, and four other delegates we considered reliable.

It was pointed out in the debates that some states had a law forbidding strikes by essential municipal employees; New York State's Taylor Law was cited as an example. Joe received a rousing ovation when he suggested with a straight face that "job actions," such as a mysterious illness that attacks only policemen, certainly could not be classified as a labor strike. In fact, he told the delegates with a broad grin there was a possibility that some department could be hit with what he called "blue flu, a newly discovered strain of influenza."

With a faint smile he let the laughter die down before he became serious again. In a ringing voice he told them that if a job action did not impress their municipal authorities they had only one alternative—to exercise the right to strike. He pledged that every dollar at his command would be used to support that right.

Then he launched into what was to become known as his famous "Listen America to Your Policemen" speech.

"And I promise you that we will defend your right to strike with every legal weapon at our command. We will fight them in the lower courts ... in the appellate courts, up to the very bench of our Supreme Court ..."

He shouted, "Do you know why? Here are the answers, and you had better listen to your policemen, America! Because he's tired of being beaten, kicked, stabbed, bombed, murdered, and spat upon by scum ...

"Listen to your policemen, America! He's aware that you have permitted every other citizen who works for a living to organize and to strike for a better living wage when his fellow unionists and leaders deem it necessary ...

"He's a new policeman, America, and you had better listen to him! He knows now that he has been conned by your mayors, your city councils, your state legislatures, your governors, yes even by the public he protects. He has been made a lesser citizen, who bows his head and accepts without complaint what is handed to him. ..."

He glared at them for a long time—God, how long we had rehearsed this scene—and I could almost hear a hundred dry throats swallow.

"You had better listen to your policemen, America," he cried. "He is through accepting handouts! Now he demands a living wage so he will no longer be compelled to grit his teeth, swallow his pride, and accept welfare to supply the bare necessities of life for his family!"

He dramatically shook the folder of case histories I had prepared of the cops receiving welfare.

"Does this shock you, America! Does this tear your heart out, America, as it did mine? Do you think it's only phony union propaganda? Listen, America! Listen to the names—the towns. I have asked permission of these men and their families and I will read them off to you . . ."

I had prepared piles of folders containing copies of the case histories—each cop and his family had been primed for the later questions of reporters—and as Joe opened the first folder Spider and Train began handing out a complete file to each reporter.

Like drumbeats, Joe read off the names of each cop, how long he had been on the force, his awards, how many in his family, his weekly take-home pay, his budget, his family's menus. As I had hoped, it was devastating.

"They're writin' like crazy," Spider said gleefully. "You ought to see the bastards! Some guys have typewriters and they're goin' like hell . . ."

"Just like the reporters at a fight, Frank," Train put in. "I swear it."

I scrawled a note to Joe and had Spider slip it to him. It read:

"Press eating your stuff like mad. End it up with something like thin blue line crap, deep unrest, politicians better listen."

After he had read off the names he stood quietly at the microphone for a moment, letting the shocking acts sink in. Then, slowly raising his arms, he cried:

"I say this to you, America, to your people, north, south, east, and west! Please! Please! Listen to the cry of your policeman! Support him in every way! That blue line separatin' you from the bombers, the rapists, the pushers, the savage militants who demand everything for nothin' at the point of a gun is gettin' thinner and weaker.

"Someday it may snap and you will find the wolves at your door! And I say to the politicians of America! You too had better listen to your policemen! Too long you have been talkin' to him from both sides of your mouth. He's not takin' it anymore, tinhorns. He's on the move. He and his brothers will sweep you out of office like dust under a new broom. You had better get with him!

"And you, judges of America! You had better listen to your policemen! They are sick of you do-gooders in black robes who give the criminal a tap on the wrist, who maintain courtrooms with turnstiles at the door. You're through. If you don't believe us, take a look at who is voting next year. It's America's new policeman!"

He threw up his arms and roared:

"Policemen of every state—city, town, and village! Join
581

us! Lift up your heads—can't you smell the winds of change sweeping across America! The giant they thought was asleep is stirring. He's awake. God bless him!"

He stood there, arms still raised, sweat rolling down his face, handsome, dynamic, magical.

He smiled and clenched his upraised fists as the delegates jumped on chairs, whistled, stamped, and cheered. Some started a snake dance and it wound in and out of the aisles. Their faces were flushed, eyes glittering, voices hoarse from shouting and cheering.

Their Blue Messiah had finally come.

52 JOE'S IN TROUBLE

During the following year our national police union grew like a snowball, becoming larger and larger as it rolled across the country picking up foot patrolmen, communications workers, and superior officers in villages, towns, and cities. In tribute to our growing sophistication, I selected Miami as the site of our second convention. The number of our delegates had tripled.

Joe and I had prepared an expensive ten-page brochure containing a forceful argument for a national police union to protect the interests of every American policeman against unscrupulous or weak politicians, and dangerous militants and revolutionaries who had publicly announced a war of extermination against the police.

That summer we had done an invitational mailing to almost three thousand city, county, and state police groups; the response had been electrifying. We had also opened a large, luxurious office in Washington and hired a veteran lobbyist at a fancy price. On the cover of the brochure was a picture I had staged of Joe speaking to a nonpartisan group of prominent politicians in the hall outside our office. On the door above their heads were the gold letters: National Brotherhood of Police Communications Workers, Foot Patrolmen, and Superior Officers.

The simple caption read: "President Joseph Gunnar and friends."

I had increased our polls until we were taking them every few months. They had begun to reveal how the pendulum of fickle public opinion was slowly swinging toward the police as assaults against them mounted and the country moved toward conservatism after the Nixon victory. But polls, no matter how good they may be in presenting a general picture and predicting elections, seldom pinpoint human decisions.

A week before our convention opened, the polls had told us how unhappy, frustrated, and bitter were the cops in the big cities. But no one expected a walkout in two Brooklyn precincts over the case of one cop. He had been found guilty of wounding a drug pusher while making an arrest and the Civilian Review Board had recommended dismissal from the department. The commissioner had announced he would accept the board's findings when Treasury agents and narcotics detectives arrested the pusher for operating a schoolyard syndicate of pushers he had addicted; its oldest member was twelve.

The cops in the precinct they called "Dodge City" because of the ghetto violence, walked out before the first tour. By noon, a neighboring precinct was empty. City Hall held the usual meaningless, frantic meetings, a hurried press conference was called, promises were made, the cop was reinstated over the commissioner's protest, and the police returned to their posts before the walkouts could spread.

A few days later three important events took place: the commissioner resigned, Elliott was appointed in his place, and I notified Pepe we would publicly announce the union was ready to recruit in the nation's largest cities—starting with New York.

Violence against the police of America, their bitter economic situation, and the abolishment of civilian review boards were the themes of the convention. Spider and his team of researchers had steadily updated their national telephonic check of police departments, and the delegates listened in an angry silence as Joe read off the results:

Twenty-six policemen killed.

One hundred and forty-one bombings in the United States in only three months.

Six hundred and fifty policemen shot, stabbed, beaten,

583

ambushed, sniped at, even booby-trapped in the corresponding months—an average of two hundred a month.

"They have made us sitting ducks," Joe cried, "and when these fanatics kill us, what do they do?"

He dramatically held up a blowup of a cop's funeral, the pallbearers carrying the flag-draped casket between the long aisle of blue coats.

"That's what they give us! A flag! A little sad music! An inspector's funeral and some heroic phrases for the newspapers! But what do they do for *them?*"

He raised another blowup of a cop's weeping widow surrounded by three small children who stared bewilderedly at the camera.

"They give those gallant, brave, heartsick women a medal! Shall we tell 'em what they can do with their medals . . . ?"

When a roar answered him Joe threw up his arms.

"We begged them. We warned them. We told them what to do with these fanatical killers," he shouted, "but what happens?"

This time the blowup showed a militant group parading with signs that read: "Off the Pigs!" . . . "A Good Cop Is a Dead Cop!" . . . "On Your Knees, Pigs."

I had told Joe this would get to them. Their chairs could have been electrified the way they leaped to their feet, waving their fists, shouting, and cursing.

When we had their adrenalin glands pumping full force, we went into economics. Joe read off the national survey we had prepared that analyzed police salaries, government reports on costs of living, including medical and insurance plans.

One of the highlights of his speech was a warning to the nation to cast aside its permissiveness and apathy toward law and morals, permissiveness which had produced the drug scene, increased pornography, and crime in the streets. We had spent months surveying churches and temples, state by state. Once again Joe made headlines when he revealed how many thousands had curtailed not only evening but day services because parishioners were fearful of walking the streets.

"How do you like that, America?" he shouted. "Your rapists, your muggers, your robbers, your killers are shutting down your churches and your temples! And what do you do? You let your children spit on your policemen! The same policemen you forced to accept welfare!"

We no longer had any difficulty suggesting to cops that they accept relief; this time we embarrassed the hell out of a number of cities that already had several financial pistols pointed at their heads by teachers, sanitation men, and employees of other municipal services. But that was their problem.

Joe ended his speech by announcing that we were now prepared to recruit in the big cities—"Give 'em a taste of blue power." The demonstration literally shook the auditorium.

That evening CBS had a full hour on national police unionization and what it would mean to the country. We were interviewed, and they ran some wonderful shots of Joe holding up those blowups. Mayors, city councilmen, even governors called us some choice names, but there was little doubt they were worried.

When Cronkite asked Elliott if he thought a police strike could take place in New York City, he shook his head.

"Never," he replied. "The police of this city realize that the orderly functioning of a society can only be maintained by dependable, consistent, unwavering law enforcement. They are responsible citizens first, policemen second."

It was during this second convention that I first noticed the changes in Joe. He was more irritable, minor difficulties made him explode, and there were times when he appeared vague, distracted. He wasn't sleeping well and he was leaving his room at odd hours. Whiskey is a staple at any convention and we all consumed our share. But Joe wasn't drinking for congeniality or even business but using booze like a narcotic. I told myself it was only his intensity, the wild enthusiasm he had for this dream, and mounting fatigue, but I knew Spider as well as I knew any man and my instinct told me he had something on his mind. When I put it up to him on the plane back to New York he hesitated, and then said:

"I've been wantin' to talk to you about Joe, Frank."

"What about him?"

"You know he's drinkin'?"

"None of us were exactly teetotalers down there."

"But he's really puttin' it away. Like it's goin' out of style."

"That's not what is on your mind, Spider . . ."

"Yeah. I know." He stared out the window then turned to me.

"This is between us, right?"

"I'll never say anything."

"A couple of nights ago he woke up Train and told him to get a quart."

"What was the matter with room service?"

"At four in the mornin'? You know Train, Frank, he would jump off this plane if Joe asked him. So the big boob got dressed and had a cabdriver bring him to an after-hours joint that sold him a bottle. When he got to Joe's room he found him with a young dame. She was a little high but Joe was stoned. Train didn't like the smell of what he saw, so he waited in the hall. After a while he heard some banging, then the dame came runnin' out. When he went into the room Joe was asleep in a chair. The dame was so upset Train brought her up to my room . . ."

I dreaded to ask the question. "What happened?"

Spider shook his head. "She wasn't a hustler, just a dame he had met in the elevator. She had seen his picture in the newspapers and agreed to do a little drinkin' with him. It started when they went to his room—"

"What started?"

"Joe can't do anything with a dame, Frank! He's over the hill and it's drivin' him crazy. The dame said it was terrible, he was cryin' and beggin' her to help him. Then he started to act up and she got scared and ran out."

"What did she mean—act up?"

"She said he turned nasty. She said if he hadn't been so drunk he would have knocked her teeth down her throat. That's when I found out it wasn't the first time—"

"What do you mean?"

"After she left, Train spilled his guts. That big bastard has been pimpin' for him. It got so bad even the hustlers wouldn't take on Joe."

"What the hell could he do to make a whore so particular? You know those Miami hustlers. They'd take on Frankenstein for a buck!"

"You're right, Frank," he said hastily, "I don't mean Joe did anything freaky, the broads said they were afraid of him. One dame told me Joe almost drove her through the wall because she laughed at him."

"Forget it. His private life is his own business."

"It won't be, Frank," Spider said uneasily, "if he blows

586

his cork some night and works over a dame. Even a hustler. It could ruin him. And us!" He added hesitantly, "Why don't you suggest he see a doctor, Frank? I think the guy's in trouble . . ."

"Okay. The next time I'm alone with him."

"There's another thing—"

"What's that?"

"Do you remember the .38 Special I stole from that cop in Brooklyn? Joe's carryin' it."

"How do you know?"

"The dame that Train brought up to my room told me he was wavin' it around."

"Can you get it without him knowing?"

"I got it. After she told me I went down and found it. Train said Joe was lookin' all over for it and was worried one of the whores had grabbed it."

"Where is it now?"

"In a flight bag back with my coat."

I gave him my attaché case.

"Take this back with you. Go into the john and when Joe isn't looking put it in my case. I'll take care of it."

"Okay, Frank. I'm afraid of that goddam gun. I should have thrown it in the river that day."

"I certainly wish you had, Spider."

"This is between us, right?"

"Sure. I'm damn glad you told me."

But I wasn't. Down deep I had kept this one fear about Joe locked away for years, now it was free again, haunting me like a grotesque, evil shadow. Spider soon came back and handed me my attaché case. We never mentioned the gun again, nor did I show it to Chena. I hid it, still wrapped in the oily rags from the CCC camp, among some old papers in a file in my closet.

I never brought up the subject of a doctor to Joe, even after what happened during the last weekend of the season he spent with us at Fishers. One night after we returned to the city, Chena asked me abruptly:

"Frank, is there anything wrong with Joe?"

"Not that I know of," I forced myself to say. "Why?"

"Well, for one thing he's drinking more than usual."

"What else is new?"

"Please don't kid about it, darling," she said, frowning. "Haven't you noticed how intense he seems when he's talking about that union? It's as if this was to be his private army . . ."

"Oh that's just talk, Chena, you know Joe."

"Well, there is something else—"

"Oh? What's that?"

"You were outside tying up the patio furniture. Joe was talking in that intense way. Then, suddenly, he stopped and kept staring at me. I asked him if he wanted a drink and he didn't answer. It was weird. We just sat there while he glared at me. I went out to the kitchen and made a drink and when I came back he was wiping his face with a handkerchief. It was cool that day but perspiration was rolling down his face. And his hands were shaking. When I asked him if he was all right, he said he was getting a tremendous headache and could I get him an aspirin? I got him two and he took them."

"Did he say anything else, Chena?"

She looked at me.

"Yes he did, Frank. He asked me not to say anything to you."

In October I saw what a police strike could do to a big city; it was a terrifying, sobering experience.

We were in the downtown office when a delegate in Wisconsin called and said he had heard from a border patrolman that the cops in Montreal were walking out. We confirmed it by phone and immediately flew up there.

For seventeen hours we watched the city run amok. Mobs roamed the streets smashing windows and looting stores. We saw kids running away with mannequins, lengths of pipe, bathroom fixtures, and appliances, while they laughed and jeered at the frantic, echoing burglar alarms.

Banks were robbed, one after the other. From a passing cab we watched four thieves casually smash a jeweler's window with a brick in a burlap bag, then scoop it clean.

After a few hours we separated to make individual tours. When we returned to the hotel to exchange our experiences, I could only come to one conclusion: Montreal's hoodlums and lawbreakers were not the principal leaders in the violence; it was the ordinary citizen who would never dream of committing a crime if there was a policeman on the corner, who was doing the damage.

For the first time I felt a nibbling sense of guilt.

I stayed a day longer in Montreal than the others in order to confer with the head of the local police line organization. I picked up my ticket at the airport and was looking for the nearest bar to pass the forty-five minutes until plane departure time when someone tapped me on the shoulder.

I turned to face a smartly dressed man with gray hair.

"Hello, Howell."

"Supercop!" I blurted out.

"I have to be that these days," he said wryly. "Are you up here as an observer?"

"Something like that. What are you doing here?"

"The same thing. And praying it will never happen in New York." He nodded to a nearby cocktail lounge. "I was headed there. How about joining me for a drink? Or is that against union regulations?"

"Not if you can get a cop to pay for it."

"Gladly."

We sat down and both ordered a drink.

"How much time do you have?" he asked.

"About forty minutes now."

"Good. I always believe in relaxing before taking off. Planes still make me jittery. How about you?"

"They don't bother me. Are you leaving for New York?"

"No. I saw one of our inspectors off. I'm leaving on Saturday. I've been invited to attend a meeting of the commanders up here."

"They'll certainly have a lot to talk about—"

"I just left the mayor. He said there are some dead and he estimates damages will be in the millions. Did you get a view of it?"

"Yes. We were on the street when the mobs hit those stores."

"I would be curious to hear your ideas."

"The public and the politicans can't go on ignoring the police. They've been nobodies for too long. There's a time when nobodies want to become somebodies and that always means trouble."

"I would say both sides up here share equal blame. The city was stupid for putting all that money into Expo and at the same time ignoring the demands of the policemen. But, on the other hand, what the police did to this city was criminal. There's no excuse and you know it, Howell!"

"You're losing sight of one important thing, Elliott—it wasn't the cops who rioted. They didn't do the robbing or driving around the city like nuts. It was the public. Let's face it—there's larceny in all of us! Cops have to make a living wage," I told him. "That silver badge or a plaque on an altar isn't going to send their kids through college or pay off the mortgage."

"You remembered the plaque."

"Why not? It was quite a story."

"The strange thing is it isn't unusual. If it happened today, there are many cops who would automatically do the same thing."

"I'm sure they would—that's why they deserve more money."

"You're not reading the papers, Howell," he said grimly. "Why the hell do you think I've been crawling to City Hall with my hat in hand? I know they need more money better than you do."

"Besides money they also want respect, to be treated like human beings—"

"We're doing the best we can," he said doggedly. "I don't have to tell you ours is a tough city these days. It's not only New York, it's every city and town in the country. Society is changing."

"That's fine," I told him. "I'm all for change but why make the cop the villain? You know as well as I do, probably better, politicians have built-in radar. They can smell a vote bloc like a dog can smell a bitch in heat. A long time ago it was the Irish they were wooing, then the Italians. Now it's blacks and other minorities. They wanted to play the big liberal role so they passed the word along to guys like you, take it easy. And who winds up behind the eight ball? You guessed it the first time, the cops. Do you know out in the west they raided the office of one of those revolutionary groups and discovered the bastards gave rewards for anyone knocking off a cop? Like in a shooting gallery. Kill a cop a day and get a kewpie doll."

"My, how we have changed," he said. "Do you remember that day on the pier when we picked up the Gimp? Do you still spit when you hear the word cop?"

"You're goddam right I do, Elliott," I told him, "and you know why. In fact you were there. To me they're a group to be organized just like plumbers, truck drivers, and coopers. I don't have to love them to do that. The way I see it they have a right to walk off their job any damn time they want to. That public service garbage is a two-way street. Any guy with a job that contains the risk

590

of saying good-bye to his wife and kids in the morning and coming home a dead hero should get paid a hell of a lot more than a guy emptying an ash can and get a hell of a lot more respect."

"I saw Gunnar on television when he made that announcement you were coming into the big cities." He added bluntly, "Are we on your list?"

"Definitely. In fact you're number one—"

"Nobody can stop you from coming in and trying to organize the police," he said, "but—"

"Why, thank you, Commissioner."

"But I hope I'm not hearing the right rumors."

"And what are they?"

"You know what I mean—a police strike."

"A police strike in New York! That's forbidden by the Taylor Law, Commissioner!"

"Oh come off it, Howell," he said wearily. "A law won't stop you or Gunnar. Not if we go by past performances."

"I don't like the sound of that . . ."

"It's no secret you and Gunnar have walked over a lot of people on the waterfront. Why the members in your union haven't kicked you out I'll never know."

"Why should they? They are getting more today than they ever did."

"Save your propaganda," he snapped. "I'm not a police commissioner now and you're not the big union leader. Let's talk man to man . . ."

It was getting a bit too warm for me. I wondered uneasily if it was a frame, was he wired for sound?

"Don't worry, I'm not wired," he said reading my thoughts. "We don't have anything on you now but maybe someday we will—"

"This is one guy you or the DA can't intimidate, Elliott. Thirty years ago I vowed I would never take any more crap from a cop and I'm certainly not going to take any now. If the guys in your department want to walk out we'll lead them and you know what you can do with the Taylor Law, your idiotic mayor, the bunch of tinhorns in your city council, and those clubhouse judges! In fact you can include your goddam public."

"Don't do it," he said quickly, "you'll regret it for the rest of your life. My God man, don't you have any conscience?" he said now almost pleadingly. "Don't you know what would happen if a police strike took place in our city? The mobs would not head for the ghettos; this time they'll come down to Fifth Avenue! Every rapist, looter, thief, and vandal will be on the loose. It would be worth your life to walk down Forty-second Street."

"That's nothing new," I told him.

He pushed his glass aside and glanced at his wristwatch.

"You have only five minutes. I'm sorry I wasted both our time."

"Thanks for the drink."

"Just one more thing," he said in a low, tense voice as he leaned across the table. "If you attempt to pull a police strike in New York City, I swear I'll cut you to ribbons. I'll put every man I can trust on those goddam unions of yours. We'll find something if its only spitting on the sidewalk!"

"Your temper is showing, Supercop . . ."

"We have thousands of cops who are second-, third-, and even fourth-generation policemen. They have a big investment in this department. They're not going to sit back and watch you and your bums come in and tear it and this city apart. There's a hell of a lot wrong with the New York City Police Department but I can guarantee you will find there's a hell of a lot right with it."

He threw a bill on the table and turned away.

Elliott was still Supercop.

We spent the next few months organizing our recruiting campaign for New York City. Joe was impatient and irritable at the delay but I insisted there could be no rush; before the first piece of our propaganda appeared I wanted to be certain of every move.

In early June we were in Chicago meeting with a group of midwestern delegates who were also talking strike, when I received a call from Chena: her mother had died of a heart attack in Stockholm while touring Europe with her cousin. I wanted to drop everything and fly over there with her but she insisted I stay in Chicago. It was a desolate ten days without her. I couldn't wait until I received the cable to pick her up at Kennedy.

I watched her come through customs, still slender, glossy black hair fixed in a chignon topped by a saucy Alpine hat. She was the most stunning woman in the airport.

However, the moment I kissed her I sensed a change.

"Anything wrong, dear?"

She smiled and squeezed my hand. "Why do you ask?"

"Nothing. Just a worried husband I guess . . ."

We had cultivated a habit of eating out once or twice a week at some small restaurant Chena had discovered and then walking up Fifth Avenue. The night she came home I took her to her favorite restaurant off Washington Square and we decided to walk home. I felt something was off-key.

"What is it, darling?"

"What is what?"

"Don't answer my question with a question—let's have it. If a big handsome Viking swept you off your feet give me his name and I'll send Train over there to take care of him."

"The only big handsome Vikings I saw were selling dirty magazines," she said with a wan smile.

I tucked her arm under mine.

"No secrets Chena."

"I saw something in Stockholm, Frank, that worries me," she said slowly.

"What was that?"

"A police strike," she replied abruptly.

"A police strike? In Stockholm?"

"I brought home an English newspaper so you could read about it. It began the morning I arrived. I found out about it at the airport when the cabdriver refused to take me to the hotel. He said mobs were roaming the streets and it was dangerous because there were no policemen on duty. I couldn't believe it. I finally found a cabdriver who agreed to drive me for double the fare . . ."

"Didn't you say your cousin had been traveling with your mother?"

"Also a niece. And thank God for that. She's only seventeen but she doesn't lose her head. Our cousin is as old as my mother and completely helpless. As I told you, they had been planning this trip for years. In fact, it was Nicky who bought the tickets for my mother's birthday. He said if he didn't, it would remain only talk—"

"Nicky didn't go?"

"No, I saw him in Palermo."

"He never wrote your mother was sick."

"She wasn't. Outside of minor ailments she was in the best of health for her age. In fact a few months before she left she made a trip to that crazy little village where we stayed during the war to see some relatives. When she came back to Palermo, Nicky said they stayed up all night while she talked about the olive groves, the changes in the

593

village, who had babies, who had died ... Nicky said she looked twenty years younger."

"Then she died suddenly?"

"My cousin said she was coming out of the bathroom when she just stopped and fell. But Frank, the horrible part of it was when I got there she was still in the room covered with a sheet!"

"My God, Chena! Why was that?"

"Because of the strike there was only one police car operating in the city," she said bitterly, "so we had to wait for the police department to bring a medical examiner to the hotel to pronounce my mother dead."

She bit her lip and blinked back the tears.

"Did anyone notify your father?" I asked quickly to change the subject. She shook her head. "Nicky said he called him at the club several times but couldn't get him. Then he spoke to one of the old waiters he knew. He told Nicky my father is seldom at the club anymore."

"I'll tell him—"

"Don't bother," she said with a sigh, "what good will it do? Nicky said he heard he was drinking heavily and chasing every tart on Broadway."

We walked home in silence. When we reached the apartment she suddenly hugged me tightly.

"Frank," she whispered, "Don't have anything to do with that police union! Please! I have a terrible feeling about it."

"It's only another union, Chena."

"It's not only another union, Frank! It's policemen. If there was a police strike in New York City it would be terrifying. Please. Please."

"We'll talk about it—"

"When?"

"Tomorrow."

Of course there was no tomorrow. When Chena tried to talk to me about the police union I changed the subject. She never mentioned it again but I knew it was constantly on her mind.

Then there was another incident with Joe. Since our return from Cuba, he had always joined us one evening a week for dinner, a show, a movie, or just a few drinks and talk. In the first few years Chena and I had eagerly looked forward to this evening; Joe had always been a witty, entertaining companion and we made a gay, inseparable trio.

He changed after our second convention. When we were preparing the New York recruiting campaign, he was edgy, impatient, more intense than ever. It became obvious to me he was beginning to get Chena's teeth on edge.

Sometimes she would just slip away and go to bed while Joe paced up and down, predicting the great things to come.

"I just can't take it any longer, Frank," she told me one night, after Joe had gone on for hours. "He scares me the way he talks—"

"Forget it, Chena. It's only talk."

"It's not only talk and you know it!"

"Okay. Have it your way. It's not talk."

"Then if it's not talk it's serious enough to discuss."

"I'm not going to discuss any cops' union at two in the morning, darling. Forget it!"

"Dammit," she cried, "I won't forget it!"

She was standing in the middle of our bedroom, a hairbrush in one hand, tears rolling down her cheeks, black eyes flashing, and a Sicilian temper ready to erupt.

I made an elaborate gesture of covering my head with one arm and crying:

"Please, signora! Don't throw!"

She couldn't help it, she had to laugh and cry at the some time. But when I took her in my arms I knew it was serious, no amount of light comedy would dismiss her fears.

"I'm frightened, darling," she whispered as she lay in my arms, "frightened sick. I'm even having nightmares about your crazy strike."

A few weeks later we had dinner with Joe. The six o'clock news had an account of a threatened walkout by an upstate police department in a wage dispute, so all we heard over our steak was cops, strikes, and unions. It wearied me and I could see it was infuriating Chena. After dinner Joe went on and on about the police union and Chena excused herself and went to bed. Joe was gleefully predicting what would happen in the city if the cops went out when, suddenly, Chena swung open the bedroom door.

"Joe—will you stop it about your damn strike? Stop it!"

Joe broke off and gave her a startled look.

"What's wrong?"

"You!" Chena cried. "You and this crazy talk of a

595

police strike. That's what's wrong. Don't you realize what could happen in this city?"

"Sure," Joe said with a grin. "That's exactly why I intend to pull it."

"Then you'll pull it without Frank," she said fiercely.

"What's all this?" Joe said turning to me.

"Chena was in Stockholm when her mother died and saw the police strike over there—"

"So what does that have to do with us?"

"Just this," Chena said coldly. "If Frank has any part of this strike I'll leave him!" She slammed the door.

Joe deliberately finished his drink.

"This is something new—"

"Chena's upset. Forget it."

"I think we had better talk about it, Frank."

"I don't want to talk about anything right now— especially cops. Frankly, at this minute I'm sick of this union and your goddam strike."

"What the hell is the matter with that dame anyway?" Joe snapped.

The way he said it touched a raw nerve end. I found myself on my feet shouting at him, denouncing his endlessly monotonous discussions of the police, and his plans for them. He listened, then silently walked out.

I poured a drink and sat at our small bar, staring into the glass. I never heard the bedroom door open but Chena was at my side, touching my shoulder.

"I'm sorry, darling. I'll call Joe tomrrow and apologize. I'll blame a headache."

"No, you don't have to, Chena, the hell with him. It was just a case of my ears were also bent. Have one?"

"Just a little crème de menthe. . . . Frank—can you get out?" she asked abruptly.

"You know it's impossible."

"Can we just drop out of sight? Go to South America for a while?"

"It's the old story, Chena, just like in the late late show when Cagney says, 'He knows too much.' I'm Pepe's boy. As he told me, 'Peppino, *su sei un mio figlio* . . .' Walk out now? It would be—you know the word—*disgraziato!* He could never give up."

"Now I'm more worried than ever."

"Why?"

"Frank, Joe's not right these days. I notice different things every time we see him. You don't want to—you

596

refuse to admit it. It wasn't a strike he was talking about tonight; it was a race war! He wants all those policemen with guns to go after the blacks if they ever come down from Harlem or out on Bedford Stuyvesant. That's not talking about a union strike, darling, that's a madman's dream!"

"You know Joe. He's been like that since the cops killed Tom. It's mostly booze talking."

"I don't think so. I really believe he is determined to have this police strike. And what worries me, he won't let anyone stand in his way, not you, not me, not anyone."

"Now you're talking nonsense." I picked up her small glass and eyed it critically. "This stuff is getting stronger every day!"

She leaned over and put her head on my shoulder.

"Frank, don't kid about this. I've been thinking a great deal lately—"

"About what?"

"About us. Especially me and how wrong I have been. Do you remember the first days of our honeymoon in Casilda? All I cared about was that I had returned to you. And *they* did it. Not the United States government but Pepe and that little fat man Don Carlo who sat in the sun eating grapes. And what they did for Nicky! If Pepe had asked me to sign over my soul I would have gladly done so."

She was silent for a long moment, staring into the shaved slivers of ice now slowly turning into a sticky green liquid.

"And I guess we both did just that," she added bitterly. Then she put her head on my shoulder and wept softly.

In the days that followed, Chena tried to put on a good front but she couldn't hide her unhappiness and fear. She called Joe and apologized but it wasn't the same anymore. Joe's visits to our apartment, his trips with us to dinner and shows, ended. We shared adjacent offices—but that was all.

Our charade didn't fool Spider.

"What's up between you and Joe?" he asked one day. "You guys act like you had a fight over a dame."

"It's nothing, just a little argument."

"It doesn't look like nothing to me." He paused. "Did you ever mention to Joe what I suggested that day in the plane, Frank? About seeing a doctor?"

"Sure I did," I lied.

"Did he take your advice?"

"I don't know—"

"You know he didn't," he said sharply. "The guy's worse than ever. Now he's hitting those Irish bars on Columbus Avenue with Train."

"Since when?"

"The last few weeks. Train said he's scared shitless. Some of those bars are rough. They have junkies who will kill anybody for a buck."

"I'll talk to Spider."

"Someone had better, Frank," he said with a sigh. "Like I warned you on the plane—Joe's headed for trouble."

The call came from Spider in the early hours of a Sunday morning.

"Joe's in trouble."

I picked Spider up in a cab and we sped up to a fleabag in the Seventies off Broadway. The creepy night clerk took us up in the elevator to the third floor where we found Train in the shabby sitting room of a dusty old suite, a six-inch nail file broken off in his chest. There were only a few drops of blood. Train's mottled, freckled face was a dull gray as Spider threw a coat over his shoulder to get him to a doctor.

In the corner of the bedroom Joe was snoring in a chair. Standing in the other corner was a pathetic-looking gray-haired woman dressed in an old tweed suit. Her kind was not hard to find on the West Side: lonely, frightened divorcees; old show girls who always had the carefully clipped, yellowing review from *Variety* that mentioned their name: the frustrated wife of some unsuspecting slob who works his heart out for her at two jobs; the desperate alcoholic only a few years from Sneaky Pete and the vagrants who gather around the fire barrels under the West Side Highway on winter nights. Easy pickings for Joe.

She had a mouse under one eye and kept dabbing her handkerchief at a split lip. Her nose had been broken before; taking lumps from barroom pickups was no novelty.

"What happened?" I asked her.

"Denny said he knew him so I went with him," she said in a trembling, frightened voice. "The big guy was drivin'. I told—"

598

"Who's Denny?"

"The bartender at Reilly's. It's only a couple of blocks from here."

"Okay. What happened?"

"He brought along a pint and said we would have a few drinks. We finished the pint, then he got nasty . . ."

"How?"

"He ripped off my jacket." She opened it—the lining was torn to shreds. Tears rolled down her face. "This is my best suit . . ."

"I'll take care of it. Go on."

"When I tried to stop him and asked him to be a gentleman"—she touched the ugly bruise under her eye—"he started to beat me. My God, mister, he was usin' me for a punchin' bag."

"What about the big guy?"

"He came runnin' in when I screamed and tried to grab me. I was frightened to death. I didn't know what they wanted to do with me. All I had was the nail file. I didn't mean to hurt him. I only held it out and it went into his chest . . ."

"I want him out of here," the clerk said angrily. "The drunken bum! If the cops hear about this I'll have to shell out plenty."

"Shut your goddam mouth," I told him. "You're operating a riding academy and you know it! For every whore that turns a trick here you get a buck. Don't give me any crap!"

"Okay. Okay," he said hastily. "I only want him out of here. I don't want any trouble."

"Nobody wants any trouble so just get out of here."

I jerked my finger to the hall.

"Blow, pal."

He tried to look tough but wilted and walked out. I counted out a hundred dollars and gave them to the woman.

"Forget you ever saw him. He can't hold his liquor. He didn't mean to hurt you."

"I'm sorry," she said hesitantly, "he seemed nice. Please mister, believe me, I didn't mean to hurt that big guy! I swear it."

"Forget it. If that creep at the desk tries to shake you down for anything tell him to drop dead."

She nodded, nervously buttoned her worn jacket, smoothed her hair, and hurried out. Alone in the room I studied Joe. The drinking was starting to tell on him. He had jowls and his hard, tough body was softening. There was gray in the yellow hair.

"Come on, buddy," I whispered. "Let's go home . . ."

A doctor who handled a big piece of our unions' medical and compensation work took care of Train in his office. A fraction of an inch to one side, he told Spider, and the blade would have penetrated his heart.

"This is it, Frank!" Spider told me. "Either you tell this guy to see a headshrinker or I'm pullin' out . . ."

"I'll take care of it."

"You had better—the next time we might wind up with a stiff."

When I nentioned a doctor to Joe he just looked at me.

"Why don't you mind your own goddam business, Frank?" was all he said.

It was this incident that finally forced me to confront myself and conclude that a police strike in New York City with Joe as its leader could be catastrophic. I was a ridiculous dreamer devastated by a forced awakening to ugly reality. I began to plan ways to circumvent a cops' walkout and still gain all the advantages we were seeking. I came up with this strategy: fly some expensive and potentially explosive trial balloons which would bring the cops to the eleventh hour of a walkout, even publicly defy the Taylor Law by announcing a strike, not a job action, then meet with Elliot alone and put it up to him to hold a gun at City Hall's head not only to get up the money for the increases but also to lick some boots and let the cops simmer down.

I knew from my reports and findings that New York had to start the national avalanche. If they settled in New York, departments in other cities would hesitate to go out. Then again, if my strategy worked in New York we could use the same gun-at-the-head bargaining technique with city halls all over the country. We would emerge with a police union of almost terrifying power, without causing a national disaster.

I realized how gingerly this plan had to be handled and what I risked if it failed. But anything was better than letting Joe pull the city—and the country—down around our ears.

We started the New York City recruiting drive before the Christmas Table.

My dossiers on the corrupt and incorruptible members of the department were invaluable. Then Hennessy reported his leak in Elliott's command was starting to feed him material; one confidential order listed simply as ORDER AAA—TOP SECRET deatiled how Elliott wanted his borough commanders to cooperate with the National Guard in the event of a police strike. Then followed a breakdown of guard units and how they would be deployed about the city. Then, to update my findings, I accompanied him on an intensive week-long tour talking to our police contacts and getting from them the inside story of what was going on; it was like putting my fingers on the department's pulse.

There are eighty precincts in the city, and my strategy called for recruiting at least two delegates in each precinct and at least four in the ghetto houses where the cops' roll-call number is as high as two hundred. To ensure success I set a goal of eight hundred out of one thousand sergeants, five hundred out of eleven hundred lieutenants, and as many of the two hundred and sixty-eight captains as we could attract.

The next Table was held Christmas week in an office above a midtown garage, one of a string owned by Tony Cupid. Joe and I outlined the national campaign, gave them an eyewitness account of Montreal, and ended with a rundown of the police units we controlled in cities and towns across the nation.

"In other words," DeLucca said, "these guys will walk out of their precincts if you give the order?"

"I would say a majority will. Of course they won't walk out unless there is a good reason."

"Like what?"

"A combination of things: a feeling they have been abandoned by the public, an impasse in negotiations with their towns or cities, the knowledge they won't receive an extra dime to offset inflationary cost of living, a poor welfare package, or if New York walks out."

"How is New York shaping up?"

"Real good," Joe told him. "We have organizers movin' around the precincts. Every tour there's a guy outside with propaganda. We're promisin' them the moon and the stars . . ."

"Are they listening? That's the thing."

"With both ears. These cops are mad, and they like what they are hearing."

"I saw you on TV," Cupid told Joe, "you guys are really movin'."

"What about the line organizations?" DeLucca asked.

"We've been working from within," I informed him; "everyone has an insurgent group screaming they've been sold out."

"Haven't you seen 'em on TV?" Cupid asked DeLucca. "The bastards are always yellin' about somethin'."

"Because some guys yell for a TV camera that doesn't mean the whole organization is ready to fold up," DeLucca growled. "Let's face it, these guys are not dopes."

"Who said they're dopes?"

"Well let's not think that way—"

"We're playin' the opposition against the leadership," Joe told DeLucca. "When we get through, both sides won't know what hit 'em. They will be smothered with radio, TV, newspaper ads, campaigns, rallies—you name it, they'll get it."

"That will cost a lot," Grossi tartly observed.

"Frank and I estimated half a million," Joe told him coldly.

Grossi just shook his head.

"Have you been readin' about that cassette business?" Joe asked DeLucca.

"Yeah. It's gettin' big out on the coast."

"We made two cassettes, all our propaganda."

"Why two?"

"One for white, the other for blacks. We promise each side everything they asked for and more. This week we'll distribute them to our organizers at key precincts. Every tour will have a showing."

"When do you sign up the cops?"

"One of the last things we'll do is distribute cards with a yes or no to the one question—do you want our union?"

"What do you think the answers will be?"

"We'll guarantee you the answer will be yes—by a majority."

DeLucca looked silently at me. I nodded.

"What about a strike?"

"You pull a cops' strike in this town," Grossi put in, "and it will mean trouble. Big trouble! I told you that before. The government will start sniffin' around. You'll have that goddam DA downtown askin' questions before a grand jury!" He waved an admonishing finger. "Remember, Sally G warned you."

"It's something we should consider very seriously," I started to say, but Grossi gave an explosive laugh.

"Ah! Now our boy Frank is not so hot about it after all."

"Maybe the cops have scared him," Grossi's protégé said with a sneer.

"Hey, what is this?" Tony Cupid said looking from Joe to me. "I thought you guys—"

"Let him talk, Antonio," Pepe snapped.

"You always said you wanted to listen to everything, to all sides," I told Tony Cupid. "Well, that's what I'm trying to give you. Just as Grossi says, there could be trouble if a strike is called. The city won't lie down and just kick its heels."

"So what?" DeLucca said. "We had the same thing in Hawaii. The big companies warned us they had the cops in their pocket and would throw us in the hoosegow and forget where they put the key. Okay. So we said drop dead and went in anyway. For every goon they sent us we sent them two. After a while when the shekels stopped coming in and every bastard and his mother went on welfare, they said okay, maybe we'll sit down and talk. So we talked. Now we own the goddam island!"

"You said it, Finny," Cupid grunted. "Here you have cops, not plantation workers. But the picture isn't that different. This city will get on its knees begging to settle once the blacks come out of Bedford Stuyvesant and Harlem looking for Tiffany's." He motioned to me. "You said so yourself, Frank. Why are you changing your mind now?"

"I've been telling you for years how a police strike will

shake this city as it has never been shaken before. But Elliott wasn't commissioner. He's tough. He'll slug it out with us. And I think we should be prepared for the government or the DA looking into the strike. Looking into me. Into Joe—"

"We've been safe for a lot of years," Grossi grunted. "But there's always a first time; there can always be a lucky bastard with the law. Remember that cop upstate? A hick. He hears about some guys buyin' meat, then goes to Joe's barbecue and finds all our guys. *Marrone!* I almost had a heart attack the night I heard it."

"No one talked," Cupid said.

"Sure no one talked," Grossi replied with heat, "but suppose that cop broke the law and put in a wire instead of just stopping the guys in their cars?"

He looked around at the Table and slowly shook his head.

"*Ecco!* I feel the sweat under my arms just talkin' about it."

"What's the matter with you guys?" DeLucca said. "What are you, children? You wet your pants because you have bad dreams? Come on! We have the cops by the balls. If Sally wants out—let him get out. We're gonna do this no matter what anybody says."

"I didn't say I want out," Grossi replied stiffly. He nodded to me, "I agree with him—let's look at all angles . . ."

"Your pal is hedgin', Joe," Cupid said.

"I'm not hedging," I told him. "I'm looking at the other side."

"Okay. So we looked at the other side," DeLucca said, "and we still want a strike. The way I—"

There was a crash. Along with the others I turned to see Gus fumbling with a handkerchief, vainly trying to mop up whiskey and broken glass from the table. A *consigliéro* hurried toward him with a roll of paper towels and quickly cleaned up the mess under the cold, unwavering eyes of the others.

"Scusa . . . scusa," he mumbled. It was the first time I had noticed Gus was drunk. Pepe made an angry gesture and two *consiglièri* helped him from the room.

There was a moment of tense silence, then Pepe said softly:

"We will take a vote later, Peppino, and let you and Joe know our wishes in this matter. Now you both go—we have things of importance to discuss that do not concern you . . ."

A week later Gus disappeared. Grossi's protégé moved into his office at the club, and the help was informed that Gus had gone to Europe for his health. At the next Table, Pepe sat in his chair; like the others who had vanished through the years, Gus's name was never again mentioned. It was as if he had never existed.

I never told Chena. Months later the Broadway columnist who had published Gus's memories of the Prohibition days idly speculated in print on why he had dropped out of sight. Fortunately, I read the paper first.

A few days after the Table, Pepe summoned me to the gallery to give me the results of the vote: the members wanted a police strike—not only in New York but nationwide.

"It is good, no, Peppino?" he said jovially.

"No," I said bluntly. "It is bad."

He put on a good show of appearing surprised.

"Why do you say this, Peppino?"

"A police strike in New York would mean trouble for us, but a national cops' strike would be suicidal! Do you know what this means, Pepe? Even if half the departments walk out in the big cities it could be catastrophic. I've been across the country several times. I've talked to more cops than a dozen three-time losers. I'm sick of talking to them. But this I know—they'll go out, but it will turn this country upside down. And when the dust settles, the public will come looking for us!"

"They don't pay their cops, the cops will walk out. Why do you worry?"

"I'm worrying because I'm not as stupid as I was a couple of years ago. I guess I never really realized what a goddam bomb I've been carrying around. You know it could mean the end of the union?"

Pepe answered me with a slight shrug.

"So we make another union, Peppino!"

"Pepe, we've spent almost a million dollars on this one. If we can force the cities to pay the cops without pulling a strike, it will be one of the strongest unions in the country!"

"*Va! Va!*" he said disgustedly, "who cares about the *polizia?*"

"It's not so much caring about them—"

"Peppino," he said almost wearily, "for years you kept telling us, 'Cops! Give me the cops! I will own them. I will spit on them!' No, Peppino?"

"That's true but now—"

"No now," he said roughly. "We want a strike."

He selected a cigar, silently offered me one, then, when I refused, he puffed carefully, flicked the tiny ash into a tray, then settled back in his chair and regarded me with a broad smile.

"Ah, Peppino, it's a long time."

"A long time from what, Pepe?"

"Forty-sixth Street," he said with a wave of his cigar. "We made out good, no? The coloreds in Harlem. The waterfront. The unions. The casinos. Now the cops."

The smile faded slowly, and the dark eyes narrowed.

"We must have a cops' strike, Peppino." He leaned forward and a finger tapped the table. "All over the country. Like we talked about, remember? You and Joe—you wanted to own the cops. They spit on you. They killed Joe's brother and his mother." His voice rose. "You forget! It is not good to forget a wrong!"

He raised his hand and closed it into a fist.

"Soon we will have them, Peppino. We say jump, they jump. We tell them to blow their nose and they take out their handkerchief. *Sente figlio mio!* It will be a great day for us."

"Why do we have to have a cops' strike? What's so important about that? We can get the same results—"

The fist slammed down on the desk.

"A strike, Peppino! We want a strike!"

I tried to avoid the cold glittering eyes that studied me as I forced out the words past numb lips.

"I don't want any part of a police strike."

"Why do you say this? You go against the Table?"

"I'm not going against anyone. I'm trying to talk sense. I don't think we should commit suicide."

"*Va! Va!* You talk like a child. We say strike, you call the strike!"

We locked eyes for a moment.

"Not me," I told him. "I'm not going to do it."

He slowly got up and walked around the desk to stand over me.

"Peppino," he said softly, "there is a reason . . ."

"What's that?"

"We have plans, big plans for the cops."

"What are they? This is the first I've heard of this."

"We will tell you," he said soothingly, "soon . . ."

54 *THE BOMB*

After the first of the year we increased the tempo of the campaign. In the last week of January delegates to the line organizations are elected. In February we virtually inundated the police of New York City with expensive brochures, personal visits, pep talks, rallies, radio, television, and newspaper ads, and promises—enough, as Joe had promised, "to make their heads spin."

Money and fringe benefits were not the only things we promised; the theme was no more second-class citizens, no more Civilian Review Board, no more turnstiles in courtrooms where the cop is always wrong. As I recall, we spent almost three hundred thousand dollars. To impress the cops with our clout, Joe shut down the waterfront for twenty-four hours protesting a New England shipping group's decision to support a state commission investigating pier pilferage. We bought some TV time and Joe made a fiery speech about refusing to let his men become whipping boys for ambitious politicians.

"We'll gladly let them investigate us," he shouted, "but only on the condition they let us investigate them! My God, do you know what we could turn up with one subpoena?"

The state's weak governor wilted, the investigation slowly died.

This evidence of raw power and the obviously expensive campaign we conducted made a strong impression on the New York police. To them it represented the two things they sought: money and enough power to force politicians to listen to their demands and protests.

I held secret meetings with the cops I was guiding and counseling and I was free with money. Every time we shook hands I made sure they received "the price of a hat," for their extra trouble. The meetings were a strong influence in the key precincts, and from our organizers' reports I could tell we were steadily winning over patrolmen and sergeants.

It didn't take very long to get the necessary ten thousand signatures demanding that an election be held to determine a bargaining agent before the State Labor Relations Board.

While the lawyers argued in Supreme Court, we went after delegates. The analysis I had done of the department showed its members were closer than they had ever been before. The principal reasons were these: some years before, after the state legislature had ruled policemen could live out of town, groups had established themselves in suburban areas surrounding the city. They rode to work together, held the same philosophy, had the same friends, the same hobbies, the same interests. This conformity of thought helped to mold their thinking, so it was not difficult to present the themes which I knew could win them over. Namely:

Money.

Clout.

Respect.

Americanism: (Church, family, country).

We announced five different rallies, one in each of the five boroughs. At every one Joe repeated the same charges of betrayal by a leadership intimidated by politicians. He promised to maintain a dues strike-off. The contract was to include all dental, medical, and pharmaceutical fees covered fully, not partially, along with the full support of our national treasury which the Chase Manhattan had certified as being in the millions; abolishment of the Civilian Review Board; full support, morally and financially, for any policeman subject to subpoena issued by a pseudolegal committee not part of the department's own investigative unit. Insiders knew the reason for the latter demand very well: the police hierarchy was well aware of its inability to crush corruption. While it did its best, most of the dirt they uncovered was swept under the rug. Independent probes—Seabury, Dewey, or Amen—never failed to produce a scandal. A few heads always rolled when hands were caught in the till by the department's investigative staff but the public was usually served a few simple facts; it was always the case of "a few rotten apples." The cop might lose his job—as cold-eyed realists they know this is the name of the game if you're caught—but his family, his pension, and his personal reputation were safe. However, it was the independent probes that the cops feared. To be caught by them could mean the loss of that fourteen-carat pension and that really hurt. After all who wants to be a bartender in Queens . . . ?

The city fought back. The mayor and Elliott held a joint press conference in which they denounced us and even hinted that federal, state, and local law enforcement agencies were looking into our union. Joe answered them on TV with a speech that shook an already vulnerable City Hall. It consisted of a whole series of broken promises, of futility, frustrations, disappointments. I insisted we keep the heat out of this one, stick to facts, and aim it at the female audience. For Joe's opening I wrote:

"Tonight I am not talking to the man of the house but to his womenfolk. They are better able to understand the price of a one-pound can of coffee, a dozen eggs, a pair of Mary Janes for a little girl, and how to put aside a few dollars to send the oldest boy to college . . .

"Tonight I will not be Joe Gunnar, president of the national police union, but I will endeavor to be the voice of hundreds of thousands of wives of American policemen.

"Please—please listen, America . . ."

It not only stirred the city but the country. Telegrams, letters, and telephone calls of approval poured into New York's City Hall and into our Washington office. I made sure the wire services took pictures of our people delivering baskets of letters and telegrams to the New York Congressional group. . . .

Then, without warning, the blockbuster fell on the city: a Supreme Court Justice handed down his decision—we had been legally selected by the cops as their sole bargaining agent. The line organizations wailed like bedeviled banshees and their attorneys ran to the appellate courts, but we didn't care—the rank and file were flocking to our standards.

Unfortunately for the city, the politicians, with the exception of Elliott, were fumblers. They were great on television but behind the scenes they could only wring their hands and ask each other what to do. In a way I couldn't blame them. The city faced a grave crisis: this was no 1968 or 1971 "sick call" but a full-scale strike by cops who were ready to defy state law and empty every precinct from Bedford Stuyvesant to Fox Avenue.

Then the governor, consummate politician that he was, unexpectedly played Lochinvar by dramatically riding out of Albany to pay a visit to the White House, personally to plead with the President for federal funds to pay the cops. To the politically sophisticated, it was a coldly calculated maneuver to strengthen the party for the not-too-distant presidential election; no matter what the means, the political ends were justified.

I told my small Fifth Column army of cops to soothe and calm the firebrands and to sell the idea of accepting the increase as a victory without a strike.

It worked. Spider and his teams of organizers reported that the cops throughout the city had suddenly become less militant as the prospect of more money became a reality. I was relieved.

I felt I had successfully walked a tightrope. No one, not even Pepe, would fail to agree it would now be impossible to declare a police strike in New York City.

But not all the cards had been dealt. One rainy April morning Hennessy phoned to tell me to expect the cops in the city to go on a rampage within a few hours; militants had committed wholesale murder in an obscure Bronx precinct and kidnapped one cop.

What would become the famous "Flint Avenue Massacre" had taken place. As a sullen city greeted the rainy, windswept dawn, five militants had walked into the Flint Avenue Precinct and cold-bloodedly killed the desk sergeant, a patrolman who had just come off duty, an old retired cop who made a habit of stopping off at his old precinct on the way home from a night watchman's job, and the switchboard man. They also severely wounded a young rookie who had just delivered a set of orders from downtown. A lieutenant who heard the shots came running out of the back room, his gun drawn, and killed two of the raiders, before he was shot in the shoulder and leg. The wounded sergeant, who had fallen behind his desk, killed another before he died. The remaining two dragged the wounded lieutenant to a car and sped away.

The rookie cop said that the militants shouted something about "pigs can't kill kids" before opening fire. It became clear that the raid was in retaliation for a routine arrest a few days previous. A radio car from the Flint Avenue Precinct had chased and captured two teen-agers in a stolen car. As the teen-agers left the car, one accidentally shot the other with a pistol he had drawn from his pocket to fire at the two cops. The boy died later at Fordham Hospital. He was thirteen.

Three hours after the massacre, while a stunned city held its breath, a television announcer received a call from the kidnappers demanding that the city turn the two radio patrolmen who had been in the stolen auto chase over to a jury they would select, to be tried for murder. In return, the lieutenant would be freed. If the city refused, they threatened, the lieutenant would be killed.

It was an unbelievable situation. As the *Times* pointed out, not since the days of the Draft Riots had the city sat on such a volatile dynamite keg. Within hours the optimistic, happy attitude of the cops in the city evaporated. They were unapproachable on beats and in their squad cars. Most of them just glared if you asked directions to the subway. The situation became even more explosive when a television newsman brought his camera into the ready room of the Flint Avenue Precinct and interviewed the cops preparing to go on tour.

I was watching the interview when the call came from Pepe; Joe and I had to see him immediately at the gallery.

I knew why we were being summoned; Pepe wanted his police strike and he wanted it now while the anger of the cops was at its peak.

My moment of decision had come.

The scene when we entered Pepe's gallery was unforgettable. Degas's graceful ballet dancers, Cassatt's thoughtful, beautiful woman, Eakins's Philadelphia burgher in his single scull on the calm river. Bellows's knowing men in that linament-smelling back room of the gym and Pepe—all staring at a portable TV set perched on the desk. When I walked in Pepe held up his hand to silence me—a reporter was interviewing a raging cop on an East Side beat.

"No deal! No deal!" the cop was shouting above the sound of the traffic. "They either turn the lieutenant over to us and come in with their hands up or we're going after 'em. No quarter! If they're in Harlem let's take it apart, brick by brick, until we find 'em!"

Then he paused and shook his fist.

"Our stupid politicians has patted 'em on the head. They couldn't give *us* more money but they had to take

611

care of 'em! It's always been *them!* What about us? I'm a second-class citizen every time I put on this uniform. I leave my wife and kids in the morning to go out and serve the public, but does the public care if I come home like those guys on Flint Avenue—in a box? And these bums in City Hall don't want to pay us more dough. They turned their backs on us while we were being spat upon and called pigs! Now it's happened! Now what are they gonna do?"

I knew this wasn't just one cop speaking, he echoed the feelings of a large segment of the department.

There was a grim smile on Pepe's face as he turned toward us.

"Now is the time," he said, slapping his hand down on the desk. "The cops are mad. They'll walk out, no, Peppino?"

"Sure they will," Joe said gleefully, "all we have to do is call a rally and plant some guys to shout strike . . ."

"What do you say, Peppino?" Pepe asked.

"This is an explosive situation. If you call a rally now it will be like looking in a gas tank with a match! It can explode in our faces! Let's wait until we—"

Pepe leaned across the desk, his face grim, his eyes cold.

"*Now*, Peppino," he said softly. "You and Joe call the rally now."

"No, I told you I didn't want any part of a police strike. Now more than ever. We would be cutting our own throats . . ."

They both stared at me in the tense silence.

"What do you mean, no?" Joe said. "Who the hell are you to say no?"

"This is my union as much as it is yours, Joe," I told him. "I say no, it's no."

"Are you crazy?" he shouted. "Your union? Where the hell do you get that? It's *my* union!"

"You've been a pretty boy on TV and in the ads," I told him, "but I put my face in the dirt with Spider and the organizers. I've been living with the delegates. They listen to me. They trust me."

Pepe gestured to the TV set. "They are ready like grapes to be picked. The cops are mad. Very mad. It is the best time! I heard from the others—now, they say—now."

"I say no!"

612

"It's Chena, Pepe," Joe blurted out. "She told him she would leave him if he called the strike."

"That is true, Peppino?"

"That's one reason. But there are others—"

"Come off it, Frank, for crissakes!" Joe snarled, "You'd do anything for that dame! Anything, and you know it! It's been that way since we were kids!"

"Leave Chena out of this, Joe."

"The hell I will. I want—"

"Leave her out of it, goddam you!" I shouted. "Mention her again and I'll kick your goddam brains all over this room. Now shut up."

He jumped up and started for me but Pepe whirled around his desk to come between us. He didn't say a word, he only looked at us, from one to the other. Then he violently shoved us apart.

"Stùpido," he said in a surprisingly calm voice. "Will you fight with your fists like little boys at this time?"

"We would be out of our minds to pull a police strike at this time, Pepe. The city, the state, the government, everyone will fall on us like a ton of bricks. If New York walks out and the other cities follow, it could be a national disaster. Someone will have to be blamed." I turned to Joe. "Use your head. Elliott will be only too happy to come gunning for us. City Hall will need victims. And it doesn't take a genius to know who they will select."

"Listen to him! He's running scared," Joe growled.

"Of course I am. I don't want to get my head in a noose at this late date. Until this thing happened we had the city where we wanted it. Washington is ready to give the cops their increase, and the governor undoubtedly will praise them as the greatest cops in the world. He's not stupid! He wants thousands of police families pulling the right levers in those voting booths. If we don't lose our heads we can come up smelling like roses with the strongest union in the country. And we would still be owning the cops!"

Pepe slowly shook his head.

"The Table wants a police strike, Peppino, New York, L.A., Chicago, all over."

"What about your plans for the cops?" I asked Joe. "What are they?"

"Drop dead," Joe snarled. "You're out. You're through. We're not gonna tell you a damn thing."

"*Pippa! Pippa!*" Pepe told him, putting his finger to his

lips. "You talk too much." He put his arm around my shoulder. "What do you want me to tell the Table, Peppino?"

"Count me out on any police strike—"

"*Si*. I will tell them." He shrugged. "Maybe they will agree with you. *Ecco!* Who knows?"

He walked me to the door.

"*Addio!* Go with God, *figlio mio!*"

Chena and I sat up most of the night watching New York teeter on the brink of disaster. That it never toppled was only because of Elliott's expert planning, his tremendous drive, and his grasp of the city, its people, and his own men. Some insurgent groups had partially emptied "Dodge City" and were shouting all kinds of threats for the TV camera, while the streets of Bedford Stuyvesant and Harlem were alive with people. Some black cops had left their precincts to return home. While a number had choice epithets for white cops, many kept calling for calm and reason.

Elliott soon proved he had outsmarted me, Hennessy— all of us—when he announced his citywide emergency plans. It was obvious that he had been feeding us phony information through Hennessy's "leak." He intended to deploy National Guard units, but in a completely different fashion from what had been outlined in these so-called "top secret" orders. The police chain of command named in that document as liaison, some of whom were our friends, were abruptly retired or transferred to outlying precincts. Within hours a new corps of police officials was appointed, sworn in, and gathered to confer with guard officers at a secret "war room" somewhere in the city.

Elliott had other surprises for us too. In a brief televised press conference he revealed he had secretly formed the department's dynasty cops—white and black—into an elite corps, similar to the department's Tactical Force.

"They offer something more important than a strong arm," Elliott said tersely. "It's dedication to the public and to their oath of office."

The leader of the corps, a handsome, gray-haired captain from the West Fifty-fourth Street precinct, was interviewed on TV against a background of jeers and taunts from the strikers.

"All of us are three-generation cops," he said, "and we feel we have a big investment not only in the department but in the city. We don't intend to lose it because of a lot of hotheads. The way we see it, there's nothing criminal that can't be settled by the law and there's nothing in labor that can't be settled by arbitration. I think this strike will be a stain on the reputation of the New York police that the public will never let us forget . . ."

There was something vaguely familiar about his face. When the announcer identified him, I remembered—Jim O'Hara, Casey's brother and Tom O'Hara's son.

The TV cameras followed the dynasty cops as they moved from precinct to precinct setting up emergency police communications centers and swiftly consolidating the department's five thousand radio cars so they could be deployed on the borders of the explosive sections of the city.

Elliott also had formed ghetto block associations, their captains moving in and out of the ugly crowds, jollying the people, calming down the hotheads, and reporting back by walkie-talkie to a central command post that linked other command posts in all five boroughs, each one maintained by the elite or "Police Dynasty Patrol," as Elliott jokingly described it to one TV reporter. He had correctly guessed I would be watching.

However, there were uneasy rumblings across the country. Chicago had a shoot-out; three cops were killed, and our delegates there were hinting at a strike. Pittsburgh was hot—"hot as a three dollar pistol," as one delegate reported—and so was Omaha. I had calls all night from Spider who reported that our unlisted phones in several states were ringing constantly with reports of delegates across the country begging to "let go," as they called it.

"Hold tight. Don't let them make a move unless I personally tell them," I warned Spider.

Rain in the early hours helped to clear the streets.

We were eating breakfast with one eye on the television screen when my aunt called and informed us that the water pump in her car had burst. She wanted to borrow one of our two cars.

"I'll drive her," Chena said. "I don't have anything else to do. I'll chew my nails off watching television . . ."

"Chena will drive you, Aunt Clara," I told her. "Come on over and have some breakfast."

After all the grimness, it was a happy breakfast. In fact, it was the first time we had laughed in days. After breakfast Aunt Clara and Chena went down together but Chena returned as I was leaving.

"Now my car won't start," she said. "I have to use yours, darling. You should have heard Aunt Clara laugh!"

"Sure. I'll grab a cab. Tell Aunt Clara it's your private vendetta with General Motors."

"What is it going to be, darling?" she asked softly as we went down in the elevator.

"I told Pepe I don't want any part of a strike." I hesitated then what had been on my mind all night came out with a rush. "Chena, I'm going to pull out."

"But you said—"

"I know what I said and it may be true. But I want to take the chance. We'll drop out of sight like you said. What the hell, South America is a big place. Let them try and find us. I have a hunch if they pull this strike we won't have to worry. They'll have so much trouble they won't have time to think about me . . ."

I pulled her to me.

"Okay?"

She nodded and tried to hold back the tears but they came.

"You go out first, Frank," she whispered when we reached the lobby. "Let me fix my face."

Aunt Clara was waiting on the sidewalk talking to our doorman. After I had kissed her good-bye and promised to take her to 21 for lunch in a few days I gave her my car keys and hailed a cab.

I turned to wave good-bye to Chena, who was just coming out of the front door. Aunt Clara was getting into the driver's seat. The doorman was running around to the opposite side to open the door for Chena, who had stopped to bend over and pet a tiny black poodle that had scampered into the street.

I had settled back in the cab and the driver pushed his flag down when the bomb went off. Its roar filled the street. The cab was blown to one side into a parked car. I was flung against the front seat. I never felt the blood running down my face. My ears were ringing. I recall lying on the floor of the cab, staring up at the ceiling, and listening to the stunned driver saying over and over: "What the hell was that . . . what the hell was that . . . ?"

Instinctively I knew. I pushed myself up and frantically kicked open the jammed door. There was a brief moment of silence in which I could almost feel the ripples of sound waves reverberating down the street. Every sound seemed dim, far off. Fifty yards or so a pall of dust settled slowly. Then a woman screamed. And screamed. And screamed. Behind me the cabbie shouted: "It must have been a gas explosion!"

I ran back toward our house. Only the chassis remained of my car. The upper part had been flung to one side as if ripped off by a berserk giant. It lay in the street crumpled and twisted, splattered on one side with blood and parts of what had been a human, clad in a torn pink rag. Aunt Clara's dress.

One glance told me the doorman was dead. Only his torso was left. The woman who owned the poodle was also dead. I had only one thought—Chena. I found her inside the lobby. The force of the explosion had flung her against the sofa that lined one side of the lobby. The body of the poodle, a tiny black mop, lay just beyond her outstretched hand.

As I bent over her she moaned and I almost shouted for joy. She was shoeless and her skirt had been torn off. Bomb experts later determined that the tremendous force of the blast had sent the door section of the passenger's side hurtling across the sidewalk like a thunderbolt, killing both the doorman and the poodle's owner. The main part had passed over Chena's head as she bent over to play with the poodle, demolishing the fake fireplace in the lobby and embedding itself deep into the masonry. However, Chena wasn't left unscathed. Her face was a bloody mask with tiny javelins of glass sticking out. I didn't have to be a surgeon to know both her legs were broken.

I pulled off my coat, placed it under her head, then ripped my shirt to shreds. As gently as I could I tried to pull out the slivers of glass.

"You better let me handle it, mister, I was a corpsman," someone said. It was a young kid with long hair and a beard. He threw aside a large leather portfolio, took off his belt and wound it around Chena's thigh. For the first time I noticed the deep ugly furrow in the flesh and the dark red blood that came out in measured spurts.

"Probably an artery," he grunted. "We'll get it stopped."

He leaned over and picked up the iron poker that had been part of the phony fireplace set and made a tourniquet of his belt. All I could do was hold Chena's bloody hand.

For the first time in years I prayed. Desperate prayers. I never heard the sirens of the squad cars or the ambulances. It was only a matter of minutes before there were a million cops in the lobby. Someone was talking to me but I pushed him aside and helped the white-coated young Puerto Rican ease Chena onto the stretcher.

"Is she alive?" I managed to ask him.

"Yeah. She's alive," he said, "but we better move fast." He yelled to the driver. "We gotta get goin', Johnny, this one's bad."

"What about the others?" the driver yelled over his shoulder.

"DOA. All of 'em. Leave 'em for the meat wagon. Let's go!"

I babbled endlessly in the ambulance on the way to St. Clare's, but the young attendant didn't pay any attention. He kept a stethoscope on Chena's chest and with swabs of cotton tried to wipe the blood from her face.

The hospital's disaster unit had been alerted and took over. Chena vanished into a group of interns, doctors, nuns, and nurses.

I let an extraordinarily calm nun take me by the arm and guide me into a room.

"We have to take care of that laceration," she said briskly.

For the first time I realized one side of my face and chest was thick with blood and it suddenly seemed as if I had just walked into the A train.

The next seventy-two hours are a blur in my memory. I recall talking on the phone to a stunned Joe and a very sympathetic Pepe. There were huge baskets of flowers from Tony Cupid and the others but they seemed obscene and I ordered the bewildered nurse to get them out of Chena's room.

I never left her side, and only dropped her hand when they took her into surgery, not once but many times. I sat, glacially calm, listening attentively to the doctors as they told me that Chena would live although she had numerous broken bones and a severe concussion. But the important thing was the arrival of the specialist, a tiny wizened Oriental so soft spoken I could barely hear him. The nuns told me he was the best eye doctor in the country.

Then it hit me. Eye doctor!

"There was a great deal of glass," one doctor explained.

Then he went into some medical gibberish which I didn't even hear. They took Chena up early in the morning and it wasn't until late that afternoon that they brought her down. The little doctor whispered that everything was fine and Chena's eyes would be all right.

The only time I left Chena's side was to bury Aunt Clara. I went through the funeral routine automatically. I found myself mumbling appropriate phrases to old men and women as we stood alongside the closed casket. Then there were the flashing photographers' bulbs and idiotic television reporters who thrust mikes into my face as they shouted questions, so stupid they were terrifying. All I can recall of the funeral itself was the Mass, the smell of hot wax and incense, and the enormous quiet of that last moment when I gently tossed a rose on her coffin and walked away.

For the first few days after the funeral detectives from the bomb squad and Homicide South were almost as bad as the television reporters. When Elliott appeared at the hospital he simply asked me if I knew who might have been responsible, or why. When I told him I honestly did not, he ordered the cops not to bother me anymore.

"Do we have your word you'll talk to us after your wife is okay?" was all he asked.

"No question about it."

"I have told the detectives not to ask you any more questions," he said. "I'll pass the word along to the DA. I'm sure he'll go along, Howell . . ."

"Thank you."

"When you're ready—you call me," he said. "Meanwhile if there is anything we can do . . ."

"Thank you again, Commissioner. There's nothing." He started to walk away, then came back, a card in his hand.

"Here's my private number—just in case . . ."

As we waited in the hospital, I felt myself slowly emerging from a twisting, foggy alley into a bright sunny avenue. I was surprised to find myself in a cheerful waiting room with wicker chairs, sofas, and a TV set in one corner.

"You okay, Frank?" Spider asked anxiously.

"Yeah. Fine." I was suddenly conscious of noises, the rattling of plates on an aluminum wagon in the corridor, the muted signals of bells, bursts of laughter, and the sound of a television set down the hall.

There was a mirror on the wall across the room. I

walked over and peered into it. A stranger's hazzard, unshaven face, forehead bandaged, with bloodshot eyes stared out at me.

"Chena is going to be okay," I told Spider.

"I know. You told me a million times," Spider said nervously. "Christ! Who would have done that, Frank? Do you have any idea?"

"I don't know. God, I don't know. What's happening?"

He held up his hand and silently pointed to the TV set. The announcer had interrupted the game to read a bulletin. It was another firebrand threat by Joe.

"They're gonna pull it, Frank," he whispered. "He's been on the phone day and night, readin' the riot act to every delegate he can find. I kept tellin' him to lay off until he talked to you but he acts as if I'm not even in the office. You don't want a strike now, do you, Frank? This city will blow apart. Even the President got into the act!"

"The President! What did he want?"

"The Attorney General called Joe and invited him down to the White House."

"And . . . ?"

"Joe refused. He held a big press conference and said there was no reason for him to go to Washington because this is a local issue for the cities and the towns to settle."

"Refusing to see the President! That's insane!"

"Sure it is. That's what I told Joe. You can't spit in their faces down in Washington and get away with it. The Attorney General announced only this morning that he would hold us accountable for crossing state lines to incite violence. You know what that means, Frank! All we have to do is shake hands with one of our delegates in another city and they could say we were incitin' violence."

"Can you get him on the phone?"

"Joe? No. I've been tryin' all mornin'. I had Train lookin' for him all night but he can't find him."

Out of the corner of my eye I saw the nurse enter the room.

"Mr. Howell?"

"Yes," I said quickly, "anything wrong?"

"No," she smiled. "Mrs. Howell is out of the anesthesia now and you can go in . . ."

Spider walked at my side as I hurried down the hall.

"Frank, I hate like hell to even talk to you at a time like this but——"

I turned and gripped his shoulder.

"Thanks for staying around, Spider, but I'm finished. Tell Joe he was right, it's his union and he can keep it." I looked around but we were alone in the corridor. "Tell him to shove it as far as it can go and then some. Tell him that!"

I silently shook his hand. He nodded and walked to the elevator.

Except for a tiny night light, the room was dim. Chena was being fed intravenously and her eyes were bandaged. I slid into the chair beside the bed and gently took her hand.

"Frank?"

"Yes, darling, it's me."

"Are you all right?"

"Sure. Fine. Don't talk. I'll just sit here . . ."

She smiled and squeezed my hand. In a few minutes she was asleep.

"She'll be out for hours," the nurse whispered. "Perhaps if you want to get something to eat . . ."

To pass the time, I decided to check into a nearby West Side hotel, shave and shower, and then return. A ten slipped to the desk clerk turned me into a member of the Four Hundred, despite my disheveled appearance. He couldn't do enough for me. A razor, plenty of hot water and soap, a double scotch, some blazing hot coffee and a Danish did wonders. The pounding headache gradually disappeared and the fog in my brain lifted.

Just before dawn I walked up Ninth Avenue and returned to St. Clare's. I was about to open the front door when someone whispered from the shadows.

"Frank! Frank Howell?"

I spun around, half expecting a shot. A man stood in the corner, a cane in one hand, the other in his pocket. All I could see were his eyes.

He limped out from the lobby into the light.

He was like no man I had ever seen before. His face appeared stiff as parchment, drawn tightly over the bony framework of his face. His lips were pencil thin, the nose strong but perfect. Too perfect. I felt as though I was looking into a face carved from marble, not flesh. He skillfully selected a cigarette from a pack and lit it—not with a hand but with a steel claw.

I knew he was Nicky before he said: "I once bet Chena

621

a buck I could walk down Guinea Alley and you would never recognize me, Frank . . ."

"Nicky! For God's sakes, when did you get here?"

"Just after you left. The nurse wanted to call you but I told her I'd see Chena and wait for you."

"Did you see her?"

"I just left her. God! How could anyone do a thing like that? Is she goin' to be all right, Frank?"

"The doctors say she'll be okay. But it's going to be a long haul."

"She has bandages on her eyes, Frank—"

"The shattered glass. The doctors spent hours picking it out of her face and eyes . . ."

"But she'll be okay?"

"The doctors guarantee it. They brought in the best eye man in the country."

There was a long, desperate pause.

"Yeah, I know it's a long story," he said as if he had read my thoughts. "When I saw Chena in Palermo she told me you knew it all."

"How did you hear about this, Nicky?"

"The papers. It was on TV in Palermo. I tried to call you but the hospital wouldn't put through the call . . . I'm sorry about your aunt, Frank. . . . I can still remember her walking over to the playground and yellin' at you to get back for supper . . ."

"Let's go inside," I said. "There's a reception room where we can talk."

Nicky looked like a skeleton in the big overstuffed chair. There was nothing about him I recognized, only his voice. Once when he was talking I closed my eyes and I could see him; handsome, with dark wavy hair, a ready grin, slacks with the usual razor-sharp crease, the V-neck sweater under the sports jacket.

"Christ, it's a long time, Frank!" he said suddenly. "Where have the years gone?"

"I wish I knew. Can you stay around for a few days?"

"One or two, then I have to get back." The steel claw dipped into the cigarettes, plucked one out, and lit it as I watched, fascinated.

"Nothing to it. It took me about a year." He exhaled slowly. "Have you seen Pepe, Frank?"

"He called."

"And Joe?"

"He called too."

"They didn't come over to the hospital!"

"I guess they have their own problems. You know about the police union? The strike?"

"I've been watching it on TV. Do you think this bombing had anything to do with it?"

"Could be. The cops think it might have been a revolutionary group who wants to make sure we don't pull any cop strike," I hesitated, then told him, "I'm out of it, Nicky."

"Out of everything?"

"Everything. I told Pepe I didn't want any part of a cops' strike. I don't know what the hell was wrong with me. I should have known it was crazy. I was up in Montreal when they pulled that one. Chirst, it was like letting a bunch of maniacs loose in the city!"

"Yeah. I know. I read about it. And Chena told me about the one in Stockholm. What will you do?"

"Get out. I don't know where we'll go—I just want out." I suddenly remembered and snapped my fingers. "I forgot all about the cop!"

"What cop?"

"The shoot-out up in the Bronx. They kidnapped a cop and were trying to make a deal with the city."

"I heard something about it when I was coming from the airport," he said. "Someone from the UN is acting as arbitrator. I think he's meeting them this afternoon."

"What are you doing now, Nicky?"

"Importing," he said casually. "I do a lot of traveling all over Europe. I want to get out too. I think maybe I'll close up the office when I get back. When Chena gets better, how about coming over to Italy?"

"That would be great. I'll make Chena show me that little village where she was holed up during the war . . ."

"She'll never recognize it. They built a factory and all the peasants have TV sets and cars."

We exchanged small talk until the nurse informed us Chena was awake. She was restless and in some pain, but Nicky was better for her than codeine. We stayed until she slipped into a deep sleep. Then I walked Nicky to the door.

"Why don't you check into the hotel where I am Nicky? It's only a few blocks from here on Eighth Avenue."

"No. No," he said quickly. "I have someone who will

put me up." He added with a faint smile, "I intend to give him a lot of business so he's real friendly . . ."

He opened the door then turned to me.

"I know about my father, Frank . . ." he said softly.

Then he limped down the steps. As he reached the curb a car drove up. He got in and, in a moment, was gone.

55 STRIKE

I didn't know they had found the police lieutenant's body in the trunk of a car outside the Jamaica railroad station until that afternoon. It was all over television and on the radio, and the hospital buzzed with the story, but I never heard it; I was in Chena's room when that little Oriental doctor removed the bandages. He kept patting me on the shoulder and telling me not to worry, but those few minutes in the dimmed room were as tense and terrifying as any I had known. He peered into her eyes with a tiny flashlight and gestured to the nurse to slowly open the blinds. Chena blinked a few times then turned over and kissed me. I knew everything was fine.

I stayed with her all day until she insisted I go out and get something to eat. I was passing the reception room when I saw a small group of nurses and aides intently watching the television. I joined them to discover what had happened to the cop. As I was leaving the announcer broke in to read a bulletin: Joe had called his rally for that night in Madison Square Garden.

When Chena slipped off into a deep sleep I again joined the crowd in the reception room. Joe's face gradually came into focus as the cameras moved across the heads in the crowded auditorium; it was haggard, intense, fanatical.

His voice was cracked and hoarse but he was still dynamic and I recognized some of my old phrases. He threw in everything: economics, racism, fears, threats, Americanism. He plucked at raw nerve ends and played

624

with their emotions until you could almost taste the hate rising in that huge, smoky place as cameras panned from section to section to catch the fist-fights breaking out among shouting, slugging, cursing cops.

Then, suddenly, Joe walked to one side of the platform and returned slowly, leading an incredible procession of a weeping woman followed by twelve kids, ranging in age from late teens to a chubby smiling boy of about two who kept waving to the audience. It was the dead lieutenant's wife and family.

The Garden watched in stunned silence as he brought the woman and her children to the center of the stage. Then, with tears streaming down his cheeks, he raised his arms and cried out:

"Listen, America! Look, America! This is the widow of one of the finest of New York's finest who was murdered by this city! Salute her, America! Salute her and her children!"

It was eerie, chilling. The fistfights ended abruptly, the shouting and cursing died away, as thousands of policemen rose to their feet. A clear, unwavering tenor began "God Bless America," and in a few minutes the cavernous Garden echoed with the words. It was staged very neatly, caught in the cold white light of a spotlight. As the bewildered woman led her family back into the wings, the first cry rose:

Joe didn't forget a prop. In the silence that followed, a huge American flag unfolded and hung from the gallery railing,

"Strike . . . strike . . ."

Other voices took it up until it became a steady, rhythmic chant.

"Strike . . . strike . . . strike . . ."

Demonstrations took place. Lines of cops snaked in and out of the aisles, their leaders holding high American flags.

It was a midsummer's prairie fire fanned by a high plains wind. It leaped from section to section, touching group after group. I did not have to wait until the end; I knew Pepe had his trike.

Before the four to midnight tour began, most of the precincts were empty. Out of curiosity I walked past Fifty-fourth Street and saw the pickets walking up and down with radio cars choking the street and crowds of cops standing about, arguing, debating, listening.

But Elliott wasn't caught off guard. I never knew if he

had cleared it first with City Hall but in a blistering press conference at police headquarters he called upon the governor to bring in the National Guard and announced that, while most of the cops had walked off their jobs, detectives, police brass, and his "Dynasty of Cops Corps" were maintaining patrols and answering emergencies.

But all anyone got on 911 was a busy signal. The civilian workers in the police communications center, all members of the union, had walked off. The few cops left were desperately trying to do the job normally done by banks of computers.

Elliott also had another ace to play. An emergency program of auxiliary police units, block associations, civic groups, and neighborhood organizations came out of nowhere, each with a few cops at their head. This was followed by the appearance of thousands of retired policemen and superior officers who had been recruited in a secret program and put through an intensive capsule training course.

In the first hours of the strike they helped to keep the city quiet while the governor and the mayor tossed the political ball back and forth between City Hall and Albany.

However, by the morning rush hour the city was chaotic. Most of Manhattan's traffic lights are progressive, one after the other to maintain a steady flow of traffic through the city's congested streets at about twenty-five miles per hour. Other lights are simultaneous. A bloc of lights from ten to twenty can be controlled by a key in every fifth light box.

Striking traffic cops changed the city's signal light pattern. Trucks were also deliberately parked on crosswalks.

By eight o'clock midtown traffic was frozen. Not a wheel turned in the garment center. Only horns blew and blew. There were no cops to move the trucks parked at the crosswalks and the lights were erratic. Nothing worked. In the Forties traffic was blocked back into the Lincoln Tunnel which had to be closed with trucks and cars diverted north to the George Washington Bridge. Then the Holland Tunnel was closed because Brooklyn, Manhattan, Williamsburg, and Fifty-ninth Street bridge traffic to Brooklyn was stalled, including the Brooklyn-Battery Tunnel.

As I watched the incredible scene on television of the solid mass of stalled honking metal, I saw a truck driver slowly crawling across the roof of his truck, then on to another.

I wondered if Tony Cupid was watching . . .

Then the mobs appeared. In the beginning they were small, they grew bolder as their size increased. TV cameras followed them up Fifth Avenue as they cleaned out the windows of the big stores. One man came running out, shouting and waving a club, but the mob enveloped him. When it passed his body lay sprawled in the street.

Not all Fifth Avenue huddled fearfully in upper floors or cellars. In the Forties several men and private guards, all armed with rifles and hand guns, silently knelt down in front of one large jewelry store and aimed at the approaching mob. It broke, swirled, and moved to the other side of the avenue to continue north.

Two small banks were hit, some personnel killed, and the vaults cleaned. Vigilante groups began patrolling shopping centers in Queens. Looters were killed as they ran from stores. Television cameras showed two men carrying a handful of clothing pushed back against the shattered store front and shot. The mobs continued to increase in size until one TV announcer estimated they were as large as the draft gangs of a hundred years ago.

Heartsick, I watched the city as it was torn apart. When the uneasy striking cops decided to patrol the streets "for emergencies," ironically it only increased the lawlessness. Black cops rushed to Harlem and Bedford Stuyvesant, and all the hate that ever existed in the department between the blacks and the whites exploded into an orgy of unparalleled violence. Then firemen talked of going out along with Sanitation. It was soon evident that only a fool would drive a car in the city or walk the streets. Fortunately a driving rain forced a lull in the looting. There was a scene on television that was unforgettable. I believe it was a Channel Five team of reporters and cameramen that slowly moved up Fifth Avenue from Altman's to about the Plaza. Soggy dresses, headless mannequins, bolts of goods, smashed TV sets, empty windows, glass everywhere, three men behind a door angrily waving away the camera and shaking their rifles; another sign in a shattered window: NEW YORK COPS—WE HATE YOU!, two men supporting a third and dragging a mahogany desk with a chair and wastepaper basket on top.

And the rain pelting down on the deserted avenue.

"What I have witnessed here today I will never forget

for the rest of my life," one awed reporter told his audience.

But if New York was quiet in the rain, other cities were only beginning their desperate days. Once the New York police went out, departments all over the nation took a walk, some on strike, others on "job action." No matter what they called it, within one morning the majority of American big cities and towns had no police protection.

Pittsburgh exploded. In Detroit private guards in a plant staged a shootout with a mob in cars. Vigilantes in Cleveland accidentally killed a black night watchman coming off duty and a race riot tore that community apart. In San Francisco the police walkout was a signal for the street people, and both sides fought each other with bombs, tear gas, and guns.

Chicago was the first to follow New York. Nothing Daley or any of the other city officials could say or promise stopped the cops. That city's big street gang immediately announced they would police the city, and while Daley begged the governor to send in the Guard, armed thugs, hoodlums, and militant groups appeared on the streets or in fleets of cars.

That was too much for the cops. They formed what they called "The Chicago Strike Force For Law And Order" and went after the street gang vigilantes. The inevitable happened. Chicago became a besieged city, and when the gang fled to its command post in a sprawling project the cops went after them, stalking them from building to building like the mopping-up operations of an invasion force. But the gang's snipers with high-powered rifles exacted a deadly toll.

A cop in combat gear, resting behind a burned-out police car, told one reporter morgue attendants were stacking bodies of both cops and members of the gang in the corridors of the morgue. As the cop said, "There's no more room in the icebox ... and when we get finished they'll have to stack 'em out in the street ..."

Every hour another city reported disturbances. The Department of Justice dispatched federal marshals to some places and the Attorney General was ordered to the White House.

It was like an epidemic of infectious madness moving across the country. It was a lot more than a demand for wages; as Joe had told our first convention that giant

American policeman had awakened from a long sleep and was stirring in the land.

Good God, the giant was a madman. . . .

Just before noon I received a call from Nicky. It was very brief, he simply wanted to know if I would be at the hospital for the next half hour. When I told him I would be, he hung up.

I waited but he never showed up. Instead a messenger delivered a bulky letter addressed to me. It was lunchtime, the TV set was finally dark, the nurses and aides were on duty, and the reception room was deserted. I ripped open the envelope and read the laboriously printed lines:

Dear Frank:

When you receive this I will be on my way to Washington to turn myself over to a guy from Treasury. For years he's been trying to make a deal with me. I have always laughed at this guy and told him to get lost. I would be still laughing at him but what happened to Chena and what I found out last night changed my mind.

Frank, Pepe and Joe pulled off the bombing. It wasn't Chena they were after—it was you. They're afraid of what you might do to stop the cops' strike.

The reason I came back to the States was for a Table, the most important ever held. I had seen Pepe before I met you at the hospital and he warned me not to say anything about the Table to you.

I found out why you were not invited: they gave a contract out for you, Frank. Two guys from out of town. They know you're at the hospital and they will be there sometime in the early hours of tomorrow morning. They said it will be in and out.

It also means Chena. Pepe sold the Table a bill of goods. He said we would all go under if you sold us out and stopped this strike.

Since the very beginning Pepe's plan was to have every memeber of the Table take over a city where a strike was pulled and really suck it dry. Big stuff. Nothing small. Banks. Investment houses. Jewelry stores. Utility plants. In Chicago, while those crazy cops and niggers are killing each other, they have it all set up to knock over the David's Chemical Company. Nine o'clock, before the payroll window opens. They have tear gas and the whole business.

In Frisco they're going to take that bank on Cornell Street right after it opens. DeLucca says they have a multimillion-dollar shipment ready for the islands.

I don't get this, it sounds crazy to me but Pepe says he has two guys from Paris who will knock off the Metropolitan. He showed us a list of paintings they will grab. He said everything is set to get them to Europe where we will demand a couple of million dollars ransom. One is an El Greco. I don't know much about painting, but Pepe said the city would pay anything to get it back.

That isn't all. The biggest haul will be in junk that was brought in last week from the coast and from Mexico. It's the biggest shipment of drugs ever smuggled into this country. It has taken them two years to get it together. Its value in hard cash is more than $25,000,000. Knocked down in the street, it will be triple that. The junk is in the apartment over Patsy's restaurant. Tonight they will use your trucks to move it out to cities all across the country.

By the time this strike is over there will be forty million new junkies and we will have sucked the country dry. This has been Pepe's plan for over twenty years, Frank. He's not going to let anything stand in his way. You. Me. Anyone.

Yesterday they took care of a cop you have been doing business with, some guy named Hennessy. Joe said he's the big fat slob we called Kidneyfeet when we were kids. Joe killed him. He told us how he walked in on the cop and let him have it. First in the legs, then in the guts and then while the poor bastard crawled on the floor he shot him in the head. Frank, Joe is nuts! Maybe they all are nuts! I just heard from Tony Cupid that Sally G and his stooge got it upstate. It wasn't a full Table, and Sally threatened to call all the Families if Pepe went through with the strike. Pepe conned him into believing he would call another Table, but as soon as they left he ordered the hit. The others are too scared to buck him. Joe came in like a madman telling us how he was going to keep the cops out for a month and how he was ready to form them into some kind of an army. Tony Cupid has been hot for the strike but I could see him cooling off. He said the government is ready to move into this thing.

I know I can be next. Pepe's not going to leave me floating around. I decided I wanted to live a little longer, even the way I am. I guess I never forgot those days in that hospital; I didn't want to die then and I don't want to now.

I will protect you as much as I can, Frank. My story to the feds will be that you knew nothing about this shipment or their plans. You were simply the union organizer, and when you didn't like what you saw, you pulled out. What Joe doesn't realize is that Pepe has him set up as a sucker. He'll be left holding the bag if the government moves in. Pepe laughed like hell after Joe left the Table.

Get out of the city, Frank, as soon as Chena can leave the hospital. It will not be healthful for you or for me after today.

One last thing. If you're wondering how I know so much about the shipment—I arranged it. I have been in charge of buying and selling drugs for the Table since I left the hospital in Zurich and was able to walk. They gave me a new face. A new arm. A new leg. You know the law: one hand washes the other . . .

Kiss Chena for me. I will always love you both.

NICKY

I tried to find the messenger but he had left immediately after delivering the letter. I was debating my next move when Chena's nurse looked into the reception room.

"Did you get your call, Mr. Howell?"

"Yes. Yes I did, thank you . . ."

"The long distance operator just rang the hospital's operator back with time and charges and she—"

I jumped up so suddenly she was startled.

"Wait a minute! Then the hospital operator would have the outside number?"

"I suppose so if it's long distance or a hotel . . . I can ask her."

"Please do."

She picked up the telephone in the reception room and spoke to the hospital operator. After an endless wait, she jotted down a number and handed it to me.

"Here's the number, Mr. Howell . . . the operator called

it back. It's the Fairmount Motor Motel, just outside Kennedy."

"Is my wife awake?"

"No, she's still sleeping. The doctor thought it would be best—"

"That's fine. If she wakes up please tell her I'll be back in a few hours. I'm going to pick up her brother . . ."

"Sure, Mr. Howell, I'll tell her . . . don't worry about a thing. She's going to be fine."

I had to pay fifty dollars to get a cab to take me to the motel. It took over three hours to get through the jammed midtown streets, to the midtown tunnel, and into Queens. The highways were a nightmare.

When we finally reached the motel he agreed to wait and take me back for another fifty.

The motel was packed with frantic people waiting to leave the city, but a harassed room clerk who looked up Nicky's name insisted he was not registered. I found the bell captain and, for ten, he spoke to each one of his bellmen, giving them a description of Nicky. The third one recalled him; he was in a room in the west wing on the street level.

I found the room. There were voices inside. For a moment I hesitated, then knocked on the door. There was no answer. The voices continued without interruption. I knocked again, louder this time. Still no answer. I tried the door. It was open. I walked into a darkened living room. A TV set was on in the corner. The governor was being interviewed and promising the end of the police strike. The city was getting injunctions. A Supreme Court justice had fined the union $500,000 a day for every day of the strike. A reporter was insisting Joe was nowhere to be found. The head of the Firemen and Sanitation unions were pleading with their men to "hold the line—stay on the job."

I hesitated at the threshold of the bedroom, something told me horror was just behind the doorway. I switched on the light, then quickly switched it off.

Whoever had killed Nicky had found him packing his valise. The heavy dumdum bullets had shattered the Nazi colonel's brilliant work of art.

I slumped into a chair and stared at the fuzzy picture on the television screen. Slowly it came into focus. It was Joe shouting into a brace of microphones. The words flowed over me like water. I sat there hypnotized by his

632

hoarse, cracked voice, his raging, twisted face, flickering madly on the screen.

Then I became conscious of a horn blowing. My cab. When I appeared the cabbie raced across the parking lot.

"I want to get back and put this hack to bed, buddy," he said. "No more for me. This goddam city has never been a tea party but now it's a goddam jungle twice over." He peered at me. "You okay, fellow? You look sick."

"No, I'm fine," I said as I got into the cab.

"Where do you want me to drop you?"

I hesitated, then gave him the address of our apartment. I had to pick up the gun to kill Joe and Pepe.

56 THE DEVIL'S OWN EXECUTIONER

Perhaps it had been in my subconscious for a long time, but the sight of Nicky had brought it spinning to the surface. During those seconds in the darkened room, with Joe's fanatical face before me on the screen, I had confronted myself, my past, Chena, my life—everything. I finally, belatedly, saw the dimensions of the horror I had created. There was only one resolution: to become the Devil's own executionr.

"Hey! What's the matter, buddy?" the driver called, studying me in the overhead mirror.

"Nothing. Nothing. It's nothing."

"Got troubles, pal?" he asked with a great show of uneasy cheeriness. "When you get home just sit back and watch TV. That's trouble! Me? I'm gonna lock my doors, grab a beer, and watch those crazy bastards kill each other!"

Good God, I thought, he's in an arena!

Just before we arrived at the apartment house, the governor came on the radio and announced that the troops were finally ordered in.

I walked through the still-shattered lobby to the elevator.

Our apartment was cool, rain had come through the open window and soaked the rug. I carefully shut the window and wiped up the puddle with a towel. The banality of murder . . .

Swatched in its layers of oily rags, Spider's .38 Police Special looked as clean as if it had come from a gun shop's shelf. I slipped it into my jacket pocket along with some extra shells and left. I tried the gallery on Madison Avenue but it was locked. One more window wouldn't make any difference I told myself and hurled an ash can through the plate glass door. Gun in hand I went from room to room but Pepe wasn't there.

I ran furiously up Fifth Avenue to the Seventies and Pepe's brownstone. The soft chimes echoed in the hall but no one appeared. The street was deserted so I found an ash can under the stoop and used my coat to muffle the sound of splintering glass. Then I unlocked the door and stepped in.

Again I went from room to room but the house was empty. Then I remembered Nicky's note: the shipment was stored in the apartment above Patsy's restaurant.

An auxiliary cop tried to stop me on Lexington Avenue but I persuaded him to let me walk to the subway to get downtown. He was a paunchy, apprehensive old guy who insisted on escorting me to the Lexington Avenue station.

"You better start running as soon as you get out, buddy," he said. "There may be a lot of trouble tonight . . ."

I promised I would run like a deer the moment I reached the street and, with a wave, he left. The subway was crowded but something was strange. Instead of glowering or staring at each other in a stony silence, the passengers, now bound together by fear, were talking to one another. Cops, of course, were the subject.

I got out at Worth Street and crossed the empty Court House Square. A team of federal marshals stood in front of the grim marble shaft of the Federal Building.

The streets behind the square were quiet, deserted. There were no lights in the windows, stores were darkened. It was like hurrying through a ghost city.

Like its neighboring buildings, Patsy's was dark. The iron shutters of the second floor were closed. I banged on the front door several times until a shadow came out of the back kitchen.

634

"No open . . . go away . . ."

It was Patsy. I pressed my face against the glass and said, "Don Vitone . . . I must see him . . . you know me."

He cautiously edged open the door.

"I have the truck down the street," I whispered, "he told me to come up . . ."

The hooded old eyes studied me before he slipped the chain off the lock and let me in. I brushed past him and made my way through the darkened restaurant to the kitchen. The old woman and the fat cashier with the moustache were sitting on stools sipping coffee. They stared at me impassively as I went up the stairs to the apartment.

The door was closed. When I knocked I heard footsteps, a lock snapped, and it opened.

Pepe was standing in the doorway.

I could tell he was startled, but he recovered quickly.

"Peppino! My Peppino!" he cried. "Come in! Come in!"

A tray of food and a silver espresso pot were on the desk. Piled on all sides of the room were small wooden boxes.

"Sit down! Sit down!" he said and waved me to a chair as he hurried behind the desk. "Have some coffee, Peppino!"

"I just came from the motel, Pepe," I told him. "I found Nicky."

He did not react, but continued to fill the tiny espresso cup. Then he carefully sipped it and made a smacking satisfied noise with his lips.

"So, Peppino, you found Nicky." He shrugged. "Our friends warned us he was talking to the federal people. What could we do? He had to be silenced." He held out his hands imploringly. "Peppino, that is the world!"

"It's your world, Pepe, but it's no longer mine."

"*Va! Va! Pazzia!* You talk foolishness. The strike is going good, no?"

I slipped the gun out of my pocket. He never blinked.

"Nicky told me you and Joe ordered the bomb. Now you have a contract out for me . . ."

"You think I would kill you, Peppino?" he asked softly. "*Figlio mio!* You are like a son to me. Did I do anything but good for you? *Ecco!* Is that not the truth?" He said fiercely, "Who says this?"

"Nicky was at the Table—"

"Va! Va! That crazy Nicky!" He shot a finger at me. "You want to kill somebody, you kill Joe!"

I couldn't help it, I had to ask the question.

"What's the matter with Joe?"

"Fesso! He's crazy! The cops keep calling and calling—Detroit. Chicago. All over. Nobody can find that bastard!" He threw up his hands. "All the time you say, 'Pepe, I must own the cops.' Now you own the police, Peppino. What do you do? Where are you? Where is that crazy Joe? *Marrone!* The Table asks me—"

He was shouting. I never noticed until it was too late that he inched from around the desk, he was holding the heavy espresso pot. Almost unconsciously as he talked he reached over and slowly turned up the French cuff of his right sleeve. Then with stunning clarity, I realized what he was about to do.

I ducked as he flung the pot. It missed my head by inches and crashed against the wall. My first shot staggered him as he lurched toward me, his powerful hand reached for my throat, the other frantically grabbing for the gun.

The spilled coffee made him slip, as he stumbled my second shot hit him in the chest. He fell against me and I could see the life fading from those cold black eyes.

"Why, Peppino . . . ?" he whispered. *"Stùpido . . ."* . . . .

He slowly slid down to his knees and toppled over.

I knew what I had to do. I hurried down the stairs. Only a night light was on in the kitchen; Patsy and the old women were gone. I rushed to the phone booth in the restaurant and dialed the private number Elliott had given me at the hospital.

"Commissioner Elliott please."

"Who is calling?"

"Frank Howell . . ."

Someone called out my name across a room and I heard hurrying footsteps.

"Howell? Frank Howell?" Elliott said calmly.

"I only have a few minutes so listen very carefully . . ."

I gave him the details of everything that was to happen that night; the Metropolitan, the banks, the utility plant, the drug shipments from New York to the West Coast.

"Stick by this phone," I told him. "I'll call in about an hour. If you can arrange to have a nationwide TV hookup, I will call off the strike. I will tell the cops, here and everywhere, how they had been made suckers, victims of a plot—"

"You'll tell them that?"

"You set it up and I'll do it." I hung up.

The next call was to Spider at our union headquarters. He was almost hysterical when he answered.

"Frank! For the love of Christ where are you?"

"I just left the hospital. Where's Joe?"

"How do I know?" he screamed. "He's nuts, Frank! I told you all the time he was goin' nuts! He was runnin' all over the city last night tellin' cops to get their guns and kill niggers. He told Train the more dead cops he saw the better he would like it! Frank, you have to do somethin'. Delegates are callin' in from every state, town, and city from Detroit to Seattle. I don't know what to tell 'em!"

"Tell every cop that calls to stand by and watch for me on TV—"

I hung up. Poor Spider. Poor Train. All they got for their loyalty was madness and betrayal.

But at least now I knew where I could find Joe.

There were less than five people on the AA Independent train I caught at Chambers Street. All of them looked frightened and two were carrying pipes wrapped in newspapers. The conductor had a baseball bat by his door.

The auxiliaries and some of the volunteer cop patrols were taking no back talk from the bums of Forty-second Street. As I came out of the subway on Eighth Avenue, a gang suddenly appeared carrying a heavy traffic stanchion. They were running toward a clothing store, ready to hurl the stanchion at the window, when suddenly a patrol swarmed out of a doorway. Guns slammed and two of the gang fell screaming. The others dropped the stanchion and fled down the street. Shouting and cursing, the cops chased after them and beat them to the sidewalk with their clubs.

"Where are you going, buddy?" one shouted at me.

"I live on Forty-sixth Street."

"Well, get your ass over there in a hurry," he roared.

I ran up Eighth Avenue. As far as I could see, sidewalks were covered with glass and store windows emptied. Several blocks north, at about Fiftieth Street, fire trucks had blocked off the avenue. Smoke was pouring from a square of buildings. A band of looters in a station wagon, TV sets, radios, and a sofa tied to the rack on the roof,

637

hurtled across Eighth Avenue headed for the West Side. Sirens wailed in the distance.

Forty-sixth Street was littered with garbage, ash cans, the slaughtered body of a collie, shattered glass, and even a heavy door. A weeping woman in a doorway called out to me in Spanish as I hurried past.

I slowly climbed the stairs of our tenement. I could see a kitchen light through the old-fashioned glazed panels of the door. Inside someone was shouting, then laughing. I carefully tried the door. It was open. As I stepped into the flat I smelled raw whiskey and sweat.

In the dim light I could make out a man seated in a chair alongside the old porcelain-topped table. There was an idiotic grin on his unshaven face. Strands of straggly, faded yellow hair fell over his eyes. He wore only a filthy undershirt, a pair of greasy work pants, and socks. His legs were stretched out in front of him and he was holding with both hands an empty whiskey bottle that rested on his stomach.

The idiotic grin faded, then his voice became a growl and he began shouting, raging incoherently, gesturing with the bottle at some invisible figure who apparently was kneeling before him.

I wondered who this strange, pathetic madman reminded me of—then I suddenly knew.

Andy Gunnar. Joe had become his father. . . .

What more is there to tell? How I made that coast-to-coast broadcast to stun hundreds of thousands of cops from New York to L.A. and end America's first national police strike? How I became the most sensational informer in the history of the FBI?

Joe has long vanished into the darkness of his own soul. Pepe is dead. Gus is dead. Nicky is dead. The Table is shattered and its members are either in jail or under so many indictments most of them will have to plead guilty. Before I talked I made a deal for Spider and Train. They both copped a plea and got off with light sentences.

I also insisted IRS come to some terms with Maxie. They agreed, and he only pulled a disbarment, a year's SS, and a stiff fine which he gladly paid. The last time I heard from him he was in Haiti, trying to persuade Papa Doc Duvalier's fat son that gambling casinos were the answer to all his country's troubles.

Every asset I have is under IRS liens. Chena has

638

pawned all her jewelry and furs; if it wasn't for Maxie's monthly checks we would be on welfare.

Except for a slight limp Chena is back in perfect health. What happened to us was not totally unexpected. From those glorious days in Casilda and Havana, we both knew that someday our bubble would burst. We offer no alibis, no weeping, no maudlin statements. We still live from day to day; the only thing important to each of us is the other.

As Chena has said many times, her only fear down through the years was that I would suddenly vanish among the Table's dead and leave her behind, like her father. That was one of my badly kept secrets. She and Nicky had known all the while that the Table had disposed of him.

I don't know what faces us. For months I exposed all of the Table's darkest, most intimate secrets; the Department of Justice was very grateful. Several times Elliott has pleaded in my behalf. But who knows what will happen the day I walk into court to face the judge.

What can I say? That I was caught up in a merciless time, that I betrayed a society that didn't give a damn? That I must accept what punishment is coming to me?

Someone once wrote that there are as many roads to Heaven as there are to Hell. Well, I certainly tried all the well-worn paths to the latter. My belated regrets and remorse may be insufficient to put me on the right way to the former place but God knows I'm trying. There are many debts to be paid but if I have the time I will square all my accounts. I have come to realize that living out your life each day haunted by the evil you have done is an act of justice only God can deliver. Mere mortals in their ignorance of what such a sentence means would only offer the gallows rope.

As Chena keeps telling me, we'll survive. I guess that's the only good part of the Neighborhood's heritage, when you come out of its depths you know how to survive—not triumph—survive.

I beg of you, don't judge me; be me.

THE BIG BESTSELLERS
ARE AVON BOOKS!

En ce nouveau siècle, Le dictionnaire historique et géopolitique du 20ᵉ siècle a été mis en page par Nord Compo à Villeneuve-d'Ascq
† achevé d'imprimer sur les presses de l'Imprimerie France Quercy à Cahors
août 2004 (6ᵉ tirage).
ôt légal : avril 2002. Imprimé en France. N° d'impression : 41719/